NEWELL GILBERT'S BOYHOOD

I. AMERICAN WINE
II. JOURNEY ON THE NEEDING
III. INFERNAL INNOCENCE

Liston Pope

MANTIS PRESS
New York
2006

Library of Congress Cataloging in Publication Data:
Pope, Liston   1943–
Newell Gilbert's Boyhood
I. American family, childhood, mores.
  First love, sports, holidays, neighborhoods.
  II. American education. Youth. Private boarding
  school life. Eastern Establishment.
  III. Public high school, education. Adolescence.
  Community and race relations. New England
  town life, government. Mafia. American journalism.
I. Title   II. Title   III. Title

Library of Congress Control Number: 2005929923

ISBN 0-9638900-8-5

Distributed to the trade by Mantis Press,
P.O. Box 237132, New York, N.Y. 10023

FIRST EDITION

Contents

In Memory of
Bennie Purvis Pope

AMERICAN WINE

STORIES

Promotion Day

I

June 1954

Past midnight Newell Gilbert tossed and turned and couldn't get to sleep: because tomorrow was promotion day, and he would probably get left back. For a long time he lay in bed wide awake; he imagined the shame. What a bad thing when his classmates heard their names called and stood up, one by one, and then marched happily out of the room to meet their new teacher. And they gave gloating glances at himself and Otter *left back* to rot in fifth grade for another year.

Oh, such would be his fate, and maybe he had it coming. D in conduct on every report card since last fall; and now you must pay the price, in shame, for your pranks and your merry ways. His teacher tried to warn him by keeping him after school again and again: Miss Kenny told him to mind his manners, or else! But he had his fun anyway, and shot his peashooter in class, sailed paper airplanes out the window, snuck up the aisle on his knees to pass a note to a girl. And now, in the morning when he went to school, Newell Gilbert must pay the price. And later on, when his dad came home from work, there would be hell to pay. Yes, sir.

He heard his mom's footsteps on the attic stairs. It was her way to come up late and make sure everything was okay.

–You still awake?

–Goin' fishing . . .–he croaked from beneath the covers.

–Are you? After school?

–This af' with Otto.

Then early morning light crept in over the window sill. It showed an active boy's cluttered space, more like a tree fort: where he held forth in his attic room and didn't give a thought to straightening up or putting things away, but left all that for Cliff to do.

Baseball equipment lay scattered about: a broken Louisville Slugger, its handle screwed and taped; two lopsided and friction-taped hardballs; a t-shirt with rust traces, and blue sleeves. Newell's Peewee uniform lay sprawled on the floor where he took it off the night before–dusty white stockings crumpled from the high-arched stirrups blue like his team's lettering: SPRING GLEN.

Across the room on a card table: action games, electric football, magnetic baseball; also, a notebook he filled with statistics. The tiny plastic players stood ready to rock 'n roll when the electricity went on: run, hit, pass, kick, tackle. Now they waited, poised, in first rays of sunlight from the window.

A low bookcase along the wall had sports books, adventure books: *Encyclopedia of Baseball, Lore & Legend of Baseball, Grantland Rice Anthology, Buddy and the Old Pro, Herman Hickman Reader;* also the Mel Martin series; also, *Hound of the Baskervilles, Three Musketeers, Count of Monte Cristo. Monster Rally, Pardon My Blooper.* There were *The Iliad, The Odyssey, Arabian Nights* in abridged editions for young people. There was *The Wealth of Nations* . . .

From a mail-order house Newell ordered pennants. He sent away. The pennants arrived in rolls, all different colors, with a felt smell. Once his sister Evelyne borrowed them for a party, and then thumbtacked them back, like she promised, in place. Now they hung in rows, the great universities of the land, across the pale green attic walls–walls a heavy cardboard, faceted at odd angles.

The bedroom looked all movement: gear and things stilled, in mid-flight, where they lay flung. Angles, clutter, a boy's workshop. The strewn objects and sense of frozen motion made a hymn to playtime, childish action, exploits.

Sunlight shot over the sill and touched the checkered quilt where the boy slept.

II

—Oh, New! Oh, Newee-e-e!

Singsong voice in the yard down below. Bit hushed: it had an urgency like someone who needs to pee.

It was The Otter, and he kept on.

A warm June breeze flitted here, there, and wafted with a few birds' chirps. The sleeping boy stretched a little and felt a quickening. What's going on? What's up today? . . . Ah! Time to *run away*.

—Oh, New!

Gravel, a few pebbles, pecked at the screen. Boy, that Otter sure is stubborn.

Newell opened his eyes: a gold ray came in past the cedar tree just outside, and over the attic sill. Then he gave a start. He jumped from bed and waded through gear to the window.

—That you, Otto?

—You all set?

—Gimme a minute!

—Geez, almost seven.

—Shh, you'll wake my folks.

—Hurry up!

Newell turned and tiptoed through the bedroom door. There were stairs, low shelves with old dusty books. He went in the bathroom. In the big white tub each morning: bugs and spiders, daddy longlegs. He didn't like to turn the hot water on them, but later Cliff would come, puffing along like he did, talking to himself, and scoop the 'poor brothers' up—he called them brothers—in a rag.

Douse face, brush teeth, comb hair. Back in his room he dressed in a flash. Then he went to the window and looked down.

From below Otter, his voice hoarse, low for a kid, the voice of sheer stubbornness, said:

—You comin' or ain't you?

—Keep it down. You'll wake the baby!

—You really going to do it? Take the rope?

—If I go downstairs, they'll hear me. I'll have to wait for breakfast.

From under the radiator, there by the window, he pulled a heavy rope knotted at intervals. The looped end he slipped over his head, and tightened, beneath the armpits, like his dad had showed him.

Then he lifted the coils, grabbed a link near the radiator, and tugged at it hard as he could. The thing should hold.

Astraddle the third storey window sill Newell tried to steady himself before the push outward, breathtaking, into thin air. The idea made his sandy hair stand on end: the first instant suspended in space . . . ! His father had set up this fire escape, but not to use for the fun of it, and not to run away.

From the ground below Otter looked up, dubious. He bit his lip a little and said in his low voice made hoarse from swigging cough syrup:

—You better use the stairs.

—Shh, they'll hear you.

—Well, get on with it.

Newell stared down. His dad would wring his neck when he found out. And his mom, when she came outside and saw the knotted rope dangling down from the attic window, would feel hurt and very anxious, just like a mother, and say: Doll, what did we do wrong?

III

He gazed down at cedar tree branches fanned along the house. A brick chimney went up the outside: wider at the base then tapered, with a letter C in black bronze, but nobody knew what C meant, maybe a curse. He let out the knotted coils in a longer loop, longer. Then, for a moment, he leaned back in and thought: can't do it, why break my neck? But he considered his D in conduct, and the fact that he would not be promoted to sixth grade today; and the shame when his parents saw the rotten report card.

For his part The Otter—Otton-Karl Zwobuchowicz—knew he had flunked a few subjects and would have to stay back. But who wouldn't flunk: who could hope to do homework in such a madhouse? Always a mess, Otter's place, and mysterious: with a hundred drawers and closets crammed full of junk and Old World stuff. Then Aunt Serenity lost his schoolwork, his crumpled papers and notebooks; she put things away here, there, and then who could hope to find them? Also his lunch box sometimes: for they made him eat his sandwich at school, in the empty lunchroom by the back entry, while other kids skipped home for an hour, by shortcuts. At all hours, in the poor boy's house: wild political discussions about Poland's past; and these flared up into arguments, violence. And his Uncle Jan called out into the quiet suburban night: 'Truutzkiij!' Then his father pounded the kitchen table and shouted: 'Pilsu-u-udskiij!' And Aunt Serenity, white curly hair, a tear in her pinkish eye, Aunt wrung her hands, gave a little cry, and feared a tussle.

Otto and his dad threw tools at one another down cellar. And their Sunday drives for an ice cream cone had a savage note about them. Newell, bundled with Otter and Bobby Zwergli in the old Hudson's back seat, waited to see what would happen. At least he used to be invited on those outings: before he threw a rock through their front window on his way home from school one afternoon. He denied it, but he did it. Why?

So no quiet for study; no softness, no quarter for anyone in the Z family: not since the day they came and took Otto's mom away on a stretcher to the hospital.

And when Cousin Henryk came for vacation from scholarly pursuits at a West Coast university: then you heard classical music played very loud, and more long discussions. Cousin Henryk shined a flashlight at night on Otto not able to fall asleep: the boy half dressed in his little room also filled with stuff.

Who could study there?

Now Newell looked down from the attic window. A final instant he fought for composure, took a deep breath, counted one . . . two . . . three,—and then off. He was *out!*

IV

Dangling in space he jerked side to side, and hung onto the rope. He kicked, swung, and tried to catch his breath. He held the top knot for dear life. Climb back in?

—Watch out!—said his friend who moved underneath as if to catch him.—Grab the next knot!

Newell tried not to panic. He began to work downward, his arms, hands on fire as he jerked, clung to one, then one.

Finally he swung like a hanged man a few feet from the ground. Otter grappled him up and helped him get free: loosen the tight rope and lift it over his shoulders.

Newell said, even as he threw up on the grass:

—Let's go.

Behind them, as they scampered away, the thick rope settled alongside the house, twisting one way, a moment, then the other.

—My shoulder hurts.

—Where to? said Otter, and took out his cough syrup.

—Brooklyn.

—Why? Too far!

—I think we could become ball boys. Hey, I don't feel too good.

In the early morning they trotted along and took a shortcut by the brook which gave Spring Glen its name. The calm suburban homes had ample lawns, neat hedgerows, garden flowers in bloom. The two boys heard the first breakfast sounds, families astir, birds chirping in the trees, a dog's sappy bark down the block. The ten year-old fugitives from justice slowed their steps, and looked around, then at one another. Lush sunlight speckled the foliage. A soft breeze seemed to rock the new day's cradle. Run away? . . . Hey, no going back now. A woodpecker *toctoctoc'd* on a tree across the brook. A robin redbreast tugged up a worm, and peered around. Bees buzzed flower to flower. These busy bees the schoolboys caught in jars, punched air holes in the lid, then watched while the yellow jackets walked up the glass, interrupted in their work. How many could you catch in a mayonnaise jar?

Newell said:

—We might get promoted.

—Naw.

By his side Otto walked along, dogged, stubborn as hell. His hard head hung a little and swung to the rhythm of his steps: as he hopped a crack not to break his mother's back.

The brook's gurgle, the grass, flowers, birds' carefree notes made the boys feel sad, and seemed to lure them back.

—Be nice if we knew . . . I mean before we run away. I'd kind of like to give sixth grade a try. That Betty Lundgren has some pods on her.

For the past month it was a restless going to and from the pencil sharpener. Alerted boys moved behind The Lunger's desk and shot a glimpse down her shirt from behind. Theresa Tyrone, called Terrible

Typhoid, had 'em too, good pods. But Jane The Pain Gluck though plain for now, had more than pods. She had a set on her already and any boy would want to get her in a corner when the lights went out at Gray-Y. As for Lily Berryer: they moved him from behind her seat to the last row: he didn't know why. So one day the arrogant girl walked down the aisle, and he tripped her: she went flying with a cry. Newell's dad, when he heard this, laughed for once over his son's pranks and mentioned a philosopher who tripped and fell in a well when he was gazing up at the stars and a peasant girl laughed.

Some older Spring Glen girls, Rose Cody, Nana Loriot, Neesie Montowese—the legendary yet never seen Makarie Straiton loved by Charlie Björnsen and also the outsider Sim Curtis who could 'mess Spring Glen up', as Ned Parigi once said to Newell in the church-yard—these older chicks gave Newell a *feeling* when he crossed their path on his way to the Glendower for Spicedrops or Spearmint Leaves of an afternoon. And this sweet, darkish, older-girl desire also tinged his sense of the neighborhood. But, among girls in his class, Jane the Pain had by far the biggest pods.

—You might pass, said Otter. Me no.

—If only we could find out . . . I bet sixth grade wouldn't be so bad. Mr. Pyat's class, what a riot!

—I'll run away by myself. You stay.

Otter took a swig of the cough syrup, and had his damn stubborn look. Pudgy, with pink jowls, squinty eyes, often looking down, he outdid other kids in the class for cussedness just as Janie Gluck did for pods. You could not win with him. For instance, he never gave up in the contest of headlocks, even after his neck creaked, and most kids including Newell would yell: go get my mom! Otter's stubborn-ness was such: you'd have to kill him to get your point across.

—Look, I know. We'll stash ourselves in the coat closet while Miss Kenny calls off the roll. Warm weather, right? No coats.

—Cut it out. You nuts?

—If she don't call our names, lousy bum: we skip town.

—Call yours, not mine.

Otter swigged.

—Okay, okay. I'll go too. But why traipse all the way to Brooklyn when maybe we got promoted after all?

So they turned their steps toward the school. And, as they went along, an alarm clock went off, a shade popped up, a screen door opened to take in the milk. Spring Glen breathed in the sunlit day, the mid-June air scented with dew and mown grass and suburban earth. The two friends discussed their plan, bumped elbows, tried to laugh. They made their way early to school today: the last time they would have to sit in a cramped stuffy classroom until September. Okay, let's go: promotion day. Hourrah! and then summer, summer every darn day: wake up in the morning with interest in Peewee baseball, bicycle rides, rambles around Spring Glen, fishing and swimming in the Water Company until that goofball Crumley, town cop, came and chased you out.

But first they had to get through the ordeal. For the moment they tried to settle on a strategy, and Newell said to his friend:

—All for one, and one for all.

They got their signals straight before a desperate squeeze play in the bottom half of the ninth.

V

All roads led to Spring Glen Grammar School, as kids shot out front and back doors from nozzles, and livened up the neighborhood in moments after eight o'clock.

—So long, Ma!

—Bye, Shorty. See you at lunchtime.

—Awright.

—Please don't sing 'Old Gray Mare' outside Mrs. Luccock's house again. She called here and she didn't like it.

—Aw, Ma. Guy can't even have fun anymore. 'Old gray mare she ain't what she used to be, ain't what she used to be . . .'

Shorty hummed.

Kids played tag, teased, called names, threw dirt balls at each other along Ridgewood and Spring Glen Terrace, Churchill toward the brook. They jumped rocks across, and somebody always fell in (with a little help). Cries, laughter, singsong taunts: nana-nananah! Boy bugged girl. Over in the churchyard two hardheads had a wrastle and grass-stained their clean shirts and pants pressed for promotion day. Ritual of the headlock: some unfinished business even now at school year's end.

Groups formed up, bantered and capered, this last day of confinement in classrooms—on past the candy store, The Glendower, toward

Boys and Girls entrances at the school. Shortly they would make the solemn yearly passage, as a class, between old and new rooms. They would see their new teacher: a strict one? Or a Tim Pyat? Could they sail paper airplanes down into the schoolyard from second storey windows? Could they throw spitballs at a girl they had a crush on? Continue their policy of accumulating eraser shavings in their inkwells? Pass notes? Whisper between aisles? Read comics beneath their school books? Horse around? . . . Could they duly inspect the progress of pods in the brief time before brassieres? Oh, today they went to school in good spirits. One seventh grader said to another:

–Hey! You know the difference between a polliwog and a boa constrictor?

–I'll bite.

–One eats its tail, and the other tails its eats.

–Say! You make that up?

–Look Ma no hands.

–Regular comedian.

Behind the school kids flipped cards in a little alcove above the slope down to Water Company property, the long wire fence: Keep Out! You caught perch and some bass down there, but more bream, sunfish; a rare pickerel. You had old swimming holes for a cool skinny dip in summer; also poison ivy galore, which blistered between your fingers, and got on your balls.

After a moment the school bell rang. Kids turned from their games, and trotted inside to classrooms and the moment of truth.

Promoted to the next grade? Parents real proud? Maybe give you a graduation gift?

Or else left back in disgrace, a name on everyone's lips. Relegated to life with the class behind you: lose a year.

–I will sing 'Old Gray Mare' if that happens. I will! And ol' gray-headed Miss Luccock, sweet sixty-six and never been kissed, can like it or lump it, if they keep me back!

VI

Miss Kenny's voice had a catch to it, sort of warbled, when she made a few comments before the formal ceremony began. After Christmas she had gotten sick, and she didn't make it back until mid-

May for the last few weeks with her fifth grade class. Related to Sister Kenny (of the cancer research foundation) she had taught at grade school level for forty years. No paper airplanes wafted from her window like they did from the sixth grade teacher Big Tim Pyat; oh no, you bet! Strict, effective, she scolded Newell and kept him after school time and again, a bad boy among her favorites. But she laughed when he called her skirt a rug. After a bicycle accident, hit by a car up there at Ridgewood and Wilke Parkway, he came back from two weeks' absence with scabs on his face, and a limp. Then he felt her kindness.

Quietly, she said:

–The following students please take your belongings and form a line by the door. Lillian Berryer, Enoch W. Brown, Jr.

–Here!

–No need to say here.–Miss Kenny paused and glimpsed two empty seats toward the back. Then she looked out the second floor window: where blue sky, almost cloudless, spread to a hazy Sleeping Giant in the distance.–Rolland Bungya, Jr. Steadman Budd Chalmers, the Third. Howland Duggan, Jr. Elizabeth Erasmus. Deary! . . . Wake up.

Miss Kenny read off the names. But she paused. At the rear, to the right, stood a coat closet, and there must be a pretty good size mouse in there: to make the door rattle that way, when there was no breeze to do it. Maybe even a rat: trying to get himself an education, among the sets of textbooks, primers, readers, desk supplies, a few old coats, and other materials. Say, besides the cramped quarters, in there for over an hour, maybe two: Studiosus Rat might've worked up a hunger if he sneaked in here early to get an extra whack at the books.

–Thaddeus Floriani. Newell Gilbert–

–*Don't answer.*

–Hey, what the–?

Miss Kenny stopped in her tracks. A few heads turned, then others. For a voice, low, throaty, unlike a kid's, had just come from the back closet. Sure as shootin' it did: maybe a poor student kept back last year? and he hung himself in there for shame? and his ghost would wait year after year to have its name called and get promoted? Yes–or maybe just a boy who didn't get his homework done because he lived in a madhouse where Russia invaded Poland night after night and the alcohol content in cough syrup had affected his larynx so he spoke in such a low stubborn tone, and wheezed, and his head wobbled side to side when he walked.

—Newell Gilbert . . . Jane Gluck. Laurent N. M. Haas. Katrina Eva Hense. Ave Hornstein. Lingard F. Hovhannes. Parnell L. Kelleher. Ronald Kong. Mary Bettina Lundgren—
—Oh no! said a voice from the closet. Not The Lunger! I'd rather get *left back* than stay in this class with her!
Then the low rasp of Otter:
—Wait. If we don't hear my name, we'll run away.
Miss Kenny raised an eyebrow, but her blue eyes had a twinkle in her wan face.
—No talking, ahem. Franklin D. Lully—Canova. Willard Steuart. Randolph Mueller—
—Mooch! It's The Mooch. You mean Mooch Mueller passed too? I don't believe it. Head always bent down, like this. Spends his life looking for pennies and nickels, a fishhook or somebody's ABC-gum dropped in the gutter.
—I said don't talk . . . Rebecca Nalgas. Ellen Mae Neuterman.
Whispers, giggles. Eyes fixed Miss Kenny and waited; but here, there, a neck craned for a look back down the aisle. Those nutty guys . . . a pair of nuts! . . . Then the teacher paused: she lowered her roll-book a moment, and smoothed her skirt, and for just an instant her grayish face twitched and looked a little funny. But Miss K. bit her lip and went on. She continued to read the names, McCarthur R. Rand, Phillip C. Starr, Theresa Tyrone, Theodore Varnhagen, Ritter N. Whittington—and these sounded like a countdown. It was the end, on this day, of a marvelous teaching career. Robert Zwergli . . .
—Otton-Karol Zwobuchowicz!

VII

—Otto Zwobuchowicz—
—Otter . . . it's Ottokins . . . the big fool!
—Here! Here!
But they couldn't get out for some reason. Stuck inside! The coat closet doors banged, shook!
The class began to chant:
—Ot-to! Ot-to! Ot-to!
Suddenly the doors flung wide in a cascade of textbooks and primers, fifth grade readers, notebooks, manila folders, school sup-

plies, coat hangers. Two boys tumbled out and grappled; they fell over one another; they tried to stand.

 –Egad, man! said Miss Kenny. You there! Gad! Katzenjammer kids! On your feet this instant. What a mess you've made of my classroom.

 She looked, she spoke like each September: so strict. And she had that reputation: strict. But when the school year ended, she had hardly raised her voice, rarely disciplined, only taught them.

 –And you call yourselves budding scholars. No, you don't. Quiet, you people. Laughter only flatters them, two nitwits. Don't encourage them! Newell Gilbert, I think I'll call your father and let him handle this.

 –Yes, ma'am. I don't want that!

 –Now take your place in the line there, sir. Let's get this show on the road.

 And so they made the procession to next year's classroom. And the bad boys' eyes lit up when they turned left and walked toward Mr. Timothy Pyat's room, because now they knew many a paper airplane would sail and lilt its way groundward, like autumn leaves, from the second storey window. And students in the back would sneak on their knees to deliver a secret message, or fire a spitball at close range. And trips to the pencil sharpener would happen often: a regular field day as 'budding scholars' did research on pods, and wore down their points. Also, Mr. Pyat told some fairly weird stories, for kids to hear: about how a certain man woke up with a rare disease, and couldn't move a muscle: not even squeeze his toothpaste tube; then one day he was okay again.

 So the fifth grade class moved on to the sixth, and nobody stayed back. They went in the new room and took a seat, while sunlight poured in the high windows, and a morning breeze smelled sweet. Pyatkins began to talk about this or that matter with a gravity, a pedantry uncommon in elementary school teachers. He was sort of a hairy man: never quite shaven, his black hair combed, parted, greased up with Vitalis. He could ramble on for an hour, talk and talk,–good! It beat schoolwork.

 A new group filed in Miss Kenny's room as well; though she knew it wouldn't belong to her. In effect she retired the moment Otto Z., last one in line, taking a swig of cough syrup, stepped out past her threshold. But she stayed with the fresh class until school dismissed at noon, and then began to clean out her desk.

VIII

Kids shot with a whoop through the Girls and Boys doors into a wide expanse of summer days and sleeping late and doing just as you please. With a wave at monitors they scooted across Gordiane and up along Spring Glen's peaceful streets toward the brook and their favorite shortcuts. Blue sky, warm June day, green grass, shrubs, summer in store.

First stop for Otter and Newell: the Glendower. Nickel raspberry soda with milk (always curdled); hamburger on toast with ketchup; popsicle. This place had racks of yesteryear's candy like an archeological dig; and you got that feeling when you went in there: too old, maybe moldy. It lived out its time, pending a visit from the Board of Health. The owner, a pale man with soft wavy red hair, telephoned Mrs. Gilbert just a month ago when her son bought not a few packs but an entire box of baseball cards, a thing never done by a kid, and started giving them out to girls. Newell had got up early, snuck in his parents' bedroom, and stolen a twenty from his sleeping dad's dresser. Then, found out, he went under their bed and bawled and carried on to avoid punishment. And later today, when he got home, there would be more hell to pay: after he worried his mother sick, ran away, and left the fire escape rope dangling down the side of the house. You can be sure Anne Gilbert called the school by now. As for Otis, he'd get due punishment the instant he stepped inside his house,—Tru-u-utzkiij! . . . Pillsoo-oo-odzskiij!—in the normal course of things, no matter why.

But first, yep, you guessed it, they lit out for the Water Company. Down the hill, under the fence they scrambled. Chose a shady spot by the water and stretched out on the grass. The two boys blew great pink bubbles, pop! and licked the gum from their noses. They discussed poison ivy, sumac, and oak; also a Peewee game, up at Lavater Field, in two days. After awhile they stripped down and went for a swim in the cool, clean water. For an hour they laughed and splashed around and had fun. A soft breeze felt so good on their wet bodies when they finally came out. Through the sunlit, leisurely afternoon the water, like a river in this stretch, lolled reeds and grass tufts along its banks. A fish surfaced, plip, plip, for an insect. The two boys napped for a spell, and dreamt of Brooklyn, baseball cards, a summer recess that lasted forever. And no meddlesome cop came to bother them. Even that dunce Officer Crumley and everybody else in town, except themselves, knew they were happy.

IX

But leave it to The Otter: nearabout wrecked the good time. Now the heat was off about being promoted he went into one of his stubborn fits. Sat there on the riverbank staring straight ahead and refused to speak! Why? Who knows! For a full ten minutes he would not touch his fishing line though there were nibbles—he just went on pouting for all he was worth. Talk about obstinate! Whew!

I know it would take at very least a few million words to give even a merest hint of a hint of Otter's absolutely colossal stubbornness which is unparalleled in human history. Maybe on another planet there is something remotely comparable. But let's face it: the infinite cannot be stated or calculated; it can only be sung.

So I would sing:—O Muses that dwell on high Olympus, now tell me. What brought on this fit of Otto's mighty stubbornness? And the Muses chorus: We don't know. Well if Clio the Muse of History doesn't know, then jeepers, how would I?

Does his stubbornness at least relate to something in this story? No, not in the least. It has nothing to do with being promoted. Otter's stubbornness was stubborn about being stubborn, that is all.

So much for our hymn to the boy's prodigious and perverse hardheadedness. We will give it a rest for now; although the 600 pages of this volume might easily be devoted to it exclusively, a legend—as Otis walks along wobbling his bowed head in defiance of the wide world.

Say, is all this boring you a little? If there is one thing on earth more boring than Otter's stubbornness, it is talking about it, which I think he loves—in others, that is: he would never admit he's stubborn.

Well, perhaps as we go along thinking of other things, the mystery will reveal itself as to why the boy was such a mule: usually in the wrong, objectively, but perversely persisting. For instance: let's say you offered to do something for Otter, to help him out in some small way. Forget it! He would hold out against being helped until the bitter end. I don't think Otto had ever read Dostoyevsky, but he would surely feel right at home in those perverse pages. It was his idea of deepest degradation ever to be helped—say by some kind soul like New-boy's mom. Otto could not abide the implications of being lent a friendly hand. Why, good night! . . . Oh he would help *others*, and act nobly here and there in future years, but that *too* was from stubbornness, I'll bet.

For now we'll just say the two boys had fun on the whole, as they lounged on the banks of the placid Water Company that day. Insects buzzed. Fish went plip! amid the sunlit ripples. Warm breeze felt good on a boy's skin after a long lazy swim. The grass smelled good too.

Hummingbird. TNT.

I

In the colorful box of fireworks: what was that cylindrical object? The mean, mysterious, lethal looking firecracker ... Was it really TNT like Newell's dad said? Could it blow up the house if detonated in the basement by mistake? Wow! TNT! Better clear out fast when someone lit that baby's fuze.

The neighbors found it a little strange when Emory Gilbert went in for July 4th fireworks displays. A professor, regimented in his daily life, a bit prone to discuss insurance policies, health problems, the burglar alarm on his front door—Emory paid a yearly visit to a store somewhere, and went wild. A week or ten days before the Fourth, Newell's dad brought home boxes filled with bright paper bags and cellophane packages: pyrotechnical devices, every type and size.

There were foot long ladyfinger strips attached by their fuzes like coats of mail. Not inconsiderable the racket they made across the neighborhood, on a quiet July night. Also called: salutes.

There were the louder Chinese, in packets with Chinese characters on the labels. Louder than the ladyfingers, more assertive, you'd better run if you lit one: flip it quick. And duds were worth collecting.

Loose in a paper bag, like (hot cinnamon) fireballs, were a few dozen cherry bombs.

—With these, gentlemen—said Dr. Gilbert—things get serious!

And then came an array of noiseless fireworks: each with its bright swirling pattern to light up the festive summer night. Spectacular skyrockets and Roman candles; also sparklers by the sheaf.

But one other, nondescript item, encased in gray, lay among the sampler of July 4th goodies.

–TNT, said Newell, and pursed his lips.

–Don't touch it, said his dad. Demolish the house.

Then the whole mess went down cellar, where Newell had his rumpus room. If those firecrackers ever caught fire they could indeed blow up the place. Luckily, the boy had passed through his fire phase: when he lit match boxes, cremated Japanese beetles, set the old doghouse alight: after Sandy the cocker spaniel died and Newell felt guilty since he never ceased tormenting the poor faithful thing– and not least by these firecrackers which murdered the dog's ears, and made the lazy fellow bark like he had a devil in him. A babysitter, one of Emory's students, once told Newell:

–Don't hurt him. A dog has feelings.

–No, he doesn't. How do you know?

–If you step on his foot, he'll yelp. Right?

II

After lunch Newell took a book out beneath a tree. Later on Otter, Thaddy, or Willard Steuart would come by; and they'd head up to Lavater Field, pick up kids along the way, and choose sides. After that: the Glendower for a few popscicles. But right now a little reading made him sleepy. There was hardly a stir in the hot afternoon, as he lay on the grass beneath a tree: only the sweet scent of lawns and hedges baked by the sun, and sprinklers' rhythmic spurt. A bee buzzed. A cricket fiddled. A breeze went among the leaves briefly, without conviction. He dozed off.

Voices woke him from inside the house, the kitchen. He stayed still a moment and listened: his mom, then Cliff, then–William Johnny! Cliff's grandson hadn't come over since the bicycle incident: that day they took an old bike to the Black section in Harmonium, and found William Johnny–riding one! So they turned around and drove back home, and next day Emory accused Cliff of lying; but Cliff chuckled and said he had seven grandchildren under his roof, and three bicycles and one tricycle to go around; but never mind, thanks for the kind thought.

In general Cliff went about his housework, dusted and swept, responded to Anne Gilbert's call. He had a lean, angular face, and grayish frizzy hair. In summer heat, in winter cold, he wore a rusted dress shirt frayed at the cuffs, a hundred years old, with suspenders and gabardine trousers half an ell too short for him. At least in his seventies, he had a hitch to his walk whether from cleaning and scrubbing, or long years he played in the Negro Leagues. Now Cliff seemed powered by a steady banter with himself beneath his breath: quiet huffs, then a chuckle in between. Get on with it; well, why hurry. Some world we got hyieh', worth a little laugh between dustings.

—You'll wake the baby!—he always said to raucous Newell; or:—I see, said the blindman . . .

In general his stories couldn't relieve a kid's boredom, but Newell followed him around as the next best thing. Yes, yessuh, he'd caught ol' Satch; and Cliff held out his fingers gnarled by foul tips, to prove it. One afternoon Newell came in and called Cliff a bad name, bad: that's right, the ugly one, something he picked up in the schoolyard and now tried it out on the workingman. So Anne Gilbert hit the roof, and Newell sort of realized; the way you give pause after you hurt someone you care for, and it might not be repaired. He didn't do it again, and they just went along as before: Cliff Gardin the same, interested in him, never moody or negative like his dad; but only going about the housework, fidgety with his duster yet calm, manly despite a few rags hung from his hip pocket. The way he said certain words made the boy's nose wrinkle: bird, third, world. These sounds Cliff said his own way; and the pronunciation, the tone seemed to contain a world.

Stories about Satchell Paige, a Stars-Cardinals benefit game probably in the late 'Twenties, compared with Jackie Robinson, Peewee Reese and Campy, Furillo and Junior Jim something like school books to the complete set of 1954 baseball cards. Reality versus the spectacular, the fetishized.

Also, an eleven year-old could only get so much mileage from curious speech patterns or cultural differences. What did tickle him, the moment he got around it, was the way Cliff related to William

Johnny. He couldn't have said why; he didn't even think it; but their easy talk, naturalness, made him feel a sort of—what? Hard to describe; a little painful, like a hunger.

—You'll wake the baby!

III

At age ten William Johnny wasn't a big kid physically; but he had something big, or big*ger,* about him. When they climbed trees, Newell hung and jumped from the lowest limb; while William Johnny, on a slender maple tree branch, up there—tilted, out further, and fell from near the summit. He hit the ground, rolled and got up unhurt, while Newell's eyes popped out. And this without fanfare, casually, the way he might play in the NFL someday. He didn't brag; though his lesser deeds beat anything you might see, unless maybe by Willard Steuart, in the Spring Glen Grammar schoolyard. Even the way he ate Anne Gilbert's lamb cake had a style to it: he even ate like he meant it, while Newell rarely had much appetite except for Bonomo's Turkish Taffee, or Milk Duds.

—How's a' go? said William Johnny, in the kitchen.

—Whatcha' got there?

Cliff's grandson looked up dreamily from a second slice. In all things, even when he licked a crumb, here, there, from his fingertips, he had that air about him Newell couldn't quite get over: like a reflection from the serene Cliff, so unlike his own crotchety dad, Emory.

Usually they went down the block to Dinghy Chalmers' bigger yard on Churchill. 'Throw the bat' for first licks: fist over fist to the knob; squeeze two, three fingers in; then swing the bat, three times, over your head, and throw.

—You gotta' hit southpaw.

William Johnny lofted a fly over the house across the street.

—Hit crosshanded. You'll break a window.

Poom! A drive plunked off the Tudor house, Luccocks', on the corner: just missed the antique front window, stained glass, worth a fortune.

Often they played together in the backyard, or at Chalmers', but maybe not today. For William Johnny had brought something of more interest along.

—Whatcha' got there?

—Gun.

—What kind? Can I see it?

—Beebee.

—Well, we got TNT.

—What?

—TNT, you know, blow up the place.

This went far beyond air rifles. But William Johnny only raised his eyebrows a little, and sketched a smirk.

—I got an idea, said Newell. Let's go hunting.

—Hunt what?

—Our neighbors shoot squirrels off the roof . . . Or else Mrs. Luccock, sunning in her bikini, on the veranda.

—You crazy.

—C'mon, we'll hunt!

IV

William Johnny toted his beebee gun as the two boys started out through the Gilberts' garage, and turned left down an alleyway between homes on this block. Here you had backyards sloped down from Spring Glen Terrace, the next street up; and, when snow started to fall sometime after Thanksgiving, and reached a boy's knees in no time, snow packed hard in the winter cold, then kids made a trail along here, and sledded to their hearts' content, and nobody minded. But on this summer afternoon the sunlight speckled among trees, shrubs, viny trellises in the spacious yards bordering the alley. Crickets sang. Flies buzzed around. Grasshoppers jumped before the boys' steps, and William Johnny said wrily:

—Boom! TNT.

Newell suggested they go shoot up Mrs. Luccock, the old gray mare, since she liked to phone people's moms and tattletale. William Johnny said maybe a rabbit; or better: pin a target to a tree—so they could get this business over and go take a few cuts at Chalmers Field:

with its hedgerow like a left field fence, its deep center field, and willow tree in right.

Toward Luccocks' house on the corner Newell stalked, an evil leer in his eye as he thought over ladies' bikinis. But suddenly William Johnny stopped, and raised the gun.

Perched on a twig, its nervous frenzy stilled just an instant, a hummingbird looked around. Then it took flight and hummed, buzzed, like a super-insect, right beside them.

–Look! said William Johnny. It can fly backwards.

The tiny bird, three or four inches high, hovered, put its needle-like bill to a flower, and sucked nectar. Then it disengaged; and the two boys saw it pick off a bug while on the fly. The hummingbird darted, wings a blur; it poised in the air a few feet away, unaware of any danger, so intense. Its underparts looked grayish-white; the chest, upper parts, a metallic green. Constantly in motion, it darted here, there. Then, the small bird's throat went a ruby red—hit, not by a beebee, but a ray of sunlight, as it turned.

–Get it!

William Johnny just stared at the bit of a thing, proud in its iridescent plumage, and held his gun.

–Gimme! Newell whispered, fiercely, and looked like he'd bust a gut.

Newell took the beebee gun and shot, shot. The bird made its sudden displacements, hovered, darted. Poom! Poom, poom! The boy sited along the barrel, and shot again. This time the bird's tremendous wings spluttered; it went sideways, and, after an instant, fell.

They laughed.

–You got him, said William Johnny.

The tiny bird spun, wobbled on the ground, like a top. It fought to rise again.

Newell shot. Poom! Poom! The kill took a few more shots, as each beebee sank into the tender skin. And the bird fluttered.

Then it lay there. Not the bright ruby patch, but a few drops of blood streaked the greenish feathers, bristly now. Newell stared at the dead thing, capsized on a patch of gravel: its eyes like two black beebees. He had never killed anything—more than pesky mosquitoes; a few hundred flies swatted like ping-pong, on the kitchen door screen, in his summer boredom; the mini-Hiroshima he conducted each year in his mom's garden: beetles doused with lighter fluid, and lit up. Bees caught in jars he usually let go after a day or so, unless they just fell out when he opened the cover. Whittington said you shouldn't kill even an ant, and got all excited when you stepped on a red ant—not to mention a whole anthill, which Newell had done, trampled the little suckers more than once, in his time. Also, he pretty much hounded the cocker spaniel Sandy into an early grave, made that dog's life a hell: that's why one night the babysitter, his father's student, posed the question as to whether a dog had feelings, and Newell answered:

—No.

Then Sandy up and died on him. And they wrote the mutt's name on cement next to the garbage cover, there by the kitchen door; also the years: 1946–1953. Let's see, seven times seven—short life for a sappy, lazy bones cocker spaniel, always to be found in the house's coolest niche on the hot days: tongue lolled out a half mile, lost look in the soft brown eyes. Yep, a brief, unhappy life for this dog grown up with Newell since a puppy—brief but heroic, and, thanks to the young master, filled with turmoil. Sandy died, and Newell burned down the old dog house. Blamed his victim.

Now he stared down at the hummingbird.

—Let's play some ball, said William Johnny.

—Shouldn't we bury it?

He scuffed a bit of dust and gravel over the ruffled feathers.

V

Ice cream for everybody: scooped out by the gracious Anne Gilbert with a smile. Kids for three blocks around showed up for July 4th festivities and because Newell boasted he had TNT and might blow up Mrs. Luccock's house. Everybody wanted to see that. Green pistachio dripped, this warm summer evening, from Ricky Williams' nose; while a few older boys sat on the curb and talked about girls. Robby Zwergli, from Newell's class, said a hot chick starts to 'heave' if you rub her shoulder—you got to do it over and over—in the movies. Also, the group noted a new girl just moved in the neighborhood, up on Lorelei Road; and then Newell heard Gemma's name for the first time. But Gemma wouldn't attend Spring Glen Grammar; no, her wealthy parents (to judge by the house they bought) had enrolled her in a private day school. But once a girl from the Children's Center, an orphan, snuggled up behind Newell in the movie theater there in Mt. Sorrel and he felt her curly hair on his neck, and her breath.

Tin cans soared up in the twilight from the impact of Chinese placed under them. Ladyfingers, or salutes, thudded staccatto in a skirmish down the hill toward the brook. Meanwhile Professor Gilbert sat with a colleague by the ivy roundel out front and discussed the political conventions this summer, Stevenson versus Dewey, I Like Ike; also something about the Korean War, and Syngman Rhee's pleading with Washington for an all-out attack on the North.

Kids ran around the yard high on firecrackers and their third, fourth ice cream scoops. Ricky Williams looked drunk; he spilled his cone, plah! like vomit on the ground; and Dinghy Chalmers laughed the little kid out of town: called him pistachio face and a dumb cluck. Big Rick had had a cosmetic operation on his ears: pinned 'em back. God, what pain he went through, what a crybaby he became just so his ears wouldn't stick out. Took all the gumph out of him. Might've made a pretty good little second baseman, too.

As daylight faded from the neighborhood, sparklers ssss-sssss'd and upstaged the fireflies. Then, at nightfall, the adults got involved. Skyrockets shot skyward with a whistle, streamed pink, yellow, orange, green, and went out. Fireballs zoomed in circles like vicious blue bugs. And cherry bombs went off, boomah! and made dogs howl and wish they had never been born.

Then came a lull. Too quickly the year's supply gave out. But there remained the large gray cylinder, TNT, held up for inspection by Professor Gilbert. Hm! Oohs, aahs greeted its menacing aspect, its size and color: this member of the bomb family. What destructive potential it must possess! What a beauty! C'mon, let's march on Mrs. Luccock's.

Naw, leave the old gray mare alone. Now who will do the honors, and light it? Maybe a good job for the fearless William Johnny? But Cliff Gardin and his grandson hadn't come to Spring Glen for the July 4th celebration. In Harmonium they had their own things going on.

—Let me, Dad!

Newell looked so unhappy then, and did a little hurdy-gurdy dance alongside his dad. So moody these past few days: his only in-

terest in life seemed that TNT canister. Anne Gilbert wanted him to
light it. She had a curious thing for a mother: out of the house,
please—she told her two sons—experience life, have adventures. One
day Gilly Posa, the bully, came by with a few friends and started to
push Newell around. Earlier, down the block, Newell had got a boy
one grade younger in a headlock, while Billy, who had provoked the
fight, just stood there; but now they came for revenge. And Anne
only watched it from her second floor window; she didn't intervene
since she wanted her son, even though worsted, in tears, to stand on
his own. Well, she already had one big baby in the house to take care
of, and that was enough: her prominent husband.

Now Emory suggested their older son light the TNT. Joey, always
aloof, into his sports, just shrugged and said he'd do it.

Then Anne brought up the time when, on a fishing expedition
out at Plum Gut, Newell hooked into a bluefish, and Emory took the
rod-and-reel away and landed the big fish himself.

—Let him light it this time—she laughed, and patted her husband's
shoulder.

VI

So the boy took the forbidding thing in one hand, a matchbox in
the other, and turned toward the far end of the Gilberts' yard.

—Just light the long fuze—said Emory behind him—and git!

—Careful not to trip! said Anne.

A moment later, in the darkness, all looked out for the lit fuze: an
orange spec over there by the alleyway. But the parents felt anxiety,
and called:

—Son, get away!

—Run, Newell!

For some reason he lingered. Slowly, he backed away from the
crackling orange fuze. As though he didn't hear people call to him
from across the yard: he crouched not very far from the expected
explosion.

Then the voices hushed, and the sky went aglow with color: first
yellow, like a sun rising at night above the neighbors' place across the
way. Then green, wow! green as money: enough cash to buy boxes

and boxes of baseball cards at the Glendower, scads of 'em. Then blue—blue color of hope, blue as the sea on a bright summer day, when life seems pure, as though ready to begin again. And then red: a full, vivid red suffused the air, and tinged everything for blocks around.

—Why didn't they make it red, white and blue?

—Just didn't, dummy, that's all.

—Sometimes they doosit, and sometimes they doosn't.

The crowd in Gilberts' yard, old and young, saw a boy jump up and down, his arms outstretched. He seemed to dance: outlined against the red aura.

What they didn't see, what only Newell could see, was a stick driven in by the spot where he lit the Roman candle. This marked the site of the hummingbird's grave.

Then the glow went out. It appeared to fall earthward, like pinkish cinders. The July 4th celebration returned to darkness. But for a moment it had an ice creamy awe, vanilla flavored, pistachio like Ricky Williams' nose, or raspberry, my favorite.

Then you saw the stars. And, far beneath them, if you cared to look, the hummingbird's funeral monument burned away silently in the summer night.

Spring Glen Boys

I

Now why, pray tell, did Gemma have a tear on her cheek when Newell Gilbert finally took her in his clumsy arms for a fox trot toward the end of Capers?

All evening long she hadn't deigned to speak with him, let alone dance; though they sat side by side at the pre-dance dinner. For some reason the organizers had fixed them up, a blind date with his true love. And then she ignored him.

Did she hold his gaucherie against him—still a Spring Glen boy, a public school kid at heart, even if his dad made him attend a private school for guys only, as she did for girls? Maybe she resented his remark about Willard Steuart, as they sat there in silence during the dinner. And after, when they got in the car for the ride to the Lawn Club, and two already sat in front, three in back including Gemma: he barged next to her anyway, in the backseat, and crushed her legs. Ow! Really now: you call that savoir vivre?

So, once in the hall, as Lester Lanin's romantic strains wafted about them, she let him go check their coats, and took off. She made a beeline for guys more her style: Jarrold Ventnor's son, Heaton, or 'Heatie', and his prim friend Albie Ford, who once, lips twisted in a vicious grin, said to Newell:

—I know guys like you.

As for the Spring Glen boy, his night didn't prove a total waste. For Ginny Barry, also pretty but older, built like a brick shithouse at age fifteen—not pods anymore by a long shot—Ginny danced close with him, not once, but twice. She also seemed a little sad, with her white ruffled dress, and lifelong burden of breasts. But her sadness, or boy weariness, didn't pose a question the same way as Gemma's tear.

Well then: to explain this mystery we must go back a year, and spend another few moments in Newell Gilbert's paradise, namely sixth grade at Spring Glen Grammar School. Let us try; although, in the last analysis, who can hope to understand—these women!

II

In the schoolyard boys were catching leaves. A warm October breeze was just right; it rippled a little; and they called for the falling leaves like fly balls.

—I got it!

—Mine, you jerk!

—I called it: make way!

—Go ahead then, selfish pig. Ah ha, nana-nananahhh! You missed it.

Leaves fell, shimmery in sunlight. The yellow, red and orange autumn leaves darted down hard to catch, off nature's bat hitting clean-up. They twisted from your grasp, they rode over your head, they wafted, dipped, spun from your fingertips. The outfielders patted their palms and settled for the basket catch like Willie Mays. Not that easy! And one, snotnosed Ritter (God! Look at him dribble snot) ran smack into a tree trunk like Pistol Pete Rieser.

Side by side a series of frantic, jerky grasps, and a leaf eluded Otter's fingers clutching air.

—Error!

—Use two hands!

—Thinks he can play ball drunk on cough syrup.

Dinghy Chalmers took caught leaves from his hip pocket and counted them like dollar bills.

Bungya bawled like an ump at Dinghy:

–I saw that one on the ground back there. You picked it up!

–I did not.

–Hand mashie! Cheater!

–Keep it up, and you'll need a lawyer.

–Liar, liar, pants on fire!

Robby Zwergli got a good jump down the bank, dove flat on his belly into a pile of leaves, and came up grinning with the leaf in question: the one that never touched the ground.

He held it high for the fans.

–How about that!

–Trap! cried Willard Steuart. You trapped it.

Mooch Mueller lumbered a few strides and called:

–Can o' corn, can o' corn.

The Mooch stretched his sweatshirt wide, like an apron, and gathered in the fly.

–Hey! Haas cried out, beside himself. You can't do that! Put it back!

–Yeah! Kelleher yelled. Go look for bent pennies.

Mooch had an uncanny knack for finding things in the gutter on his way home from school. He took his leaves home.

Other kids flipped new football cards in the alcove. Around the schoolyard girls skipped rope or played hopscotch; they talked and giggled and exchanged glances. Everyone made the most of these few free minutes. Ran, yelled, laughed.

But Newell stopped. He called to Willard Steuart:

–Me 'n Otis went up to Gemma's last night. Snuck around in the bushes. We saw her through the window.

Willard Steuart turned away, and dove desperately down the hill after a leaf. But Zwergli, Kelleher, Hovhannes took interest. For they had gone up there to Lorelei; they too sneaked around in the bushes for a glimpse of Gemma. And now they paused, and looked up the hill at their classmate; they squinted in the bright early afternoon, still warm enough for shirtsleeves, another few days as Halloween approached. Bungya, Kelleher, Lenny Hovhannes, Robby Zwergli seemed to see the new girl then: her few freckles and smile, her hair light brown, with an autumnal sheen seen, in the lamplight, by those who lurked in the bushes beneath her living room window. What was it about her? How did she do that–bring all this new stuff up in a boy, and make him dream? Gemma's image made a lovable russet

leaf caught high above their outstretched palms by the fall day and
the wind.
    –Come up to my house on Halloween!–her smile said to them.–
I'll give you a trick, and a treat.
    The school bell rang. Lunch recess ended. Here and there hard-
caught leaves fell to the ground from distracted fingers. Spring Glen
boys were falling in love left and right at mention of Gemma's name.

III

    She lived on Lorelei Rd., just off Newell's street, Santa Fe, in a
large red brick home with Tudor touches, amid the tall trees, artistic
garden plots, shrubs. Her father looked like a good guy, one day,
when Newell saw him in Floriani's Pharmacy: bit of a Scottish high-
lander with his green felt cap, burst capillaries on his reddish cheeks,
and something upbeat, family mannish, in the voice. But her mother
had not developed a fondness for Spring Glen boys, and called the
police on Willard Steuart and company, marauders lurking in the
shadows to ravish away her daughter. Luckily Gemma gave them a
sign from the living room window; and so the sixth-graders, led by
Steuart, hightailed it down to the brook. There they watched for coppers, the truant officer Crumley and his cronies; they whispered:
'shifting lights!' as a car bucked over a rut down the hill (all cop cars
had shifting lights). Then, after an hour's hiding out in the duct
where the brook flowed under Santa Fe, the boys reemerged covered
head to foot in grime. A good thing these suitors, Steuart, Kelleher
and Haas, didn't pay their calls in evening dress. And then, after ten
p.m., they scattered toward their homes like hunted men, in and out
of the shadows along the quiet suburban streets. But Gemma's mom
wouldn't spare them. And it didn't thrill her when Spring Glen boys
called the house, and had nothing better to say for themselves than a
giggle, or some other sound. Worms, snails, and puppy dogs' tails!
    Yet she should have been grateful. Her daughter's effect on them
created a diversion; it softened, or sentimentalized, their idea of Halloween. Who could describe, besides a war correspondent, the destruction done by these juvenile delinquents on the nights before

Halloween? For example on clothesline night, the year before, Newell and an Otter soused on cough medicine cut lengths from 72 clotheslines. On garbage night, the Tuesday before Halloween, Mooch Mueller and Bungya dumped garbage on the wrong person's front porch, and got themselves soaked with a hose for their efforts. Hardly a Spring Glen doorbell escaped pinning. But what shall we say about the quiet, aloof sixth-grader called Rand? He suddenly went berserk and javelin'd someone's clothesline tree on top of their garage! And Dinghy Chalmers teamed up with Enoch Brown,—both good boys—unheard of!—to vandalize the Craylings' new house on Ridgewood; and they got Newell to join in the second day; and so, innocent for once, or almost, he became 'accessory after the fact' when the police got involved, and his parents had to pay money.

Hopefully, this year, Halloween wouldn't get so out of hand. Gemma's presence had a civilizing effect, by and large, on these young hoodlums; and so they might not 'mess up Spring Glen', like bad news Sim Curtis, the outsider, when he tried to impress the inaccessible beauty, Makarie Straiton. No; this year they had higher things in mind, and they hardly observed the twelve nights before Halloween: streetlamp night, parked car night, pets night, mail slot night, garage night, telephone night, Old Gray Mare night, fire alarm night, phony deliveries night, clothesline night, garbage night, doorbell night. No, Halloween '54 they cooled their act, good boys, in love with the new girl. And what thanks did they get? They left the neighborhood in peace these evenings, and Gemma's mom sicked the goon squad on them, and pooped their party. Yet they only wanted a glimpse of Gemma: to bask in her smile and marvel at her auburn ponytail, her few freckles, where they huddled under the window sill, in the glow from a living room lamp. For Gemma was sweet and lovely, unlike their female classmates in Mr. Pyat's classroom: The Lunger, and Terrible Typhoid, and Janie who bought a brassiere just to spite her admirers, so now they couldn't see anymore, on their trips to the pencil sharpener, those superior pods become full-fledged female breasts. Such Spring Glen girls, or crows, merited all the noogy attacks they got on their way home past The Glendower after school. But Gemma, the new girl far above all that: her they wouldn't tease. Oh no. For she had a smile that grabbed a boy where it doesn't hurt: not in the place where puberty occurs, like a polliwog eating its tail; but at the heart, the boyish goodness also shyly eager for a way to develop, somehow.

IV

One day Newell came within a few feet of her: passed her by just as free as you please, on his way home from Lavater Field. At the corner of Lorelei and Santa Fe Avenue she straddled her bike, a skinny kid, just another girl at that distance, in broad daylight; and he could easily have started a conversation if he had anything to say. Just another girl, and so he had nothing special to tell her. Now if it had been Rose Cody, or Neesie Montowese with the derrière—whew! That might have loosed his tongue which some already called 'glib'. But no, it was just a nice kid sister type with light brown hair and a few freckles, so he coasted past and on down the hill.

Still, he took her image with him back to his attic room, and dedicated his action games and his little studies to her. He thought of her presence three blocks up the street when he went to sleep at night, and got up in the morning, and felt more eager, because she existed, for another day.

In the schoolyard, on Halloween day, the boys caught leaves. They flipped cards in the alcove.

—Leaner! I win.

The girls ran about too, and talked in groups, and ran some more. Haas let a leaf fly past and said to The Zwerg:

—I feel kind of hard-up since The Pain got a bra.

—Katy Hense's coming along well.

—Yeah, but I like Janie's. Maybe I could offer her candy.

—Careful, said Robby. Don't do that. They'll take you away like they did Wiley DeWitte.

Hm: a name nobody said anymore. Wiley DeWitte with the strange thing about him . . . better not say what he did. And he disappeared from view, in Spring Glen, a few months ago; but everybody knew his older sister went down and hung around the train station. In a minute the worldly wise Robby Zwergli would start talking about the big kid named Gil McQuinn: another Spring Glen scandal, phew! some years ago. And McQuinn disappeared from the scene too.

Haas said:

—You heard about the pictures with you know who? She got in trouble.

Zwerg:

—Naw, only rumors, exaggerated. She's nothing like the famous Susie.

Whittington joined them:

—What Susie?

Zwergli often spoke suave words about girls: how they 'heaved' in the movies, if you could get your arm around them, and rub 'em, in the right spot. Now he preened his maturity, and started to explain for Haas, Lenny, Teddy Varnhagen, Rand, all about the famous scandal involving a teenage girl and a bunch of Yalies, undergraduates.

—She performed 'lascivious carriage' on them.

—She what?

—What-what?

Chorus of whats, aahs.

Newell, breathless from running, joined the group to listen. And Willard Steuart took in a few words, but then saw a leaf, wafted high, high by the year's last warm breeze. Steuart called it: mine! I've got this one! and then dashed down the hill, dove, rolled, and made a miraculous grab. As for Newell, he went to his afternoon classes wondering about Zwergli's words, and the girl named Susie. What did she, and the sad story about Wiley DeWitte, have to do with Spring Glen? What did such things mean? It made him blush to compare what he knew about sex: how his dad came up to the attic, one night, after Newell had said the word 'sexy' at the kitchen table during supper. And then Emory Gilbert, the public speaker, the man never at a loss for words, gave his son the most awkward talk punctured by silences: all about 'sticks and doughnuts', and women's breasts (you must never, ever hit them). And that, somehow, was as it should be: things difficult to say, between father and son, things with an aura about them, when you really meant them. And, next morning in the schoolyard, Newell beckoned to Thad Floriani:

—Psst! psst! Listen to this!

Birds and bees, a first lesson. Not at all like hacking around after school, when the long confinement made you say any old curse word and then laugh:

> *Fatty and Skinny had a race*
> *Round and round the pillowcase.*
> *Skinny stole Fatty's underwear,*

> *Fatty's flabby ass was bare.*
> *Fatty told Skinny: Me no care,*
> *Me go buy another pair.*

Or else:

> *Lady of Spain I adore you,*
> *Pull down your pants I'll explore you.*

Or:

> *Oh! The monkey wrapped his tail around the flagpole*
> *To sniff his a-hole, to lick his a-hole.*

Or:

> *Here comes the bride*
> *Fair, fat and wide.*
> *Here comes the groom,*
> *Skinny as a broom.*

Or:

> *Happy birthday to you,*
> *You belong in the zoo.*

Etc. No big deal, just kidding. But this stuff about Wiley and his sister, and strange McQuinn, and notorious Susie: this made Newell think. Such things were not as they should be, for Spring Glen boys and girls.

V

Early on Halloween a few young mummers met at the Gilberts' house. Costumes counted less than in years past, or else in a different way, as persons began to emerge from the ghosts and goblins of childhood. Really these rough and ready boys had outgrown trick-or-treating, though not free candy; and so they turned the event into something a little bit different.

Otter came dressed in a shabbiness: old beat-up hat and grease-stained work clothes. He swigged cough syrup, tottered on purpose, and called himself The Bowery Bum.

Bungya wore Farmer John overalls and carried a rake. Commercial signs hung front and back to advertise his family's landscaping business.

Dinghy, or: Steadman Budd Chalmers, III, related to the House of Chalmers, investment bankers at Broad and Wall, in New York, took a notion to dress up like a homeless man, and panhandle for his candy.

But Thad Floriani's costume beat all, for authenticity, a macabre beauty. Thaddy, already beginning to feel himself as an artist, dressed up like the Sistine Madonna copied from a reproduction on his bedroom wall. Now I ask you: is this suitable for a twelve year-old on Halloween? Leave it to Gertruda 'La Furia' Floriani's son to go trick-or-treating as a transvestite. No joke for the conservative 'Fifties! But Thaddy always had his own ideas.

Phillip Starr, Flipper, the future astronomer, went as—well, what else? A star. The blond Flipper's five luminous points went out from a silken black outfit with sequins to look like the night sky.

Whittington came in boxes painted silver, a robot. He could hardly walk: much less run, if some homeowner roused by events the past twelve nights had a mind to pour boiling water down on these little devils from a second floor window.

Lenny Hovhannes put on his baseball catcher's equipment and called it a Halloween costume. From his mask hung a pair of big dice since he spent his after-school time playing dice baseball.

Believe it or not: Robby Zwergli, the sex fiend who knew all about why women 'heave', came dressed up as a book—*The Kinsey Report*.

And then Enoch and Kelleher, Teddy Varnhagen, Mooch Mueller, Ronnie Kong, Haas, et al, showed up in turn with white sheet, skull and bones, broom, witch's mask, snake hair. Newell Gilbert, tarot cards in hand, put on a mask and a sign: Fortune Teller.

Last to arrive was Willard Steuart; and his costume was a surprise. In real life Steuart, descendant of Scottish highlanders like Gemma's dad, had wavy auburn hair, rugged features, a reputation for manly courage. But here he came dressed up, with help from Thad Floriani, as a lovelorn clown, Pierrot from the Commedia dell' Arte. Lips arced, a tear on his pale bluish cheek, Steuart had a pathos the way he mooned about and laughed sadly to himself. He put a hand to his heart as though it had an ache.

VI

Anne Gilbert gave them a little party, cider and hot crullers, and each boy got a Polaroid photo of himself. Then Newell's sister Evelyne had the boys bob for apples, and play a few quaint little games: old pagan practices that survived, as she told them, from the Middle Ages when Hallowmass, or All Hallows, marked winter's beginning.

Then the Spring Glen boys piled out the door, one after another, like a stampede. Laughter, cries: they went into the chill night and felt November's breath on their scruffy necks.

Jack-o'-lanterns flickered in front windows along Santa Fe. High in the sky a sickle moon hung from a cloud's frayed edge. Amid the houses, trees and shrubs, the wind sang its doleful song like a Celtic rune. A frazzled cry, a haggard shriek! Masked bands lurked among the lurid shadows tinged with orange.

Witches, ghosts flitted. Set loose on the suburban neighborhood with its ancient tribal superstitions, these dreadful spooks hallooed. A few pre-schoolers, hand in hand with their parents, lingered late and hoo-hooed, like vexed spirits from the pallid cerements of their diapers. And the moon looked down, like a wise man's lean visage, with a wisp of beard, and seemed to frown at such a deal of candy.

But a few older boys waylaid the mummers on their way up the hill toward Gemma's on Lorelei. They stepped from behind trees and peppered the sixth graders with pea shooters. The heartsick clown Steuart counterattacked, quite out of character for Pierrot, and drove the bullies back. But he caught a pea in his right eye, and went to one knee, while the ambushers fled because maybe they had really hurt someone, and done a bad thing.

VII

—Uh, hullo, uh—

—Ma'am, so sorry to bother you.

—I, hm, could we trouble you for a, um, trick or treat?

—Of course, if it's any inconvenience, Ma'am, we could come back.

Meekly, at Gemma's doorstep, they stammered a greeting and waited to hear their fate. Her mother frowned from the foyer at them, tapped her foot a little, and didn't offer candy. But then she saw the clown, Pierrot in pain, as he shook his head, a hand to his face.

—What happened?

Newell said:

—Big kids with pea shooters. Hit 'im in the eye.

Her face softened.

—Really? We'll have a look then. Alright, you can come in.

One by one they filed into the magic house that held such loveliness in the being of a girl. Well-to-do home: oriental carpet, family pictures along the mantelpiece. Logs crackled in the fireplace; and, alongside, Gemma's father pipe in mouth, cheekful of burst capillaries, looked up from his evening paper at the troop in his living room.

—Have some punch, men. Corn candy for you in the tureen.

—Dear, come have a look at this boy's eye.

The boys stood around, on their best behavior. And some might have liked to get back outside, and rove some more, marauders, Quantrell's candy bar raiders, in the wild night of Spring Glen.

But meanwhile some giggles came from the next room, an indoor porch or solarium, where, under other circumstances, they had caught glimpses of Gwynna when they hid out. Wait, it sounded like a group in there: girls, more giggles, secrets! Once, over at Theresa Tyrone's house (I'll tell you, she has some pods on her: big as her nose almost), Newell, Otter and Thaddy had crouched in shrubs outside the back porch and heard a regular gossip session. Whew! The cattiness at twelve years old. The slander! What ideas these women have! How can we ever forgive them?

Now Lily Berryer stood in the living room entry, and made an announcement:

—Line up, children. You're going to get your treat!

Hey, what the–? What is a Lil Berryer doing here? You mean she belongs to the same planet as Gemma? The same species? She dares to leave her own sphere and come here to associate with an angel? Next we'll even see The Lunger . . . Look! Well now, if that ain't the limit! It's Lunger herself, Bettina Lundgren, also up here on Lorelei for a Halloween party among girls. Welcome Gemma to the neighborhood? And there's Betsy Erasmus, and El Neuterman! And–oh god! You don't mean–no! no! Terrible Typhoid Tyrone here as well?! Shouldn't we call the health department right away? Yes, yes, it's Terrible Terry, pods and nose. And–oh, oh, oh! I can't stand it anymore! Jane The Pain Gluck with her first flying buttresses. Now, really: is this some sort of a trap? Have we been set up, gentlemen?

But wait a minute. They all have something in their hands. What? To tell the truth, it looks a little like a you-know-what, the stick that goes in the doughnut. Pale green color to it, with a purple tinge; and kind of furry, fibrous. And look! A little milky juice comes out if you squeeze it, and seeds. Milkweed! That's what it is: milkweed.

What are those bratty girls doing now? Here they come: filing into the living room, like some sort of runic procession? And Lillian Berryer gestures at Newell Gilbert arrogantly (that's why he tripped her that time: after they had faced off as the last two in a spelling bee and *he* tripped up over 'tobacco', spelled it with two b's, so the girl won). And she says:

—Here you are, dahhling. I give you your very own–pod.

Ah, so that's it. So they, these women, know the why and wherefore behind repeated trips to the pencil sharpener, and all this new business about their what's-its. Milkweed pod, ah ha.

And then one by one the Spring Glen girls presented the Spring Glen boys with their pods: as in a ceremony, or rite of passage.

The gallant Willard Steuart came in with Gemma's mom, and he looked a little the worse for wear, red-eyed as a parakeet.

And Gemma, last in line, handed the poor boy his pod as well. And she curtsied. Oh, no words can hope to describe the grace of Gemma's curtsy: when she offered Willard Steuart the milkweed pod. I think she actually went beyond Makarie Straiton, for beauty, when she did that: in her genre, anyway.

But she didn't stay there, by the corn candy tureen, to chat with the stricken lad. No; because maybe she knew, and could feel, what she meant to him: more than the usual crush by a sixth grader in Mr.

Pyat's class. And thus too intense for her present tastes: she liked the Heatie Ventnor types, at the Capers Dance. Yea, Willard loved Gemma as though he would have to make this one do: the love of his life. Look at him: a healthy, strapping kid, courageous, smart, not the least bit unhealthy except for some passing eye irritation.

But you never know. And he loved her deeply, at least for a grade schooler. He loved Gemma truly, as though he might not have time to love again.

VIII

The following year Newell's dad decided the boy must change his ways, and get the 'finest education available'. So Newell left the paradise of public school and went to an old, exclusive day school in the area. While his friends moved on to bigger and better things at the new, chaotic junior high, replacing Spring Glen's departmentalized seventh and eighth grades, Newell learned to loathe a conservative preparatory school with six 'forms'. So his life of larks, his evening forays with Otter, Thaddy and the others, his cavalier attitude and freedom from homework, came to an end. Gemma attended the sister school, but he never saw her. The philosophy in those days was: keep 'em busy.

But Newell's thoughts still focused on his childhood friends, and he met them at every opportunity: weekends when permitted, holidays. In October the next year, 1956, he helped Willard Steuart, Haas, Rand, Bungya, Otto and the others organize a football team; and to this effort he brought knowledge gained from club football at the private school: how to number and call plays, and align a defense.

Remarkably, on a weekday, all eleven boys played hooky and went up to Lavater Field where they took on a team from Cedar Rock across town. Thirteen year-olds, they took care of everything: equipment, field dimensions and first-down poles, a timer, a fair referee.

They won the first game against Cedar Rock, 26-0.

But they played again: an away game, over at Cedar Rock Field, there behind Galen Street sector. And this time the Spring Glen boys had a surprise.

For three periods they dominated, and kept the ball in enemy territory, but could not carry it across, into paydirt.

Then, on that sunny morning in late October, the week of Halloween, a Cedar Rock player showed up late on the scene.

Tullio Trecastagne.

—What?! Newell cried. But he plays varsity at the High School.

Just a year older, but physically a man: Tullio The Slug suited up on the far sidelines. Big, hefty body; but strange: his short, chunky legs with a bandy air; his upper torso so developed as to look deformed. His younger brother, Louie The Limp, had a club foot.

The Slug.

The Cedar Rock boys rubbed their hands and said to one another:

—Rock 'n roll.

Time out.

A meeting at mid-field.

Newell, there alongside Willard Steuart, said to the other captain:

—You just want revenge. Kept Tullio in reserve in case you needed him.

—No way.

—Saw you couldn't win this time either, with home field advantage. So you sent someone to call him at home. Had it all set up.

—He plays. You quit, we win.

—Win then. Hope you enjoy it. Close, hard fought game, does both teams honor, and you ruin it. Cheater cheater, pumpkin eater.

—Sore loser.

—Why not call Denny McGill and Al Ward to help you win? Why not call up Sid Luckman or Bobby Layne?

Newell shrugged. He walked off the field. He said: let the babies have their bottle.

But Willard Steuart had another idea. He wanted to play against Tullio The Slug. He wouldn't quit.

And so the game went on.

And Tullio Trecastagne's short, chubby legs churned through the Spring Glen defenses. And Willard Steuart tackled Trecastagne and The Slug dragged Wil Steuart another ten yeards, before Otter hit them both sideways, and Canova and Kelleher crashed into them from behind, pushing the whole rout another five yards downfield. And Rand and Mooch Mueller leapt into the fracas, and gang-tackled the spectacular Slug, and Laury Haas jumped on top of that great human mass, as they all fell in a sluggish heap across into the endzone, Tullio T. and his tacklers dragged over the goal line along with him before he could be made to fall down. Whistle, play dead: another touchdown. But Bungya piled on top even at that late date, and put on the finishing touches: unnecessary roughness, fifteen yards. But the sportsmanlike Slug forgave him, and gave Bungya a little pat on the rump, and said:

—Way to hit, kid.

Cedar Rock 28, Spring Glen 0.

Newell stood to one side and watched them all jumbled together, human limbs, like a bowl of spaghetti. And he laughed, good and loud, so all Cedar Rock might know how he viewed this farce. And the Cedar Rock captain called him a chicken, and clucked. And Newell rushed at the Cedar Rock captain, and the two began a wrestling match right there on the grass, in their helmets and football pads. The other players took it up, and tussled too. Everybody fought, flailed, floundered on the ground, forgot about the game turned into a fiasco with only a few minutes to go in the fourth quarter. But Tullio and Willard Steuart didn't fight. They just stood there, panting for breath, and looked at each other.

Later, in early afternoon, Newell walked with Haas along Wilke Parkway after they bought blue popsicles at The Glendower. And there across the way, alongside the brook where it flows on Enoch Brown's property, went Willard Steuart on his way home. He limped. He still took his usual long strides, but with a limp: sort of had his left leg in tow. Hurt the hip?

Newell wanted to call across the street: nice game, Wil! But something in the other's aspect, by himself now, into his thoughts, discouraged this.

A warm sunlight fell on Willard Steuart's auburn hair. He sort of strained forward, against the limp, and didn't look to either side.

Ten days later he was dead.

IX

In February, the next year, Newell found himself seated beside Gemma at the pre-Capers dinner. There they sat in silence, while around the long table their private school classmates chattered. Why had the organizers put them together? Because he sent her a Christmas card this past December, signed in his neatest handwriting? Now to save himself he couldn't come up with a word of conversation.

After awhile he leaned and said to her averted face:

—You know Willard Steuart died last fall. Remember him? He swallowed his tongue in a footrace at the new junior high.

Gemma didn't respond. She said nothing.

Then, after he crushed her while squeezing into the back seat, that cold evening, they parted in the Lawn Club foyer never really to meet again, except for a moment. He hardly knew enough to take her coat, and check it at the coatroom—he was such a heathen: not to be confused with Heaton—if she even desired his services. And so they parted on the threshold: she to her Heatie Ventnor and Albie Ford; while he would have a few dances, through the evening, with the exciting if somewhat lethargic Ginny Barry.

But then, toward midnight, he felt an urge to return and ask Gemma for a fox trot. And she said yes. While they danced, one-two-three-four, to Lester Lanin's romantic strains, Newell thought: Well, they fixed us up tonight because I'm a prep schooler now. Not a Spring Glen boy, not like Lenny and Kelleher, Bungya, Otter, Mooch Mueller anymore. They must think I'm respectable! Not the Loch Ness monster from Spring Glen Grammar: lurking outside, in the bushes up at Gemma's, for a glimpse of her . . . No longer free, happy, a wild man like Willard Steuart—ah—!

He drew back, for an instant, and looked in her face. Bold move; but he felt loose enough now, freed from a spell, after Ginny Barry's dance floor embraces.

Newell looked in Gemma's eyes, and hers met his for the first time all night; though he still didn't notice any feeling on her part, any encouragement he could go by.

And then he saw the tear on her cheek, and thought to himself: why? Not for himself anyway, Newell the neighborhood vandal, this he knew; and never mind if he had given up night forays with Otter and grown civilized, and wore hated suits and ties to school. For these notwithstanding he would never be comme il faut enough for a beautiful girl like her. Already he had gotten in a peck of trouble at the elite school. They sent him home one day because of the way he wore his hair, all greased up in a Chicago duck's-ass. So no, not for him, Gemma's tear. And . . . not for Willard Steuart either, or not exactly. For what had she ever really felt about the poor guy, the Spring Glen boy so awkward, tender, undignified in his clown outfit, that Halloween evening they all went up to Gemma's, on Lorelei, and her mom tended to his eye made bloodshot by an older boy's pea shooter? She hadn't loved him the way he loved her, that's for sure, or anywhere near it! Why, she probably only gave him the ceremonial milkweed pod to cheer him up a little, after a nod from her mom, since the poor kid was hurt. No, she hadn't loved Willard Steuart any more than Makarie Straiton ever gave Spring Glen's own Charlie Björnsen the time of day; or Sim Curtis either, incredible as that may seem since he could mess up Spring Glen. No; la Makarie had bigger fish on the line.

But Gemma cried now, a single tear—for herself perhaps? She felt the love, gone forever, she had inspired in those wild Spring Glen boys, not only the late Willard Steuart, but a dozen others, even Bungya. For nobody ventured up Santa Fe anymore, and lurked outside Gemma's house these cold February nights, you can be sure of that. The excitement died down pretty soon after their Halloween 'reception' when Gemma's mother, maybe on her husband's advice, put an end to the nuisance with a little more forbearance, more openness. Nothing solves a mystery like familiarity.

But tonight another boy, Steuart's friend, looked in Gemma's eyes. And she looked back, just for a moment, and saw, reflected in Newell's gaze, Willard's love that lived on though the poor boy had died. An idea now, a memory, it wouldn't grow old, or fade, lose its beauty someday. Only when she herself died could it ever go away, and be forgotten. But not even then, not totally: if another Spring Glen boy like Newell happened to survive, and remembered their brief young time together.

Meanwhile, as they danced at Caper's, Willard Steuart lay in his grave up there in the town cemetery, off Crest Road. From there you can see, westward, all Redemaine to Maldoror Drive, West Hills, the parkway toward New York City. Eastward you gaze out past The Dump—where trains make their way up into New England, and whistle sadly at the distance.

After awhile Gemma danced again with Heatie, as this year's Capers dance wound down.

Tomorrow, and the next day, Newell would carry on a struggle against the 'finest education available'; against straitlaced schools and people not charmed by a Spring Glen boy's wildness.

Newell turned from Gemma when Heatie approached. He sensed what she wanted. But he would remember her. Her beauty would help him, in his long campaign to survive, and tell the story.

Flipper

I

Afternoons, the school bus coasted downhill from the secluded institution, and wended its way through surrounding communities. It left young scholars at their doorsteps.

After a half hour Phillip Starr, Flipper, got off on Crest Road and ran in his house to change into play clothes. The race was on. Could Flipper make it down to Santa Fe before Newell eluded his grasp? Newell stayed on the bus another ten minutes: for its circuit by Dyre Club Lane; then scooted up to his attic room, ripped off necktie and itchy tweeds, jumped into muddy football gear, and lit out by himself for a game of tackle in the churchyard.

Sick as hell of prep school, in a state what with the daily academic pressure, he didn't want to see that smiling face any more today. So he brushed past his mom in the front hall without a hello, and didn't even bother to throw a crossbody block on his little sister in the living room. He burst in, did a quick change into pads and jersey, and scampered out.

But there stood Flipper waiting for him, with a wave, by the ivy roundel out front. Or, if Newell tried to slip away, through the kitchen door in back: then the other had an uncanny sense and was usually on him in a flash. Flipper stuck to you like glue as he chattered about this and that. Flipper tagged along and tended to stifle any free-as-you-please feeling, any escape. Also, Flipper's presence made for a constraint between Newell and the old public school friends. Bungya, Otter, The Mooch just shrugged; but Newell felt embarrassed as The Flip came along sooner or later and hung on the sidelines: rosy cheeked, prating on about some trivial detail from his private school day. He butted his nose in where he wasn't wanted. Little gaper.

As a result Newell had to prove himself, in some sense, again and again, and bridge the distance. He could play a gritty brand of pick-up football, yet not shake off a kind of separation: even as he butted heads with the stubborn Otto, or held his ground when rough Bungya tried to run him over. Day after day Newell felt a frustration now, misunderstood by his parents, kept from what he needed to feel happy. And why? So he might end up like Flipper Starr, and suck up to masters like the dainty Mr. Morbleu, mythology teacher, whom they referred to as *Thor! God of Thunder!;* or Mr. Kent, whose dronings over Eliphalus Hopper in *The Crisis* put his class to sleep: as though the sandman sprinkled that dandruff on his shoulder; or Mr. Bornierte whose red face and salt-and-pepper crew cut, whose complex science lessons and red marking pen made his students wish that not only Bornierte but also the subject of biology had never been born.

II

Both boys' fathers, university professors, wanted a better education for their sons than Redemaine Junior High could give. But whereas Flipper submitted cheerfully to the new regime, with its strict discipline, Newell resisted. The former actually liked to wear a starched white shirt, cufflinks, necktie; while the latter, allergic to wool, felt crucified by charcoal gray suits, flannel slacks and sport jackets, tight vests required by the code. Pretty soon Newell's revolt became more open, as he combed his hair outrageously in a Chicago-style 'd.a.', and carried a sneer through each school day, and wore white silk ties over dark hoody shirts. Once the provocative, flitty Shellnitz taunted Newell right there in front of the headmaster's office:

—Gilbert, you couldn't fight your way out of a wet paper bag. Then he punched Shellnitz in the stomach, and The Shell doubled over and wailed like an actor on stage, and the incident turned into a big deal. Miss Burton, the English teacher, passed by and said: —Seems like his own worst enemy. Newell didn't understand this comment. But the pressure to conform brought other bad traits out in him. For instance the bus ride home, in the afternoon, became a free-for-all. Flumczyck, the monitor, could not control the boys. And so a few of them badgered and bullied the blubberball Milford Stith until it grew pretty serious. Word got out. An ugly thing; and Newell, though not the ringleader, played a part. Result: the headmaster decided Flumczyck's calling in life was not school bus monitor. Also, he talked to students' parents. A little longer, and this respected institution founded over a hundred years before the American Revolution might have a first-class scandal on its hands, like 'Lascivious-Carriage' Susie, of Yale fame.

Perhaps you have an inkling by now why Newell felt such a need to avoid Flipper's clutches, and join in a game of tackle, the muddier the better, at the churchyard.

—Heu. Good riddance to bad rubbish!

He catapulted down the stairs. All day long the woolen trousers pricked his pores, as he sat through Mr. Kent's tedious English class, and stared dreamily at the man's dandruff. O the paper airplanes sailing down from Spring Glen Grammar's second storey windows . . . O the good times at Redemaine Junior High, missed, heard about secondhand, later on, from Thaddy . . . O Jane The Pain's superpods in bulged brassiere, beneath a tight blue cashmere sweater, and duly felt up when some young gentleman, a Haas or a Bungya, turned out the lights during Gray-Y in the Congregational Church basement . . . O life! O opportunities lost forever!

Now he lurched past his mom, like a halfback's slant off tackle, and plunged across the front hall. All day, hour after hour, the starched dress shirt made him feel like a roasted pig with an apple, not tempting as Eve-Ginny Barry's, stuck in his mouth.

Out the front door he flew, and muttered a curse word for those nitwits who didn't know that when someone says you can't fight your way out of a paper bag you must show them you can. Even a seven year-old understands this, but you won't learn it during the finest education available.

Newell ran outside—smack into The Flip.

–Uh . . . hi.

Today, as usual, Flipper stood waiting, in his baggy khakis and tennis shoes, a flitty smile on his flitty face. And now he would follow Newell to the churchyard, and stand on the sidelines, and poison his friend's moment of freedom.

III

A sneer came on Newell's lips as he ran across the field toward his friends. He did a few calisthenics and tried to ignore Flipper parked on the far sideline, toward The Glendower. The sissy in his tennis shoes, khakis and warm pea jacket, gaped, through burnt-amber glasses frames, at the game in progress. Now Bungya was sure to include Newell, if only a little, in his contempt for this rich kid with his rosy cheeks and well-scrubbed neck. The others, Canova and Kelleher, Lenny, Rand, even Otter would sense this, and lose respect.

It was a cold, lusterless day in mid-November. At shortly past four the sky began to darken. Winter hovered in the air: from a distance you could smell the first snow. A few leafless trees bordered the field; and, beyond these, cars sped along the avenue or pulled in at The Glendower.

The players cupped their hands, blew on chapped fingers; huddled; ran off another play. Newell still did jumping-jacks on the sidelines. For some reason they didn't invite him to play right away like other days. Even teams: hard fought contest. Across the muddy field the boys played with a will; they ran and blocked, they tackled, they completed a pass. Despite the cold they sweated in their chin-strapped helmets, hip and shoulder pads. Nobody seemed to notice the newcomers.

Flipper sidled up to his best friend, and said:

–How about a Clark Bar? I'll go buy us a couple.

Newell didn't answer, but then took thought: alone, he would shake this feeling, and just go barge in the game.

–Okay, yeah. Take your time.

When the others called a brief time-out, Newell sauntered up and asked no one in particular for a chance to play.

For a moment they sort of ignored him. Then Bungya, who sat on the football above the dark muddy grass, said:

—Where'd Cutie-Pie go?

—For candy.

—Why didn't you go together? You could hold hands crossing the street.

—What's that?

Plenty of times Newell made solo tackles on Bungya or anyone else. He played tough as anyone, and now they included him in banter for the cream puff. Right there he would have gotten into it with the rock-like Bungya, but Kelleher said:

—Aw, c'mon. Getting dark.

IV

So now it wasn't enough for Newell to miss all the good times, Janie at Gray-Y when the lights went out, evening forays around Spring Glen, or over at Redemaine Plaza, the Music Box, the bowling alleys, where he might see Cynthia Landis, queen of Redemaine Junior High, a Makarie their own age. Now he must stand idly by while his friends, Canova and Kelleher, Haas and Otter and Rand, Mooch Mueller, Robby Zwergli and Lenny turned away from him.

Stunned, he stood there and stared at them. He almost looked ready to cry, or else punch somebody. All week long he had to scramble and keep up with the 'course contracts' handed out, each month, by teachers who seemed to demand everything of students and nothing—no vital interest, no realism, let alone spirit, wit, of themselves. Mediocrity was packaged, expensively, as the finest education available. And then, right away, Newell stayed up late and hammered out those lessons in a rage, all at once, so he wouldn't have them hanging over his head the whole time. At 2 a.m. he felt better, relieved, when he finally lay down his head and tried to get a few hours' sleep.

Look: over there, in the tall grass, Neesie Montowese once grappled for a softball with him, and snatched it away with a laugh. Ah! What an ass that Neesiekins had on her. That was some ass. And see the maple tree over at the churchyard's edge, by Wilke Parkway? In its shade, one summer afternoon, Ned Parigi talked about how his friend Sim Curtis could 'mess up Spring Glen' because of Makarie Straiton, whatever that meant. Was it to impress her? And Newell thought he himself might mess up Spring Glen, or at least his own undies, for the older girl named Rose Cody: she gave him such a feeling, sweet, dark somehow; she tinged the whole neighborhood . . . Well, those were the days, but they were gone now. And all he had in exchange were hated neckties, itchy woolens which jabbed into your pores, ouch!, but he couldn't even cry out in the stifling classroom of a pale, dainty yet strict Mr. Morbleu in his sixties. And this *Thor! God of Thunder* gave the first-formers snap quizzes, like a mythological punishment, to see if they had done their homework. On these and other Morbleu tests Newell always thought he did well: now I've got a B, he told himself halfway through; I've aced this sucker, he opined, at the end. And then came a C, always a C for Newell Gilbert, C decreed by Zeus and Mr. Morbleu, like the fall of Troy.

V

Play went on: a bruising contest, in the mud.

Flipper returned from The Glendower and handed his friend a Clark Bar.

Newell, distracted, hurt by a rebuff from friends, began to unpeal the wrapper. Then he realized what he was doing, and tossed the candy bar on the ground.

—Look, go on home. I don't like to be a bully, but if I see you at my house once more, or down here, you'll know what Shellnitz' stomach felt like after I fought my way out of a wet paper bag . . . Git!

He gave Flipper's baggy ass a swift kick, and sent him on his way.

Newell turned his attention to the game and looked for a way to get in it: if only to jeer. He didn't much care what happened right now. People he thought his friends had turned against him, and he would give some back.

As light waned from the churchyard Bungya's side trailed by a touchdown. In the twilight you couldn't pass very well; so in these last few sets of downs before the boys called it a day, and made their

way home for supper, the tough Bungya just said hup! and took the
snap from center. He lowered his head and chugged forward. Mooch
Mueller dove and hit him low. Otter got him in a bear hug, and
down they toppled, runner and gang-tacklers. Bungya had grown in
a spurt this year, and hardened physically, but he was no Tullio
Trecastagne.

Then it was fourth down and goal from their own thirty or thereabouts. You couldn't make first downs. You had to cross the field in
four plays. Bungya's team huddled and decided to try something
different.

All this while Newell had remained on the sidelines. Unbeliev-
able. Such a thing had never happened in the past. But his new status
as a preppie, plus the effect of Flipper Starr, had managed to get him
left out by his childhood friends. The Flip had gone to Spring Glen
Grammar with them; but there he pal'd around mainly with Steady
Chalmers, who also went away somewhere: to boarding school. As
for 'Dinghy' Chalmers, a scion of Chalmers House, the Wall Street
magnates; he had a world of privileges, but he would never have the
honor to attend Redemaine Junior High, or feel up Bettina Lundgren at Gray-Y when the lights went out, or dream about Cynthia
Landis, teenage queen, up at The Plaza.

Bungya cried:

−79! 24! 42! Hut-hut!

Last play of the game. He took the ball from center and lateraled
off to Canova in the backfield. Canova began a sweep around end,
and drew Mooch, Otter, Lenny right from scrimmage. But then he
stopped, and tossed a short pass back to Bungya drifting left toward
the church. In the gloaming Bungya caught the ball somehow, and
now found himself wide open for the long run downfield.

His teammate Haas gave a laugh, threw up both arms, and called
out:

−He's to the fifty! . . . he's to the forty! . . .

Off to the races Bungya strode free and chuckled to himself in triumph. Now with the extra point, which he could drive home on a
quarterback sneak, they would win.

But just then a dark figure, a phantom tackler darted out at him:
from the avenue side.

−What the−?!

−Hey! whattayaknow! Newell laughed crazily, charging off the
sidelines.

Remember the poor boy named Tommy Lewis who jumped off his bench in the Cotton Bowl and raced on field to make a mad tackle? Like him Newell streaked out from the sidelines with a war cry, and threw himself at Bungya with all the force he could muster. Like Tommy he only wanted to play.

The runner fell with a cry, and lay on his back a moment, stunned. That was some tackle: so hard, the ball squirted from his hands, a fumble.

The Mooch recovered it. He scooped up that ol' pigskin and ran back the other way, but nobody paid any mind.

All eyes focused on Bungya and his tackler. Both shaken up, they got to their feet slowly, and then stared at one another. Newell held his shoulder, and felt nauseous.

Bungya said:

–That the way you play, pipsqueak?

Newell looked at him, darkly:

–Jerk.

–Maybe you better stick to playing with your sissy-wissy friends.

Bungya shoved the injured shoulder.

Newell's brow contracted, and he said:

–You couldn't fight your way out of a wet paper bag.

Bungya jolted the shoulder again, and then threw a few punches at the other unable to defend himself, before Otter and Haas, mainly, could get them apart.

A moment later Newell went to his knees, on the cold muddy grass, and threw up.

VI

His dislocated shoulder involved a trip to the hospital, and there was some pain. Also, his face had bruises from Bungya's punches, plus a split lip, a cut over his eye; it didn't look too good. But Newell considered himself ahead of the game since he hadn't gotten unsightly zits, like a few others. If you saw the zits on Shellnitz! Shellnitz's face looked like Pompeii after the volcano erupted. Shellnitz's cheeks and chin looked like a pizza pie with the works.

Newell's dad threw a tantrum. What a scene they had: faced off in the kitchen. Professor Gilbert shouted about a person's duty, honor bright, and you have to serve humanity. Newell, in tears, screamed back and wouldn't budge: he didn't care about humanity but only wanted public school again, Gray-Y, play baseball, be happy! Then his father threatened him, and held up Dinghy Chalmers as an example.

—Watch out, Bud. We'll send you away to boarding school, like the Chalmers. The way you're behaving lately: you have your mother worried sick.

—I want my friends back! I want life in Junior High! But no, you couldn't leave well enough alone—wise parent, with your finest education available. Gray-Y gives the education, not those nincompoops, Mr. Morbleu.

He didn't tell them what happened when the lights went out.

Newell left the room, his ugly beat-up face all teary. What a mess! Puberty. His dad, Emory, ordered him to come back, young man, this instant! But he wouldn't come, despite threats, and his dad's shouts meant to cow a boy. In such times the house got very quiet, Newell's older brother and sister, Joey and Evelyne, up in their rooms, away from the fray. But his little sister, Lemon, as he called her, had started to cry too, and snuck down the stairs, cute little kid, humble, in her pajamas.

Later, Anne Gilbert went wearily up to the attic. Once again, she sat on the edge of the bed, and tried to console her younger son so shaken up, in tears, angry at his father. She also tried to speak a little reason, and mediate.

But long after his mother left to go downstairs, Newell lay awake in the darkness and turned the self-justificatory words over, and over, and over in his mind. It wasn't fair; it was not. His father blustered, threatened, and waxed mightily indignant over the son he had produced. But he would never understand.

VII

Then came—a reward! Thursday, Friday plus the weekend, Newell got to hang around and enjoy himself in his attic room. A prisoner (he couldn't go out, or even show himself downstairs supposedly) but how happy! Oh boy! He had a big electric football game: LSU versus Ole Miss. What runs, passes, what stats Billy Cannon amassed, and

Jake Gibbs. Newell played, and daydreamed of Gemma just up the hill. He listened to the Friday Night Fights. To hell with monthly course contracts, *Thor! God of Thunder,* Mr. Kent and Esyphilis Hopper's 'simplicity'—whatever that was,—and dandruff on Rainer Kent's shoulder like a ten-inch snowfall. As for Bornierte's biology course: why was it born? why is it living?

Cliff came to the attic on his round of chores. Cliff puffed, and chugged, duster in hand, a rag or two in his threadbare suit trousers' back pocket. Newell told Cliff about Bungya, and Cliff came back with a story of his own, days long ago, down South.

—White high school in my hometown, state champs that year in football, challenged a group o' black lot players who'd built up a repi'tation for themselves, to a game. Well, we'z older, men against boys, but didn't hahdly have no pads o' nothin', like them. Whole town come out to the high school field, and watched us roll to a couple touchdown lead. Then, I 'member, the Mayor came down from the stands and had a wuyhd wid' the referee, 'n this, 'n that, 'n pretty soon they managed to get one across.

—Cheaters, Cliff?

—Well, things like that, y'know . . . We just thought: least nobody'ms gettin' huyht. So, late fourth quarter, they on'y sent out ten men. But the eleventh, he come off the bench, after the play started, to catch a long pass. TD: they win.

—But, Cliff, they didn't play fair.

—No, it wuyhn't. But things like that, y'know. Let'm have they way. We just shrugged, on 'm, 'n walked off the field. Why get distuhybed?

Cliff gave a chuckle, and puffed, dusted some more, chugged forward, ever forward. But he paused an instant, even then with a little laugh; and Newell saw something in his eyes he hadn't seen before. And a vein sort of stood out on his bony neck, beneath the old, old dress shirt, with its buttery sheen.

—Anyway, you were better.

—Well, older. But . . .

—What, Cliffer?

—We played hard, we handled ourselves well, that's the main thing. I jus' couldn't understand why you'd wanna' win a game like that. Absuyhd.

Cliff didn't often tell stories, but you knew he had them. Usually Newell was just too rambunctious to listen, and Cliff puffed, polished and rubbed up a table, whispered:

—Shh . . . you'll wake the baby.

Boring, more of same: for a boy stirred up by sharp words with his dad, on the lookout for action. Sometimes, though, Newell paused long enough from harassing his kid sister to hear Cliff's anecdotes about ol' Satch and the Negro Leagues, and look at his fingers gnarled by foul tips. Cliff Gardin bent over his pail; Cliff cheerfully at some menial task, talking to himself . . .

Later on, Newell thought it over a little: sneaks . . . dishonesty. Why win a game like that? But, Cliffer, that's unfair . . . We handled ourselves well: that's the main thing.

Sometimes, at the detested school, Newell thought about Cliff for a moment. He didn't know it, but he looked to him for something.

Saturday afternoon Otter and Haas came over. Anne Gilbert decided to let them visit a little while; and so the two boys, shaking their heads over her funny southern accent, tumbled their way up to the attic. So Newell got to hear all about Rand and Bettina Lundgren in the Congregational Church basement when the lights went out at Gray-Y. Bittersweet experience! You bet Jane The Pain made herself scarce then; insofar as that brick shithouse could ever be called scarce! When the lights went out, and it was time to sneak a feel, The Pain knew herself to be a prime target, two prime targets, so she crawled beneath the table. But Robby Zwergli followed her down there, like a caveman, and began rubbing her . . . shoulders. He tried out his method. But, would you believe it, she didn't heave according to theory. Instead, The Pain slapped him, jeepers! and hollered for all to hear:

—Get off!

How embarrassing.

Such were the fascinating accounts given by Otter and Haas the Saturday after Newell tangled with Bungya in the churchyard. In part Newell felt dismay. He was missing out. So with Otis he made plans to climb down the rope fire escape one of these nights and attend Gray-Y if it killed him. But one thing came up, and another, and so he never did.

VIII

What a sight he made, on Monday, when he made his triumphal return to the private day school on the hill. Black eye, facial marks from Bungya's blows, split lip, arm in a sling: he looked like *Monster Rally*—a zombie in a charcoal gray suit, with a Chicago-style 'd.a.' He didn't grimace from aches and pains so much as the wool suit sticking pins and needles into his skin, the starched shirt and necktie that made him feel like a stuffed scarecrow, the misery of another hour spent with *Thor! God of Thunder.*

That day Newell Gilbert made a decision. When he came of age, and could decide things for himself, he would never again wear a necktie. No matter if his dad disowned him, whatever that meant: he would become a tramp first, and ride boxcars, before he'd wear a necktie.

Shellnitz sidled up to him, took a long look, and said:

—One tough wet paper bag: that's what you are . . . like Millie Stith, blubberball. Ha ha ha!

—Watch out, Shellnitz. When this sling comes off, I'll flush you down the toilet.

—Gee! Let's see you.

Newell bristled, and stepped back to kick Shellnitz in the balls. But he thought of something, and moved with a shrug along the corridor.

—Small fry.

Uh-oh, here came Flipper Starr.

—Uh . . . hi.

Newell had never ignored The Flip, a former Spring Glen boy like himself. But now he cut him dead. His split lip hurt when it curled with contempt. Absuyhd.

Through that day he sat quietly, and the next. No, he wouldn't beat up Shellnitz when the sling came off, or tease Milford Stith on the bus anymore. Why? For one thing: his father might send him away to boarding school, like Dinghy. But more important: it was okay to take on Bungya, and roughhouse with his equals, Haas, Otter, The Mooch. But forget about these sissified private school specimens. Leave them to their fate. Because you had to handle yourself well: that was the main thing.

Also, he might try to please his dad and avoid trouble if possible. But for how long? He was stubborn as Otto. He knew what he knew. And the dignified Professor Gilberts never will approve of the Bungyas and public schools and Chicago-style duck's-asses of this wuyhld.

White Christmas

I

—Dear Lord—Newell prayed for once—let her not come here. Don't let Grandma come and spoil my Christmas vacation this year. I'll have to spend the whole time in tweeds and a necktie, with her around. Please, Lord, please, do this thing, keep her away. I promise you I won't sin anymore: tease my little sister Lemon, steal, sneak out to Otter's at night, act up in class by day, torment the dog. I'll shovel the walk for my dad! But let Anne-Green spend her Christmas down South and not come here and wreck everything. Let her stay away, or she'll show up and stick around forever. Okay, God? It's a deal? And I promise I'll pray to you everyday for the next four weeks, like one of these damned course contracts, homework. Square deal, shake on it then. She's a wrecker! ... As an added bonus I'll even take off the playing cards clothespinned against the spokes of my bike, and not make such a racket in the neighborhood.

Newell's maternal grandmother, Anne-Green, dominated any get-together. And she took up half the dining room table, with its wings in use, when the Gilbert family sat down for a light supper on Christmas Eve.

A large fleshy woman with a bulldog air, a little like Winston Churchill, she had that statesman's massive blond jowls. Often a strand of luxurious silvery hair strayed down over Anne-Green's broad forehead etched with wrinkles.

She always looked pale, but tonight paler than usual: the hint of pink roses faded from her marshmallowy cheeks. Still, she talked such a blue streak, in her strong eastern Carolina accent, Newell looked at her and thought: what's going on?

When Anne-Green arrived at Redemaine Station the week before Christmas, she swooped down on her grandchildren. One by one she nailed them, with her great repulsive hugs, and broad face full of dripping kisses. She could bark, and she could coo. She gave a boy the most elaborate presents, purchased at a department store in Goldsboro, and not only at Yuletide. But she also made him pay: in hugs.

Thus Anne-Green, at Redemaine depot, had imprinted her mad grin, her fangy kisses on their young brains: first Evelyne, Newell's twin, then Joey, who held aloof as usual, and let it happen; then little Lemon, made afraid, but she didn't cry; then Newell lastly:

—Oh you bad boy, oh you good boy!

Anne-Green smothered him. For weeks he had hoped against hope she would 'feel right down', as she liked to say, getting attention, and not show up here and poop the party. More than any child she always had to be the center of attention.

Now, at table, her voice flew up in a siren. I declare! She resembled, she sounded like a fire truck on its way to a blaze. So even Professor Gilbert could hardly get a word in edgewise to say grace.

Newell stared at Grandma's wrinkles: dry, not rhythmic, not gracious somehow. Then he compared Cliff's lean, angular face: the dark eyes clear and calm, the brow lined, carved it seemed by Cliff's life story: wrinkles of manliness, character, so you didn't think of them as wrinkles.

Newell always liked it when, as a little boy, he waited for Anne-Green to come settle by his bedside, hum, and rub her hand over his head for a long while, in a tender mood. And, if she paused, he shook his head, wiggled a little, as a sign between them: more, Grandma.

But it takes tact to win a boy's heart, and too quickly she frowned. Often she showed an angry impatience. When his wool suit jabbed into his pores, ouch! and he wanted to stick a hand in there and find out what caused such a sharp pinprick, she held him in her gaze,— Don't you move, young'un!—and he just stood it.

Over fifty years a widow, since old W.T. Purvis passed away at the century's turn, Anne-Green entered the work force only briefly. She had a millinery store in Virginia City while her daughter Anne (Newell's mother) attended finishing school at Goucher before transferring to the Women's College in Durham. From old W.T., the banker, Anne-Green had stocks to live on comfortably; and so she contented herself with coupon clipping for the rest of her days. Emotionally she made do by a decades long feud with her son-in-law. A dark thing: deep undercurrents, between those two. Anne-Green, opinionated, racist as hell, never gave the liberal Emory an inch. And lately the situation grew bitter due to certain practical matters: namely, her will. For Anne-Green would leave her money, when she died, in trust to her grandchildren and not directly to her only child, Anne, who agreed with her; or, thereby, to her son-in-law, Emory, Newell's father, who didn't.

II

Now Emory said a lengthy and sonorous grace over the Christmas Eve supper. Tonight he looked grave and didn't turn on the charm, Pop's corn, as he served a pâté de foie gras with salad. The adults sipped a red wine; the kids had mulled cider with a cinnamon clove taste. Newell and Lemon kicked in the traces and thought only of opening Christmas presents heaped high, within view, round the splendid tree across the high ceiling'd living room.

But first they had to pick at fancy French food, without appetite, and listen long-faced as Anne-Green launched into a detailed account of how she along with Aunt Sootie, Ninaway, Ruby Bruton and Ruby's sister Pauline, from Bristol, Virginia, drove out in Aunt Sootie's buggy one Sunday afternoon looking for the old Pittmann place in Grifton, farm country ten miles outside of Kinston, where Anne-Green née Pittmann grew up.

—Ah' declayyeh'! After an hour and half a tank o' gas we still couldn't find Uncle Joe's spread. Passed the red church, y'know, on our way to Sutter's Well: jes' like Raz told us to, then on 'round again. Same red church, same gas steshin'—could not find the house, ah' declayyeh'! Twice 'n again we stop and asked some....... by the roadside: say, boy, where's the old Pittmann place?

At this Newell turned to his mom and said, under his voice: —You told me not to use those words, and she says 'em. —Hush up! said Anne Gilbert, as if something was going on. Anne's southern accent deepened when she got around her mother, after twenty years in the North. —But it's an insult to Cliffer. —Shush.

While the harangue went on, Newell fingered pâté crust, toyed with a beige doily, and glimpsed his older brother. Joey gazed to where snow fell, peaceful snowflakes, in the frosty windows hung with a few holly sprigs. Through the day snow had made a drift on the window sill, and lined the bars between the panes, where it condensed. Now the snow twinkled with warm, cozy light from the dining room chandelier, and lent a fresh, cold, northern scent, laced with fir trees, to the rich dinner scents of this plush interior.

Joey liked to gaze out windows. How come? Not the dreamy type really ... But during the years at Spring Glen Grammar, and now in his sophomore year at Redemaine High, he almost had a reputation for it. Distracted in class, uninterested, he stared out the window and thought maybe about baseball. Newell's older brother, though sociable enough, never said a whole lot to anybody. Why? He just went his way, absorbed in his thoughts, and didn't argue with Dad.

—Ruby's sister, Pauline, y'know, I think her mind 'z agoin' the way she cries out: oooooweee! real high, lak' that. And sometimes she farts ... right loud. For another hour we rode the back roads, out there in Grifton, alookin' for the old Pittmann place where me 'n Aunt Sootie grew up. But you jes' won't believe what we finally found, oooooweee! ...

Newell hoped she would find it soon; otherwise, Grandma might have to croak before they ever got those Christmas presents opened. For weeks, almost since Thanksgiving, he had seen wrapping materials, ribbons and bows, bright red and green paper with Santas, reindeer, decorated trees, quiet villages in the wide snowy evergreen night where airborne sleighs veered our way from among the stars.

December days passed, and the pace quickened toward Christmastime. Here, there: red leaved poinsettia in fancy pots. Mistletoe hung in a few strategic spots. And holly, plus Santa's pink bearded face, or an electric candle, trimmed the windows. Anne and Evelyne decked the halls, and lined the mantelpiece with the most artistic Christmas cards received, while fifty others cluttered up the front hall table, and hung taped to the walls. Emory took the boys to buy a big Christmas tree: perhaps the most impressive in Spring Glen, since the Gilberts had the highest ceiling.

Then Newell passed up his Friday Night Fights, Sandy Saddler versus a lightweight contender, to help dress the tree. Tinsel streamers, gurgling icycles, blinking lights; a host of ornaments storebought and also crafted after school by Evelyne and little Lemon; seasonal cookies sugary like new snow, with red and green sprinkles; mini-gingerbread men, hand-painted paper wreaths and cutouts, cranberries beaded on a string; also some small packets, mysterious, provided by zany Lemon: all this and more dangled from the branches. One afternoon Evelyne turned her second floor bedroom into a classroom for Lemon and a few other little kids from around the neighborhood; and together they played school and made Christmas trinkets and a lot of nice things.

III

From where Newell sat he saw the tree's upper branches, and star on top. Anne-Green's bulk blocked the rest: all those presents heaped up like a big snowdrift. Anyway he knew the packages by heart: far better than Master Bornierte's science lessons, too boring to be borne. He even knew the contents: since he held them up, and took a penlight to the package, and managed to read through the wrapping paper.

From mid-December presents piled up beneath the tree, while excitement mounted. The shrewd Emory refused to put tags on his gifts, and made Newell's sleuthing more difficult. But Lemon snuck downstairs all by herself early one morning, in her p.j.'s, and undid a dozen packages. This did not thrill her mother who had to rewrap them, with Cliff's help. Anne already had enough on her hands, more than enough, with Anne-Green's visit.

Gifts, gifts, gifts! Childish excitement, Yuletide carols, busy hands, around the house. Also tension, and expectations, as Christmas Eve approached. And now, only a few more minutes! If only Anne-

Green would finish her story about some old house in some old god-forsaken wilderness down in North Carolina–then they could clear the table, and get started. Let Evelyne play Santa Claus this year. Oh boy! How Newell would help his mother in the kitchen, and dry the dishes. What a good son. What a good, helpful fellow, that Newell, tonight: unlike the other 364 days of the year–the times when he refused to obey his dad and shovel off the walk, but only stomped his foot and shouted:

–It's going to snow again! Wait till it ends!

–What do you mean, snow again? said Emory. Snow this winter?

–Sure! Why shovel the walk at all? Warm weather'll take care of it.

Without exaggeration a hundred and fifty Christmas presents had appeared this year beneath the tree, and spilled halfway across the living room rug. But Newell couldn't see them now because his grandmother had been drinking muddy water, as Emory said; Anne-Green made a better door than a window.

But say: why was she so worked up tonight? All about some durn' fool house down in Grifton; and nobody else could get a word in for love nor money. She seemed so worked up: you'd think she might never get to speak her piece again, and needed to say everything once and for all, right now. Anne-Green so excited: did she expect some very special Christmas gift this year too? That's why she looked so nervous? And her voice flew up with an: oooooweee! like Ruby Bruton's sister Pauline from Bristol, Virginia, and it's a wonder she didn't fart. She like teh' shout at her son-in-law as though she wanted to start a brawl. So nervous her hands trembled. So exalted. But why? Real pale, too. Well, no doubt she was happy about her Christmas presents which she couldn't wait to open. Hm. If so, if she had any of the Christmas spirit in her, she wouldn't talk on and on, like old dandruff-head Mr. Kent once he got onto Esyphilis Hopper in *The Crisis*. Instead, she'd rub her hands and say: Let's get down to business.

So Newell just sat there, and twiddled his thumbs, and sighed. He endured Anne-Green's ranting, and thought about different things: how his dad, who liked cherry pies, gave a dollar to anyone that found a seed in one. An easier way to supplement one's allowance than shovel the walk! And so he was always asking Anne to have Cliff's daughter bake a cherry pie . . . Then Newell glimpsed the gold star, lit up atop the Christmas tree, and wondered if he might have to attend boarding school next fall.

Emory threatened:

—Don't burn your bridges, boy!

And Newell, snide:

—I didn't build them. I don't like private school.

Emory blustered:

—That so, bub? A privilege any boy in America would want. The finest education available!

Then, away at boarding school, he wouldn't get to meet Cynthia Landis, maybe ask her to dance the jitterbug, like on New Haven bandstand. No, he'd never even see the Queen of the Junior High, but have to go by what Robby Zwergli said about her, since that lucky stiff saw her and talked to her everyday. One afternoon last week Newell had snuck over to Redemaine Plaza, along with Otto, and heard 'Santa Make Her My Bride For Christmas' on a loudspeaker outside the Music Box, where the gorgeous Georgette Delorio worked, a bleached blond. Georgette married hockey player Dirk Crayling and went to Florida on her honeymoon, and all I can say is: be glad that wasn't your honeymoon. The handsome young couple didn't stay together long. But Dirk's brother Brent was a hockey star and had a tryout with the Blades, and Indian Joe Nolan checked him and decked him, pa! . . . pah! . . . because Brent skated head down when he had the puck and just couldn't change.

But this song gave Newell such a *feeling* for Cynthia Landis. When he heard it, 'Santa Make Her My Bride For Christmas', he wanted to marry Cynthia sight unseen, and spend his Christmases with her someday. At least *her* mother wouldn't have such a wild look in her eye, like Anne-Green tonight. On the contrary, Mrs. Landis must still be pretty, to have such a daughter; also, she wouldn't devour a boy in one fell swoop: with her big white teeth and sloppy saliva; a loose strand of silvery gray hair that tickled his cheek when she kissed him; a crazed grin on her flabby jowls. But why did Anne-Green look so pale right now, her skin a little grayish? Why did she get so darned excited, and use nasty words which made you feel sorry for Cliff? . . . Newell's father, who liked to talk too, and could do it, especially at his own table, hardly said a word while Anne-Green's story about her childhood home in Grifton was going on, and on, and on . . . She brought up other subjects, too; she might never finish. So Newell just sat there and mulled over Cynthia Landis up at Redemaine Plaza; and this made him feel Christmas differently— sweetly, brightly, not quite like Rose Cody and Neesie Montowese somehow; not like that time Neesie plumped her nonpareil derrière down on him, umph! in the tall grass at the churchyard, and snatched a softball from his hand with a laugh. But first he made her work for it a little so he could—well, you know . . . But Cynthia Landis was more like Gemma: a popular, regular, junior high rock 'n roll version of the girl up on Lorelei Road.

IV

—Same . . . . pumpin' gas there by the red church, you know, Annie, at the fork in Grifton. Many a drunk driver ploughed into that old church Saturday nights, and a few on Sunday, in broad daylight, durin' meetin' . . . . say he don't know nuttin' 'bout no ol' Pittmann place roun' 'dese pahts. Unless it be . . . So we rode a ways 'n Ninaway 'n Aunt Sootie mentioned Betty-Hodges, y'know, cute thing moved in next door to me there on Carey Road. Betty Hodges tells her poodle: jump, Gigi! Jemp, Gigih'! Such a cute thing! . . . I declayeh! Ah do deeclayeh! Well, we rode the country roads, and rolled down the window when Pauline farted, pewwwee! never mind your hair-do! . . . Raz has tobacco land out there, y'know . . . And down that old dirt road we drove, five old ladies takin' the bumps. And all the while, jump, Gigi! jemp, Gigih'! Betty-Hodges' doag. And Pauline not quite right in her mind, I don't think, oooooweee! and fartin' too. You added up our ages I guess it'd be over four hundred . . . And then, doncha' know, ah declayeh! we drove through a grove of trees, like the . . . . . . told us, 'n up the old gravel drive—and I'm lookin' around, tears in my eyes to be there again, out there, and cryin' over this, that, t'other. And then I saw the old front porch grown crooked now, warped, paint flaked. Gray, unpainted, the place sagged to one side. So many good times . . . (Anne-Green sniffled.) Love amongst us Pittmanns, in those days long over with . . . But can you rightly imagine what we saw then? Can you? It beat the devil 'n I don't know what-all! Jump, Gigi! After so much drivin' around, that Sunday afternoon, we came to the place I was born in, and growed up, a girl in days back there durin' Reconstruction. And I had so many beaus hangin' around me you couldn't figure 'em all out and get 'em straight, which was which, no suh! We had nice places to court then, too, green spots with a view, if you could trust a fella. But I waited . . . a long time for the right one to come along, ol' W.T. Purvis, good man, twenty years older than I was . . . But then what, Gigih'? What y'all think we found out there, that day in Grifton, at the old house?

Flippant Newell, anxious for his presents, said:

—I'll bite.

But everyone, even the fidgety Lemon, listened to Anne-Green in those instants. The old woman grown so excited, her voice risen toward a climax had a kind of fascination. And Anne-Green's eyes went wide; her big jowls gave a quiver; her face took a bluish-gray tinge by warm Christmas lights from the blinking tree in the living room, the bright chandelier above their heads, the dark evening outside the frosty window panes.

Lemon chirped:

—What, Grandma?

Anne-Green groped for breath. She paused, as the bit of lace on her big breast rose and fell. A large, womanly mass, in disarray somehow: she had not one but two luxurious, silvery gray strands strayed down from her temples now. Her eyes appeared to flare up, weirdly bright, and filled with tears.

—Oh, Precious, what do you suppose? Just a group o'. . . . . . settin' outside, and rockin', the way my father, Earl, and the rest of us used to do, in our day—

Silence. Finally, Anne-Green stopped. She grew quiet. She had found her childhood home.

And now Anne-Green's blond cheeks, etched with unlovely wrinkles, sort of settled, the way ice begins to melt. Her lips closed, and made a warped line, like the front porch of the old Pittmann place in Grifton. Her pale, grayish blue eyes seemed to understand something; her features grasped at some bit of truth; and she would ruminate this knowledge, in her jowls' pale, saggy, grayish flesh, like a third stomach, for a long time. Maybe, in the far place where her fixed, unblinking gaze had gone, the old Grifton site she looked for so long and finally found, oooooweee! jemp, Gigih'!—maybe out there they all know such a truth firsthand: about how we're all only just people around here, no matter what color, all basically the same with our day to day struggles, and our bigger problem together: life, survival.

Anne-Green's story came to an end. She didn't talk anymore. Her southern drawl, her ah declayehs and y'alls and Betty-Hodges's fell silent, strangely. Then she sort of settled there, hunched in herself a little, but didn't budge. Her pale eyes stared, stared past everything, far away.

Emory met his wife's gaze: the way they did sometimes, over their children's heads.

—Alright, guys. Almost time to open your presents. Evelyne plays Santa this year. But first I want you all to go upstairs, wash your hands, and then rest for a half hour. Till seven. Lady, I put you in charge. Jojo, you stay here.

Emory's voice had a different note then, even more deep-toned, like a church bell, a knell.

But not Newell's:

—Thirty minutes! Aw, Pa!

His mom said:

—Scoot, while we clear the table.

Joey's gaze came back in from the darkened window, and fell on his grandmother.

Evelyne, ever so thoughtful, frowned, and said softly:

—Is Grandma okay?

—We'll let her rest awhile, Lady, in the guest bedroom.

Emory liked to call his oldest daughter, the favorite, Lady.

—It ain't fair! It ain't.

Newell said 'ain't' to provoke his dad, and gave him double his money's worth tonight. In the same spirit he used double negatives sometimes, 'I don't want no . . . I ain't got no . . .', or talked like a hoodlum from the streets of Brooklyn.

—Jump, Gigi, jump! said four year-old Lemon to her grandmother, and giggled.

V

That year Newell's Christmas haul surpassed anything previous; though it also included new itchy suits, sport jackets, woolen slacks to jab his pores. And a dozen neckties, the thing he hated most on earth besides monthly course contracts: neckties hardly qualified as a present. Well, he had all the Christmas loot he wished for, some fifty packages; but did it pay him back for the fun and adventures he missed out on at Redemaine Junior High?

The gift distribution went off without a hitch, once it got started; although Anne-Green couldn't participate, and lay stretched out, fully clothed, in the downstairs bedroom. Quietly, Professor Gilbert closed the door, and hugged his wife, who was crying, in the front hall. Then, after several phonecalls, they went hand in hand into the living room to enjoy the Yuletide season with their children.

Young voices, led by Evelyne mature for her age, sang a few carols. Say, how sweetly that little devil Newell could sing once he had a mind: about to receive his ton of stuff. What a bad boy, what a good boy.

Then eager, childish fingers (I almost wrote: greedy) attacked the cheery packages, ripped, tore apart, shredded; demolished ribbons and elaborate bows in a jiffy.

—Santa, make it snappy!

—Aw, fooey, more ties?

A kid hardly had time to glance at the tag, in that mad scramble, and say thank you. But clearly Anne-Green had made an inspired visit to the department store in Goldsboro this year. Don't you find it amazing: how the same person could be so generous, bighearted in some ways, and so darn bad in others: when she said ugly words, and disrespected Cliff. Scat!

A cozy fire sizzled and crackled in the fireplace. Kids whooped a bit longer, fussed over the nice new things, and made a neat pile as their parents began to move them toward bed.

But in the guest room downstairs Anne-Green, her eyelids closed now, slept through the cheery evening, as snow fell. She didn't stir. Her big form, her womanly chest lay still, a contour in the darkness, like Sleeping Giant out there in the distance, and wide night of new-fallen snow. The silvery gray strand on her wrinkled cheek didn't rise and fall to the rhythm of regular breaths. It was hard to imagine: all her bustle, fuss, to-do, all that agitated life like a ruffled flounce, aflutter the day long from room to room; so many projects, visits, purchases, opinions, angers, tendernesses; so much chatter, in her strident eastern Carolina drawl, her ah-declayehs, her y'alls—all stopped, silent now, ended.

Softly the snow fell over Spring Glen. It drifted along Lorelei, Spring Glen Terrace, down Santa Fe from Crest Road to the brook, on Churchill where children would go sledding tomorrow, Christmas Day. Pure snow enchanted the suburban lawns and gardens, the still unshoveled streets where no cars passed. Snow pittered and whooshed a little amid the eaves; it filled the wide, silent night with whispers, the cold crystalline air with its secrets.

Upstairs, Newell snuggled in his warm bed beneath three quilts. Even in winter he kept a window open, so the attic room got cold during the night. Now only his snout stuck out from under the covers, and it tingled when a snowflake drifted in and lit on his nose. He thought there must be people somewhere, like the poor section of town, Harmonium, who didn't have such nice warm homes and a big pile of spectacular Christmas gifts to take their breath away. What were those people, Cliff, William Johnny . . . doing right now? How were they feeling?

Finally he fell asleep. He had a strange dream. This year Santa took gifts to people in the cemetery: up there beyond Crest, where you could see West Hills in one direction, looking across Redemaine, and The Dump in the other, where long trains chugged past. Then he stirred and nearly woke: sounded like quite a commotion downstairs, as Santa's helpers opened and closed doors. He heard their voices, movement; they got ready to go back up the chimney hung with care. Don't forget your milk and chocolate chip cookies!

Santa really did right by the nice, good little kids, who went along with the program. In Newell's dream his grandmother figured among the nice ones; though she often acted bad-childish, for a woman in her sixties: she cheated at cards, and wouldn't talk to you if she lost. Yet she would get sugarplums. Himself he included among the naughty ones: charcoal and switch in *their* stockings. Lately he had acted so hoody at the private school, hair greased up in a d.a., dark shirt with white silk tie, pants tapered like a zoot suit—he already knew his dad meant to send him to boarding school next fall. So he would have to go away like poor rich Dinghy Chalmers, whose mom (a rumor in Spring Glen) fell ill like Otter's. Well, what do you expect? a woman confined to her room for years on end by her husband, old C.V. Chalmers, the Wall Street magnate. Only they didn't come in white coats to take Mrs. Chalmers away, like Mrs. Zwobuchowicz. No, she made her escape one day on the New York New Haven & Hartford. She ran away to live high in Manhattan, and make up for lost time: away from all those millions which 'suffocated her', far away from her philandering husband, old C.V. So, at least, she told her neighbor, Mrs. Luccock, one day before she left Spring Glen.

VI

Through Christmas morning Newell played in the living room, and then took the new stuff upstairs. He had a feeling: is this all? Nothing more? Enjoyment in the glittery gifts dissolved in his mouth, like three bags crammed with Halloween candy, and left a cloying sense. Once Evelyne attended a social function, at school or somewhere, to do with 'underprivileged' children. For some reason he remembered the intonation his sister gave that word: 'underprivileged'; as though she had an uneasy feeling, and laughed a little. He felt kind of punchdrunk on presents, punchy on privilege.

After lunch his parents held a family council. Emory said Anne-Green had died last night, but it was alright because she had a long, full life, and everybody would miss her, and still loved her, and she went to heaven.

Newell thought this over a moment, and said:

—All people can go to heaven, right? if they're good?

—Pipe down, said Anne.

—Grandma may not want to see the people on her porch in Grifton.

—Shush up.

Joey smirked, but Evelyne sat quietly, sadly.

Lemon chirped happily on Christmas Day.

Emory went on for awhile: a kind of stick-and-doughnut lecture, for his children, this time about death. Also, they would all travel South tomorrow by train for Anne-Green's wake, funeral service, then burial at Shine Street Cemetery in Kinston's Black section, ironically.

What a life! thought Newell. My vacation, too, spent in tweeds and a necktie.

VII

Christmas Day always brought an anticlimactic mood. After lunch he went outside into the bright day and the snow. Snow up to your waist, drifts over your head in some places; it sparkled in the sunlight. Adults shoveled their walks and called to neighbors across the way. Kids trudged along pulling Flexible Flyers, or stopped to pack a snowball. Here, there; a snowman with a derby hat, charcoal eyes, carrot nose. A crow cawed. No cars made their way down Santa Fe.

Newell went along to the brook: frozen over, its banks nearly snowed under, like everything else. He continued on to the Glendower: closed not only for Christmas, but for all time, by the Board of Health. Serve its proprietor right, the snitch, after he blew the whistle on his best customer: that Robin Hood who gave baseball cards to girls.

Then he decided to go round up Otter.

—Oh, Oh-h-h-tis!

He called outside. For years they wouldn't let him come in: ever since he broke their window with a rock.

Out came his friend hardly dressed for the weather. Otto took pride in wearing just a sweater when it was freezing outside. In his stubborn, hoarse, cough syrup voice, he said:

—Where to?

—I don't know. Go sing Old Gray Mare at Mrs. Luccock's?

The boy shrugged.

—Naw. That ain't a carol.

—My grandmother died. I have to take a train tomorrow.

—Sorry. Is it far?

—North Carolina.

—Too bad. Party at the Junior High this Friday. You could've gone.

—See that? I always miss out. I would've seen Cynthia Landis.

—Yep. The Zwerg knows her.

—Maybe even danced with her . . .—In disgust Newell kicked up some snow.—What luck: doesn't it just beat all? . . . Well, what if we go call on some snooty girl right now. Ring Terrible Typhoid's doorbell here on Wilke Parkway. Or go up to The Lunger's on Crest Road.

Otter flushed red, shrugged. He had a bad crush on Betty Lund-gren.

–Naw. Let's shovel walks and make some money.

–Hell no. Just snow again tomorrow.

–So we'll shovel again and make more.

–Not me. Darn, I have to go South . . .

For a few hours the two boys tramped around Spring Glen with nothing to do, and nowhere to go. They bumped shoulders, and dove into a snowdrift, and splashed around. Mush! you huskies. They threw snowballs at a streetlamp, or a neighborhood dog. Newell made believe they explored the Arctic Circle, where there were no private schools. He muttered to himself:

–Eskimos don't wear neckties.

The midafternoon light turned golden, and began to wane. As shadows spread toward evening, across the clean high-drifted snow, the two boys said so long. Otter turned his steps toward home and flapped his sweater sleeves out in front of him, since he kept his hands drawn inside for warmth.

Tell me: do you think he would ever wear a coat on a cold winter day? Hell no. He was much too stubborn to do a sensible thing like that. Newell stared after him a moment, and so will we, asking: O Otter, why so perverse? Why are you so prone to a mood of *no*? Again and again your weakness puts you in the wrong, and then you must defend that position until the bitter end . . . Why, sir? Is it with an eye to your place in legend–since no one on this earth was ever so stubborn? Well, don't think we condemn you, or even pretend to understand you. For never in the whole history of humanity was there such a convoluted stubbornness as yours, Otter; never such contradictions defended with such a tenacity, such obstinacy. You know what? I think this stubbornness of yours is a religion. You believe in it!

Make no mistake: we are sympathetic to The Otter. A bit impatient at times; but we like him. Yet in the interests of truth we must point out that deep down, in regions beneath that bullhead of his and that spirit of contradiction, there was a mainspring of–envy! Ow. It was the bourgeois spirit balled in a fist. Otter was envious of the world about him, which he wrongly saw as sane–at least by comparison to life at his house. And so his noble deeds, helping friends, were done from a motive of envy. Well who wouldn't be envious in his position? Tell me.

I think he may have been profoundly envious that some other American, somewhere, could ever be deeply and sincerely happy with a good conscience. I am (envious, that is); though you and I, Reader, know this to be impossible, a pipe dream. What say? You deny it? Then you better close this book because I'm afraid of its effect on you.

In any case, Otter wasn't happy. But he *was* stubborn. Oh yes. And he would live.

Maybe it was a lifelong war with him for self-respect. But he chose his battles badly: always in the wrong, always defending an untenable position with an irrational stubbornness never before seen in the annals of Redemaine, or Mankind, or the universe for that matter. Three universes!

Of course all this is just a guess. I surmise. For who can fathom a boy's soul? It is nature's soul.

Minimum Requirements of a Man

I

If you asked Mrs. Luccock her opinion about the neighborhood, life in Spring Glen these days, as the 'Fifties wore on toward the 'Sixties, she would tell you things had changed. When, not long ago, Newell Gilbert hurled a crab apple up at her second floor veranda where she took the sun in a bikini, she laughed it off and called the culprit a bad little boy, but cute. Last Halloween, however, someone ran a hatpin through her Siamese cat, and killed it. This shook the good woman up, as well it might: to find Dearie that way outside the garage, Dearie stuck through with a hatpin.

Then Mrs. Luccock said:

—Spring Glen has changed.

For awhile suspicion played over the small New England community, since no one had been caught. Nobody came forward to claim responsibility for such an act. An eyebrow raised here, there, some folks raised both of them, whenever Professor Gilbert's younger son strode past. But Newell, with an uncharacteristic thoughtfulness, rang at Luccocks' one afternoon and said he felt sorry for what happened, but he didn't know who done it, and couldn't imagine. None of his friends. Of course, this didn't put him in the clear, not completely. Lil Berryer's dad would believe till his dying day that Newell, the other Halloween, had dumped all eight burlap bags of hard raked autumn leaves back on not Berryers' but their neighbors' lawn, on Neighbors Night; though I know personally, for a fact, that my hero never did such a base thing, at least not to his recollection, among so many similar deeds. Maybe Rand did it. Yes, ask Rand; this prank, about the leaves, has Rand's name all over it. He went berserk that time after staying aloof from such things through his childhood. By now most Spring Glen boys had outgrown Halloween.

But tell me: wouldn't the cat killer have scratches up and down his arms, like a candycane, dealt by the Siamese? An occupying army's intelligence service triages enemy among a civilian population by such signs, a chafed elbow, a scuffed knee, a blister.

For over six months, no clue. Was Spring Glen haunted? Must we speak no longer of boyish pranks, but rather something demented, and very mean; a violent act made worse by its ability to go unpunished? For a time some town fathers suspected Teddy Varnhagen, a twelve year-old demon and surefire bet for a future pyromaniac, when he went to Harvard.

But then another event occurred, even more spectacular than a hatpin in a cat—far more, unfortunately. And then nobody needed to look any further.

II

On a sunny day in April, 1957, a fifth grader named Hershell Fitchew took Ricky Williams' baby sister hostage. Hersh, or 'Curly' to friends and associates, calmly rolled the fourteen month-old girl in her baby carriage from the Williams backyard, and took her down to the Gilberts'. There he unstrapped her pink stumpy legs, grabbed her up like a bale of laundry, somehow didn't drop her, and went inside the doghouse alongside the garage.

The child, named Faye, did not howl for some reason. But a moment later something else happened, and caught Evelyne Gilbert's attention where she sat studying by a window in her second floor bedroom.

A loud crash, a cry, outside: in the garage! Curly, emerged from the doghouse a moment, had gone in the garage for something, and pulled Professor Gilbert's toolbox down on his head.

Evelyne glanced out and saw him dash, face dripping blood from the hairline like in *Monster Rally,* back into the doghouse. He carried a tool in his hand.

Then she saw the baby carriage.

—Mom!—cried Evelyne, and made for her parents' bedroom.—Come look! There's something going on out back.

After a glimpse Anne Gilbert went downstairs, through the screen door by the kitchen, and approached the doghouse.

Kindly, but with a frown, she said:

—Hershell, are you okay?

—You're it, and I quit.

—You've been playing tag? . . . Then you must be hungry.

—Gotcha' back!

—I . . . I just baked a pan of gingerbread. Would you like some, with whip cream?

—You're it, and I quit.

Anne thought a moment, hesitant.

—Or thirsty. How about some soda? sarsparilla? . . . Why don't you come in the kitchen?

—Let's not, and say we did.

His curious low voice had a quiver, a tinge of—what?

—You can bring the baby. Or . . . or I could bring a tray out here for you?

Anne leaned to see more clearly what was going on inside the doghouse. A makeup artist couldn't have done it better: the boy's face grim, features set, humorless and pale, not a good color; his shock of hair straight, sandy, all Curly's hair one single cowlick—like the dead Siamese cat's, his victim.

Anne drew back, stunned by the sight of blood on his forehead, cheeks; also by his dark expression, the tinge of—just what, in his eyes?

—Well, let me know, okay? . . . Okay? Come on out now, really. Come on, please do—

—Make me—he sang out at her, so strangely.—You're made, and what a mess! Make me—he said again, as though to himself this time.—You're made, and what a mess.

Then Anne straightened, and, slowly, moved away. For she had seen, in the boy's hand, a pointed instrument: an awl kept in her husband's toolbox. And the sharp point Hershell held, with an intentness, to the small girl's heart—just as he had a hatpin, six months ago, to Mrs. Luccock's Dearie: maybe using a pair of elbow-length gardener's gloves that time, since a cat could defend itself, or else stealing up on the languid, pampered house pet where it slept. But Ricky Williams' little sister gave Curly a kind of pucker, as though happy with this attention beyond her immediate family, and said:

—Pwowwup. Dada!

III

Anne Gilbert, shaken, tried to remain calm, and collect her wits. As she retreated back toward the kitchen entry, a fact dawned on her, something rather terrible. Young Hersh Fitchew had his mother Adele's eyes, a languid, catty green; eyes, in her case, too much for this staid suburban community: where so far the juiciest piece of gossip concerned our Congregational minister's running off with the assistant pastor's wife. What attendance the following Sunday: you'd have thought it was the Second Coming. What a hush when the bridegroom of Christ ascended his hard-won pulpit, like a man with a cross. As for Hersh's mom, the sensuous Adele: she should have ridden a barge down the Nile instead of raising three kids, by herself, in this gossipy town.

Another thing Anne pondered, as she picked up speed, once past the screen door, toward the telephone. Mrs. Luccock's sleek blue-gray Siamese always received VIP treatment. Everyone knew this. A local wit said it had to do with her brother-in-law's high government post in the nation's capital. Like some millionaire's mistress the female cat lived on fishy morsels, sturgeon, if not caviar. In winter Mrs. Luccock dressed Dearie in sensual little dickies, a bejewelled collar when guests arrived. Like Hersh's mother, Adele Fitchew, this cat went about self-contained, full of her sex, lewd at times in her posturing, strutting, arching her rump up, when an electric impulse bristled her velvet fur.

Just a word, in passing, about the Williams family. They too had a way about them: also well pleased with themselves, pampered; they sort of beamed, and they stuck together. Look at Ricky Williams: his ears wouldn't stick out after the expensive operation, but he'd never amount to much as a second baseman either, hypersensitive to the slightest touch, a whiner. Can you picture Rickykins bowled over, spiked by a runner breaking up the DP? I could sooner think of the Seven Blocks of Granite performing entrechats in their ballet tutus. So there it was. Hershell Fitchew, Curly, a Spring Glen kid under-privileged when it came to mother love, maybe crazed with depriva-tion, stared out from the doghouse with a glum look. He didn't care anymore: Newell's mom or the town police, Crumley and Com-pany—he'd thumb his nose at you, too. Why, this guy was even stub-borner than Otter, and I for one have never seen such stubbornness as that before or since. But whereas the motherless Otis spent his days at Redemaine Junior High drowning his sorrows in cherry cough syrup—Curly had more of 'the mothers' than he knew how to handle. It went beyond. And so the time came when he snapped. And now he hung on the verge of an act far worse even than the fa-mous Susie giving blow jobs to Yalies; though I think that's pretty bad, don't you? It was the worst scandal we'd had, around here, up until that time.

Little Curly's act went beyond. Plus he felt no guilt, not a dram. He would stick out his tongue at Officer Crumley, or Professor Gilbert for that matter; he would give President Eisenhower the voodoo hex: thumb, index to lips and eyes, then draw them together to distort your features, all eye whites. Fearful! If Curly made such a face at Ike, the Allied Supreme Commander would quake as though he saw a communist. It made you wonder how the boy could wear his double Western belt buckle on the side, like everybody else.

What a sullen, mulish little outcast, this Hershell Fitchew! Oh, Adele, I admired your *short*-shorts, cuffed even shorter, tighter, in line with your . . . oooooweee! I lusted for you, Adele, beside other Spring Glen boys, Zwergli, Parnell L. Kelleher, spinning on our stools there at Floriani's soda fountain, while Flumczyzk spun our malted milks and poured an overflow lump into a five cent coke glass, for himself, like a kickback. And suddenly you came in, a Spring Glen woman, and then some. You took our pubescent ids by storm, Adele, and knew it, and I snorted like a horse and wished you'd go away because a boy has enough troubles without women getting into the act.

In those days I gaped at your too apparent charms. But now I say:

—Shame on you, Adele. You should have looked after Curly a lit-tle better.

Such a morose little character, this Hershell Fitchew—and now a Spring Glen outlaw. He peered out from the doghouse at a world lacking in affection, kindness, parental guidance, truth. I know you and I may argue, Reader, but somehow I just can't blame the weird little kid. See how he stares out at us, blood on his freckled face, and even now craves the love and affection he deserves despite his penchant for the macabre?

Also, I have a weakness for Adele Fitchew, and, on second thought, don't like to blame her either. She didn't emerge fully formed like Venus on a seashell. Free will exists, and responsibility for our actions. But social conditions also made Adele and molded her will to such a degree we may ask: how free was she? Would a free person treat a child as she did? What is freedom?

Ah me: who is to blame? Curly? His mom? Spring Glen maybe, that boy's paradise?

IV

Anne Gilbert usually called her husband at the office when something came up during the day. But not this time. The professor could not abide little Hersh or his provocative mother: Adele who liked to tie her blouse above her navel, so her breasts jutted more than an Atlantic City pier. Those things, let me tell you, were not crab-apply like the bikini'd Mrs. Luccock's; no, Adele's were two ripe mangos, the reddish kind, a bit overripe. Well!

But why must her bad seed of a son come to the Gilbert's doghouse, and not someone else's, to pull his dangerous stunt? Did he choose it because it was new? Newell burned down the old one after Sandy the sappy cockerspaniel, whom he mistreated, died . . . Anne, phone receiver in hand, wondered what to do. Call her husband? The police station? The infant Faye Williams' mother, Claire, three doors down? or Adele Fitchew up on Dorsal Drive? Anne paused. While she thought a moment, Hershell's reason for coming here grew more clear.

When springtime came Newell organized whiffleball games with little kids from the block. His older brother Joey went out and played Babe Ruth League ball, but Newell—like Evelyne when she turned her room into a schoolhouse—liked to coach and teach the neighborhood squirts. He never forgot a day when he himself was small, seven years old, and some older boys used him, Thad Floriani and Enoch to play a game called 'torture' in a garage: hung them upside down from beams, he remembered, and would've done worse, but Dinghy Chalmers' older brother vetoed methods that really went too far. Finally they let their victims go home, crying and choking for breath after such a tension. You wondered: what will happen next? . . . Another time, Newell arrived home from fourth grade to find blocks above the brook in an uproar, kids fleeing here, there, in tears. The same bigger boys had gone about creating a war atmosphere along these placid suburban streets; they ambushed, they terrorized the smaller ones; a miracle nobody got hurt . . . Anyway, Newell remembered. By and large it was in his nature to do good by little kids, not bad; though I'm not saying he didn't tease them sometimes, and especially his sister Lemon, best kid on earth.

The Gilbert house on Santa Fe had curious traits: gray with a long black roof, quaint roundish eaves, like an elves' house. We've mentioned the high living room ceiling, and cardboard attic walls at odd angles. Also, Emory used to drive the Packard right under Evelyne's room to the garage: before he had a downstairs bedroom built on, and then you had to drive around by the alley. But the old cement driveway still bordered the backyard, and here Newell staged whiffleball games, when spring came. And, as always, he bugged his dad: if this latter home from work found the game gone into extra innings, Anne's flowerbeds a wreck, shouts and infield chatter, arguments with the ump, Newell, as kids got hungry and cross toward suppertime.

They enjoyed playing here. You hit from the garage toward the house: lofted 'short porch' homeruns onto the tall sloping gable, its dormer window (the attic bathroom where Cliff wiped away daddy longlegs with a rag). High drive off the second storey: a triple. First floor, or else dead center down the bank: a double. On this bank Newell and Otter once fought all afternoon, the day after they met in third grade, without a decisive headlock. Grounder not fielded cleanly off the cement: a single.

In late afternoon the kids talked it up, cried out, insulted each other over a disputed play. Baseball sounds filled the backyards down to Luccocks'. Before long moms would intone their familiar calls, Bill-lee! Rick-kie! and the game would revert to the previous inning for a final score, despite Durocher and Stanky's furious protests. Last week a hard-fought whiffleball game entered the fifth inning, and a few parents and siblings leaned out neighboring windows to watch. Tension mounted, as the hitter measured his swing with the yellow plastic bat, and Newell, who pitched for both sides, wound up grandiosely. Newell fooled around a little too much for such a clutch moment: he might pitch behind his back, like Tommy Byrne; or he'd wind up, kick high, right arm whipped round for the high hard one, zii-i-i-ip!—but meanwhile he slipped the ball to his left hand and flipped it in, blip! . . . as he made the follow-through. Talk about a change-up! The Newb scared a little tot half to death and then had a laugh about it . . . But what a wicked roundhouse curve you could throw with a whiffleball: wickeder than . . . than Adele Fitchew's . . . well, I'll let you complete this sentence.

—C'mon, you kid! Sock 'er a country mile!

—Well, uh, yes—said Newell, low-voiced, professorial, like that nurd Mr. Morbleu rock 'im, uh, sock 'im, and, er, mock 'im.

—Hey! Pound that sucker, Benny kid!

—No batter no batter no batter!

—Hawn' you kid! Lambaste that baby!

—Can o' corn, can o' corn.

—Slugeramile, you babe!

—Blast that pill!

—Okay, said little Benny Haas. I will if I can!

In came the pitch.

Whiff!

Newell, pitcher and umpire, roared and jerked the batter out with a showmanship:

—Steee'! Sit'tit'it downuhhh!

Talk about overkill. Little Benny, without a word, slunked away head down. He fought back tears.

In stepped the next hitter. With conviction he tapped the plastic bat on home plate, and stared out defiantly at the pitcher.

Newell cried:

—Mechanical men on second and third! Two gone!

—Jump on 'er! Over the house with that pea! Into orbit!

Newell said, thoughtful:

—Anyone breaks a window . . . they win.

—C'mon, Stretch. Tie up the game!

But just then the players became aware of a somber, a moody little personage who stood in foul territory on the grass by the swing set. Hersh Fitchew inspected a stray glove tossed there by the team at bat.

—Hey! Get away from my mitt.

—Yeah, ya' little skunk.

—Doesn't even know how to play.

—Yeah.

A few laughed at him.

For a moment Newell stared at the sad little boy. The future missionary in him took a hand, and he said:

—Hey there, Buddyroll. Wanna' get in the game?

The others looked at their coach, umpire, friend, mentor, hero, Newell Gilbert, then at one another.

—You got bats in your belfry?! He can't play here.

—Not on my side!

—What a jerk!

—What a 'n-i-c-e'!—said the little kid Doedoe, too small to play. For awhile this Doedoe got on a kick and called everyone stinker; so Evelyne Gilbert said to him one day: Do you know how to spell stinker? N-i-c-e.

More protests.

—He can't even catch.

—Look at 'im, a nervous wreck!

—I know, said Newell, but I don't care. Look, nobody kept you from playing. Why should he get left out? Say hey, Curly, you've got to play the field before you get your ups.

—If he plays, I quit. He can't even see straight.

—Yeah, nutty as a fruitcake.

Hershell stood there, and looked at them, darkly. He still held onto the other boy's glove.

—C'mon, ignore him! Let's finish this inning.

—Naw, I quit.

—If you do: no cards.

After the game Newell distributed baseball cards from a box he had up in the attic: cards worth a fortune someday, complete sets; also football cards, airplane cards, pro boxers, movie stars, Hoppalong Cassidy stickers from Bond Bread wrappers. Sick of 'em.

Now here, there, neighbors leaned out of upstairs windows like grandstands to see whether Curly would get in the game. One adult gave a catcall:

–Send that nut to Middletown!

–Where Wiley DeWitte went.

The batter kept tapping home:

–Hey, pitch 'er right in there! I gotta' go in soon.

But now somebody else arrived. A much respected figure strode across the lawn toward the delayed game. His heavy gait, in a gray business suit and homburg hat, compelled everyone's attention. Professor Gilbert approached.

–What's going on here? Newell, if I've told you once I've told you a thousand times: no ballplaying in the driveway! Look at your mother's flowerbeds. And you'll break a window.

–With a whiffleball?

–This isn't Yankee Stadium!

One little kid raised his hand and said to Newell's dad:

–Will you please tell Curly to get out of here.

Professor Gilbert frowned at the strange fellow: Hersh Fitchew, where he lingered in foul territory by the swings . . . The grown-up, ponderous, intimidating, got a hostile stare in return. Seems Curly would brave all Spring Glen if he felt like it.

Deep voiced, the professor said:

–He can't play here because none of you can.

–Oh, hell–Newell glanced skyward and threw up his arms–always so high and mighty.

Newell looked disgusted by the tight game's delay in late innings. In fact, he felt pained by his dad's presence. Next fall, almost a certainty now: private boarding school.

Professor Gilbert made a sweeping motion which included his briefcase. He turned to go inside the house, and shouted behind him:

–Begone! Next time find somewhere else to play.

But now suddenly, like a tempest, Adele Fitchew arrived. Out front, along Santa Fe, her sedan screeched to a halt. She flung open the driver's seat door and left it open. Menacingly she moved across the lawn toward Curly, who looked scared.

Maybe Adele also felt afraid, by this time, of her son becoming a problem. His behavior made her wonder, and begin to sense she had a problem, and then some.

Here she came, hands on hips, a female demon, across the grass. She didn't deign to greet her son; oh no, in a minute she would yank Curly by the forearm and drag him after her toward the lair. But such a look she gave the learned academic: as though she had Emory

Gilbert's number! Ah! Those really were *short* shorts Adele Fitchew wore. Why, I believe the posterior she had on her was a thirty-five year-old version of Neesie Montowese's. And the professor must have seen it before, that still shapely bulge, the world's eighth wonder: maybe down at Big Jim Floriani's pharmacy when their paths crossed one afternoon; so that now their eyes met, for an instant, like lightning on a rod. But as for Adele's curves . . . well, words fail me. Again I refer to my reader for the details.

Adele shook a finger and yelled at the well-known intellectual: —What did you say? I heard you. And the time I caught you staring straight at my crotch inside Floriani's? Oh yes, don't deny it. A married man—say, where's your wife? I want a little talk with her.

Parents could be heard calling their kids home for supper. For another moment the whiffleball teams stuck around and watched the scene develop between adults. But then they winced: when the female phenom (as ol' Case said) from Dorsal Drive lost control of herself, hauled off and slapped her son so his head snapped back, and his haystack hair ruffled a little bit.

Then Curly jumped away. He avoided her grasp. All eyes watched Adele move, like a tigress, on her son. He backed off. And now, yes, Curly looked scared. His mom looked deranged in these moments: husbandless as she was, without emotional support. It all boiled over. And she did not enjoy the trials he caused her.

And now, in Curly's gaze, something dark, a strange note, fearful: it played on his features.

And, as she stalked him with the sleek movements that were hers; as she raised an arm like a paw to slap him again, grab him up by the scruff, drag him into the car for the ride to Dorsal Drive; as she moved on him, slowly, because she too, even his mother, had to be careful:—there! oh, there it was, it appeared, long and deadly, glittering in the April sunlight begun to wane toward West Hills beyond the treetops. A pea shooter. He had bought it at The Glendower, and now he put it to his mouth, and: puh! puh! A pea hit home and stung his mother's cheek.

Well, Adele gave a snort. But I've got to give her one thing: she had balls, beneath her short-shorts. Whew! She pounced on him and took the evil thing away.

All this may explain, partly, why Curly went to fetch an awl a few minutes ago, and pulled the toolbox down on his head in Gilberts' garage. And now he bled like Boris Karloff from the hairline.

Now, also, you can see why Anne Gilbert has asked the town police to come, hurry! and not her husband at the office. Gracious! Emory would pitch a fit (spitting image of his mother, Wilhelmina, down South) if you so much as said Adele Fitchew's name in his presence. He didn't like her! Too provocative! And don't ever mention her son either, Curly, a would-be psychopath with his pea shooter.

V

Inside the house Anne wrung her hands and tried to think. She had a panicky feeling since she knew a tragedy might be in the offing. Something told her little Hersh would not respond too well to the police. The sight of a man in blue could lead him to do this mad thing he had to do. And no way, probably, they could steal up on him from behind: he'd hear the metal fence rattle.

Right now things looked bad for Claire Williams' baby daughter, Faye, and not only for her. If a child got kidnapped, if a fourteen month-old girl got stabbed, maybe to death—then a national news story. A trauma for Anne Gilbert's family as well, since the horror occurred on their property. Then her husband's name got dragged in, a blot on his career. Heaven knows what that Adele Fitchew, hysterical on her better days, would say.

Legal implications, liabilities, lawsuits, attorney's fees, slander, infamy, ruin, despair—Anne's thoughts ran away from her for an instant.

What to do? She had phoned Redemaine police, and brought them into it, with a sinking sense. For what officer would show up to handle this delicate situation? The bumbling Crumley, a regular lummox? There were no female police officers, but say a squad car arrived with a guidance counselor. What then? A woman? Good idea: we've seen how well Curly relates to women. Maybe he stuck that she-cat in the first place because Dearie belonged to a seductive female, the bikini'd Mrs. Luccock.

Well, Anne phoned the authorities to protect her family. But, as the minutes ticked past, she felt hope wane for a peaceful resolution. Maybe the terrible thing had already been done out there; though she heard only silence, no infant's cries. A human child: so much more helpless than a Siamese cat.

Anne kept her head. She didn't call either of the mothers in question. Claire Williams, beside herself the moment she missed Faye's baby carriage, would not help matters if she came rushing over here. As for Adele Fitchew: that woman's presence was all the situation required. Such a squinting mistrust Anne had felt in this boy barricaded in their doghouse. And Anne had always treated him kindly enough, offered him cookies, a glass of milk once.

After her call to the Police Department, she moved upstairs. She went in her elder daughter's second storey bedroom, and there, by the window, stared out.

What she saw then amazed her.

VI

Behind the Gilbert garage stood a round cement burner, old as the house, but it still served. Cliff had made a fire from bushel baskets of last year's leaves, which he raked to prepare Anne's flowerbeds. He took no notice when Curly pushed a baby carriage into the fenced off doghouse area. But he did look up when the toolbox crashed down inside the garage.

—Hey, man.

Cliff peered in and saw the boy's bloodied face. Curly knelt and grabbed an awl from the metal tool chest.

It took a moment to react: Cliff in gardener's gloves, tending the fire. Plus, at his age, somewhere around Satchell's, you didn't turn on a dime. So by the time Cliff drew near the doghouse, with his rake, Curly had dug in with the hostage and stared out grimly.

—Freeze! said the boy, and held the awl closer to the baby's neck.

Cliff gave a little laugh, beneath his breath, and raked some odds and ends, a candy wrapper.

—Play some ball? he said.

—Can't you see I'm up to my elbows here? said little Hersh, self-importantly, in a grating voice.

Cliff did a double take as he glimpsed the baby carriage, the child, the awl in the boy's fist—and began to understand.

—Gimme a sec', he said. Got to finish my wuyhk.

And so Cliff went about, hummed, talked to himself under his breath as if nothing had happened. Got to clean 'my' garage, he muttered, sweep 'my' walk, then into 'my' house to wax the floors . . . Rags dripped from the hip pocket of his old gray gabardine trousers. Worn shirt frayed, shiney—batiste, I want to say, fine fabric. Lean, lean face gnarled like his knuckles and fingertips, from life's foul tips. He mumbled and chugged along, only movement in the house most days until the Gilbert kids came home from school. A steady eye, never mind his age: Cliff handled the rake like an athlete. Even now he kept up his cheery rhythm. The day long he dusted, swept, cleaned, sort of fidgety, with an upbeat commentary under his breath.

Cliff Gardin had a hint of the old high-pockets hitch to his walk: from days when he consorted with Josh Gibson, and they took some town in the South by storm. But his sad suit trousers, too wide, too short, his suspenders over a rusted dress shirt with a threadbare shine: some things didn't change. And where did Cliff's money go? It went, such as it was, to the children and the grandchildren: to a fund for his grandson's college, since William Johnny could hit the books, as well as burst past tacklers in the broken field. As for the rag in Cliff's back pocket, it hung there twenty or thirty years ago when he caught Satchell Paige, since you'd suyhch pretty hard for an umpire's brush in the Negro Leagues.

VII

—Rough stuff—said Hersh to himself: something he heard in the schoolyard.—Rough stuff.

—Say hey.

—Don't come no closer. I'll stick 'im.

—What's your name?

—SBD, said Hersh.

—SBD?

And then Cliff caught a whiff of a boy's anguish.

—Silent but deadly, Hersh croaked.

And then he sang a note to himself, and held it, and gave his voice a little quiver, the way kids do at a certain age: just to hear himself.

Cliffer gave a little laugh. Inside the doghouse the bloodstained face looked afraid.

—Cuyht'nly. I seen you round here before. Play some ball, don't you? Just wanted to know a ballplayer's name.

—Curly.

—Cuyhly.

—And Hershell, my real name.

—Heuyshll, good. Whatcha' got?

—Nothin'. Cats have no feelings.

—Don't they?

—My momma said. We put our cat in the bathtub.

—With water?

—N-no. First we put marbles, run 'em up and down the sides. Cat crazy trying to catch marbles with its paws, this way, that. Then water.

He gave a sort of laugh: more like a distressed miaow.

Faye Williams, slung in Curly's left arm now, across his chest, began to squirm a little, and raised a first cry. Luckily her neck, at fourteen months, had some muscle tone, since her kidnapper didn't know to support it.

—Look out, said Cliff. We woke the baby.

Curly said:

—If she knows what's good for her, she'll shut up.

—Sher' kinder cross at that.

—Stand back, I mean it.

Then Curly maneuvered, and propped the small girl on his knees, facing out. He bounced her easily, and had a nice way with her for a kid. But all the while the deadly awl stayed held in his right fist at her heart.

Cliff paused by the fence. He sort of leaned on his rake.

—Why, son?

—I don't like him.

—Who?

—Newell's dad.

—Ah.

Cliff thought this over. When he focused on a problem, something important, his wrinkles smoothed, curiously. His clear eyes had a look to them; they wondered. All the servant's bearing, rough hands and features, short breaths, brusque movements, wuyhds mur-

mured as he went along, calm responses: all had a happy-go-lucky look, except the eyes, virile.
Curly said from the doghouse:
–You hate him too?
–My wuyhd . . . he done a bit for my family. I don' 'xatly hate Mister Gilbuyht.
–You like 'im.
–Now, I didn't say that.–Cliff gave his laugh.–Diff'nt wuyhlds, 'zall.
Curly thought about this. His bloody face gave a grimace, like a mask, and he said:
–Oh. Rough stuff.
The baby got more restless. Thrust out a stick arm. Squirmed. Cliff said:
–Seems a bit hungry . . . No, Mr. G. employs me. That's good. I don't 'xactly count him as one o' mah friends.
–Oh.
Cliff said:
–Friends are equals.
–SBD.
Curly struggled a little with the baby. And now she had done something in her pants, yes, shitted up the place. So Curly began to lose patience. He kept the thing next to the infant's heart, her little yellow outfit, which stank.
–Mistuh Gilbuyht not the wuyhst.
–I killed a cat.
–Did you?
Cliff paid less attention to this than it deserved. He leaned 'his' rake against 'his' fence, and then sat on haunches at the boy's level. Still seven, eight feet away, in the opening.
–Stuck 'er.
–Say . . . Why's that?
Little Faye didn't like the stink either, and started to cry. Her wail came out like necessity, and she wasn't afraid, she asserted her rights. She pushed away the other's clutches, as babies will. And you tell me what chord this may have played in Hersh Fitchew. For hadn't his mother sunk her claws, for ten years now, into him too? And didn't he squirm?
Now Curly tried to quiet the child, but he got nowhere.

–Tst! he said. Tst!

Bad to worse. Crying. Stinky. 'N-i-c-e'.

Yes, things got more tense. In a moment–snap, stop her mouth for her.

–Say . . .

–Once a tiger pissed on me, at the zoo.

–Did it?

–Momma said: get away from that cage. So I went closer, and it lifted a hind leg, and pissed. All over me.

–Good for you, said Cliff, distracted.

–Good for you,–Hersh chuckled.–Good for you.

From his shirt pocket Cliff took the five-cent candy called Nik-L-Nips. He had bought this for William Johnny there by the bus stop at Floriani's Drugstore. Small red carton with lettering: five wax milk bottles size of an index finger, with syrup in them. Red, yellow, green, orange, purple. You had two ways to eat them, two choices: put a milk bottle in your mouth whole and chew it, like gum; or bite off the top, suck out the sweet liquid, and afterward chew the wax.

Cliff laughed a little and took out the red bottle.

–Baby woke up hungry.

–Tough shit.

Curly mimicked his mom. But he had an eye on the red milk bottle.

Cliff said:

–This'd calm her. If she could suck it.

–I want some, said Curly, and shook the baby a little.

–Okay, we'll share. Equals. You huyhd?

–Equals?

–Yessir. One for you: what color you want?

–Green.

–So. You green. The guyhl can't decide for herself. What color for her?

–I don't know.

Curly wanted his own, but he hadn't a free hand to take it.

–How about yellow like her dress?

–Wish she'd shut the hell up.

–I'll have the puyhple, and we'll save the orange for my grandson, William Johnny.

–And the red?

–Maybe we could find a reason for you to have the red.

—What reason?

Cliff gave his low laugh.

—You tell me why you desuyhv' the red milk bottle.

VIII

The baby flailed, and hit Curly a good one right in his sour puss. Little Faye Williams writhed, and cried, and stank, as though she knew the gravity of the situation.

Cliff, on his haunches, chicken-walked in reach of the doghouse, and said:

—Who drinks fuyhst?

—Me.

—Ah,—Cliff laughed, low.—Thought you might want to propose a toast.

Now Curly wondered what to do: awl in one hand, Faye in the other. He stuck out his fingers, took the green bottle, popped it whole in his mouth, chewed. He almost smiled, and said:

—Don't say I never gave you nuttin'.

—Hm, said Cliff, and waited. Here's the yellow for her. Hold on—

He hesitated to break off the top with his soiled workingman's fingers. Okay for Curly: you could throw worms and snails down a kid's gullet. But the small child?

—Gimme the red.

—No, you have to open this one, fuyhst, for the guyhl. Euyhn it.

Curly kept an arm around the squirming infant. For a moment he thought what to do, and mumbled:

—Equals?

—Hm, Cliff nodded.

—I saw a Dodger game.

—Did you?

—Randy took us down there. Erskine beat the Jints 3-2 under the lights.

—Randy?

—Mom's friend. He gone.

Curly didn't have three hands. For the baby to get fed, and him to have the red, he either had to give her up, or the awl.

By now Faye was becoming agitated. She bawled, off her rocker.
Cliff tensed: ready to spring forward since he felt Curly might
simply drop the infant from exasperation.

Cliff said:

—You can give me that hole-punch and feed the baby, or give me
the baby and I'll feed her. You choose. When she's fed, I'll give you
the red milk bottle.

—I'll get in trouble.

—Nothing like what you'll get if you huyht that guyhl.

—Will you tell on me?

—I won't.

—Honest Injun'?

—Give you my wuyhd.

—But . . . if they come after me, will you say you did it?

—Did what?

—Stole the baby.

—Listen, Mister Cuyhly. Should I lie? Even for a friend?—Cliff
grinned.—Twuyhn't be equal.

Faye ranted, and clipped her captor's nose.

Curly stared.

—Not equal?

—You'll be okay. Still young. But if I kidnapped a white guyhl,
they'd lynch me from the tree over there. You don't want that, to a
friend?

—N-no. But they'll punish me. My mom hits me.

—Does it huyht? A woman?

—Y-ye'—naw. But it scares me.

—Alright, I'll help you wuyhk this out. I'll tell them you don't
need no mo' punishment.

—You will?

—My wuyhd on it.

—Cross your heart and hope to die?

—Yessuh.

—If you don't, after I give you the baby, I'll stab myself.

—Now now.

—Then cross it.

—Huh?

—Your heart—

—Oh. Yessuh.

Cliff crossed his heart.

Curly clutched the awl. He turned, with the infant's stubby legs kicking, her mouth screaming, her head going redder than the milk bottle, and her arse shitting.

—Here, take her. Gimme the red—

But just at that instant three police officers including flat-footed Crumley came into the yard. They were led by a woman in plain clothes, not Mrs. Gilbert. They marched, tall, imposing, toward the doghouse, and they meant to have their way. You could tell. Apparently it was the best thing they could think of: a child psychologist in the lead?

—You lied! Curly yelled. Crossed your heart, and kept me busy till the coppers came.

—I did not, said Cliff, and his eyes narrowed as he tensed forward.

—I don't believe you anymore!

Curly's right arm went out with the awl: to stick it through Faye's side. Cliff sprang from his haunches to grasp Curly's forearm. The baby tumbled down, headfirst toward the doghouse floor, and Cliff sprawled to catch her in his catcher's quick hand: a wicked curve in the dirt.

Too late?

The three police officers, the woman in her business suit, charged forward.

IX

When Emory Gilbert arrived home, all in a fluster as usual after his day at the office, he had a fit. He threw a tantrum you could hear all the way from The Dump at Sackett's Point to Maldoror Drive over there at West Hills. In other words: the whole town heard the professor's invective against—his younger son.

Anne let him rant. As the evening wore on she would work to restore peace.

Her husband's second impulse, after he lowered the boom on Newell—since Newell included Hershell Fitchew in whiffleball games—was to hurt Cliff.

—Well, he's fired. Have they put him in jail at least?

This gross unfairness Anne didn't like to see in her man. She said in a curt tone:

—No, the hospital.

—Why?

—The awl went in his arm. He lost a lot of blood.

—What a damn fool stunt! I swear to you: it's boarding school for Newell in the fall. He caused Adele Fitchew's sick son to come around here in the first place. Military school!

—Not military—said Anne. And Emory didn't contest it, because he knew his wife had her limits too. Where her favorite was concerned, she might yet, for the first time in their married life, turn and confront him. She repeated, softly:—Not military school.

As for Cliff Gardin—Anne knew what they owed him tonight. More than they could repay. Plus she felt guilty. For her first thought that afternoon had been anger: when, from the second floor window, she saw Cliff chatting with the child who had taken an infant hostage in their doghouse. We may call Anne well-bred, well educated; we may not call her intellectually capable, à la hauteur. She was spunky in her way; she was not in the least confrontational, like Adele. In Anne's delicate role as mediator in a bitter, longterm father-son conflict, she often felt overwhelmed, and tried to rely on instinct. Love for the two men involved, a desire for peace, must see her through. So when she saw Cliff out there in tête-à-tête with little Hershell, her first response was bad: Cliff couldn't handle it, Cliff didn't understand, Cliff's presence would bring on disaster, and ruin her family. Cliff thought this was playtime ... So she felt. This southern woman knew Cliff Gardin only as her servant, in no other way: not as a family man himself, not as a ballplayer, catcher of Satchell Paige, not as a man, and an equal. But then, in the next instant, Anne's intuition came into play: Anne ever gracious, modest, able to appreciate the underdog's position. Her character may have been inadequate, but it had no lying in it. And so, wonder of wonders, she had felt hope suddenly; she believed in Cliff; she feared the town police would arrive and barge in and bring on disaster. Take your choice. Is it Cliff? Or Officer Crumley with his blustery authority, his insensitivity in a crux: toward a ten year-old who held an infant at knife point?

Cliff dove, and his grasp missed Hersh Fitchew's thrust, but caught, like a foul tip on his forearm, the awl in mid-flight toward the girl. He caught Faye as well; sort of cradled her half on his other arm, and eased her down: a good thing, she might have broken her neck.

Then the wild affair ended in what seemed like chaos—chaos in Spring Glen. Claire Williams, hysterical, arrived at the scene. And, a moment later, Adele Fitchew came and screamed swear words and threatened to tear out her own hair.

Curly they subdued. The cops had to strap him down, so the child psychologist could administer a sedative. They led poor Curly away toward Middletown—as they had Wiley DeWitte once, child molester, whose sister spent her days at the train station. And Gil McQuinn. But let's not talk about him.

Violence, chaos, our town. But not a tragic outcome, this time: thanks to Cliff Gardin—whose own thanks was Crumley's offer to arrest him, and take him to the police station in Centerville; though Cliff's open vein bled.

Then the urbane Crumley said:

—Next time mind your own business, jig.

Well, too bad for Officer Crumley.

But I wrote this story to say:

—Thank you, Cliffer. Thanks, friend, equal, more than equal.

—Hey, Billy! You comin' out after supper?
And Billy Holmes:
—Hope so! If my mom lets me!

The Great White Laundry Bag

I

Ethridge School. Colonial architecture. Red brick student houses lined the quadrangle on either side. At this end, Settlers Hall: administrative offices, classrooms and library, freshman quarters on the third floor. On the far side: a long dining hall called The Refectory with high windows done in elegant tracery, chandeliers, a wide entry fronting the Senior Path. Beyond the quad: infirmary, gymnasium, Headmaster's residence, also the Atelier, art studio.

At this hour, after evening study hall, then bedtime, Ethridge lay quiet. Seniors had all-night lights and prolonged their reading. Masters corrected papers by a cozy fire in their quarters down the hall. But nobody moved between dorms unless it was a raccoon sniffing the day's garbage.

In the darkness a river flowed, the Needing, past the idyllic campus. High above the dozen quaint and neatly arrayed buildings with their colonnaded walkway, the stars shone in the cold northern night.

Wind moaned like a wolf in winter at the windows, and sighed in the barren trees outside. Two friends tapped imaginary ash from chocolate cigarettes, bit them off a little at a time, and chewed. Silent for a moment they listened to a New York station turned low, since their all-night lights were illegally wired, and this would cost them detention hours, or worse, if the floor counselor found out. No footsteps in the hall . . . A desk lamp shone.

On one wall hung a pin-up: Joanne Campbell poured into a low backed, pink, sequined affair–three-quarter profile, turned away, for the full effect of her glorious rump. Record albums lay strewn here and there. On the covers: rough, surly teenagers lounged by souped-up cars, arms draped on a chromeline hood, or a buddy in black leather also chromelined, a gang deb with blond ponytail like Joanne. Teenage Dance Party. Rumble. The Paragons. The Jesters. The Charts. Troubadors of the slums.

Granny Zammet looked plum tuckered after his day: seven classes, club football, Refectory duty, evening study hall. He screwed his eyes at the pin-up, dreamily, and remarked:

–What a luscious young ass.

–So you conclude–Newell yawned–every night.

–And prove it too–said roommate Bernard, still not asleep, from under the covers.

–You mean you can hear me whacking off across the hall? asked Granny.

–You or Schmied–said Newell–alternate rhythms.

–Play a record, said The Bern. Play 'Chip-Chip-Chip' by the Mello-Kings.

–The fabulous Mello-Kings from Mount Vernon, New York. On the Herald record label.

–Shhh! The counselor–

–Lights out! Shh! Zip it.

Outside, footsteps paused by the door.

–Gilbert, Rathschilde, you guys settle down in there.

In the dark Granny Zammet raised his middle finger, making a point.

–How I do detest this place, said Granny, after a moment.

–Finest education available, said Newell, yawned.

–My cinnamon exactly, said Big Bern.

–You know what–said Granny–I'm serious, let's get out. Let's blow the joint.

–Sure, said Newell, hit the City.

The Bern was here on scholarship and not one for adventure. Often enough his roommate Newell made him nervous. The Bronx had spawned Bernard Rathschilde: a scientific genius, which he proved by brewing yeast wine from grape juice. And, as his homesickness began to abate, he felt little nostalgia for East 166th and Grand Concourse. Bern said:

—My faculty adviser won't sign my checks.

—He takes your allowance, said Granny, and goes whoring in Hartford.

They laughed. For Berneth's adviser, in the general opinion, was . . . not likely to womanize.

—Just for a weekend, Granny insisted. We'll use a weekend pass.

They only had one 'extended' pass (included Friday) per semester, and one regular. Home, they yearned for, home.

—Hm, said Newell, I'm not sure. We could go look up Ben Bolt. But how to buy the round trip ticket?

—No sweat! said Granny. Hide in the toilet.

—Leave me out, said Bernie.

—Party pooper, said Granny.

—No, I got lab work.

—Listen, said Granny, I mean it. First, pick up a few platters at Colony Records, or Tin Pan Alley. 'Down the Road' by the Neons. I want it bad, Joanne!

—With whose allowance? said Newell.

—Naw, we'll steal 'em, like we do here in town.

That was true. They had become pretty good shoplifters.

—Then . . . then we'll hunt a few choice quail. Pick up a deb or two each, and . . . and head for Coney Island. Not bad!

—And get rockin' pneumonia, in the process.

—Or something else, said Bernard.

—Hm, said Newell. I got twenty-three detention hours already. I lead the league.

Granny laughed:

—You hold the record: a Saturday detention great. Then . . . then we'll go find Ben Bolt, and play some basketball in the park, Sunday morning, before we come back. How 'bout it?

—I'd like to see Ben Bolt again.

—Sure! said Granny. All the 'reet guys get bounced. The good ones leave. Whaddayasay? C'mon.

—I can hardly stand this grind. I'm being robbed of my youth by a tweed suit. You know, I sort of don't care what happens anymore. Okay, I'll go.

–Hourrah!–Granny jumped up on Berneth's bed, with Bern in it; he trampolined.–We'll join a gang, we'll become Amboy Dukes. Pah! pah! zip-guns! No more whacking off over Master Glebe's fat wife. No more counselors, they can go cornhole themselves. No more dining hall duty, no more pop quizzes, no more detention hours! Hourrah! We'll meet Joanne Campbell and–
–Listen, said The Bern. Shh, hear it, next door? It's Schmied.
–Hey! Schmidlap, stop that!–Granny jumped down and knocked on the wall.–You're a bad boy to do that! The first Ethridge commandment: thou shalt not whack.

II

That Saturday, after lunch, Newell Gilbert walked into town and turned right along the main drag to the train station. At the last minute Granny begged off, for all his enthusiasm, and said he had better make up three hours in detention. And so, alone, without a ticket or much money, Newell hopped on board the New York New Haven & Hartford and hid in a toilet while the conductor passed through punching tickets and issuing seat checks. Anxious, in no very jubilant mood, the prep school student's heart pounded when a knock came on the bathroom door.
–Tickets!
At first he didn't answer.
–All tickets!
–You took it already. Be out in a minute.
For awhile he cowered in there, smelly place, and kept silent when people tapped to use the facilities. Newell tried to raise his spirits with thoughts of Ben Bolt, a regular guy with a blond d.a. (full and greasy, not crewcut or Chicago-style). Ben Bolt got expelled from Ethridge on purpose after he threw all The Refectory silverware into the lily pond out behind The Atelier, where a yearly mixer with the sister school was held. Newell wanted to see his friend again, though he didn't have a phone number for him, and only remembered: West 84th Street. But the idea of arriving by himself, at nightfall, in the great forbidding City made a fourteen year-old feel sick. Also,

this would cost him at least ten detention hours, but he didn't care anymore. He was working hard to get kicked out, booted, like Ben Bolt; only he had to work much harder because his father served on the Ethridge board of trustees.

Newell had journeyed to New York before, a few times, with his dad. Twice he saw ballgames; then almost two years ago, in January '57 when he still attended the private day school, he got his first experience of Manhattan. First, he angered his father by asking in Brooks Brothers if they had zoot suits, and then refusing to choose anything at all, calling the place 'hell in a wool suit'. But worse was in store. While Emory went to collect a million dollar foundation gift for a construction project at the university, a quad of married dorms, Newell snuck out of the wainscoted men's club where they were staying, in the shadow of Grand Central, and made a foray to buy a certain platter he was obsessed with in those days: 'The Wind' by the Four Diablos. So obsessed, he later read a thick novel about public school, *Harrison High,* while the song played over and over, a hundred times, until his parents thought he was crazy. Well, when Emory returned, and found his son missing, he had his usual caniption fit, and made the front desk phone the precinct and put out an all-points bulletin. But Newell showed up, his trip a success despite the men's store fiasco, no zoot—since he had found Colony Records and bought not only 'The Wind' by the Four Diablos, but also 'Going Down the River' by The Students, terrific! . . . Back home Emory told a colleague, with pathos:

–I think I've lost my son.

The co-faculty member replied:

–But you've gained a million dollars.

Emory laughed and said:

–I'd rather have a million dollar son.

III

The train rolled along through the cold January afternoon. Still in the bathroom Newell listened to the clickety rhythm of its passage over the rails. The whistle blew into the distance of Connecticut farmlands. Lights inside were dimmed and went off for an instant. Sounds muted through a tunnel. He mulled over Granny Zammet's big talk about 'hitting the streets', and then collapse when it came to action. Well, what else was new? You could search awhile before you found a regular guy at Ethridge: someone like his friends back home. After all he felt set up by Zammet. For he must return from his weekend pass with word on Ben Bolt's life in public school down there; also detailed accounts: how he hunted quail, picked up a few chicks. And don't forget to bring back new hot tunes, by the Mint Juleps, or 'Nite Owl' by Tony Allen and the Champs, or 'Strange Love' by the Native Boys, duly hocked (stolen) from the racks at Tin Pan Alley. Plus he had to play basketball in a playground somewhere, Sunday morning, for this escapade to be a success. Right now he hid out a moment longer in the lavatory; shook his head, and thought: Granny Zammet, what a drip; and tried to muster courage for the arrival at Grand Central.

But a long way yet from here to there. And first he had to go out and try to steal a seat check.

So he went forth, wandered through the cars, and felt the other, paid-up passengers' eyes on his guilty person as he moved down the aisle. 'Down the Aisle' by The Paragons. Like a tracked beast he looked out for the conductor, and just knew he'd get caught if he tried to palm somebody's seat check.

Unfortunately, Newell had made a big mistake. You explain it: he brought along a white laundry bag abulge with dirty socks and underclothes, shirts and hankies. He meant to drop it off at home on his way back tomorrow night. But how did you act suave (pronounce like wave), pick up chicks, hound quail—how do you enter a store unnoticed and clip rhythm 'n blues records when you have to lug around twenty pounds of grungy socks and soiled undies? Cool! And the damned thing swung over his shoulder; it drew people's attention to his coming and going through the train. The Ethridge laundry service could have starched those shirts: so stiff you'd think you were a robot. Instead, he brought them along for his mom's careful hands.

IV

He scoured the cars and found no hint of a stray ticket. Anxiety gripped him. We are sorry to report this of the fourteen year-old adventurer, but he felt ready to break down crying, and give himself up. What a gang member he would make, what an Amboy Duke.

But just then someone said his name.

He turned and saw a classmate named Royall Lambert, sitting in a window seat with a grin on his pale zitty face.

—Hello, Lambie-pie! Going home on a weekend pass, Lambkins dear?

Relief flooded into Newell's soul. For The Lamb was a born dupe, a total flit, and would be almost anybody's flunky who went in for such things. Why, Newell might snatch Lambert's seat check before the drippy dip knew what happened. Newell forced a laugh and said:

—You know, The Bern wired all-night lights. So I want you to come tomorrow after lights-out and do my mechanical drawing assignment.

—Sure thing!

Royall Lambert, his sallow face marred by inflamed pimples, flushed with pleasure at the idea of working into the wee hours on someone else's difficult project.

Newell kept up the smalltalk, like a man with more serious matters on his mind. And the other looked so delighted by this bit of attention from a classmate, he didn't notice when the hand slipped casually over his orange seat check, covered it an instant, and removed it.

—Well, Lambster, see you back at school! Don't forget about tomorrow night.

—Sure thing!

—Have a blast. Enjoy your weekend pass.

—My mom's sick.

—Oh, sorry. Say hello to Genevieve for me.

—Sure. Someday a mom's got to die, you know. I thought: better go see her.

—Heck yeah.

Sometimes, on the hall, boys called each other by their mothers' names. So Newell sent greetings to Genevieve.

—Gee! It's fun to talk. This seat's free: can't we ride together?

—Naw, I got business to tend to, up front. Accompanying a chick into The City.

With a manly wink Newell turned, and sauntered along the aisle in the crowded train. For the moment he felt pretty relieved, happy with himself, and fingered the classmate's seat check in his coat pocket. The big white laundry bag bumped along, swung, hit one or two heads.

V

But as the train neared Redemaine Station his anxiety rose up again. Worse than before! Gone the heroic pose for Royall Lambert's benefit. Gone the bravado needed to see through such a trip: more than he could chew. How would he confront New York City alone, this cold winter evening, and hope to find a long lost Ben Bolt, expelled for the silverware stunt, on some West 84th Street out in the middle of nowhere? Now he felt dread, a keen sense of regret. The idea of passing up Redemaine, twenty-four hours in his own room—after he used a weekend pass, and only one remained for the year—this scuttled his willpower. He wanted to see his parents, and Joey and Evelyne, little sister Lemon; maybe make a phone call to Otter, CHestnut 8-1378, he still knew the number. Otis was no longer a chunky little kid with slit eyes set deep in his pink face, shy and evasive yet stubborn as hell, with a chip on his shoulder the size of Spring Glen. No: Big O had become harder, short but sturdy and tough, a second-string center for the Redemaine Junior High Redmen. Once last fall he got the nod to start after the first-stringer broke training; but Coach repented such a decision, and so Otto rode the bench again. Yep; he'd do well if he ever got in.

Now Newell hefted the laundry bag which weighed him down a lot, and cut into his shoulder. Yes, the dirty laundry was a factor too: he couldn't see himself hauling that mess into The City where he had to pick up at least three hot chicks if he wanted to save face back at school tomorrow night.

Sunday night . . . The mere idea made him sick because he had boasted to Schmied, to Big Bern, all about how he would snow-job some broad in a bar, and hock *'reet* platters in Tin Pan Alley, and play b-ball with Ben Bolt in a schoolyard on West 84th Street. He must do some big thing so he could tell the prepsters when they came flocking into his room, expecting something terrific, on Sunday night. Probably they were thinking only of him this very moment, as they tied the necktie noose round their necks, and donned their woolens for another rotten dinner in The Refectory, and then on to dreary study hall for an hour and forty-five minutes. Oh! how they stood awed by his courage, out here on his own; how they shared his City romance from afar, while they spooned the insipid soup, and chewed lukewarm peas with a grimace, and rotten meatloaf, and spooned tiny nips from their small pudding portions—size of a chocolate cigarette, or a piece of crud—to postpone the moment when they headed back toward evening study hall.

But the fear rose in his throat, and now he wished he hadn't told anyone about his plans. Why not simply take off for a few hours at home, telling no one, and then pay the price when he got back? He had amassed so many detention hours already: what more could they do to him? Only kick him out—and this he strove to achieve.

He read and reread dime novels of the city streets, *The Amboy Dukes, Knock on Any Door, Reefer Kid, Let No Man Write My Epitaph.* Instead of doing assignments he daydreamed gangs, The Egyptian Kings in Harlem. What a heaven! He imagined rumbles and life on a block in New York. How would he handle himself? Gain acceptance among those lucky city kids? A slum tenement looked like paradise compared with Ethridge School, where his few friends were misfits trying to conform, Schmiedikins and The Bern. And now how could he read his books, or play his records anymore, 'Up on the Mountain' by The Magnificents, 'Zoop' by The Charts, after he chickened out on his plans. What anguish he felt in these instants, trying to decide.

VI

The train slowed and then halted, with a gasp, along Redemaine Station platform. Before Newell had time to decide his own plight, and weigh the consequences any further, he had lunged down the aisle like a wild man, his great white laundry bag battering heads on the way, and flung himself outside into the wintry, intimate Rede-maine air. His pain vanished as he began to make his way from the station, and he thought: what a scene when Dad sees me arrive like this, without their permission.

Then a strange thing happened. He no longer thought about his father, or the return to school tomorrow night when he would have to confess all, and go from hero to goat, and Granny Zammet's grin would say: see that? you're no better than the rest of us. No, Newell didn't think about this now; instead, he recalled Lambert still on the train. In the sudden flush of happiness, to be home, Newell felt pity for poor Royall Lambert, whose mother was sick, and someday a mom's got to die, you know, so why not be kind to her now?

Newell dug in his pocket for the classmate's seat check, and then stood staring at it. Lambie-pie's image smiled out at him from the small orange seat check.

The next moment, to his surprise, Newell found himself confessing the theft to a conductor who happened along the platform.

—All ah-boa-ahd!

Before he realized the boner he was pulling, Newell gave up the stolen seat check and paid two dollars, a week's Ethridge allowance—four slices of seven layer cake in The Snug, or else two 'reet platters from the store in town, though he could steal them anyway—for a train ride he had already taken.

But even this humiliation was gone at once as he trotted from the station into the chill, familiar Redemaine evening. Already he blessed his attic room, and the warmth of his mom's smile: the gingerbread she'd bake him despite his dad's anger and rantings; the criminal got rewarded with a triple portion of whip cream! How happy he felt suddenly: after months of misery at a school he detested. Merrily, merrily the laundry bag swung over his shoulder as he ran along toward home.

VII

Sunday night, after lights-out, here they came: Granny and Schmied snuck along the corridor like mice in pajamas, and darted in Newell's room to hear a real life story of New York exploits. Reet!

While the senior counselor, Hillyer, fingered his zits before a mirror, the young Ethridge delinquents huddled to hear a tale of gang debs, Ben Bolt's public school life in New York, hoods in zoot, while they spun a few of Newell's new platters. Shh! Real low, so that suck-up Hillyer, Hilly-babe, wouldn't hear them and inform the dorm master down the hall.

Well, it always happens. Hillyer's one chance to do some good in life, instead of screaming like a cunt at sophomores, dishing out detention hours, running to the master to tattletale: Hillyer gets his big break, and look: the zitface is nowhere to be seen. For Newell had no idea what cockeyed story to tell his friends, and would gladly have taken six more detention hours or a dozen to get off the hook.

How he disliked bullshit in others! And now he had to lie, and hate himself for it. So he feared them when they came in the room, his superiors; he cringed like a convict paraded before decent people. For the moment he would gladly have exchanged one of The Hill's zits for each baldfaced lie he was about to tell.

Then, to make a long story short, and because he felt ill, Newell skipped over the details with a manly frown. He told his listeners not to ask too many questions; no, they were too young, too sheltered, as preppies will be, to hear of such things.

—Curiosity killed the cat.

Chorus of protests.

Schmied:

—Aw, come off it.

The Bern, disgusted:

—Give us the real dope!

Granny:

—I don't believe you went to New York anyway.

Newell dug in:

—Alright, you asked for it. Now you're going to get it. Every last horrible detail: hold onto your hats.

—Okay, so go ahead already!

—Stop stalling!

—Can the crap.

Granny added:

—He didn't even go. Hid out at Cormac's here in town.

Newell raised a hand. He commanded silence. Fateful, he said:

—Outside Tin Pan Alley a guy came up to me. Started talking, low. Gold blond hair, wavy, sort of . . . maybe . . . a little overweight, yeah. Dressed rich.

—And what did he say? said Granny.

—Asked me if I wanted to get laid.

—Good gracious! Schmied blushed.

—Really? said Bern. Get laid?

—Reet.

—Sure he did, said Granny Zammet. And who was the babe? Joanne Campbell I guess.

—Wait. I said to him, Look Mister, I said, you'd have to pay me to get laid. I need cash to buy some platters here in Tin Pan Alley, or across the street at The Colony. I need . . . a double-sawbuck!

—Reet, said Granny, and sneered. A double-sawbuck. And what did the well-dressed overweight man with wavy gold hair say then?

Newell, hand up, self-assured, made them wait.

—Oh, my goodness! said the big, blond Schmied, who looked like he couldn't hold it.

—He said: reet.

The Bern thought hard:

—Probably . . . you know, like my faculty adviser.

—Guess again.

—Well, what? said Granny.

—He said, uh, no sweat. She's an older babe, see, a rich one in a nearby skyscraper. And she needs it bad. She has to have it right away!

Schmidlap turned crimson:

—Honest to goodness! And did you, um, er—?

Schmied cleared his throat; and, though in pajamas, made to straighten his necktie.

Newell, lips pursed, bowed and threw up a palm: as if all this were in the natural order of things.

—So I asked him if she had big ones, like Mrs. Glebe.

Bern:

—What did he say to that?

Granny Zammet cackled:

—Said he didn't know any Mrs. Glebe, you idiot.

—So I explained . . . that Ramona Glebe is our history teacher's wife, which is why Master Glebe teaches such boring classes, all fagged out in the morning since she has curves like the Coney Island rollercoaster.

Bern whistled under his breath.

Granny:

—Did you visit the older rich woman in the nearby skyscraper? Did she have big ones?

–They're big alright, said Newell, but they sag pretty bad when you unfasten her bra. At least so her . . . her pimp told me.

The Bern:

–So do Mrs. Glebe's. They would hang down almost to the cellar. Nipples as long as Master Glebe's you know, when he, uh, you know–

–Talks about the French Revolution, said Granny. But look: that's not what a pimp does. A pimp makes *you* pay.

–I know that, said Newell with contempt. I know well enough what a pimp does. We had a discussion as to whether most prostitutes have big ones or small ones.

–Boy oh boy, said Schmied, and stared.

–So who was the well-dressed stranger with wavy hair who hires prep schoolers to satisfy an elderly nympho millionairess with big saggy ones in a nearby skyscraper right away?

Granny giggled and shook his head.

–Who was he? I'll tell you who he was. Are you ready?

–Ready as I'll ever be.

–Well then, he was . . . her grandson!

–What?!

–Oh, no!

–Goodness gracious me! cried that blockhead, Schmied, red as a beet beneath his short blond curls.

–How perverse! Granny shook his head. So did you earn your reet platters by bringing joy to the rich grandmother whose big ones sag to the floor?

Schmied:

–You must've brought back a lot of new records! Let's play them now while Hilly-babe's busy squeezing pus out of his blackheads.

–Yeah, where are they? said The Bern. I haven't seen them.

–Well, here's what happened, said Newell. Are you ready?

–Ready! they cried in a chorus. Very ready!

–Okay then. I made a list of all the 45 rpms I lust for: 'Chapel in the Moonlight', 'So Strange', 'Sunday Kind of Love', 'Ruby-Ruby' . . .

–Earn one per orgasm, said Granny.

–Piecework, said The Bern.

–Then, would you believe it? We went looking in Tin Pan Alley and Colony Records, but neither had 'Ruby-Ruby'. I felt sorry about this, and shook my head sadly, for her sake. I had to tell the man I couldn't help his grandmother. But if she wanted to make a trip up here to Ethridge, then I could introduce her to an entire study hall of horny guys. Get it? Stud-y hall, that's a pun. Only, she'd have to supplement our skimpy allowance checks. Right, Berneth?

–Reet. I can hardly afford a piece of seven layer cake in The Snug.

–I'll do it! Schmied burst out. I don't care if they sag or not. She won't even have to pay.

–She will, said Newell, because I get one reet platter per pop. Get it? Pop.

–*That's* what a pimp is, said Granny.

–Okay, okay, just get her up here, said Big Jay Schmied. Get her here quick! I can't wait much longer, I need it right away!

–True love, said Granny. Made for each other: the raunchy prepster and the old lady with wrinkled bezooms.

Granny hummed: 'Born Too Late'.

–Both grateful–The Bern gave a goofy grin, all braces, zits.

–I want to get laid! Schmied shouted.

–Shh, said Newell. You'll bring Hillyer in here: three hours apiece.

–What about Ben Bolt? said Granny. No doubt you found him on West 84th Street, and played b-ball in the schoolyard.

–Look here, men. Wouldn't you rather hear about Ben Bolt some other time? I need Lambaste to get in here and start on my mechanical drawing assignment. Otherwise I'll flunk out of this elite shithole.

–Now! I want it now!

They chanted:

–Ben Bolt! Ben Bolt! Ben Bolt!

Schmied mumbled to himself:

–Right there in public high school . . . Lucky so-and-so.

VIII

For awhile Newell had to tell all about Ben Bolt's free life in a Manhattan public school, Ben Bolt's family: he lived in an apartment with his dad, and Newell made up some phony story about his mom; Ben Bolt's own true-life adventures when he hounded quail in

Times Square; Ben Bolt's collection of reet platters; and all sorts of other nonexistent bullshit concerning Ben Bolt until the mere mention of Ben Bolt's name made his biographer feel nauseous. Ben Bolt: the only regular guy, with a greasy bleach blond d.a., who ever attended Ethridge, and got kicked out.

Then finally, sometime after eleven o'clock, the friends gave a sigh and rose to leave.

Granny laughed, and said:

—So all this happened to you in one night down there.

—Reet.

Just then the door creaked open. The boys gave a start, fearing a visit from the meddlesome senior counselor. Douse the lamp! Hide under the bed! Slowly, cre-e-eak! a head peeped in. Royall Lambert, compass, t-square, drafting paper plus other materials in hand, gave a sorry grin. What a prissy kid it was, pale, sickly, with gentle manners more like a girl—The Lamb came to perform the difficult, meticulous mechanical drawing assignment. It would take him two good hours, but he didn't mind since he liked Newell for some reason.

Newell said:

—Where you been, Lambskin?

Schmied chimed in with a beaming, angelic smile, all white teeth, pink cheeks, curly blond hair:

—Whacking off.

Schmied said this the way a cannibal might say: meat.

—Well, go on. You can use my desk. The lamp works.

—Wait till they leave—said The Bern afraid all this racket would draw Hillyer from his cave.

—Hell, said Newell, impatient. Get started.

But first Lambert had to pipe up and have his little say. He just couldn't help himself. There was admiration in his soft whiny voice when he said:

—Gee! You played a swell trick on me last night in the train.

—What?

—Magic trick. Made my seat check disappear.

—Hold on! said Newell with a spastic gesture. Just hold your horses: enough said about that. I shouldna' done it. Sorry, kid.

—No, it's okay! The conductor made me pay for another ticket. But then you told him about your practical joke—

—What joke? I don't know about any joke. Listen, zit-ass, if you want to stay in here you'd better zip it.

—No, I . . . I just wanted the guys to know what a fun thing you did.

Royall persisted. For once in his life he showed some willpower. Why, you couldn't shut the fellow up as he went on with the story and did honor to his best friend, his host for this mechanical drawing party tonight, Newell Gilbert. Well, it did the poor boy good to get some attention.

—Lambcake, I'm warning you.

—You're too modest, Newell. Really, guys, we're living here side by side with a future great man, and don't even know it. What a cute thing to do. I'm still shaking my head over it.

—I said shut up! Now I mean it, I'll boot you out!

—Then who'll do the mechanical drawing assignment? said Granny.

Royall, happily, went on:

—Listen, guys! The train conductor said *a young man with a white laundry bag, getting off in Redemaine,* had stolen my seat check, but felt badly about it. He offered to pay.

—How noble! said Granny.

—Don't you think it's swell? Nobody ever treated me that way except my mom. You know she brought me up by herself, an only child, and now she's too sick for me to live at home, and—

Lambert's head went down a notch. He sniffled.

Newell looked around, disgusted:

—Look, Royall, get the hell out of here, before I become excited. Blow my pad, out! Boy, you've really made my night.

Big, blond Schmied gazed wide-eyed at all this sentiment, while The Berneth just shrugged. Granny Zammet, however, gave a peal of laughter. And Granny may have laughed too loudly because here came the senior counselor, Roger Hillyer, like a rhinocerous along the wainscoted hallway.

And then Hilly-babe laid about him with Saturday detention hours:

—Schmied, Zammet, three hours! Out of your room after lights-out. And three for you, Royall, I'm amazed to find you consorting with these low-lifes.

Newell needed an outlet for his frustration: back in this jail after the brief bliss at home; and so gave it back to The Rog with vigor:

—Oh! Hilleth, you peckerhead, you devil! To hell with your detention hours.

–Eternal detention, said Granny.

–Go jerk off a zit!

–That's three for you, Gilbert, six! Disrespectful of your superiors.

–Nine, twelve! All good children get to heaven! We're trying to get some sleep in here, and you come in, you dork! Guy can't even sleep without Hilly-babe screaming like a cunt in the middle of the night.

–Stop swearing, Gilbert. Three more.

–Forty, fifty! You think I care anymore? Everybody get out! You too, Schmidlap, go whack off.

–Okay! Schmied beamed.

–As for you, Zammet, I know you now: abject nullity . . . Set up a friend, and then have a good laugh after you let him down. Go on, run along . . . Hell, now I gotta' do my mechanical drawing assignment.

–In the dark? said Hillyer.

–Damn thing's due in the morning. See that, Lamprey, what a little wussy you are? You spoiled everything.

–Sorry!

And now, if this wasn't enough, here came the fond dorm master. That Hercules emerged from his bachelor quarters at the end of the hall. Taken aback by such high jinx, such a hullabaloo as midnight was nigh, the master came on. Sternly, with a frown, he said:

–You're all docked your allowances for the week.

Such a show of force excited Rog Hillyer. His whiteheads and blackheads glowed redder. His protuberant Adam's-apple stuck out further. Why, you'd have thought his throat had a hard-on.

Newell said hell with mechanical drawing, and withdrew under the covers. He muttered:

–Screaming like a cunt in the middle of the night . . .

For a few more minutes he mumbled to himself, and swore. His last word, before he fell asleep with a smile on his face (the sleep of the righteous) was:

–Reet.

Vufflens-Le Château 1970
New York City 1974, 2002, '3, '5

JOURNEY ON THE NEEDING

NOVEL

Chapter One

I

One day in October, at the private boarding school known as Ethridge, a boy did not show up to take his assigned seat in morning chapel. There it was: an empty place. Of course he felt sick and went to the Infirmary; so his classmates thought that day, if they did think about it. A master on hand took notice only because this boy, the foreign exchange student, came from a country in the news due to political unrest. But he would hardly have sensed any tie between those faroff events and this secluded New England campus.

A spell of bright fall weather had settled over the region. The first chilly days seemed tailor-made for a prep school's vigorous routine. One day passed, and another: the missing student did not show up in chapel. Still he didn't come to class; appear at mealtime in the Refectory; or suit up for club football in the afternoon. The poor guy must be sick; or no doubt homesick, like any new arrival: worse in this case, so far from home. Depressed: a psych case over in the Infirmary? Maybe he left campus: snuck off to a day student's house in town—a thing very much taboo, going in town, and punishable by detention hours. But if he had run away, then where to? He didn't live a train ride away like the other students. Say, what really happened? Was the foreign exchange student still here at school, or wasn't he?

Administration knew the answer, perhaps, but so far they weren't talking. That is: the Headmaster and Dean of Behavior knew the boy was not in the Infirmary, and pretty soon the Ethridge faculty would begin to discuss this piece of news as well. But nobody, as yet, gave any clear idea as to where the sophomore might have gone, or why. And, into the third day of his absence, it began to look like the exclusive school must take action: contact the family, in the faroff country; also tell local and state police; seek early legal advice. Probably the Headmaster had phoned certain Ethridge trustees.

But so far no mention was made by the Chaplain when the student body met for morning chapel. Nothing official was told the students. There was only a rumor: to the effect that their schoolmate had a nervous breakdown, and was taken to a nearby hospital.

II

Newell Gilbert, who lived on the same hall as the missing student, couldn't sleep well. He awoke in the early hours; he seemed to hear a voice coming from the chinks of the old student house. Or did it come from his dream? Did it wake him up and stay in his head like the fumes of sleep? Beneath his pillow the voice whispered, rustled, from deep under the floorboards: a sigh seeped up into his sleep. He awoke with a jolt.

Then, on Sunday afternoon, one of the week's few free moments, he just wanted to lie in bed. Newell dozed off to the plunk, plunk from tennis courts down by the old gym. And then he dreamt again . . . His body gave a jolt, like an electric shock, but the images had him in their grip; they scared him. Now he saw Manuel, the foreign exchange student, who went away . . . And Manuel came to the surface with a faroff glint in his dark eyes; he emerged from the depths of the Needing River. First the head: the curly black hair dripped, dripped. And Newell saw those eyes, so sad you knew something bad had happened. Well, the poor boy went mad without a word to anyone? He flipped his lid in evening study hall, where you could not talk.

In the dream Manuel's shoulders hunched: such an odd posture, not like in real life. He got used to being in the river; but now he came out dripping and covered with a reddish slime. Even in the depths of the Needing River he wore a charcoal gray suit and a striped necktie, maroon and blue. Manuel's lips made a distant sound, plunk, plunk, as he strode onto the riverbank where no student ever went.

And then:

—Tap!

Again Newell's body gave a little jolt. He saw the look, so sad, haunted, on the boy's soft girlish face.

—Tap-tap!

III

Newell woke with a start. He turned, looked over his shoulder— and there, in the window, was the day student named Cormac.

—Psst!

Cormac stood chest high in the shrubs. He pressed his nose against the window pane, tapped again, bongoed a little on the sill. The townie looked strange too, sort of bedevilled; a same lurid light fell on him as in Newell's dream. Tousled, features puckered as usual, The Corm stared in. His sandy hair took a greenish gold tint at midafternoon, and his face had a cute irony, like someone in the know, with a piece of news. Mostly Corm looked like an eccentric in full puberty: eyes kind of wild, cheeks pouty; sandy mesh down over his shy, guilty grin, you know why; and cowlick up, in full erection. Now he was excited, but maybe no more than when he went into a solo drumming on his desk in history class, and Master Glebe got in a stew and told him not to do it.

Corm whispered, a finger to his lips:

—Shh . . . You been into town?

—No.

—Then you don't know.

—No. I don't want to know.

—Well, Mingo saw him.

—What?

The small New England town had one hobo, a man named Mingo said to have graduated from Ethridge and gone on to Yale many years ago. May we believe this? He spoke like a master, only more to the point; he liked to ask questions, and behind his words there seemed a deeper meaning. Also, he listened. In any case Mingo slept in Cormac's basement when The Corm's dad and stepmother were away on trips they took, to foreign countries. Sometimes they left the fifteen year-old to fend for himself, with a maid's help, in the big lonely house.

—Him, Manuel.

—Where?

—Along the riverbank. Late Friday afternoon Mingo saw some students get in a rowboat and row across to the island.

—I don't believe it. Who?

—Well, how would he know? But one of them was dark skinned, sort of pudgy. Charcoal gray suit.

Newell gave a shiver, and propped on his elbow. For a moment he seemed to peer out from the bad dream at his real visitor. And he wondered: that voice, the whisper he heard coming up through a fissure in the floor—had he only dreamt it? Or was it real?

IV

Newell yawned and looked around. These hours, after church service and then Sunday dinner, all in tweeds, were among the week's few free moments. Each day had its busy routine; each of eight periods brought more homework, more stress; each master knew the Ethridge motto: keep them busy, noses to the grindstone. Don't let 'em think: no time alone, no play; not much laughter. A few little pleasures; a risk of detention hours . . . Follow the rules. Ah, have your own idea? Then pay the price; then Saturday afternoon study hall. A nosy senior counselor, a concerned faculty adviser, namely Pastor Geeter, kept an eye on the corridor.

And now, if this wasn't enough pressure, a student turned up missing. It had a strange effect on your thoughts, on your dreams, as you wondered: what happened? What's going on around here? What next?

But Cormac, the day student with a bit more freedom, the boy genius able to do homework in class while a master droned on up front, Cormac said:

–Let's go.

–Where? Newell frowned.

–To the island.

–You're mad, Cormeth. Hey, why not? We'll swim across.

Corm cast a furtive glance. Face pinkish, nose to the screen, he sniffed a little. He looked like a ferret.

–Isn't Manuel your friend?

–A brownnose.

–Don't he and his roommate stay up till all hours doing our mechanical drawing assignments?

–Manny and Jeffers like mechanical drawing.

–Not that much. They like you.

–Oh, Cormer, go along. I'll see you in class.

Newell yawned and shooed his friend, the dayhop, away: a pesky fly at his nap. But the boy just wouldn't go, and said:

–We've got to row out there.

–Do what?

–Mingo told me there are two rowboats tied up in a cove, a ways downstream, toward the Bartlett turnoff.

Corm talked on about what the hobo said that morning. There was an old cabin out on the island of tall trees: where the Needing made a bend in its course through meadows and forest near the school . . . Newell made a wry face. Then he sighed. He had his own guess as to where the foreign exchange student might have gone. He felt a pang for the poor kid, Manuel, but more than this he shared the fear of a few others, on this floor–and asked himself: who is next? Simply go away, disappear one night?

Newell had an active nature. Optimistic, adventurous, he missed his friends back home and their forays around the neighborhood. Now his sense of things told him not to stay here in his room and wait for the next bad thing to happen. Don't worry yourself silly; no, get out there, on the trail . . . But if he wanted a sure way to get thrown out of Ethridge, and displease his parents bitterly, then it was to row with Cormac out to the island of tall trees.

V

A few minutes later the two friends were trotting down a path behind the school laundry. A strange light slanted along the windowless red brick building where boys took their dress shirts to be starched: the school laundry run by the wife of Astarte, head custodian. It seemed a student's disappearance could change the way sunlight fell on things. Weeds in cracks of the concrete steps, a loading platform round back, had a sad, neglected look.

A service road went round the Ethridge quadrangle. The two boys crossed it on their way toward the embankment down to the river. To their left, a mile away, lay the small New England town off limits to prepschoolers except with a special pass.

The October sun hovered over trees along railroad trestles which bridged the winding road to town. The afternoon light began to deepen; it glinted on the spire of the Protestant church in the distance. Warmth faded from the air as Manuel's rescuers scampered down the bank with its wild grasses, and weed entanglement.

—Corm, this is crazy.

—Na! Fat Manuel's out there, and he's scared. He's ready to poop his pants.

—Not my problem.

—You'll poop yours too, when you see—the Beast of Ethridge!

—Cut it out. You're nuts.

Cormac gestured, grandiose, as he slipped on a patch of skunk cabbage.

—We've got to save our brother.

—Look, he ran away. Got fed up with Refectory food, that's all. He skipped out.

—Mingo saw him. Mingo doesn't lie.

—A tramp.

—A scholar. He went to the best schools.

—And became a wino. Well, that's something to look forward to. At least I won't have to wear a necktie.

—Where's your school spirit? Honor bright.

They made their way into the forbidden zone. Few came here; in springtime a town fisherman after shad, a trespasser further downstream, in some secluded spot, out of view. Also one Ethridge master liked to canoe. Now the tangled undergrowth, sedge grass, weedy thickets checked the boys' steps. And now Newell Gilbert began to realize, with a frown, what he was up to, and what his father would have to say about this, if he ever got wind. Newell didn't want to let down his mom and dad; he had promised to do his best here, and he stuck to Ethridge regimen as best he could. Well, he wanted success for his own sake as well as theirs: high grades, a good record so they could feel proud and happy with him, the future look bright for one of tomorrow's leaders. Last semester he put in an honor roll performance, and went home to enjoy the summer with his friends in Spring Glen, Otter and Bungya, Thad Floriani, Haas. How he liked to play and read in his own room; and tease his little sister. Home to a good healthy sense of things, to his toys and books, and his dog. But now, out here, he felt so rebellious, and unhappy: perhaps it was fear which made him feel this way. Of late his Spring Glen self took the fore: strong willed, fun loving, wayward. A knot had formed in his stomach these past few days: something wasn't right, something was not as it should be. And so his bad boy side took over, unruly instincts, and he went to the river for an escapade with the mad townie named Cormac.

VI

The Corm beckoned him forward like a scout leader. Down to the muddy riverbank they went: where it fell steeply to the water. And then, for a moment, the two boys stood and gazed at the dark current. Last year Newell never paid any mind to the Needing River; though he could see it from his room on the freshman hallway, third floor Settlers.

—Not much further—said the excited Cormac, as he hooked a finger in his greasy hair, like a spastic, and tugged.—By the Bartlett turnoff there's a cove with a rowboat.

They neared the cove. Newell never heard of anyone crossing over to the island. He paused, out of breath, and took in a vegetal smell, like the year's dying breath. Across the river ran the island's eroded banks. Tree roots coiled and jutted like long snakes above the water's surface.

–Look–Newell pointed.–Bartlett's over there. Let's forget this and go meet girls.

Bartlett Academy: the sister school. But you'll need a derrick and crane to get Cormac anywhere near a girl. During the yearly mixer at the Atelier, next weekend, he will lurk outside in the shadows and make wry faces. Bet on it: he begins to tremble when he gets around a girl. Any normal person would ask some hot Bartlett chick, probably with zits, to do the fox trot and make a couple: try to beat the odds and have a good time this one night, per year, of open season on chicks. Not Cormac.

Now the boy gazed across the river. In a tense tone he said:

–Big Manuel, our classmate, is in a peck of trouble.

–Good for him.

Newell wedged his mud-caked shoes one against the other, as though making cement; he thought a moment. On the sidelines at a soccer game he had seen a striking girl. Not like other Bartlett honeys; a foreigner maybe, with a strange look about her, and a woman's figure. Oh, she didn't drown you in it like a Ramona Glebe, the history master's stout wife. No, this girl had an exotic air, dark eyed and pensive, a rough note, somehow, to her features. All in all, a knockout; also older, a junior? hard to tell her age. That afternoon Newell sort of sidled closer, but he didn't dare go up to her. Now he gazed off toward an evergreen grove this side of wide playing fields. Up an incline stood administration building and girls' dormitories.

–Look there!

Corm pointed: just up ahead, in the cove he had mentioned, a gray rowboat floated by the edge. Corm slogged along the bank; jumped in nimbly; sloshed bilge water and tilted side to side.

–No can to bail 'er?

He reached for an oar and, laughing crazily, nearly capsized the old boat.

Newell, breathless, moved forward. So this thing will happen? Then he too leapt from the soggy bank into the rowboat.

VII

From the helm Cormac shouted:
—Man the poop. Undo the rig, mate. Come come!
—Shh, you want to announce our arrival?
—Topsails, ahoy! Jump in! Starboard and aft.
—Go ahead. Tell everyone.
—The Beast! Corm laughed. The Beast of Ethridge!
Newell stared out at the island. So there was a chance Manuel really did get kidnapped, and taken out there? But why? Who would do it?
Corm rowed, scraped bottom, and laughed his mad laugh as both oars jumped the oarlocks. Newell thought: this isn't play.
Toward late afternoon a cool breeze blew along the Needing River. Autumn painted the ripply surface: red-orange, bright yellow puffs amid patches of green, lavender and burgundy. Sunlit shafts pierced the border of trees, overhanging boughs, and cast a speckly net here, there, over the dark water. The air was tinged with fall and its burnished leaves, but also a sense of danger: as the stern skewed round, and Cormac still punted in the shallows. Beside himself with excitement the day student stood up, tilted the boat steeply and nearly went over the side. Anyone with that boy's nerves should not go in for adventure.
Newell said:
—We both have to row.
In the silence their voices sounded eerie. Down stream a mallard or wood duck gave its yearning call. Newell stood up too, splashed his way from the stern, sat abruptly. The boat dipped to the oarlock.
—I hope Manny-kid thanks us for this. I don't expect to do any more mechanical drawings.
After a moment Corm said, his voice spooked:
—He's over there, in the cabin.
Newell's arms ached as he rowed.
—Sure, sure. He ran away, is all. Got so homesick he hopped a plane.
—Dead, in the cabin. Ouch!
—Cormer, you're getting me in trouble.

Some bird, or small animal, sent out its thin despondent call: winter soon! winter soon! Vapors, cooler pockets, had a tang to them like the river. A loon cried out; its call echoed a long way from up stream. Sometimes after lights-out Newell heard the same bird cry, cry; and then, in the day's few free moments, before sleep, he thought of home.

Corm grunted in time, like a cockswain. Breathless, he said:

—In trouble? Hey, take your pick.

—What do you mean?

—He's our classmate. Lives on your hall. But what do you care.

—That's not why you brought me out here.

—Oh no? Why then?

—Because you're mad, Corky. Your parents leave you alone too much in that big house, alongside a cemetery. You and Mingo, village idiots, senior and junior.

The rowboat scraped on something. It groaned with an ominous, an almost human sound a stone's toss from the far side of the island. As the boat edged nearer, the rowing grew easier.

Over here things looked dim, hard to make out, as dense foliage curtained the waning sun. Newell peered ahead and tried to spot a landing.

Leaves floated down from the tall trees and spangled, red, orange, yellow in a last shaft of light, like butterflies in a breeze; they hit the dark current and drifted past the bow. From the abrupt riverbank hung underbrush, which gurgled. A chill air breathed from the depths: its riverine tang hinted at another sort of life out here. This Needing River, this lonely island had little to do with a prim, eccentric Headmaster, with a serious, snooping Dean of Behavior who would dish out detention hours in the nick of an eye; with a kindly but tense Chaplain, his gaze, his thoughts haunted by things far beyond Ethridge; with a stern school code that kept you busy from the first stunned instant when a reveille bell rang out on each hall, around the quad, to lights-out when a boy tried not to sleep, and have a few minutes to himself.

—Look! said Newell, keeping his voice low.

Cormac gave a lurch. Once again his oar jumped.

—I told you Mingo wasn't lying.

A landing—among the trees.

A second rowboat. So somebody else was out here?

Cormac moved toward the bow while his friend rowed the last few strokes. In those instants Corm made a figurehead: snout stuck out in the breeze, rodent-like, under a furious cowlick. He stood poised for the leap ashore; and then, mooring rope in hand, with a war cry to let Manuel's kidnapper, the Beast of Ethridge know they were coming, he sprang. In the shallows his sneakers sucked slime, as he grabbed at a root, and clambered up the bank. But the unsure Newell, mumbling about how his dad would disown him, got out more slowly.

Before them the island, silent, mysterious, posed the question of a boy's disappearance from school. Corm tied the rope to an overhanging branch.

VIII

The two boys went into the twilit forest. High overhead leaves were lit in patches by the waning sun: where it sent up a last few rays from the far side beyond the railroad trestles and the town. There was a clatter of bark: a raccoon, some small animal's claws skittered down a trunk and rustled a bed of leaves. Pine needles crunched as Corm trudged forward and set the course.

–Cabin's halfway across. Mingo comes out here when the river freezes.

–By himself? said Newell.

–No, he has a thing going with Ramona Glebe.

–Stop it. We're risking expulsion if not our lives.

–Reet, said Corm.

As they went along, in the strange setting, Newell began to grasp the reality and feel his hall mate's absence from campus. What did it mean? What happened to the soft, pudgy, well-dressed foreign exchange student whom masters and brownnosing types made a fuss over? Headmaster Smithson singled him out with a good word in the Refectory of an evening. But now he was gone. Where to? Did his rich parents make him a kidnapping target like Charles Lindbergh's son? Was this a political kidnapping? Would it make headlines? Would it involve the exclusive private school in a scandal?

Newell shook his head, as they went along, and mumbled:
—There's no cabin. You believe a drunkard.
—Mingo drinks, but he went to college. He's cultivated.
—He cultivates fleas, said Newell, tripping over a root.
—Oh yeah? said Corm. Oh yeah? Look there—
Shingle roof, half hidden by trees. In the window: a light, or stray beam of sunlight, flickered. First the cove, the rowboat; then the landing with signs of other visitors; now a cabin with a foreboding look, in a thicket under the tall trees. And nobody seemed to know these things except a gray scraggly man, a human wreck who spent his days tramping about and frightening the schoolchildren—when he wasn't holding Socratic dialogues with himself in Cormac's cellar. Newell caught his breath: yes, there it was, the cabin.

Half-crouching they made their way on a slow incline. Nearing the thicket they used a tree trunk or underbrush to keep from view. Then as light on the island grew dimmer they went on hands and knees and imitated the war movies. But there was a change in roles: Cormac, with his cute look when excited, began to hang back; while Newell's interest, on the rise, forgot about things like Saturday detention and his dad's strictness, and he took the lead.

He said, low:
—That a light?

Dry, dripping sound: a sort of hush, as the forest fidgeted, and settled in toward nightfall. And Newell thought of nights the year before when a senior counselor told ghost stories on third-floor Settlers, the freshman corridor. Then did the living dead roam an underground passageway between the student houses. For those Frankenstein types hated laughter; they detested footsteps heard just up above them, any sign of life in progress. And then did Newell first hear the name: Beast of Ethridge; and it made him think what might happen to a boy, far away from home, in this secluded private school where everybody, masters and students alike, seemed not 'regular'. And after lights-out he lay listening to wind groaning in the window casements: as strange sounds seeped up from underground into the chill autumn night. Century old ghosts, headmasters gone off their rocker, students visited at midnight by a master turned werewolf: all ridiculous, all made-up tales meant to cow an Ethridge student, and make him adhere to the harsh routine out of fear. But now something real had happened.

A limb snapped or fell with an eerie knock. The two boys stopped in their tracks, glanced here, there, and looked at one another. They crouched in a tense quietude, near the cabin now, as dusk drew over. Was Manuel inside there? Alive? Trussed up, tied hand and foot, like an animal? What to do? Go find him; knock on the door, and ask: have you seen our floor mate Manuel? . . . In the moments before action Newell thought of his first night at the school, a year ago. Some twenty of them, new arrivals, in those first stunned hours on their own, far from parents, had formed up in a band behind a student named Redge. And they went about the quadrangle in a strange procession, like they had a demon in them. There was something wild about this, barbaric, worthy of some old myth they might study in class. But in following days and weeks the rigid schedule took hold; such instincts faded quickly along with the leader for a night, named Redge. In fact, what had become of him? No doubt he knew right away this wasn't his cup of tea? Redge asked his parents to take him out in the first week—didn't he?

—I'll go have a look.

Leaning forward, one hand to the ground, Newell went to the cabin.

Then, straightening slowly, catching his breath, he peered over the window sill. The curtains were drawn, and he heard nothing. No sign of a flickering light: probably that was sun on the window. The place seemed empty, so he glanced around and waved to his partner. But The Corm hung back. Corm had begun to shiver: something took the starch right out of the boy.

Newell saw and heard nothing. But he did smell—what? Not the rotten odor of the exchange student put to death by his captors, but rather—perfume. A woman's perfume wafted on the air, an adultish scent which reminded him, with a pang, of the older girl he had seen at the soccer match.

On tiptoes he slipped round the brown shingle cabin and ducked under another window. Then he shrugged, went up to the front door, and knocked. He tried the knob, turned it, pushed. Locked. His teeth chattered from nervousness, or the air turning cold.

—Let's go!—He skipped away toward Cormac.—Nobody home. But why do I smell perfume? Whew.

IX

Suddenly, behind them, there was a sound. What? A twig snapped underfoot, close by; the boys' eyes met. And then, an instant later, they both saw—what? Him, or *it*. Was that a mask? A broad shouldered figure rose up as though from nowhere and came toward them. The face ashen, disfigured, more horrible because unclear in the forest light. Newell thought: what on earth?! And then there was a pause, the instant before a plunge, in the silence ringing with fear. The thing stood there another second with no life, no features on its face in effect, but only a putty-like mask, a sadness that looked inward. Mask? The rest was a big male form, on the verge of attacking; but still it held back.

—Ah!..

Newell gasped, unable to breathe, as his heartbeat clutched at his throat. It was hypnotic: the way the dark figure took a step forward, toward them, and another. Its eyes turned inward: nothing human left in the torn features. Fascination, panic held the two boys rooted in place a few more seconds. Newell felt a wave of nausea before he turned and started running for dear life.

At first he lunged back and almost fell. Each man for himself now: at once he lost sight of Corm, and could only dash away from that cabin and sprint wildly beneath the trees. Like an animal in a hunter's path he plunged and leapt over underbrush and tried not to fall since that could be the end. The huge urge drove him on: the fear. Brambles scratched his cheek; a root did send him headlong. Now up again, shivering, whimpering. There was a ravine. There was a brook where he fell again and twisted his knee. Never mind: he flung himself madly and guessed his way back toward the rowboat. Or maybe find the Ethridge side? Try to swim the frigid river? And get lost! All alone with that thing as night drew over the island. Tracked down, caught, like Manuel.

As he slowed down, his sides aching, unable to breathe, he heard the steps come on behind him. They plodded: not far behind. The steady stride shuffled up leaves, crunched pine needles, a twig. And then he felt the breath of the pursuer on his neck. He was overcome with panic, a witless frenzy. For darkness was creeping across the island; it veiled the tall trees, and distorted the look of things. Again he tripped and fell sprawling and got up somehow; he was losing his hope of escape. The steps of the other came on, there behind him, steady, maybe a dozen yards back. In the big, inhuman figure he sensed an ill will, a snide horror of life. He glanced back and saw—close enough now to *see* in the shadows—the Beast in those features, flesh in decomposition. But the body lived on, vigorous; it menaced, and pursued.

Groping, flailing his way through the maze of bushes, tree trunks, webs of branches, Newell tasted blood; he had bitten his tongue when he fell. And now he felt on the verge of losing all control. He would risk anything, smash against a rock, jump from a cliff, if only he could be done with the panting, grasping terror of this other. Its image in his mind made him cry out.

In the headlong flight he threw himself forward at two tree trunks, side by side, wide like a gateway. And that was when he felt the big, brutal hand pound down on his back and grab at his shoulder, his neck. And that was when, after a panicked dash to the edge of the island, he knew his own fate would be like poor Manuel's. As the beastly hand latched on, and stopped him from running, he knew it was time to give up hope for escape, and stop struggling.

X

But he jerked away once more. He slipped from those clutches, and wriggled through the two tree trunks, with a cry. And then, all at once, the obstructing roots and the underbrush, the clinging bushes gave way. They were behind him. And there he was falling, legs first and kicking, freely, through the air. Suddenly an icy cold stunned his senses, his body, arms, legs. It took his breath away, as he gasped, choked, over his head in the river. The water had a tang to it, like a rotten thing given up to winter, like the breath of the Beast of Ethridge.

In the frigid current he floundered, and looked around. Cormac? Now there was light. The sun was down, but a weird, luminous twilight played over things. Newell blinked, and his senses throbbed and tried to regain some kind of focus. He stretched down and touched bottom; his shoes sank in the cushiony bed as he strained forward. He glided, pushed forward in the numbing current because he had spotted the landing, and made out the rowboat where they left it tied to an overhanging branch. Its dark hull tipped a little in the shallows. The gloaming spread deep blue-gray shadows over the river.

There sat Cormac. From the rowboat Corm's tousled, marten-like face looked around. Stiff-armed, he began rowing with both oars. So he had lost hope for his friend, and only wanted to clear out? But in his frazzled state Cormac didn't think to untie the moor line, and so the old rowboat tugged and made the branch bend double, like a fishing rod hooked into a big one.

But then The Corm glanced right and saw his friend: just the head gliding toward him, not twenty feet away, like a ghost emerged from the river's depths. And Cormac's eyes went wide; his greasy hair stood on end, and he gave a sound like someone on a rollercoaster: wah-h-h! Then he rowed harder, jerking against the moor line. Big Corm went nowhere fast as the oars flailed up from the locks.

A moment later Newell lifted himself over the side, dripping like a ringer. Blue with cold, wracked with shivers, in a voice not his own, he said:

—Untie the knot!

Then, after a shove with the oar, another—the current caught them up. The boat began to swing out downstream: back the way they came. Cormer was in no state to row, so the rowboat turned sideways, on its way now. Were they safe?

But no, behind them—what? They heard something, a laughter of sorts, or a cavernous cough. Maybe the dead cough that way when they catch a cold.

Now the two boys looked back across the glimmer of the river's surface. They stared, afraid, at the density of the island of trees.

By the landing, above the abrupt riverbank, stood the big, dark figure that had chased them through the forest. It almost caught Newell, and added him to its collection of Ethridge students, after he ventured to the cabin and got too close to its mystery. There stood the thing, lingered a moment, and laughed at them, if you could call it a laugh. And then it turned a hulking back on them, and made its way again into the island bleakness, among the trees. It went about its dark business.

Newell still had a strange odor in his nostrils. Did the Beast of Ethridge wear perfume? Did the dead make love?

XI

That night Newell Gilbert lay in bed feverish, sobbing at moments, in a bad state. His roommate Bernard, a city product on scholarship at Ethridge, looked at him and didn't want to ask what went on. The senior counselor on the floor, Rog 'The Dodge' Hillyer, came by with good news of another six hours' detention: absence from Sunday night chow, a cold cut buffet on stale bread, but you had to sign in; then study hall over in Settlers. Three hours per unexcused absence. Newell didn't tell The Rog about his outing with Cormac: off campus without a pass, ten hours.

–This could cost you the mixer next Saturday.

–I'll c'contest it at the D'Detention Office. I'll talk to Wart.

–Dean Wart, to you.

–Yes, Hilly-babe. Now run along. Go s-s-suck up.

–Make it nine hours: disrespect.

–Then go lick Dean W'Wart's ass, since you like him so much.

–Twelve! Offensive language . . . Anything else, Gilby?

XII

Later, it must have been toward midnight, he jolted awake. Some kind of pounding, inside the cabin on the island, turned into footsteps on his corridor, which woke him. Again he heard–not one voice this time, but more; a dirge moaned up through chinks and crevices of the old student building. Then, in his senses, he heard only the wind's lament in the window casement by his bedside; and footsteps, as someone, no doubt a master, paused by his door, then went past. Those steps: such a sadness they had, in the late hour.

Quietly, Newell drew back the covers, and got out of bed. On cat's paws, not to creak the old floorboards, he snuck by the sleeping Bernard, and put his ear to the door. A low mumbling, out there, two doors down: by Manuel's door! If he wanted to hear, he would have to crack the door, and go into the hallway. Did he dare? Who was this? Who spoke in low, tense tones and had a late night look in the missing student's room? Had The Beast come here on campus? With a slow movement, trying not to creak, Newell opened the door a little. He stuck his head out, into the hall, where amber light glowed from the stairwell. And he saw, but didn't recognize, yet. A big, adult figure, like the one on the island, paused a moment by Manuel's door as though to listen in. Then a slow tap, tap, with one finger; and the door opened. When the late night visitor spoke, it was a bit impatiently but with a warm, deep voice:

—Jeffers, not asleep?

—No, Sir.

—I have told you about this.

—Yes, Sir.

Newell went into the hall and took a few steps. They spoke in low tones, he could hardly hear; also he wanted to see and try to identify who it was. In pajamas, folding his arms, he drew closer; the wood floor felt cold on his bare feet. Closer now, too close: he stood beside the doorway, right behind the large, menacing figure, and peeped in.

—I'm going to ask you a few questions, Ethan. But first get up from there, boy. Snap out of it.

Ethan Jeffers, the exchange student's roommate, was not in bed. He sat on the floor with his legs crossed, and he didn't blink. Perhaps from that position he saw the face of the person who had entered his room; but if so, only a glimpse. The man snapped his fingers, but Ethan still did not stir, blink, seem to breathe. The boy's very pale, bevelled features looked lit from within; they just hung there, apart from his body, in the near darkness. The play of bluish shadow round his deep, gentle eyes told the vanity of all things Ethridgian: of eight daily classes, the horror of intramural sports; of eating Refectory food, and being in one's frail body, and sleeping, too.

—It is blasphemy. Please stop at once.

—Yes (sigh), Sir.

The boy had a kind of provocative pause, which didn't charm masters. Maybe it was ironic; it could put off the person trying to talk with him, no matter who, a Headmaster Smithson.

—Now when was the last time you saw your roommate?

Pause.

—Yes . . . (sigh) . . . , Sir.

—Look, just answer. I haven't time.

Moon Jeffers gazed in space. He didn't seem to care what went on anymore. He looked up at this master who came to his room at midnight: who bit off the words, curtly, in a hurry.

From the hallway Newell peered in: so close, he could almost reach out and touch them. But who was it? Master Glebe the history teacher? Turned into a zombie by the caresses of his wife Ramona, queen of the Ethridge Refectory? Or maybe Coach Roentgen, gymnasium dictator who would slap you with ten detention hours faster than Jack Robinson? Master Roentgen looked tall when he got angry, and pulled in his paunch. Or was it the Beast of Ethridge, who kidnapped Manuel, and now returned to the scene of the crime? In a minute he would take away poor Jeffers too: sling him over his shoulder like a sack of flour, and lug him out to the island, where the dead wore perfume.

—When was the last time you saw your roommate?

—Yes-s-s . . . s-s.

Ethan left him hanging. The good man might have waited a long time for the 'S-Sir' which was due a master.

—Did he seem strange? Look funny? . . . Did Manuel say anything telltale to you?

—Om-m-m-m!

Ethan chanted.

The other shrugged broad shoulders, and crooked his head a little, in frustration.

Newell, just behind him, tried not to breathe. But he gave a start, where he lurked in the hall shadows just beyond the doorway, because now he knew who it was. He knew from the man's lisp, a big virile man with a sort of burr to his speech. The awareness sent a shiver the length of Newell's spine; and his hair felt like it rose up in horror, like Cormac's greasy mesh in the rowboat that afternoon, after they saw a master turned werewolf? . . . And now Newell shivered, and backed up in fear that The Beast might sense his presence: wheel around and face him with those corroded features. But this time it smelled more of men's wear, perhaps a dash of cologne, not women's perfume. And so Newell knew this person had a real face, very much among the living, and the one on the island was surely a phony mask. No, this man wore an everyday face, with short, curly, graying hair; a strong jaw, a ruddy complexion which looked tanned even in winter: once a handsome face, but now it had a hard, sort of crimped look to it, from a life spent disciplining students and worrying about school security. For the man who stood over Ethan Jeffers, and tried to browbeat the poor boy but got only a hummed chant in response; the big, impatient figure who stood there, and hovered over his young victim; this monster who had caused such terror out on the island that afternoon, where he kept Manuel hostage, if Manuel in fact still lived and breathed and didn't have perfume sprinkled on his body so he wouldn't stink; this Beast of Ethridge, this madman out of control, who deserved ten times ten detention hours—was none other than the handsome, graying, lisping Ethridge Dean of Behavior.

XIII

Do you believe that? Newell Gilbert did, because Ethan's late night visitor gave off a same scary aura, seeming to stalk and overwhelm his weaker prey, as the lanky pursuer out on the island. There was a same fierce note to his behavior, which wouldn't get him an A in conduct on his report card. After all what was he doing here: past midnight in a student's darkened room? Why choose this hour to ask the boy a lot of questions—and in such a tone, at once concerned and highly irritated, a tender sort of growl? Up to no good! Beast of Ethridge.

–When did you last see your roommate?

–Thursday afternoon, Sir, after eighth period. Om-m-m.

–Was he okay then?

–Om-m-m.

Then, for a moment, Dean Rivington Wart didn't speak. He stood over the boy before him, Ethan, and thought about something. And behind him Newell lurked in the shadows, and mused over the master's strange behavior on past occasions: the way he went about campus testing locks; the way he had his spies, his suck-ups like Rog 'The Dodge' Hillyer, senior counselor, on every floor; the way he was said to install listening devices not only in student rooms but also in classrooms and in the masters' quarters as well, though this was hard to believe. The Detention Office was a small space, a cubicle at one end of second floor Settlers. There the devil kept his records; and any poor sinner, even a senior, feared to go and ask about his case. Dean Rivington Wart looked out at you from that hole in the wall with dark eyes and a scowl. Watch out: you were lost, if little misdeeds piled up and began to loom large. Everywhere sins, infractions of the school code—a necktie on sideways, a cufflink missing, a pencil sharpened at the wrong end, a handkerchief untidily folded in your breast pocket— Dean Rivington Wart saw all, noted all, knew all, reckoned all in detention hours. You lost your one Saturday mixer of the year with Bartlett Academy; you forfeited your one 'extended weekend' per semester, and then your regular weekend, 24 hours in the paradise of home. Maybe you even lost your Christmas vacation. Oh dear!

Such was Dean Rivington Wart: a man of the law.

And you are telling me this Ethridge pillar, this righteous, respected and feared upholder of the school code, went around acting like a gorilla? He abducted fifteen year-olds? He took them out to a lonely cabin and performed some sort of devilish rites on them? You mean this conservatively dressed, softspoken individual in his late forties, peer of our Headmaster, colleague of Master Roentgen the athletic director, was a psychopath? Those two men, Wart and Roentgen, could not stand one another. But never mind. You can't accuse a man obsessed with locks and school security of kidnapping the same people he was supposed to keep safe. From whom was he trying to protect this academic community off by itself in the New England wilds? From himself? Well, that's a good one: talk about fox and chickens! Of course Dean Wart did have an irrational fear of strangers; but could you really call the brown-skinned foreign exchange student, Manuel, a stranger? Dean Wart kept his eye peeled at all times for outsiders, any unwanted element on campus. In a new face he saw a troublemaker: maybe a man who had an idea for its own sake, like Mingo, the town bum, who spent the day chattering instead of getting on in life. But Manuel Higuera was a guest at the school: sent here by his parents, from one of the Latin American countries, to get the finest education available.

XIV

—Om-m-m . . .

—Did Manuel tell you anything when you saw him, after eighth period on Thursday?

—Y-yes . . . (sigh) . . . Om-m-m, Sir.

The busy Dean Wart waited patiently, each time, after a question. But he flicked his hands downward, and turned his noble head a little, and grew more annoyed. It was no easy thing to keep tabs on a couple hundred adolescents: little devils in full puberty, violators of the code. Now he didn't have time to fool with Ethan: not a moment to waste in his effort to keep the lid on things. Hadn't Ben Bolt thrown all the Refectory silverware into the Pond out behind the Atelier? And hadn't Ethridge expelled Ben Bolt for that act?

—What, Ethan? What did he say to you?

—He said . . . om-m-m—

—What?

—He said . . . om-m-m . . . said . . . om-m-m-m . . . said one of the boys made him stay up late . . . om-m-m . . . Wednesday night to do mechanical drawing assignments. Om-m.

—Who did?

In the doorway Newell drew back. Ah! Don't tell on me, you little flit! Snitch!

—Newell Gilbert, Sir. Made him do four. One for himself, om-m-m-m, one for Bernard, one for crazy Schmied, one for the townie, om-m-m, Cormac.

—Ethan—

—Yes, Sir. Om.

—Ethan, tell me this. What else did your roommate say? Was he worried about anything? Did he—did he say anyone else's name?

—Om-m-mmmuh!

—Did Newell ever threaten him? Would there be hell to pay if he didn't do the drawings?

In the hallway Newell crouched in the shadows, and thought: I see your game! So I'm the Beast of Ethridge. Me it is, eh? You rascal, Sir!

—. . . 'ringeeee padme . . . om-m-m!

—Or did Manuel say somebody had scared him? . . . said something strange to him? Did anyone . . . maybe a master, to your knowledge . . . threaten your roommate?

Slowly, the boy's tender gaze made its way back from outer space. And, so sadly, with a glint of suffering, he stared up at the big, tense master hovering over him, and said:

—Om-m-m-m-m!

And this went on. Locked into his chant now, Ethan gazed straight ahead and hummed. Maybe he didn't want to answer the last question, about the master. And so all Rivington Wart's intimidation tactics, all his expertees in boarding school law enforcement, his tradecraft, so to speak: all went for naught faced off with Moon Jeffers' meditative trance, when the boy didn't wish to answer a question and cast blame on someone, perhaps Dean Wart himself! The spiritual Ethan didn't wish to dig his own grave. Om-m-m it was, from now on in, and neither earthly affairs nor the laws of physics, not even the Beast of Ethridge in person, right alongside him, in his room, could lure Ethan Jeffers' gaze back in, this time, from the divine efflatus embodied in the chant. Nothing mattered to him now: not mental pain, not threats, not worldly presences like a Dean Rivington Wart enthralled by earthly affairs. Ethan sat in the lotus position and hummed calmly. Wart stood over him, anguished, it seemed to Newell poking his nose back in the door for a look at them. But it was Ethan who, in fact, hovered above, in nirvana.

And then Dean Wart, at a loss, did a strange thing. Very strange; maybe a stroke of genius. Well, he showed a mind which went beyond your usual Dean of Behavior: as when he rerigged the system of locks, bolts, alarms which made your everyday walk about campus something of an adventure. Newell couldn't believe his eyes when the master, in conservative tweeds, starched white shirt, a necktie his ancestors may have worn when the Mayflower came over—when that serious master got down on his knees beside Moon Jeffers, and crossed his long legs in lotus position, and sang out:

–Om-m-m-m-m . . .!

There he sat: the distinguished Dean of Behavior in lotus position. Why? Had his decades' long obsessive-compulsivity about Ethridge security interests, locks and bolts and special devices, heard the mating call of the eternal Buddha, and gone on its way in quest of nirvana?

–Om-m-m-m!

The sight made Newell wonder. For a few seconds the man's imposing features, carved in granite, had a childish look. And then the high and mighty Dean Wart seemed to submit, a good boy now, to the cosmic spirit. Was he fooling around? Never in his years at Ethridge had Dean Rivington Wart been known to crack a joke, or give a high sign: do some little thing to relieve the tension between himself and students, underlings. Never. Why, you must be mad to think a serious man like him, a pillar, could be hacking around. Never, I tell you, not on this earth. In his Harris tweeds and his shally necktie the Dean of Behavior sat down there on the floor of Ethan Jeffers'—and Manuel's—student room.

—Omm-m-m-m-m.

Soulful! And the Dean gave a weird tremulo to it, as he made the switch from earthly passions, illusions, to a heaven far from his J. Edgar Hoover always-get-his-man karma. He gave a little laugh, under his om. He seemed happy.

—Dean Wart? said Ethan.

—Om-m-m-m . . . rengy-y-y . . . kyo-o-o!

—Uh, Dean Wart?

Now Newell Gilbert, all the while lurking in the dark hallway, a few feet away, felt mixed up. For this seemed to upset the natural order: a master sitting crosslegged with a submissive smirk on his face—a man so often, in normal times, ready to attack. Dean Wart looked like a bad boy gone to confront . . . Dean Wart! Gone to the Detention Office on the second floor of Settlers. And there, yes, he would have his one 'extended weekend' taken away for some small breach of the code. But he would gain salvation, a loss of self. Hm! Does this mean the good Dean Wart had a soul, and not a mere disciplinary reflex?

More probably the Dean of Behavior chanted om-m-m as an undercover disguise. He must follow Ethan into the empyrean in order to get an answer to his question: whether the boy knew the truth about his roommate's disappearance.

Ethan Jeffers stopped chanting. He looked around. Dean Wart kept on chanting, but Ethan had stopped.

—Uh, Sir?

—Om-m-m-m.

Newell thought all this was pretty ridiculous. It reminded him of the time, last year, when he saw Dean Wart talking with Mingo the town bum, of all people, on the drive before Settlers, where it led out to the winding road toward town. And Newell looked down from his freshman room, on the third floor, and tried to imagine Mingo in a suit as Dean of Behavior, and Wart in rags as a tramp. And this made Newell laugh, and feel a bit better, in his homesickness. Maybe he sensed that, without laughter, this Ethridge ordeal would be too much. Without a good laugh now and again you might not make it through.

But Ethan said quite clearly for once:

–Sir, Manuel did receive a threat.

–Om-m-m-m-m, said Dean Wart, and stared into space.

–My roommate received a threat the night before he went away. Uh . . . Sir–

–Om-m-m-m-m!

–Jay Schmied said he would make him roll a marble, with his nose, the length of the Senior Path, if he didn't stop being such a flit.

Chapter Two

I

Clangalangalangalanglangalangeruh!!!
Early morning bell at Ethridge: 6 a.m. campus-wide, on each corridor. Like birth trauma: jerked from warm covers to a dark room. A boy's feet ached on the cold floor, since freezing temperatures caught the head custodian Astarte off guard. Bodies shivered. Hands clutched at lamp switches, bathrobes. Goosebumped legs did a hurdygurdy dance toward the bathroom with its icy tiles. Then did a student welcome itchy woolen trousers and jackets over dress shirts starched stiff as a brickbat. Fingertips paled as a boy stood before the mirror trying to clip a bow tie on straight, or fiddling with cufflinks.

Outside, in the first light, the campus lay in a frosty silence. One by one they emerged from the student houses, and went along the colonnaded archway the length of the quadrangle. Ethridge playing fields to the west, wide farmlands bordering the Needing to the east: all lay in a blue mist.

Here came the slight form of a freshman looking dazed: made afraid by the rumors? He emerged from Settlers. And there went a jaunty sophomore blowing on his fingertips: he banged the Hampton House door behind him as though he meant to scare away ghosts. Here, there, an antique lantern began to fade and be snuffed by the pink glow of sunrise.

On the breakfast line. Eggs swam in a vat of grease, like sinners. The toast was charred, hard, dry: no more buttered up than the stern Dean of Behavior. At one table Jay Schmied handed Newell and Big Bern a cube of cocoa from the last package sent by his mom. Then, in the Refectory, boys lingered for a bit of smalltalk before the day's ordeal. Newell looked around and saw Jeffers, moonfaced, a flit; but there was no sign of Manuel.

II

By morning chapel the sun had risen; it flooded the eaves, and cast shadows across the silvery grass. A few birds chirped. A lone mourning dove sang the plight of the descending year, as masters and students filed in and took assigned seats along the pews. No Manuel. A vacant place. And today that empty seat spoke more eloquently than the sermonette of Geeter, or Reverend Geeter to you: the Chaplain.

–Popularity is cheap, he said, and undiscriminating . . .

Newell had a fever, but he didn't want to go in the Infirmary. All alone over there, away from the others? In his pew he held himself upright, looked around a little, and thought: no Manuel . . . He glanced at Rivington Wart, a madman. Big Schmied stared at The Geet, and gave a wide obstreperous yawn which drew a bit of laughter from students. Pastor Geeter: another nut. It seemed they all got together, Headmaster Smithson, Coach Roentgen, Master Glebe the history teacher, Wart, Geet. They made up a code of rules for Ethridge School to live by; it was strict and comprehensive. But if you got close to them, if you ever saw under the impeccable men's wear–like Dean Wart on the floor in Ethan's room last night–who knew what you would find?

The high Venetian windows of the chapel brightened. Spears of sunlight cleared Warren House and shot through the airy casements. Pews, altar, balcony were an off-white hue with mahogany trim, the walls white too. And now one place was empty. And a demon ran around chasing people out there on the island of tall trees. And who could say what else he did? Newell gazed out the tall windows past birch and sycamore trees losing their leaves in late October. Gymnasium, tennis courts, the Atelier where the yearly Bartlett mixer would be held this Saturday evening; he might see that girl from the soccer game, but would he have the nerve to say hello? Beyond the Atelier: a rolling lawn, a pond fed by the river, autumn foliage, willows; and then further, out along the winding road to town: the small bridge where a train passed each morning as Rev. Geeter went into his climax.

The long train whistle blew over meadows and forests of the New England countryside.

Newell drew in his gaze and looked again at the empty pew seat. In his fever he gave a little shudder, and remembered the cabin, that scent of perfume, the cold, cold tang of the river.

Later, the sun heated up the classrooms, and then would a boy itch, itch, beneath his woolens. And Master Glebe droned on the length of third period history class. Tell me: how could a man whose wife had such flesh be so stuffy? The birds, blackbirds and starlings, chirped, hopped outside the closed windows: not for their likes to get trained and molded into tomorrow's leaders. Grackles flitted in the locust trees donated by Class of '46 for quad beautification. Please tell me: why did Newell Gilbert feel, not think but feel that one of life's great things, an education, was being done to him like a hostile act? Why? And why did Master Glebe make Little Mallet take pieces of waste paper from the basket and crumple them, over and over, next to Garvey Sackler's ear, after The Garv had crinkled a sheet of paper from his looseleaf notebook? And then that flit Sedgewick asked:

—Sir, may I remove my tweeds?

And the witty master replied:

—Certainly, but not all of them, please.

Master Glebe, bald, rolypoly, stood by the blackboard and droned on, on, on. He and Ramona, The Ram, were childless, and one day he had said in class:

—You're all my children.

Now why so? How could this be? The master's words, the sound of them, seemed a little strange at the time. Newell who, after his trip to the island and shock on Sunday, tended to see a Beast of Ethridge in every adult, thought Glebe didn't fit the bill. He was not as tall as the monster they had seen out there; was he? Maybe so; maybe it was the vicious attack, not physical stature, which made The Beast look so big. Anyway the curious words remained: 'You're all my children'. Might the barren couple kidnap a boy in order to play mother and father? No, ridiculous. But one other thing, now he thought of it, drew Newell's suspicions to the history teacher. The previous week—in fact Wednesday, the day before Manuel disappeared—Master Glebe came to class with a shiny forehead and a flustered look. Well, he began as usual, boring everybody to death, as though all human history with its convulsions, wars, great social movements and struggle for freedom had only happened so Master Glebe might hold forth today in a monotone and put his students to sleep: like at the dentist, only what got extracted here was a boy's mind, his curiosity. Same spiel last Wednesday; but then something happened. Suddenly Master Glebe flew into a fit talking about some old Frenchman, a certain Chalier, from the time of the Revolution. You might have thought a student laughed at Glebeth: the way the master began to rant and flail his arms and fling his person around. Then he was like the Beast of Ethridge; it electrified the classroom. Jeffers came out of his trance, almost, and Granny Zammet looked a little less depressed. And Boz Krips, Ethridge's great athlete, drew his gaze in from the window for the first time in history. And Cormac, the dayhop with his cute look, seemed in his element as, for those five minutes, the noted Glebe went in a frenzy over the fate of a long forgotten man named Chalier. Then, for a moment before the bell rang ending fourth period, Glebe came to his senses; he came back from the distant planet where people acted that strange way: alive, involved, taking sides on the day's great issues, trying to survive with their loved ones. Glebe cleared his throat with a weighty: ahem! looked a little embarrassed, and again tended to business as usual, homework assignments, threats of pop quizzes. But his upper lip still trembled a moment. And his forehead shone: it shone. One thing about Glebster though: he was a natty fellow. His suit looked like he'd just had a romp in the sack, fully clad, with his bosomy consort. And his shirt, wrinkled at the navel, bunched, in need of laundering, stood out half untucked the way the blousy Ramona left it. This was Master Glebe's trademark: his rumpled shirt in front. Only on that day, last Wednesday, as the master lurched around and flailed in front of the astonished class, there at world history's podium, it came all the way out: one glorious shirttail flapped, for all to see, like the tricolor of the victorious Revolution.

    —Uh, Sir—said Fred Butterworth, 'Butterball', when the storm had calmed—tuck your shirt in, Sir.

—Sorry, said Glebe; and, nervously, after the outburst, reached for his rollbook to take attendance before the hour ended; though a glimpse told you everyone was there, and Manuel too, still. As the sunlit autumn morning rose toward noontime, an odor of corned beef hash wafted over the quadrangle. What a pathos in the smell of Refectory food, those dishes seasoned with saltpeter: said to help a lad control his doggy instincts.

In fifth period all grew hungry, but not for knowledge, as the scent of corned beef hash embalmed the quad. Yet Newell perked up and had a rare moment of interest. Juvenal's satire on women had a few scabrous lines not translated in their bi-lingual edition; so the young scholar got more Latin, more declensions by instinct in a few minutes—as the Latin master passed over—than he could put to memory the rest of the semester. One day Newell had complained:

—Sir, I can't remember them. My mind won't do it. I mean what's the use to me: bellum, bellī, bellō, I can't bung it in, Sir, I don't care about it. Maybe I'll have to fail.

The master rose to his full height, defending his subject, and livelihood:

—A nation's prominent men are formed, boy, on the battleground of Latin grammar. How many young people have this chance? Only a few, handpicked, one in a million. And with future success, riches, happiness at stake, you tell me you can't learn a few Latin words by rote. Fie.

Newell nodded and didn't answer back: because he wanted to succeed, not fail; please, not hurt, his mom and dad. So he toiled over pure i-stems and mixed i-stems and got nowhere; but the moment it was forbidden, like the Juvenal, and the subject matter caught his eye, his brain came alive. For example, he would have liked to know more about that man Chalier who had such an effect on Master Glebe.

By twelve noon, when the lunch bell clangalanged, there were seniors strolling in shirt-sleeves along the Senior Path toward the Refectory. Woe to any underclassman who set foot on the Senior Path, and trampled a sacred institution. Then would the elite of the school—Jon Holbein, protégé of the headmaster; Josey Kipnes, future matinee idol; Paul Rhodes; Tim MacDonald called 'The Captain' or 'The Square'; Herbert 'Toad' Wingate, who could crush you with a comeback: then would those seniors, all members of *Self-Furtherance*, a secret society, punish a poor boy who set foot on The Path. I tell you: don't do it. Why, they will make you roll a marble, with your nose, from Settlers to the Refectory and back again, until you learn to respect your betters. Respect senior privilege! Look what happened to Ben Bolt who (with Big Schmied, Boz Krips, and Newell Gilbert, it was rumored) overturned the science teacher's sports car right there on The Path, horrors! This symbolic act–along with the school silverware incident–led to Ben Bolt's expulsion.

And so, through the long morning of classes, at lunchtime, and into the afternoon, sixth, seventh and eighth (lab) periods, a seat stayed empty. And Manuel didn't come back to take his place with the others, and bend to the yoke of Ethridge routine. He did not complete his lessons. His cries weren't heard from the athletic fields when intramural teams Hereford (the green), Montrose (the blue) and Rushworth (the red) fought valiantly for The Cup. The foreign exchange student was not seen at dinner; nor was he at his place in evening study hall on first floor Settlers. He no longer slept in the bed that had been his. And he wouldn't, it appeared, anymore. Not today, not tomorrow, not ever again. Rumor had it, as first days of the boy's absence passed, that he got too homesick and simply went back to his country. Hopped on a plane–without saying goodbye to anyone? or bothering to pack his things?

Few were the hours of warmth that remained in the descending year.

III

Was it possible the administration would call off a yearly mixer with the sister school, Bartlett Academy, scheduled for that Saturday? Not at all: the show must go on as in normal times, appearances be kept up. But rest assured of an even more stringent school security. Look for special measures to see Ethridge through the crisis. Enjoy yourselves, boys, with Dean Rivington Wart as the chaperone.

That Saturday evening Newell returned from the dining hall and stood a long moment staring in his dresser mirror. What a barefaced zitty guy he was: but never mind. He rubbed a green pomade, gooey stuff he sent away for in New York, over his duck's ass hairdo modelled on Ben Bolt's. Gingerly he daubed acne lotion on a blackhead blooming like a poppy by his lip. How could he, a lowly sophomore, compete with snobbish seniors and hope to impress a deb like the one he saw at the soccer game? Comb, deoderant, clothes brush: he tossed things behind him among parts of a radio, like debris from a wrecked ship, on his bedspread. The fine portable radio sent by his mother made no sound: it never had worked; and Newell suspected Dean Wart's office of tampering, since they opened all packages, and didn't want any radio playing after lights-out. Newell smiled grimly at the mirror and threw a few cool moves. He blurted, jerkily:

—Reet, New-baby, yer' cool!—He glimpsed Big Bern in the mirror.—Berneth, the idea is to meet her, reet!

—Well—said the scientist, a skeptic—there is the small matter of seniors, also hounding quail.

Newell postured. He gave a manly frown. But try as he might to make himself look good, he felt insecure. He sighed:

—To catch her eye I'll have to find Manny's kidnapper, and make a hit in the newspapers.

—Sure—said Bernie, tired of hearing about it—catch the Beast of Ethridge.

—Cormac'll help.

—Reet. A maniac on his better days.

—Hey, he's cool.

—As long as he takes his pills. Milltown: breakfast of champions.

Berneth clung to the view that Manuel ran away. If Newell and Big Corm could be believed, and there really was a monster living in a cabin out on the island, then it must be Jon Holbein or some other *Self-Furtherance* member smooching with a town girl of a Sunday. To The Bern this kind of talk meant a threat to his scholarship, if he got involved.

—Big B, I will ask her to take a spin.

—Josey Kipnes'll tap your shoulder. Bug off, soph.

—I wait for her by the Atelier door. Uh, hi! Tonight I hound quail, see. Tomorrow I make a trip to Bartlett, I announce myself: cousin from out of town.

—Sure thing. What's her name?

—Ever the pessimist, Bernikins. Well, what do you suggest? Stay here and jerk off?

—Okay! I'll make a smear and analyze it in eighth period lab.

For the occasion Newell donned his favorite heliotrope shirt open at the neck, and a blue blazer. Corm would show up at seven: the dayhop grew lonely by himself in that mansion by the town cemetery, with only Mingo's smelly socks for company.

–Bern-boy, c'mon. Get ready!

–Naw, I'll stay here. Get drunk on my vintage yeast wine.

–Get sick and barf.

–Those Bartlett girls are too stuffy. And I don't mean their brassieres.

For another moment Newell agonized in front of the mirror. If anything could make her notice him, it was the heliotrope shirt. Don't you think so? But his t-shirt neck was crooked. Oh, hell. Sometimes he thought he was handsome, a sure bet to make it with chicks. Most times the mirror didn't agree, and he felt like crying, a frustrated child.

Now he sat on his bed and fiddled with the small electronic parts; but not long, since he knew the radio sent by his mom would not work. No, its chances were scuttled by the Dean of Behavior or whoever looked through boys' packages from home. Suddenly Newell thought of something: a powerful thing; his face flushed red with the force of such an idea, and then went pale.

Bernard looked over at him and said:

–What's up?

Newell shook his head. He got up and began to clear his desk. Then, neatly, he laid out mechanical drawing instruments: compass, t-square, pencils, eraser. He went to his closet and, from a portfolio, took four sheets of a large, heavy drafting paper. Then he told his roommate:

–I may not sleep here tonight. So don't get excited.

IV

Outside, the air was crisp and cold, tinged with a burnished scent: the New England autumn. Good weather for bears; or small animals roaming the fields and woods surrounding the school. Or beasts. Stars shone above the colonnade connecting the student houses; stars flickered high over the Settlers cupola with its garlands and swags atop a Georgian Revival facade. The roommates crossed the Senior Path: at its far end the Refectory had a shadowy look from two lanterns by the wide main entry in the center.

—Wonder what's keeping Corm.

—What if I have halitosis? said Bernard.

—Here's a jelly bean.

—I've got zits, and my glasses fog.

—Berneth, you'll be a great scientist someday. They'll give you society women to dissect.

—But what to do in the meantime?

—Go to the mixer, like me.

There was a stir round the quadrangle with scents of cologne and talcum powder, strains of rock 'n roll from a room on third floor Nye House. Inside Settlers freshmen sat for evening study hall: at work over math and English assignments; no mixer for those flits.

Bern nudged his roomie:

—Look.

Past the chapel, down the steps to the service road they went: toward the Atelier lit up beyond the tennis courts. But up ahead stood a familiar figure, tall, imposing, graying at the temples.

—Good evening, said Rivington Wart. Going to the mixer?

—Yes, Sir.

The Dean gave them such a bizarre look, grayish eyebrows raised, that Bernard who already wore a craven air from the upcoming encounter with chicks, asked for another jelly bean, popped it, and then bent over to cough and choke when it went down the wrong way. Newell slapped his back and said with a shrug:

—Nervous, Sir. Afraid of girls.

—Enjoy yourselves, said Dean Wart, his voice deep, wistful. But Newell's heartbeat also churned at the sight of Jeffers' late night visitor, down here by himself in the dark, looking sort of sheepish. Newell thought: will I do it? Can I carry through this thing tonight? What a plan to catch the Beast of Ethridge. What a risk!

V

Out there in the darkness the Needing River, its strong silent current, ran tangent to the winding road into town. Newell sniffed in a fresh forest scent and recalled with a shiver his outing last Sunday, and dip in the freezing water. For a moment he thought of horror stories told by a senior counselor on third floor Settlers, before lights-out, meant to befuddle a flitty, zitfaced freshman and browbeat him into conformity, as if he needed it.

Berneth snapped his fingers and said:

—I've got it. Reet.

—You do, baby, you really do.

Bern's face had a hangdog look as he took in the Atelier. He mumbled something about Einstein hounding quail and bowed his head. In store for his ego was a head-on collision with the female sex.

—Let's go back, he said.

Just up ahead a small crowd gathered by the glass doors of the Atelier. They stood on a porch lined by six slender columns. There were plots of ivy, a low relief of the Graces, set in white against the light blue walls: four on either side of the sliding glass doors.

Boys awaited the first busload of meat. Meanwhile they swaggered, acted cool: many were the worldly remarks, by these scoffers, and then an insecure little laugh. They were brash alright, for a bunch of zit-ridden underclassmen: before they saw the whites of a Bartlett girl's eyes. A do-or-die affair! the single day of open season on quail in the school year. Many were the sex objects due to arrive any minute on the clanking Bartlett school bus. All dogs.

In the first blinding glimpse: such a quantity of honeys would be dismissed—too serious, too pale, too zitty. Too flat chested. Too angular, all elbows, knees, goofy grins. You'd come away with bruises if she deigned to dance with you. But those braces! Good Lord, you'd need a trip to the emergency ward if you kissed her. Of course a few *hot* chicks might show up, worthy of an Ethridge student's cool moves. But you had to be fast, boy. You had to pounce and sink your teeth into that meat! That is: you needed luck and a plan of attack if you didn't want to end up foxtrotting with your pillow, alone in your room, not only tonight but the rest of the year.

Then, count on it, there would be one knockout among that motley crowd. The pick of the crop: oh my aching gonads. Naw, forget about it, zitface, go crawl back in your hole. She is not for your likes. No way! For here come the superb seniors of the *Society for Self-Furtherance.* Look at 'em saunter on the scene, preening like cocks: I mean Jon Holbein, peer of masters, the one they call Bossman; and Josey Kipnes, the golden boy who has played in summer stock; and Herbert 'The Toad' Wingate, able to stick his ugly mug into places it has no business being. Yes, sir. If you dared ask a hot chick to work out, they would tap your shoulder with a sneer, and say:

–Move it, flit.

VI

In a moment the Bartlett Academy bus would rattle up the drive with its batch of debs. Here they come: the sweethearts arrive for the slaughter in a chorus of giggles. Hearts jump, thoughts race. Work fast! Snap up tasty morsel!

Bernard tugged his friend's sleeve.

–Let's go in. 'snot cool to stand out here, looking so baldfaced.

Newell gazed down the rolling lawn. A squib of lantern light reflected from the winding road onto the Pond. During the soccer match he had edged closer to the beautiful girl; and his eyes met hers, once, and he thought she might not snub him. Now he would have a chance, if he was lucky, before Holbein and Rhodes came late to show how suave (rhyme with knave) they were. Yes, he had to move in and ask her to dance.

The art studio was a large room cleared of easels and gessoed canvas. Bunting and baloons hung from the cornices: WELCOME BARTLETT. Already a three-man combo got in gear. Reet! Folding chairs lined the walls. A refreshment table had punch, unspiked, and cookies.

–Where I come from, said Bernard, jiving, a few dozen virgins *get it* every night.

Big Jay Schmied ambled up, blond orangutang whose arms dangled to his knees. Dance with me? Schmied's mug, his curly blockhead, and steely eyes revealing a sinister purpose, made him quite a catch for some young honey. A funereal look on his great pinkish jowls, he glanced at the glass doors where hot chicks would soon crowd in, and said:

—My parents are rich.

—Good line! said Newell. And you've got a big dick too.

—Reet, said Schmied. Big dick.

Coach Roentgen detested Jay Schmied because Schmidlap refused to go out for varsity football. What a contrast between his gawking, apeman ways, the symphony of springs you heard from his room every night when he beat meat with a wild abandon—and the prissy, mincing way he had of speaking. But don't mess with him: even those arrogant seniors didn't bait Crazy Schmied. When they wanted to give Newell's greasy Chicago-style d.a. a haircut whether he liked it or not, Schmiddeth told Tim MacDonald, the Captain, to his face:

—You shan't snip Newby's hair or my lob.

VII

The bus arrived. The music started: velvety, revamped, from an earlier time. Now Newell sat in shadow against the far wall and began to feel sad.

Berneth strolled past, one hand in pocket, jiving. He popped jelly beans with a power, man.

—Mean chicks. I'm flipped.

Girls came in, plain ones, past triage by the glass doors. They slung coats over chairs. They stretched and looked around.

The Bern bent forward and said:

—They're everywhere.

—Sure.

—Look, let's split. Get drunk on yeast wine. Puke guts.

Newell shook his head, and stared. Groups of girls took seats at a few tables to one side. The combo wore dark suits, check neckties, spitshined shoes. They played intently, with beady eyes. Their music seemed just a bit hesitant before the hepped-up tastes of a younger generation.

Bern jived past, muttering:

–The Kid . . . from the Grand Concourse. Oldest son of Dottie and Moe . . . Not a WASP. Cool, Daddio.
Newell shook his head some more, in disgust:
–Oh, okay.

VIII

He saw her.
She came walking across the dance floor with a reckless air. Boys stared after her. A friend followed her, petite, freckled, maybe good for Bernie, though he liked them brazen and voluptuous, like Ramona Glebe. But the other one–phew! A dozen chairs away from him, she stared at the cattle market by the entry, and didn't take off her coat. How she ever made it through that gauntlet of sex-starved flits, who wore their horniness on their sleeve, he would never know.
At once the flit Sedgewick went up and asked her, *her*, for a dance. What? No way! Are you kidding, Sedgewick, you nebbish! Shite!
She danced. She took off her coat, handed it to her homely friend, and what Newell saw, sitting there on the sidelines, made him ache. Then another flit, a junior named Wellingham, took the place of Sedgewick, who stood looking stunned. She didn't seem unkind: not like the fantastic Mrs. Glebe who held 'em out there, in public, for boys to ogle in the Refectory–but cut you dead on the quad, and gave not a hint what had gone on between you. O Ramona Glebe! O pubescent nights, when a boy lay in bed, his thoughts smothered by your too ample charms.
Newell sat glued to his chair, and thought: off my duff and go meet her, now, when this dance ends, or I'm a flit. Only chance, all year. A cool hood would do it, a townie, lucky high schooler. An Amboy Duke would put the reet moves on her . . . He winced at her womanly figure, the heavenly curve of her cashmere sweater, as she danced with that goofball Wellingham.
Then Newell stood up. His heart jumped in his throat when he saw, past the wide glass doors on the cement patio, the elite group of seniors who in some ways ran the school. Holbein, Kipnes, Rhodes, MacDonald, The Toad with his pudgy face full of nasty thoughts. In a moment Josey would spot this hot chick and move on her. Good

night, sweetheart. Okay, okay, mused Newell: when this hip tune ends I will ask her to dance, or I'm a zitty flit.

IX

For a moment the words wouldn't come. Brought before her by a force sort of beyond him, Newell stood and stared. Calmly she smiled up at his fumbling, and waited. For one thing she seemed older than the others. But how old? Her face looked foreign: unlike any Bartlett girl he'd ever seen. Also her clothes were different: stylish bluejeans with the gray cashmere sweater; her suede coat, with a silk lining, lay draped on the seat beside her. Where did she come from? Did she have a name like normal people? Her black hair was done up in a maroon scarf: more like a peasant woman than a daughter of New England gentry. No prim dress like the others; no makeup applied with a spatula; no giggles. Unlike the rest of them she looked blasé, carelessly rich, a wee bit snide. Now she rose with a yawn, scratched her head with one finger under the scarf, as if she had fleas, and said:

—Phyllis, watch my stuff while I dance with this gentleman.

Then he held her in his arms for the first slow dance of the evening, and she moved in closer! Oh, this beat Cotillion classes back in his hometown: there all callow laughter, cracking jokes with a smirk; here a well developed older girl pressed against him free as you please, and she gave a low chuckle. Her voice was throaty, a little rough. Did she smoke cigarettes? If he looked beyond the paradise of her body, he felt others' eyes on them. How to impress her? What to say that she would remember? She was his height with curly hair at the temple, which tickled his face; he seemed to sense something careful, a little unsure, in the touch of her hand in his. Now, instead of enjoying the dance and this wonderful event, maybe introducing himself, keeping it light since he had just met her, Newell said:

—Did you know a boy is missing from Ethridge?

At this she drew back.

—Really?

—On my corridor. It's a mystery. But I'm trying to—

—Did he run away? she said. Go home?

—I don't think so. To South America? He's the foreign exchange student.

She stared in Newell's eyes and thought a moment. He looked in her face so different from the others: her exotic features, high cheekbones. Say! Did she come from Manuel's country? Her features weren't cute, 'pretty' the way he might find this or that girl pretty back home in public school.

—Are his things still in the room? she asked.

—Well, I . . . I'm going to find out more tonight after lights-out.

Newell felt a strangeness in the look she gave him. Yes, she was taken by what he said to her; and this made him want to brag more. But there was another thing in her dark-eyed gaze. Somehow, she might know more than he did: the way she nodded, and looked thoughtful.

—Is the missing student your friend? she said.

—Uh, yes. I help him sometimes with his mechanical drawing assignments.

At this baldfaced lie he blushed to the roots of his hairline.

She frowned. Her voice had a twinge of sadness when she said:

—Do you?

Newell shrugged.

—It's just . . . well, I don't like to see anybody in trouble. I'm on his floor, and I feel a . . . a sort of duty to look after things, since our senior counselor Rog the Dodge is such a flit.—Here Newell drew up; hey, go the whole hog.—So I think from clues so far he's been kidnapped. Something bad's going on: Hound of the Baskervilles type thing. And, if this is true, then I'm going to find the kidnapper, and save Manuel.

The name gave her a little start, as though she knew it. Her smile at Newell's boasting became a frown. For a moment she held him from her as they two-stepped. Yes, she wasn't pretty in the soft, wily way of girls. You might see a face like that in a dream at night, and feel an anxious kind of yearning. Then a lad might shy away from the haunting image: even while he felt its charm. When she spoke her voice was low, a bit rough like her features, and sad at instants.

—How long has it been?

—Over a week.

She moved in close again. Timidly he held her while they danced: ever so gently because, somehow, she seemed fragile. Well, he had impressed her, but he still felt out of his league. So he said:

—Don't worry, I'll get to the bottom of this. Last Sunday me and my friend Cormac took a rowboat out to the island . . .

X

Again she drew back and looked in his eyes as though she meant to read something there. While he began telling her about their trip to the island, and how he wanted to visit Bartlett instead, and meet her after seeing her at the soccer game—this strange girl's eyes narrowed to two slits. She peered into his depths and noted the boyishness, the bravado; and he feared she would say so long the minute she took a whim. Her eyes were dark, dark. And when she drew him close, her opulent body pressed close to his: so warm, so tense. She spoke in a throaty whisper.

—What is your name, sir?

—Newell Gilbert.

—Hm. Tell me, Mr. Gilbert, would you happen to know those gentlemen by the door?

The dance ended. She turned him, and he felt his fears take shape. In a group by the entry stood the tall, imposing seniors; and with them, like a mascot, The Toad.

—You mean Paul Rhodes?

—Which is he?

—Lighter hair.

—And the one in the center?

—Holbein.

—What about him?

—Mean guy, a bully. He's the headmaster's suck-up, so he just about runs things. Holbein wants to send thugs some night to cut my hair, but I have my own thugs: Schmied, the big blockhead you see over there, with short blond curls; and Boz Krips, a sophomore like me, but the best athlete this school ever had, by the time he's a senior.

At Newell's side the girl screwed up her eyes with interest. Her voice had a catch:

—And that other, with long hair, who looks half asleep?

—Josey.

–And?

–He's an actor: been in plays. But a shirker, real lazy. He skips classes, and Dean Wart lets him off.

–Shirker, eh? And would you say Josey's a . . . a regular guy?

She said Josey's name like she knew it too.

Newell gave a twitch. But he was fair:

–He'll say hi at least, and leaves you alone. Some of them, like The Toad, the short ugly one next to Holbein, are skunks. Steer clear of The Toad.

–Why? What does he do?

–Well, they have a secret society, called *Self-Furtherance*. They'll put the hex on you, and make things harder. Maybe you'll disappear, like Manuel.

–This Josey fellow: would *he* put the hex on you?

–Not on me, but a girl or two. Last year there was a rumor he got a town girl in trouble. But Cormac, my dayhop friend, thinks it was Holbein.

XI

Now after nine o'clock those couples meant to pair off had done so. A few sat and talked at tables to one side of the combo. Stags like the gangly Schmied, jiving Bernard from the Bronx, or that flit of flits Garv Sackler, made tours on the rim of the dance floor, and gaped. The wallflowers sat dreamily alone and awaited their knights in shining armor. On hand as chaperones were Master Glebe and his wife Ramona, who taught mathematics classes at Bartlett. Would you believe it? That flit to end all flits, Warnickie, a junior, had asked the immense Ramona to take a spin on the hardwood, and she said yes! So there she was, grinning ear to ear and having herself a grand old time as arms and legs gyrated.

Newell's roommate came by looking unhappy. His pace had slowed.

–This is Bernardo. Should we introduce him to Phyllis?

–Hello, Mister Bernardo. My name is Katya.–She held out her hand for a frank handshake. Then she turned and said:–Could you get me a drink?

—We have yeast wine, said Big Bern. Want to come get drunk in our room? Puke up your guts!

Newell thought: have Berneth get the punch? But that would look gauche, and what else could he say to her while they stood waiting? And so it was that he entrusted his dream girl to Mister Bernardo. He went toward the refreshment table, and there was a bounce to his step after dancing with the Queen of the Mixer. All around him beady gazes had looked on with envy and devoured Katya: those poor souls who hadn't found true love, as he had, at the hop. And then Newell caught the dark gaze of Jon Holbein where that future statesman stood by the door . . . And outside the darkened glass lay a prospect of cold autumn night, the rolling lawn, the Pond, and Needing River beyond: with its island of tall trees, and its secret. But all this, including Manuel's disappearance, held no interest for a Newell Gilbert on the brink of first love.

XII

The studio space was crowded. Things had loosened up, and voices were raised in laughter. Classmates called out above the music, as Newell went among the bouncy dancers. He glanced back at Katya: would she wait? He tried to hurry, but there were people ahead of him at the refreshment table. He inched forward and was finally able to get four cups of orange soda which spilled on his fingers. Sticky hands! Charmed, I'm sure. Now how would they dance? Then someone clipped Newell's elbow and the liquid sloshed down his heliotrope shirt onto his pants. How embarrassing! Dance close with her? snuggle up when he was all wet? Newell stopped in his tracks, holding the four paper cups, and swore. His face felt hot, and by now his nose must be good and shiny, his zits on fire like little demons' eyes. Zits! There were mornings when he stood before his mirror and wanted to dig his fingernails in his face.

When he returned, she was gone. Bernard held up his two palms: empty. So he stood there a moment in silence, and looked around, and his worst fears were confirmed. There she stood over by the glass doors; she gazed into the handsome face of Josey Kipnes. It seemed they knew one another; there was something between them. And then they danced, and Newell looked across at them, beady eyed, and felt envy. He didn't think it but he felt it: they were made for one another. Not only because they were both older: he saw a hint in their eyes, in the way they danced.

Still he went to her, feeling stunned, and said:

—Here's your drink, Katya.

Rhodes stood nearby, and said:

—Sophomore, how uncool. Don't you realize you're not wanted?

But Josey took the two cups.

—Thanks.

Newell turned and walked away. A moment later his roommate said to him:

—Yeast wine, anyone?

XIII

There she was: across the dance floor in Josey Kipnes' arms. Nevertheless Newell sat in her spell, and thought: of course the elite seniors would yank her away. But a hard thing: to be in action a moment ago, and now the bench. Tall, gangling Jay Schmied was out there having a go with some stumpy thing. Even Garv Sackler, a mental case, did the stroll; though his glances at the ceiling, and lack of rhythm, were not suave (rhyme with grave). Moon Jeffers did the Zen boogie by himself to one side; but Cormac, the townie, hadn't shown up for this prepster rally.

—Let's split the scene—said Bern with a high sign.—Dullsville. Reet.

—Not yet.

Newell shook his head and thought: what to do? He had tried to turn on the charm and win her the easy way; but now he would have to act. He frowned and asked himself: play the hero and find Manuel's kidnapper? Last Sunday with Cormac, en route to the island, that struck him as a crazy idea. It would get him disowned by his dad who wanted good grades from him this year, the honor roll, on his p's and q's: not a wild escapade which could even put his life at stake. What to do?

Lately he had heard a rumor that *Self-Furtherance* was going to extend bids to underclassmen. Any student, even a flit, would want to join and hobnob with Jon Holbein and become a big man on campus. This Society for Self-Furtherance went back in Ethridge annals as far as anyone remembered, like Skull-and-Bones at Yale; but Holbein had taken it over for his own purposes, with The Toad as secretary. Well then: what if they tapped the foreign exchange student for membership? And they took the boy out to the island where they held their secret meetings. They hazed him. They abused Manuel and took it way too far, and he had a heart attack, or fell and hit his head. Manuel died. And they made a bonfire on the far side of the island, and cremated him; they buried Manny-babe's ashes, charred bones, in a hole beneath the autumn leaves. Yes, they killed a sophomore by accident and turned the whole thing into a kind of ritual so they wouldn't have to feel guilty. And now nobody knew where the missing student went: not the school administrators, Headmaster Smithson and Dean Wart in a stew to find out the facts, maybe hush them up; not the boy's parents far away, if they had been informed; not local or state police, who must know about it by now; though no squad cars had come to the school. For there would be the devil to pay if the story got in the press and became a national news item. Who were Manuel's parents? Were they well connected? Were they political?

And so Holbein went out to the island and minded the store. He scared away snoopers by wearing a corny Halloween mask, and throwing a scare into them. All this made sense. Many knew Jon Holbein was not, like other Ethridge students, of a genteel background; rather, he grew up in an orphanage. And Laurence Smithson, a former merchant banker, and a philanthropist, took Holbein under his wing after the boy drew attention to his plight by saving someone from a fire.

For another moment Newell sat on the sidelines at the yearly Bartlett mixer. In dejection he kept one eye on Katya and Josey enjoying themselves in each other's arms; but with his other, his mind's eye he mulled over the case. As things stood, the monster who chased him and Corm last Sunday must have known who they were: two of Manuel's fellow students onto a clue. From somewhere (Mingo) they had heard about the rowboats tied up in a cove, and the boating party the previous Friday, which included Manuel.

All this meant that, like it or not, Newell Gilbert was involved. Either he or Cormac might well be next on the list. So he couldn't just ignore the thing, as his dad would have demanded; he couldn't go calmly about the Ethridge routine. Too late simply to conform and blend back into the woodwork: if he didn't go looking for trouble, it could come looking for him. And this wasn't so much a matter of playing the hero for Katya's sake as keeping his wits about him, fighting back, surviving, for his own sake. Such were Newell's thoughts as he sat there and looked on. He was sad, but curiously excited. Plus he had an afterthought: Manuel might still be alive, in trouble, and need someone's help.

Berneth came along once again, jiving the night away. With a big grin, all full of zits and braces, the suave (rhyme with brave) Bern waved hi with a circular motion, and said:

–Reet!

XIV

After awhile Josey escorted Katya out the glass doors of the Atelier and into the darkness. The time was a few minutes past eleven o'clock.

–So ends a perfect evening, said The Bern. All got mixed.

–Hm.

–Uh, Katya's with Josey. They went out together.

–Gee, I hadn't noticed.

Newell glanced up at his roommate. Exasperated, he thought of the dark river with its island, and cold loneliness. Why had his parents sent him here? . . . He almost felt like crying; how cool: cry in front of everyone, at a mixer. You had one chance, per year, to hook up with a deb; if you blew it, baby, then you had Geeter's chapel talks to fall back on.

–How 'bout a nightcap? said Berneth.

–Let's go.

Down the rolling lawn lay the Pond in its silence. An antique lantern on the road to town reflected across the dark surface. The night was cold. A misty scent came from the river: distance, the deep forest. Red foxes nosed their way on campus in the late hours, along with muskrats, raccoons, and skunk. A near full moon went riding high up among clouds and stars. Newell shivered and thought of Cormac in his big empty house by the Protestant cemetery, with only The Ming for company. A night bird called out across the meadow, off toward the Ethridge sister school.

Newell led the way past the headmaster's house, or Ethridge Homestead, by the front circle. The two boys entered the dim Settlers lobby and passed the study hall with its portrait of a boy in a tennis sweater; he died in a car accident last summer. Then, on the Warren House side, Bern tiptoed:

—Shh, hanky-panky.

A creaking, a murmur came from inside the faculty lounge. Someone sighed: a woman. She heaved a sigh. The cushions of an old sofa seemed to breathe as well. Bernard bowed his head to the keyhole. A low, animal voice gave a few short gasps. The female gave a little cry. And then . . . then . . . There was an odor of perfume.

Bernie lingered by the lounge entrance. But Newell drew away from those sounds, that scent; there was something he had to do.

XV

First, though, he lay in bed. He breathed in air from the window slightly open. Burnt leaves, dew. His thoughts hurt him: so people acted that way, a few dances and zingo, down to business. Through the daylight hours they played their masquerade, reality, and waited for night to fall. Like a light switch: life had two sides. Oh, Katya . . . Newell started crying. His shoulders shook and the warm tears burned his eyes. The tears hurt him, but they also helped him.

Then he sat up and stared into the darkness. He didn't want to fall asleep as Bernard had at once. He had to do something.

Suddenly there was a tapping on the wall. In the dead of night it gave him a jolt. Then he heard Schmied's voice:

—Stop that. I heard you! You're a bad boy to do that.

Schmidlap's laughter.

—Quiet, Big Jay. Down, boy.

—You guys jag off all the time!

Newell had to chuckle. Schmied accused others when it was he, Schmied, who led the league in jagging off. Why, he tied the record of four homers almost every night.

XVI

—Ethan?

—Om-m-m-m.

—That's some style you showed at the mixer, Ethan. What do you call it: the levitation rag?

—Om-m.

—You really balled the jack tonight. I know you must be tired, but I need you to get up from there, and come with me.

—Om.

—Come on.

He helped him to his feet.

—Huh? said Moon Jeffers, rubbed his eyes a little, and looked around.

—Let's go.

—Where?

—Don't you know, Ethan?

—N-no.

—Kid, it's like this. A few of us, Berneth, Cormeth, Schmiddeth, Boz Kripseth, and meeth, we held a meeting. We decided to form our own secret society, and make you president. We will call it the Mechanical Drawing Club, and since you were elected president, by unanimous vote, you will have certain responsibilities. Yes, Ethan, as our Mechanical Drawing Club leader you will have a few assignments to do, after lights-out, once or twice a month. Beginning tonight. Okay? Each of us has a job to do: The Corm will get us blind dates with hot chicks in town. Would you like one?

—Y-yes.

—I thought you would. Cormer even offered his house so we'll have a place to take them. Boy, are they hot.

—Are they?

—Yes, sir, they'll smootch. As for Schmidder, he'll be your body-guard, Ethan, so the Beast of Ethridge won't kidnap you, like it did Manuel.

—Gee, thanks.

—And my job will be to find the Beast and catch it, sort of like Peter and the wolf.

—Will you?

—Yes, I will. And that's why we brought Boz in too: it won't be easy to tie that monster down. By the way, Ethan, do you know who it is?

—N-no.

—Not Dean Wart?

—Oh, no!

—Easy, kid . . . Or Holbein? I sort of like him as the Beast of Ethridge.

—Dear me.

—Well, we'll see. Anyway tonight you start with your duties as President of the Mechanical Drawing Club. Okay? Alright, buddy? I laid out the materials, and you can just turn on the lamp. Bernard wired us for all-night lights. Hey, you'll like it! You'd stay up till dawn anyway with your om-m-m. C'mon now, let's rumble.

—But—but—

—But what, buddyroll?

—Dean Wart said I shouldn't talk to you. Or anybody, without his permission. The headmaster might be mad at me.

—Don't worry.

—He came to ask me questions.

—I see. Well you can tell me what Dean Wart said when you finish the assignments. Right now you've got a job to do. Let's go, Mr. President. Just pretend your t-square is a hot chick from town, and you're feeling her up, you know, in a dark room at Cormeth's. Care to chacha?

XVII

Fully dressed Newell lay down on Ethan's bed and drew over the covers. In one hand he had a penlight, in the other: a jackknife. He waited. He blinked and kept his eyes open since, in the darkness and campus wide silence, he might fall asleep despite his excitement, and fear. Why do this stupid thing? Why play the hero? Would Katya be a little more impressed with him, if she knew he had a plan to entrap the Beast of Ethridge? Three doors down Big Schmied also lay awake—hopefully! Schmied, if he hadn't drifted off, was on full alert and ready to pounce: if the Beast paid another late night visit to the floor.

Now something Katya had said made Newell wonder; though he took no notice while they were dancing close together. She said: Are his things still in the room? Well, why had she asked that? Did she know before he told her there was a foreign exchange student named Manuel who had turned up missing? And when Newell bragged: I will find the kidnapper—she only stared at him with her strange eyes.

So were his things here? Was Manuel an Ethridge student in good standing, or had Dean Wart come and packed up his clothes and personal effects? On the boy's desk, yes, there still lay a few books and papers; but messy, as though he hadn't bothered to take them, in the last-minute rush. If Manny ran away, throwing a scare into Headmaster Smithson and everyone else, then his stuff might stay here until he showed up somewhere. Right? Yet ten days had passed since he was last seen on campus . . . And, if he was in fact able to get on a plane and go home, then why didn't the Headmaster say so and put people's minds at rest?

Maybe the school administration was playing for time. Maybe an investigation was going on behind the scenes. But then why had no one come around Warren House asking the students questions? Only Dean Wart came, secretively, late at night, in order to meditate with Ethan Jeffers, and go down on the floor and chant.

XVIII

Then Newell couldn't help himself: he fell asleep. In a dream he stood before the headmaster and said: aw shucks. He held a certificate, in mechanical drawing block letters, which read: Ten Hours. Katya gazed up at him with weird, dark eyes from the audience. All applauded, but the applause was also strange, more like—

Footsteps! He heard them: someone's footsteps, outside the door, along the hallway. Newell jolted awake, raised to one elbow, and stared in the darkness. Someone came slowly, past Schmied's door—hopefully Schmied heard them too—past sleeping Berneth, and Moon hard at work on the assignments. Quiet, thoughtful, almost sad they sounded, these slow footsteps, as they came closer.

Newell held his breath. Beneath the covers he opened a pocketknife, as whoever it was began to knock, slowly, on the door.

—Ethan?

Whose voice? Low, adult. Dreadfully serious, and, yes, sort of sad. It occurred to Newell this wasn't a dream with Katya looking on. The stakes were higher than ten detention hours. Eyes wide, heart pounding, he lay back and pulled the covers over his head. He gripped the knife. Give the signal he and Schmied had agreed on? a loud sneeze . . . Oh, he wished the rough and tough Boz Krips was on hand, the football player; but Boz lived in Nye House across the quad.

The door creaked open.

—Ethan?

From under the bedspread Newell tried to imitate Jeffers' pitiful, whiny tone. With a childish accent he said:

—Yes, Sir?

—Ethan, you and I need to talk.

—But, Sir, I'm sleeping.

—Are you, boy? Are you really?

What a grim sadness there was in that voice. Each sentence trailed off, like the voice of a dead man. Also, it felt oh so sorry for what it had to do now.

—Om-m-m-m.

—Yes, it is time we talked. It is time . . . for us.

Was it Dean Wart who stood there and breathed, sighed a little, like a dodo? Newell waited for the lisp that would give the Dean of

Behavior away. Newell was afraid to lift the covers, ever so slightly, and try to see. He didn't dare move, or even catch his breath: what if the man had a weapon, a club—and rushed at him, fell on him, hit his head, knocked him out? What if the Beast of Ethridge stuffed him in a sack and took him out to the island to keep Manuel company? Locked him away in that lonely cabin, where the dead were playmates? But, Sir! Please don't do that.

In a thin, puling tone, like a child, Newell said:

—Sir, I'm sick . . . to my stomach. Sorry. In the morning I'll go to the Infirmary. But if I move now I'll throw up. It's the Refectory food, Sir. Don't come near me unless you want to get thrown up on.

—Ah. Refectory food, eh?

This visitor said each word so weirdly, so distinctly, like a mind produced in the lab of Master Sippel, the science teacher who once had the students write an essay on 'How a Cow Walks'. However, the tone had something so bitter to it—when he said: Refectory food, eh?—that Newell guessed this might be the Ethridge cook, Bill Hastings. But still he didn't know for sure. He couldn't quite tell.

—Sick, Sir. Could upchuck, all over. Om-m.

—That's bad,—said the other, in a hush, as though disguising his voice.—I'm sorry to hear . . . that.

—I better lie quietly, Sir.

—No, tonight you must come . . . with me.

—Not tonight . . . Sir. Too sick. Om-m-m-m!

Then, slowly, he lifted the bedspread just a bit to see if this was Dean Wart, or Geeter, maybe that maniac Coach Roentgen; or even Mingo the town bum; or else the senior Jon Holbein putting on a show. And Newell stared out, like a small animal from its lair, sensing grave danger; and he blinked. And in that instant his heart darted up in his throat and it was all he could do not to jump out of bed and start yelling which would have been the end of him. For there, its big frame outlined in the dim hall light from beyond the door, stood the creature from the island, the Beast of Ethridge. The shoulders sloped in their bulk and stood ready to pounce. That was him. The face, or else mask, was the same horror, like putty dripping around two dark sockets, the eyes. Its features looked decomposed in death, like human rot.

—Come.

Newell's heartbeat was so wild he could hardly breathe. But he said:

—I can't . . . tonight . . . Sir.

The other, coldly:
—Are you sure, Ethan?
—Very . . . sure.

And then, suddenly, Newell tried to sneeze loudly; but instead he gave a loud retching sound, stuck out his head a little from the covers, and threw up his dinner in a big spew, on the floor. This retching noise was not the signal; still it might have brought Big Schmied running to the scene to save his friend. But no, there was silence. And then Newell threw up again: a fountain of it spattered the Beast of Ethridge's shoes, as Beast drew nearer to the bed.

The big, disgusting figure stood there a moment. Perhaps it saw this was not Ethan, its next victim. Or perhaps it was a squeamish Beast, which liked the smell of women's perfume better than that of upchuck. In any case the big ogre turned from the messy sight before it: a boy dripping goo at the lips, and hiccuping. Rather than soil its hands, or claws, The Beast walked with slow, measured steps back into the hallway. And then you heard its footsteps, slow, sort of thoughtful, creaking, along the dim corridor. And the Warren House door opened, with another creak, cree-e-eak! And then The Beast was gone—outside, into the night from where it came.

XIX

Silence.

In the wee hours no one had been woken up, it seemed, by the noise. Not Crazy Jay Schmied; not Rog 'The Dodge' Hillyer, senior counselor on the floor; not the dorm master, Pastor Geeter, at the end of the hall.

Newell pushed back the covers and sat on the bed a moment. He shook. He felt feverish, but he also felt like crying. Manuel's kidnapper had paid a call, returned to the scene of the crime, and gone again. So that's how it was: he came in the middle of the night all ready to drag away a second boy. And if the timid Jeffers had been here, that flit? Then what would have happened?

Newell turned on his penlight and went to Manuel's dresser. It was still full of the boy's clothing. Piece by piece the detective took out socks, underclothes, shirts, and looked for bloodstains, a hidden note or some other clue. Even while his hands shook, teeth chattered, the sophomore played detective and removed a few articles from the top drawer: glasses case, comb, pack of chewing gum, a tie clasp. What about fingerprints? Could Bernard see them in a microscope? What about his own fingerprints, which he was leaving all over the place?

In Manuel's desk drawer he looked for a note or a letter. An address book? A phone number? He did find a two-page letter in Spanish, but who could read it? Newell delved. A leather bookmark. A small wind-up clock, stopped. A checkbook for the school bank so the student could get his weekly allowance and buy a slice of seven-layer cake at The Snug in Hampton House basement, if only Geeter would sign their checks. An old photo yellowed at the edges: happy family. Then one of a girl, a sister perhaps? She was dark complected like Manuel, grinning, sort of cute. If the missing student left of his own free will, on the long journey home—wouldn't he take this picture? and other stuff? Would everything be left neatly like he was coming back?

He wasn't coming back.

XX

With his penlight Newell went to the closet. He rummaged through shirts, pants pockets, shoes. No notes, nothing at all telltale: except the fact of these things left behind. Was that why Katya asked about Manuel's belongings? because he would have taken at least a suitcase if he ran away? . . . And then, in her hypnotic eyes, came a glint of . . . of what, when she asked the question? Was Katya in the know? Did she have something to do with this? Maybe she knew more than he himself did, but wasn't telling. Maybe Katya had also made a trip out to the island.

He closed the closet. He went to lie down on Ethan's bed, but there was vomit on it, so he turned to Manuel's. Should he go fetch Jeffers and call him in here? It was late, past three a.m.; the mechanical drawings must be done by now. The hall was quiet except for a clock which clipped off two, three minutes at a stroke.

For a long time Newell lay eyes open and couldn't let himself drift off to sleep. Cold wind moaned in the window casement by the head of the bed. For a long while he tossed and turned; the pillow grew hot, and when he flipped it over he felt a crinkle. Then again, moving his head, a crinkle. He reached around, and his finger touched something inside the pillowcase.

He rose to one elbow and again turned on the penlight. Inside the pillowcase was a piece of notepaper folded twice: like an invitation, in gothic script.

> *Sophomore:*
> *You are called to the high rites*
> *of the Society for Self-Furtherance.*
> *Await further instructions, and be glad.*
> *Show this bid to nobody.*
> *Be wise.*
> *Watch, wait, obey!*

Chapter Three

I

Each morning, in the overheated chapel, the student body sat as one to hear Geeter give his talk. Inspiring! Sunlight filled the high windows. Boys stared at the chaplain from assigned seats the length of each pew. Now and again a stifled cough; but rarely did a head turn. Rarely a hand strayed to scratch an itch beneath the stuffy tweeds. They sat. They listened. Geeter said: Tomorrow's leaders have a brief childhood. Destiny calls upon those few to play in a world arena, not a nursery. In this higher sphere, this *oberen Welt* (Geeter cast a bit of German before them), one must not grumble or think of self. Don't backslide! Meet the challenge, and become a man.

Each morning Newell took a look around. From his place on a raised pew along the wall to Geeter's left, facing the congregation, he could see who was absent today: who had gone to the Infirmary. Manuel's seat stayed empty, like an extracted tooth. In the fifth row from the altar, toward the center: Manuel was not. No one. This lent an eerie sense, as Newell asked himself: who's next?

Geeter spoke on:

—You must not falter, but meet each test as it comes . . .

One day Ramsden Mallet, The Ramlet also called Little Mallet, did not appear for morning chapel. The next day it was freshman

Owen Crinshaw. Then Frederick Butterworth, 'Butterball', missed three days in a row.

Who was next? Would there be another Manuel? Would someone else disappear from school, as the foreign exchange student had done?

—Well then, a man doesn't tarry among childish things. Man goeth forth to his labor . . .

Newell had his fears. He based them on two meetings with the Beast of Ethridge.

And these fears materialized.

On a cold morning in early November there was a seat empty in the sixth row to Geeter's right. And it stayed empty, day after day, into the next week. The boy didn't return: he didn't show up for classes, meals in the Refectory, athletics, study hall. Newell went and tried the knob, a few doors down, on first floor Warren. Locked! When he saw his faculty adviser, the same Geeter, who lived at the end of their floor, the Chaplain said:

—Ethan has left.

—Where?

—To a hospital. He had a nervous breakdown.

—And Manuel, Sir?

—Gone home.

—But his things are still here.

—No, they've been sent to him. Ethan's also. The room is vacated.

—Oh. Vacated.

So Ethan Jeffers was gone from Ethridge School.

II

A curious change took place in Newell Gilbert during these cold, sunlit November days. All last year, as a freshman, he walked around campus with his head down, eyes on the ground. He was depressed. He felt betrayed by his parents, who sent him here: like an attack on his childhood. No more attic room at home; no more Otter, Haas, Thaddy Floriani: his friends in Spring Glen which was a boy's oyster; no more free life, and roaming the streets and lawns at night with his sidekick Otto, paying visits on girls, getting into trouble. All that ended when they sent him away to Ethridge with its iron routine, its conformism to the Dean of Behavior's code, its itchy tweeds and tasteless food. And so he shuffled his feet and walked along the colonnade with his head down; he did his dining hall duty with a sneer. Newell's posture, his facial expression became a sort of provocation; more than once a master took him up on it and said, out of the clear blue sky:

–Gilbert, I don't like your attitude.

–Yes, Sir.

–It'll cost you three hours' detention, smug boy. I'll see you in study hall this Saturday, two to five.

So it went last year. He felt stunned, and hung his head.

But now his head came up, and his gaze cleared. With the disappearance of two students from his sophomore corridor he had to begin keeping an eye on things. Oh, the routine went on, and nobody was talking about what had happened right here among them. Masters and students alike kept on with their affairs and didn't talk too much about things they couldn't hope to change. Anyway, there was the schedule of classes, studies, sports and chores; so no need to waste time on suspicions, on vain imaginings. No distraught parents had come on campus to demand an answer: where is my son? Of course Manuel's mom and dad were far away. Ethan Jeffers' parents were divorced; his father, a concert pianist, spent most of the time on tour. Also, it seemed no shocking articles, exposés of life in an elite preparatory school, had appeared in the newspapers, not yet. So you might as well take the Headmaster's word for it: nothing was rotten at Ethridge; though a look at Dean Wart's style these days, a bit harried, with a furrowed brow, seemed to hint at another story.

As for Newell Gilbert: he became a bit more cheerful, more alert. He seemed to come alive–partly because of a certain girl in his life? Even though she loved another? He lifted his head up. He talked more, and took some interest in others. For one thing he began asking boys on his hall and elsewhere what they thought about the situation; though he only told those few closer to him about The Beast. Whether between classes, during sports or in the Refectory, he started talking more to fellow students; and one evening during study hall it occurred to him that the schoolmates fell into three categories. There were the mute ones, who avoided him, or maybe glanced at him with doubtful eyes: Sedgewick, Jeff Kemeny, Wharburton; guys like these might go tattletale to a master, or tell Dean

Wart how the flit Gilbert was asking a lot of questions. Also, they gave little signs of being envious—yes, that was it: envy—maybe at his dance with Katya, maybe the fact that he made the honor roll last year though he was a shirker. Category I had the informers, the envious boys. Category II, by far the largest, had those with nothing to say about the fact that two boys now had vanished from Ethridge. Here he placed the busy or vague ones, like his friend Boz Krips; the crazy ones like Jay Schmied (also Cormac who had backed off since their Sunday outing to the island); and all those too afraid to get involved, or talk about it much. There were plenty of these, who didn't want to know about The Beast: Bernard Rathschilde for one, his roommate, a poor kid on scholarship and also a foreign exchange student, in his way: from the South Bronx. Such students just drew in their heads, beneath the turtle shell of Ethridge routine, and hoped the mad thing—come to be known as the Beast of Ethridge—would go away and leave them alone.

And then, lastly, came the Category III students who had to ask themselves: isn't it amazing a schoolmate could go pssst! into thin air? Isn't there something wrong here? How did this happen, and what can be done? . . . Well, Category III wasn't full. Newell was looking for someone who felt this way: a regular boy, a friend, who knew what any five year-old child would know; who didn't need to twist the facts around, or deny them, for the sake of success in a high-pressure Ethridge environment with its need to conform.

III

On a Wednesday morning in mid-November the students flocked to the overheated chapel. That day Rev. Geeter stood at his pulpit giving the usual pep talk before their day of studies began. He looked after school morale. Everyone sat perfectly still and listened, as, promptly at 8:35 a.m., a train clattered on the railroad bridge over the winding road to town. Newell wondered: Why does Virgil Parker (a junior who lived in the old gymnasium for some reason) dislike Geeter so much? Most students went for Geeter in a big way because he acted more caring than other masters, and had a kind voice; though he prided himself on being a strict grader in re-

ligion class; and you better know the difference between Isaiah and
Hosea, if you know what's good for you. Well, why did Virg Parker
avoid Geeter?

Suddenly the chaplain paused in his chat—as though he overheard
Newell's thoughts. But no, something was happening. You seemed
to hear the real Geeter for the first time when he stopped speaking.
First a few students, then others, looked around and saw a small
blond boy, curly haired, pinkish, with a funny walk coming down
the aisle. Oh, you could tell this one was new to the school, a spectacle to everyone in these instants. First, he was late. But what struck
you was how unruly, how wild he looked, what a strange uneven
walk he had, though not a limp. His walk had a sort of hitch to it, as
he charged down the aisle right at Geeter. The lad's charcoal gray suit
was not on straight, much less his necktie; maybe we could say his
mind was not on straight, but time will tell. At least he was different.
The boy's shirttails were sprung from his waistline even worse than
Master Glebe's—Glebeth who at least had an excuse for being such a
slob, namely his voluptuous wife.

Here came the new boy, looking all shook up, with flushed
cheeks. But there was more. He didn't know where he was: the quiet
order of this place, a private school which had formed U.S. Senators, Governors, not a few Wall Street financiers become major
donors. Ei, ei: the mad little fellow with his shirttails flying, un-
combed hair, and features pulling this way and that as he strove onward toward the goal, his seat—the little devil had no sense of himself, much less the Ethridge setting. He just came on, with a twitch,
and took a seat in the fifth row from the altar, toward the center:
Manuel's vacated seat. And then he threw one leg (drowning in
those oversized suit pants) over the other, as Geeter looked on
amazed: no one ever crossed their legs in the Chapel before. Like a
law unto himself the newcomer looked around, and gave a wan
look at the pastor.

And what? What was that?! He had on pink socks, pink and black!
Pink with black polka dots. And he swung his leg a little right there
under Geeter's nose, and started to whistle.

For a long moment nobody spoke. All sat agape. I think mainly
they wanted to laugh, because this new boy was a scream. He sat
there hunched in his charcoal gray suit three sizes too large; and then
looked at one of his hands, put it to his mouth, and bit into a hang-
nail. Then he craned his neck, and cracked it, like a knuckle.

But into the silence came a voice. Yes: from the raised pew to Geeter's left, facing the congregation, someone blurted out what must have been the new student's name.
–Shellnitz! Is that you? It is! Oh ho! There'll be a hot time in the old town tonight. Ha ha! Shellnitz!

IV

–Gilbert, you still can't fight your way out of a wet paper bag.
–Oh, can't I? Well maybe we'll see about that, m'boy!
They carried on this talk between pews. Amazing.
–Ha ha!–said Shellnitz, his voice fluty.–Look what the cat dragged in, it's Gilby!
–Uh, ahem! said Geeter. Gentlemen, no talking here.
The chaplain took up the thread and droned on a little more before the closing hymn. He put them to sleep again with his nice voice that had such an effect on Virgil Parker.
But Newell beamed, where he sat, and suddenly felt happy. Why? In the private day school they both attended before Newell's parents sent him away, Shellnitz had been a misfit. And one day outside the main office The Shell, or Shellfish, said to The Gilb: You can't fight your way out of a wet paper bag. So Gilber hauled off and punched him in the stomach, because when someone says you can't fight your way out of a wet paper bag, you must show them that you can. Well, Shelly doubled over, and said: oh-h-h. And, as luck would have it, a flitty teacher came along just at that moment and took Newell into the main office for a talk with the powers that be. At the time Newell was unrepentant, happy to be out of his wet bag; he seemed rather self-righteous about the act. This led to suspension, and at year's end he was asked not to return, which prompted his dad to remark: you have burned your bridges. Goodbye, home. Hello, Ethridge.
For a long time Newell held this against Shellnitz: the way Shelly seemed to stage their fight right in front of the main office; the fact that it proved the last straw and helped get him sent away. For a good while Newell, even though he had fought his way out of a wet paper bag, felt worsted, and didn't understand. Then he looked at the cagey

Shellnitz with other eyes, and asked: why me, Shelby? What did I do to you? Why did you get me in trouble? For weeks after the event Newell went a little bit in awe of Shellnitz, and thought: who won after all? Who fought whose way out of a wet paper bag? Then one day something dawned on Newell. It was nearly a year later; he was already up here, in his freshman year at Ethridge. Once, in morning chapel he was thinking things over while Geeter rambled on: Geetie's syrupy words, you could almost pour them on dry, tasteless French toast in the Refectory. And then the time with Shellnitz came to mind, the one that got Newell sent away. And you might say an idea clicked in, at that moment; and he seemed to light up for no reason, there among Rev. Geeter's flock. And then he understood something.

Everything was strange about Shellnitz, and he also had a strange first name. Nimrod. Nimrod in Genesis: begat of Cush. Nimrod a 'mighty one in the earth'; Nimrod 'mighty hunter before the Lord'. Well, like any other sickly 90-pound twirp who showed signs of being a flit, Shellnitz wanted you to call him Rod. He sidled up to you with that hitching walk he had, drowning in his tweeds even as one pants leg rode up on his calf, and his pink-and-black or red and white striped socks sagged, and bunched up over his shoes. In this way he came up and said, in a friendly tone:

—Call me Rod.

But Newell did not call him Rod. In those days a bullying streak had shone itself in Newbeth: I think because he was so unhappy to be away from his old friends in public school, sent to a private day school with its hard schedule, its rigors. Well, he had always teased his little sister Lemon, but that year he also joined in the bullying of Milford Stith on the school bus home, and it was no good.

Anyway, Newell did not call Shellnitz 'Rod', and say: Hey, Rod! What's up, Rod? when he saw him along the hallway. Instead, he called him: Nim. Or Nit. Or Nitwit. Or Nimby -Pimby. Or: Nit the Flit.

And Shellnitz had wanted to be his friend, and start a friendship. But in those days, yanked out of his Spring Glen element and made to wear wool suits to which he was allergic, and do scads of homework which he saw as worthless—Newell wasn't himself. At times he knew not what he did.

Now something had gone wrong for Shellnitz in the old school; and so Shelleth, Rod, had followed his would-be friend to this elite prep school in the wilds of New England. Newell felt a little laugh starting up, like a gurgle, in the area of his kidneys. And he wondered what Shellnitz's arrival here meant.

Next to Shellnitz, as the chapel talk went into its grand finale, sat the athlete Boz Krips. Newell thought: Look at Boz, a muscular 180 pounds, four-letter man as a sophomore, greatest promise ever shone by an Ethridge jock; and yet Boz wasn't in tune most days. Unfriendly. Boz wasn't solid. And now look at tiny Shellnitz sitting next to him, in Manny's seat: The Shell weighed half of 180 pounds after a full meal with second helpings, even if he won the extra dessert when the master played 'choose a number' because someone was in the Infirmary. And Lord help him when he showed up at the Gym, this world's least coordinated person, for phys. ed. class. Coach Rocntgen would harrass and hound his little ass until Roddy soiled his gym shorts—ten hours! Ouch! All over Rocntgen's, or The Runt's, shiny gym floor. Not only was Shellnitz a puny kid, he was also the least well adjusted person mentally you will ever meet: I mean he made Cormac look like a model for All-American boyhood. And yet Shellnitz had a way about him that tickled Newell, after the wet paper bag stunt. So The Newt found himself thinking: what if this little guy, epitome of flittomy, as The Toad, an original thinker, once called Sedgewick: what if Rod the God, not Boz Krips the star in the backfield, proved to be Category III of Ethridge schoolmates, namely the frank and honest ones?

Shellnitz, after the stir of his arrival, gave a loud yawn, in the stuffy chapel, and threw the good Geeter off his train of thought.

V

—Pssst!

Newell glanced around and surveyed the nearly empty study hall on first floor Settlers. Delvig, the English teacher, looked after Saturday afternoon detention from a raised desk on the quadrangle side. The young master made a wry face over his volume of Dickens, gave a little cackle, and then cleared his throat in the silence.

—Ahem.

The wide airless room made a boy want to nap, but this was not to be done by the dozen or so delinquents paying their debt. The place smelled of old books and wainscoted walls revarnished a hundred

times. High window casements behind the master had prim mold-
ings and framed the gray quad deserted of a cold November afternoon. Outside, the sky had a pre-snowfall look. An early twilight descended over the red-brick colonial student houses.

–Pspspsss!

–No–whispered Bernard, like a hiss.–Go.

The Bern was not thrilled to share his roommate's time in the
slammer: after Rog the Dodge caught them in their post-lights-out
pranks to which he was a party.

Newell glanced around. Then he gave a phony sneeze, a signal, and tried to get Schmied's eye. Goldilocks Schmied gazed back
and nodded. A grin spread over his blond jowls: as the sun might
come out from behind a cloud, and light up snow on a mountain-
side.

Heads turned.

Slit-eyed Schmied waited for his cue.

Then Newell slipped on one knee, crouching by his desk. Into his
back pocket he stuffed a paperback novel about city streets, romantic
jackrollers, teenage gangs, sex. Crab-like he went along the aisle but
paused to untie Sedgewick's shoelaces. While the laces were then being tied together, Wickie, who rarely knew what was happening,
whispered:

–Gilbert, you fool.

How did The Wick ever come to share an hour with bad boys? He
had dozed off during Geeter's chapel talk.

The junior Butterworth, 'Butterball' to his friends, gave Newell a
kick as the latter shuffled along on all fours.

–I'll get you for that . . . Butterball!

The Butt was a flit. Buttercup would love to create a disturbance–
ask Delvig if he could go to the bathroom, for example, and get the
sophomore caught.

Newell reached the far end of the hall and rose to one knee. He
cast a glimpse over the sea of desks at the droll master; then reached
up and tested a curved, gilt handle on the old door. Cre-eak . . . Just
then was heard a loud sneeze:

–Ah-ah-ah . . . hunka'–shite!

Schmiedeth doeth sneeze. And then the blond gorilla, wiping
away snot with a finger, got up from his desk and went to the raised
platform where Master Delvig looked up. And Schmiedikins draped
himself all over the young master, breathing in his face, obscuring

the view. He mumbled something into his ear; until the amazed teacher, trying to free himself, said:

—Mis-ter Schmied. Are you mad?

VI

Newell skipped down the concrete steps by the chapel, and turned left past the old gymnasium toward the new one, Coach Roentgen's pride. Basketball tryouts were today. And some impulse drew Newell to have a look; though after last year's fiasco, he would not go out. Not that he was cut; he never got to show what he could do. When he came to the gym for what some thought would be a duel between himself and the talented Terry Caldermann, Coach Roentgen pointed:

—No long pants. Out.

On the sidelines Newell watched Caldermann sink a jumpshot from the head of the key. Then Caldermann drove for a layup. Newell looked at Roentgen in disbelief: how could you keep a boy from trying out just because he didn't have on a pair of shorts? Or else tell him where to get some: help him. Coach, how could you do that? . . . At home Newell played outside in the dead of winter until his fingertips split open, but here you had to wear the prissy gym shorts. And Roentgen strutted on the sidelines, stuck out his big belly, and gestured at the boys running up and down the floor with his hand which was missing a finger. Caldermann shone: Caldermann who once put a crushing tackle on Newell during club football, blindsided him, from behind, when Newell ran to fall on a loose ball. Oh, my aching back.

Roentgen had played some ball in his day: Minor League pitcher, a lefty, until he lost the finger in a lawnmower accident. As Ethridge Athletic Director he coached the three major sports, and he loved the boys who were his favorites, senior Tim MacDonald, basketball captain; and Caldermann, at first sight. The fact that Jay Schmied refused to come out for football broke Coach Roentgen's heart. He pleaded with that big goofball to play for the school, and make his parents proud. But Schmied laughed at Roentgen stuffed up as a turkey-cock, the great man. Roentgen looked so flushed from his last rich meal: you thought he might bust a gut. Poor Schmied only shook his pale blockhead a little and told Newell that, as a virgin, he would be proud to get his 'head broken'; but not playing varsity football. That was too much like work.

As for Newell Gilbert—well, Coach Roentgen may have seen him as a bad influence on Schmidlap, an All-American tackle who refused to go out for the team. And maybe this was why Coach liked to yell at the sophomore when he saw him:

—Ten hours' detention! Report to the tennis courts!

VII

Newell planned to walk in town, and go to Cormac's on the chance Mingo would be there. He meant to ask the hobo a few questions. But first he went for a glimpse of this year's basketball tryouts.

Warm air, a locker room smell met him at the service road entrance to the new gym. Coach Roentgen stood on the sidelines watching boys run up and down the court and fire off shots. Few passed the ball. Tim MacDonald, the captain, acted as ref.

But suddenly, as Newell went in for a look, all the players laughed. At him? You might have thought it was the Globetrotters: the way players stopped here and there to laugh at something. What? It was that flit Shellnitz again, a midget, a spastic, who took it in his head to try out for basketball. Everybody laughed except Roentgen, who looked so pompous, in those moments, it brought tears to your eyes. For Shellnitz had gotten hold of the ball, and he wouldn't give it up. He dribbled with both hands at once, caught the ball and ran a few steps, dribbled again. He zigzagged across the court holding the basketball and faking passes here, there, but he would not pass off, or shoot. Roentgen looked too offended, in his self-importance, to react. MacDonald laughed with the others, and blew his whistle. Shellnitz was a one-man basketball game, he jumped, he ran, he threw up a running one-hander like a bullet off the backboard. Zingo! Then he put two fingers to his lips and gave his own shrill whistle. What a crazy guy: look how he runs around, with his gym shorts on backwards; socks bunched over sneakers a few sizes too big. Shellnitz put his head down, zoomed after the rebound; and, when someone else got the ball, he ran a few steps and jumped with his hands held out and called, in his fluty voice:

–Me! To me!

Oh, sure, Shellfish. I'll pass off to *you*. The Shell looked so eager for the ball, you thought he might pee on Coach Roentgen's shiny new floor. And then he kept running about like a dervish: so small, so light, he might take off and corkscrew through the gym ceiling. What seemed clear after a moment was that Shellnitz didn't know how to play; he didn't know the rules. And Coach Roentgen was in no mood to tell him, and teach a whirling dervish how to dribble. Coach never had much time for boys, except his pets, and right now he had even less. He stood on the sidelines looking so puffed up, he might explode. And Shellnitz kept on leaping here and there; he made a mockery of tryouts and the noble game of basketball. Really you could hardly blame The Runt for getting angry when he saw this screwball ruin his tryouts. And Shellnitz ran in a circle with his head down. And Shellnitz gave his little hops and leaps for his lone bene-fit. And Shellnitz waved his tiny hands and screeched for the ball. He was the first perpetual motion machine.

And then, so out of it was Shellnitz, that he ran smack into Coach Roentgen, boom! hit 'im right in his breadbasket. Runteth stood fuming by the bench and wondering how many detention hours to slap on this nut. Oomph! He plowed into him.

–Ooh!

Coach, no longer a young man, doubled over. His ruddy face went livid. And then he raised his arm, pointed toward the door where Newell still stood, but couldn't get his breath to roar as usual.

Rod Shellnitz stood facing the Ethridge coach, a few feet away, and his body still gave a few little leaps, sort of on its own. His stick-like arms had more spastic movements, like afterthoughts, as he gazed up in surprise at Coach Roentgen. Yes, Shelly looked sur-prised: could it be that someone wasn't charmed by his antics? And then he gave Coach Roentgen such a hurt look. Shellnitz gave the master a hangdog stare, as if saddened, and disappointed in him. How on earth could anyone treat his sweet little self that way? It was truly amazing. And sad! I think in those instants Roentgen may ac-tually have felt guilty. Ha-ha! Talk about blaming the victim.

And then Coach's face went a fiery red. You thought the man might combust, as he stood there and stared at lowly Shellnitz. The high and mighty dictator of the gymnasium gave a bellow, and said:

—You there! You, I say! Out!

Coach shook his shoulders a little, like a hosed off tomcat. There were tears in Rod's eyes as he made his way, in a silence with chuckles, across the floor to the gym exit. He glanced back at the ogre who had yelled at him. Shellnitz sniffled, and wiped his eyes. But then he saw his old friend Newell Gilbert who stood there gaping in the doorway. And at once he perked up, and gave one of his little hops: but not too sure, with a look back at Roentgen who glared and puffed his chest for all he was worth, on the far side of the basketball court, while waiting for this scourge to be gone.

—Shelleth—said New-babe—you can't fight your way out of a wet paper bag.

VIII

Outside, it was cold. Cold wind came off the Needing River and sliced across the winding road which led toward town. Shellnitz still in gym shorts and jersey followed after his friend and wouldn't take no for an answer. Newell shooed Shellnitz away but Shellnitz stuck to Newell like glue.

—You can't come in town with me. It's against the rules.

—You're doing it.

—Look at you. You'll catch pneumonia.

On their left the Pond was frozen over. To the right were meadows bristling, a gray tan color, beneath the wintry sky. Silently the river flowed along its banks.

Shellnitz skipped out in front and still leapt around and waved his arms, as though possessed by the demon of basketball.

He squeaked:

—Don't leave me! I hate it in the dorm.

—But I've got things to do. Business at Cormac's.

Behind them someone gave a whoop. Oh hell: it's that flit Delvig calling me back to study hall. But no, another sort of voice—a woman? with her hair in a bun? Newell caught his breath and forgot Cormac, Mingo, the frigid weather, the pest Shellnitz gone a ways up

ahead as proof he would not turn back: Shellnitz shaking side to side
as he ran in place. For it was Katya. She had followed them out along
the winding road. Say, what was she doing at Ethridge today? Strictly
off limits to Bartlett debs!
  —Are you *deef*? she cried.
  —Where are you going? said Newell.
  —I saw you walk by. I was in Tildon when you left the gym.
  —Oh.
Newell looked in her dark eyes. He thought: Tildon Hall, Josey's
dorm.
  Katya's eyebrows gave a twitch as she pointed at Shellnitz.
  —Who's that fellow? Sir, you must be frozen stiff!
  —Not yet, said The Shell.
  She took off her jacket and sort of descended on little Shellnitz.
She wrapped the shivering boy in her suede coat; and then, while
Newell looked on, gave the guy a big maternal hug and buttoned his
buttons for him.
  —Won't you be cold, Katya?
  She laughed and shook her breasts at him.
  —We've got oodles of fat. But what about your friend here? Why
not take care of *him* a little better?
  —Ah.
Newell couldn't hold her dark, steady gaze then. He frowned and
looked down.
  —Hm, said Katya. Well, I know you're gallant . . . But say, we
haven't seen each other since the mixer and you promised to tell me
a story. Remember? Something or other about a missing boy, and
you wanted to find out the truth about it.
  —That's where I'm going now. I just thought it might not be a
good idea for my friend here to tag along. What if we meet up with
the Beast of Ethridge?
  She laughed:
  —Why sure, he might eat him. Sir, what's your name?
  —Rod.
  —Rod, eh? Well, tell me, are you afraid of the Beast of Ethridge?
  —No.
  —It seems he kidnapped a boy, she said.
  Shellnitz walked along in Katya's coat which reached his ankles.
In his high voice he said:

–Well, if the Beast comes to kidnap me, I'll–I'll–

–You'll what?–Katya's features seemed to light up at sight of Shellnitz.

–I'll say: Beast, you can't fight your way out of a wet paper bag.

Shellnitz gave a little laugh, and a hop, though dwarfed by Katya's warm coat.

Katya gave a hop too. But Newell said:

–Watch out: he may punch you in the stomach.

–And get expelled! said Shellnitz.

–The Beast of Ethridge expelled? said Katya.

They told her how Shellnitz got Newell kicked out of the private day school back home.

–Anyway, it's what I wanted, said Newell. Only then they sent me here.

–What if you get kicked out of here? said Katya. Where to then?

–Well, said Newell, give me your advice. I'm trying to figure it out.

–Shoot! she said; and all her face, high cheekbones, dark hypnotic eyes, showed pleasure.

–I don't want to let my folks down. I want to make the honor roll again, be a success, a big wheel on campus like Holbein.

–You'll never be like Holbein, she said.

–But now this thing . . . Me and my friends are in danger, I think. And more bad things will happen, I can feel it. So what should I do? Stick my head in the ground like an ostrich? Be a good little boy so I won't let my mom and pop down? Or come into town for a chat with Mingo, the town bum, and ask Mingeth a few questions since he may know something about what's going on?

–Even if it means you could get kicked out, said Katya.

–That's it: even if.

–Well, she said. What do you think about this, Mister Rod? I ask you to help with this gentleman's problem, because I can tell right away you're *my* friend.

–Okay! said Shellnitz. I will. Newell here, whom I like–

–Who*m*? said Katya.

–Whom I like, even though he bullied Millie Stith on the school bus that time–

–Millie Stith?

Newell hung his head:

–Chubby kid, like Butterball here. I didn't mean it.

–Ha! Katya shook her breasts again. So you don't like fat people. By her side Newell blushed crimson.

Shellnitz finished his thought:

–I think young Gilbert should prove he can fight his way out of a wet paper bag by catching the Beast of Ethridge.–Shellnitz squeaked:–Please, Mister Beast, don't eat me! Ha ha ha!

IX

Side by side the three friends went along. They bumped shoulders. They called out ghost sounds which echoed as they walked under the railroad bridge. Katya wore stylish bluejeans, kind of tight, and a turtleneck sweater like at the mixer. Her face had an oriental look unseen in Bartlett honeys, and it was darker, almost like Manuel's. Her black hair, done up in a scarf, curled on her temples. She looked exotic, like a peasant girl; she had sensuous lips, and a willful air. Also she wasn't very shy, and drew the two boys to her, rubbing against them, so she too could keep warm.

–Take my jacket now, said Newell. Turn about is fair play.

–No, you keep it. I'm warm.

Pausing beneath the bridge they hallooed and made noise.

Newell said:

–After I got kicked out of the private day school, because of my friend here, I wrote a poem. Would you like to hear it?

–Sure! said Katya.

–Don't applaud until it's over.

–Okay.

Shellnitz's teeth chattered as he snuggled up to the taller Katya.

Then Newell's words echoed under the heavy concrete:

> *At an early age I*
> *have joined the select crew*
> *of the well-to-do*
> *who are kicked out, expelled, booted—bye bye!*

–Gee, that's good! said Katya.

–Like it so far?

—Not, uh, too bad, I think, said Shellnitz.

> *Saints and similar chaps*
> *and Sakyamuni perhaps—*

—Hold on, said Katya. Who's Sakyamuni?
—I'm not sure. That's why I said perhaps.
—I see.
Shellnitz said:
—It's cold as a witch's tit!
Big hypocrite: he pressed up against Katya with a snigger.

> *And that good little brother, J. Christ*
> *who pulled the greatest heist*
> *in our whole upstanding history—*

—Wait, said Katya. Why upstanding?
—Well, because maybe it isn't. All the upstanding ones called Jesus a bandit, right? But who was the bandit?
—They were.
—When I showed my dad this poem, he hit the roof, as usual. Face got red: you'd think I called *him* a bandit.
—Proceed—said Shellnitz, and snuggled up to Katya's lovely sweater.
—Almost finished:

> *When snubbed, rejected, spat on, he*
> *said prep school is for flits, a bore.*
> *And then he turned,*
> *and shuffled toward the door.*

Beneath the railroad bridge they applauded.
—Hourrah! cried Shellnitz, and threw up an imaginary cap.
Katya said:
—Hm, shuffled. I do that . . . see?
She shuffled a few steps; and then turned back toward the two boys, smiled, and curtseyed.

X

On into the small town they went, bumping shoulders, giggling. It reminded Newell of life in Spring Glen, good times with Otter and Thad Floriani, Haas and Willard Steuart–boyhood, the old freedom gone now it seemed forever. Then Katya bumped tiny Shellnitz into a pile of autumn leaves.

–Hey! said The Shell.

And then she jumped in after him!

And then did Newell Gilbert wring his hands with indecision as to whether he might pile on after *her?* Well, she did act like a boy, didn't she? So he went in the pile of leaves too, and crawled around and squealed the way they did. Yes, Newell piled on after Katya, but not too hard. And mostly both of them mauled Shellnitz, who deserved it: after the way he had treated that poor, longsuffering Coach Roentgen, Runt the Runt.

After their romp in the pile of leaves they got up with leaves in their hair, leaves in their clothes, leaves in their mouths, like a fishbone from a cat's.

Evening was coming on in the town. It went among the elms graying toward winter. It dimmed the town commons with a church at either end: one dark stone, stolid as old New England virtue, the other white and gossamer as a Puritan's faith. Library, town hall, Maspeth Needing Homestead, other pre-revolutionary structures gazed from their distance, amid the tall trees, at a chintzy row of stores, hardware and Five-and-Dime, Plaza Theater, across the main drag called Mather. These children of a less heroic age had to endure the stare of their more solid but prim and intolerant forbears. Town pharmacy, tailor, barber, luncheonette: a mess of neon signs, show windows, cheap color framed in red brick and pasteboard.

–C'mon, said Newell, I'll introduce you to Cormac. He says Mingo saw–

–Who's Mingo? said Katya.

–A tramp, who once got the 'finest education available', as my dad says.

–Like us, said Rod Shellnitz.

Katya said:

–So we can get civilized and bore each other to death.

—Mingo sleeps in Cormac's basement when the cold weather comes: if Cormer's parents are away, that is. Mingo said he saw some people get in a rowboat the day Manuel disappeared.

—Who's this Cormac? said Katya.

—Well, said Newell, he's kind of different.

—Join the crew! Shellnitz piped.

—He told Mingo about Manuel, and The Ming said there was a kid like that, pudgy, dark complexion, getting into a rowboat.

On the far side of the commons they came to a filling station with a sign: Shepherd's. By the gas pumps round a souped-up car stood three high schoolers, and they looked Katya over, and Shellnitz. One said:

—She's fuel-injected.

They lounged. Another had a blond d.a.; and he had that way of talking, like spittle in the words, plus a freckly smile. Regular guys: heads like a jukebox, rough enough, but okay. They reminded Newell of public school friends back home, enjoying themselves in Junior High while he was up here missing out on the fun—tracking, or being tracked by, some Beast of Ethridge who made two students go away from school. Newell gazed at the blond one; and it gave him such a twinge, such a sense of . . . yearning. It was like a momentary vision: normal life.

The three teenagers stared after Katya, and Newell felt a pang. One of them said:

—Burns rubber like a junkyard.

Or something to that effect. And they laughed, easily, in the cold, gray late afternoon on winter's threshold.

XI

Night fell. Lights glittered in the spectral trees. A few last autumn leaves fluttered down. Shrubs and front porches went a twilit blue. The suburban earth, all portioned off in blocks and sidewalks, front lawns, backyards, all neatly geometric and enclosed, had its little sinkings and settlings: as if ruminating after a meal of daytime.

Down a side street called Engadine the three friends stood on the edge of town by the old Puritan cemetery. Newell said:

—There's Corm's. We can go through here, or take the long way around.

—Brrr, gives me the spooks, said Katya, folding her arms.

—I'll hold your hand—said Shellnitz with his spooky grin.

He took Katya's hand.

Across the cemetery stood the old, rundown mansion where Cormac Flynn lived. Its gables, shutters, front porch sat back at the end of a walkway on a slight incline. Lawn and hedges were untended. The place had an air of affluence in abandon: not money, but something else, was its problem. Elegant window casements, long eaves of four stately gables gave the place a forbidding air, like an old age home for ghosts from colonial times. But old ghosts found no rest here, and something about them was still unsettled. The mansion where Cormac lived, by himself part of the year, when his father and stepmother were away, stood there at nightfall like a detail from one of Master Glebe's history lessons. Once Glebeth told them of the county where they had come to school: in one of his sudden eruptions, more vital in five minutes than the entire course curriculum, though understood by no one. He told the big, ruthless freedom of those early struggles: when the 'barbaric Redskin' pointed settlers to a fertile river valley, well watered, liberal to husbandmen, named for Maspeth Needing. Those trailbreakers of the eastern frontier went and gained a foothold after a few gruelling seasons. The Dutch of New Amsterdam, the Massachusetts Bay Colony compatriots struggled with man and nature for the prize of land, liberty, wealth, the great natural resources. And did they win? They built the house where Cormac lived, but had they 'found favor in God's eyes'? . . . In the back row Newell perked up when Glebeth threw one of his fits, spluttering by the blackboard like an oracle; though the inspired words flew over a student's head. Now he paused at sight of the oppressive note to that architecture, shadowy contours in the darkness lit only by a streetlamp, and *felt* if he still didn't understand.

Then, holding hands, they went among the headstones and the tombs.

—Don't trip!

—Shhh.

—Hoooooh! said Shellnitz, and pressed Katya's hand.

—Are you an owl? she said.

—Hoo! hoo!

—Shhh, said Katya. What if there's a ghost?

—Ask it to dance, said Shellnitz. Lady's choice.

Newell said, shivering with cold:

—Shelleth, I don't know about this 'Rod' business. I mean I'll call you 'Rod' if you want, I won't call you Nimmeth anymore, unless you'll get me kicked out of this school like you did the other one. But I think a good name for you would be 'Owl'. I won't call you The Owl without your permission, but it suits you. What do you think, Katya?

—Hoo, hoo.—But at that instant Katya looked back over her shoulder. Her eyes widened as she saw a dark figure stand up from behind one of the ancient, moldy gravestones. The boys didn't know at first, or see her eyes go wide. Then her voice flew up:—Hoo-oooh!

Katya gave a throaty scream, and, breaking away from them, began to run among the tombstones. This was dangerous: she could fall and hit her head.

Shellnitz glanced back, threw up his arms, and also went leaping like a human toad among the old, moss-grown headstones. But Katya's suede coat, much too large for him, got in his way and so, yes, he clipped his leg on a headstone, sprawled forward and lay on the ground, conked out!

Newell looked back and saw the big, dark figure stalking slowly forward as though it had chosen him of the three. Like the Beast of Ethridge out on the island! Oh, the empty gaze, the same wasted features, same sad, haggard, plodding step, like a robot from beyond the grave. Newell stood frozen in place, unable to breathe, move, and gaped at the evil thing on its way toward him: because . . . because it *seemed to know him* and he had thought this the first time he saw it, that Sunday, and then wondered, yes, when would it come for him? . . . Finally, with the thing ten yards away he turned and began to move. He ran in the direction of Corm's.

Katya was up ahead. He heard her crying. He watched as she threw up her hands. Now Newell stepped among the tombs and made out Shellnitz's puny figure, out cold, like a sack of grain with some spilled on the grass: his blond pinhead. Pick him up! Save Shellnitz! But there wasn't time and if he stopped they would both just get caught and clubbed senseless, stuffed in a sack, dragged out to the cabin where who knew what horrors would happen to them, before death, like Manuel and now Ethan Jeffers as well. Newell slowed and gazed down at Shellnitz' limp form, in a dark mound covered by Katya's coat—and then he gave a cry and kept on going past.

XII

They arrived together on the front porch. Katya beside herself fell into his arms. With a free hand he banged on the locked door and hollered:

—Open up! Cormac! Open the door!

He rapped the old bronze knocker. It gave a hollow sound—deep, echoing inside a little, like a fist pounding on a vast drum. Behind them, across the street in the cemetery darkness, the grisly thing made its way. It strode. In a moment it would appear, and pass over the stone barrier toward them; then cross the street at its own sodden pace. Those vacant eyes, that dreadful gaze would freeze them with horror and take away their will to escape.

—Cormac! Come to the door! I'll break the window—Please, Cormac! Cormac!

Frantically Newell rapped the knocker; again, again, looking back over his shoulder into the darkness. Poor Shellnitz already at its mercy!

Inside, a foot away from them, someone undid the latch, calmly. The lock turned. The door opened, slowly, with a creak. And there stood the Ethridge dayhop, who blinked, and gave them his pouty grin.

For a moment Cormac stared out, his brow knit, eyes screwed up, as though from the inner chamber of a conspiracy. Tousled as always, Corm's massive cowlick seemed sprung from the impetuous whirr of his brain. But his gaze changed. You might say it came undone at sight of Katya.

They brushed past him. They pushed by this half mad Cormac left alone week upon week by his industrialist father flown off to South America.

—It's coming! Newell shouted. Hide! Save your life!

Katya stood there shivering head to foot. Her scarf was half off, hair in disarray. Her features were strangely mobile. The eyebrows jumped.

Corm looked her over, sniffed, nodded, and said without blinking an eye:

—What's the word?

—Close the door! Newell pleaded. That *thing* is after us. Hurry! Slam it!

Corm just kept staring at Katya up and down, and grinned at some secret. He shook his head a little, and said:

—I think you could use a drink.

—Don't joke, Cormeth! Didn't you hear me? Shellnitz is out there right now in that monster's clutches. The Beast of Ethridge has poor Shellnitz!

—Poor Shellnitz?—The Corm still grinned, cuter-than-thou.— Shelly is never in *any*body's clutches, I thought you knew that by now. 'Poor' Beast of Ethridge is in Shellnitz's.

—You're crazy.

—Well, this is true. But I think the occasion—Corm shook his head again, marvelling at Katya—calls for a toast, don't you? Let us take a nip from my old man's private stock.

Calm, hospitable, Cormac took his frazzled friends into the living room and turned on a lamp. The idea of an impending attack by a psychopath, a killer of children, didn't seem to bother The Corm. He gave his cute grin, and said:

—Make yourselves at home.

Corm laughed a little. And then he grabbed his sandy hair. The Corm tugged at his cowlick in full erection. Was this the way he showed delight at having guests? Then, fingering it with an intensity, he went from the room to have a look in the liquor cabinet.

XIII

After a moment Cormac came back with a bottle and cocktail glasses on a tray. Katya sat on the sofa staring straight ahead, in shock at the awful vision. Never mind, Cormer said to her with a wink:

—I brought an extra glass . . . for the Beast!

And he looked at her, slyly.

But then it was no laughing matter as there came a knock, slow, fateful, on the door. There it was: the sound they feared most, once, twice, heavy and slow, like a knell. Katya gave a small cry.

Cormac, happy to play host, said:

—I'll see who it is.

—Don't open that door, said Newell.

—I thought you wanted to solve the mystery, Sherlock, and find the Beast of Ethridge. Well, here he is.

And before they could stop him, the boy pranced out of the living room. He undid the latch.

—Wait, Corm, no! Don't do this thing.

—The more the merrier—

He opened.

And then to confirm their worst fears: they heard a fearful noise in the foyer.

And then The Beast's footsteps, its trudge in the front hall, toward them: it came on, solemn, like the assailant's steps before a crime.

Newell and Katya stood up, as, into the living room entry came a tall figure, hard to say how old, with weatherworn features and some gray in his hair. Clothes the worse for wear, hand-me-downs: this Beast had been to the Salvation Army.

—Ah! gasped Katya.

In the man's brawny arms lay cradled the frail remains of Shellnitz; even as the man carried, in one hairy paw, a brown paper bag.

Was Shellnitz dead? Apparently not, because he opened his childish eyes, raised a hand to the man's thick beard, and said:

—Doggy, wolf-wolf.

Shellnitz turned his curly head a little, and looked at his friends. Those innocent eyes had a wicked glimmer in them, as he tugged The Beast's beard, and talked baby talk:

—Da-da!

It seemed Hot Rod Shellnitz had gotten the best of the Beast of Ethridge, like he did Coach Roentgen earlier that afternoon, and everyone else who got in his way, fighting their way out of wet paper bags. Back in the gym he had provoked the master. But here it looked like a case of seduction: as the craggy features of the monster lit up in a smile.

XIV

Well, you guessed it, Reader, long before I wrote it: that wasn't the Beast of Ethridge at all. That was only the town bum, Mingo, who smiled at the tray of cocktail glasses, and elegant bottle of booze like a cozy fire to warm a man's heart. For The Ming knew at a glimpse that his lukewarm can of beer, which cost him a day's panhandling in this hick town, would now make way for the good stuff from the liquor cabinet of Cormac's old man. The beautiful girl, who looked so shaken, must be the cause of this windfall; otherwise, the cupboard would have stayed locked.

Gently, Mingo tried to stand Shellnitz on his two feet, but that little wiseass didn't want to be stood up. With a contented yawn he spread out on the couch, his head on Katya's lap. Cormac, however, went to pour out triple shots for these teenagers who had never sipped much liquor, let alone been drunk. Just now Katya and Newell could use a drink after their scare in the cemetery.

Before long they were all sprawled like Shellnitz across the plush furniture, and took their first swallows of alcohol with a grimace. But Mingeth took his dram with a more thoughtful look, for he knew life's changes, and it was best to seize the moment. His drinking partners had begun to giggle, and say the first thing that came to mind. They made faces at each other, and swore. Corm had a cute grin to beat the band when he looked at Katya: her features kind of puffy, but gorgeous. In her honor he made a fire with the birch logs meant only for show, and which cost his folks a lot. Newell wanted to ask Mingo about Manuel down by the river that Friday afternoon, but he could hardly get a word in, once Cormac began on the subject of Nazis.

—Oh, Cormeth. Let it rest.

Newell tried again. Here and there, as the talk flowed, he asked his questions:—Minger, what did you see that day?—But The Ming wasn't having any; he shook his head; and tossed down a swallow of bourbon. He turned their chitchat onto 'the meaning of life', God and existence. For some reason, as if he had his own idea of the matter, Ming was not saying what he saw that day by the river. He wouldn't tell what he knew.

Katya's face was very flushed. On the sofa she made Shellnitz slide over a little, but that imp only kept his head on her lap.

—Oy! she said. Whiskey in my nose.

Tears mingled with strong drink ran from her nostrils like a drowning person. Cormac crossed over and gave her a slug on the back, and she started to hiccup.

—Tell me, Mister Mingo (hiccup!), what is the reason why we humans live? Is it biological?

The Ming had been staring benignly at them, and at the bottle by now half full, or empty, depending on your point of view. He nodded wisely. For a moment he looked at the Bartlett girl, to take in the full, um, meaning of her question; and then his gaze tilted up toward the ceiling. This act lent a view of his neck beneath the wooly beard. Then he came down again, and worked his thirsty lips, and the thumb and forefinger of his free hand, preparing a response. And then Mingo spoke, in a high voice quite unlike the profound gaze, and craggy brow, of the drink'—thinker.

—Why life? Well, I will tell you . . . if my friend here, Cormac, will agree . . . that the chaser must, um, be chased.

And with this he stood, Katya's words as his cue, and went to the tray with its bottle of whiskey, that elixir. Then, like an act of justice, he poured for himself a shot or three, and mumbled to himself something like:—All history is a shot or three . . . —and then, going against his principles, quaffed the lot at once. But this error he must make right again, like any man of conscience, a thinker of thoughts. Besides, it wasn't nice for young people, sons and daughters of the nation, to drink whiskey. And so Mingo thought he would spare them a hangover, the side effects. And he poured out more than a thimbleful, yes, rather more, of this good stuff, into his glass. Then, dotting the i of this righteous act, which spared others, he put the cork back on, gave it a neat tap with his palm, quite pleased with his decision, and returned to his seat. Oh, if you saw the dignified bearing of this wise man so apt to follow the golden mean, 'nothing too much'! The armchair where Mingo sat might have been a chair at Plato's academy. And then, ex cathedra as it were, The Ming said to his young listeners:

—The meaning of life? Abstinence, sobriety.

And he sipped, after uttering words worth their weight in gold.

Katya stared at him. Life has its surprises. A bum, the town drunkard whose one goal in life was to find his next drink, had spoken out against his own vice. How noble. What an effort it must cost. And then Mingo lowered his head, modestly, to do the very thing he detested so much: drink 'the good stuff' for *their* sakes, so they wouldn't have to poison their young bodies and minds—ay, he saved them, he took their sins upon himself, so to say, a regular Jesus.

Mingo waved a finger at Katya, as he had a moment before when he preached what he practiced so well. Then Ming stood up and went back to the table: in order, this time, to hold the whiskey bottle up as an example for them. And then he said, and didn't even slur the words, or lose his train of thought:

—Don't touch it. Think I'll just guard the bottle so you'll be safe from temptation. I found the meaning of life when I took a vow not to let others drink whiskey, if I could help it. Hey, I'm a martyr.

Katya wrinkled her nose at the big man looking like he swallowed a mouse as he went to the armchair with his prize. Then she started to tickle Shellnitz. She found Shelleth's ribs and he kicked his stick legs and carried on as though he didn't like it. But do you think The Shell really fended Katya's tickling? Hell no. He only made it worse by reaching up to get her back. And his hand landed in the wrong spot, you know, which wasn't hard since most of the space over his flitty little head was taken up by two such wrong spots, if you get my meaning. Shellnitz hollered with his mouth wide open and jerked his legs at the ceiling and grabbed at her any which way; though he didn't make a serious effort to stop her tickling. The boy just wanted a cheap feel, and he did get his money's worth.

—I'll pee in my tweeds! he cried.

Then Newell, deep in thought, showed a sign of life.

—Schmied once asked his folks if they go to the john.

Cormac:

—He should ask himself why he plays with his hog so much.

Tears streamed down Shellnitz's face. He heaved a sigh like a small child calming down, and said:

—I know for a fact Coach Roentgen doesn't go number two.

—Doesn't he? said Katya.

—No, the passage is stopped up.

—Is it? she said. By what?

—His head. He wears eyeglasses on his belly button.

XV

All this time they drank what Mingo meted out to them, while he gulped the lion's share, for their sakes. But it was enough. Newell unlaced his shoes, and kicked them off. Then he turned around in the Chippendale chair, and let his feet climb the wall while his head lolled off the edge. He gazed at Katya upside down, and touched finger to lips, chin, nose. He thought: Nosy-nose; Katya looks weird from this angle, frizzy hair, kind of wild. Those you-knows slung over her shoulder. What was she doing at Ethridge this afternoon? You don't see hot Bartlett chicks on campus. With Josey Kipnes? Tildon, she said. But she came running outside for us.

Then, though high on the liquor, Newell made an effort to pump Mingo, and do what he came here to do, breaking the rules.

–Mingeth! Come, tell me, what did you see that day by the river? Manuel's kidnappers? Were they students?

Again Mingo frowned, and tossed liquid down his parched throat. Then he turned away. He wouldn't even look at his questioner. And Newell thought he saw a wince in the hobo's pleasant features, drunk as a skunk. Hm, a conspiracy? . . . Had they silenced this man who could be so talkative when it came to 'the meaning of life'?

Across the room Cormeth leered at Katya with his cute grin. She made Shellnitz take a sip, but The Owl, choking, swung up his hand and liquid splashed her. Katya laughed; she spit a shower down on the delighted Shellnitz. Cormac stared hard, his face taut with Cormackian irony. Mingo sat back and blessed these antics since they left him alone to compose, mentally of course, his Ode to Sobriety. Newell walked his legs up the wall and thought: How many hours would Rog the Dodge hand out if he saw us? He doesn't have that many. Say, somebody kidnapped Mannikin, and Moon Jeffers too. What if I don't go home for Christmas? What if they keep me here because I led the league in hours? I broke the all-time record, but I want to be good.

Katya sat sloshed by a 'waste of good whiskey', as Mingo said, since this lowered his chances of saving others from the vice he had come to terms with; he only drank now for humanitarian reasons. Katya dug into Shellnitz and tickled his ribs and he screeched: I'll pee! And he grabbed her hair, then her sweater, a bunch of it, more than a handful, in Shellnitzian terms. And then together they tumbled down on the carpet. And Cormac came out of his trance and gave a whoop; he poured the rest of his drink on them and then jumped on too. Opportunist! Someone, was it Katya? reached out and pulled Newell off the chair where he sat upside down and so he too was dragged into the mêlée. And the four of them made a jumble of arms, legs and other things; they thrashed about on the rug, flailing, shouting, swearing. And for just an instant Newell's hand found its way somehow to Katya's breast, would you believe it? But he drew that sucker back as fast as he could, as if he didn't really mean to feel her up, the baldfaced flit! And then for a good while those four young people lay on the floor grunting, climbing on top of each other, swearing, swinging their arms and legs, gasping, spitting, bellowing remarks about parents, teachers, Runt the Runt Roentgen, Dean Rivington Wart, Master Glebe, Bill Hastings the Refectory cook, and even, horrors! even Headmaster Smithson whose name should have been sacred. It was a free-for-all. It was a rumpus. It was a mess. I know you would not want said of you what they said about the senior counselor on first floor Warren House, namely Rog 'The Dodge' Hillyer. But oh what a tenderness Newell Gilbert felt for the exotic Katya in those moments: which goes far toward explaining why he felt her up, but then drew back his hand quickly, like a moth from a flame. But does it, this tenderness, also hint at why her own hand followed along, and clutched his an instant, and seemed to press his very adolescent soul just then, yes, his very essence against her too, too womanly breast?

—C'mon, Mingy-Ming! cried Newell, his head emerging from the scrimmage. Tell us what you saw by the river. Who is the Beast of Ethridge?

But all the while, as they howled crazily, cackled, and gave themselves up to the effect of liquor—all this time Big Ming sat stonefaced, and drank. He got hold of the key to the liquor cabinet, which Cormac had left on a coffee table, and then went in for spirits in a big way. Mingo swilled. He took it in until he stank. Mingo didn't rumpus with the kids—oh no, a serious man, about his business. He just sat there and lapped it up, sipped it, and dreamed great dreams. Mingo thought over his mission to save the world by drinking up all its bourbon whiskey. He would die for this cause. He would drink such a quantity it would etherize him, as a saint transcends to heaven. And his spirit would soar up, in fumes not quite like incense. And humanity would sing his glory in a chorus to the four corners of the earth: Mingo Redemptor.

Chapter Four

I

December days receded. The reveille bell rang across the sleeping campus. Students took toilet kits and towels into the bathroom, with its cold floor, and brushed their teeth eyes closed. They fumbled with a necktie. Outside, in the darkness, a trail of white smoke rose from the Refectory; as a few starlings and blackbirds still chirped at dawn.

Boys chewed the dry toast and spoke, if they did, in a drowsy tone. Ready for the logarithms test? Look out: pop quiz in history. Glebeth, you flit. But, Sir! But, Sir! Eleven more days: then Christmas vacation. Oh, when I come home my mom stocks the pantry with pies and cakes. And you should see my dog when I walk through the door. Hey, Schmiedster, you tease your little sister a lot? Ha ha: never, he says. I'll bet. Now get along with you and shovel the walk: aw, Dad! At least you could pay me.

Then they trudged across the quad to hear Geeter's inspired words. Jackfrost bristled as the sun cleared a treeline across farmlands to the east. Long rays slanted through the greenhouse between Warren and Carlyle Houses; flushed the red-brick facades, and colonnaded walkway; shot inside the overheated chapel where Newell sat itching in his tweeds.

The pastor was stirred up today.

—That boy, he said. Do you know the one I mean?

Geeter's voice went low. His young congregation, far away from parents, ate it up—all except Virgil Parker, who detested The Geet for some unknown reason, and sat in the back row scowling.

—You know the one: he went off, alone, and hid his talent in the ground.

A column of lint sifted above the pews. Outside the high window behind the altar a beech tree shivered in the wintry wind.

—Now this second boy, said the Ethridge chaplain. What of him?

Then the train, same time each morning, rumbled on its trestles over the winding road to town. In a minute organ notes would flow down from the balcony and send Geeter's flock to Math and a pop quiz, but Sir! English book report due, History put to sleep by Glebeth, Latin declensions, Religion, corn beef hash for lunch, Mechanical Drawing, Science and Science Lab where Master Sippel made Ethridge stink like hell; athletics, dinner with dining hall duty, lights-out, sleep, clangalang! wake up. Through it all Newell dreamt of Christmas holidays, the blessed ride home, ten days in his own room, or roaming Spring Glen with Otter and Haas.

But at the moment Geeter went into his closing. Wow! He roused them. Geeteth, quite beside himself this morning, read the versets.

From the raised pew Newell looked down at Manuel's place: now taken by Shellnitz, who worked his features the weird way he had, and stretched his neck as he glanced around. Moon Jeffers' seat had not been filled. But something about Shellnitz, as he sat there: the boy looked alone in the universe, like The Beast's next victim.

Geeter's voice was intense. He seemed to grit his teeth.

—They were full of envy, deceit. They were gossips . . . insolent . . . disobedient to parents. Why does Saint Paul write these things, and even make a list? Do you know how the first chapter of Romans ends? I will read it to you. 'Though they know God's decree that those who do such things deserve to die . . .'

Newell stared down at Shellnitz, and felt worried. A devil entered Rod Shellnitz each time he went to the gym, and got in sight of Master Roentgen. It amounted to a duel between them, as Owl provoked hell out of Runt, and Runt piled detention hours on Owl. Well, Shellnitz couldn't help himself. He was a bad boy alright, but did this mean he 'deserved to die'?

For a few days, as Christmas approached, Newell went through the routine in a strange mood. Elated by the idea of going home, he worried another awful event might come between now and then: a third hallmate turn up missing. Still the days passed, and the nights. Only two more to go! Excitement ran high on campus, and boys packed their bags in advance.

Then something did happen. It made Newell wonder who had more to worry about, himself or Shellnitz.

On the eve of departure he came back from evening study hall, brushed his teeth, put on his striped p.j.'s, and turned in.

Lights out. Clunk!

–Good night, Berneth.

Big Bern, roommate to Ethridge's rebel in residence, pulled over the covers, and said:

–Reet.

Newell snuggled in and made to daydream awhile before he drifted off. But just then, right by his ear, he heard—a crinkle.

He reached around, and felt a piece of folded note paper. He took it in two fingers. Switching on his penlight he saw this was identical to the one he found in Manuel's pillowcase the night he slept in there while Jeffers did the mechanical drawings.

He read it. And, for the first time, he wondered whether he would be going home for Christmas.

> *Sophomore:*
> *You are called to the high rites*
> *of the Society for Self-Furtherance.*
> *Await further instructions, and be glad.*
> *Show this bid to nobody.*
> *Be wise.*
> *Watch, wait, obey!*

II

Toward noontime that Wednesday the long, chromelined automobiles began to arrive. They parked along the service road and down the drive from the circle in front of Settlers. Parents, siblings, liveried chauffeurs got out and stretched after the parkway ride up here. The sky was overcast: snow later on. Patches of snow lay here and there;

but the cold, gray December morning couldn't chill the warmth of hearts, the joy of a boy eager to go home. Mom and Dad strolled the walkway while waiting for the half day of classes to end. They lingered beneath an arch or went to their son's room. They were proud. They were satisfied. They wanted the best for their child away on his own, at this exclusive, highly competitive school. And they paid for it.

Inside classrooms on second floor Settlers the young scholars sat ready to erupt. After the weeks and months of stringent routine they counted off final minutes before a glorious ten days at home, in their own rooms. There the very air had an intimate scent; the clank of a radiator made you feel safe, and cared for; the whine of a sappy dog, the chirp of a little sister at play made you want to give a laugh and hop, skip, jump across your mom's newly waxed kitchen floor—into the pantry stocked with goodies in your honor. Yep! Ten whole days. Sledding, ice-skating with friends back home; non-Refectory meals, pantry raids; a bowl of maple syrup over newfallen snow. And then Christmas with its fun, its carols, gifts: a bright tree up to the ceiling, and cute little ornaments you made, being good for once, with your bratty sister; tinsel, angels, gurgling lights, a star. And look! all the cookies you can eat—just gorge yourself, young man, eat yourself silly! And oh, oh, no more morbid stories if you please: about the missing foreign exchange student, and pale, depressive Ethan Jeffers also gone away, and nobody knew where, or why, or who might be next! No, sir. No more of that. Dad? Ma? Here I am: let's go home.

III

The noon bell rang. A cross between a sigh and a cheer rose up along second floor Settlers, and you heard a closing of notebooks. Then the chorus of hearty goodbyes among fellow students: you might have thought they were journeying to another world. Such pathos, with a slap on the shoulder: such happiness. Suddenly the desks before Master Glebe were like those blank pages which figured, for Hegel, as the happier epochs of history.

Then, outside, it was: Hi, Dad! Hey there! Gee whiz, Ma! It's time to hit the road. We'll stop off somewhere for lunch, okay? No, not here. Oh, what fun it was to ride home together in the car. More boys, more handshakes out by the front circle, in the dorms, along the walkway. Holymoly, gee whizzakers. Let's get the heck outa' this joint.

Newell Gilbert was packed and ready. For a month he had laid off seven-layer cake in The Snug so he could save up and buy–with his own money–Christmas gifts for his older brother Joey, two sisters, and his folks. Now he wondered who had made the drive here to fetch him, and bring him home.

Newell knew someone would be at the room in Warren House by this time. He glanced around the quad and saw 'The Wick' Sedgewick whose Belgian shepherd dog was so excited it went and peed right on the Senior Path. Whew! A good thing Jon Holbein, the Bossman, as they called him, wasn't on hand to see this, or the brains behind his crime organization, seedy Toad.

Nope: Newby's mom and dad were not at the room. So he said so long to Crazy Schmied who also had parents, somehow, like a normal boy; as well as Bernie-Bern off with only a backpack to the train station in town.

–Wait, Berneth, you wanna' ride? We'll fit you in.

–Naw, I'll foot it.

–Okay, kid. Give 'em hell in the Bronx.

–Sure thing, said Big B, with his grin full of zits, and fogged up glasses. Cool ass!

–Bye, Bern. Bye!

Then Newell paused. Such a silence. Stay here and wait for them? Go back to Settlers and look? He went out in the quad again, and stood there by himself. Boy, it didn't take long for this shithole to empty out. The excitement ebbed away. The noise seemed to drift into the distance: sort of funnel through the Settlers main entry, and flow out along the road toward town and the parkway.

He paused another moment, and then decided to go look for his people by the front circle, or maybe at the Ethridge Homestead to one side, where Headmaster Smithson lived, since they were old friends. Professor Gilbert was a trustee of this school.

Thud went a trunk, closing over Wellingham's luggage. One by one the long shiny vehicles pulled out and moved from the front circle. Then down the slow incline, past where the Needing ran tangent, onto the winding road which led across the meadow.

For a moment he stood on the steps outside Settlers Hall. He gazed off at the river flowing with its mystery beneath the leafless trees, the gray sky in winter.

But then he spotted his dad's car parked in the driveway outside Smithsons'. He started running toward that car, but then heard, behind him:

—Ah, here he is. Newell, come back!

Geeter. The chaplain stood in the front entry and waved for the boy to turn around, and come inside. Just the look on Geeter's face, the gesture he gave, was enough to dampen the boy's excitement.

Newell had a wondering look. Then he saw his father who came out and stood alongside the pastor. Geeter had been Emory Gilbert's student at university, some years before. Newell frowned and felt a sinking as he walked back toward them.

—Where's Mom?

IV

Professor Gilbert stood there in the gray suit he was born into. Something about him looked more ponderous than the stuff of mortals. In his late forties he was no stockier than most prosperous men his age, but there was a gravity about him. Author, academic; there was an air of boardrooms, of high places. Yes, Emory Gilbert had a sort of aura, as he spent a moment in this micro-world of Ethridge so far from his busy round. But the aura weighed him down.

Now he shook his son's hand. He didn't lean to hug him, and Newell could tell something was wrong. This wasn't the pleasant errand it should have been for a father and a son. Why weren't they tossing his bag in the backseat and driving away?

Geeter drew back, and held out an arm: this way, into Headmaster Smithson's office, if you please. In that instant Newell seemed to see why Virg Parker didn't cater to the softspoken pastor.

As they went in—Newell heard a last shout from the circle behind him. He turned and saw a bright scarf, some adults in furry overcoats. The junior Warnickie beamed. Oh, Warnickie, you flit! What did you ever do to deserve a family?

The Settlers main entry closed behind Newell Gilbert. It closed on a harmony of voices, Wally Warnickie the flit and his flitty parents. It was the best Christmas gift a boy ever had from his father and mother: to go home.

–You may go in–said the Headmaster's secretary with a smile.

V

And then there they were. He sat in a heavy silence, a space charged with adults. In the plush quietude of Headmaster Smithson's office he had a sense of distance: the wainscotted walls, the bookshelves seemed far away. Newell sat with hands folded. He thought something about 'values' must be coming. What were the 'values' his dad always talked about? What about Christmas? . . . He sat still. At times, back home, a slightest movement might anger his dad; so now he waited, very still. The problem was they could never sit and discuss those 'values', man to man, calmly–since their opinions differed. Go home today? . . . Maybe this was why they sent him away, he didn't have 'values'. Well, his mom didn't want him punished but she had to go along with her husband. Sometimes at home it was electric; there were scenes over the kitchen table when father and son both lost control, shouting, accusing one another, Newell crying; and this hurt his mom a lot, and scared his little sister . . . Head bowed, Newell sat in the Headmaster's office and waited to hear his fate. Then he thought of a trip he and his dad made once: the night they saw the Northern Lights, far out over the lakes and fir trees of Canada. And then he slept tucked in a warm bed at a lodge, and he heard a train whistle.

The Headmaster began the meeting.

–This fall, Newell, your behavior has been a subject of concern to us. (A pause; maybe ten seconds.) Should it be? What do you have to say?

–I've worked hard, Sir. I tried to be good.

–Tried? You went in town and got drunk. Two grave infractions of the school code. When you came back, you were rowdy after lights-out, and abused your senior counselor. I quote from his report: 'Gilbert called me Hillie-babe, and said I was a flit. Then he vomited on my monogrammed pajamas, even though I am a senior, and he should not disrespect me this way. He said I have zits, which is not true. It was after midnight but he shouted and swore, using words like 'zit-face' and 'cunt', and he woke up the hallway. So I gave him ten hours.'

The Ethridge headmaster fell silent. In those instants Laurence Smithson's eyes had a sort of twinkle. His lips, as he shared a glimpse with Emory Gilbert, then Dean Wart, almost smiled.

Newell sat huddled in himself. A curious thing: among these big men his dad was the biggest, but he felt humiliated seeing Emory there. Not for himself, somehow, but for his father. Why? Fingers crossed, Newell flattened them against his stomach which had begun to ache. But he glimpsed Dean Wart who sat squinting at a title along the bookshelves, as if testing his eyes. Newell didn't dare look at his dad, but he said:

–I'm not failing any subjects. And . . . he does.

–Does what, boy? said the Headmaster.

–Hillyer has zits, that's all.

–Lad, you have accrued forty-nine detention hours in half a year. A school record: it beats your performance of all last year. I am told your grades are, yes, in the mediocre range. But they are off from last semester when you made the honor roll, also without really trying, so your adviser tells me. What do you say to this? Shouldn't we worry about you?

Newell had a tear in his eye. He wanted to give them what they wanted. He didn't care what he said: just so they let him go home for Christmas. And yet, in a small, strangled voice, he said:

–Hillyer is a brownnoser, Sir.

Silence. The gentlemen thought this over. Not a diplomatic response . . . not sorry.

Softly, Laurence Smithson spoke.

–This is not about Roger Hillyer's motivation.

Newell's eyes filled with tears. He gave a shrug, and managed a glance at his dad who sat brow creased. Goodbye to the holidays at home.

And then–you explain it, for I cannot–then Newell dug his grave deeper, when he said:

–It is if he's unfair.

At this the debonair Dean Wart raised an eyebrow. Rare sign of emotion from that man.

No, Newell Gilbert was not going home today: after a three month wait crossing off each day on a calendar.

The Headmaster came back, with an edge to his voice:
—When you behave like a child, you will be treated like one. You don't express regret now. You balk, and answer back. Please, then, enlighten us further. Is there anything else you'd like to say.

Newell looked out into the driveway where all but a car or two had gone. Then he bowed his head, and a tear ran down his cheek. He murmured:
—I'm sorry.

But, would you believe it, he shrugged his shoulders again, as he said this.

And then he looked up at them—not impish, like a Shellnitz, but . . . but . . . but, Sir!

—Your attitude will need to change, Newell, quite a lot. Ethridge is generous, and Ethridge will give you one more chance. No misconduct, or else; no liquor, no forays off campus, in the presence of a girl. Your behavior this semester merits expulsion many times over. But we will continue to work with you, and believe in you, out of respect for your parents. We expend a special effort (Laurence Smithson nodded at the Chaplain) on the one in a hundred, who goes astray. Which is why we're doing something rather different this year for Christmas. There will be a small group of boys staying over, here on campus, for the holiday break. Besides partaking of Christmas dinner with us at the Homestead, they will work, study, pray together. They will form part of a work group for special projects under head custodian Astarte's direction, and with Jon Holbein as foreman. Thus you will have a chance to mend your ways, Newell, and show respect to our school. We'll either gain your loyalty to Ethridge, or give up trying. There . . . You are not expelled today. You won't have to go home to stay. Are you happy? (Pause: maybe fifteen seconds.) Well, aren't you?

Newell looked up at them: at the smooth Laurence Smithson; at the Dean of Behavior more like a block of granite; at Geeter so kindly, and caring. By now Newell's eyes were glazed. His cheek quivered. He felt like blurting the truth: You accuse me? You punish me? Well, what about Manuel? What about Jeffers who also went away? Why do masters sneak around the dorms late at night, and sit on the floor acting like madmen? And dress up in corny Beast of Ethridge costumes, and wear masks? . . . Tell me that!

But his stomach ached. He had cramps, and couldn't catch his breath. He only tried not to start sobbing.

VI

Beneath a bleak sky lay the town commons with its elm trees, bronze eagle monument to war veterans; its patches of gray snow across the blanched grass. A crow cawed and veered over the stone steeple of old Grace Church on the far side. Later on snow would fall.

Father and son walked under the maroon awning of Maspeth Needing Inn. A hostess showed them to their table at the rear of the white gabled structure, a landmark converted to the town's one fine restaurant. Through a bay window you saw railroad tracks; and, beyond the low-eaved train depot, a fenced-in complex: the dog pound.

–That's where this place gets its meat, said Newell.

Emory Gilbert let this pass. He said:

–Your mother feels badly. This autumn her health has not been up to par.

–Why didn't she come today?

–She's busy at home.

–Ah, for Christmas.

–No, your sister has a school play today. She needed her.

–Lemon has her everyday.

–Listen, Bud–Dr. Gilbert spoke quietly–they let you get away with it up here. I won't.

Newell frowned and looked away. Around the restaurant: silverware clicked, conversation hummed. Out beyond the Dog Pound lay the meadow with its mauve tint in winter. Trees lined the river. That way lay Bartlett; he wondered if Katya left already for the holiday.

–Get away with what?

–Showing off.

–I'd like to spend Christmas with you and not at this crazy place. That's showing off.

–We pay handsomely so you can have the finest education available. Your older brother hasn't had the privilege.

–Joey wanted high school to play ball. You let him, but me you
didn't ask.

   Dr. Gilbert looked tense. Lips pursed, he glanced for the waitress;
then said to his son:

   –You don't know the way we've worked for your sake. Your
mother and I sent you to private school so you could make the most
of it, and make us proud. How many boys get such a chance?

   –To stay here over Christmas? And now I have to sleep by myself
in an empty dorm. What you don't know is that two boys disappeared from campus. When I do too, maybe you'll wish you stood
up for me and took me home.

   Dr. Gilbert glanced at the ceiling. Again he tried to hail the waitress, and then shook his head.

   –I guess you'd say anything to get the blame off your shoulders.

   –Manuel, a foreign exchange student, and his roommate Ethan
Jeffers. Gone. And they didn't come back. And no reason is given by
the Headmaster. I don't know how they can keep it a secret, out of
the newspapers. When I went in town that day, I was trying to find
out something. Mingo the hobo saw the kidnapper or kidnappers
take Manuel out to the island, so I thought Mingo might be able to
describe them. How many were there? What did they look like? I try
to find Manuel and Jeffers, and now I'm punished for it and have to
stay here. Well, I think it is somebody right around here who took
those two boys away, and now he knows I've got an eye out, on his
trail. Maybe a psycho from town; maybe one of the masters . . . gone
mad. So I asked Mingo about it, but he wanted nothing to do with
such talk and said he didn't know anything about it. Shook his head
at me, and took a drink quick, tossed it down. Because it's bad. I'm
telling you, Dad, somebody has kidnapped those two boys and has
them locked up, if he hasn't hurt them even worse. Now I think it
might be Jon Holbein, and his friends in a secret society they call
Self-Furtherance: took Manuel out to the island for a hazing ceremony and got carried away and maybe even killed him. Me and a
townie named Cormac, we rowed out to that island one Sunday, after Mingo said he saw them go there; and we went to an old cabin,
and a man wearing a mask chased us away. Wanted to kidnap us too–
after he came and got two boys right from my hallway in Warren
House! And now he knows: now the Beast of Ethridge knows I saw
him, and I won't rest until I find out who he is and report him . . .
For all I know it's Dean Wart who's gone crazy and ended up killing

a boy; and that's why he wants me kept here: so I won't go home for Christmas vacation and spill the beans. But I'll spill them. I will.

During this outpouring Professor Emory Gilbert's look changed. It was no easy thing to have such a son. Uneasily he glimpsed the other tables to see if anyone was listening. But his features also, for the first time since his arrival at Ethridge, seemed to soften, and show concern. For the crazy one here, or so it seemed to him, was his own flesh and blood. To adapt words from the Bible: people must get married and have sons, but woe unto them that do it.

Emory's voice went low, something like Geeter's:

—Don't rave.

—Where did they go? The room was empty until a new boy moved in.

—If a room was empty, they transferred to another school. That happens.

—Both?

VII

After Newell's outburst there was a lull. He looked out the window and avoided his father's eye. Then he spotted Garvey Sackler across the room. The Garv, who set records in the flit league, was seated at dinner with his parents. Was he also assigned to Headmaster Smithson's work detail? Lord knows what would happen now: at the mercy of that bully Jon Holbein for ten days. Of course, they could all expect to be eaten by the Beast of Ethridge; unless The Beast was on its own way home by now for Christmas vacation, like any other normal Ethridgian.

The waitress came and went. Professor Gilbert's brow softened as he worked on a cocktail. Then he spoke in a changed tone, but the same meaning:

—I've worked hard, Newell, all my life. In a few days I fly to Geneva for a speech, next month who knows where. Larger issues.

—So you don't believe me about The Beast.

—I think you're making excuses.

—That's what hurts me, Dad. Say it actually has happened, say I was right about this—would you stand up for me? Or for your friends: the Headmaster, and Geeter? Tell me, I'd like to know.

–When you do right I'll support you.

–Gee, thanks.

–Son, I'm sorry you're so unhappy. But you made the choice to come here: when you got yourself expelled from the day school at home. You burned your bridges. Newell stared. Tears welled in his eyes. He shook his head. For now he couldn't take any more.

The fine food came, and he picked at it in silence.

VIII

They went out into the cold, gray afternoon of the small New England town. A first few snowflakes fell on the green with its church at either end, and row of dingy stores across the street.

Back at Ethridge there was a last car parked by the front circle: a limousine. Seven, eight pieces of luggage lay on the pavement: for ten days? Little Mallet seemed to emerge like Jonas from the great trunk, while a snappy chauffeur stood and stretched. Ramlet, who looked like a cherub, had made a name for himself by giving out goodies from his packages. Ten Little Mallets could have fit in that black hearse they sent for him. And now the happy freshman was going home.

It was time to say goodbye.

Dr. Gilbert, feeling easier after drinks and the luncheon, tried to comfort his son as they sat a moment in the car.

–Your mother and I will drive up before New Year's with your presents.

Newell nodded and watched Little Mallet talk over some pleasant matter with the uniformed driver. Newell felt like pleading with his dad to be taken home as well. Ramlet's voice was birdlike as the boy made a point, then tried to reach the top of the trunk to close it, but couldn't, so the chauffeur grinned. Newell felt such pain, but he wasn't crying; he would shake Dad's hand like a man, then get out and walk away, head up. Alright, he would deal with Ethridge and face the bad thing by himself, if that's how it was. It was there, this Beast, now choose your category: deny it, ignore it, or fight.

He opened the car door and slid from the front seat.

–Okay, Dad. Love to 'em at home.

He nodded. Emory smiled at him and started the motor.

—You're our son. We believe in you.

His father drove round the front circle and past the Ethridge Homestead with a wave. Newell watched the car move slowly along the winding road across the meadow, and then go beneath the railroad bridge. In a minute it would be on the parkway.

—Hey! Merry Christmas there! cried Little Mallet, as the tall driver, in livery, bowed to open a rear door.

—Okay, Big Ram, said Newell. You too.

And then they were gone.

Not a soul in view. Off past Headmaster Smithson's house, down the embankment, the Needing River took on an early twilight. In late afternoon snowflakes drifted down from the cloudy sky. Snow fell on the island of tall trees; on the cabin over there; on the river's surface frozen over.

Newell turned, shivering, and went inside an overheated Settlers. He wondered who the other students were: taking part in a dismal work project run by Holbein. All flits. Well, he didn't care anymore if they threw him out. Christmas Eve he would go in town to Cormac's and get drunk again. Right now he couldn't think how to get through this day, let alone ten more days, by himself on an empty campus.

But as Newell stood in the wood panelled hallway on first-floor Settlers, he thought he heard something. Alongside him hung that boy's portrait, in a v-neck tennis sweater, who had died the summer before, and the study hall was renamed after him. Did it—could it be this picture? Newell listened closely. Down the hall a clock struck, the minute hand: as if to protest being left alone, abandoned by so much routine. No one else in the building. No one visible outside the study hall windows, in the quadrangle. And yet he heard something, like the wind in a shutter: the low moans he heard in his dream, so he believed, the Sunday in October before they went out to the island. But now he wasn't sleeping. This wasn't any dream. Yet he heard, or thought he did, those same voices issuing from fissures in the wall. Rustlings, sighs: as though generations of Ethridge students might graduate, but their souls did not. Their spirits died of sadness, of conformism. Their lives had moved on to the next stage, while their consciences, denied what was required to grow, develop, make good choices, were sent to an early death beneath the Settlers floorboards—a long, long confinement. And so you heard them:

moans, laments late at night. And these echoed, in his mind: older echoes, more recent echoes, echoes unable to be stilled because *no one had heard them in real life*. No one was able to hear. But now, after all the noise and bustle fled campus and went to its Christmas holiday: now Newell heard those sounds–ghostly echoes with a rising tone, a spirit of inquiry forbidden to them this year, last year, a hundred years ago, as living students. Ten hours' detention! . . . Newell shook his head. He felt dizzy as he stood there in Settlers hallway: dizzy with sense of loss, and with fear. So much pressure on him; such anxiety for these two months since Manuel went from campus. Now, also, there was a strange light over things. Everyday surroundings, objects, looked strange. Was he going crazy, like Jeffers? Too much stress here at Ethridge, too much fear–of the unknown?

No doubt there was an investigation going on, into the two boys' disappearance? No doubt detectives had come on campus; and, while everyone was in class or down at athletics, or maybe asleep, the law enforcers went about looking for the truth, preparing to report on clues, leads, their findings? But you didn't see them. No investigator, no outsider came to the student house asking questions–only Dean Wart, and perhaps Geeter a little, offhand. And so it all remained a secret, hushed up, contained: the *Secret* of Ethridge.

Newell stood there listening. He heard what sounded like a chorus of muffled howls, but so low you couldn't be sure. From within the woodwork, behind the wainscotted walls, beneath the floorboards, they came. What was happening? So many spirits he seemed to hear: souls bitter at being cheated of life. Souls confined to darkness with no air to breathe, so they went bad. It must stink in there! Oh, so many, such a multitude, damned by the finest education available. And Newell stood there all alone, and wondered how he could ever fight them all.

Chapter Five

I

The same day school let out for the holidays Dean Wart met with the Head Custodian as well as Jon Holbein. They made up a work schedule for the two seniors and seven underclassmen who were staying on campus. Long neglected maintenance chores headed the list.

An underground tunnel ran on both sides of the quadrangle from Settlers to the Refectory. In recent years few if any people had set foot down there; though the space served as a possible air-raid shelter during World War II and through the mid-'Fifties. The Steam Tunnel, as it was called, also formed part of Ethridge lore and legend; and senior counselors, on third floor Settlers, liked to tell incoming freshmen a ghost story in moments before lights went out. Here you had the origin of the term: Beast of Ethridge.

In the late 1700s an Ethridge master studied and performed alchemy, secretly, down in the Tunnel. His wits turned. In some rare old volume he read how the conversion to gold needed 'a human element'. And so he took it in his head to bring live boys down there, knock them out, like white rats, and boil down their mortal remains for the retort. Ouch! It was all in good fun of course; but the story could help set the tone of a boy's first year at the school. Often the senior counselor's voice took a hushed tone, as if he too was moved by what he was saying. Waiting for lights-out he told a more recent story, not a Beast of Ethridge tale, but a true one: to do with some Ethridge teacher. What was it? Which master did it concern? The Glebes? What was the strange story, also about the Tunnel, that Newell could never quite bring back; though it still seemed to hover in his mind, before the lights went out?

Students, on their way to morning chapel, gave a tap at the Steam Tunnel door across from the Study Hall on first-floor Settlers. Many were the jokes made about what might happen to a lad if he failed Master Sippel's science test; or ogled Ramona Glebe too openly;—if the day ever came, and the hour, when he had to pay the price for his sins. For there were ghosts and devils at the bottom of those cobwebby stairs. There were trap doors opening on gory sights: corpses, dry bones, gray dust. There were skeletons dressed in tweeds and a necktie, propped upright beneath a bare bulb. Manuel sat in a tea party with the vampires, and he was the tea, he was the crumpets. Oh! What a nice young neck the foreign exchange student had, what heady blood! Further on, where the Tunnel passed underneath Hampton Hall, there were secret passages leading to the upper levels of hell.

Surely no one, unless it was the Head Custodian, a man named Astarte, knew the dark secrets of the Tunnel. But the Dean of Behavior, on Headmaster Smithson's orders, had told the Headmaster's protégé Jon Holbein to put a crew of students into that pit and clean up any mess they found down there. But, Sir! Oh, yes, they would work their little behinds off, and leave the Tunnel spotless. So said Holbein.

II

—Alright, sucks! You, Shellnitz! And Gilbert, you flit! Come, little puppies, lowly frosh sucks: Hinton, Butterball, all of you, hear me. I am leaving you with Mr. Gar Stanton, a senior, your superior. I, Master Holbein, to you, am the bossman. Got that, suckies? If not, then Santa will give you a switch for Christmas, and not in your stocking. Okay! Let's go in.

It took Holbein a moment to insert an old key. He got angry and shook the door. Finally it opened with a cry: maybe the first time in years.

—Follow me, suck-ups.

But then Holbein paused, and hung back. Over the old wood stairs, which looked warped, there were streams of cobwebs like Spanish moss.

—Shellnitz! You're small, you go in first. See the light bulb hanging down? No switch, you have to twist it.

Down went the fearless Shellnitz—made to stay on campus by Coach Roentgen—into the dust and the darkness. Passing Holbein onto the top stair he shined the crew's flashlight into the senior's face, and chirped:

—Holbein, you flit.

But laughter turned to awe when Shellnitz paused, and gazed down into a darkness which looked without end. The small light he held before him showed a chaos.

At the bottom of the stairs a bare bulb hung on a cord. It needed replacing, and this gave the Tunnel crew a minute to think what they were in for. Shellnitz came out laughing but wound in cobwebs. No wonder the leader, Jon Holbein, would not go in: he had loathed the sight of a mop or dustpan since his days coming up in a state-run orphanage. He hated dirt of any kind. A twist of fate had led him to this old phobia, as he meant to make the Tunnel a showpiece: see what our holiday work detail got done? He wanted to take the credit.

While the rosy cheeked lads in work clothes looked on, and rubbed the stirred up dust from their eyes, Shellnitz shook himself out like a wet dog. It made him laugh to get good and filthy, and shake off dust and cobwebs on Holbein's neat clothes. Then the bully might have given little Shellnitz a good shaking, but he only scowled and didn't care to touch him.

They went in.

From the door Holbein peered down and said:

—This little work-job will take today and tomorrow. Farnsby, you and Butterball go see Astarte and carry pails, rags, soap, things we need here.

Overhead a steam pipe dripped dust and lint on their heads. Boys wheezed and hung back on the steep narrow stairs, which were bent; but Shellnitz seemed in his element and moved deeper among a mass of furniture jumbled on the murky edge. Broken desks, chairs, bedsteads. It stank. Why? It stank a lot. Whew, putrid! Was nothing ever thrown away at Ethridge? All kept, except the essential. More old desks, lamps, lamp shades, lampstands; more three-legged chairs, rotted mattresses leaking their stuffing; more tables, dressers, book-shelves. And over it all hung a sweetish rancid smell. Poor Garvey Sackler hung back, and his teeth began to chatter.

—Gosh! said The Garv.

What a flit.

—No use dusting, said Stanton. We've got to run a hose or else haul water. Wharburton, go find Farnsby, even better the janitor, and tell him we need help.

—Any spiders in here? said Hinton the freshman.

Sackler looked on. He shook a little. Maybe he had to pee?

The bare bulb cast a stark light, among shadows, and did tricks with the boys' features.

—We can throw out most of this stuff, said Stanton. But where? Lug it up the steps?

III

Work began. By midmorning they used every mop, broom, pail the custodian Astarte could supply. Newell dawdled; he hated this work detail. But all the boys worked, even Sackler in a trance. Rod Shellnitz splashed water, mopped, scrubbed, like a man with a goal.

Holbein checked on them from time to time. He called at the top of the stairs:

—Sackler, you nebbish. Come up here at once.

Newell said:

—Go on, Garveth. See what the senior suck wants.

—What say, Gilbert?

—I said why bug us when you don't do diddly.

—You'll pay for that remark.

The Sack trudged up the stairs. Then the shy boy met the crew chief's gaze. Besides a pale face full of zits, he had a pair of thick glasses always on crooked. Poor Sack: only son of rich parents, he made a picture of neglect.

There was a cruel, a sensuous curve to Holbein's lips, as he took Sackler by the collar and raised him on tiptoes.

—Going to do what I say?

—Yes, Sir.

—I asked you nicely.

—I know.

—You know? What does that mean?

—Yes, Sir.

Holbein slapped him. Not too hard; but Big Garv's glasses flew off.

—Ready to work?

Sackler was ready. He shook.

—I kn—yessir, Sir.

Holbein let him go. And Sackler fell, limply, to the floor, like his clothes had nothing in them.

With a chuckle Holbein, the wrestler, took Sackler by one arm. He pulled him upright.

—Go get 'em, champ.

Pat on the rump. He pushed the poor boy toward the stairs. Back to it, Garv. Aw, you know you love it.

IV

Dust balls formed like tumbleweed beneath the students' feet. Holbein went and came. From time to time he urged them on with a look of grim pleasure. He pushed back the lunch break an hour.

Newell sweated, wheezed like the others, and said:

—Time to knock off.

—No way, said the senior. Lunch at one.

Finally, done in, dusty head to foot, they made their way to the Refectory. What a gay parade. Holbein hardly gave them time to wash their hands; and then, after a sandwich and glass of milk, he said:

—Let's go, men. Back to it.

And then they were down in the Tunnel again. They itched. They sneezed. They thrashed about them like a bunch of drunks. And the dust rose into their eyes, nostrils, mouthes. Holbein badgered and threatened and bullied them with no pity. He sat at his post, the top of the stairs, in a silent fury at the sloth of these flits! He sent Farnsby and Hinton to the custodian after more mops, more rags, while juniors Wharburton and Beauregard made up the trash barrel team.

Gilbert, Shellnitz, Sackler and Butterball stayed in the hole. They drudged like slaves as the afternoon wore on, and Holbein's eye was on them. In a big way he had it in for Newell, the rebel, who was at wit's end by now and began to talk back. Also Holbein wanted to punish Shellnitz for the way Shellnitz treated the good Coach Roentgen: the knack this sophomore had of mocking the Coach, mimicking him to his face. But Hot Rod looked like he took to the work down there: the dust, stench of dead rats, filth; even as he liked to defy Roentgen during gym period when The Runt hollered: ten times thirty push-ups! fifty laps around the gym! two hundred sit-ups! As for Marvelous Garv, the senior gave him no quarter. Oh, how he goaded The Sack. He drove the boy and made him cry.

–Shirker! You lump. Work faster or I'll tear you to pieces when you come up here.

–Yes, Sir–piped Big G.

–How would you like to spend the night down there by yourself?

–No, Sir.

–Then hop to. Stop slacking off. Gilbert, I'll lock you in–good Christ, I swear it! You'll starve to death, you'll eat one another. Ha ha ha. That's what slothful little flits should do.

They worked like a bunch of young demons, but nothing could please him. When Holbein stepped away for a moment, they paused and sat among the old furniture, all that fluff of lint, hairs, upholstery and mattress stuffing. For a moment the boys sat in silence, after the hours of hard work–what? what was that? In the sudden hush they heard a sort of moaning from deeper in the Tunnel, like the wind trapped down here. Or else a boy was crying feebly, losing his strength, as he moaned, and pleaded to be set free? In sleep you might hear such voices, whisperings, buzzing about your ears. Now in the Steam Tunnel they listened. Silence. Then murmurs. Murmurs reached them, like a whirring of winter wind.

Suddenly, bursting the silence, a great clatter made their heads jerk. On the steps a trash barrel, then another, a third came vaulting and crashing down at them. Big things, heavy cardboard, metal-rimmed: they bounded down on top of the four boys spooked already by strange noises from deeper in the Tunnel. And, up there, in the entry, Holbein stood laughing low. The bare light bulb, lighting his face from below, made him look like a leering devil.

–Share the bins, he said. Take turns with the dustpans.

But he didn't come down. There wasn't a spec of dust on him.

V

—First, little sucklings, we will douse the furniture from pails. Have you got that, in your brains? Then rub it dry with rags. Make it shine piece by piece. Every square inch of this tunnel will be made to glisten, and then we will put things in order. We'll make the place look like your mummy's living room.

More gobs of lint and stuffing and hairball. More sodden strips of mattress and rotted upholstery. Oh! how it stank down there. But they hardly noticed.

Down the crooked steps came Farnsby and Hinton with pails brimful of water.

Holbein crowed:

—By New Years we'll sweep and clean the whole damned length of it thanks to you sucks!

—We need a hose, running water, you suck!

—What? What did you call me?

—I said you can't fight your way out of a wet paper bag, little suckling, pee-in-your-pants.

Rough 'n tough Shellnitz bit off the words.

—You'll wish you weren't born.

—Oh yeah? Come down and get me, fartface.

Shellnitz clucked like a chicken.

Newell paused to stare at Rod; though nothing about that guy could surprise him anymore. Rodikins was without fear whether of Runt Roentgen, or the bully Holbein who would beat Shelby to a pulp when the crew went back up at the end of the day.

Cluck-cluck, cluck.

—Holbein, you flit!

Mad Shellnitz gave his chirpy laugh.

Newell picked up a first pail and, would you believe it, sloshed water all over Shellnitz. Why? Well, he laughed, but he was afraid of what Holbein might do to the boy. Then Newell took up another pail and, while Holbein shouted at him to stop, he went after Butterball. He had simply had enough, and wanted this crazy business to end. He didn't care any more than Shellnitz what came next. He went after a squealing Butterworth deeper into the Tunnel, and let fly.

They paused. Bossman couldn't believe his eyes. He stood speechless.

Drip-drip. Drip . . . , in the silence.

Onto the old chairs, tables, bedsteads, desks, cracked mirrors, sinks and toilet bowls, more water was poured.

But then, suddenly, a dark thing darted from beneath one of the brownish mattresses. Not so small: a rat the size of a shoe wriggled right at Garv Sackler who let out a shriek.

Newell flung his water, pail and all, on the rat and stunned it. It paused. It squealed, snout high, sniffing, by The Garv who rubbed at his pants, and cried:

—Get out! Get out!

—There's another! yelled Shellnitz, with a whoop.

While the first rat wobbled off, a second ball of fur came out, as if for its brother. There was a panicked squealing, rodent and human, in the cluttered space.

More came. They came. Gray, bristling, feeling themselves attacked, they flew at the boys' shoes and nipped. Sackler, Butterball, Shellnitz, Newell shouted at the top of their lungs and hopped on tiptoes toward the stairs.

Rats, rats! They shot here, there, after years of breeding and feeding on the rotted-out bedding of Ethridge. A diet at least as delicious as the Refectory's.

Rats scooted over the intruders' shoes. Did they fight for their flooded home among the furniture?

Yow! Look at Butterball go! Who ever saw the soft Butterworth move so fast? Not in club football, I can tell you: where he fell over himself, tangled in the pads which rode up on him.

—You there! Holbein shouted down. You stay!

But only Shellnitz had a notion to stay on the scene. The crazy guy leapt about and kicked back at rats and seemed to enjoy himself.

Hey! What's that smell? Has Sackler wet his pants? Drip-drip . . . Honour bright! I do believe he has. The Garv stood stock still: he was in shock. And now rats bit at him and nicked his ankles. In waves they came and attacked. The rats went after Garvey Sackler; and good night if they knocked him down. It was Newell Gilbert, shouting, kicking a path, who took Garveth under the arm and led him to the steps; though just then a grinning Holbein did a mad thing.

Holbein gave a big horse laugh, seeing his pet project go up in smoke, or dust. And then he—shut the door on them!

But Newell shouldered it open in no uncertain terms; and, brushing past Holbein, said:

—Senior suck! You'd lock us in?

Holbein would have decked him. He'd have ground him into the kind of mush they were wading in—Shellnitz was still down there—; only Newell in those instants looked—what? too upset to be afraid. Covered with soot, rat hair, also some blood on him, he said:

—Suck, watch out. I'll play another way.

Newell brushed past the senior and made for his room and a shower.

Meanwhile the other 'work-jobbers' had grouped round the Steam Tunnel door. Farnsby, Hinton, Wharburton, Beauregard—all saw Butterball come away from the scene looking the worse for wear. The Ball stared at Holbein, as though looking to him for mercy.

But Sackler stared straight ahead: the way Jeffers had, in a trance. The Sack slumped down, and no one broke his fall. He simply lay on the wood floor, there by Study Hall on first floor Settlers. He gazed in space like a dead rat, and trembled.

But here came Shellnitz. The others managed a laugh and cheered him. But Shellnitz thrust his filthy fingers, like a cat's paw, into Holbein's face.

—Hssss!

Well, Bossman fed up with Gilbert's antics just couldn't let this pass. So he got the little sucker in a crushing headlock, flung him down, and, legs pinning Shellnitz's spindly shoulders, laid a juicy fart.

As for the rats: maybe they would go like nomads deeper into the Tunnel—which went to who knows where beneath the Ethridge campus.

VI

There was no work detail on Christmas Day. Besides, two of its members were in the Infirmary; they missed Christmas dinner with Headmaster Smithson at the Homestead.

That afternoon Newell Gilbert went slipping and sliding, shin-deep in snow, behind the school laundry and out along the road to town. If anyone shouted his name he would break into a run because there was simply no dealing with Jon Holbein anymore. Holbein had made them spend Christmas Eve setting out rat traps in the Tunnel. Deck the halls! Then back upstairs, the boys heard the traps begin to snap, as rats didn't seem finicky when it came to Refectory food.

As Newell went along the winding road to town he asked himself:–Should I care? . . . Dad, you said I was a disgrace to the family, but what is that? I ask you one question: who gets to say who is a disgrace?–Under the railroad bridge; then past the town library; he went along the main drag called Mather Street. At the Plaza Theater a war film called 'The Hunters' was playing, at two and eight p.m. But he had no money to go in and see it. So he went along: not a soul in view; only white snow across the town commons. He thought:–We could slave in that hole until doomsday and not scratch the surface. Holbein is killing us, and he calls us snot-nosed and 'little shirkers' after we worked so hard . . . A madman; even if his legal guardian is Headmaster Smithson. But say, why not adopt him? Why not the same last name? Why doesn't he live in the Homestead? . . . Another mystery: in this Ethridge under a curse.

He took the side street, Engadine, out to the old Puritan cemetery. The day was cold, cold. Houses looked lifeless in the gray midafternoon. Going through the graveyard he passed Maspeth Needing's mouldy headstone in the snow.

At Cormac's the blinds were drawn. Shutters of the old place looked like a gallery of crooked pictures. On Cormeth's front porch, full of snow as well, Newell rang the bell.

The door opened a crack. A long face peered out: the servant, Pullver. Oh, hell: Corky's parents picked this moment to come home.

–Sir, is Cormac here?

–Wait.

Newell needed to come inside from the icy air. But the zombie gave a nod and shut the door.

So Mingo must be out here as well in the near zero temperature?

In a moment the young master came to the door. Corm was a sight: all got up in a tweed suit, a maroon and blue necktie. What a flit! Cormer had had his greasy mesh washed by main force, and brushed back neatly, with a part. Poor Corm looked ridiculous. At sight of Newell his face was more cutie-pie than ever: the ferret eyes, the snub nose, sort of like . . . a rat!

–Yes, sir, he said, in a nasal tone.

—Say, Cormeth, you look worn out.

—By a visit from my parents.

—But you said they couldn't stand *you* anymore, and ran away.

—Came in last night for the Yuletide. Dad all riled 'cause we burned the birch logs that day with Katya.

—Oh. Sorry. Hey, you seen The Ming?

—No.

A woman called from within: stepmother of Corm, complaining about the cold draft.

—He must be cold. Icy wind.

—Must be.

—Gee, it would've been swell to have the house to ourselves. When are they clearing out?

—Not till New Year's at least.

—Heck, I can't come in for a minute? Too cold.

Pullver came down the front hall. The dayhop just had time to whisper something, and slip an envelope into Newell's hand. With a grin the manservant shut the heavy front door.

VII

Where to? He had better make up his mind because it was just too cold out here, in late afternoon, with no sun in the sky. Wow! he thought: Cormeth's folks will drive him off the deep end if they stick around very long. Then Newell got an idea, and broke into a run. Ten minutes later he stood in front of Bartlett Academy's main hall, and looked for a light inside, or in the red-brick girls' dorm. Newell—trying to be good and please his parents—had not snuck over here, or seen Katya since that Saturday at Cormac's. So he didn't know if she went home for Christmas. Or maybe to her roommate Phyllis's outside of Boston?

No lights. He went round the administration building, and from a patio gazed across playing fields, and wide snow-covered meadow: toward a grove of trees and the Needing. This was the best way back to Ethridge, and he had to get going, or else frostbite.

Down an embankment he slid on the seat of his pants. Then up, high-stepping, he left a long line of footsteps toward the river. Behind him, over his shoulder, he glimpsed the stone spire rising above the town commons. Afternoon waned toward evening as the sky went a deeper gray. This was the shortest way back; but wind whipped and whirred in trees along the riverbank, and Newell didn't know if he could take much more cold. It stung his hands and ears. What to do? Ethridge seemed a long way off. He passed the cove where Corm and he had found the rowboat that Sunday last fall.

Far down river, in the direction away from Ethridge, he saw a light, or thought he did. Mingo trying to keep warm beside a fire? A town fisherman? Too far to go and find out.

He moved along the riverbank, tripping over roots, raising snow dust. It occurred to him: why not walk on the frozen surface? So he did by the edge. But then he walked out further: toward the middle. It felt eerie out on the Needing River. What a silence. Would the ice crack? Newell walked and listened: only the wind whirring among bare branches, only the crunch of snow under his steps. Was that Mingo by himself down there on the right bank of the Needing? Or was he huddling in a doorway somewhere, freezing, as night came on?

Then Newell had an idea. This was dangerous: he couldn't make it much further, with the cold numbing his hands despite mittens his little sister knitted him. The cabin must be close. Now in winter he could probably see it from the far riverbank. And so he went across. He grappled roots up the bank. No light; he saw only tree trunks black to the windward side. But the cabin was there: he could find it.

Now he didn't feel the cold so much. He felt fear, a strange excitement; no longer sluggish, not sleepy with cold. He was going, by himself this time, straight toward the lair of the Beast of Ethridge. Well, he had to get inside pretty quick, and curl up under any covers he could find. But he also felt spurred on by a need to find out what was inside; and—strangest of all, but he felt it!—maybe see his lost hallmates, Manuel and Jeffers, again. Then, too, after his father's visit, the news that he would not be at home for Christmas, he just didn't care. He had nothing to lose. Why should he try to please them, his parents or anyone else, when they treated him this way? He felt kicked out from his own family.

Newell went on: past trees, ruts, down a slow incline. The island's twilit aura took him in its arms, as he walked along, tripped, caught his breath, got up. Now he didn't feel the cold; though his teeth chattered. His mind was on Katya, and how brave she would think he was to do this thing. His mood lifted after these past days, weeks of walking along looking at the ground, an old habit. Newell's steps firmed as he plodded forward across the snow: over his knees in places. He didn't realize he was crying.

VIII

He saw the cabin. No light, no sign of life. He stood by a tree and panted for breath after the trek. What if Manuel and Jeffers were still alive and being held out here? Had there been a manhunt across the state in the days after Manuel went away? Or Jeffers? Nobody said so. Nobody talked about publicity; though boys on this secluded campus didn't see newspapers, and wouldn't know either way. But no outcry? No repercussions after two boys' disappearance from an elite private school? What if he found them? What if he saved them? The story went that Jon Holbein had been just such a boy wonder: a poor kid in a state run orphanage, Holbein dragged someone from a fire. The heroic act got national attention and also caught the eye of Laurence Smithson, a well-known merchant banker at the time. As for Newell, he only wanted to show the world how bad things were at this place; so his parents would have to take him out of here, and send him to public high school, his dream. And he wanted Katya's praise.

But still alive? Could the two students still be saved after all these weeks? In Manuel's case nearly three months! Didn't the school and town authorities know about this out of the way cabin? Wouldn't they come out here and check? What a spooky air the place had: all by itself, crouched in the snow beneath the gray tree trunks. Who could have built it, long ago? And why? What purpose did it serve?

In the pure air a scent wafted to Newell's nostrils.

Perfume.

IX

He drew close. Then he leaned to the wood shingles and listened. No sound. Nothing but the smell of a woman's perfume . . . Newell rose up and looked over the window sill.

Dark inside. Not a stir, past the blinds.

He waited and tried to hear a movement. But no; silence, empty. Still he couldn't wait too long because of the cold. So he went round to the front—at each step expecting to see that big, evil man, or ghost, step out from behind a tree trunk, and attack. Only this time Newell wouldn't be able to run away, since he hadn't the strength to go any further. This time he would be at the monster's mercy, a victim like Manuel and Jeffers. Oh, it was a mistake to come out here today. But here he was: so he must try to get inside, and find blankets, covers, a coat, a rug, anything to curl up and warm himself before he really did freeze to an icycle.

Hm. Hm. Who *was* that madman who went around kidnapping teenage boys? Was it some faculty member gone crazy? though still sane by day—or at least as sane as Ethridge? Was it the science teacher who performed alchemist experiments on himself by night in his lab—Master Sippel? Hm! . . . who *was* it? Maybe Bill Hastings, chef in the Refectory, trying to improve his menu, and put a little more beef in the beef stew? What living ghost haunted the restless dreams of Ethridge students, and could step any time into their wakeful lives as well? Who? Holbein and his crew? Tim MacDonald, the cleancut captain of three sports? Josey Kipnes, the actor, who played in summer stock? Not likely: the Beast of Ethridge wasn't as lazy as Josey. Or Paul Rhodes? Maybe Herbert 'The Toad' Wingate, tomorrow's Wall Street big boy? With help! Who was doing this dreadful thing? And who, among the students, would be next?

No sound or stir from inside; no footsteps in the snow; no sign of anyone being on hand. Newell grew a little bolder; he straightened up, and, going to the front door, turned the knob.

Locked.

He would freeze to death out here.

What to do? Hurry. He poked about for something to pry open a window, and found a broken branch. Though he wore mittens, his hands were in such a state he could hardly hold anything. The day was winding down, and he must get inside, somehow, or else. With the branch he tapped on a window, tap-tap, and then tried to heft it up. No, locked, frozen shut. So he butted his stick harder—the glass broke. Now with numb hands he cleared the frame of glass splinters, and hoisted himself over the sill. Headfirst down he went onto the floor. He was inside.

X

He took a first look. In the dwindling light he expected to see the Beast of Ethridge, shaggy and terrible: all ready to pounce, eat him. Still no sound, no breathing, only his own. Only that smell, a rich perfume . . . Neither was there any heat or electricity; although the place looked neat. It had a small sofa, two chairs by the fireplace. On an end table: a kerosene lamp; and, in a second room, a mattress made up on the floor, with army blankets.

Heaven.

From the sofa he took a cushion to block, at least partly, cold air in the window. Then he looked around for matches, and found a pack; took kindling from a rack by the hearth, an old newspaper, two logs; reached in to see if the chimney was opened. It must have been a half hour, as the forest grew dark outside, before he settled in beside a fire and warmed himself. For a while this was painful after the cold. He rubbed his arms and legs, shivered, and tried to make himself at home: here in the Beast of Ethridge's den.

But what if the thing came back and found him? What then? It dawned on Newell he had better get a weapon of some sort, and be ready. So he looked around, and picked up a kitchen knife from a pantry area off the second room, at the rear of the cabin. There, in a cabinet, he also found a tin of biscuits. These he opened, and saw—mold, a disgusting mush, like what the rats left in the Steam Tunnel. It looked like worms, by dim light from the fire.

Also: plates, utensils, a few drinking glasses, coffee cups, an opened packet of paper napkins were there, in the cabinet and on the counter. There wasn't a sink, or running water; yet the glasses had no rings from liquid left in them, the plates no grease stains from eating.

Newell gave a little laugh. Ghosts don't eat or drink; but he did, so he melted some snow from the window sill and drank thirstily.

If Holbein and The Toad used this place for a clubhouse, they weren't careless enough to leave a sign. Despite the note Newell found in his pillowcase—a bid to *Self-Furtherance* like the one in Manuel's—he hadn't heard any more about The Society since then. Boys knew it was active in the period before Christmas vacation; and any underclassman would welcome a bid since this meant privileges, a place in the sun with elite seniors. Still nobody talked about it. Lately, since two boys had gone away and no one knew where, the students didn't thrill to rumors, secrets, ghost stories.

At nightfall, as a moonless darkness drew over the cabin, Newell played detective a moment. Kerosene lamp in hand, he went over the two rooms in search of a clue. One thing he meant to do was skim through old Ethridge yearbooks in the library. He just couldn't remember the details of a strange story he heard last year about an Ethridge master: something told by a counselor on the freshman dorm . . . But who came out here? Who used this secluded cabin and for what purpose? There weren't any crumbs, cigarette butts, signs of recent use that he could find. There weren't any notes in code; but only a few knives and forks with a gloss to them, like they never were used. On his way here he had found no footsteps in the newfallen snow, besides his own left on the way from the river.

Wait: there was a closet . . . Open it? Now he felt afraid; he hung back, staring at that closet door. What if—? What if, after all, they had brought the exchange student out here and overdone it: killed by mistake—and Manuel's skeleton, still dressed in a tweed suit, hung from a hanger in this closet? And the bony skull would grin at him, those black cavernous eyes stare out when he turned the knob . . . and opened the closet door?! Oh, c'mon, Newell, there's no dead body in that closet. Now be a man, and open it.

He didn't want to. He shied from knowing what was inside there, what horror he would have to spend the night with here in the cabin: since he could not go back out in the darkness, in sub-zero weather. No; he didn't want to open it, and know the secret. But was there a secret? Maybe. Maybe there was. For as a cozy fire warmed the cabin Newell began to sniff another scent beneath the perfume. It seemed to come from the walls: this tinge he had in his nostrils. What? A rancid smell, sort of restless, if you could say so, like something gone bad . . . He paused. He hung back a moment.

But he had to open, because he thought: Katya will not admire me
if I chicken out now.

Then he stepped forward, reached and turned the knob. And . . .
Did a dead boy come swinging, lurching out at him, Manuel's lifeless
body, Manuel's face ashen and decomposed, eaten by maggots? . . .
No, there was no body. But what Newell saw made him wonder.

One garment hung in the closet: a white sailor's pinafore with a
bib and blue trim.

Newell thought a moment and remembered. It belonged to Ethan
Jeffers.

XI

Newell's heart beat fast. Quietly, he closed the closet door, as
though he shut it on poor Jeffers. Backing away, Newell gave a yawn
and felt sleepy even despite the setting. It was clear he had the place
to himself, in the silence with only the wind's whoosh and moan,
some animal's call off in the night. He added a log in the crackling
fireplace; and, as the cabin warmed a bit more, a musty odor seemed
to come out of the woodwork, and grow stronger. There was no bathroom. Did people just go outside the door?

Yawning, he spread the army blankets out neatly and lay down on
the mattress. Of course he knew it wasn't wise to fall asleep here. But
what else could he do? So tired, so sleepy—he sat up again, reached
for the kerosene lamp and set it closer. What could happen when the
lamp, and fire in the other room, died down? Soon this lonely cabin
would fall in total darkness.

He was just so beat after Holbein's mad work detail, 'work-job' as
the senior called it; oh so dead to the world after tramping in the
snow to Cormac's where he got shut out, and then all the way here
to the island . . . Newell lay back again. Not even in his room at
school: how far away he was from his own room in Spring Glen—at
home, in the attic, where he felt so active and happy, into himself, he
just liked *to be* there—with his action games, his books, daydreams . . .
He thought of Katya with her dark smile, a witch's smile as her features got turned in, crimped, and her body tried to tell him a sad
fact. Why had she pressed his hand to her breast that day when they

got drunk on the floor at Cormac's? Why did she do this when she really loved Josey Kipnes and went to Josey's room on third floor Tildon?.. Also, whose light was it he had seen far down the river-bank? Was that Mingo trying to make it through the cold night? Mingo had high times when he drank the good stuff from pa of Corm's liquor cabinet. But now had come the era of Pullver, and good luck to you . . . As Newell hung on the verge of sleep, he saw his mom beckon and smile: Anne Gilbert said goodbye, hello or goodbye, going home or on a long, long journey . . .

After a few minutes the warmth, folded in sweet blankets, had him drifting off to sleep. The bad odor tweaked his nose, but it didn't matter anymore. Nothing did except sleep, this sense of Katya's arms . . . And so he slept.

XII

What time could it have been? How late? Past midnight?

The fifteen year-old boy lay sound asleep in the darkness. Then, like a fishing rod bent double, something yanked at him from the depths of the river . . . He heard a sound: creak, cre-e-eak! . . . This came first from a dream: rhythmic, as he reeled in a big one from be-neath the dark surface. It made his wrist ache as he reeled, as he yanked . . . creak, cre-e-eak! . . . The thing rose in the water. It was hooked . . . a fat yellow carp his friend Otto hauled one day from the Water Company in Spring Glen. And then he looked, and saw him-self reflected in its dead yellowish eye.

He awoke with a jolt.

By now the smell was bad, an acrid rot; though the fire had died, the cabin grown cold again.

Cre-e-eak . . . He was awake now. And that was real.

He sat up listening. All was black, so dark he couldn't see his hands. All silent, for miles around, except the creak, creak, like springs of a glider. Where was it? Very near . . . In the room where he slept? No, but inside the cabin. With him. Something was hap-pening, right here. But where? Could a rat or maybe a mole make such a sound: rhythmic, but heavy too, like a squeaky rocking chair?

Over and over, but not hurried, slow . . . as though controlled by someone's hand: creak, cre-e-eak.

Newell got up. He rose from the mattress, quietly, and reached for the kerosene lamp. Felt on the wood floor for the pack of matches—but paused, afraid to light one, afraid of what he might see. At any instant some disgustingly ugly thing, with a face like moldy biscuits, would jump out and grab him. And then his turn: Manuel, Jeffers, Newell Gilbert, missing.

Quietly he put on his shoes and tied the laces. He reached for his coat but didn't find it at once and was just too shaken up to get it on. Time to leave here—no matter the cold, the dark; no matter what. Yes, it was late; how much longer till dawn? On tiptoes he made to go in the other room. And still he heard it, closer now, ever so close, by his ear. Yes, now he knew he wasn't alone. He must flee the cabin and light out for the river; though it was still pitch black outside, and he might lose his way, run around in circles and turn into an icycle trying to make it back to school.

The grating sound went on. Same rhythm: the creak hardly varied. Nothing else stirred: the wind didn't whirr in the bare boughs now, or moan in the cabin chinks.

Newell snuck into the first room. There his eyes grew aware of a faint glow. Light from where? Above? He frowned and rubbed the sleep from his eyes. And then his heart leapt like a bird in a cage. He shuddered because there, in the dark, he saw a trap door opened from the ceiling. It hung down, like a flap of shadow cast by that dim light; and, alongside it, a ladder. So there was an attic, a storage space under the sloping roof. And that was no squirrel or raccoon trapped up there, making the eerie sound, over and over.

Holding his breath he moved to the ladder. What he wanted to do was run out the door and through the forest as far away from here as he could get. Wait: was the door still locked? What should he do: unlock the front door? or else go out the window as he came in?

It, the Beast, could be just up above him. With a candle. But what was it doing? What awful thing was going on up there? And, all the while, it hadn't grown aware a person lay sleeping in the other room? Didn't notice the fireplace had been used? a window broken? Maybe the Beast was dead, and only saw what it wanted?

With both hands Newell steadied the step ladder. And he thought: boy, you must be crazy, get the hell out of here. At the same time he wanted a look and felt drawn onto the first rung, then the next . . . In a few instants he would see the Beast of Ethridge, and know who it was. Third rung, fourth, his head almost to the opening . . . And then he must escape at once, without making a sound or being noticed, if he could. He must run back through the night, slip away and scoot down the riverbank, onto the iced-over surface of the Needing. Go back to campus where he would tell them what he had seen: all about the Beast of Ethridge. But would they—Headmaster Smithson and Dean Wart and Chaplain Geeter—would they believe?

XIII

Shivering with fear Newell raised a foot on the first rung of the ladder. At close range the flickering glow from above grew clearer and gave more light. He tried to take each step, sure to make some slight sound, in time with those creaks from the attic. Luckily he didn't have his coat on: his movements were freer.

Up he went: a fifth, sixth step, and then one more. He stretched his neck. His eyes just cleared the edge.

He saw. He peered up—at the long, broad form of the Beast of Ethridge. And this was when, by the light of a candle to one side, he saw the horror.

There was a child's swing set up beneath the slanting roof. Its poles took most of the attic space. Two boys were swinging. That is, they were being swung, pushed from behind by the same madman with a ravaged face who had given chase to himself and Cormac last fall.

The two boys on the swing went about their play somewhat stiffly. They weren't having much fun. One sort of half sat: his pelvis thrust up the way a child may squirm in a high chair, refusing to eat. Also, they were both dressed for classes, in white shirts starched stiff as themselves at the Laundry run by Astarte, the head custodian. And, even in playtime, both boys wore neckties.

Neither of the playmates looked like Manuel.

The first boy was pale, so pale. His body, not too athletic, had bloated until it seemed his cufflinks would pop off. Oh, the gaze was deep, deep, om-m-m-m . . . , with no white to the eyes but only a wormy, crawling darkness, merged in the shadows.

A charcoal gray suit hung loose on the second swinger's limbs. So loose, he must not be getting enough to eat: neither he nor the maggots he invited to dinner. The poor guy was all skin and bones, or only bones. But he looked more relaxed than his friend. Instead of a face he had a black and white photograph, in a frame, set above the buttoned collar and fastened on somehow. It was weird to see an old Ethridge yearbook photo blown up and used as a mask.

One, then the other, swung out right above Newell. Then back— they seemed to stare down at him. Forward again, looking far, far away, in space. Back: the first one's legs so rigid, bulged at the calves and thighs—his dark gaze went in orbit somewhere, far out in the night. That one's head looked shrunken, like a turnip: the features sunk into the skull, which jutted out, past the flesh.

Ethan Jeffers.

He still had an almost human look: a face more or less like the one he carried through his brief life. The wormy cheeks were ashen, but the forehead kept a bluish blotch. One eye had a yellow dot.

Newell wondered who the other boy could be. Had he ever seen him? Looking hard at that old class picture, that mask, he seemed to remember something, but not quite . . . What was it? A student died by a tragic accident. When? How? Was it the one in a tennis sweater: whose color photo hung outside Study Hall in Settlers? No, another. Well, who then? . . . He couldn't quite recall; but he must leaf through old yearbooks.

What a smell, phew! Down below the stench was kept in check by the cold, but up in the attic it was sickening. Hey, the Beast of Ethridge didn't seem to mind. You'd have thought he sat in a children's nursery filled with sunlight and flowers. Calmly, a smile on his gory face, he sat there and swung them in the dim light. Next he would start to sing: 'Frère Jacques, Frère Jacques, dormez-vous . . .?'

Back and forth, cre-e-eak! . . . back and forth, he pushed them with a tender note, to this horror, as if they were his own children, whose future he must look after.

XIV

For a long moment Newell frowned up at the two playmates. He held his breath.

But then suddenly the big man turned, sort of cranked his neck round, and seemed to come out of a spell. For an instant Newell met the flickering dark eyes of that murderer, who snapped to from his daydream.

Not a scream but a gasp, a cry of surprise, came from Newell who made the mistake of pushing backwards. The ladder swung back, tilted, and fell the other way across the cabin. By reflex Newell turned, as the ladder fell, but he banged forehead and shoulder against the stone hearth. He was out cold. He lay on the floor, as, from the trap door, the Beast of Ethridge looked over the edge: stared down at him, and knelt in position to hang before jumping. Spry movements for a zombie.

The student lay sprawled unconscious as the other, The Beast swung its big legs, body, in stages from the attic, hefted down, and made to let go.

A moment later Newell Gilbert, head ringing from the fall, woke to a groping hand on his shoulder. Opening his eyes he stared point-blank into that terrible, lifeless face. Then he screamed. He shrieked with all his might, and also spat. He spat in The Beast's ugly face; and, in the instant when it shook its head a little, turning away, Newell wriggled out of its stone cold grip.

He rolled over and his hand probed, in the darkness, for a poker he had used at the fireplace. He grabbed it and, swinging round, swiped the attacker who had reached out to grasp him: to pound him senseless again, kill him.

Thwack!

The Beast let out a low sort of yowl; you might almost think the dead feel pain. It was more like the surprise a Dean Wart would show, when a student had the gall to talk back and say: But, Sir! Maybe it wasn't pain. The Beast's cry had a dull note to it, of deadened senses. It shied, and fell back just a second. This gave Newell the chance to jerk away.

He got to his feet. And now he meant to hit the kidnapper again, for keeps, in the head, and try to finish him. He swung viciously, but the poker missed its mark, slipped from his grip and went clattering across the room.

The Beast rose toward him. On one knee, it held out both arms to catch this boy who dared come into its lair, and upset the order of things.

But Newell made a dash. He slipped past those outstretched arms, and dove for the broken window. There he knocked away the cushion wedged to block the cold wind, hoisted himself on the sill, and fell over, head first, into the snow.

Upstairs, the boys had stopped swinging.

XV

Into the arctic night he flew without a coat. He darted beneath tall ghostlike trees tinted with a first light of dawn. He tripped on a root, and fell in the snow; thought of the other on his heels by now, not fifty feet behind; got back on his feet, scampered further; ran smack into a tree trunk. He tottered, eyes rolling; and maybe now he would have fallen and given up the fight, except for his fear, and the attacker coming toward him with long strides, breathing deep and slow, if it did breathe. Panic kept him on his feet. Like the last time, in October: only now there was snow on the ground, and the air was so cold, so cold, in moments before daybreak. Arms held forward he ran on, and tumbled forward, and got up again. A branch scraped his face, neck; he felt a rough hand grab him from behind—and tore himself away with a last effort, and then lost his footing, arms and legs in a tangle, lost his balance and fell down, down from the high eroded riverbank and over the jutting roots and onto the ice.

Out.

But he came to. He got up again. Slipping and sliding, he cried, and ran.

Where to?

Only one place: his room, which didn't have a lock. Well enough The Beast knew its way to first-floor Warren.

He ran.

XVI

At the end of the hallway, hiccuping, trying to get control of himself, Newell beat on Pastor Geeter's doorway. No response. His faculty adviser must have gone away for the rest of the holiday.

—Sir! Please open! Sir!

Run and tell Headmaster Smithson? Oh, great: I went out to the island, Sir, I crossed the frozen river and went to the cabin and saw the Beast of Ethridge with two dead students, Sir! Ethan Jeffers and one other from long ago but only a skeleton now with a class photo instead of a face, Sir, but I didn't find Manuel the foreign exchange student out there . . . Why, of course. It sounds likely. The Headmaster would surely believe him; and admit such facts so helpful to Ethridge's reputation: Ethridge doing its utmost to avoid a scandal . . . Well then, what? Tell Glebe? Tell Sippel? Runt Roentgen? Tell any of the masters? Who would believe such a tale? Who would stand up for him and take his side? Would his own father even do it? Yes, that's why they brought him home to enjoy a warm Christmas in Spring Glen, no matter what Dean Wart and the Headmaster and Geet the Geet said about his behavior.

Maybe he should write a note and give it to the town police:

YOU WILL FIND TWO MISSING
ETHRIDGE STUDENTS, BUT NOT MANUEL,
IN A CABIN ON THE ISLAND WHERE
THE NEEDING RUNS PAST THE SCHOOL.
THERE IS A FRANKENSTEIN TYPE
MONSTER OUT THERE WITH THEM.
TOGETHER THEY ARE PLAYING AND
SWINGING ON A SWING IN THE ATTIC.

Good! Everyone would believe that. Why, they would come and get him, and take him to the nearest mental ward. Then he might never get home again.

Newell went to a student room in Nye House, across the quad, and lay down for awhile. Later that morning he walked to the Infirmary. He had a high fever.

He slept. He lay quietly beneath the covers. He drank juice, and glasses of milkshake a nurse brought him; and thought. No, he wouldn't tell the fond Geeter whom he couldn't trust any more than the others. He wouldn't even tell Cormac; or his roommate Bernard who didn't want to hear it anyway; or Big Schmied too in love with Ramona Glebe to hear what you said to him. The only person he might tell, since he did need to tell someone, was Shellnitz. Oh, how nice: scare him to death too? . . . No, Shellnitz didn't scare, even though he–if not Newell himself–was next on the list.

The day before students came back from Christmas vacation, Newell returned to first floor Warren and found his coat, which he had left behind in his flight from the cabin, lying on his bed.

In the coat pocket was an envelope Cormac had placed in his hand, as Pullver came like a Dracula in uniform along the front hall to end their chat.

Newell read:

–'To Whom It May Concern: Let me tell you a thing or two about a girl I know. She has black frizzy hair, black eyes, high cheekbones, and a secret. A secret? Read on to find out. You may also see a book called *What the Creature Knew About Spence,* if you want more info . . . Well, this secret–you may call it a riddle–drew responses from far, far away, and she did not always know herself. (She wasn't too bright, you see, oops.) Well, the girl's parents parted ways. Then her mother died. So she went to live with her father, a Wall Street person, but he sent her away to a school in Switzerland. (I forgot to mention how she and her little sister, Anne Pia, liked to stay up late at night and hold séances.) So at the school in Rolle this secret girl fell in love with a boy, not a student but a foreign worker, and they–well, you know how it is, oops. Then, each time, after . . . you know . . . she got sad and didn't know what to do with herself. Please note: only kind people may read this theme paper. Well, it didn't work out with the boy. Ha ha. So her dad said to her: let's try a finishing school, so you can get finished. And now I am at Bartlett Academy. Where to next? . . . I made a friend or two at least, but the same thing goes on here too, like with Spence, you know. The story doesn't have an end yet, but once in a while I think: Wouldn't it be swell to have a place to go for Christmas–Phyllis's is 2nd best–and feel happy for once?'

Chapter Six

I

The snow fell. The students crammed for exams. Snow, snow: a sweet freshness in the air, a scent of Canadian forests. Midyear exam week.

Newell Gilbert lay in bed. He had one eye on a math equation he wouldn't ever solve; one eye on a dime novel, the life and loves of a hood; and a third eye on his slightly opened window and the dark night outside. This Beast of Ethridge stuff had done his normal good spirits a bad turn, not to say his wits. He was a healthy well-balanced kid when he left Spring Glen to come up here, but you can only take so much. And so he gave a lurch at the slightest creak in the Warren hallway. He shot his glance and saw a pale, worm-eaten face in the darkened window: his own, reflected there. And be sure the room-mate, Bernard, had had his fill of The Beast too: after Newell held a meeting and told his few friends, Berneth, Schmied, Boz Krips from Carlyle House, Shellnitz, what happened when he went out to the cabin. Newell had always been one to fool around; so whether they believed such a story was open to question. Maybe The Newb had spent too much time alone during the holidays. Lococito, as Manuel would say. But if what Newell told was true–then worse, a hundred times worse. Steer clear! In any event Big Bern was spooked and went to ask Geeter for a move to another room. Denied. Now he spent any free time in the science lab.

Newell took this amiss. He felt sorry to see his roommate not in Category III, the frank and honest ones, but rather in II, the conformists, thinking of themselves. Lemme' alone!

One evening the two boys walked back from the Refectory before evening study hall. Turning on the light, in their room, Newell gave a start.

On his bed lay a mitten, knitted for him by his little sister, which had fallen from his coat pocket during the night out in the cabin. First the coat, now a mitten.

—A thoughtful Beast, said Newell. Brought it to me.

Without a word Bernie took up his books and left. He had a standing pass from Master Sippel, amazed by the boy's scientific aptitude, to spend time in the Science Lab.

New rumors flew around campus.

II

In the morning students made their way along the walkway toward Geeter's chapel talk. The winter sun spread a carpet of gold across snow fallen during the night.

The custodian, Astarte, was hard at it. He shovelled off walkways, driveways, the steps in front of Settlers and the Refectory; while the town sent out a snow truck to clear the winding road across the meadow, the front drive and service road. Snow drifted chest high beneath the eaves, and out along the Senior Path. Snow sparkled amid the bluish early morning shadows. There was an unseemly hint about the Ethridge custodian, when he raised his head from the task, and gave you a toothy smile. Sandy hair neatly brushed in a wave with hair oil; a bit gangly, with a few freckles, angular features and Adam's apple: Astarte had played some basketball in his day. But now, Newell felt, there was something not quite right about him, as he watched you pass by. He looked lonely, an adult flit.

Inside, the chapel vestibule was overheated. Boys pattered their feet and left streaks on the linoleum.

−Oh ho! said the junior Warnickie. I just gotta' ace trig. If I don't get a bid to *Self-Furtherance*, I'll die!

Warnickie was showing off: such a flit, it made you shake your head.

Holbein's secret society was all the rage since underclassmen began to get bids in their pillowcases. All sorts of rumors went around campus. If you got in *Self-Furtherance* you would also get a . . . kiss, etc., from Ramona Glebe.

−What makes you so hot?−said sophomore Royall Lambert, for whom the term 'flit' was high praise. The Lamb and Granny Zammet were roomies on Newell's floor.

Yes, bids to *Self-Furtherance* were all the rage. With one of those you were among the elite, the chosen few. There would be privileges. You could hobnob with the famous Jon Holbein, the colossal Toad, the haughty Rhodes, the All-American square MacDonald. Faculty members, plus your flitty peers, saw you with other eyes; as you became rich in a thing so rare at Ethridge: respect. Hell, it was better than a letter sweater.

But get a load of Geet the Geet this morning. He's pretty worked up! Go, Geetie: get off your rocks from the pulpit.

−And didn't stress, lads . . . didn't pressure to perform help Joseph find out the fine and godly power within himself? And didn't dear boys . . . didn't Saul suffer a sort of anxiety attack, nay a nervous breakdown! during his great midyear exam along the road to Damascus?

It was a weird sort of pep talk, thought Newell Gilbert, to be giving students during a week filled with three-hour ordeals. But we must say about our hero that he was not doing well at this point. He didn't study, but only reread his dime novels, *Knock on Any Door*, *Reefer Kid*, and *The Amboy Dukes*. After his shock out on the island he drew into himself, more and more, and walked across the quad now with his head hung down again. He felt so alone. He couldn't explain to a soul among those faculty members who sat in judgment and so airily took away his Christmas vacation−not to them, and not even to his own parents. Runt Roentgen liked to say about a boy's parents: If you don't stand up for them, who will? . . . And, among his classmates, only Shellnitz−who adored Newell−stuck by him and tried to rally his spirits. The others didn't want to hear any more about the Beast of Ethridge: Boz Krips so strong in sports and so weak, like a wounded person, in life; Schmidlap such a sap, too deep in masturbatory fantasies to care; Bernie-Bern busy saving himself for great things, like Galileo from the Inquisition. No, Newell moped. He felt himself under attack. And good luck to you, when you feel this way, and Shellnitz is your psychiatrist.

Geeteth:

—For, dear young lads, we must come . . . come somehow to savor our trials, like oysters on a silver tray!

Around the stuffy chapel, the radiators hissed a little. Then came the train whistle as it went over the railroad bridge. Oh, would this Beast of Ethridge nightmare ever end? Would he see his own room at home again, and feel so good in its familiar scent: there with his toys, books, action games, pennants on the walls, old radio for Friday Night Fights, bratty sisters, brother Joey, friends Otter and Thaddy? With his dog, backyard, bicycle, all Spring Glen his oyster?

After Geeter outdid himself—oysters on a silver tray? now really—the congregation sang:

> *For all the saints*
> *Who from their labors rest . . .*

Then the 'dear young lads' filed out toward the next three-hour test. Maybe they felt more like convicts, despite their charcoal gray suits and neckties, than tomorrow's leaders.

III

After exam week the campus was astir with bids here, there, to the Society for Self-Furtherance. Newell held onto his from before the holidays: when would he be called to a flitty swearing-in ceremony? By now there were a number of new bids; though it wasn't easy to learn which boys got them. Rare the guy who would blab when each note said clearly: Show this to nobody. Newell thought the arch-flits Kemeny and Sedgewick, both in the 'envious and telltale' category, must be among the lucky. You saw them whisper to one another with a knowing look, a little smirk. What flits, those two juniors, Holbein's suck-ups. Also, Newell knew two freshmen had gotten bids, 'Dippy' Romulo, and Little Mallet, since Ramlet told him so. And then Shellnitz got a bid.

Lately Newell had been worried about The Owl, and amazed by his behavior. Shellnitz *had it in for* Coach Roentgen; and he went after him; he took it to the gymnasium dictator; he did what he could to be the bane of The Runt's life. In the gym, at the Refectory Shellnitz waited for Coach and then went into his act. For one thing he mimicked him in front of everyone: The Shell, scrawny, with a chirpy voice, stuck out his paunch and made slobbery grunts. In gym class he would do it: bellow at the other boys and slap hours on them. What a card! Look at him go into his act, and laugh at Master Roentgen. Puffed up, strutting like a cock, Shellnitz stepped from the line and, without a smile, right in front of The Runt, started to roar like 'Thor! God of Thunder!' as he called him. Yes, he called the poor man names. He insulted him to his face. You'll recall Coach Roentgen had lost a finger to a lawn mower. Well, Shelly liked to point *with the missing finger* at a boy, and scream:

—Young vandal! Ten hours!

Shellnitz had fastened onto his victim. He irked that pompous man. He stung him like a gadfly where it hurt the most: his vanity. Shellnitz ridiculed Runt the Runt, and then paid the price, which could be severe. During gym class one morning Runtie made his nemesis 'shimmy the rope'.

—Ten times to the top knot!

In other words: until Shellnitz's hands blistered. But Shell the Shell, who had a wiry strength, and a mad courage, kept going up the rope, up, up, until he reached steel ceiling supports high above the gym floor. What's worse, what took everybody's breath away, he swung on the rope like a blond monkey, and, *letting it go,* grasped a girder in the nick of time. He hung there a moment before pulling himself up to a perch. Very scary. Headmaster Smithson and Pastor Geeter were called to the scene and had to plead with the boy to come back on down and 'rejoin the human race'. This went on for some time: Shelleth way up there, laughing, enjoying himself at Coach Roentgen's expense. He screeched for the fun of it, like a little chimpanzee, as, outside the gym, police arrived from town, then a fire truck, then a child psychologist all the way from the city. When it was over, hours later, the psychologist went with Shellnitz to the Infirmary. She asked him:

–Don't you think we care about you?

–He doesn't.

–Who?

–Runt.

–Who?

–Runt of the Runteths. Coach Roentgen. He wouldn't let Newell Gilbert try out for basketball without gym shorts.

–Don't you need shorts to play in a gym?

–Shows how much you know. Call yourself a psychologist and you don't know anything. The Runt isn't nice. He's mean. I can't see why he took it into his head to work with boys, when he hates us.

–He doesn't hate you. He's trying to do what he thinks best.

–Oh, hell.

Shellnitz looked away. He gave up on the child psychologist. But she said:

–Not everybody is your mother.

Shellnitz thought this over a minute. Then he sort of bucked his head, and said more to himself:

–Aw, yer' mudder eats fertilizer.

And that was that. End of conversation. He wouldn't respond to her questions, her softer, caring voice, like 'Quicksand' Geeter's. That's what he nicknamed Geeter: Quicksand.

Soon as Shellnitz got out of the Infirmary, the duel went on. Roentgen stared daggers at Shellnitz, and Shellnitz put thumb and index to his mouth and whistled shrilly in Roentgen's face. Mercilessly Roentgen gave it back, and Shellnitz looked pretty ragged after the gym class—which was hardly a class anymore: but rather a spectacle, as Shellnitz made cracks, acted out, bent over and had a belly laugh at Roentgen; and Roentgen leaned on the boy more, and more, with calisthenics, with fifty laps round the gymnasium, *roll a marble with your nose* the length of the basketball court and back again. And Shellnitz did these things, to the letter. He didn't do them because he had to, but because he wanted to, while the other boys looked on. Maybe he just liked to be the center of attention. Maybe he sopped up *any* attention, no matter how cruel, even from the hated Runt Roentgen. Hey, maybe he liked to suffer–'take it, and dish it out' he said–and by going the whole hog seem to win versus his enemy; put the poor man in a bad light; show the tyrant for what he was. Yes, Shellfish was as pitiless, in his way, as 'Clump' Roentgen. That's what he nicknamed this one: Clump. Shellnitz made a farting sound with his lips in lieu of a hello, when their paths crossed along the quad. He said to the Ethridge Athletic Director's face:

 —You bag of hot air.

Such a remark did not jibe with the Ethridge code. But Shellnitz didn't seem to care. Bashful, head hung like his hero Newell, Shellnitz—or Shellklutz as Master Sippel called him—went about campus with that uneven walk of his: hunched forward, a cuff rolled over one ankle, sort of humpy, ever forward. He was the lowest of the low, but he didn't mind taking on the highest of the high, Coach Roentgen, or Headmaster Smithson for that matter; and he would say to God Almighty, if he felt like it:

 —You can't fight your way out of a wet paper bag.

And yet they didn't expel him. Why? His dad was a partner at House of Chalmers on Wall Street, a major donor. Baby-sitting at these rates is good work if you can get it: even with a bad seed like Roddy Shellnitz.

And then, in early February, came Shelleth's tour of dining hall duty. As luck would have it, he must serve at The Runt's table.

 —What may I get for Your Excellency?

 —Black coffee—said Runteth, working his lips.—Full cup, no saucer.

This was Ethridge tradition. After dinner boys brought masters their coffee—the hot liquid filled to the brim. Then all eyes watched as a lad came slowly through the swinging out-door from the kitchen: would he spill a drop? The 'no saucer' was a sadistic little touch by Roentgen: to scald the boy's hands. Well, in this instance a loud crash was heard: so many plates broken, it made you think of Ben Bolt's dumping the Refectory silverware in the Pond. There was applause across the dining hall.

After a moment Shellnitz came out. Despite the crash he used the wrong door: the *in*-door. There you have him: he goes on with it, he wants to have his way no matter what. At sight of him, the flit, more applause. But what had happened in the kitchen? The poor kid didn't look too good, doused with hot liquid, ooh! Well, it serves him right. Didn't he bring this on himself by using the wrong door? Knowing Shellnitz, how perverse he is—don't you think he did it on purpose? Plus he bugs our good, our kind Master Roentgen all the time, and makes the man's life a curse.

But there was something wild in Shelly's aspect as he neared Coach's table. His hands were red, red, burned by spilled coffee. And his face was pink, pink; he looked serious for once. Filled full, no saucer,—Shellnitz's hands, arms, body shook as if *he* might flow over. And he moved toward Runt the Runt. And that scorching liquid had become a weapon.

Shellnitz's high fluty voice had a tremor, as more drops spilled on his blistered hands.

—Sir, I brought your coffee.

He paused. And Roentgen's face had a note of fear. Would this young fool douse him with hot coffee? Would Shellnitz, a law unto himself, do something foolish? Take revenge?

—Okay, put it down. Have a seat.

—Sir—Shellnitz's glistening hands tried to hold the cup steady, not spill a drop—Sir, you should have let Newell try out for the team that time, when he came with long pants.

—I said I run basketball tryouts, not you!

Shellnitz paused, pink-faced, and held the coffee cup over Roentgen's pink balding pate.

—Badly, Sir, you do it badly. He's as good as Caldermann.

—He is not.

—We'll never know. But even if he isn't, you should have let him try out.

—That's not your affair. Now stop standing over me.

—Every kid deserves a chance.

—. . .

Slowly, Shellnitz lowered the cup in front of Coach. He met his eye. And he said:

—Sir?

—Sir what?

Roentgen gave him the evil eye.

—You're what my old man used to call a 'nyuhnyuh'.

—Come again?

—A first class nyuhnyuh.

Shellnitz put down the cup, spilling not a drop on Coach, and went to his place. He moved the dessert dish away and bowed his head on folded arms. Maybe he was crying, his head turned away from Roentgen at the center of the table; you heard Shelleth sniffle a little. What he needed was the Infirmary, since his hands were inflamed. He laid his small blond head on the table that way, contrary to proper etiquette, because he felt nauseous. Well, Roentgen said nothing about the Infirmary, but only pressed his lips.

−Stop it, Shellnitz. Do your chore.

−Nyuhnyuh.

−I may be a nyuhnyuh, but you, sir, are a shirker.

IV

Self-Furtherance was all the rage. Those underclassmen tapped for it moved through classes, athletics, evening study hall, waiting for word of initiation rites. Meanwhile the elite seniors, Holbein and company, asked certain boys to their special table in the Refectory. Seated with The Bossman and Paul Rhodes, Josey, Tim MacDonald, The Toad, were a few young flits who didn't look too at home.

A spell of cold weather came, New England in February, and lingered. Snowdrifts from exam period looked gray beneath a murky sky, as a thin snow fell through the day. Winter plodded across the calendar in snowshoes.

More than once Geeter joined the *Self-Furtherance* men for dinner. Another time it was Ramona Glebe without her husband: explain that one! Astarte, the head custodian, came to join the fun. Also, Rivington Wart dropped by, though briefly; he did not sup with them.

Then, one evening the first week of March, there were murmurs round the wide dining hall. Whisperings, stares. It was an event. Katya, that Bartlett Girl, came in on Josey Kipnes' arm, and the two made their way toward the *Self-Furtherance* table. They entered beneath the clock on Tildon House side while the student body watched. For this girl, or young woman, made Ramona Glebe look dumpy. Not a blubberball like la Ramona, but truly statuesque, she was stunning in red velvet with a strand of pearls on her breathtaking corsage. Her jet black hair was done up in a bun; a fringe of ringlets on flushed temples framed the oval of her exotic face. There was a sort of wild tenderness in Katya's dark eyes.

She and Josey made quite a couple, as, ladylike, she took her place between him and Tim MacDonald, the Senior Class President. MacDonald, a buttoned-down achiever, came from Scottish lineage associated with Ethridge School beginnings. His friends called him The Squire; others, The Square.

Then a bottle of red wine made the scene—not home brewed with yeast like Bernie-Bern's, but imported, the good stuff, la-de-dah! What a shame Mingo couldn't be here to taste it. He would do it justice. The Ming hadn't sipped such vintage wine since his days at Yale when he attended seminars in the Temple Bar. But oh! what a new age must be on the way if spirits were served in the Refectory.

Ooh, aah. A sigh of wonder greeted Katya's arrival.

One of the waiters, freshman Owen Crinshaw, a bug-eyed flit, shot a glance back at her, and lost control of his overloaded tray. Just at that moment another lad—you guessed it, Shellnitz—came out the in-door, and a huge collision was heard. The crash was long, as plates, glasses, dessert dishes cascaded and broke into bits. Hourrah! That Shellnitz should become a stunt man when he grows up, if he ever does. But you know what, Reader? I don't think he ever will.

A few tables away from where Katya sat, Big Schmied gave Newell an elbow and said:

—Look! Thar' he blows.

V

Headmaster Smithson had just come in the Refectory—drawn here by Katya? Beneath the big clock he paused, took in the crowd of faces, and gave a nod. Laurence Smithson looked like—I don't know a better way to say it—like a rich man's Charlie Chaplin. Same brushed hair, same chewy mustache though with a bit of gray; same jaunty air about him even while he liked to mug it up and act like one of the boys. He sought a humble pose, a good way to relate to students, but he was not humble. He was elitist. The Ethridge Headmaster tried to be down-to-earth, but he was patrician to the gills. When it came down to it: a snob. This two-facedness was known to boys who had been around: for example, Virgil Parker who lived in the gym, and couldn't stand Headmaster Smithson any more than he could Pastor Geeter. Yet The Virg was unfair, because Smithson was more complex than Geetie.

For one thing the current man at the helm lent a strong contrast to the last one, Headmaster Castlereagh, who held the post for forty-minus-one (as the Bible says) years. The Castle was a man from the old school so typical of his generation of New England headmasters. They made a gang of perfect unfallen Adams in their prep school paradises.

Headmaster Castlereagh, Mister Ethridge: upbeat as a frosty day in January; cordial, cold, narrow, right witty, above all effective; the compleat pragmatist when it came to getting them into Yale, Harvard and Princeton, like robots in neckties. Had the good Castlereagh's heart ever beat for the weaker man? the underdog? the worker? No. He was arrogance itself except for his own class, and those who had the luck and sense to gain entry. Self-righteous as hell the instant any boy's mood, let alone behavior, showed the least bit of originality, which he called 'deviation': Castle got piffed when anything squeaked in the well-oiled routine. Well, long live Master Castlereagh.

Headmaster Smithson was not like this. Smitty liked to concern himself with a boy in trouble. Not a Ben Bolt of the greasy d.a. perhaps, but a Sackler, a Jeffers, a Royall Lambert, superflits, he would invite to dinner at Needing Inn in town. Then he sat talking with them in his car: after he had pulled up in the Homestead driveway, and turned off the lights. Oh yes, he could take an interest, and raise a boy's spirits.

Bred and dressed like an Etonian thoroughbred, the Ethridge Headmaster had fine features tinged with gray, but softer, less rugged than Dean Wart's. He carried an air of influence, a worldliness brought to this secluded school from the boardrooms of corporate America. He had spent two decades helping to make big financial decisions (this ended not long after his wife's death). And then Ethridge School, where he had served the past seven years, became a toy in this big boy's hands. He needed a pastime. Still vigorous, capable, he went along toward later age with a twinkle in his eye.

If we had to sum Laurence Smithson up in a phrase, it would be: noblesse oblige.

VI

From a few tables away Newell Gilbert saw a shadow seem to pass over the Headmaster's gaze: when he nodded and said hi to the beautiful girl from Bartlett. Didn't he like women? Katya had charmed everyone at the *Self-Furtherance* table, and indeed across the

Refectory, with its community of faculty and students. The place came alive. And poor Ramona, Glebeth's consort for life, now sat in her proper niche; she looked more or less like what she was, a lump. True, an ample lump, but a lump.

Newell looked at the Headmaster. And, as he did so, a knot in his stomach seemed to tighten. It had been there, in his gut, since the night he spent out on the island, inside the lonely cabin, where he saw ghastly things he didn't want to speak of, think of, repeat. He felt so alone in the knowledge that an awful thing had been done—was still being done, and hushed up, here at Ethridge—that he tried to blot the facts from his mind. But he couldn't. His nerves took up those facts, and acted on their own, and gave him an ache. Yes, the worst had been done: at least one boy's murder, Ethan Jeffers'. And it could, it would be, again. So when Newell stared across the dining hall at Headmaster Smithson, a man so in control, so impeccable on every level—it seemed hard to imagine *him* as the Beast of Ethridge. And yet Newell did. In his mind he dressed the dapper man up in haircloth, old clothes, a death mask, and thought he saw a likeness in bearing and gait. Headmaster Laurence Smithson as the Beast of Ethridge! Surely you jest. And yet that might explain, at least in part, how the thing was hidden from view for so long: two disappeared students; and how Ethridge business could go on as usual even while the school's very existence was threatened. The Headmaster loved boys? His repressed instincts finally went off the deep end? And now by day he ran one of the country's most select private schools, but by night he turned into a werewolf. Did it fit? Yes? No? Was it Smithson? Was it Geeter? Geet the Geet? Could it be? Or Runt the Runt? Dean Wart ? Was it Sippel who done it? The science teacher a bit too caught up in his experiments? Who did the grisly act? Was it Astarte the custodian? Bill Hastings, the Ethridge cook, serving up Manuel as cornbeef hash? Which one of them? thought Newell. Lord, preserve us from these masters. What a crew. And: my parents will disown me if I don't behave, and make my grades. Will I ever make it out of this place alive? Will I ever go home?

VII

A chandelier overhung the Refectory, while elegant lights, like gaslights, shone on the long wall between high arched casements. Beyond, in an aura of lamplit snow, the Senior Path extended in shadows toward a lit up Settlers Hall. Squibs of light reflected over the snow from antique lanterns.

Newell gazed out those high windows into the wintry darkness; then back at Katya and Josey, Headmaster Smithson, Holbein and the others. His mind was in a riot.

Schmied spooned a tiny nip from his dessert dish, prolonging his Hastings pudding, like a little chunk of turd, but sweet. Schmied said:

—Looks funny to me.

—What does?

—Something going on.

Katya smiled at the Headmaster; she made some remark, and all laughed. MacDonald and Rhodes laughed. The Toad laughed, sort of; his squashed features, his head full of Toadness, tussled with a cackle. Josey smirked. Josey had swallowed a mouse.

Newell turned his gaze away. He couldn't watch them. If she was Josey's girl then why did she run after himself and Shellnitz on the road to town that Saturday? And why did she press his hand to her breast when they were on the floor at Cormac's? Newell, in his thoughts, stared at lamplight on the blue expanse of snow. He felt a tension: in the pit of his tomach but also over there, at the senior table. Something going on . . . He heard the voice of Katya, her sensuous laugh, but it didn't sound right. For a moment he felt low-down and jealous, angry at her, and he couldn't look.

The Headmaster's presence made for a merry time. But under the chatter there was a tension; and, though Josey Kipnes still grinned, he looked ill at ease. Katya raised her voice in an offhand tone, and eyed her lover. What did it mean? The senior table grew quieter, as the week's waiters went about their chore: through the swinging indoor, then out again.

But then Schmiddeth's eyes went wide. He poked Newell:

—See that?

Katya was on her feet and staring down at Josey. She might have been on stage, in an opera: her pose so grand, her eyes fiery.

Brusquely she turned from them and moved, stumbling, righting herself, toward the foyer. All eyes watched as she opened the door and swung herself through.

Now Josey Kipnes had a frown on his handsome face; and, standing up he traded a glimpse with the Headmaster.

Newell sat forward in his chair, and said:

—Sick to my stomach, Schmidikins. Tell him.

—Oh, okay.

Newell nodded at Master Sippel who sat talking with the senior Marendl, also called 'The Tyke', about an Eastern wood peewee he had sighted this winter; about birdseed, and greedy bluejays which he couldn't refrain from calling Cyanocitta Cristata. Marendl was charmed.

—Gotta' go—said Newell; and he slipped away from the table.

VIII

Up ahead he heard their steps beneath the archway.

On the Tildon portico Katya moved through a patch of lamplight: in such a fury, she hadn't taken her coat. Where was she going? Off beyond Settlers the moon was rising. The evening sky, clear and very cold, was filled with stars.

Katya slowed her pace. She could hear Josey's steps behind her.

Newell stepped down from the walkway, so they wouldn't see him; he went along half-crouching in the snow.

Then Josey broke into a trot and caught up with her by the last column before the chapel. He grabbed her arm, but she drew away as if she meant it. Katya had snapped; she looked dishevelled, wild. They struggled a moment, as Josey held her at arm's length, and shook her.

—That's right, he said. Be a little fool: you think I care?

—Go back to Holbein.

—No way.

—Dammit, let me go!

She wrenched free.

—You're wrong about Jon, he said.

—Josey-Josey, pocket full of poseys.

Katya laughed, shrill. She stood there shivering, her face half lit by lamplight. She resisted tears: oh, if he could just say a tender word to her . . . He said casually:

–You better come back inside.

–No, I won't–her tone was low, a warble, her features contorted.– There's something missing in you, Josey.

–Righto, my custard.

In the background the Refectory murmured. Spoons clicked on dessert plates. Newell hung back by a pillar, out of view.

The Bartlett girl said:

–It's so easy for you. All you have to do is smile, and then–

–You spread your legs.

–Tst.

–Sorry.

Her hair was mussed. Her features looked out of kilter. She stood arms folded trying to control the trembling. It wasn't her beauty Newell saw so much as the look in her eyes. She was in some sort of trouble. She needed help.

–Go ahead. Your master calls.

–What's the use?

Josey shrugged.

–Someday maybe you'll grow up, but I don't think so.

–It's cold.

–No, it's warm, she said, and started to cry.

–I'm going back.

–Go.

–You're not coming in?

Katya paused. Then she said, in a broken voice:

–N-no. Leave me out of it, do you hear?–Then, to his back:– You're a coward, Josey Kipnes.

IX

He left her there. Arms folded, shoulders shaking, Katya turned toward the Settlers entry.

–Wait up.

She looked back with a frown. She saw no one. But a shadow,

curved on the last column of the walkway, gave her a start. Who had
heard them?

—Someone there?

—Just me. You okay?

—Huh?

She stared at Newell as if she didn't know him.

—Gee, you don't have a coat on.

He came forward, a bit hesitant, but dared to touch her shoulder.
Then he managed to coax Katya inside Settlers with its clanking radiators.

—I feel dizzy, she said.

He guided her. And then, together, they went in the chapel and
sat side by side in the last pew. In front, above the altar, a gleam of
light played. The pew creaked beneath its cushion as Katya sat. She
breathed in starts.

—What's going on? he said. What was that all about?

—Nothing. Josey's a—

—A what?

—Skunk.

She laughed, like a spasm, and brushed back a tress of black hair.
She sniffled.

—Gee, sorry things turned out that way—said Newell, and he
meant it, almost.

He felt her closeness in the sudden warmth. Her hair touched his
brow as he leaned to catch her low, throaty words.

She said:

—If I asked you to go somewhere with me—would you go?

—Y-yes.

—It might not be nice.

—Why not?

—It might be ugly. Even against the law.

—Really? My dad is so fed up with me. Last chance, he told me.
And: you burned your bridges, boy. But I don't care, I'll go with you.

Katya, trying to get control of herself, gave a little laugh:

—What will he do?

—I don't know. Send me somewhere else. It couldn't be worse
than this.

—No.

—I'll go with you, said Newell.

They sat in silence. He felt her shoulder against his own, and stared straight ahead. He didn't feel jealousy now, as he had back in the Refectory; but only love for Katya and a desire to stand by her come what may. It was awkward when he lifted his arm around her shoulder, and tried to comfort her. She was older, more mature, as they always said about girls; but she was also crying softly, like rain in springtime, and she hung her head, and didn't seem to notice the arm. After a minute he took it back.

–Even if, she murmured, I told you–

–What?

–That I'm going to . . .

Her voice trailed off. She leaned forward, her forehead on the next pew, and sobbed. But she sort of bucked. She threw up her head and stared at him through glazed eyes. Newell felt her emotion enter him, and go tingling along his spine.

Up front the lamplight from outside, with its spidery shadows, hovered over the choir and altar. Now dinner hour was drawing to a close: in a moment the students would drift this way, across the quad toward evening study hall.

She sighed deeply, and fought for control.

–If I hate him, I might as well hate myself. He's made me pregnant.

–He what?

–I'm going to have his baby.

–Gosh.

Newell's jaw dropped. The idea was so enormous, pregnant without being married, he drew back into himself a moment. Beside him Katya trembled, and made small, pained sounds. He thought she was waiting for him to recover, and say something else. So he said:

–During vacation I had to stay here. It was bad, but I won't tell you about it now. To keep my spirits up I daydreamed how we, you and me, lived in a farmhouse. We adopted some orphan kids.

They sat together, heads bowed, in the quiet darkness.

A pair of voices were heard along the walkway.

–Rotten deal, she said, and cried softly.

–Does Josey know?

–Nobody knows, not even Phyllis. Only you. And you're not to tell Cormac, or Shellnitz. Nobody.

–I won't, but you should tell Josey,–Newell paused; he frowned, in thought; then said:–We could get married. Will you?

At this she gave a chuckle, and hiccuped.

–Too young. They wouldn't give us a license.
–We'll go somewhere, Canada, and live together. I'll work.
Katya turned and looked in his eyes.
–You can't get work yet.–She patted his shoulder.–No; when you're eighteen, or after college . . . if you still love me.
She leaned, and kissed him on the lips.
–I'll love you.
She wiped a tear with her finger, and drew a breath. Her face relaxed a little. She looked around, as if realizing where she was.
–I hope God didn't hear all this.
Katya gave a laugh, and brushed away tears. She sniffled and laughed low.
Newell took out his handkerchief, inspected it, and handed it to her.
–Here.
–A gentleman–she said, with a glance at the hanky. She sighed.–That's what I want, in a future husband . . . Will you walk me home?
–Sure. Here, take my coat, or you'll be cold.
–No, go get mine. I left it in the vestibule.
–You'll wait here for me?
–Sure.
Katya gazed up wistfully at the altar.

X

In a rapture he went trotting off toward the dining hall. Two seniors chatted along the walkway in front of Hampton.
–Gotta' go, Gilbert?
–The sophomore needeth to pee.
He skipped along and nearly fell on a slippery spot.
Then he burst in the side entrance of the Refectory and scanned an empty foyer. Not there, no more overcoats. No suede one with a silk lining and fur collar. So Josey took it to his room in Tildon to keep for her. Go ask him for it? . . . Sure thing.
The week's waiters raised their heads from cleaning tables as Newell sprinted the length of the dining hall leaving his tracks.

—Hot date, eh? said one.

—Ramona waits, said a second. She swoons!

Then he broad jumped a puddle and landed slip-sliding on the Warren House patio. From his closet he took another coat he had, grabbed a sweater from the chest of drawers, and flew out again. Back through Settlers toward the chapel he ran, so fast his sides ached. A few underclassmen paused along the first-floor corridor by the study hall. Across from *that* door they stood: the one to the Steam Tunnel which ran beneath the school.

At the chapel he stopped short, gasping for breath. He opened, peered into the darkness, and saw—no one. Where was she? Lying down on the pew? He went the length of the center aisle, and whispered:

—Katya?

No response. A bough scraped: outside the high window behind the altar.

She wasn't there. She hadn't waited for him.

Where to?

He stood before the altar with the second coat over his arm. Then he turned and scooted back through Settlers, out across the front circle: past the Homestead where the Headmaster lived, with its plaque: Built in 1708 by Roderick Etherege, a Puritan judge.

Newell ran down the slow incline toward where the Needing made its wide bend around the school. A pale sliver of moon sailed in the night sky out over the bleak meadow. Dimly he saw the tall trees of the island. Wind whispered in the icy boughs, in the frozen reeds by the river.

XI

Later that night he lay in bed and couldn't get to sleep. Bernard and he didn't talk much to each other these days; they no longer shared things; and Bernie had spoken to Geeter again about wanting his own room. Now, sometime after midnight, the hall clock ticked, pretty loud, every few minutes.

Was it the wind moaning in window casements? in the old woodwork? Another bad night . . . sleeplessness. The loneliness was there, a presence in the room with him: ever since the night he spent out at the cabin and saw—what he saw.

And now, again, he heard the murmurings: from down below the floorboards. Maybe there were ghosts along the tunnel that ran under the student houses? They moaned, they whined like wind in the skeletal trees by the Needing. Beneath his pillow voices lisped some secret about the past; they buzzed round his ears on the verge of sleep. Oh, there seemed to be so many of them, and he was alone; he wondered how to fight against so many. During the day they were there too; but you didn't hear them then. You only felt them. Were they really there? Did he hear their voices now? Was he going crazy? Sometimes a sudden loneliness came over him as he went along the arcade between the student houses; or when classes let out in the afternoon: when everyone went down the steps by the chapel to the old and new gyms.

Yes, he heard sighs, sighs without hope, like a bad breath of the soul. You could die up here at this school, like Jeffers, and no one would ever know, or care, or ask where you went, like Manuel. Voices, sighs, groans, down below . . . they rose into his sleep . . . wingflaps, hear them? soulflaps . . . trapped.

He started awake.

Who knows what time it was. The window by his cheek was just open. A voice seemed to prod him from his dreams.

—*My doll . . . they took my doll.*

What's that? He opened his eyes. The voice was real.

—*My son. I lost my son.*

Then weeping. A grown man was outside his window, out there in the frigid night, and cried about a lost son.

Newell lay still, afraid to breathe, or turn his head to look.

Then the voice was right by his bed, a few inches from his ear, It breathed its coffin breath on him, and said its hopeless words. So a man came and lurked outside, after midnight, and mumbled puzzle words to the boy who had been out there, and seen him, and had a look at the horror. Now there was some kind of pact between them: the sophomore who led the league in detention hours, and the Beast of Ethridge. The Beast sounded needy tonight: please, solve the mystery, catch me so the curse can end, and more boys won't have to go away.

Newell lay in the dark. And then, without moving his head, he shot a glance out the window.

There it was—the decomposing face, the dead stare.

Newell sat bolt upright, and screamed.

The next Saturday Bernard packed up his gear, clothing, books, notebooks, all his scientific apparatus. He moved across the quad to a single room on second floor Tildon: right beneath the floor occupied by elite seniors.

Chapter Seven

I

A week passed. Flu was on campus in mid-March. Geeter's chapel talks were punctuated by sneezes and coughs, as he spoke of springtime on the way.

—Upon my bed at night, said Geet, I sought him whom my soul loveth. I sought him but found him not. I called but he gave no answer.

Shellnitz turned in his seat and hissed back at Schmied:

—Don't do that! Thou shalt not beat meat in church.

Shelly slipped an envelope in Warnickie's hand, next to him, and gave a nod at Newell Gilbert. But Warnickie handed it back.

—I will rise now—said Geeteth, crooning—and go about the city, in the streets and the squares. I will seek him whom my soul loveth.

Snow streaked the lawn behind the Atelier, but it was in retreat. Long tracts still glittered on the meadow across the winding road.

There went the train over the railroad bridge, clickety-clack into the distance: same time, every morning.

Shellnitz, big fool, was on fire to have a word with Newell, so he went into his act. Shelleth started to bellow like a sick calf even as Geeter sang out versets from the Bible. What a duet! Those groans went pretty well with Geetie's choice of a text today, love poetry as spring came on.

—Stir not up, nor awaken love, until it please.
Shellnitz, that reckless madman, undid a grave taboo by leaving his seat during morning chapel. You have to be dying to do such a thing. He clutched his stomach and made loud vomiting noises, as he went doubled over up the aisle. On the way he flipped a small cream colored envelope at Newell—evil act duly noted by Geeter at the pulpit, even as Geet-Geet swooned to the sound of his own voice. The note turned out to be Shellnitz's summons to initiation rites of the *Society for Self-Furtherance*. And how did The Owl take such a piece of news? He only seemed to care because Newell did. More on his mind was a plan for a practical joke on Geeter: how to sneak in Geet's quarters at the end of the hall, and short-sheet the randy master's bed.
—He's too horny! said Shellnitz. A preacher shouldn't be so horny.

II

Returning from the Refectory, in the few free minutes after dinner, they held a council.
—Schmiddy, you wait outside in the bushes. The signal will be a sneeze, loud, very loud. Do not come in if you don't hear it. I'll go to the third floor with The Owl, but first we'll give the code knock at Boz Krips' door, on first-floor Tildon, and put him on alert. See, Shelly? You've got two big bruisers behind you, who can deal with what may come up. I'll sneak in the bathroom next door, ready to jump in.
—In the toilet? said Big Schmied, blond jowls grinning.
—No, you oaf, into the fray: if Owl gives the signal.
—Hunk-o'-shit!—sneezed Shellnitz, in his small, squeaky voice.
He looked a little ill at ease.
Schmiddeth, from his pocket, took a switchblade and flicked it open.
—Holbein, you flit!
—Put that away, said Newell. You and Boz can handle this without a knife. Shelly, you go through the ceremony, and see what you can

see. The question is: does Holbein's secret society have anything to do with the Beast of Ethridge? Is Holbein himself The Beast? We all know what they say about him. We've heard the story how he grew up in an orphanage. Who knows what the boy went through there: maybe went nuts, and nobody found out. Then he saved someone from a fire—knowing him, he started it. He made the newspapers, and Headmaster Smithson became his legal guardian, turned the tough kid into a son. And now here he is at Ethridge: also an orphanage, if you ask me. Only here *he* has the power, and picks on smaller boys the way he once was abused. He got carried away, that's all, and killed young Manuel by mistake that day out on the island, after Mingo saw them; and then kidnapped Jeffers because Jeffers knew too much, and ended up killing Ethan too. And now he has a taste for it: the blood of Ethridge boys. One leads to another. And this guy named Holbein right here in our midst has become a killer even though he's the golden boy and the most likely to succeed. Now me, or Rod here, or who knows who else may be the next to go, before this school year ends, with its horrors. So we'll play along with the madman, and have Roddeth go to their swearing-in ceremony. Okay! We're more apt to make it through by cunning than open rebellion. But we need a clue. We need proof. That's why Rod must keep an eye out and come up with something, so we can track this Beast of Ethridge down. Who is it? Holbein? One of the masters? See what you can see in there, big boy. Into the breach, Roddeth! Now let's move.

Newell ended the pep talk and gave Shelly-Shell, pale as an eggshell, a pat on the rump.

Schmidlap, blond gorilla, hefted the pearl handle switchblade in his big mitt. He refused to play varsity football for Runt Roentgen, but he was ready for a rumble.

III

After study hall the three boys went out the Settlers front entry and doubled round by the service road to Tildon House.

Schmied chuckled:

—We're sending him into the lion's den.

Beside them Rod wasn't his usual self. He looked even tinier, floating in his charcoal gray suit. He went along with that jerky walk of his toward his fate.

Outside Tildon they left Big Schmied to lurk in the bushes: a good place for that social deviant. Then, on the first floor, Newell gave the code-knock at Boz Krips' door; and Boz, most promising athlete in the history of Ethridge, knocked back.

By the hall light Newell glimpsed Shellnitz's face, sort of screwy, with its tics. The poor boy had been cool up to now.

The student house had a scent of incense.

On the third floor Newell whispered:

–Go ahead. Get something on them. Do your best!

As Shellnitz, tail between his legs, went to the room of *Self-Furtherance*, Newell ducked in the bathroom. There he heard voices: from where? A girl's, and familiar. Next door? Or through a duct? It was eerie. Newell went in a stall, took a seat, and listened.

Yes, he smelled her perfume amid the incense.

A little laugh. Then a voice, Josey.

–You look wild.

–What were you boys up to?

Katya.

So she went back to him. Couldn't help herself. His baby in her belly.

–Something of The Toad's.

–Must be important.

–Not really, said Josey, listless, as ever.

Then silence. Newell listened. Were they kissing?

Katya:

–I couldn't wait till Sunday. I want you, Josey, body and soul. I need you.

From his hideout Newell heard–their silence, a long moment. Then moans, sounds of pleasure. Lovemaking. The male prodded, surged. The female gave a whimper: as though hurt, but her being needed this hurt, to live. The two voices rose, a kind of agreed-on violence being done; and something fell, maybe a desk lamp they reached to turn off. Her moans and groans, Josey's locomotive throes, his frantic panting–her cry, ah! as he entered her. Swoosh, swoosh, like a strong wind. Newell felt tensely alert, too amazed for shame, now, or jealousy. Wasn't there a faculty adviser on the floor? Newell listened, his heart pounding. He tried to keep his wits about him, and waited for Shellnitz's SOS, Shellnitz's yell of distress: if they began to hurt him in there; or worse, if they got carried away . . . But it wasn't easy to keep an eye on what he came for, when Josey and Katya were huffing and puffing, slurping kisses maybe not two feet from his ear, on the other side of the wall. And then she cried out:

–Hold me, Josey, hold me!
–Oh! . . . oh!
–Ah! . . . ah-h-h!

They climaxed. Katya fairly shouted it out, in the silence of this hall where no girl had ever penetrated, much less been penetrated. An Ethridge first. Just leave it to Josey Kipnes, the darling boy who was a ne'er-do-well: he did with people as he pleased.

Then quiet.

Nothing, so far, from the other room: where the show went on. Nothing from Rod Shellnitz. Only the wind. Wind moaned as an afterthought through the window frames–chill wind, off the Needing River, but with a first hint of spring. The wind groaned as Katya had a moment ago, like someone being punished.

Woman's perfume mingled with the scent of incense, and radiator heat. Suddenly she spoke, throaty. Somehow it didn't sound right, off key:

–Hold me, Josey.
–You make love, he said, like you were taking revenge.
–Do I?

Silence.

A minute later he said:
–Ow, that tickles.
–Really? Where, here?
–Don't, I mean it.
–Just wondering if you're still there. You draw away.
–Stop.
–Please, be tender. Don't you love me?
–Watch it. If you tickle, I'll start on you.
–Will you? Spoiled Josey, spoiled little boy.
–I can bite.
–Really? Wolf, wolf.
–If I tickle you, you'll wet my bed.

She laughed, but her laughter trailed off. You could tell she wanted to coo. But Josey, turned off, gave a clucking sound.

–Poor boy, she said. Spanked too hard by his mama, a neurotic.
He can't get it up.

–Oh, no? Cock-a-doodle-doo!

–Poor kid. Went all limp in a pool of goo.

–Cluck. Clu-uck.

Katya paused. But she said:

–I take the risks, coming here. Why does it all have to be on me?
From the bathroom Newell listened, and thought: Tell him.
Haven't you told Josey you're pregnant? Why don't you tell him?
There was a lurking sense between them, as though Katya would
light into her lover.

–I think Sookie wants to get in here.

–Sookie?

–The Toad. We call him Sister Sookie . . .

–Are you kidding? Let him wait.

–Well, this is his room. It's only fair.

–Only fair . . . Tst, such a good little Josey. Wears a bowtie on his
weenie.

–I'd rather wear a bowtie on my weenie than be Bartlett Academy's first nymphomaniac, who goes parading in her birthday suit
on an all-male floor.

Silence. At his post Newell listened for Katya's reply, and Shellnitz's cry of distress from the *Self-Furtherance* room.

–I mean it, Josey. Take me to your mother sometime, I'd like to
learn from her. How she spanked poor ittih' boy and made him into
a wimp.

–Wimp meets nympho.

–Screw you, Josey.

–Me?

More silence. Outside, the March night, still biting cold. In here,
anger–when those two should have felt such a tenderness, thought
Newell, and held one another close, and whispered in each other's
ear.

–I'll leave, she said. Sorry I came.

–Why be sorry? said Josey.

–Never again. This time I mean it.

–My roommate will be glad to know.

–I thought I knew you better.

She must be on her feet in there. Dressing. Her lover said:

–Some stuff. Too large for my taste.

—You're hard.

Her voice quivered.

Another pause. Then the sound of her blouse or sweater swept across a desk top: notebooks, papers, pen and pencil set sent on the floor.

—Hey! What the—?

—Goddamn you, Josey! Why—her voice broke, in tears—why are you doing this?

—Make way, men. It's a hysterical female. In her knickers.

She yanked open the door.

—I'll get out. To hell with you.

—Bye bye, he said, in a weary tone.

—Out of my way—Katya, with a sob, shouted into the third-floor Tildon silence.—All you high and mighty seniors with your hush-hush Society for Self-Furtherance! That's right, little Joseykins, do you know what I think? Do you? I think—it's not nice!

IV

Newell wanted to run after her, comfort her, take her home. But what could he do? He had promised Shellnitz, and he must wait here, in the bathroom, and see that his friend got out in one piece. But Katya was in trouble; maybe she needed him more ... Well, maybe she did, and maybe she didn't; but he had no agreement with her; he made no promise to her. She hadn't wanted one from him. She ran away that night in the chapel ... Yes; but she also told him about her baby, something she wouldn't even tell Josey, the father, or anyone else, but only him. Even if it's dangerous? Will you go with me? Oh, Katya, yes. Just say when. But right now I promised my friend Shellnitz, that flit, and so I have to stay here. Whether you want me or not, I can't go ... Oh, how he wanted to go after her, down the stairs into the cold night, and save her, love her, cherish her. But just then he heard a voice along the senior corridor. Shellnitz.

—Say: I have seen! Ha ha ha! I have seen, you jerks! Ha ha! Sacred presence, debased divinity in the darkness—you bunch of clowns! I won't kneel for you or anyone else in this crazy place. The whole mess of you, mad seniors, couldn't fight your way out of a wet paper bag!

That was Shellnitz. Newell went out for him, and together they ran down the three flights of stairs. From a nozzle they shot into the quad. The two boys were halfway across the Senior Path when Newell stopped short and said:

–Hey, what about Schmied?

He turned and flew back looking for Schmidlap in the bushes outside Tildon.

No sign of the boy.

A minute later, inside Warren, Newell listened to Shellnitz tell of the ceremony.

–Some flit spoke in a muffled voice, The Toad, I'll bet you–all about the 'debased divinity' . . . and how I lit it a little with my 'puny light'. And 'you: low one . . . say it: low one . . . Submit yourself, kneel!' . . . Well, that was too much for me, I wanted to get the hell out. But there was one more thing. It was dark. And in the background they had a . . . I don't know, a . . .

Rod's pale face gave a grimace. It twitched. The brave boy had just been through something; though he made light of it, and laughed at the senior flits. He didn't let on.

–A what?

–It looked like a dummy dressed up in a charcoal gray suit.

–Manuel?

–I came after Manuel left. I never saw him.

–Ah, right. Well, sort of pudgy, dark skinned, short curly hair, a flit?

–No, he . . . he–Shellnitz swallowed and worked to get out the words–he was gray, dead as lead, or a pretty good wax doll. In the background, the darkness, about halfway through the show: he started to glow, with a goofy grin.–Shellnitz shivered.–I guess he was what they meant by 'debased divinity in the darkness' . . . Just a little light on him, or it, like a candle.

–Did he smell? Did it stink in there?

–I don't know. Maybe: like somebody's socks. The room reeked of incense.

–Right.

–So anyway I . . . I had to go.

A tremor passed through Shellnitz's wiry body. He bowed and shook his blond curly head, cried a little, then looked up at Newell and laughed. He giggled, teary eyed. The Owl cried and laughed at once, as a ripple of fear went over his scrawny shoulders.

But where was Schmied? Next door there was no sound of mattress springs tonight: Schmiddeth rock 'n rolling to the tune of Ramona Glebe. The boy left his post. In his defense: it was cold, out there in the shrubs. Still, that's no good, thought Newell; what if we needed him? . . . Well, there was Boz, and he would've come. But where was Big Jay off to, after he left his friends in the lurch? Too ashamed to come back here? Hm, it's quiet next door.

V

After lights-out Newell drifted toward dreamland with a last thought for Jay Schmied: we'll see if he's in his place at morning chapel tomorrow . . . What with the long day, and night of excitement, Newell needed a good rest so he could do it again tomorrow. But this was not meant to be.

Into the late night silence a voice said his name.

—Newell?

It sounded low, and pained. Was it in his dreams, or a real voice? The sleeping boy gave a jolt: it was there, in the room with him— where he slept alone now, ever since Bernard moved out. He thought: The Beast. But, by a reflex, he said:

—Sir?

—Newell, I . . . I want to speak with you, please.

The Beast said please?

—About what, Sir? It's late.

—No, come.

Pause.

—Uh, where?

—Into the lounge, with me. I insist.

The voice was familiar yet so strange, sort of charged, in the late hour. Newell rose on one elbow and stared straight ahead. He was afraid that if he had a good look, the thing might come closer . . . Open the window, right now! Jump out and run before the other crossed the room, and attacked?! . . . But it said the lounge: why into the lounge?

—Shall I put on my charcoal gray suit, Sir? Like Ethan?

—That won't be necessary.

The voice was so sad.

Newell risked a glance to his left. Was it the corroded death mask from out at the cabin? He couldn't stand to see that anymore.

In the doorway, by the dim light from the hallway, the man's eyes gleamed. A harsh yet pitiful gaze glinted in the shadows.

Geeter.

VI

Inside the darkened student lounge by the stairway they sat in silence. By the glow of hall light Pastor Geeter's features looked haggard, even wasted, though he wasn't old. Did he look like the Beast of Ethridge? A little; since he was big, vigorous, also a bit bowlegged like The Beast. Newell's parents once said the Ethridge chaplain served in the Korean War and made it back home only to divorce his pretty young wife.

Now, in the early hours, The Geet's eyes were strange: guilty, it seemed, and kind of frazzled. How often this intense man was seen going about campus with the long strides of a Puritan possessed by a devil. So intently did he strive toward a higher faith, Geeteth might break his neck on a transom someday. Once Boz Krips saw him talking to himself and pointing up at the sky from a grassy mound beyond the baseball diamond. 'Sinning!' he had cried, when he thought no one but God could hear. 'I am sinning!'

Now he only said:

—What is it, son? Why are you so unhappy? You go around with your head hung down.

—. . .

The student waited for more. Perhaps it wasn't Newell who, among the two of them, was truly unhappy.

Geeter knit his brow and peered into the distance. He might have been posing.

—There were things I saw . . . and did, in Korea . . . I shall never forget them.

The tone of his voice was so sad: it made you feel like crying.

Why? The words trailed off into the silence . . . What things? . . . What had Geeter done? What awful things, in Korea, fit for a future Beast of Ethridge? Had a beloved friend been killed? Had he himself, a man of God, killed someone? Maybe a child? Maybe a boy about Manuel's age? Manuel who also came from a foreign country, and had a different color skin? . . . Well if so then why not just come out with it? Why deny the truth all your life, and have to feel guilt? Ah, because you were a coward? You did something you just can't face up to? live with?

Silence. What time of night could it be? The grown man sat there tensely. Did he want to confess his sins to a teenage boy? He was unable . . . So it was he, Master Geeter, who spoke solemn words in the shrubbery outside a student's window? He was the Beast of Ethridge: in an agony to atone for some terrible past crime, but only damning himself further. Only hurting others who were weaker. For he had no choice. He had to carry on this mysterious ritual of his faith gone awry. Even more mysterious, even crazier than *Self-Furtherance*. To kidnap two boys? To kill at least one of them, and then keep the poor lad above ground: for that grisly pastime out at the cabin? If such things really happened: could it be Geeter didn't believe in God? Could it be he was angry with Him for not existing? Well, what fault was that of Manuel? of Jeffers? And now he came to call in the middle of the night—but didn't have the heart to harm the child of Professor Emory Gilbert, his onetime mentor?

VII

In the Warren House lounge the chaplain stared into space. In a trance, a faroff look in his eyes, he hardly seemed to breathe or know where he was. At length Newell, forgotten, rose from his seat, stretched, and gave a yawn. Then, passing the pastor by, he said:

—Good night, Sir.

—. . .

It must have been after two a.m.

Back in the hallway Newell gave a start. He stood in his tracks and listened. Was it raining outside? There were sounds: like a lot of people walking somewhere. Where? In the depths of the school: down in the long Steam Tunnel beneath the student houses–thcy wenl in a procession, like mourners in a cemetery. He heard them go. He stood rooted to the spot because there could be no mistake this time; he was awake, in his senses. And he could hear their moans, late at night, seeping up from beneath the floorboards. Newell stood there by the stairwell, listened, and wondered: could the secret voices, Ethridge ghosts, come up here and take over things and mingle among the living?

VIII

The reveille bell stunned the gray, quiet dawn. It clangalanged down each corridor, loudly, and took a boy by the scruff. Twenty minutes later the students began to emerge, one here, another there, beneath the porticos, and make their way toward breakfast. That morning the sun didn't shine, as the student body swallowed the dry toast, lukewarm eggs, unsweetened juice, and then made its way toward an arduous day.

In the Refectory Newell was looking for Big Schmied, and he didn't see him. Along the colonnaded walkways to chapel: no sign of Jay Bird. Had he disappeared forever? from his post in the bushes last night outside Tildon? Not so easy to kidnap that big bruiser, the apple of Coach Roentgen's eye, if only the boy would go out for the team.

From his place along the raised pew, inside the chapel, Newell awaited the appearance of his neighbor. Would the seat be empty, and stay that way: like Manuel's last fall, as the school year got underway, and then Moon Jeffers' a few weeks later?

Today the chaplain was not on hand. Now where had he gone? Headmaster Smithson took the pulpit amid a silence which seemed strained to Newell. And the Headmaster didn't look too good either, distracted, a bit less dapper, after a sleepless night; and, wondrous to tell, his bow tie on crooked. For a few minutes he talked to the Ethridge community about standing up at times under strain, making it come what may through the more difficult moments. This he called: 'a matter of principle'.

Newell looked straight ahead. He frowned, as if he had bitten into a bad thing. Something sounded wrong about the Headmaster's words; he felt this, he didn't think it.

Suddenly, at the back of the chapel, a door swung open. And now here came gangly Schmied, all goofy grin as usual, blond jowls, pink cheeks beneath his slit eyes, short curly blond hair: here came the guy down the aisle. What a flit!

Everybody forgot Headmaster Smithson's fine words and turned toward Schmied, Smiley, who gave a little wave and sat with a creak that sounded boisterous, in the silence.

Newell took a breath of relief and tried to focus, like the others, on what was being said.

But wait. Now, as Schmied settled in and heads turned back to the pulpit, there was still an empty place. Whose? Newell should have known at a glimpse, but because of some trick played by his memory, or because he didn't want to see, the fact didn't come home to him at once.

At first he thought: Manuel. But no; that wasn't Manuel's place anymore; not since last October had the foreign exchange student taken his seat there. Who then? Who replaced him?

Shellnitz.

Of course: no Shellnitz today. Absent. Had he failed to respond when the wake-up bell rang around the school? Had he gotten flu and gone to the Infirmary?

Newell sat forward tensely. Where was Shellnitz, that nut who had no fear, who always said what he thought, and challenged Runt Roentgen, 'Coach Sir', gymnasium dictator?

The chapel talk ended. Organ notes flowed forth as the students stood up and filed from the chapel toward class. But Newell didn't go to his first period class; instead, he went to the Infirmary and asked for Shellnitz.

There the nurse in charge wouldn't tell him anything.

—Is he here?

—We don't give out such information.

—But he's my friend. I need a word with him.

—I suggest you go to class.

At this Newell took the law into his own hands. He walked round back, looked in windows, and began to yell:

—Owl! Oh, Shell-ee-ee!

No response.

Knowing Shellnitz: if he didn't yell back, he must not be there. Where then? Where had he gone?

–Shelleth! Oh! Shell'llnitz!

The same nurse came to the back window and shooed away this pest.

–Shh! What are you doing? People are sick here.

Newell skulked away toward Warren House for a look in Shellnitz's–Manuel and Jeffers'–room.

Chapter Eight

I

On Sunday afternoon Newell drifted off to the plunk, plunk from tennis courts down by the old gym. He dreamt. He saw Shellnitz, who went away . . . Shellnitz, face a mess, rose from the depths of the Needing River, drip . . . dripping slime from his blond hair. And those eyes, no more laughter and high spirits in them: you felt some very, very bad thing was going on, for a long time. Newell's body gave a jolt, but sleep still held him, with its images: Shellnitz, covered with a reddish slime, emerged from the dark water. He wore his charcoal gray suit, with its perfect crease, a white dress shirt starched stiffer than Dean Wart's grin, and a maroon and blue striped necktie. Shellnitz stared, walking on the surface, but he didn't see. His ears worked like gills, plunk, plunk, as they took in air.

And then:

—Psst!

Again Newell's body jolted as he saw the poor boy's face which had once been so merry, so full of life.

—Psst . . .

—Huh? What?

—Wake up, sleepyhead. Sleep your life away.

There was Katya. By his bedside she stood over him: in her tight bluejeans, gray cashmere sweater, same maroon scarf tied up like a peasant woman's. No suede coat though: wasn't she cold? There was a tender, vulnerable look to Katya's features, pudgy, but even more beautiful. And she had a funny smell: was she on medicine?

−Remember? she said. You promised to go with me, if I asked. Now's the time.

He sat up in bed, and shivered.

−What's the matter?

−They say I had a breakdown. They're wrong. Wanted to keep me in a sickroom over at Bartlett: sadistic nurse guarding me, face like The Toad.

−The Toad?

−Or a mushroom. All night long she kept fussing, this, that, the other thing. They say I'm crazy, but they're the ones. So I escaped.

−Really?

−I fooled them. When the day nurse went to lunch, a guard came to watch me. I went in the bathroom, climbed out the window, and ran down by the river. Now I'm here. You said you'd go, remember? Today's the day.

Katya smiled down at him and ran her fingers through his hair. She sat on the bed beside him, caressed him, kissed his forehead. She seduced him. He didn't want to go anywhere, but she could make him do what she wanted with a kiss. Katya's face made small fluttery movements; her eyebrows twitched. His head lay on her shoulder, as they cuddled a moment.

−I think I've got a fever, he said. Geez, I'll bet they're going berserk over at Bartlett.

−Sure, call the cops. Bring the men in white coats.

Katya's hair was thick and wild, as she swayed a little, back and forth, holding onto him like he was her child.

−I love you, said Newell.

−Let's go. We've got a date.

−Where? I want to stay here with you.

−The rowboat is waiting.

−Rowboat?

Drawing back he stared in her eyes.

−Do this for me, she said, and pressed his head to her breast, and stroked it.

−It's cold out there, Katya. And I feel sick.

She kissed him on the mouth and took his breath away.

−For me . . . Could be we'll have the cabin to ourselves.

Newell frowned and wondered what all this meant. He didn't want to go, but his will was no longer his own.

II

They made their way behind the Laundry, which also housed the school's power plant. The red-brick windowless building, Astarte's domain, reflected a weird light . . . They crossed the service road and then, hand in hand, passed over the wire fence onto the grassy slope down to the river. So Katya had been out at the cabin before? Did she know what they were going to find there now?

Leaving the school and its shadows behind, they felt an unsure March sun on their backs. A crow cawed. The two teenagers slipped over the soggy ground, as brittle twigs and loose-ends of winter crunched underfoot. Then Katya lost her balance and drenched a leg in an icy bog.

He helped her up.

—Never mind, she said. Keep on.

On the riverbank they paused, and heard the gurgle, the quiet swift current of the Needing as it flowed, in its wide bend, this side of the island.

They went along the edge with Katya leading the way. And Newell remembered the first trip he made out here last fall, and then his night in the cabin during Christmas holidays. He felt alert now, not so dizzy with fever. The air was cool and fresh. Earth reawakened beneath the dead matted grass, and decomposing leaves. The river took a deep breath after its icy months.

Any minute Newell expected to hear voices from a search party, angry adults in cars, or coming toward them across the meadow; police and Bartlett people looking for Katya who ran away.

—Look, she said.

There it was: the rowboat moored to a tree trunk, in the cove.

She broke into a run, and slipped again.

—Wait, he said.

She nearly fell headlong down the steep riverbank, but was able to right herself, and pointed across.

—It's getting late. They won't expect us. We have to drift downstream then row with all our might.

—You've been there too?

She didn't answer, but ran on to the cove. There she grabbed the rope, and jumped in the old rowboat, as he followed after. She leaned to push off with the oar, as one side dipped toward the water. Grabbing up the rope she laughed:

—Help me, heave ho!

Katya's face was flushed and eager: childish, full of life.

—This is crazy, he said.

She rocked back and forth:

—Your oar!

III

And then they were on their own, adrift, upon the water. The current was swift in mid-river, as it took them in its hushed embrace. The old boat turned on itself in a slow circle while Katya tried using her oar to steer. Newell stared off at the high eroded bank on the island side, its tangled roots like snakes, and got ready to row.

Past the tip of the island they drifted. Newell heard a branch snap in the silence, and bird call, lonely and sad, a loon down river.

Katya pointed. She said calmly:

—Over there's the landing. Okay, row now, your oar only.

At first his thrust skipped off the surface, but then he caught hold and pulled with both hands. She joined in beside him and soon they were making headway against the current. His arms ached, and his head hurt. He thought: Katya must be strong to row that way. There! There was the post and the tree, fifty yards upstream, where he tied up with Cormac last fall.

—You were out here with Josey?

He paused in his rowing.

—Forget him—she said; and then, after a moment:—We'll row past, and coast back in.

—Manuel came out here with the Society. Never seen again.

—Hold your oar in. Put on the brakes, easy . . .

Katya stopped rowing and stood up. She poised to reach forward for the single post, but gave a lurch and nearly fell as the bow bumped and spun off.

—No rowboats—said Newell, and he thought: are we out here by ourselves? Only the skeleton in a tweed suit, with a class photograph for a face; only Jeffers, and maybe Shellnitz now, brought out here to be a dead boy's playmate.

—There's another place, downstream, where they tie up. You can see it from the cabin, so we came here.

—But what for? he said. Why did we come?

She jumped on the bank and held her hand down to him. Their feet were soaked from the leaky rowboat. It was cold out there, as shadows began to creep across the island.

IV

They moved into those woods: beneath the tall trees bare of leaves at winter's end. Their steps sank in the underbrush, twigs, humus with its tinge of rot as the thaw went on. A pale sun shone off gray bark on all sides.

Newell went along unable to get his bearings, but he sensed the cabin up ahead. Katya moved forward; she was eager, but paused and took his hand again, as the ground rose toward the center of the island. It surprised him when she turned, drew him close, and, smiling, kissed his lips.

—Shh, she whispered. Don't talk.

There was a stillness. The light went a deeper tone toward late afternoon; and, behind them, the Needing flowed on in its shadowy silence. For a moment they stood there and hugged.

—Have you told anyone? said Newell.

—About what?

—Your—you know.

He blushed.

She drew back from him, a tear on her cheek.

—Josey still doesn't know?

—No. And he won't.

—Why do you let him off the hook that way? Everyone lets him off the hook.

—Tst.

Newell thought a moment, and said:

—I'll help you, Katya. I'll bring up children with you.

He said this brusquely: the way a man, one who does what he says, might propose. She gave a little laugh and kissed him again and said she loved him too. But the next instant she was urging him forward, and pressing his hand for only one reason: so it would do her will.

Then he saw the ravine, where it ran alongside the descent to the cabin. And there it was: the homely structure; the shingle roof sloping over its horror, two dead boys at play; the single window with a flicker of light either from the dying sun, or inside. Now Newell remembered, and shuddered. He crouched beside this mad beautiful girl he loved, and stared at the quiet scene: the cabin which held his fate as a student at Ethridge. Go on, he thought, kick me out: I burn my bridges. What do I care about anything else, if I have her? We'll run away; we'll find a way, somehow, to be together . . . Vaguely, he felt his one goal in life was for her and him to make it through this day alive. For the rest, for the 'finest education available', as his dad liked to say, he didn't care anymore. He couldn't think about such things when it was time to stand up and show he was a man. He would follow Katya, since she came and got him, and made him bring her out here . . . For a long time he had felt such pain at not knowing what to do, being torn between his duty as a son, an Ethridge student, on the one hand, and what he thought was right on the other. But now he knew. He didn't believe or trust the school authorities anymore. And, as for his parents, they would just have to understand, if they were able.

—This way, she said, low.

—Why? he said. Tell me why come out here.

Always, at the mixer last October, at Cormac's when they got drunk and rumpus'd on the floor, in the chapel when she told him her awful news: she would not hear a word. She decided what to do, and that was that.

—There's something I've got to see.

—And then what?

—I'll be free.

—You don't want to see . . . , he mumbled.

But she was moving ahead with steady strides, and urged him onward. And he thought: what if there's no one? What if it's just us? And then the creak, cree-e-eak . . . above the trap door to the attic . . . ?

Now Katya led the way with a fierce look. Her face was flushed. For the first time since he had known her, she looked not languid, non-caring, provocative, but vital and alive.

V

Sounds of the forest: a damp settling, the March thaw. They heard the rising call of a wood duck up river. There was a vague scent of skunk in the days before springtime; and, also, the smell of wood burning in a fireplace.

Bending forward they went the last few yards to the cabin. Side by side they huddled a moment beneath the window. Were there sounds of movement inside? Newell had a sense of something grave and impending. He crouched beside Katya and wanted to plead with her: leave off this thing right now; give it up; let's go back to Bartlett and decide what to do: plan our future together. And then he would never leave her, and they would be happy . . . But it was too late for such words, as, slowly, she stood up and peered over the window sill.

Katya gave a gasp, and her eyes went wide. Her sudden emotion sent a shiver along Newell's spine, as he rose beside her and also took a look.

The room looked cozier than he remembered: pair of facing divans, end tables with what looked like a decanter of brandy; chairs, oriental throw rug in the center. No lamplight, but a wood fire smoked and crackled in the hearth; its flames glowed warmly against the fading light of the forest. It took Newell a moment to focus and see what was going on. There were shadowy figures. A woman, who was not from Bartlett, lounged on the near sofa: older, thirtyish, she had her dark hair pinned up, and wore a kimono. Beyond the other divan stood Jon Holbein naked at least from the waist. He flicked his wrist, which held a riding crop, and someone gave a cry. Nearby stood Herbert Wingate, The Toad, whose ugly face had an angelic smile on it; he seemed to do a slow dance, sensual, ridiculous. At the window Katya, staring in, had the look of a tigress. She breathed in starts, but Newell didn't know why until he saw that Todd Bennett, a sophomore, was on his knees before The Toad. Also, on the far divan lay Josey, naked, like a Greek god; and in his arms lay a town girl who looked in her teens; maybe the other's daughter? They were in coitus: their bodies rocked slowly and shimmered with the firelight. Josey sipped brandy; he gave a chuckle even as he thrust, into the girl. Meanwhile Holbein dealt his unseen partner a series of stinging taps with the whip, and there were more cries.

Newell straightened for a better view. The scene inside lent a sense of hopelessness; it all seemed so anxious; and he thought: so this is *Self-Furtherance*, they come out here and do this. But they got carried away with Manuel, Jeffers . . . Holbein had a devil's look on his face when he flicked, and made his partner yelp. Josey's pleasure began to crescendo, and his handsome head lolled back, his body arched.

Another surprise. At that moment, from the other room, Paul Rhodes appeared. He was in skivvies. And then behind him, also framed in the doorway, stood Tim MacDonald also called The Captain, or The Square, in all his nudity.

Golden tremors played on those arms, legs, glazed eyes, an orgy.

Holbein stood tall and seemed to survey it all. Then he glimpsed the window. His eyes narrowed, and he tensed.

But just as Josey's passion peaked, and his torso shook, tossed about, there on the divan, a piercing scream rang out. And Newell, stunned from his somber fascination with what was going on inside, took a second to know it was Katya. She too rocked her body, there by his side, and shrieked in horror.

She struck at the glass. Her fist fell back as if afraid, at first, to make its full impact. He reached trying to stop her, but the second time she splintered the window pane. And then again, her dark eyes on fire, she lashed out at the jagged glass, as a long piece fell and tinkled on the floor inside. And then her blood began to spurt.

VI

With a look of disgust Holbein shoved Little Mallet back with his knee. He gave Ramlet a kick and sent him sprawling.

In a furious bound Holbein rushed outside and came round the side of the cabin. With a sneer he raised the riding crop to Katya.

—Slut, I thought I smelled your perfume.

But she thrust her bloody fingers in his face, laughing wildly, and The Bossman shied a step back. The blood made streaks on her forearm and dripped from her elbow as though a vein was cut. The skin of her high cheekbones and forehead seemed drawn tight by her fury. In the dusking light, out there in the forest, she herself looked like some kind of beast.

She moved past them, half laughing, whimpering. Holbein, in his half-zipped bluejeans, glanced with contempt at her escort, the sophomore. Katya tripped, nearly fell, and ran around the side. A moment later her shrill peal of laughter came from inside.

Through the broken window Newell saw her standing over Josey, who, stark naked, still in the embrace of his girlish lover, gave a grin. Sharing a glance with Paul Rhodes, he shrugged and said:

—Look what the wind blew in.

Katya glared here, there, as if at bay. She sobbed and, putting a bloody hand to her face, besmirched her cheek. Josey only grinned up at her, sheepishly, while the girl beside him looked afraid to move. With a last effort to control herself, eyebrows popping on her forehead, face twitching, Katya said:

—Josey, I hate . . . your guts.

Her voice flew up.

—No kidding, he said, calmly.

His words seemed to jolt her. She screamed, lunged with her fist, but lost her balance and fell to one knee. Josey chuckled.

Then Newell lost sight of what was happening. Holbein grabbed his arm, wrenched it back, and pushed him toward the cabin door. He growled:

—Come where you're not wanted, eh?

Katya hurtled out past them, her hands, face, dark hair streaked with blood. Now she looked out of control, and bolted away toward the Ethridge side of the island.

Holbein shouted:

—Wingate! MacDonald, get after her. Bring her back here!

Something made Newell glance up at the attic window over the front entry. Had a hand, a face flitted there and then drawn back? Who was up there now, and doing what? But no: there was no one, only reflected sky, trees. And no odor anymore, despite the fire downstairs—so Jeffers was no longer on the swing, a playmate for a skeleton? Playtime ended?

Holbein pushed Newell forward, twisting his arm, inside the cabin. But the captive jerked loose and tried to dart off after Katya. No go: the wrestler Holbein was quick, agile; he caught his shirt and got him in a bear hug.

Just then one more participant in the Sunday orgy showed his face: sophomore Jeff Kemeny, Holbein's protégé, came from the inner room.

—Kemeny, you go with them. Catch her and hurry up about it, dammit, goddamit!

Tucking his shirttails the sophomore went trotting off, among the twilit trees, after MacDonald and The Toad.

But there was a hint of fear in The Bossman's eye. Found out in his lair, in his fun and games: what must be done with this new one, to keep the secret?

VII

The broken window glowed with firelight like a shattered sun. Newell breathed in the lodge scent and thought, for an instant, what might have been if he and Katya were alone. Then he said:

—You brought Manuel out here and hazed him until he died. Then you didn't know what to do so you put him up in the attic, as if nothing had happened.

Holbein looked at him curiously, and then laughed:

—We never had anything to do with Manuel.

—You sent him a bid. I saw it.

On the divan Josey, thinking of something, glanced out the window. Little Mallet and Todd Bennett, both afraid, stayed in place on the floor. The woman and girl were in the other room dressing.

In the fireplace a log fell, throwing up sparks. Outside, someone called high-voiced across the forest.

–Little twirp, said Holbein, you've caused us some trouble, not much. Since the year started you've pretty much had your way around here.

Logs in the hearth snapped and sizzled in the silence following Katya's mad dash. Holbein smiled with his lips, but there was a twinge to his features, unlike Josey who stayed aloof even in a crisis. Standing there naked from the waist with a small–what? a mermaid? tattooed on his shoulder, the senior looked muscular. His grin was cruel as he shoved the sophomore in front of the fireplace.

Newell said:

–You better watch out.

Off beyond the Ethridge campus, winding road to town and railroad bridge, the sun was going down. It was setting above the parkway which led over the hills, into the distance toward home. Light deepened inside the cabin. Newell caught his breath and wondered what happened to Manuel and Jeffers. Home never seemed so far away as at this moment . . . Now Katya was running, all alone, hysterical, toward the river.

–Gilbert, you've got some nerve. One stubborn little twirp, is all I can say. What ever shall we do with you?

Newell waited on The Bossman whose gaze held a threat. And now he realized there was no use trying to conform any longer. What sort of crazy game was this? Boys gone no one knew where. Wild goings-on among the most respected members of the community . . . In these instants the conflict building all year in Newell Gilbert came to a head. All the pain of not going home for Christmas; having to work long hours in the Steam Tunnel; Dean Wart so arbitrary, Roentgen so arrogant, Geeter so caring yet refusing to sign his weekly allowance checks:–all this seemed hopeless now, too sad for words. He let his parents down; he tried to be good but something conspired against him all the while. Months of misery, Saturday afternoons spent sitting in detention, homesickness . . . Newell stood there feeling stunned, lost. He thought of his father's anger, and how Emory was right no doubt: how his folks only wanted what was best for him. And if you didn't stand up for them, then who would? as Coach Roentgen liked to say.

Holbein's lips twisted:

–You simply do not . . . realize.–It was sexual, it was primal: the sound of Holbein about to take revenge. Suddenly, the pampered adoptive son of Headmaster Smithson had the coarse accent of a street kid; he was back in the state-run orphanage fighting for survival, eating flour and who knew what else, lying his way out of one scrape after another. Now he sneered:—Who runs this school, Gilbert, you or I? Maybe you think you're better than me, is that it? Well, why don't you just get down on your knees.

There was terror in the air. A heavy beating was about to occur: the kind of hazing that went beyond all bounds and could end in tragedy. There was a tremor in Holbein's voice. He grinned.

Strangely, Newell felt like laughing out loud. You might say he snapped, as Katya had. Week after week living with the idea of kidnappings; and unable to ask anyone what was going on, or he'd get himself in more trouble . . . Oh, he knew this senior hated him: it was probably Holbein who urged Dean Wart to keep him on campus for the holidays.

All, in the cabin, held their breath: Josey and Tim MacDonald, Todd Bennett and Little Mallet, the two town women standing in the doorway.

Newell went down on his knees, slowly, like a sprinter.

Holbein stood over him grinning.

VIII

All waited for the hard blow to fall: the whip.

Newell was hardly himself in these instants. It felt like someone else: as he coiled, and his body seemed to clench in a fist, acting by itself. He drove up at Holbein's genitals. With all his might he erupted, punched, and again. He lunged up, into him, and shouted something. And now it was the senior who doubled up in pain, and fell sidelong against a chair.

Newell scrambled past the sofa and grabbed a piece of jagged glass. Like a young savage he screamed and held the glinting fragment to Holbein's neck. It dug in his trembling fingers. That felt good. For an instant he wanted to drive it into the other's face. Newell gripped the glass tighter, and drops of blood fell from his hand.

But he paused before plunging his dagger into the senior's face.
Josey Kipnes smirked, gave a wan gesture at the window, and said:
—What about her?
This broke the trance, the rage. Newell flung his piece of glass into
the fireplace, and, flying from the cabin, heard Holbein's choked
words behind him:
—Gilbert . . . I'll see you . . . later.

IX

He ran twenty, thirty yards into the forest before halting. He
looked at his hand: on fire, sticky. Where was Katya? She had lit out
for the Ethridge side like she knew where she was headed. But could
he find that landing?

Daylight was fading; it evaporated from the floor of crunching
pine needles, the mush of dead leaves and underbrush. Newell stood
there trying to think. Which way? On all sides the tree trunks enclosed him and could make him lose his bearings. But heaven help
him if he got lost, or thrown back on the cabin, at Holbein's mercy.
It was getting cold: after dark it would be below freezing.

He heard a rustle and thought he saw something white scurry up
ahead amid the trees. Katya? He said her name out loud, but she was
long gone by now; she had found the other landing and untied a
rowboat, by herself . . . Maybe it was the dying light which played
tricks among the tree trunks, foliage overgrown and rugged—but
again he thought he saw a flutter up ahead. Was it The Toad's shirttail, starched stiff by the school laundry? And Wingate hadn't tucked
it in, as he ran around in circles?

Newell leapt over a fallen branch, caught his toe and sprawled
headlong. Up again he tore off through the forest, making his way
along the lower end of the ravine: back toward the far side. The dwindling light made it hard to gauge distance. But he ran on, panicked
for Katya; he stumbled and fell in a tangle of branches, briars that
looked further off.

He struggled up and rubbed his grazed cheek and eye. His palm
was burning, with dirt and bits of leaf stuck to the cut. How would he
row? Newell tripped over more roots and clambered up a bank. Then

he saw the river. There amid overhanging branches stood the single post and the landing. More slowly he moved forward now. He listened for sounds, and looked around. There was the rowboat where they left it: still tied up, tugging on the line.

So she had gone for the other landing. She knew how to find it since she had been here before, and taken part in their orgies? But he shut out such thoughts. She was in trouble: on her way downstream by this time, in a boat from the other side? maybe so distraught she wouldn't make it back across. And then where would she go? Bartlett? Cormac's house in town?

Finally Newell climbed in the rowboat. He spent precious seconds to untie the rope, and shove off. With one oar he poled and helped the old rowboat sidle, sluggish at first, out into the current toward midstream. The bowline came trailing after, like a snake in the dark current of the Needing.

X

The river flowed beneath him. Quickly he got oars to oarlocks and sat in position to row. But his hand was a problem; he couldn't get his stroke. Then began a struggle for control: one oar jumped, the other flailed at the surface. The boat went drifting along, and twisted toward the far bend.

Dusk lingered. Evening mantled the river, riverbanks, tall trees a bluish mauve. Newell maneuvered the oars and seemed to stroke against a rising sense of dread; but not for himself now, for her. It was hard to control the course, but he pulled, grunted, glanced over his shoulder at the tip of the island. Another few minutes, flowing with the current, brought him in view of the small cove near the turnoff to Bartlett—where they started from earlier.

Newell swung back upstream, against the current, and almost at once his whole body began to ache. His hurt hand was on fire. Another twenty, thirty yards—and there, at a gap in the eroded bank, sat a boat tied up on the Ethridge side of the island.

Then he saw Kemeny. The sophomore stood wiping his eyes with the back of his hand. He gazed out at Newell, who said:

—Where is she?

It was so quiet on the water: no need to shout. Kemeny sniffled. His features looked childish as he pointed off downstream.

–That way.

–And The Toad? MacDonald?

Kemeny swung his arm back toward the cabin. He said:

–Take me with you!

–No time.

–Please! Holbein's gone mad!

Newell lifted the oars.

The rowboat angled away in the current at mid-river. His arms and chest flooded with relief as he headed back downstream. Soon it would be dark. Behind him Jeff Kemeny stood crying, and staring after. It would have been a good idea to bring Kemeny with him, unmoor the other rowboat, and strand the bunch of them out there. Then tell the whole story when he got back to school–but to whom? The proof was there, but those masters would deny, cover up, in the face of facts: to 'save Ethridge', and cover their asses. Anyway there wasn't time.

Newell scanned the gloaming river for a sign of Katya. His gaze went to the far bend bathed in a purplish mist. Now the rowboat coasted along swiftly, stern first, without any sound.

He stood up but couldn't see much: the river ran too low between its banks. Far across the meadow stood a grove of evergreens, a dark mass at the edge of Bartlett grounds where the girls played field hockey. He imagined her walking toward it by now, though he couldn't see over the riverbank.

Newell dipped the oars, and stroked more easily to slow the rowboat's course. To the left–a web of scraggly branches; and, above them, a cloud jutted up in the twilight. Now the last light was fading; nothing held firm. He called out her name, softly, and listened to it seem to skip over the surface.

All was silence at nightfall. The far bank was a wall of darkness. Oars groaned in oarlocks; he raised them, and let drift toward the bend. What to do? Westward a red glow hovered over the small New England town.

Surely she made it to the other side and didn't take time to tie up her boat. So it went drifting away down river, and no use now to chase it and retrieve the thing. No point going after a phantom.

XI

But then he saw it: he spotted her boat. He tried to call out her name, but the sound stuck in his throat, like a sob. The boat had turned over; its bottom shone dully in the dark water toward the edge.

–Katya! he cried. We're safe, Katya!

He called her as a bird calls its mate, but she was gone. She had headed back to Bartlett since there was nowhere else for her to go—at least not to Josey, the boy she loved, who didn't love her. Maybe she went along to see Cormac who was alone in the big house again. Those two seemed to have something in common; they hit it off as friends.

The overturned rowboat dipped, and turned slowly, in the shallows. It scraped, like a groan, on a rock beneath the surface, and drifted a bit further. Night fell. By now the Needing was a vale of shadow with a last gleam of sunset from above the bank. Where was she? Which way . . .? He was trembling as he looked up and down the dim riverbank, and rowed a few strokes to keep his boat from drifting.

Then he saw her. She was doing like her rowboat a ways back upstream. Katya's sweater ballooned, a spot on the surface, as she swung, slowly, in the current which gurgled a little into its wide bend.

He stood up. One oar went flying over the side.

He yelled at her, shivering, crying. He couldn't control the boat any longer, but only wanted to go to her. And he had to. Still holding the one oar he dove, head first, and felt the convulsive shock of cold as his body sliced in the water. He tried to kick toward her but was held back by his clothes, and the stunning cold. Behind him the rowboat glided off downstream; its contours began to merge with the deep blue gloaming.

Newell paddled his arms and tried to swim toward her. He wanted to call out her name but the cold took his breath away. Cold went through him in spasms. When he tried to get his footing, the water was still over his head, and he swallowed a sickening mouthful.

Up ahead he saw the back of Katya's neck, a white patch, like a fish's belly. Or her face? The freezing current was enough to quell any struggle, but he kept on, splashing toward her. In another moment he would be borne down, go under, and stop swimming as she had.

Then, hardly knowing what he did anymore, Newell let himself float helpless a few seconds. But his head dunked under, and this brought him back to life. Again he tried to stand and his feet sank in sucking mud on the bottom. He gasped for breath, choked, and with a sodden effort began to push in, heavily, toward the bank, and her.

XII

Dimly he saw her floating, bottom up, snagged on something. It wasn't over her head there: why wasn't she okay? Why didn't she move? Wading to her Newell groped for her arms; he grabbed Katya and caught her up, clumsily, in his own arms gone numb. Breathing hard, a low rattle, he lifted her out and towed her into the shallows, and then clutched at roots on the riverbank. He dragged her from the river, and then up the muddy, crumbling bank, somehow; she was such a dead weight. Again, again he slipped back on the water pouring from their clothes.

There was still some light up there, above the riverbank. Her face was so bloated you couldn't tell it was her. Slime oozed from Katya's mouth, nostrils, ears. It dripped from her hand clenched in a fist. Her eyes were wide open beneath the wild, matted hair. Those dark eyes gazed past him, as they always had, but now with a sort of hurt wonder. No more defiance. There was a little girl look in Katya's eyes, at odds with her terrible puffed up face. But her jaw was rigid, clamped down, for the onset. He put his numb fingers to it, and pried.

With a cry Newell tried to wedge his knuckles between her teeth. It broke his skin; no matter, he didn't feel anything. Too cold. The mouth made a slight crunch, and hung open. Then he took a deep breath and put his lips to hers; of course he didn't know how to do it, only guessed he should breathe air into her. Katya tasted like the river, a tang of decomposed things . . . She had an earthen flavor, like last year's vegetation after the inhuman cold. But it was laced with a chemical taste, her medicine.

His body was shaking. He pressed his mouth to hers, and his thoughts seemed to get tangled in her hair. No one, ever . . . his lips to hers . . . when they lived in the country, in a red barn . . . orphans. They might have had a chance but now no one . . . again . . . never.

XIII

There on the riverbank, as darkness drew over, he threw up his Sunday dinner. Soaked to the bone he knelt drooling, as the taste of the river brought up more. Wouldn't she come to life? So alive an hour ago, when she challenged them and shouted at Josey—now it's over? He tried to revive her. He kept blowing in air, but the look of Katya, when he drew up to breathe, made him cry and rock his body.

After a while he just embraced her. It didn't matter how bad she looked, he just loved her. And one thing he knew: he couldn't leave her out here alone for the raccoons and foxes. He had to take her back to Bartlett and get her inside.

He couldn't lift her body. Getting her up the bank, a few minutes ago, when beside himself with fear, was done with adrenalin. Now he caught her up beneath the wooden arms and began to drag her backwards.

Newell stumbled, as he pulled her along, and she bumped over the tufts. He whimpered:

—Sorry . . . I'm sorry.

Slowly they went on the path toward the grove of evergreens, and Bartlett playing fields. There was a quarter mile of meadowland, tufts of last year's grass, rushes. He talked to her, and she seemed to answer as her dark hair brushed his cheek with a tingle.

—I won't leave you.

Water trickled down from her hair, into her face; she didn't blink. Step by step they went. He had to rest, get his breath, so he sat down next to her. He talked.

—We'll be there soon. I'll take you home. No one, again . . . ever.

Then the cold drove him to his feet—onward, making their way, slowly, past the grove of evergreens, over the dark playing fields.

Nobody in sight outside Bartlett: only dorm lights, curtained windows lit up in a neat row. Beyond dark contours of the administration building, beyond streetlamps and trees, a last wink of sunset.

As they drew near he grunted. He tugged, hauled her halfway up the embankment, fell back, and again. Then for a minute he lay there, sprawled on the damp grass beside her.

Glassy-eyed Katya lay still. She had two streaks from her nostrils.

XIV

No one in view on the walkway. None came out and stared wide-eyed. All in evening study hall.

—I brought you—Newell cried, trembled.

He put a hand to Katya's face. Stone cold. She lay there muddied, wild. She didn't budge.

In a moment people would come out. Newell knew this; and his instinct told him to get away. Before long someone would happen by, see them, and run off with a cry. Then a nurse from the infirmary, a security guard, teachers, the Bartlett headmistress would appear—and then students standing in a circle around Katya, staring at the girl. They would whisper and ask questions and frown. Some would start crying, at the sight.

Newell didn't want them to see him with her: catch him, put him where he couldn't get out, or make a move. He felt afraid 'they' would get hold of him; though he didn't know just what he meant by 'they'—not Holbein anyway, he wasn't afraid of him, and no longer thought he was The Beast. Jon Holbein liked to play with live boys, like Todd Bennett and Little Mallet, not dead ones. No; The Beast was an adult, a faculty member who lost his mind, but kept on functioning as if nothing at all was the matter. Which one? That was what he had to find out—if he meant to save himself. And he might not have long to do it before the Beast of Ethridge struck again.

So he rose on one elbow. He leaned to kiss Katya on the forehead, and knew this was the last time he would ever see her. He was crying as he got to his feet and walked off toward town in his sopping wet clothes covered with mud.

XV

At Cormac's the heavy front door opened, slowly, as though left unlocked since no one was on hand to answer the bell. Anybody home? The empty mansion seemed to ache with loneliness. Inside, the warmth was not pleasant to Newell, and made his legs go cushiony. He didn't want to vomit again. Up the main stairway he trudged: up those carpeted steps, in the silent darkness, he made his way toward Cormac's room. He had to lie down soon if he didn't want to collapse.

First he undressed; then found a towel and dried off. In the dark he shivered. Then, at last, he lay back as the room went tilting up, up and over the moment he closed his eyes.

Someone was calling him through a fog. The words sounded warped.

—This is more, please. This is more!

There was a whimpering but it sounded false.

Sulphurous fog moved over a meadow. Far across, on the other side, the sky looked like burning paper. Again the same voice: gurgle gurgle. It wanted help. A cork popped, and the river began to fill with yeast wine. Wine rose, deeper, over his head. His feet were caught in her hair, and now he must drown. He reached and tried to pull her up by the hair—like a black jellyfish. No use. He jolted awake. Strange bed, silent house.

Again he drifted off. He waited in a cove overhung with willow branches, a green niche shaded from the summer sun. There in the swirl of an old stump dividing the current, the sunspeckled surface: there was a baby, tiny, shrivelled, turning slowly on itself. Dead or alive? It eyed him with fish eyes, and wore Josey's languid smile: hey, no problem. But tied by a white cord was something dark, large beneath the ripples. A woman turned slowly round, in the brown water; she spread her arms toward him. Her posture was a horror, as she emerged, toward him, from the dark river. He cried out.

XVI

He opened his eyes in the gray light and saw sandy locks, a cuter-than-thou grin. Cormac.

—What time is it?

—Early. Before six.

—Geez, I'm thirsty.

Steps creaked. Outside the window a motor idled, a bird chirped. As daylight snuck in beneath the drawn shade, Newell sipped water and then lay back.

Through the morning hours Cormeth sat by the bed.

Newell was feverish. In the afternoon he swallowed a greenish soup Corm had found somewhere, and then slept some more. Later he heard voices in the room.

—What time is it?

—After five.

—They'll be out looking.

Mingo sat across the threshold. He wore a faded work shirt, and old pants with the cuffs rolled up. A curving line across his forehead made him look baleful. The Ming rubbed his thumb and index.

Corm looked upset now: his elf features seemed to bristle. Did he know about Katya?

Cormer stood up and paced. He mumbled to himself.

—There's a limit. We shouldn't . . .

Feverish, in the silence of the old house, Newell didn't want to re-member. A wave of sadness broke over him, and he sobbed. In his mouth still: the tang of wintry earth, the river depths.

Cormac broke out laughing but stopped abruptly.

Then Mingo said:

—Funny thing death. Ever notice? Goes on, inside us. Only one antidote: have a drink.

Newell, eyes closed, shook his head a little on the pillow. A tear fell on his cheek.

Cormac stopped pacing. He thought a moment, and said:

—Freud means joy, content. Do you believe that?

Corm stepped over the tramp's lank form and went in the hallway where he stood talking to himself. He lost his train of thought and then took up the tirade from another angle. Evening shadows mingled with the wallpaper and gathered round the gray immobile Mingo.

–Takes some patience, said The Ming.

–What does?

–To waste your life.

Cormac gave a peal of laughter. He cried out names of Nazis through the silent mansion, and then laughed with an exaggerated irony. At the top of the stairs he delivered a historic address, and listed terms of surrender. Master Glebe, the history teacher, was small stuff compared to the grandiose Cormac; except for the time or two per year when Glebeth got excited.

Then there was silence. Mingo worked his thumbs a little more.

Newell held out an arm for his clothes draped over a chair. They were filthy, and stiff. The warm room smelled rank.

Suddenly there was a bloodcurdling yell as Cormac went leaping down the stairs:

–It's the bunker!

With a clatter he fell, rolled down the steps, and lay still at the bottom.

Then Mingo raised a finger, and said to himself:

–Strange thing. It has implications . . . for the future.

XVII

In the old mansion Cormac lay with a cute grin at the foot of the stairs. So he knew? He loved her too. Cormeth never talked about girls.

Slouched over the bedroom threshold Mingo looked like a broken statue. His gray face was cradled in his gray sleeve.

Newell waited in bed another five minutes, but it was time to go. He swung his legs to the floor, tottered, and then reached for his dust-caked pants and shirt. He fumbled with his socks, shoes, things of grime.

He stepped over Mingo who looked up at him.

Downstairs, Cormac had crawled into the living room where he sat on the rug. To each of his temples he held a framed photograph. Corm's look of sly cuteness came and went like a dappled sunlight.

–I know it's my fault, he said. It must be.–He cupped the pictures to his temples.–If not, that's where the trouble starts. Don't get me wrong, we're all God's little bastards, I won't complain! But there's a limit.

A tear rolled down his nose.

–Cormeth.

The clock on the mantel struck three, four, six times.

Corm thumped the picture frames on his cheek, and one gave a little crunch. Then he flipped them toward the fireplace. He tried on his smug grin, but that didn't seem to work. So he sat back against the divan and stared, blankly, straight ahead. Loneliness flowed like a current through the spacious, high-ceiling'd rooms; it eddied round a lamp, and plashed over the wallpaper.

–I've got to get back there, Cormer.

–Ah ha! You heard me.

Newell stood a moment: like a scarecrow in his muddy clothes. Each movement shed a fine dust on the carpet and furniture.

He gazed at his friend. He leaned and brushed the greasy mesh from Cormac's bewildered forehead, but it fell back, like a broken spring.

–Thanks, Corm.

He patted his shoulder.

Night was falling as Newell made his way through the small New England town. He turned left past the library; then underneath the railroad bridge, and out along the winding road toward Ethridge.

Chapter Nine

I

Arriving back on campus he was amazed to find the usual routine. No police swarming around the quad. No note on his door: 'Report to the Ethridge Homestead at once. Signed, your Faculty Adviser.' Not even a sign of Dean Wart lurking on the hall to read him the riot act. Everything went along its normal course for a weeknight, as though the girl named Katya never existed.

Dinner had ended. In evening study hall the students toiled over their lessons until 8:45. Then time to do a few things, straighten up your room, get ready for bed. Lights-out promptly at 9:30. Let your eyes close, and then—clangalangalang! Get up and do it again.

So Newell went along to his room. It was so quiet . . . No Geeter, or Rog Hillyer the senior counselor; only a deserted first-floor Warren House—a peculiar silence, campus wide. At any instant Newell expected to see that dreadful face, or mask, again, as though suspended in the darkness outside his window. But no. Though he felt sad, very depressed, he was so exhausted he began to calm down. His mind and body seemed to melt as he went in the bathroom and had a hot shower.

Then he put on a t-shirt and pair of old corduroys. Thinking he might read for awhile, escape into one of the dime novels he liked so much, he propped on his pillows and turned a few pages.

But he was done in. His head lay back. The book closed by itself and fell by his side on the bed.

He slept.

II

The student houses were darkened: all but a few lights in the masters' apartments, and on the senior floors. The school lay quiet.

On first-floor Settlers the hall clock struck back, then forward three or four, at a clip. Radiators, set in the wainscoted walls, made their small noises like the thoughts of the old.

At a few minutes before midnight the long Settlers corridor was deserted, dimly lit, with its musty bookish scent. The wide study hall, a hundred or so desks, lay empty in the shadows. From ground level windows spread a view of the quadrangle with a glow, here and there, of antique lanterns.

Now, campus activity stilled, the silence had a life of its own. Creakings; stirrings of a vent; settlings–these had a live accent, as though a second Ethridge community carried on its affairs, behind the walls, or down in the underground tunnel, while the daytime Ethridge took a rest. The faint whoosh of a draft sounded like sighs from somewhere. A breeze off the river groaned in the windows; you might have thought a choir of ghosts sang a hymn in the chapel at the end of the hall. But this hymn wasn't in any sacred hymnal.

And now, slowly, a door opened: the door to the Steam Tunnel. A big, male figure emerged, stepped from that darkness into the amber light of the corridor, and turned toward the Warren House side. Whether or not by design, he didn't shut the door: just as he didn't bother to brush a cobweb from his brow.

That face must have been a mask: unless it got burned in a fire some years ago. The skin was drawn, with a glazed look; it had a shine to it, hard to imitate with makeup. The features were horrible enough, with a smooth knob, a tumor to one side of the deep, dissolving eyes; and another, larger, in the flesh of the neck.

The big, awful man went along, with a solemn stride. Behind him, the sighs, moans, rustlings rose in pitch, still low but seeming to gush through the door left open; as if the dead might cry for help to the living, but didn't know how, so they just kept singing their song. The Beast of Ethridge looked pretty bad. Yet it had a sure step, as it moved down the empty hallway and turned right past the faculty lounge. There was a dull force in that measured gait, as it went along, on the verge of action, in the moments after midnight. In my opinion it looked a bit too fit, and purposeful, for a normal ghost. Also, it had some flab, just a hint of paunch perhaps, beneath the sort of smock, like filthy sackcloth, which it wore over a pair of suit trousers.

III

Calmly, sadly, the large figure moved past the lounge and out the door on the side of Astarte's school laundry. It knew the way. Then, on cat's paws, it entered the first door along the walkway.

Warren House lay silent. A light by the stairway cast a dim aura on the student hallway, the half dozen doors: one, at the far end, where Pastor Geeter had his quarters, an inner sanctum not entered by other people; one, in the center, where Manuel the foreign exchange student and his roommate Jeffers had lived, and Shellnitz after them, but there was no one in the room now; and one, at this end, first door to the left from the front hall, where Newell Gilbert lay sleeping alone, since his roommate moved to a single room across the quad.

The plodding figure paused by that first door, and turned the knob, slowly. It grated a little in the late night silence.

The Beast of Ethridge looked in, and saw the boy asleep on his bed by the window—but still dressed, with the bedspread pulled over his legs. What's this? A sound in here? A radio played low, a distant station in and out of static. What? The grim visitor stepped in, and switched on the desk light. Hm, a sophomore with all-night lights. Ten hours! But, Sir!

Strewn on the desk were school books, a loose-leaf notebook, pens and pencils, mechanical drawing implements in a pouch. Lined neatly on the shelf, like valued possessions, were paperback novels: *The Amboy Dukes, Knock on Any Door, Reefer Kid, Gang Deb, Harrison*

High, a dozen others. This student prized such works, but not the course books where his future was written.

On the bed the boy stirred. He raised a hand to fend the light. He rubbed his eyes.

The light went out.

—Newell?

The voice was sad.

—Sir?

The boy sat up—someone in the room with him.

—It is time.

—Time?

—Get up. You must go with me.

—Go where?

From the stairwell a touch of light showed the large, dark contours of The Beast, its slightly hunched shoulders, powerful legs, its terrible face, and unblinking stare. The thing stood there. It waited. No movement; no rasp of breathing. Only the feel to it of an evil purpose: in its deep, insufferable eyes melted into dark night.

On the hall clock, outside the door, the minute hand struck.

IV

Newell, on his bed, jolted awake. His heart pounded wildly. After all he had been through he tried to control himself and not show fear. He thought: cry out for Schmied next door? The big nitwit could not be counted on and probably wouldn't respond. Well then scream: make a racket and wake up the whole hall including Geeter? What if The Beast *was* Geeter? A religious man possessed by a devil? no wonder Virgil Parker couldn't stand him. Oh, what to do? Of all the boring flits Newell had to live with day after day since last October, only Shellnitz had the spunk to come running at his call; only The Owl wasn't selfish to the core, too hurt by life to be otherwise— but he was gone now, and what could he have done anyway? Boz Krips was also a friend: Boz would have tried to do something about this Beast. But the jock lived all the way across the quad . . . So what to do? Jump out the window? He would have to turn, and open it wider, and then there was the screen. The Beast would be on him with a bound. And then no mercy, no more delay: strangulation, or a heavy blow on the head: how ever it had happened to his hallmates, Manuel, Jeffers, Shellnitz, bye bye.

He saw The Beast: those disgusting features, maggoty, with a smooth knob tucked in the drooping skin. And yet the face glowed, in the shadows—lit from within? Hell's fires, inside him? Yes, the time had come. The wait must have been a long one: for nature to make such a face; for Ethridge to produce such a monster. But here it was. It stood poised in his room, and stared right in his eyes. It nodded: oh yes, the time had come to fulfill a long desire. And, even in such a moment, under attack, an idea dawned on Newell, namely: Manuel was different, in his way; Moon Jeffers, in another; Shellnitz even more different, nothing if not different, a regular nut; but I am the most different of all because I just don't care anymore, you flits! I won't conform, or play along. Expel me if you like. Disown me, Dad, if you have to. Good! For I am not afraid of what you think.

Newell spoke to it.

—Hello, Sir.

This seemed to take The Beast aback. It said:

—Hello.

That voice . . . such a kindly, quiet tone, one moment; it would beat you to death in the next. He knew the timbre of it, quite refined . . . Well whose? Geeter's? Dean Wart? Or, horror of horrors, the Ethridge headmaster's? That would explain why nothing had come of the killings: why there was no sign of an investigation, but only cover-up. Maybe Master Glebe, the frustrated husband, childless despite the world's most voluptuous wife? That figured. Or Runt Roentgen, gym dictator, who deemed ten hours' detention a trifle? Astarte, the head custodian? Bill Hastings, Refectory chef, who made his hasty puddings from an original recipe? Who? Who could it be? Who was The Beast? Newell had its name on the tip of his tongue, but it just wouldn't come, yet.

Those dark eyes, so sad, so sick. Did they lead to a brain, a soul, the way human eyes did? The look they gave was hypnotic. But Newell had been through so much in the past two days, in the past six months, he only said:

—Give me a minute, Sir. I'll come with you, but I want to put on my shoes.

The Beast didn't answer. But, maybe impatient, afraid of a trick— oh, he knew their little wiles—it took a step forward, then another.

–Time to go.

Such a weary voice . . . And then? What of the story a senior counselor told to incoming freshmen on third-floor Settlers? What was it he said about the Beast of Ethridge, a legend? Now here was the real one: it took another step, and looked on the verge of springing forward, as Newell laced his shoes, and got ready.

Newell stared back at it, and wanted to say something. He gulped down his fear.

–Are you . . . are you looking for your son, Sir?

Now it came on, rigid, slow. Arms hanging down like an ape's, it passed by the other bed stripped except for the cover. Almost over the prey, the Beast of Ethridge said:

–You're my son. All of you . . . all my sons.

For an instant the two seemed to hang there: the psychopath, the rosy-cheeked teenager. In the glimmer of light from the hall, they looked hung by a thread.

Then Newell turned, and dove low, like a lineman, in an effort to lunge past the other's shins. But this Beast was a nimble beast, and grabbed him, shoved him back. Newell glimpsed the ghastly mask: no life in those eyes, no feeling.

As suddenly as it began, the fight was over.

The other was on top of him, and had him in a death grip. A powerful hand took Newell by the nape and jolted his head against the wood bed frame, once, again. And that was all.

V

No one, in the deserted quadrangle at two a.m., and no one inside Settlers saw the big, stalking figure carry a boy slung over his shoulder. Steps sounded down the long corridor, past the faculty lounge, front lobby, but there wasn't a soul to hear. The boy rose toward consciousness like a fish on a hook. And now, in his willless state, jostled on that cold broad shoulder, the key to it all was just a thought away. A name . . . it was there in his throbbing brain filled with sulphurous fumes like the science master's lab. For an instant it did come to him: the name spelled out in a mechanical drawing assignment so intricate, so hard even Manuel couldn't hope to do it for him, after lights-out. The Beast's identity was clear as a vision, but faded as the boy's mind rose back among the living. It had come too late anyway, since nobody else would ever know. The madman, who had kept an eye on him since that Sunday afternoon last fall, when they saw one another at the cabin, did not mean to let him tell the secret. And so they came to the door, across from the study hall, which led down to the Steam Tunnel.

Pausing, The Beast reached for a key chain, a master key that fitted every lock at Ethridge. The old door, left open, gave a whine, like a boy crying, alone, in the middle of the night. Inside, in the darkness, The Beast locked it. Then the two went down those rickety steps into The Tunnel. And the door was locked behind them. And no one saw, or heard. Nobody knew.

Thump, thump. Newell felt the plodding motion, but still from a distance. His kidnapper stumbled over something; a small jolt, in passing, served to alert the boy's senses. He had a warm salt taste on his lips. Blood. And then he got a vague awareness: is this the end? Carried along, his mind began to hone in, and he blinked.

A flashlight went on.

Further, further in they went: past where Holbein's work crew had left off, after starting an impossible job. Newell, fully conscious by now, felt a need to scream and pound the monster's back. But he had better play dead, since no one would hear if he cried out. No one? He listened. Those voices, those moans, laments he had heard from time to time through the school year; the chorus of muffled howls that seemed to filter from the aged foundations of Ethridge: up through chunks in the floorboards—secret voices, whispering things about the past, buzzing round his ears in sleep: he heard them now, but closer, clearer, as though firsthand. There was a murmur of many, many spirits, like leaves which rustle in the cold autumn wind, and they say their hour is past. And then he heard, further into the Tunnel, ever further—wingflaps, roused by the steps of the Beast of Ethridge. Wingflaps with a distinct sound, as if in a vacuum: there were bats down here?

What a strange glow The Beast's flashlight cast over things, the scene like an endless mausoleum caked in gray dust; a landscape of death. But it was a practical Beast, wasn't it? Rather a handy madman: first the master key, then a flashlight: pretty soon he'd stop for lunch in a favorite niche, a scenic spot where he stored some kind of wormy picnic . . . Newell tried to remember the name, and the sad,

sad story attached to it. But his head bumped along upside down, slung over that brawny back, and he just couldn't think. He did keep enough presence of mind to hang limp, play possum and not rouse the thing to a fury which would mean a good pounding, like meat on a marble slab, and then the end.

Was it the head custodian, Astarte? Had it been Astarte's kindly voice, but toneless, back there in the student room on first-floor Warren? The janitor was a moody man, but sometimes of a sunlit morning his eye had a hearty glance; and he would give you a pat on the back as he passed along the walkway, jovial on his good days, not like the masters. Could this maniac be him?

They trudged deeper, deeper into The Tunnel. No hope of ever getting out now: after they had come so far in. After the battering Newell's head had gotten, the shock: was that old story coming back to him? . . . They went along the narrow passageway where immense spider webs, lit up like wonders by The Beast's flashlight, looked more complex than Mechanical Drawing Assignment XII, which no normal boy could hope to do but only a Manuel, only a Jeffers. Filth hung down in wreaths from the cornices, as The Beast and its prey went along, and stepped past objects, the world of Ethridge refuse, which cast fantastic shadows.

Then they stopped.

VI

Amid the dust and clutter Newell was dumped, banged down with a force contained only by the fact that it wanted him alive a little while longer. And then playtime; then to swing, back and forth, whether down here or out at the cabin, forever. Then to become a playmate for the lost son: the one who had been buried in the Puritan cemetery across from Cormac's, dressed in his Sunday best and lowered in a grave with a neat headstone–but dug up again, no matter how far gone, and given a change of clothes like a doll, and a swing set and toys to play with and even a few little friends to share his games, his childhood hours. As for the choice of such playmates: they had to be different, misfits, not at all missed, not the blue-blooded Ethridgians, tomorrow's leaders.

Again the key chain clinked. The master key was inserted in an old, old lock. It was the door to a side room off the Tunnel. Dropped like a sack, shoved roughly by a strong leg, Newell lay still. He smelled an awful stench. It stank so bad in this storage room off the Tunnel, he thought he would faint again from it. The dead don't smell that awful; this was a live stink. He wrinkled his nose at the peepee and doodoo smell. And now he knew the idea was to leave him here until he died of thirst. His screams would never be heard except as sighings of the breeze in early spring, when it fluttered amid cherry trees and dogwoods in the first warm days. And all the while just up above, not ten feet over his head, the Ethridge student body would pass from classes to the Refectory and back again, and then down to the gym and playing fields for athletics in the afternoon. They would go about their day as though nothing had ever happened: no boy turned up missing, his place vacant on the raised pew beneath the high Venetian windows, in morning chapel, as Geeter droned on. No, his soul and body too had gone away, that's all, to a place of less privilege. And he would be forgotten soon, not talked about, and life would go on without any fuss, as Dean Wart preferred.

Now just another instant: the door would close, and the lock would turn. Then how long would he last, by himself, down here in the darkness? And there would be rats the size of a master's cordovan shoes. There would be big spiders like the ones that did those mechanical drawing assignments all along the Tunnel. After all might not this psychopath be their mechanical drawing teacher: the one who taught Ethridge's spiders to spin their complex web?

In another instant Newell would be shut up, caught in such a web, forever. And then the days would pass, the weeks and the months, until Ethridge let out for summer vacation. Then all, except Newell Gilbert and a few others, would go home and enjoy themselves, and none be any the wiser.

VII

Backing a step, pausing a moment to view its good work, The Beast shone the flashlight at Newell's body heaped, with head turned away, in a mound of gray filth. Whew! How it stank in here. The

Beast seemed to gloat. Maybe it thought of the fun in store . . . And then Newell, risking a glimpse, saw his friend Shellnitz huddling, deeper in, on the edge of light. The Owl's eyes stared out from his face caked with what looked like droppings. Shelleth's blond hair shot this way and that like an electrocuted cat. Was the boy still alive? Wasn't he dead yet? Shellnitz squatted in his poop. He didn't move; but Newell thought he heard breathing, yes, slow, rasping breaths, like a dying animal. How many days had he been down here? The Beast just left you alone for nature to take its course. The Beast relished death.

—Shellfish! Newell spoke. Is that you?

—Shell*nitz*, croaked a voice. My name is Shell*nitz*.

Now the door began to creak . . . creak closed, never to open again, for them. But, before this happened, Newell spoke again. Maybe he got the guts, or presence of mind, from his friend being there. He said in an unsteady voice:

—So it's true . . . what they say about you, Sir. And everybody knows it too . . . all the boys, and all the masters. How you killed your own son.

—No.

From somewhere Newell produced a low sort of laugh, devilish, and said:

—Good work, Sir. So you were the one. You plugged it in, you did it.

The other sort of bucked.

—No talking in class.

Again Newell gave the laugh.

—That year, Sir, when the Needing rose up and flooded the campus . . .

The Beast seemed to get upset. The Beast had feelings. It ground its teeth.

—Pipe down. No talking, I said. Three hours.

Newell chuckled, low, while he racked his brain. He was bluffing because he just couldn't remember the name—which the senior counselor spoke in a spooky tone, during those first stressful weeks at Ethridge, when Newell was a freshman on third-floor Settlers. Was it Reginald Glebe, the childless history teacher, who flew into a rage once or twice a year during a lecture? Was it Master Delvig, the youthful English teacher who lived in a world of his own? Lord, what antisocial characters they hired to help form tomorrow's leaders.

Who? Who was it? Newell saw that his words struck home, so he kept on:

—And then, Sir, when the river went down again . . . then your son, Sir, what was his name? What was it?

—. . .

Teeth grinding, there in the doorway, the Beast of Ethridge glared in. Was it the science teacher, Master Sippel? Truly it would take a scientist to cook up such a mask as this rascal, this kidnapper of boys wore when he went about his dark deeds. Last summer there was some other kind of scandal about Sippel, though Newell had seen him as almost human because of it. What went on? What had he done? Something about a teenage girl, in the back of his car, sex! Sippel parked on a lonely road; and he petted, felt her up, like a high school Harry. But the cops found them, her half naked, him unzipped.

—What was your son's name, Sir? Go on, you can say it.

—Rodney.

—Ah that's right. Rodney Like my friend Nimrod Shellnitz here, whom you've been so kind to have as your guest . . . Your son Rodney was down in the cellar, wasn't he, Sir? And then it was you, his father, who—

—I'm warning you, you little fiend.

That voice sounded alive. Teeth gnashed.

The little fiend stared at the flashlight.

—We all know about this. The whole school knows. And we talk about you, Sir, after lights-out. Yes, we do. Rod . . . what's his last name? I can't seem to remember.

—. . .

—Rodney was a brilliant student, a quarterback in football. All-around boy. And he stood down there knee-deep in water, putting the basement pump in place just like you told him. Didn't you, Sir? Well, didn't you? And then from up above, on the first floor, you had the bright idea to turn on the pump. Why, Sir? Why do such a stupid thing? Shame, Sir. You own son.

—Oh!

In a curious display, the Beast of Ethridge howled with pain.

—I think you deserve ten hours' detention, Sir.

—Oh! . . . oh!

—You electrocuted Rodney. I'm sorry but it was you. Why? On purpose? Wasn't he the son you wanted?

Now The Beast waded in. The Beast came on, and meant to shut the little fiend's mouth once and for all. But this was what the little fiend wanted: for The Beast to stop blocking the door. Newell jumped around. He laughed wildly. He darted in and out of the bright beam.

—Oh-oh! . . .

The Beast roared.

—Over here, Sir! Ha ha!

Newell kept laughing and tried to see a way past the kidnapper, to scoot by him and out. But no use. It didn't work. Newell laughed and talked it up, but the Beast of Ethridge cornered its prey, and stayed between him and the door. On it came, like a one-eyed Cyclops with the bright flashlight, agile, arms wide, and full of hate. And now Newell Gilbert felt this was it for him, the end, death at an early age. And fear took him in its grip and wouldn't let him move anymore, resist the pursuer; he couldn't stir an inch though his life depended on it. He stood there half crouched, bristling like an animal caught in a headlight beam on a dark highway: unable to budge, break the spell, about to be run over.

The Beast, arms wide to prevent escape, grinned. The Beast was on him. It reached out. It raised a hand to knock him senseless. Then it stopped grinning, and roared, on the verge of a death blow to the thing it hated most on earth: a bad boy, like his son with a flaw—to be human—his son everybody thought was so good.

But suddenly there was a scream. Oh what a scream that was, from deeper in the cave; why, the Headmaster must have heard the scream where he slept his sleep of the righteous, dreaming of Ivy League admissions, inside the Ethridge Homestead. How is it possible the entire campus, just overhead, didn't hear Shellnitz's ear-splitting cry for help? The boy leapt forward, an awful sight in his charcoal gray suit tattered to shreds, caked with human waste, his clip-on bowtie gone crooked, his cufflinks half undone. Mad Shellnitz's blond curly hair fanned out stiff as a stingray. His young eyes bulged with horror. He sprang out of the dark, two little fists in the air; it would have been funny but for the look on his face, truly terrible. And The Beast couldn't help but glance away, and stare at Shellnitz an instant—as Hot Rod windmilled his arms and rained punches on the Beast of Ethridge's ribs and midriff like gnats round a floodlight. And this jolted Newell from his trance of fear. As The Owl screamed and flailed, and The Beast turned and shone the light here, there, distracted from his prey, Little Fiend jumped forward and yanked the flashlight and tried to grab it away! This loosed the thing for an instant, and Newell got hold, and pulled it free. The light fell on the floor, spinning to one side, and went out.

Total darkness.

VIII

Newell crouched. On his own now he gasped for breath, and got ready to pounce for the door. He moved left. He tried to stay out of reach and only hoped The Beast would squat to its right in search of the flashlight. Shellnitz had fallen back, onto the floor, and sounded asthmatic, or like he'd gone into his death rattle. But the attacker took slow, deep breaths as it groped about, its arms used as feelers, in the blackness. Then Newell felt its paw on the scruff and gave a yell and lurched away.

Staying low, one hand to the mouldy floor, he crept back. He tried not to give himself away by puffing for air.

Then he came to Shellnitz. The poor kid crumpled in a heap, spent—all his high spirits, crazy pranks and laughter, all his revolt against Runt Roentgen had climaxed in his fury of just a moment ago.

Newell whispered:

—I'll come back. I won't leave you.

Then he picked up the wasted boy, who couldn't have weighed seventy pounds after the ordeal down here, and lifted him up. He held the little guy under the arms, in front of him like bait, sort of propping him with his knees, and said:

—Over here, Sir! This way!

The Beast grabbed Shellnitz with a violence. The impact sent Newell sprawling back. But then The Beast gave a roar, different this time, like physical pain. What? Had spunky Shellnitz rallied a last burst of energy and grabbed onto The Beast's paw and bit it? Newell took his chance; he bounded round on hands and knees; he groped his way toward the door; and out.

IX

There was no time to stop and think. He knew to his left lay the way back, but the exit onto first-floor Settlers was locked. Now in the middle of the night he couldn't yell for anyone's help; he would only be trapped if he retraced their steps and went that way. So he had to take right and go deeper into the Tunnel, without a light. Hands out in front he felt his way along. What things did he bump into? Under his feet he heard stirrings—the rats, the rats. What did he touch? Who can say what spiders lurked down here, in a maze of webs spun year upon year? It is hard to think how such a place could ever get cleaned up. But Newell Gilbert learned about it the hard way, groping with his hands, bumping into ghastly stuff with his body; he had a look, so to say, in the dark.

Behind him the flashlight went on. He ducked. It searched in the other direction first, and then swung around. Maybe he tried to hide too late, or it saw movement. The thing had seen him and now here it came. The Beast moved forward now, and The Beast knew its way around, down here, the ins and outs of hell. It came on in a solemn rage; it didn't mean to let the little truant get away.

But at the same time it lighted the way, somewhat, among those mushy contours. And Newell's eyes, and reflexes, began to get used to the place. He went along. He gave little cries as he kicked at the rats, their scurryings underfoot; he gave squeak for squeak and felt them leap and nip at his shins, the intruder. He stumbled and fell; he got back on his feet. What horror would jump out at him next? Closer now, ever closer he heard the moaning, lamenting sounds which came from deeper in the Tunnel, like wind on a winter night. This was the murmur and stir of many, many young people trapped down here, like Shellnitz, like Jeffers and Manuel, held against their will and tortured by the Beast of Ethridge, in a Self-Furtherance Society of the Dead. The sound of them, as of wingflaps about his head, bats, and the strange light now cast on the passageway and the weird echoes of his own steps and also The Beast's, coming on behind him,—all this made Newell so alert, so tense with fear, he did things he couldn't have hoped to do elsewhere. Perhaps fifty feet separated the pursuer from the prey. Newell turned with a shrill laugh and called back:

–Ten hours, Sir! You killed Rodney! Ha ha ha! Good work: the Honor Roll!

Beast didn't respond, but only plodded after him, and shone the light.

On and on they went deeper into the Tunnel. Bats flew up in flocks with a thunder of wingflaps. And the groans and howls grew louder–from somewhere in the dark distance far up ahead: much, much farther than the real distance between Settlers and the Refectory where they must be right about now; somewhere along there, he thought, since he couldn't recall a turning. Or maybe they turned while he was being carried like a sack on the other's shoulders? before the room, and Shellnitz? Say this stretch was beneath Tildon: there would be reentry at some point, maybe unlocked. Maybe at The Snug in Hampton House basement where the seven-layer cake was kept! . . . But he couldn't be sure; he didn't know where. And the Tunnel was so mossy with dust, with stinking mold, so filled up and cluttered with age-old shapeless things, masses of filth bred of filth and more reeky filth, woolly ghostlike forms from the time of Maspeth Needing and the first Puritans ever to come this way, centuries ago–how would he know? How would he find an exit? under these layers upon layers of gray dust and cobwebs and who knew what else left by the generations of rats, bats, other pests which fed on furniture stuffing and soiled mattresses and on one another. A horror house. And by now he was wound all around by spider webs; and no doubt he had poisonous spiders and every sort of horrible insect on his skin, worms, white beetles, tics, crawling things which had never seen the light of day. Newell struggled, groped onward, spit out furry bits, and thought of Shellnitz back there covered with droppings, his face bloodied, a texture of rat bites.

X

They did come to a dead end. He ploughed into a wall, which might give way, as it flaked down about him. He gave a cry. His eyes were on fire, swollen, nearly closed. Refectory just above? Behind him the flashlight no longer lit the way, its beam drawn in, kept at closer range on purpose. And then, suddenly, there was no light at all.

Still Newell made his way forward. He had to. Hope or no hope, what other choice? He coughed. He spat dust. He was running from a man, if that's what it was, who wanted to murder him, end his life, and make some sick use of his corpse. The man wanted to revive the shock and horror of that moment long ago when he had made a fatal mistake and put out the life of a beloved son on whom his hopes rested. And so all Ethridge and its grand tradition, its beautiful campus and elitist reputation, all this 'finest education available' for future leaders had become no more than a place to fixate on his dead son, a boy killed by mistake. Now for years the Beast of Ethridge had felt a rage against the living, an envy to end all envies; yes, envy had turned it into the thing it was, a man into a beast; and its face, that gory mask, gave a good look at the soul. And while the son, the best of them all, an Ethridge star, lay turning to dust beneath a cold stone out in the Puritan cemetery, the father lost his mind with grief, and guilt, and knew he could never accept this. And then he went out there with a shovel one night and dug him up again—worked over the grave site so no one would know, closed the coffin, put back the cut grass, and brought Rodney home again, in his Sunday suit. What law was it, or broken law, in the mind of man, that caused such a thing? And it would go on. It would continue until some boy, Newell Gilbert or another, had the daring and rare luck to outsmart the full-grown man become irrational and tragic. And somewhere, in its deepest being, the Beast of Ethridge must have wanted this too. It longed to lose, in such a dreadful contest, so the nightmare could end, and life go on. It yearned to be seen for what it was, identified, and made unable to harm any more people: no longer at liberty to stalk them, in the dark night of Ethridge, and pounce. Through the school year Newell had felt something like this, though he didn't know what to think: Newell often sleepless, always nervous because aware of a lurking presence night and day, a pale mask hung outside his window, eyes—eyes upon him, which envied his normal joy in things and good, healthy response to Dean Wart's injustice, Coach Roentgen's arrogance, Geeter's two-faced concern, Headmaster Smithson's . . . system, played for all it was worth. Those eyes boded no good; they did not love a boy who refused to conform for better or worse. But if, overcoming fear, you looked deep into them, you would see—a beast, the Beast of Ethridge, itself aware it could not go on like this, could not hold life back, and take innocent lives to meet its own sick needs, forever. Perhaps it had had enough, too, of such a grim game, and wanted to be caught; it craved to be put away where it could no longer hurt others. But until that moment, of its release, it would go on with its game of death.

And so it did. All through the school year, since that afternoon out on the island last October, The Beast had been in a life and death struggle with the boy. This one, the one it chased tonight: it hated him truly for being not like other Ethridge boys,—alive, which is what Rodney wasn't; still free in his mind, which is what The Beast wasn't;—and also for being onto its secret, its crimes. It watched over the boy's comings and goings. It hovered close; it looked in his window late at night; it breathed its foul breath, its obnoxious sighs on him. It meddled in his everyday affairs as well; the holiday work detail was just a way to keep him from going home, and in its loving clutches. And all the while it tracked him, in silence. And it loved him. And its beady eyes looked quite self-righteous when they marked the rebel, the rebel despite himself, a good cheerful kid really, with a sign.

This happened. These facts, stranger than fiction, came to pass. But The Beast and the boy are in their last lap now.

XI

Behind Newell, back down the Tunnel, there was no more flashlight: no jittery beam seen one moment, gone the next, like a ship's light in a gale. But up ahead now, it was hard to say how far, he could see a dull sort of glow. An orangish aura had begun to play over the dark surface of things, if things these still were, tinged with charcoal gray. Somehow it looked like a curtain of flames; or let's say the ornate chandelier of the Refectory, seen from afar.

But not only this. He also heard something; that is, he heard what he had been hearing for a long time, though the sound was muffled beneath his breathing as he threw himself along the Tunnel. Long drawn-out moans and laments sounded louder now, closer at hand, up ahead round the next turn, or a few more turns. Here they were, yes: those secret voices that rose through chinks and fissures of the ancient Ethridge 'plant', through walls and floorboards late at night, and buzzed about your ears in sleep. Strange echoes round the quad when you least suspected, echoes of laughter at times, like tired voices in a spree of high spirits, in a ghostly fiesta. Maybe one of the masters had cracked a joke. Ha ha. But, in general, the murmur of many, many people unhappy over something; and they seemed to threaten an advance: threaten to take over the quiet campus and step into the role of the living, if Headmaster Smithson and Dean Wart and Coach Roentgen and Pastor Geeter weren't a little more careful in their dealings with the boys. Still, and ever, like wind moaning in the old window casements: the undertones sounded whipped up to a pitiful wail down here, in this Steam Tunnel, closer to the source. Also there was a submissive note to them; and a kind of abandon, vaguely sensual, like the orgies conducted by Jon Holbein with his baton out on the island, in that lonely cabin: when there were town women on hand, along with underclassmen privileged to become a member of *Self-Furtherance*, receive bids, and do those seniors' bidding.

Newell went on. He turned at a dead end and forged ahead because he had no choice. All sense of direction was long gone, so he made his way toward the distant glow; though it looked like no light of this world, and didn't promise an escape. The reddish glimmer was more like an entry into a place from where no one got out. Had he reached the far end of the quadrangle by now? Or gone beyond? Beyond Ethridge?

There was an odor. A bad smell came to his nostrils, which might have been Bill Hastings' fine cuisine, in the Refectory, if it weren't more like the one that night last December, out at the cabin. But he didn't have time to sniff the bouquet, and think about it, because suddenly the flashlight was there right behind him.

The Beast came on. It took the last corner and tripped among the jumbled clutter, the dark shapes so dust-covered they no longer looked like anything human. The Beast came: it shambled along knocking things from its way; it shone its torch on this house of horrors, this place beyond the grave, and gave a low growl to say it didn't like so much fuss caused by a mere boy.

Then Newell fell. He lost his footing. The ground rolled from beneath his feet, and he went down heavily, breaking his fall with an elbow. Electricity shot through his arm, his body, as he lay there stunned. And the pursuer got closer.

With a cry Newell climbed back on his feet. He wheezed dust; he had become a thing of dust. Dust filled his five senses and entered his body at every step, every breath, swallow. And the other grunted and drew nearer, nearer. And in a moment The Beast would be on him. Then lights out. Then the end. Newell Gilbert stopped. He stood where he was, where he had fallen. An idea came to him, and he stooped to reach for the thing that brought him down: a length of lead piping.

Then he went on, and paused at a turning. Here the Tunnel forked, and he must choose between two directions. A right turn seemed to lead nowhere: darkness. To the left, still far off, in the starless night underground, he saw the eerie glow but bigger, somehow, big, as a cosmic flicker. How far did this Tunnel extend?

Far.

So he kept to the left, and went on another twenty yards perhaps. The Beast was close behind, ever closer. And here the odor was more pungent, even worse than Master Sippel's science lab, worse than Ethan Jeffers out at the cabin, that night: Ethan so rigid he might rip a seam in his tweeds; Ethan decomposing as he swung back and forth, back and forth, with a creak.

But here Newell no longer found old furniture, or anything manmade. Here he saw only nondescript things, a maze of shapes with no clear relation to the human. If the definition of hell is—neglect, then this must be it.

XII

And then Newell neared the Tunnel's end: the Steam Tunnel, as such. Another thirty, forty yeards? so hard to gauge distance down here, in the murky darkness. There was some sort of cave, or a falling-off place, a great vat, where shadows seemed to ripple up from the earth's bowels. Were his eyes playing tricks on him? Was it Astarte's boiler room? Was it a fire? Flames lashed up from some volcano-like underground space. He felt the great heat, and knew he couldn't go on any further. But here came the light behind him: it got closer, closer. The Beast of Ethridge knew one thing only; it wanted its prey.

What to do? Where to hide? How to get out of here? How to survive?

Back, back he pushed himself, into the flaking, crusty wall with its layer on layer of cobwebby dust. He meant to merge himself with the dust, so the other couldn't make out his form, or see where he hid. Standing there, stiffly upright, pressed back against the wall, he waited for the flashlight to arrive.

He waited.

Like a batter at home plate, in his stance, he waited for his instant to swing out with the lead pipe. And here it came: the big ugly thing that had tormented and bullied him, and done such a job on his friend Shellnitz.

It came. And the powerful form came on behind the light. Well, let it. Please, step this way. You are welcome. Here, here—the ugly mug was only a patch of darkness, a hint of horror behind the light which trudged on, on. Now—now—

It went past him a step or two. Newell lashed out. With all his might, all the strength left in him, he swung the length of metal pipe at the back of its head, first a glancing blow, then again, smack! this time more solidly, and the angular figure reeled, and dropped the flashlight, which went out again. Down the Tunnel there was a stir of wingflaps, the bats, in a huff. A third blow, a fourth—Newell bopped that head which didn't want to fall, and never made a sound, never gave a slightest groan. Didn't it *feel*, after all? Whether stunned, or from sheer impact, The Beast went to one knee and shook its head a little, as Newell in a frenzy, crying, shouting, pounded down again, again.

And then he writhed, cursed, sobbed over The Beast lying sprawled in the ashen dust at his feet. Wildly he hammered down at its horrible face, its knobby neck, its chest, ribs—and gave himself up to the violence. Newell pounded down, down, down, with an animal grunting, a grinding of teeth.

And then The Beast lay still.

XIII

The boy crouched by the broad-chested body to pull off the mask. Who was the Beast of Ethridge? Finally, now, he would know. But he wasted precious seconds with the flashlight; he shook it, trying to make it come on again. No luck; and, while he was busy with this, The Beast opened its eyes, and stared up at him; but then closed them again, and waited. Newell fiddled with the switch some more, and then gave up, and put the flashlight in his belt. How would he ever find his way back now, out of here? A dim orangish flicker lit this final section of the Tunnel. But deeper in, with its colossal jumble of old furniture, and blocked turnings, and rats waiting for him to fall, once, so they could attack and make a meal of him—back there, in the total darkness, how would he find his way?

Then he had a shock as the light, stuck under his belt, went on by itself. Why? He was afraid to touch it: a devil's light! But now the moment had arrived when he would find out, and know, who was this legendary Beast of Ethridge. No, no! Get away while the getting is good! What do you care about The Beast's name? Just clear out of this hateful place, go away, bye bye! . . . So he told himself, and yet he knelt by The Beast and leaned to pull off its mask, expecting to see he knew not what. And try as he might the name just wouldn't come back to him: the name he had heard when the old story was told in his first weeks at the school two Octobers ago. Rivington Wart? The imperturbable Ethridge Dean of Behavior? Dean Wart was at least crazy enough to get down on Ethan Jeffers' floor and chant *om-m-m-m!* in the middle of the night while sitting in lotus position in his three-piece suit. But Newell had hardly been aware of Dean Wart when the story was told that time on third-floor Settlers. And did the senior counselor even say the name then? Rodney: yes, he must have said the son's, since Newell knew it. But the father's? Did the counselor even know the father's identity? Or was this person never mentioned perhaps: a long kept, and long festering, *secret of Ethridge?*

Newell reached, and touched the skin. Ugh! . . . The mask felt like real flesh! Maybe it was a permanent mask? But no; he pulled on it, he gouged, and it gave . . . Some sort of putty perhaps? It sort of squidged.

Newell positioned himself so the light, still under his belt, would shine in its face. And then, slowly, his clutching fingers made runnels in the skin. His nails made welts in The Beast's cheek. The nose bent crooked. One eyelid drew down, over the evil eye. This must be some kind of putty.

Newell jolted back.

The Beast's other eye had opened, and stared up at him—on the verge of attacking. The Beast's upper lip drew back into a silent growl. But no sound from it, never a moan or groan, while the plastic surgery had gone on. Inhuman. No blood. Nothing but a vague hate in its movements, its assaults from time to time: taking away boys from their rooms. All like clockwork, as though wound up a long time ago, and then it ticked, ticked.

Newell huddled in the darkness. Get away? Turn and run? He gripped the piece of lead pipe.

Boom!

He crowned the Beast of Ethridge.

Bing!

The pipe crunched the skull. It sunk into the clayey flesh. It closed the unblinking eye.

Then Newell, trembling, leaned forward. He put out a hand, and slipped it, even as he shivered head to foot, into The Beast's pocket. There! The master key. His fingertip touched a key ring—Astarte's? and quickly tugged it out.

And then the boy stood up, and made to leave.

XIV

But first he paused, and gazed on down the Tunnel to the end. Was that fire? What was happening? He went further. Against his better judgment he simply had to look over the edge: where the Steam Tunnel turned into something else. He wanted to see. What if that thing back there got up again, and trapped him—cut off his way back?

From a distance it looked like the opening to a huge space. A mine? And so he crept forward. He drew nearer to the end of the Tunnel. And now the howls, the clankings, clatterings sounded loud, loud, all around. And the orangish light had a whiplash to it, like sheets of flame. And the stench, in this last section: who could endure it? Like the cabin odor times a thousand. But no woman's perfume here.

And then Newell Gilbert came to the far edge. Grimy face bathed in the hellish aura, he leaned over the threshold. And he saw.

Dead students, dozens of them, sat stiffly at their desks in a study hall. They sat to their assignments: the finest education available.

Their worm-eaten features stood in different states of decay, eyes ge-latinous, skin bunched down on the jawbone. But they didn't know it. Eyelids, nostrils, mouth: all crimped, rotting away, with a shock of hair. In the overheated space,–was this Astarte's boiler room, also ac-cessible from the Laundry on the Warren House side?–the stench made it hard to breathe.

Tomorrow's leaders sat at their lessons. Dressed in wool suits they seemed to daydream a moment: maybe of home when they were smaller and still had time to play, like normal kids; maybe of sum-mer, and freedom to fish and swim and act like boys again; though judging by the looks of them, so serious, so aware already of their destiny as future statesman, Wall Street magnate, corporate execu-tive, captain of industry, noted academic, their proud parents would probably find a way to *keep them busy.* Don't let them think! The *people*-people may play and waste their lives away: we, the privileged, must look after the tasks of civilization. Noblesse oblige! as Head-master Smithson would say.

Here it was: an entire world recreated as it once had been: Rod-ney's world. The past; or, you might say: life missed, like Rodney's. Look at them: wow! what application! How they do memorize, and get it all by rote, and stuff their skulls full for Master Glebe's, Master Sippel's, Master Delvig's pop quiz! Carry on, young scholars! Go on: agonize over that eternal math equation. Take t-square and compass to that infinitely complex mechanical drawing assignment. Cram exam, score high, make honor roll, enter Yale! We believe in you, our future! What a bunch of geniuses! I'll bet one of you will be Presi-dent someday!

XV

Newell had the Ethridge master key in his hand.

But still he stood there. He stared at the scene.

Where did all the noise come from: the moans and the howls? Of course they didn't really scream and send up lamentations? They were too dead for that, dead and quite contented with their state, quite comfortable–like Manuel and Moon Jeffers both seated placidly among them. A bit maggoty, yes, with a rictus grin on them:

they wouldn't have complained for the world. Hey, they were at Ethridge.

Newell stood there, another moment, and gazed his fill. Did he know any of the other students? Why, there was Deforest Morris from the year before, a flit! And there was Inman Brainerd who dove naked from Nye House balcony onto a massive snowdrift two winters ago while beating his meat over Ramona Glebe. And–and wait: wasn't that Granny Zammet from just across the hall in Warren? Why, he disappeared without anyone even noticing, since he sat in the balcony during morning chapel. What a flit! And–say, hold on a minute: isn't that Redge? the mad guy who led the march, from one student house to the next, that first night Newell ever spent at Ethridge? And it was lucky such a wild band of boys, led by the little devil named Redge, hadn't gone over to The Snug in the Hampton House basement and stolen all the seven-layer cake: just gobbled it down. Of course they'd just gotten on campus, and didn't know about The Snug yet. But look at poor Redge . . . Whew! he hadn't lasted long at all, among the living–the Beast of Ethridge came and got him, a bad element, right off, even before the boy had time to serve his first three detention hours.

Newell stood reminiscing, and looking with awe at students who had turned up missing from campus through the years, the decades, the centuries. So they were brought down here to serve Runt Roentgen's idea of ten hours' detention. But, Sir!

Newell stood there. His jaw dropped, about as far as Ramona's chest will in a few years, while he feasted his eyes on the sight. And so he didn't notice–when the thing, the Beast of Ethridge, sat up–rose to its feet again, silently, and came toward him. Arms held out like a zombie, since its gouged flesh, putty or whatever it was, covered the eyes–Beast strode slowly behind the boy who had swiped his key ring. It moved near him. It must have been able to see something, because it came straight on, and didn't stumble over the godawful mess all over the place. And then it raised one of its grayish paws–

Newell felt the strong, ponderous hand grip and clamp down on his shoulder. He lurched back as though from an electric shock. He toppled backward and then stared up at those clayey cheeks, those sad, sad eye sockets bunched like silly putty. All in all it looked quite a lot like Geeter in the throes of one of his moving sermons; his breath stank enough, not unlike the spiritual halitosis Geet the Geet's morning chapel talks gave off.

On his feet again Newell Gilbert swung out, with all his might, and pounded his length of metal pipe. Conk! Conk! Then he drove it—drove it deeper, deeper into the other's head! The pipe sank into The Beast's eye socket, and came out the other side! Now if that doesn't take care of the sucker, nothing will. One thing I'll tell you though, and it is for sure. The Beast of Ethridge may have had its faults, it certainly wasn't a perfect beast, but it was no flit.

Newell had the master key. He had the flashlight attached to his waist. And he ran.

XVI

He ran. And behind him, strangest thing of all, he heard laughter. More distantly as he bumped and stumbled along, taking the first turning, then the second, back toward the entry to Settlers—he heard a cavernous laughter, as though the dead could be glad. Hm! Who was it? Who did it sound like? Headmaster Smithson, on a rare occasion, when that worthy waxed merry over a good joke, maybe a good dirty joke, with an old business associate? . . . Hm. Laurence Smithson as the Beast of Ethridge? Well, you heard the laughter. You decide. You tell me who done it. But I must say: this would be some sort of hanky-panky for the headmaster of a top private school.

And so the long chase ended. What began out on the island, that day last October, was over. Newell escaped this time. But right now his thoughts weren't on Headmaster, Pastor Geeter, or any of those weighty adults: so certain they'd found the best of all possible systems in the best of all possible . . . hells. No, Newell's thoughts were for Shellfish now. He must run and free Nimrod Shellnitz from the dungeon. Yes, and please be quick about it: if the precious little guy, with the brave spirit, is to survive.

But still, going along, he heard the laughter: as though he might hear it the rest of his life—during moments of a lucky escape. Or maybe not so lucky: a time might come when he would not get free.

And then he'd hear it again: that deep hollow laugh like a revenge, Ethridge laughing last.

It echoed along the Tunnel. It wasn't nice, not a ho ho ho, oh no. Its possessor could hurt you. And then he'd have a good belly laugh at your expense—to himself of course; though a few devils do gloat in public over their successes.

Chapter Ten

I

Newell was suspended from Ethridge. Then word came the private school had decided to expel him. The reason given was: being off campus again, after a first warning, without a pass.

Back home in his attic room, a prisoner, Newell felt guilty and ecstatic. He let his parents down and yet was deeply happy. One day men came: two detectives asked him questions and more questions, then went away. He told the truth, but the story was just so bizarre, so unlikely: can you blame people for not believing?

There were bad arguments with his dad. Emory Gilbert didn't want to hear a word of it; he was angry with his son and in no mood for excuses. He called all that about a cabin out on the island, an underground tunnel, a Society for Self-Furtherance, a Beast of Ethridge, nothing more than a lot of cock-and-bull.

Anne Gilbert grew thoughtful when she saw her son get so excited and splutter out the hair-raising tale. She wanted Newell to speak and her husband to listen; she knew there had been a nervous breakdown in a family just up the street a few months ago, and that family never could talk to each other.

Who did believe was Newell's little sister. Lisa Mona (Lemon) put hands to ears and made a face. She shook her head at him: please, sir, no more.

For days at a time, alone in his attic room, Newell enjoyed himself. He thrived under house arrest among his action games, his books read because he wanted to, and daydreams. But late at night he lay in bed trying to find out why life was so unfair. He still loved Katya. He would always love her, but those thoughts hurt too much. As long as the two of them had a chance to go together, holding hands as they made their way through the forest, he would rather be at Ethridge with her, in misery, than at home contented by himself. But hope ended. She died. So when news came he wouldn't be going back, he tried to put thoughts of all that, and her too, behind him.

Anne came to visit her son the prisoner. She glanced around the attic, a healthy boy's setting: with its pennants on the walls, sports equipment, and fresh air tinged with spring blossoms through the window he always kept open, even in winter. Anne frowned with concern, and her voice was soft.

—Are you okay?

—Yes. Dad hates me.

—No, he doesn't. You're our son. But the expulsion is hard for him to accept.

—Another boy would have died, Shellnitz. I saved him, but that doesn't matter . . . Ask him, ask Shellnitz if you don't believe me!

—I want to believe, Newell.

Anne Gilbert looked away. The fact was she didn't know what to think this time. Newell had always gotten in trouble: in grade school his teachers kept him after school. Yes, he was a bad boy, but he also told the truth.

—Mom, you don't believe me, that's all. It's the first time. You think I'm either lying, or gone crazy like that kid up the street. But you're wrong. What I told you, and those men, is what I've just been through at the mad school where you and Dad sent me. Well, we won't talk about it anymore, if you don't want to. But I will tell you one thing: no more private schools. That's two too many: two strikes, one more and I'll be out, I really will go crazy. Next year: public high school, Redemaine High for me, where my friends are, if I have to go there while living in an orphanage; since Dad likes to talk so much about how he'll disown me.

One day Newell snuck out of the house. Dangerously, he dangled down a rope fire escape from his attic window. Then he ran off to find his old friends in Spring Glen: Otter, Thad Floriani, Haas, Zwergli and Kelleher. They were in junior high by now, and, as dusk settled, they took him to sneak in the shrubs outside windows at a few girls' houses. But all the rage that year was Cynthia Landis, queen of the hop at the Junior High. Next time the band of teenage boys would go over to the Music Box at Redemaine Plaze, and the bowling alleys there, to get a glimpse of the lovely Cynthia Landis. But you must be asking: what came of the investigation? Was there no publicity? Didn't this affair of Manuel the foreign exchange student, Ethan Jeffers the Zen Buddhist, a Bartlett girl named Katya Karamzin, and Granville Zammet, a flit, lead to a national scandal? The answer to this question you know already: it did not. You never heard the story until now. One day the truth may come to light: in the meantime those four young people will have died of a strange virus, related to pneumonia, rarely seen in these climates.

II

On a warm weekday in May of that year, Newell and his mother made the drive north to fetch his belongings. In those days Anne seemed to tire easily; and, by the time they turned off the parkway, Newell sensed her weariness.

Slowly they rode through the small New England town: Plaza Theater, drugstore and five-and-dime, wide commons with a church at each end, and tall elm trees rustling in a breeze. Newell pointed the way, and Anne turned left: past the town library, under the railroad bridge, out along the winding road across the meadow turned green again.

The afternoon was warm and bright. Still the breeze had a nip to it, like winter's last dying sigh. There was crocus in bloom.

As they approached the school, Anne said:

—The girl who died: did you like her?

—Yes.

—I mean . . . did you care for her?

—Yes, Mom.

—Why? Can you tell me?

Seeing this place again, glimpsing the Needing River as they turned up the incline toward the front circle, Newell felt a shiver. He frowned.

—Well, she . . . she was kind. And unhappy.

—A few of us are unhappy, said Anne.

Newell gestured:

—Over there . . . You can park in front of Settlers.

Anne Gilbert thought a moment, and said to her younger son:

—You just didn't get along up here.

—Mom, nobody's regular.

By the Ethridge Homestead there were yellow and white daffodils, pert, fresh, like a schoolgirl's blouse. The dogwoods and cherry trees had blossomed, and the forsythia.

Afternoon classes were in session: science lab, mechanical drawing; art workshop in the Atelier down the grassy slope, across the service road. Young brains buzzed on second-floor Settlers, a studious murmur and shuffling of paper, as Newell and his mom got out of the car. Plunk, plunk went a tennis ball from courts by the old gymnasium. A tractor droned over farmlands to the east of the school. From one of the classrooms came a master's voice.

Clearly nothing had changed here except the season. Ethridge was even more the same than before, if sameness permits of degree.

III

Together they walked to Warren House and began packing the old green trunk which had seen many a family journey.

With a grin Newell took a fistful of flitty necties and flung them in too.

—None of these in high school. My one ambition in life: not to wear them.

—Don't say that.

A face appeared in the doorway: Big Schmied. Short curly hair over his gray pellet-like eyes, pink droopy jowls, a choir boy's smile, though he would beat meat while singing a hymn: what a goofball. Such a gorilla, yet so affected: how do you explain it? Just shrug your shoulders and say: a flit.

—Uh, hi, he waved.

—Hey, Schmiddeth. You skipped eighth period? Meet The Moms.

—H'lo.

—Well, what's new, Schmidlap? What's the latest and the greatest?

—Not much. Exams soon.

—Uh-huh. Cormac around?

—Naw, he dropped out.

—Oh. What about Shellnitz?

—Naw.

Schmied shook his big blockhead.

—Hm. And Berneth, my old roommate?

—He's around.

—That figures, the flit. Future Nobel Prize for Fliterature.

Schmiddikins helped Newell carry the trunk back through Settlers to the car. Then he said goodbye.

While Anne waited to have a word with the Headmaster, her son went to walk around a little.

IV

The schoolwide bell rang across the quadrangle. Classes ended. Students came out from Settlers in shirt-sleeves, books in one arm, tweed jacket slung over the other. They chatted a moment before heading down to athletics; they enjoyed this warm afternoon after the long winter. Seniors strolled The Path: clean-cut, cocky, they basked in their privileges, and thought about the Ivy League campus they would go to next fall.

Just as Newell went out on the Settlers patio, Toad Wingate came the other way. For a second they faced one another.

—Holbein get expelled?

The Toad, pudgy-pussed, glum, but very clever, waved away such a notion.

—You know, Gilbert, uh, it's about your flittiness.

—*My* flittiness? Newell laughed. If I was as ugly as you, I'd hang myself. Say, come over here, Sookie—that's what you like to be called, isn't it?—come out here, I want to tell you something.

—You can't go on the Senior Path.

—Oh no? I'm booted, your rules don't apply to me. Come, come, I'll tell you a secret.

—What?

Then, as they stood there face to face, Newell kicked dirt on the
senior's penny loafers.

—Hey! Don't do that.

—Ha! You flit! Look, everybody, it's a flit!

He kicked up dust. And, when The Toad turned away, Newell followed him and kicked some more on the back of his suit trousers,
with their perfect crease.

V

Newell picked a daffodil on his way, across the service road, for a
last look at the river. There was a sweet smell from the meadow, dew
in the new grass, a damp scent of warming riverbank. Insects buzzed;
a butterfly went its carefree way. The sky was blue above rustling treetops filled with sunlight. Behind him, as he went along, the pure
voices of choir practice came from the chapel.

Despite everything spring had come to Ethridge. And, gazing out
over the Needing's surface, Newell felt a twinge of the sadness that
had been with him these past weeks. He wished Katya were here if
only so they could keep struggling in the same desperate way, side by
side. Hadn't they been getting closer to one another toward the end?
He believed she cared for him but just couldn't get free from what
kept dragging her down.

A bird hopped in front of him and then shot off toward the tall
trees of the island. Why couldn't they laugh and be happy and hold
hands when they came here to study for final exams together? Still
the Needing River went its way, murmuring secrets to the eroded
bank, long roots like snakes in the mud. Newell sniffed the warm
breeze, the wildflowers and earth and life of the river. A loon called,
far downstream . . . Newell loves Katya.

He stood a long moment staring at the ripples, cool and blue. Then
he looked across at the island, and the whole thing came back to him.
He shuddered, standing on the bank. And then a big figure seemed to
appear, ah! The Beast of Ethridge lit up, phosphorescent, emerged
from the Needing's depths. Its putty head, still with a hole from the
lead pipe, broke the quiet surface as it strode out. Water streamed
down from its charcoal gray suit. Ah! So this was where the Tunnel

ended; so this was where, deep under the Needing, all the victims sat stiffly at their lessons lit by hell's fires. The devil was a master teacher. Now The Beast came on the riverbank where Newell stood hypnotized. In its charnel paw, which stuck out from starched cuffs, gilt cufflinks, it took the boy's hand and led him, slowly, back into the water. And now there was no more effort to their steps. The Beast led the promising student (who made the Honor Roll without trying) away, back into the river. They strode. And, as their feet sank into the slimy bottom, The Beast gave a low, gurgling laughter, without bubbles. For it was laughing last.

And then it pointed at something which horrified even more than all the rest: at what looked like a slanting desk, down in the dark depths, with a strange glimmering effect, like all-night lights. And set out neatly on this drawing board, unstirred by the strong current, were a compass, t-square, pencils of various hardness, an eraser, and a broad sheet of mechanical drawing paper, still blank.

VI

Newell shook his head. With a shiver he thrust that vision from him, because he had summer, sports, good times to look forward to, and public high school in the fall. His parents were afraid now, worried about him, and so they let him have his way. Somehow he had a warm feeling in his stomach: as if, this time, he had won.

But then, coming to his senses, he thought of Katya. He remembered the tight bluejeans she liked to wear, her gray cashmere sweater; always sensuous, provocative, her black hair done up in a maroon scarf, like a peasant woman's. Her eyes had depths like the Needing River, depths of love; and her features, with their high cheekbones, and Slavic cast, told of faroff times and places. He saw the sunlight in her hair, in her dark eyes when she laughed at his childishness. She challenged him. But she also kissed him, once, and pressed his hand to her breast that day last fall. She made him yearn for her. Oh, she was so unhappy, yet she thought of others.

It was Katya he saw now in the depths of the Needing. Her eyebrows were calm; they no longer twitched, in that way they had, when she got excited.

—I won't forget you, he said.

And he seemed to hear her murmur, as the river gurgled past:

—I love you . . . love you . . . you . . .

He tossed the daffodil he had picked onto the water, and watched it begin to drift, slowly at first, on its way downstream. The delicate white blossom turned on its stem; it hesitated, catching on a reed, at the edge of the current, and then broke free.

1974–'78, 1982, 1993, 2003

INFERNAL INNOCENCE

RÉCIT

Полусмешных, полупечальных,
Простонародных, идеальных

—Pushkin

Chapter One

I

–Hey.
–Hey.
–Hey. New-boy.
From my post as 'decorator' I stared at Art Kilroyne working the oven. Art-boy looked like a red devil where he stood by the firebrick oven, 800 degrees hot, which hadn't gone out as long as anybody knew: since Redemaine Pizzeria existed.
–Art-boy, I said.
–Hey.
–Hey . . .
–Big New.
Killer worked the peel, sliding pies in and out. He didn't have time for smalltalk: just then the place was pretty busy, plus takeouts. With thirty pies cooking, in the fourteen-by-fourteen foot oven, Art-boy had to be quick or those masterpizzas could curl up and char along the crust.
–New–he said, shovelling.
–Big A–I said, chopping anchovies coarsely; slicing mozzarella; sprinkling grated Parmesan on a Pizza Classica alla Romana.
The Arch slid the peel, in and out, in and out. And his air of a devil in hell, working sinners, jibed with the sight of lit coal deep in

the firebox. It was an infernal landscape that looked endless. Vivid reds, flickering orange shades led away toward shadowy depths in the back. You sensed a great black pit in there, but out of view behind mountains of coal.

Kilroyne sprinkled liquid on the farina as it browned. Now in springtime, with the warm weather, it was 130° where he stood five feet from the oven. He used a broad wooden peel to slide the new pies. Then he took a metal one, like a shovel, and brought them out again: once they were done.

II

–Hey.
–Hey.
–Where to, New-boy?

He saw my restlessness, as I strewed mussels and clams, drizzled oil, laid tomato fillets and diced mozzarel' on a *quattro stagioni*. He knew I couldn't wait to leave.

–Hey.

They had asked me to stay later since the place was busy. But I said:

–No can do, Mr. C.
–Alright, Newell.

I came by after my day at the high school: when practice ended. I helped out Mr. C. at dinner hour and earned some pocket money. But now things had changed. I had to go.

–Hey–said Art, again.

And that was mostly what he had to say–hey–even before the thing . . . But you'll hear in a minute. And I liked just saying hey back to him, and hearing his: hey, thirty times per shift at the pizzeria. One reason was that Kilroyne's 'hey' was high school, hang-around talk; and I had struggled my way into Redemaine High, and the right to hang around and enjoy life like any kid needs. Well, I made it. I won this battle with my dad.

See the way Kilroyne shovels pizzas? Sort of gunning from the chest: the way he used to shoot a jumpshot, with a little hop, stumpy legged, during CYO days. Then I was home on holiday from boarding school, and went to watch them play basketball at the high school gym: Kilroyne, John-O Kogan, Rawl Paepe, Resca, Jame Hayes. Back then my heart was filled with yearning: I was missing out.

The second reason I savored Art's 'hey' brings us to the point. His 'hey' was a world—usually lighthearted, contented with itself; funny, when it shrugged off stress, heat, pain while helping produce 300 pizzas in a day; also deep, a deep 'hey', like a high school philosophy. It addressed the day's burning issues, girls and sports: a sort of *dixi,* a last word on human affairs.

But tonight it had another task. I don't know about you—but I cannot say my youth found too much sympathy. From my mom, sure; but friends? One didn't look for it, expect it. All was banter, a brashness; all competition I guess, self.

Yep.

But tonight Art-boy's 'hey' meant—sympathy.

Why?

—I'm going up there.

—H-hey, he said, hefting an *all 'ortolano* on the peel.

—I'll hunt for a clue. Newell Gilbert, private eye. I'll find out who did that.

— . . .

—Thaddy'll help me.

That's Thad Floriani, my friend. Because he grieved for her too. He loved and admired my twin sister, a beautiful girl, like a star in her high school class. Well, she was murdered, up on Maldoror Drive, where she went parking with her boyfriend, Jame Hayes. It was ten days ago: April 7th, 1961.

—Hey, said Art K., face fiery red, by the oven.

Evelyne Genia Gilbert, 1943–1961. 'Lady'—our dad called her. Evo, to you.

III

My senior year in high school I drove a Willys Jeep painted two green shades. It was much dinted up, much joy-ridden with classmates as I made up for years of strict private school.

Outside the pizzeria I got behind the wheel and pulled into traffic along Gordiane, the main drag. At sunset a strange, it seemed unnatural light played over the row of plazas and malls, chain stores, fast food places; all new in those days, and called by townsfolk the Miracle Mile, or Miracle 'Strip'. A red gloaming came from the sky above West Hills: where Maldoror Drive ran, and where I was headed. Well, I felt a little dazed in the days after my sister's death, and spooked by the idea of what I meant to do, namely look for a killer. So I wondered if the red aura wasn't hell's glow pouring forth like the brick oven in Redemaine Pizzeria.

On I drove along familiar streets so dear to me. They got taken away when I was sent to prep school. I'll never forget the night, in September '60 after my return, when we rode in Nino Braggi's 327 Chevvy to the sorority meeting at Coralie Panducci's. Oh what a night! It was paradise regained: et ego in Arkadia. But there's work to be done now, on the trail of a murderer. Later for nostalgia.

I cruised through Redemaine Plaza past the bowling alleys, then hung a right and made for Thorndale Avenue. This was where Nazzarro and his ZBK frat brothers held their drag races: a long slow incline with a slight curve to it, and room for three hot rods snorting fire like dragons.

Twilight enfolded me as I turned onto Thorndale and saw not a car, no headlights but my own on the long stretch heading up toward the Maldoror Drive entry. Maybe I should try this during the day?

I turned up the radio, though it drew a rhythmic static from the engine: AM radio I bought for a buck at the junkyard and threw in the glove compartment.

So I was going by myself up there, no help, no weapon: to poke around in the darkness by the radio tower, where the thing happened. Why? It isn't so easy to say what I was thinking: about my sister Evelyne, about the town of Redemaine, about many things as I rode along. I stepped on the gas, and the Willys responded since Nazzarro had souped it up: bored and stroked, you know, fuel-injected, overhead twin cam, gear from the Moon Goggles catalogue. Cost me a couple hundred from part-time job money. Boy, you should have seen my mom's face the first time she turned the ignition—it was her car after all—to go for groceries.

IV

If there was a squadcar at the Drive entry, I'd sweet-talk them: hey, let Evelyne Gilbert's brother go in and look around . . . But no; not a soul in view. No one in their right mind would come up here now. Even high school kids, parkers looking for a niche to kiss and pet in the fragrant Redemaine springtime, would steer clear for awhile. Wait for the fear, the town's sense of shock and tragedy to wear off. And the attacker? Would he strike again?

The Willys fenders scraped shrubs. I went in the winding 5-mile course of Maldoror Drive overhung with trees. My sister and Jame Hayes had come this way: you went up a kind of approach with a railing to the left. It was dark on the unlit drive: a state-owned park with scenic overlooks. No one lived here except a legend, a town boogeyman called the Maldoror Mon. Also Nazzarro Zummo, the Town Comptroller's son, had a cottage.

So I entered: the same way they came ten days ago.

Here and there a sharp turn: speed limit 15. Wild kids did 50, and there were wrecks, cars falling into the valley below. A gray, spectral branch reached and touched the Willys' windshield; it gave me a start, as I cruised, slow.

Now over here Jame—so he told me—pulled into the first circle, with its scenic vista, and paused, motor idling, on the far side. That night there were parkers. He knew the cars but didn't beep or say hi if both heads weren't showing. Tonight: no others, only me. For a moment I turned off the engine, doused lights, and sat looking out over Redemaine at night. I thought about my sister up here gazing far out at the town beneath the stars. There were other clusters of lights along the valley: rival towns we played in sports. There would be bluster about a rumble after the game: frats, voc. training guys. In the night sky a pinkish glow rose from the city in the distance. I thought about Evelyne staring out at the far ridge, a dark line by now beneath a sliver of moon. An hour left to live. And then the dreams, the promise, early acceptance to an elite women's college, Evo's fine mind moving easily among academic matters toward the profession she chose; then love, life's abundance, a world to experience:—all blighted, in early springtime here on Maldoror Drive. All erased. At age seventeen.

I imagined her, that night, up here with Jame Hayes.

V

—It's pretty, she said.

Jame looked at his date and then dully back at the dark panorama. He felt impatient with her that night: so he told me, in his anguished grief, when I called at his house after the funeral. They were falling in love. And for him this meant more than strolling the hallway between classes, hand in hand, with her wearing his letter sweater. It meant more than a double-date at the ice-cream parlor, a drive-in movie, or Sunday picnic by the river; and more than their shared excitement when he set state records, the Friday before, in the 440-yard dash and the broad jump; and newspapers called him the area's greatest track and field athlete ever. Jame Hayes wasn't thinking about the Olympic trials just now. No; he had an obstinate desire in him, the desire in the blood: when a woman attaches you to her, and then plays moody, hard to get, not ready yet for caresses. And so he felt irritated, as they sat there, looking out from the parking circle at lights across the valley. Was he being treated unfairly? Maybe she just needed time, sorting out her feelings like any teenage girl; maybe she was afraid what could happen; what had happened more than once, up here, amid the rocky coves and woods of West Hills.

For the moment she held him away. He could say or do nothing right.

—What are you thinking about? she said.

—Not much.

—How foolish men can be?

She chuckled.

Jame's voice had an edge, perhaps a hint of anger:

—What's wrong, Ev? Damn.

She stayed, slightly huddled, by the window. But he reached over, took her hand and said excuse me with his own little chuckle.

The ignition turned over in the car beside them. Rear wheels scraped dirt—headed for home or a less populated area.

VI

Then they too wended their way along the Drive, looking for a secluded spot to park. Now she moved toward him on the seat and his
arm went up and around her, resting on her shoulder. His right hand
touched her breast while with the left he drove. Of course both were
nervous. There was a Maldoror Drive mystique, and every high
school student knew the stories: old horror tales, the ghosts of those
violated by the Maldoror Mon.
   Where to stop? Is this a good spot? No. Well, what about here?
N-no . . . It was the indecision early in relationships. Not here? Then
where? Evelyne kept saying no; and Jame felt thwarted, and didn't
care about the logistics so long as they pulled off the road, and nestled among the trees, and smooched.
   Then down the dark winding road came a break in the overhanging boughs. And the young lovers saw, up ahead, two red lights high
in the night sky. The WRED radio tower.

That's where I was headed: the local station's radio tower. The
murder occurred there. I wanted to search for some sort of clue,
something to go by, a way to start my 'investigation', playing amateur detective.
   But suddenly I was jolted from my thoughts, as I tried to reconstruct the night my sister died. Suddenly a pair of headlights lit up
my rearview mirror.
   Those lights: they were on bright, not lowered. And . . . strange
. . . they seemed to have a personality of their own. I mean it wasn't
the cops following me; it had another feel. But who came up here at
such a time: in the days after our town's most grisly crime? What
were they trying to find out? or prove?
   That car was coming on. So I gunned the Willys around a sharp
turn. Darkness, back there, for a minute maybe. Then there it was
again: the phantom car with its brights reflected by the rearview mirror, in my face.
   Then I had an idea worthy of the private dicks I was getting ready
to imitate: all those hardbitten sentimentalists, quiet men with a
clipped wit, loosened neckties and a mesh on their forehead after
drinking too much the night before, loving a gun moll carried over

from the last case. I thought: ah! so you return to the scene of your crime?

I slowed. I wanted a glimpse at that car. No go: brights on.

I threw the Willys in second gear, and challenged the guy to come nearer. All bluff of course: I didn't even have a heater.

And his response? Did he gun it then? Did his four-on-the-floor roar up beside me and force my Willys off the road? Did he ram me down the steep side of West Hills?

No; as you see, I'm still here. But the bright headlights went out. Blink!

I didn't believe the mirror. I turned to look back.

Dark.

VII

Hm. A pair of sweethearts looking for a niche? They must have an awful itch: to come up here with the Maldoror Mon, killer of Evelyne Gilbert, on everybody's mind. Well, it was springtime in Redemaine; the pink and white puffs of dogwoods and cherry trees made suburban life smell sweet. Apollo had touched our town with flourishing goldenrods. Life went on because nature has its rights, you know, and when a guy's got it bad, he could become a dad.

I drove on. I rode the Drive those few miles to the radio tower, just as Jame Hayes and my sister had—he all the while saying: Let's try here. Why not, Evo? Aw c'mon, one's good as the next . . . But she wasn't able to tell him: okay.

At the highest spot on West Hills, I came to the tall relay tower of our local radio station, WRED. A bit of gravel path leads in to where it rises from cleared ground. In the last twilight glimmer mixed with stars, the tower looked like a huge spider web spun downwards by two gleaming eyes. Those red lights, perched high above the treetops, could be seen from towns up and down the county; on clear nights, that is, like the one when my sister . . . but wait.

So it was here Jame pulled off the Drive. He hit the brakes and swerved right, onto gravel. And it didn't matter what she said now. He killed the ignition. But she in her fear, in her doubts, forced a concession: leave the radio playing low, and parking lights.

With his long, strong athlete's hand Jame mussed her hair a little and tried to keep it light.

–What's wrong, Fella?

She had nicknames. Dad called her Lady. I liked to call her: Ever. At the high school she was such a crackerjack: our POD (Problems of Democracy) teacher Mrs. Hebbel called her 'Swell Fella' one day, and it stuck. But since childhood me 'n Joey–older brother–had yet another name for her: Report Card. Never, on any report card since kindergarten, had Evelyne Gilbert gotten a grade below A. Wait, take it back: she got a B in conduct in sixth grade for correcting the teacher, Mr. Pyat. Tim Pyat said affect was always a verb, effect a noun; but Report Card said: 'What about: effect a change . . . ?' Anything like that, she won. Spelling bees. Prize essays. You'll say I exaggerate, but she could imitate Chaucer in a grade school composition.

–What's wrong, Fella?

–I feel strange, Jamie. Maybe we shouldn't be here.

He took his girl's hand and leaned to kiss it, poke fingertips to lips; he felt her tense in his embrace. Back by the first circle she seemed to warm a minute, among the other parkers. Now the isolation, off by themselves, alone at the radio tower, made her nervous. She felt trembly, with a chill, like tinsel which shimmers to the touch. On the radio an old tune played: 'At Last'. She said:

–This song makes me think of the war.

As anyone can tell you, my sister was real pretty, tallish, like a leader, besides being such a whiz. She could debate rings around Marsden Dale, the history teacher who wrote *Annals of Redemaine* containing, in fine detail, all but the essential. The he-spinster, Dale, had a crush on Evelyne Gilbert despite her wit at his expense and quips in class.

So, as I said, my sister was a stunner; oh, not a voluptuous babe like some of them in Miss Jollymeier's homemaking class; not a hot chick, either, she couldn't be bothered to lead cheers or twirl a baton; but pert, fresh, intelligent. She could more or less choose her boyfriend, though fate chose him for her: one of the most promising athletes our town ever produced, also a good student headed with full scholarship to an Ivy League campus in the fall.

I must add, however, that she could be a tease. Oh, yes. A tease with a difference: she might seem to look down on a boy who meant no more to her than a smile. In saying this I ask: was she the target?

or just any girl, wrong place wrong time? Fine mind and good looks:
a challenge to the male ego.

Well, there were issues. And one other big one, in particular, we'll
get to in a moment.

VIII

In Jame's defense, it must have been a temptation: parked with
her in the darkness on Maldoror. Hell, he might have spared his girl
a scene she wasn't ready for; at least waited till Senior Prom when
spending the night with your high school sweetheart was a rite of
passage.

–Let's get in back, he said.

–No, Jayvee.

Glib girl: is this the nickname, Jayvee, you call a boyfriend like
Jame Hayes?

Her voice sounded distant.

He nuzzled her hair. He craned his neck to kiss her earlobe. His
hand caressed her rising breast.

–Oh, Evo.

–N-no.

She slumped toward the window and gave a little laugh. Yes, yes.
No, no. They laughed low, as he smothered those little no-no's with
a kiss-kiss. And his fingers undid a button of her blouse: her rather
full blouse with its self-conscious modesty. Who could have thought
these precious minutes, when a man's hands first found and cherished her breasts, were to be the last?

In the front seat he tried to maneuver. For a moment he didn't
seem to care what she was feeling, but bowed to kiss her and urge on
her the next step.

–No, Jame. I will get angry.

By the window she struggled to keep her head. She felt what it was
she had stirred in him. She felt a force which boded no good for the
love they were both looking to nurture.

–Oh, hmm.

–Too fast–she said, pushing him back.–Cool off, boy.

Boy?

–Mmm.

–I'll scream, I mean it.

–Mm.

–No! Time to go.

She pushed him away. In the faint reddish glow from the radio tower she must have been a vision of loveliness: her pure features with a fleeting look ... indecision. Loving her guy she had to tell him no; so she pushed him back. But something in her wanted to say yes, so much, to him; and he might really have taken her, then and there, if this was his deepest instinct, Jame Hayes' goal in life. Who knows: if he went ahead and did this, then things could have been different.

Evelyne's head leaned against the window. Her blouse was open. She pushed back his broad shoulders, and gave a whimper. Yes, they were going too fast; it just wasn't it. So she threw out an elbow against his caresses, and clipped his forehead. This made Jame draw back and look at her: maybe come to his senses.

With her free hand she rolled down the window on a chilly April evening. She breathed in the freshness of reawakening nature, and shook her head.

Jame, beside her on the front seat, hunched head to hands, and didn't speak for a moment.

IX

–Take me home, Jay.

–Don't worry. I will.

–Please take me home now. We'll talk tomorrow.

–I've got to go outside.

–You ... Don't leave me alone.

–Just be a moment.

–Wait–

–Be right back.

Then he opened the car door and walked away. Nervous energy propelled his steps. He had to leave her a moment and calm down. Jame went up to the radio tower and stayed there what may have been—so he told me—ten minutes. He felt sick to his stomach from the tension between them. Well, let her cool off too.

X

My sister heard her boyfriend's steps on the gravel. She sat by the window, alone now, shivering. She felt cold, and suddenly afraid: as though someone were watching her button her blouse, then smooth her ruffled hair.

She called his name softly as he moved off in the darkness. Well, he needed to relieve himself: then he'd drive her home. But why keep on walking? The radio tower was half a football field away . . . Now she would have gone out after him, but he was angry. He wanted to shake off the thwarted desire. Also, she didn't quite trust him, or herself, in these instants: by themselves on Maldoror Drive, beneath the stars.

So Evo sat brooding, and confused. What to do? As the last seconds of her life ticked away, she thought of how she would be kind to him when he came back; how she would kiss him and hug him if he still wanted; how they would live their lives together and raise a family like other families, yet not like them: until age ninety, side by side, a pair of ancestors. People had spats. Lovers quarrelled. The point was to learn from it, clear the air, and go on loving.

Again she said his name . . . because she sensed something. Was there someone outside? She sensed a presence. Near the car? Evelyne sat upright, alerted. She stared at the dark windshield tinged with red.

—Jame?

Well, was he playing games now? Was it a trick, sneaking around the car to get his little revenge? He shouldn't do that. Feeling cold she folded her arms over her breast, and hunched her shoulders. Fear welled up in her, she didn't know why; then it went away. She glanced around, through the back window; saw no one.

Then impatience blent with a tremor of anger. Ah! he asks for too much; I say no, and he leaves me to stew here all by myself . . . He makes me go through this too?

A few more moments, and the door on the driver's side opened. Her brow knit with a twinge of anger, she didn't look at him when he got in. She stared straight ahead, leaning away, and waited for him to turn on the ignition.

—Take me home, Jamie.

But there was something—what? Something about him now: the way it felt sitting beside him. So distant, cold. And Evelyne thought perhaps: it is serious.

And then she turned, glancing up as he moved across the front seat toward her. And then she knew, she realized, that it wasn't him. There was a strange smell in the car. Medicinal. (I'm telling you what Jame Hayes told me when I went to visit him after the funeral.) Evelyne's fear was such: she couldn't scream. At least, Jame never heard her cry out: where he stood a good fifty yards away from the car. Maybe she just fought, in silence.

At last the track star took a deep breath, and turned away from the shadowy relay tower. He walked back down that bit of gravel drive.

XI

—Sorry, Ev. I'm okay now.

He opened the driver's side door and got inside. Ashamed at his behavior, he didn't look at her.

Silence.

—I love you, he said.

Jame reached for the keys to turn on the ignition.

No keys.

And now, his eyes a question, he glimpsed her: where she sat slumped down on the front seat, and stared upward, curiously, through the windshield.

—Are you asleep? Evvy, what's—?

But her eyes were wide open. And from her throat came a sound: like a straw when it sucks the last drops. Her arm gave a small, sort of resigned movement toward him. Then her head lolled, on her shoulder, to one side.

He reached and took her hand. Then he saw the shiny substance on her blouse, tinged reddish by the tower lights. And his heart lurched up in his throat. A low scream came out of Jame Hayes as he realized her hand, blouse, her entire front were drenched in blood.

And so my sister lay there, half upright, slumping further. I imagine Evelyne in the moments before death . . . our father's favorite, Lady. Not the mythic Maldoror Mon but a real-life psychopath had grabbed her light brown hair in his fist and yanked her to him for a kiss of death since no one had ever given him the other kind. And he bored his mouth into hers and the taste was strange, medicinal, repulsive. She bit him. She clamped her teeth on the killer's lips, teeth, tongue, the bad taste. That was when the blade of a hunting knife went in her soft skin, into the heart. Her flailing fists, and kicking, and butting kept on another few seconds, as she grasped for the door handle, as her hand fumbled on the door, went limp—and the hunter plunged the knife again, again. He shook her, thrust at her, though the struggle had ended . . . A moment later she was alone again with waves of nausea and a numb uneasiness, half-conscious now, as shock came on. Her pupils began dilating beneath her eyebrows' horrified arc, a wrinkle like a question mark on the bridge of her nose. And then Evelyne went slack by the window. For an instant her murderer went loose too having discharged his hatred into her: the girl they called 'The Genius', Swell Fella at the high school; sure bet for Most Intelligent in the '61 Yearbook Hall of Fame. He took the ignition keys. He slid out as quietly as he had come and shut the door, calmly, and walked off along the Drive toward his car or wherever he had come from. Maybe he felt a release then, even a morbid joy. Behind him his victim, the girl, waited on the front seat of Jame Hayes' car while blood formed small, sticky pools on her blouse, round her navel, trickling along the abdomen. After the explosion a silence like a vast cocoon gathered over her mind. A high-pitched electric tone was the only connection she had left. She felt a slow descent in smooth, relaxing circles, death's carrousel. Grab the ring? Our dad, Emory, came toward her in a black tuxedo; he made to greet her on her wedding day, but then kept on past. His eyes were transfigured; he was going the other way; no expression on his face . . . Oh, oh, this would kill her mother, Anne, whom she loved so; but it was too late to think about that. There was only this slower and slower drift, the tenuous signal from her mind, her fine straight-A brain reduced to a wavering tone, thin, for another few instants. Evelyne Genia Gilbert's life flowed away in a last few timeless seconds, blinks. She had the wondering look of a hurt little girl, as she waited in the darkness for her lover to return.

XII

When Jame drew away from his girlfriend, his fingers stuck to her, the blood. He tried to stay in control, but he couldn't start up the car. No keys. Just a moment before he had been so happy to come back to her—he daydreamed a huge Olympic stadium cheering him into his kick, as he left the other runners like a wake. She sat in the crowd, thrilled and silent . . . Forgiveness was easy when you loved someone: her point of view was valid. When he got back in the car, he just wanted to hold her close to him for an hour, no funny-business.

Now, as he pulled away, crying, she seemed to follow and fell sidewise on the seat beside him. She stared down beneath the dashboard. He panicked.

—Don't die . . . Evo, please don't die.

What could he do? Carry her on his shoulder the five miles back into town? There were no cars, no other parkers this far in. Every second was precious as he sat there trying to decide. He dug in his pockets. He felt around on the rubber matting, beneath the seat. No keys. The low rattle came from her throat.

He touched her again, but this time drew his hand back, as if burned.

Hesitating, sobbing, his tone pleaded as he opened the car door:

—Please, Evvy . . . I'll be right back! I have to leave you here . . . please!

So he got out. A last time he stared back at her pitiful form curled, in the darkness, half off the seat. Such a beautiful girl . . . Jame Hayes gave a sob, turned, and ran.

He ran off beneath the trees back along Maldoror Drive.

Then he screamed—a scream the stars must have heard. Oh! If only there were a car . . . He hit his stride, his long graceful runner's pace. The time he made that night, when his high school sweetheart died, must have broken the record.

There was one car. One. It passed him by going the same way. Who knows: maybe even then it wouldn't have been too late to save her. But that car didn't stop. And—curious thing—its lights were on until he turned and waved, waved. Then they went out, and stayed out until it passed him and got round the next bend in the Drive. And then—on again.

XIII

Jame ran along with his strong regular stride; and, even in these moments, his body didn't forget it was that of a great runner. In a broken voice he cried out for help. What he felt could not be said; it was part of the nausea, a stabbing cramp as he stepped up the pace. His love was back there, alone in the dark, the life flowing out of her while she waited for help. Should he have stayed with her? His long legs churned over the Maldoror Drive blacktop back past the parking circles, the scenic lookouts, where he looked for a car but saw none. He must find someone and go back for her and take her to the hospital. There was no one. What time could it have been? No cars on the Drive; none left at the first circle. Once and again he lost his line and brushed past an overhanging branch, scraping his face, scratching his cheek and eye. As he went down the slow incline, past the railing at the entry, he turned his ankle on the road shoulder and fell. Up again, limping badly, he hopped and stumbled—how badly had he sprained it? Not broken; no, but he panicked. If he let himself stop he wouldn't get started again. And so he limped, like a svelte deer wounded by a trap, the pain shooting up his left leg. Down the sloping side of West Hills and then into the long slow bend of Thorndale Avenue—he ran. There was the rare car, at this hour, but it didn't stop for the big, wild figure waving his arms in a frenzy and bawling out beside himself. He rang a doorbell. No one opened. Would you open? Jame ran along back toward Gordiane, the police station there by the town hall, in Centerville. By now Evelyne had bled to death? She lay in the front seat of his Chevvy Impala parked beneath the radio tower. Her terror and despair were over . . . ? Oh! What if the psychopath, the devil who did that to her, came back, and—Jame Hayes burst into the heart of Redemaine crying out his

terror, gasping, half hysterical as he gestured at traffic along the main drag; he seemed to clutch at stars. The quiet houses, smooth lawns and trim hedgerows, then stores and neon lights along Gordiane—all had a deaf and dumb air, gaping at him.
—Somebody help her! Somebody please help her!
Here were people, houses, telephones, passing cars. But nobody opened. No one stopped for him: not a soul. If it was too late now, then it was too late, and she was gone. And if she was gone, then he was gone, yes, his race over before it began, before he got out of the hometown starting blocks. And now the shame was such, the despair was such, he might as well end his life too, and go be with her. It was no use. He might as well topple over, and lie there, die too. Evelyne Gilbert was gone. But he kept on screaming and windmilling his arms, there along Gordiane Boulevard for all to see. His senses spun in a furor of panic and hysteria, as he neared the police station and the end of his marathon. She was dead up there. And the world was dead. And he was dead, in the terrible, sudden knowledge.

And still none, among the many who saw him from their cars—none would stop, open a door or window, ask what had happened. None asked why he was carrying on that way. And this despite the fact that they knew his face, his form, his picture often in the local sports pages. Hal Duggan of *Our Town News* ran a special feature on Jame Hayes just two weeks ago, as spring sports opened at the high school. So why didn't someone stop? you ask. Why? Is it possible? Is Redemaine an unfeeling, an uncaring town? Why did no one stop and give this man a lift when he so obviously needed help? Precious minutes might have been saved.

Well, now I must tell you something else. I mention a detail which will play a part in this true story. If no one would stop for Jame Hayes, a track star, an honor student headed for one of the posh colleges next fall, then maybe that's because he made an even more terrible spectacle—out there along the brightly lit boulevard waving his arms, shrieking hoarsely, pleading—than I have described. You see, Jame Hayes was a young black man. His family was one of the first African-American families—Negro, as we said in those days—to move out from the city to the Greenwood or working class section of Redemaine.

XIV

Late night sirens wailed through the placid streets. Our tranquil, not unhappy town gave first cries of pain.

Police sealed off Maldoror Drive. There were roadblocks on Thorndale Avenue and other outlying thoroughfares: never seen here before. A sinister note rose on the air fragrant with lilacs, this clear, inviting night in early spring. Suddenly there was such a tension. You didn't know why as yet, but you felt . . . on the spot.

Something had happened. What? A fire? A heart attack? Rush old So-and-So yet again to the hospital? How many times will he get people worked up?

No. Something had happened.

Something bad. Nobody, least of all Police Chief Roscommon, was talking. Everybody was feeling. On the spot.

There was a flurry of police activity. Roscommon, interrupted in his nightly call at his brother's restaurant, came to our house in Spring Glen with the news. My older brother Joey was away at college; my younger sister Lemon asleep in her room; but I, from my room in the attic, heard the car drive up, footsteps on the walk outside, then the doorbell. I came downstairs to see what was going on . . . But I will not describe the scene here, its effect on my mother. A sensible woman, and not a weak one—she would not recover.

Then Roscommon and my parents crossed the front lawn in the quiet, dew-scented suburban night. I stared after them, and saw my mom put a trembling hand to her forehead, as they got in the squad car for the ride to the hospital.

There was still hope. Later my dad told me a nurse who greeted them at triage desk looked upset. My mom said:

—Can we go in?

No; they must wait in a family room to one side of the swinging doors. They were choked with fear; but, my father later told me, not only for Evelyne or for themselves—it seemed a world was beginning to split apart. Of course the mask of the man, contrasted with his wife's features, must remain steadfast, impassive, in tragedy.

XV

By this time, the wide treatment room where my sister lay looked like the path of a tornado. Paper and plastic wrappers, tubes strewn on the stretcher and floor, syringes and used gauze strips, and blood, blood. Half a dozen doctors worked furiously, consulted in clipped phrases, made requests to which several nurses responded with quick movements. A young intern pumped the ambubag as Evelyne's stomach bloated like a pregnant woman's, but not with life. A chest tube had been put in: to drain off massive hemothorax, or chest hemorrhaging.

They shocked her with 200 amps. Her body grew taut and straightened—convulsed, in a frantic dance, on the stretcher.

—400 in a minute. X-ray! Where's the neuro attending? He was paged, right?

One ran a hand over her skull.

Another:

—E.k.g. shows some fibrillation.

—Alright, another amp of epi.

—Maybe a rhythm.

He peered into her eyes behind his flashlight seeking a response. When Evelyne's dark pupils were expanded, insensitive to light, unable to focus, then no blood was getting to the brain. Then night closed over.

—Give her 400. All hands off.

The body, abandoned to the shock, convulsed.

The paged neurosurgeon showed up and got a brief account.

—E.k.g.'s a straight line. Pupils fixed and dilated.

—I'm sure she's tamponading. Let's open her up. Drain her; give open heart massage.

But a feeling, known to them, had come over the scene.

This patient was lost.

The tension, the combined effort ebbed, in an instant. And that was it. Unpleasant to persist: when you knew. Now they took a last look, and started drifting out. They went from the treatment room in chaos toward a chart to write, then a cup of coffee. Then something trivial, if you please.

One of the doctors said, softly:
—Ballgame.

XVI

Chief Roscommon had stood in the doorway watching. Now he backed away also: toward his sorry task. Also, he must look to the deposition of the medical report, and make sure, personally, the chain of evidence wasn't broken. Now a town crisis. On the spot!

After a few minutes a nurse's aide came in and began swabbing the body. The pale breasts had come through unscathed; the dark nipples jutted upward as though opposed to the abandon of her torso bathed in blood. Hair bunched beneath neck and shoulders seemed to cushion her head. The nurse's aide washed her and drew over a clean sheet.

A nurse came back in. She began by taking the airway from Evo's throat, opening the mouth with two hands. A dark clot with mucus slid from the lips, along the chin.

I tell you these things as I later heard them, after starting to play detective, because I want to bring home what happened to us, that night, in my hometown. Why did it happen? For what reason? We'll try to find out . . . Right now you need to feel the depth, the immensity of it, as I did: how life seemed to change, in our small New England community, the night Evelyne Gilbert died.

The nurse taped the eyelids shut, but one reopened: the glazed pupil dilated, reflecting the overhead lights. She closed it again, pressing the white adhesive to the long lashes, the bluish brows.

Then the nurse drew the clean sheet over my sister's head. Now the corpse was ready for the morgue, and for viewing.

Before long an orderly came and wheeled the stretcher from the treatment room: past the triage desk out front, toward the elevator.

Through the ward there was silence.

XVII

These, you see, were the things I remembered, as I stood a long moment in the darkness at the base of the radio tower. I tried to reconstruct the scene, and replay those events in my mind, before I started looking about for a clue, an idea. First, I knew what Jame had told me. Then other people told me things: the Police Chief; also a detective on the case. Plus I went to the hospital. It was something for me to have those conversations. Upon coming to the high school after a bad time in boarding school I was pretty much the lighthearted teenager with his mind on sports and girls.

I paused in thought by the radio tower. Down the gravel path stood the Willys Jeep, its dark outline looking ridiculous: slung so high on its chassis, with a slight tilt, the way Nazzarro made it when he souped it up. I parked it just where Jame had his car the night of the murder. I tried to think myself in Jame Hayes' shoes, lingering by myself, sulking while I looked in my heart for forgiveness. Then, slowly, I walked back down the path toward the girl I loved ...

Crunch, crunch, went my shoes on the gravel. There was such a silence, such a loneliness up there, on Maldoror Drive.

With a flashlight I inspected near the car, just poking about for a sign, a hint. This was silly enough; the police spent days here with their expertees and equipment. Of course such work needed daylight hours. But I felt a yearning, you explain it, to get started and go through the motions.

So I ranged a ways toward the Drive: inspecting the gravel, dust, grass. I crossed over the paved road, flashlight still on, senses alert, and stared a moment at dense foliage on that side. Poison ivy afflicted me in childhood: you know, a good bout, blisters between your fingers, on your balls. Well, I gave a sigh before going in: up to my waist in underbrush. Now I'd endure poison oak, or sumac.

My flashlight touched on a strange sight. There was a bush, wild shrub, that looked manhandled, beat up. Some madman, or animal, had a notion to thrash a bush and break branches and crumple its leaves? A curious thing: to take out one's anger, hatred, on nature.

For a good half hour I stayed in that patch of West Hills forest by the roadside. Maybe this was the killer's escape route? If it was the Maldoror Mon, he had spent decades roaming the woods up here;

he knew the geography . . . ? But I couldn't go in too far: I'd get lost. So I shuffled about, nudging dead leaves with my toe. Brambles prickled on my skin. One scratched my cheek. Then, a bit further in, my light picked up something: only because it was white, and there by my waist. A spot of something, like cream, on a leaf. I took it in two fingers and sniffed—what? So familiar that smell, medicinal . . . What did it remind me of? The scent came from my memory as far back as childhood, but I couldn't place it, yet.

Carefully, not folding, I put the leaf into my shirt pocket, and made to grope my way out of the briars.

But I heard something. What? No mistaking: a human sound, nearby. From the road? It had that edge to it, as against breeze in the trees. Click—

I turned off the flashlight.

XVIII

To be out there by yourself in the darkness of Maldoror Drive, where a murder has just occurred . . . and to know you're not alone—

I stopped in my tracks, crouching a little. Silence; don't move. My young nerves met the big fright, but I wanted to scram.

When I got back to the Willys, if I did get back: would Jack-the-Ripper be in the driver's seat, waiting to give me his grisly kiss, as he did my sister?

Then my heart sank. Clunk! I had left my keys in the ignition just as Jame Hayes did. Elementary, my dear Watson.

So I shrank back among the prickers, since they were the best friends I had right now. Ah! I thought I placed that sound: it was like a cover closing, a woman's compact. So the Maldoror Mon was a female?

I paused, holding my breath. What if The Mon was right alongside me, or behind the next tree trunk? Now the flashlight was off: too dark to tell anything. After a few minutes I began edging forward, not backward—in unknown terrain, and unwilling to make my escape down the steep side of West Hills.

Finally I got tired waiting in the bushes to find out my fate. Also I was itching like mad and unable to scratch without giving myself away. So I ducked low and moved along thinking at any instant I'd fall into a pair of hairy paws. Watch out!

XIX

By the Drive I crouched, in a tuft of tall grass on the roadside, and stared in the dark. Directly across from me, a stone's throw away, sat the Willys Jeep also looking on the defensive: raised, tilted, like I said. Then half a football field further, up the slow incline, the WRED radio relay tower with its two red lights looking out over Redemaine. I peered left: the Drive, in darkness, to the next turn. I peered right, and—tick-tick, my heart started pounding a mile a minute.

For there was a car. Low, sleek job, lights off. Just dark contours; but those contours seemed ready to pounce. Was it the car I saw when entering the Drive? and suddenly, pffst! it had disappeared, no more headlights behind me. Anyone in the driver's seat? I couldn't tell. Ah, ah, was that Nazzarro's 'Vette, up here on a spooky mission near the site of my sister's death, when all others stayed away? I couldn't tell! Rumor was, at the high school, that Nazzarro Zummo had his reasons for not loving it when the popular Evelyne Gilbert went out with Jame Hayes, future Ivy Leaguer and perhaps Olympic athlete; while he, Nazzarro, was a vocational shop student with no such glory on his horizon, though he did lead a faction at Redemaine High: namely its illegal fraternity, the ZBKs; and though his family was influential in town, Mr. Zummo our Town Comptroller.

Could it be Nazzarro waiting alone in the dark? He loved another girl, not Evelyne; but more of that in a moment. Well, had he come here impersonating the Maldoror Mon, and—no, I wasn't ready to believe such a thing. Didn't he soup up my Willys in fine style, so I could be a regular guy, a hotrodder, after my personality wasn't helped by the years in private school? And he only charged a few hundred dollars. Now I could burn rubber with the best of them and even have drag races if I wanted—rev 'er up, roommm'rrooommm! at stoplights along Gordiane when some pizza pie face in his parents' Buick gave me the evil eye; and, laughing at Willys with one hand on his girlfriend's tight sweater, ow! and the other on his stick shift, revved 'er up as well.

The low car sat there on the asphalt and appeared to coil on itself; while the grill and headlights had a look to them, like a snarl. Was there someone behind the wheel? If so, he sat blocking the lane, free as you please; though traffic wasn't too heavy on the Drive at this hour—even taboo for now. Ah! What if he was at my Jeep now, crouching in ambush—having swiped my keys? That key chain had my name and address on it: 80 Santa Fe, in Spring Glen! Ah, so the Maldoror Mon had my family's address now, and had the keys?! Carry on, amateur detective.

If I felt an urge to run away before, scoot in my Jeep; if I'd have chosen jumping off West Hills over hand-to-hand combat with the Maldoror Mon—then how could I act the coward now when not only my safety was at stake but also my family's?

XX

From the bushes by the side of the road I chicken-walked—didn't burst out into the line of fire, staying low, and then across. No, I waddled in plain view—pretty briskly, onto the gravel road, and across.

Bending down I took some gravel and put it in my pocket. My hands found a couple goodsized rocks. I could hurt him before he got to me with his knife. Nearing the Jeep I hit the dirt, down in the dust, sort of a jungle crawl.

On the driver's side I jumped up cocking my right arm with a rock. Nobody! I opened and climbed in, reaching for the keys. Then I sat behind the wheel trying to catch my breath. But before I could do that, I had another jolt. Brrrrmmm . . . an engine started up: the car parked over there on the Drive. So I turned over the Willys ignition: brrrmmm! 'r'roooommm! What a roar it made—for a Willys Jeep. Nazzarro Zummo had souped the sappy thing up out of its mind, and with a glass-packed muffler to match. Yes, my poor mom, whose car it was, had a jolt when she heard that roar amplified by garage accoustics; and then in her southern accent she called me a damn fool. But the din sent my old man through the roof, which was something to see: the weighty man, nerves on edge from his high-powered job, had a personality like a jack-in-the-box. He threw fits on a dime; and so, as Willys went berserk in the garage, he blew his top too; it was a duet.

Now I made a racket in the Jeep station wagon perched on its shocks like stilts slightly out of kilter. And Maldoror Mon in his mean buggy gave a low growl: all set for a test drive.

I threw 'er in reverse, swerving round; but I hadn't mastered all that power under the hood. The transmission played tricks, and the Jeep jerked and reared like a bronco onto the Drive. It seemed to buck at sight of the other's smooth body without a dent. Mating season for hot rods. But can you imagine the Mon's rage if I put a scratch on his chassis? He screeched back. Then at the last instant I lurched past, missing him by a hair. And we were off: back along Maldoror Drive toward the Thorndale Avenue entry.

But for a split second, on the verge of plowing into him, my headlights picked up his face. I say face, but . . . Now you're thinking, ah, it's a werewolf, bloodshot eyes . . . Guess again.

You may not believe this. But there will be one or two other things you don't believe as this true story unfolds. The Maldoror Mon wore a mask. So it appeared. Well, alright: a Halloween mask to scare the daylights out of young lovers? Not at all. He wore a sort of grinning mask. But I sensed the grin as tragic. Imagine the ancient masks of comedy and tragedy—combined in one. That gives an idea of what I saw. Also, in itself, that mask looked businesslike; or, let's say: medical, maybe a prosthesis . . . for a face.

XXI

And we were off. Willys Jeep in the lead: I gunned it in third gear round a turn, doing fifty in the 15 mph zone. So far I didn't see The Mon's lights in my rearview mirror. And why would I? Unless he wanted to run me off a cliff, and have done with my snooping. But I had another idea: I'd pull in the first circle and let him pass—and then, whoom! get out behind the sucker and see his license plate.

This I did. For a minute, engine off, I waited. Here he came; he too turned into the parkers' circle. And, coasting in silence, he moved slowly around, slipping behind me, and—phewff! On went his bright lights! He flooded my ass with his brights! How embarrassing!

Vrooo-vroooom! I put 'er in first and pounced back onto the Drive. And he followed, tailgating. One thing's sure: I didn't get his plate number, but he got mine. Hey: in Redemaine there was only one two-tone green Willys Jeep looking like it had back spasms. The Mon knew me anyway: Evelyne's brother. The Mon knew about our town; or so I concluded from the nature of his crime. Be sure that, in the year 1961, there had never been a pair of high school sweethearts like Jame Hayes and Lady Gilbert.

It rattled me to have him back there. I might've stopped short, and then—smack! But then what?

Toward the Drive entry we speedoo'd. And then, all shook up, I made a mistake. Swinging onto Thorndale Avenue I turned too wide. He pulled up side by side on the inside lane; and there I was, caught across the divider lines, and the son'bitch wouldn't let me back in. He wedged deftly. Thorndale Avenue, a country road, is not wide; and he had me trapped to face oncoming traffic. I went faster: he went faster, fender to fender. I slowed: he slowed. I stopped: he stopped! Luckily no cars in the other direction—not yet.

I glanced right and had a better look. I saw the mask: or perhaps plastic surgery, in its grinning smoothness more gruesome than a mongoose with a shave. So the devil has a driver's license, I thought; and quaked at the idea he meant to run me into the next oncoming car. Get along little dogey.

Shrrrrrr! I burned rubber, I took off trying to leave him behind. But the Cobra was so powerful, so agile, it laughed at a Willys Jeep. Then, into the long slow curve where Nazzarro and his ZBK frat brothers held their drag races, I opened her wide up—'rrnaaaangggh-hhtrr'! 90, 100, 110 . . . He stayed alongside: no sweat.

And now here came a car the other way: some suburbanite on his way home from downing a few at Roscommon's Tavern while he watched late innings and talked rot. Round the curve he came and couldn't believe his eyes though he might have because the whole town knew Nazzarro Zummo and his gang used this stretch for their own purposes.

Rrrraaaeeennnggghhhh! Here we come! And there the other came, blowing his horn like doom. But do you think he'd slow up? Hell no. He flew along Thorndale Avenue and didn't give a hoot what happened next. In his cups. Hey, his right of way, so . . . bleep ya'.

Then, at the last instant, I hung a left and rocketed off the road doing 120 plus. Up, down, I bounced around. My head hit the roof. Like a plane in an air pocket the Willys plunged, soared; it took my breath away. Thankfully no trees! I hung on, hit the brakes, and came to a skidding halt midway along the drag strip: where the tree-line recedes a ways from the road shoulder. Any further and I was a goner.

—Okay. But you know, that crazy boarding school made me start doubting myself. Now I feel so good with you, like you saved me.
—Hm.
—No, really. I . . . I feel like I want to serve you. How can I?
—Take your time, she laughed. You'll think of a way.

I just marvelled a girl like her would want anything to do with a ne'er-do-well like me: a boy kicked out of two schools, moody as hell, an outsider. I guess we were alike somehow: both 'regular', yet different. Anyway life by Thani's side—'Thani', her friends called her, or Thania—was an enchantment. But it was painful too at moments, since she knew the art of not making things too easy.

III

When I arrived at Redemaine High in September 1959, I found my childhood friends from Spring Glen, whom I missed so while away, along with teammates and old rivals from across town. They filled the college prep classrooms. I suppose a sociologist would say I went from upper-middle to a mix of middle- and lower-middle class environment; or from our financial aristocracy to the petty bourgeoisie. No one seemed to notice I was Professor Gilbert's son, coming from four years of 'finest education available'. So I was placed in a vocational training program, and homeroom. My classes were changed after a few weeks, to my chagrin; but homeroom remained the same: Mr. Gags' misfits. We never learned to spell his name, but we knew he could be a rough customer, and was there to keep the homeroom of juvenile offenders in line. What a joy for me—what an honor! From an exclusive private school to the shop crew and the dropouts. I promptly got a crush on one of the girls; though it cooled when I saw she had no teeth at all.

In days after my sister's death, and the funeral service, a quietness greeted me in Mr. Gags'. This was from sympathy. There was Mills Brooks, a native American: olive skin, black hair in a Chicago d.a.; he must have a hard home life, I thought, the way he got me in a chat and put his arm around me.

There was Louie 'The Limp' Trecastagne, who looked like Byron, handsome with a pouty cast to his features, black wavy hair, and a club foot like the poet. The Limp arrived in homeroom with a regal air, if he did; there always seemed a bustle about him; he had more important things to do than go to school, perhaps involved in things beyond the ken of teenagers. He hadn't the slightest status or clout at this high school where sports and dating reigned supreme. But there were rumors about him, and he didn't stay long with us.

Two madmen, Ray-Guy Beatty and Cuckoo Kiernan, tested the limits of trouble you could get into and still hang on. Others were sons and daughters of Greenwood section families, working class, headed for the military and the factories: Francescuccio Camposaldana; Rawl Paepe with his 100-yard dash style, windmilling one arm; Nino Braggi. But Beatty and Kiernan were another breed, wild, disruptive. Like a connoisseur I looked on their stunts, from afar: myself a good kid now, since I got my way to attend public school. For months, after I finally got kicked out of Ethridge and came home, I liked to play and play in our backyard, like a little boy again, making up for lost childhood, convalescing from that sickness.

Once, after baseball practice, half the team climbed in my Willys for a ride home. When I turned on the ignition, there was whistling, smoke. Whew! if you saw Franny Fofanna, Bo Wurzel–Beaufort Wurzel, the catcher–haul ass out the back! Maybe Beatty or Kiernan did it, I wouldn't put anything past those two: you saw them lurking in the hall between classes, devising ways to get in trouble. I saw no advantage in getting booted from high school, my paradise; but they seemed to court expulsion. They specialized in breaking, entering, pouring sodapop down Mr. Petrocchi's gas tank, flatting The Rhino's (our principal's) tires. They came from middle class families, one Centerville, one Cedar Rock section. But turn to their pictures in the yearbook, and they're among the missing.

Many in Mr. Gags' homeroom wouldn't make it to graduation day. For we were the outcasts, the pariah types, and I felt the distinction. For me such antisocial elements made the place sacred by their presence: when they deigned, that is, to come to school.

Among Mr. Gags' flock were black students too: Roy Jarvis, Whit Wendell, rough kids, quiet; Cathy Knowles and two other girls, also rough–seven or eight Blacks on a given day of the perhaps 90 in a school whose census was some six hundred.

The unspoken leader of that homeroom, as he was of the illegal ZBK fraternity, was Nazzarro Zummo: the one who souped up my Willys beyond recognition. He was the real Byron of Redemaine

High; but more about Naz shortly, much more. For now I'll just say he dated Beth Engstrom—she had a thing for wildmen—before I did. When they broke up, he got wilder.

IV

The Cobra I rumbled with on the Drive didn't have a student parking pass. And no one came to school in a mask with a macabre grin. But I went through that tense morning with an eye out, a sleuth's eye, for any sign. Of course every guy cast a glimpse at Thani Engstrom when we came in side by side, and then stood a moment by her locker. She wore a delicate green top, filled with fresh spring-time, and straight skirt above the knees. Once, at Floriani's Pharmacy in Spring Glen, Danny Leopardi said to me all excited: 'Do you know who will be at the dance tonight? Beth Engstrom!' The whole town was talking. I had a plan which couldn't be used; no use even telling her: you don't ask your high school sweetheart, sure bet for Best Looking in the Yearbook, if she'll go parking up on Maldoror Drive and act as bait for a killer. Beth was so full, tender, so rich in life, as Evelyne had been. Besides mothballs she had a soapy scent, like nature on Redemaine's best days: pure lakes of the Water Company, our Dray River in that less polluted epoch; the sallow green and pink of new leaves and flowers. She was perfumed by her innocence, and immense potential.

There was an uneasy feeling up and down the long hallways between morning classes. You knew something could happen. Why now? Why today? A week after the murder? Maybe because the first shock and numbness had worn off after a trauma to all the town—putting us, for one thing, in the national news. But more than that: this was Jame Hayes' first day back in school. Of course everything is thought; all the possibilities are mulled over by people; no doubt there were those who saw Jame Hayes as the murderer. Don't think there was no racism in our town: far from it. And, if I take pains to write this true account, it is partly to show what racism does to all concerned, white perpetrator, black victim. Racism. Also, it is to show we're all just people around here, so far as I can tell: with our problems and sorrows, aptitudes, hopes; all alike in the joy and hurt, difficulties and pleasures from cradle to grave, whether black, white, or somewhere in between, which we all are. The police had not held the star athlete and honor student whose story rang true and whose grief was deep. It didn't make sense to subject him—his despair, his insistence he was to blame, with a dignity amid the ruins of his young life. But there were those who did accuse him, in their minds, words, soon in their deeds. As for suspicions: who didn't have them? I don't exempt myself. Sometimes it isn't easy to keep a level head.

V

Before fourth period I saw students talking outside their classroom doors. It wasn't the usual talk, sports and girls, clothes, hit tunes. So I sensed from a distance. I wasn't included; though in general, yes, I was: as a jock wiling away hours of my senior year, on a pass to the nurse's office where we liked to hang out, getting our ankles taped. Psspsspss—whispers, murmurs, rumors. I thought the teachers seemed jittery too; and I'll mention Penny Grich, a youngish English instructor who ran a Greek Club after school and invited me to join when I said something to her in the cafeteria one day, really to impress Thani, using the Latin I had from private school: jejunus raro stomachus vulgaria temnit. Rarely does an empty belly pooh-pooh institution food. Academically I learned nothing in high school except how to type; and every teacher, not as person, but as teacher, left me cold. So conformist! Disassociated civilization; the classics by rote. But after school one day, in the auditorium, Penny Grich gave a lecture on 'Image and Symbol' which had a charm: her words so clear (too clear) unlike her lungs filled with cigarette smoke. In class once or twice Miss Grich almost made me think abstractly. But usually I watched the poor woman pull a wrinkled hanky from her brassiere as she spoke, and cough her still virginal guts out even while inspired by romantic verse.

By a classroom door, as I did the stroll with Beth, stood a few ZBKs. It was almost funny—it wasn't—the way they couldn't decide whom to look at: my humble person, or the beautiful girl. In both cases the psychology was complex. Evelyne Gilbert's brother they approved and disapproved, perhaps. You see, Redemaine had never seen, in public, anything resembling an interracial couple, as I said before; and these ZBK frat members were not what you'd call liberal. It stunned the town to see Jame and Evelyne going out: eating an ice cream together at The Mall, or walking hand in hand by the brook in Spring Glen. Heads turned. Minds seethed. And yet Evelyne was such a popular girl: a great kid, always kind, generous, concerned for others, especially the less fortunate. Now that she was gone, however, I took on a social meaning: a rallying point, as her brother, for racial prejudice; since some ZBKs blamed not only Jame Hayes but all Blacks for my sister's death.

Then they glimpsed Thani Engstrom as she glided past them, too fine for words. But they had to watch their eyes. Why?

−Hey, Gilby, what's the word?

−Bragg'. What's new wich'oo?

We moved past toward fifth period, last one before lunch.

Up and down the third floor corridor with its linoleum flooring, and dreary walls lined with metal student lockers, there was a hush like no other morning in the school's history. Usually an exuberant scene: young America; today a war zone. We were on the verge of something, and almost knew it. An assistant principle moved onto the stairwell−toward a stir on the second floor? The AP went quickly, with a purpose, unlike an AP: more like a militia fighter trotting across a field.

ZBKs eyed Beth, or Thani, warily. They didn't 'grade' her, with a guffaw, as they did girls coming down the ramp at lunchtime toward the cafeteria: Trisha Manteuffel, B+, Charlene Buffe, B−, Coralie Panducci, C. In their midst stood the de facto leader Nazzarro Zummo; and in his eyes today there wasn't too much impertinence. You heard no lighthearted remarks as Thani passed by, like an apparition in a boy's daydreams. At sight of her Nazzarro took a posture of superior sullenness; but he couldn't help himself: there was awe. For Nazzarro loved Beth: not as I loved her, but a different way. I had come to the high school shaken by my experience away from home: in need of regular kids, maybe some attention, if I got lucky. And I found Beth; or, rather, she gave me a signal, taking the first step. I'd never have dared to ask a cheerleader for a date. And the result was a magic renewal; also an initiation, in its innocent stages, to the ways of men and women. But I thought about other things too. I went my way from one experience to the next; whereas Nazzarro, son of Italian immigrants whose father became Comptroller, could only keep his distance, after they broke up, and wonder in glum silence—wonder, or plot. Fate is unjust. For she had been his girl before she was mine. And he loved her the way what's best in us loves and dreams of a higher faith, a better future. I don't think he ever would have hurt her, but he did frighten her a little: when he dedicated his grandiose drinking sprees to her, and his outlandish grandstanding. In a great public display of drunkenness, seated at the wheel of his speedboat on its trailer, he had himself towed back and forth before Tony Eden's up at The Mall where Beth worked parttime; and, through his Moon-Goggles, he stared in past the glass at her, as she in her gray uniform served customers along the counter. Yes, he loved her the way we do once in life: the way Antony loved Cleopatra, and Lenny Hovhannes's older brother loved Spring Glen's own Makarie Straiton, who shot him down; the way tragic Willard Steuart loved the new girl in town, Gemma. Well, I loved Beth too, a lot! But Naz cherished her in the future, as his best chance; and then she broke up with him for me. I loved her in the present, my first love, living each day with a zeal, and 'letting nature take its course' as I liked to say in those days.

VI

Students chatted by the cafeteria doors. They relaxed after morning classes. Voices went lower as I passed by; maybe they felt that, until my sister's killer was arrested, I held everyone in the school, in the town, responsible. On the spot.

—Hey.

I met Kilroyne's eye by the entry.

—Hey, I said.

—New-boy.

—Art-boy.

—Hey.

He shrugged. But today's 'hey' was no everyday 'hey'. Today's 'New-boy' seemed to say: careful, something afoot. And his second 'hey' seemed to say: don't go in there; go to the nurse's office and get your ankle taped. My 'Art-boy . . .', with raised eyebrow, might have asked him to elaborate; but not for nothing did Kilroyne have as caption beneath his picture in the 1961 Redemaine High School Year-book (*Cupola*): 'A hey to the wise . . .'

Beside him was Beatty from my homeroom. The Bait smirked: —What's the latest and the greatest? I guess I gave Ray-Guy a withering look. I didn't mean to: like when we were on our way to the cemetery to bury Evelyne and the chauffeur started talking about litter, beer cans messing up the town . . . Now there was such a silence around me. What's going on? It wasn't clear, as I passed into the cafeteria.

VII

The high school was a red brick building the length of a city block. It fronted busy Gordiane Boulevard where traffic might jam up at rush hours and also lunchtime. This affected what happened next— an event that seemed to cast light on my sister's death, and would also go down in the town's annals. In those days there was no drive-around to the pillared main entrance, but only a cement walk across the grassy front lawn. It would take squad cars besides the two on show more time to arrive, and then precious minutes to deploy. Once on the scene, one police team could secure the avenue side, administration office, hallways; while another rushed through the parking lot toward the rear. Inside the school, two long ramps led past the auditorium to the gymnasium entry, and cafeteria in back.

Unlike today: student violence was rare in those old days with their lingering 'Fifties conservatism. On the verge of a new era: did we know it? The 'New Frontier' was nice enough, fresh, acceptable; it had nothing to do with the body of a black 14 year-old named Emmet Till found in the Tallahachee River after he said 'Bye, baby!' to a white woman in a store. That was 1955, as was Rosa Parks' historic gesture in Montgomery. All that took place far, far away from Redemaine; and so did events in Arkansas, where anger, racial hatred, harassment greeted the Little Rock 9, black students entering an all-white segregated high school in September 1957. Hey, we were the North. No ugly racism around here, right? To prove it we had, besides Jame Hayes, an African-American girl named Samantha Esmonde who became our school's first black cheerleader. Greensboro, the lunch counter sit-ins, the Freedom Rides the previous spring, the bombing of a black city councilman's house in Nashville: such things didn't concern us. Such violence was a southern vice—a few pistol shots left over from the Civil War. Am I right?

Beneath the Redemaine High cupola, in the center, a golden garland draped over a rose window to form the word: MOM.

VIII

One by one, or in groups, we passed into the cafeteria. As I stood in line for my tray, I glanced around and fixed on the 'black table', or group. Catherine, Roy Jarvis, Booker Best, Wendell, a few others; also Sammy Esmonde, so lively before the tragedy affecting Jame Hayes and Evelyne, so bright with her twinkling eyes. And, sitting beside her was the man himself, Jame in his first day back at school. Well, he didn't look good, head slightly bent over the untasted food, brow knit. He was in grief, and he had told the editor of our local weekly, Hal Duggan, that he was through with track. For this year? No, forever. Think about it, Duggan replied, in print: life goes on, terrible at times, but oh so sweet too. You've got the world before you; you're greatly talented and a bit young to retire. So wrote Duggan; and, when I read the article, it occurred to me I might go see him at the *Our Town News* offices. He could have a more professional opinion than my friend Thaddy on the masked dragracer of Maldoror Drive. And he, Duggan, must also be wondering what had happened the night my sister died: who did it, why, and would the horror occur again in our community. Yes; I had it in mind, as part of my detective role, to go ask for a chat with Hal Duggan. Plus there was another idea in my head, put there by Thad Floriani—but more of that in a moment.

Speaking of Thaddy: he joined me now in the tray line, and stood looking around the crowded cafeteria.

—Sort of weird, he said.

—Weird?

—Too quiet. And look at the black table.

—Mills Brooks is with them. So?

—Look at the next table. Who's that?

–Momino.

–They usually sit on the other side.

–True–I said, in my thoughts; but I was coming out of them, because Momino Postella was a ZBK subcapo; and his taking up a post by the black table was not like a peace pipe.

–Now look, said Thaddy.

–Huh?

–What's that idiot doing? Is he ZBK?

Ray-Guy Beatty from my homeroom sat down with his tray beside Momino. Ray-Guy never looked too with it; but now somehow he did: up to no good. Evil enthused him.

We paid for our trays, and Thaddy said:

–I know what to do. Follow me.

IX

Thad Floriane was a little guy with a big acne problem and reddish hair all over the place. His eyes were so keen, so expressive: what he felt gave a glow, and he felt a lot, happy or sad. He had artistic blood but made nothing of it: he just did it. Nobody like him for decorating a room, a school play décor when he also made fantastic costumes; he came into his own for a big production: the way Florentine artists of the Renaissance took in hand the city's festival days. Thaddy was the furthest thing from an athlete, in a high school where sports were status; also, he had that apartness of the artist, into his own onions, in his life work already though he didn't know it yet, as a teenager. He was a runty, zitty little guy. But I would follow him where he led that day because he had a knowing heart rare among adolescents, and balls. He had a thing much missed in my other childhood friendships: call it sympathy, concern.

So we took our trays and, Thaddy in the lead, strode across the wide room. Then, yes, I came out of my thoughts about the masked rider–there was just such a tension, not diffused by the full lunch room space with its pale green walls, and high windows sunlit on the avenue side, its sea of tables. Something felt ready to happen, and it wasn't nice. The ill-feeling had been building throughout the town since the night of my sister's death. She was so popular, and admired.

People couldn't believe what had happened to her; that she was no longer with us; that such a thing could come to pass here. Jame Hayes had pluck coming back to the high school. Did he know the ugly rumors trying to implicate him? Well, here I am, his presence said: tell me to my face.

Eyes, eyes were on myself in those instants as we crossed the cafeteria; not on Thaddy, whom I followed. My twin sister was the first to cross the color line; she and the track star were the only mixed couple our town ever saw in public: proud of it. Heads nodded one way when it was known Jame and Evo went out together, and now they nodded another. Even my dad the professor, with his liberal enlightenment, kept to a heavy silence. This man, Professor Emory Gilbert, had written a book of methodology for good race relations within a community. Now his silence, public and private, seemed to me like a turnaround: a gloomy 'I told you so'.

X

By now you've guessed where Thaddy was headed. Modest, mangy sort of fellow; but he had a demon in him, and a flair, at moments, for becoming the center of attention. He was showing off like Nazzarro! Crazy Italians.

There we went with our trays of lasagna. All eyes were on us.

A wiser course would have been avoidance, at that point, much wiser: taking a seat at neither ZBK nor black table. That's what my father would have done. But it's not what Thad Floriani did. He steered me straight to the latter. A grand gesture. I guess it suited me too; though I'd rather have sat with Thani Engstrom. There was no question of joining those ZBKs looking for trouble; but we might have tried to calm them down. Sitting with Jame made things worse.

All in all I thought they were good guys. I liked them. Nothing could be neater to an ex-prep school exile than regular hoods. They had olive complexions, slick-down hairdos, beady eyes, saliva grins, a fresh free-as-you-please laugh. Non-deviants, friendly. But right now they were not laughing. And alongside Momino Postella there were: Vinny Resca, Jimmy Bella, Tory Fallon called 'The Anchovy'; Francescuccio Camposoldana from my homeroom; Biff Modena; oddball Smagowitz, The Smags; also Ray-Guy and Cuckoo. Others. But the ZBK leader, Nazzarro Zummo, was not on hand. And I had a twinge of jealousy to think he was waiting for Thani on one of the corridors, Beth Engstrom, A+. He'd try to make up with her, and ask for a date, and she would tell him—what?

For a moment no one spoke. Whites didn't go to the black table. But now we just sat there together.

At the next table sat a dozen ZBKs, gaping. Jame's lips pursed. Who could have read his thoughts? All his life he will feel the hurt, the guilt, the horror. Still he didn't like this situation. It was not in Jame Hayes' nature to take shit from anyone, but Samantha was on hand, and Catherine Knowles, besides the others.

How quiet the cafeteria was in those minutes. Even Thaddy didn't know what to say: another first. There was a hush before the storm.

Three staff members stood by the wide entry: Mr. Souvarine, Coach Wieboldt, and Penny Grich coughing up her lungs after a quick cig in the teacher's lounge. They might have tried to do something, though nothing had happened yet. They could have sent Miss Grich to telephone for help, namely reinforcements of town police. Too late.

XI

We sat there. Mills Brooks, the American Indian from my homeroom, made a wisecrack. But it didn't relieve the tension; if anything it sounded awkward. I glanced at the cafeteria clock: another 17 minutes before a bell called us to afternoon classes. I looked at the ZBK table, sort of scanning it as if to ask: which of you wiseasses is the masked rider of Maldoror Drive? Gentlemen: who is the Maldoror Mon? And one other little item: who—but no, such a question was gross unfairness to the likes even of a Ray-Guy, a Cuckoo, a Smagowitz.

I felt it was my task to say a good word, and forestall the hatred which hung in the air.

—I want you all to know—my family appreciates your kindness.

Momino dropped his napkin and stood up: as though provoked by my voice.

–Also, that my sister would not have wanted, that she never would have condoned any violence–

No use. Something was on the march, and these were not the words to stop it. Probably there were no words that could have defused the bomb all ready to explode. Where were the police? This was what I wondered in those instants: why didn't the Police Chief, Roscommon, have a presence inside the high school when everyone knew racial passions were running so high? There were patrol cars and two vans parked along Gordiane; but those manning them were not in evidence. I must say that all through the crisis, in days and weeks after my sister's death, our local and statewide media, and then national media, did not help matters. In the newspapers no attempt was made to play down the racial aspects; instead, they were sensationalized, it didn't take much: as 'free' expression was given not only to the town's grief, the tragic aspects, but also to undercurrents of rage–in a word, a gesture, a suggestive photo. Also, there was a late night talk show on WRED, 'The Loner', which under a guise of frank exchange could hardly have been more reckless.

When Momino got up, he was staring beyond us: off toward the cashier and tray line. He seemed to await a cue. Whose cue?

–Look–Thaddy spoke low, as my words, trying to play the peacemaker, fell of their own weight.

I saw Nazzarro standing with his tray alongside Thani, and they were talking. Nazzarro might have been a knight pausing with his lady before entering the lists. I thought she hung back from her ex-boyfriend, and listened reluctantly.

Then he turned from her, and came our way.

XII

As I said, Nazzarro was a leader. But, as he came nearer, it wasn't clear how he viewed the situation. Momino, Vinny Resca, Ginoli, Tory Fallon, Ray-Guy and Cuckoo, Smagowitz–they had a devil in them; they wanted a rumble for different reasons. But I don't think Nazzarro was in the same mood. When he saw me sitting at the black table, playing the hero, he felt a twinge of rivalry. He needed to upstage me. He must obey his nature, and show off. And so the wild child couldn't just come on the scene calmly, and give a soothing gesture to Momino Postella: wo big fella. No, he had to make the impact he had just failed to have on Beth Engstrom, asking her for a date maybe, being rejected. One way or another he had to impress her; and he would, at the absolute worst time, cause an explosion and be right there in the center, laughing, thrashing. So what did he do? He looked at his ZBK friends gathered across the room from where they usually sat. And then he looked at us—not so much like bad guys, as a group of people beneath contempt. And then he raised his lunch tray a bit, for all to see, coolly threw out his hands, and let the thing crash, in the silence, to the floor.

This seemed a cue. All hell broke loose. Suddenly, on this side and that, tempers flared. It went so fast, let's say the deterioration—I'm not sure how, why it happened. Ten days of tension came to a head and erupted in fistfights, violence. There was shoving. There was the usual filthy language which I won't repeat; though a national magazine did, the following week: it cast the whole affair in racial terms and reproduced photos taken by a reporter from *The Scoop* our school newspaper. But I just didn't feel that; and I can't call it racist. Yes, the ZBKs rose and came toward us like a wave; but there was also shoving and shouting at adjacent tables: whites and whites. And why? For what purpose? Things were thrown: milk containers hurled between tables and lasagna portions like blood and gore and chocolate cake and handfuls of vegetables. Luckily knives and forks were plastic. People lunged between tables, and punches rained. Why? So suddenly! Was everybody fed up with the tasteless food? Servings barraged between tables across the wide cafeteria. Shouting, deafening war cries, bad names: degrade the enemy! An untempered wind raged—a force more elemental than racism which it seized on as pretext, or even all the bad stagnation in our town. I saw whites battling whites from table to table; it was anarchy in the school cafeteria. And no one, I repeat no one seemed eager to take on Jame Hayes; though they rushed at us. No one escaped hits unless it was Thad Floriani who got up on the table and began haranguing for 'peace' and pleading for 'love and understanding', hollering anything that popped into his head; and his picture made it into the national magazine and came to symbolize the Redemaine High School Race Riot of 1961. Thaddy had that about him, and left even Nazzarro behind when it came to taking all the light unto himself.

Punching, fighting, flinging food, shouting, screaming. I saw Coach Wieboldt wade in among it, but his voice wasn't heard. For godsakes! yelled Coach at a bonehead play. But he didn't have the authority here. Jame, Whitney, Roy Jarvis, Brooks, a dozen of us stood in line trading blows with the ZBKs. When the blood began to flow, it was red on both sides. More Blacks came on the scene, a few dozen grouping, fighting together against the more numerous but less united whites. Black girls were tough as nails. I didn't see many white girls fight. But the devil, you may say, was in all of us. Peaceable ones, even the non-athlete, non-student government non-cool types consigned throughout their high school life to the woodwork: even these went at it, if not hog wild. Guys jumped between tables, hurled food trays, in a real scuffle. Now on every side there were fistfights. Students grappled one another to the floor. Girls flailed, grabbed hair, bit, scratched at a peaches and cream complexion. Tooth and nail! Our high school cafeteria was turned into a battlefield. Bloody noses, black eyes, cracked heads. Some sprawled on the floor. Here, there, one bent over and vomited up the lasagna lunch. No knives as yet. Cuckoo Kiernan jumped table to table, kicking people till someone upended him and he fell backward, heavily, lucky if he didn't bust his skull. Wieboldt, the French teacher Souvarine, Miss Grich, Kurt Bergan the AP, Petrocchi the tennis coach and biology teacher: none had any real effect on that chaos of teenagers seeming to work off a young life's frustration. Where were the cops?! And all the while Thaddy up on a table gave his tirade, shouting this and that about peace on earth and good will toward men, like this was Christmas. He gestured wildly and called for social justice. He looked half mad with happiness as he surveyed the chairs, trays, books, you name it: all flying back and forth so that he seemed to direct traffic as the world ended, and gyrated both arms. The future bureaucrat Smagowitz also looked out of his mind as he threw vicious punches at the air, simulating a fight, until somebody—I believe it was Rawl Paepe—decked The Smags.

There were screams. There was an explosion of some kind: maybe a firecracker? or gun? on the far side. AP Bergan went about shrieking and dishing out detention hours (he wrote them down) which looked pathetic; in fact, you seemed to see a generation gap opening up beneath our feet, as the 'Sixties got in gear. By now there was no center ring; it wasn't black table versus ZBKs. Resca, Bella, Fallon leapt about planting punches on anybody in their path. It was a field day for repressed instincts, a revelry of violence. Francescuccio Camposaldana, future Golden Glover, went about methodically knocking people down. For him it was like a running of the bulls. Koko laid about him with kicks, elbows. Ray-Guy spat, laughed, gave a hex sign, twiddled fingers, pulled down the skin beneath his eyes. Demented lad: he spat, cackled.

I could go on and on, detailing this craziness. I seem to remember that, of all my homeroom mates, only Louis 'The Limp' Trecastagne was not participating; indeed, a high school riot may have been innocent enough compared to his after school activities. A good thing he was absent from school as usual: The Limp might have smuggled in a semiautomatic weapon under his trenchcoat. He looked down on Nazzarro, a callow youth.

So no Louie the Limp, and no police whistles either, yet. I never heard them. No town patrolmen arrived in a van and began plowing up the high school cafeteria with billyclubs. They stayed out. Is that possible? Well, it seemed much longer than it was, a mere fifteen minutes from when the first blow landed to the schoolwide bell ending lunch hour and ushering in the fifth period. And then people looked around, and took stock, and perhaps a few began coming to their senses.

I thought the law might have showed up in advance of the ambulances: when nearly thirty students were taken to the hospital with injuries beyond Mrs. Aylmer's capacity to treat in the nurse's office. And who, of all the brawlers, was taken into custody? Why, it was five black males, for their own safety; later, a dozen or so others. Mills Brooks managed to slip away; good for him, serving a term on probation.

Then the violence flowed out into the halls. You heard girls' screams. You saw fighting on the ramp back to classes, as an old score was settled. A group ganged up on a student by his locker. I saw Coach Wieboldt with blood on his face from a gash by his eye. It seemed the elements were loosed. And for a good half hour until school was dismissed early, as a dozen police finally cleared the halls, no adult had the moral authority to restore order. Where was our principal, The Rhino? Where was Police Chief Roscommon? Where was Mayor Tomao Simiglione?

Redemaine youth, good boys and girls without a blemish on their record, not an afternoon detention, suddenly went berserk with a great urge to hurt, destroy, overturn school order. Was it because something in each of us, whether or not conscious, identified with my sister Evelyne cut off at an early age? Go in any American high school and you will find, among other things, a world of beauty and promise—but how much is fostered and directed into its proper channel by caring adults? How much developed? someday realized? Tell me: who survives?

Or, maybe, our student body went into convulsions that day because Evelyne's killer had not been captured, and so he might strike again? People were afraid. Terror was in the air not in some faroff place (where we, in our innocence, imagined barbarians) but right here at home, among us: coming out of our midst, and pitiless. It had happened once. It could happen again. Why wouldn't it? unless racism, and the oldtime phobia of miscegenation, had provided a crude motivation for the crime? Unless that talented young couple's happiness, in the fragrant Redemaine springtime, had sent some sick soul into a fit of jealous rage?

Along the corridors there were more vicious attacks, and none of us felt safe. At 12:15 the town police had still not come on the scene. I find this the most mysterious fact of all. Why hadn't they arrived within moments of the initial confrontation there by the 'black table' in the cafeteria? Miss Grich had gone to the office and called; but the forces of law and order in our town took a long time to respond. Why? Had someone given an order to that effect? Hold off? Did a powerful person or group have some interest in seeing racial violence at the high school? The Redemaine mayor, Tomao Simiglione—or more precisely his father, Zu Girolamo—was rumored to have New England mafia connections; though no one ever saw Zu; and the old style *uomo d'onore* from the Sicilian mountains was more like a bogeyman to Redemaine youngsters: more a creature of legend hovering on the horizon of town life. Anyway: what possible advantage could the Simiglione clan reap from teenage violence at the high school? I'll tell you one thing: Mayor Tomao hated that dramatic photo—Thad Floriani haranguing on a cafeteria table with flailing fists, falling bodies, projectiles in flight all around him.

Once again I ask: why no police on the scene right away? Why did their response come so slowly when a few dozen teenagers, and some teachers as well, had already taken a drubbing?

XIII

At last police units came and mopped up inside the high school. They cleared the halls. Now, yes, order was restored: in an empty building. Silence.

Outside, on the wide lawn before the school, students lingered in groups. They spoke low; or just stood around looking at each other, in wonderment. There was a charm to the mad half hour they had just passed: when fighting spread through the peaceful school. No such thing ever went on before. This wasn't the city with its street gangs and rumbles. This was Redemaine of the tranquil neighborhoods: kids, pets, manicured lawns; Peewee League in summer; sledding, maple syrup over newfallen snow in winter; Christmas, the 4th of July.

What happened?

AP Bergan came out on the long steps before the front entrance, and said, using a megaphone:

−Go home now, everyone. Cool off. That is an order.

A girl called to him:

−Will there be school tomorrow?

−We'll announce it on WRED as soon as we know.

−Where?

−Listen to WRED. Now all of you go on home. Those with cars may come around back. Others must walk or catch a public bus. Please leave the high school.

−Have there been arrests?

−Yes.

−How many?

−I don't know.

−They just want to scare us.

−Will there be warrants issued? cried someone.

−I don't know about that aspect, said Bergan. Go home!

Still the students lingered, talking among themselves. Few seemed eager to leave. Who wanted to be alone after a bloody riot?

Chapter Three

I

When Bethany Engstrom led cheers at the football games in the fall, at hockey games in the Old Arena during winter, she drew spectators' eyes away from the players. In her senior year she blossomed so nicely it was hard to be around her—hard for me at least, the poor boy she gave a signal via one of our classmates, and decided to date. Through each school day the desire gnawed at me: baseball practice became a bore; I could hardly wait to get away. And then we drove home together. You can't imagine—or, yes, you can—what it felt like and what it meant: the first time we kissed, and held one another close, and her full breasts swelled against my chest. And our legs touched, and . . . well, you supply the . . . images. Love was growing day after day as springtime rose all aound us with its tide of snowdrops and crocuses, early tulips, daffodils, Japanese yews and azaleas. The weekend before my sister died, Thani and I went for a picnic by the river, in a cove among the willows and cherry trees in flower, all to ourselves. I thought I was in paradise We lunched and napped together; and I was so aroused, as we walked hand in hand on the sandbank, it seemed a blowfish had inflated in my khakis. I was king of the cove, as we marched shoulder to shoulder, but how embarrassed. Yet she didn't seem to notice.

I said my girlfriend led cheers, and was a sure bet for Best Looking in the yearbook. I didn't say how different she was: in her vulnerability, her deep response to things. She wasn't the usual distracted teenager; though maybe no one is. Perhaps her father's death when she was eight years old, a key moment, left her more open, more sensitized; more likely to feel pain, and this life's potential for loneliness, than was altogether healthy. I don't know. But she did have a restless personality given to uncheerleaderly throes of anxiety. And she had a phobia for, of all things, romantic poetry. Once, Coach Wieboldt's son, Chic, happened to see her crying in a telephone booth as he drove past; and so he stopped, loaded her in the front seat and took her home to her mom.

II

When at last I got away from the cafeteria in shambles, I had only one idea in mind. Find Beth. Over my shoulder I glanced at the wide area—graffiti'd pillars like teenage totem poles, metal ducts along the ceiling. A dozen sunlit windows looked over the scene: students fighting in groups, or down on the floor; students throwing things, shouting, cursing. Some waded in; others scattered amid the littered space toward the wide entry, and ramp back to classrooms. No sign of Thani.

Concern came over me, a kind of spasm. I loved her. After what happened to Evelyne there was a big fear in the town; though people tried not to dwell on it. I think they didn't want to admit that something was dreadfully wrong, and had not been righted. So what next? What further horror might catch us on our blind side? Well, Redemaine High had erupted in a fullscale riot. And now anything was possible, in these moments, as terror and panic seemed to whoosh down the long corridors like my sister's violated spirit, her ghost which wouldn't be laid to rest until the mystery was solved, and something was done. The thing had to be addressed by our community. But we were slow, slow facing up to the situation. We didn't see a way as yet. Maybe change—I mean change from our accustomed ways and thoughts—meant a risk worse than the Maldoror Mon. In those days our town seemed to fall from paradise yet still held fast to its notions of innocence.

III

I glanced around. I turned and ran up the ramp, but my destination was not fifth period class. Strange noises came over the public address system: left on in the main office, it caught snatches of office staff. 'Police . . . an insurrection! . . . FBI . . . suspensions . . .' There was our principal's stuffy voice. The Rhino, a historian in his more scholarly days, said in a vexed tone:

—I need a lawyer to suspend a student now.

Another voice, in the background –blurred.

Rhino:

—I blame the Warren Court for this. Civil liberties? Why man, they confuse liberty with license. These wreckers! . . .

Thus the principal, 'our pal', for all to hear. Please adjust your fig leaf: those voices, at such a time, did not inspire confidence.

Where was Beth? To understand my anxiety you had to see her. She lilted through the school days like an Eve among snakes. A girl so sumptuous, so well developed you'd think she might play it down, rather than up; well, she dressed modestly enough in winter, but when the warm spring days came she couldn't be bothered. Was there a blemish to her physical wonder? Her hips were a bit slender: not a pair of provocative haunches swinging like Sammy Kaye.

I went to her second floor locker; then combed the third floor classrooms; and back downstairs six steps at a time. No sign. As her steady date maybe I was overreacting. But who could say what might take place in this school gone mad? We had my sister's tragic example. Some fiend disguised as a high school student: a masked psychopath who got his kicks on Maldoror Drive, might strike again. He could seize on the confusion to drag Thani Engstrom into a bathroom, bang her head on the tile so she wouldn't scream, and do the undoable.

I ran about frantically but I didn't find her.

IV

—Everyone must leave at once. The school day is ended. All students must evacuate the building immediately. Anyone caught loitering will be suspended.

The principal's voice came over the loudspeaker. It tried to give a sense he was at the helm—in the main office.

The school corridors had become a no-man's-land: you went at your own risk. Here, there, a scuffle; but mainly you felt hostility like hell's vapor through the floorboards. Fear, hate. People were afraid of one another: Whites of Blacks, the sudden influx this past year or two from the city: Whites afraid for their property values and their daughters—in that order?—as of a new black militancy spreading across the land. Blacks of Whites: Blacks still an island in a white sea; Blacks fearing blame, scapegoating, for the Evelyne Gilbert murder; fearing reprisals by white town fathers or perhaps the Klan with its presence in our northern state. Black antennae sense racism. And across the land there were black folks building an awareness and getting together to fight for their rights and organizing. I got a sense of it from the senior thesis I was writing—on Little Rock from material in my dad's files—for Mrs. Hebbel's POD class.

I didn't know what to do. Thani wasn't here, not in view at least, so I might as well leave. But before going out the sunlit entry I glanced back down the long first floor corridor, and saw a vision. I saw a lone student: an Italian kid with the unholy name of Santo Poponé whose parents had emigrated to America and found themselves living here in the workers' section. Not for them the stunning upward mobility of mafia's own Mayor Tomao and his dad Zu Girolamo, the capo di famiglia. Not everyone can be a Simiglione. No; this Santo Poponé looked scruffy, poorly dressed, a bit bewildered. He was beneath the ZBKs. But what was he doing at this moment? In a rage he kicked at his locker and shouted racist curses and would slug The Rhino himself on the flabby pink jaw if that man came his way. Well, Santo Poponé felt small and frustrated. He wanted to hurt somebody for it: somebody *under* him, on the Jacob's ladder of immigrants. Hurt Blacks! But the Blacks weren't having that anymore. They fought back.

In our community a moral dam had burst that day. The violence surged forth and carried all before it. Why? Who was behind this? Who stood to gain? Guilt, fear, anger–gut talk, fists. What did it mean? What was happening to us? I went outside into the bright light.

V

I found her in the back parking lot. We stood in the shadow of the football stands: I had my arms around Thani Engstrom who was crying, trembling. She said: It's my fault. I held her close and soothed her like a child, though not very calm myself.

The fighting had stopped. Groups of students lingered on the wide front lawn before the high school and talked it over. They caught their breath after the thrill. Then they gazed at my outlandish Willys set high, tilted slightly on its oversized tires. Evelyne Gilbert's brother and Beth the sexiest cheerleader rode slowly along the front drive. By now there were a dozen squad cars with flashing lights; there were ambulances and stretchers. Police, medical personnel, town politicians moved into the building.

Without looking back I turned left into traffic along Gordiane. If the cops noticed me, a student at the riot's epicenter, they might hold 'the dead girl's twin' for questioning. I don't know how they didn't; but it was good because I needed my freedom. In those instants, mourning for my sister, I was borne along by a sort of dark swift current: as I resolved to play detective and find the link, if any, between masked drag racer on Maldoror Drive and Evelyne's murderer.

But maybe you've known the way grief, with its somber stare, may give way to a soaring sense, an elation. We're not supposed to feel such sadness day after day: the healthy personality has its rights. And so now, as I sat beside Redemaine High's loveliest girl in my Willys Jeep, even savored the scene as all eyes watched us turn into the busy avenue: now suddenly I felt flushed with my teenage élan and with love . . . How lowly and miserable I had been at the morbid boarding school, after my parents sent me away. I despaired of ever getting to Redemaine High where every scent and imagined situation held such a romance for me. Now here I was in the thick of things; and I had just enjoyed a moment, despite the bad time and circumstances, like High School Harry's apotheosis.

Oh, I loved my sister deeply: she was so kind, and brilliant! I would prove my love by solving the mystery of her death. But just now I couldn't help myself. I was young and in love with life. There was a second reason for my strange joy then. The cafeteria mêlée had released a terrific nervous energy, as fighting will, if you aren't hurt badly. And now here I was with a free afternoon—there would be no baseball practice today—until 5 p.m. when I went to work at the pizzeria. A distraught Beth Engstrom sat by my side: so receptive, like putty in a lover's hands. What with the violence back there; and now a warm sunlit spring day on every side: the excitement turned to a tender sexual arousal fresh in our seventeen year-old veins. I reached and took my girlfriend's hand.

VI

She sniffled a little. Her shoulders trembled. But I felt an exuberance—on an impulse I hung a left into Redemaine Mall, zoomed the wide parking lot diagonally, and stopped in front of Tony Eden's, the ice cream parlor.

—What flavor?

I kissed her hand.

She looked at me sideways, and said:

—My stomach's in knots.

—Butter crunch! Just the thing.

—No, thanks.

—We'll share one. Don't be a square!

I bowed and sucked her finger: made like I'd eat it!

The first time she noticed my humble person was at a basketball game last winter. Thaddy and I sat at courtside, and, when the cheerleaders took a rest from jumping around, he started using big words on them, for laughs, and I took his lead. So now I trotted out some pedantry from my dad's shelves.

—Butter crunch! It is good, and pleasant to the eyes. In the day you and I eat thereof . . . our eyes shall be opened. And we shall be as gods, knowing good and evil!

Well, Redemaine Mall was not paradise, though some may think so. But butter crunch beats sin. It was her favorite, and she couldn't resist it. She looked at me like I was crazy, after what just happened. I leered.

–N-no, Newell.

–Ah c'mon, kid, we'll share a cone. I didn't get to eat my dessert.

Ha! A devil was in me this warm glorious spring afternoon.

VII

–Don't leave me here long.

I kissed her with a little laugh, opened the car door, and with a hop, skip and jump went in Tony Eden's. She worked here part-time and didn't want to go in and see anyone.

Out front, on the long Mall walkway, I greeted Mills Brooks and Rawl Paepe from my homeroom, also Franny Fofanna. I guess those three bravos cleared out when the rumble began, Brooks a bit later, as a matter of conscience. They were juvenile offenders–once more, and reform school across the state. Fofanna we called Mouse due to his snout and sparse black hair teased with Vitalis to a longish crew-cut, also 5 o'clock shadow in his teens. Franny was a 'fine little athlete'; once, at practice, we wrestled in the outfield grass after he said we two were just high school pitchers; and Coach Wieboldt shouted out at us from home plate: Godsakes! But his dad, local athlete Lon Fofanna, was a Cincinnati scout; and so Franny, who could hit too, would probably sign and be sent for a year in the Rookie League. For now you often found him up here during class time; he hung around; he shot a rack in the pool hall by Tony Eden's, and waited to see who would show up.

Someone always showed up: from lowlifes like myself, Ray-Guy and Cuckoo, to the legendary Cynthia Landis–the one girl in our class as beautiful as Beth. In truth, Miss Landis should get Best Looking, and Thani Most Desirable, if that was a category; but Cynthia was not a cheerleader, or *in*, in any way: she just had fun at the hop, and called up WRED to read a dithyrambic chant in praise of rock 'n roll.

Time didn't touch us at Tony Eden's. Suddenly you found yourself in debate with the intellectual cheerleader, Spring Glen's own Lil

Berryer: my first crush on a woman, as third graders. Or here came head cheerleader Bärbl Hebbel swinging nature's pompoms; she was the daughter of my somewhat interesting POD teacher. In POD I learned to use Kierkegaard's alternation method, focusing on some other attribute . . . s . . . besides the lofty matter at hand, and then wasn't so bored. But wait! Here comes Tony Eden's star: it is Nazzarro Zummo in his 'Vette souped up with all the latest Moon-Goggles gear. That red and silver striped buggy looked like a hornet gone mad for his queen. And Nazzarro in the town's hottest car—unless it was a certain black plateless Cobra—Nazzarro sat low in the cockpit, head resting haughtily on the driver's seat as he peered out at life, girls, with a long cigar in his mouth. He gave her the gas; the 'Vette lurched before Tony Eden's, like a farting god. All looked up from their ice cream; but Naz didn't stop to say hello. Having made an appearance, achieved his effect, he spluttered on down the Mall pickup and delivery lane before the glittery stores into the distance.

Everybody who was anybody showed up at Tony Eden's for a sugar cone with two sticky scoops and a napkin. Have a ball at Redemaine Mall! croons 'The Loner' over WRED. It was the all-time hangout spot, and center of the universe; although, as Thaddy used to say, I didn't have the patience to waste my life. But for a spell after the ordeal of boarding school, I tried. I cruised and boozed. I cropped up a lot at the hot spot where the clock stopped, and everything happened, and nothing. Hello, you! Be cool, and drool. Hey, Nate the Great. Never too late for a date with fate. Twist 'n shout: it's the 15-round bout of hanging out. But look. Here he comes in the flesh. Say, is it? Is it Louis 'The Limp' Trecastagne, babyface with double dropcurl: come for his favorite butterscotch sundae with pistacchio ice cream? And if that weren't enough, he's got a limousine for wheels since The Limp's dad is a chauffeur to the Simigliones. But who's that by his side? Marrron'! Can it—could it be—the one and only Francescuccio Camposoldana who once belonged to the fan club of the late, great Johnny Ace!?

VIII

Then Thani and I in the souped up Willys drove along Gordiane Boulevard, and we owned it. There would be time to grieve for my sister, a lifetime. But right now sunlight poured through the dark clouds into my adolescent heart. I couldn't help it. Thani and I kissed as I drove. We put the violence behind us. We took turns licking the butter crunch. Going along, I remembered the night 17 of us piled into the Jeep, and I overturned it doing figure eights across the Mall parking lot while shoppers watched beneath the arcade and applauded. That was before Nazzarro took a battered Willys into his garage; it went in a virgin, but came out bored, stroked, and fuel-injected. Hot stuff! Only cost the kid—well, a pretty penny in those days. But hey, wasn't it worth it? Now our garage had one of the loudest, fartingest, fastest accelerating hot rods in town. Cool hack! But my poor mom called me a damn fool and couldn't get over it.

Now suddenly, after the excitement, it seemed like a holiday.

—Hey! Chic kid!

I honked, and waved out the driver's side at Chic Wieboldt and his girl. Chic was first pitcher, All State; Fofanna and I second and third pitchers. From the awake look on Chic's face—nicknamed 'Nap'—I saw he didn't regret baseball practice either.

—Big Jay! You Jay!

Smooth John-O Kogan drove by in his used Studebaker; and he didn't need Wordsworth's *Ode* to have a blast. Rumor had him going out with Cynthia Landis, on the rebound from Roby Hurteau.

Now the Willys swerved between lanes as I gave a high sign at Hen Scagliese who played some infield for Fungo-Amapola back in Pee-wee League days, and had a stacked older sister. But I was with Beth, so I didn't yell at the top of my lungs: Hankee! Fix me up with your sis'! No, I'm not that stupid—I only hailed the boy while leaning to lick Beth's dripping cone after she bit off the soggy bottom.

The Jeep ranged over the dividing line. A few cars beeped. Then a voice rang out in the traffic, echoing:

—Hey-y-y!

You guessed it: Arty Kilroyne, with his hundred heys, on the way to another day as oven-man at Redemaine Pizzeria.

Thani nestled her head in my neck. Not like her: shook up from the riot. She held the sugar cone for me to suck, O the sweet butter crunch. Ooze, ooze from the hole in the cone. Roll, ocean.

Kilroyne yelled:

—New-boy-y-y . . .!

Well, I had come a long way. From the lowest of the low, most antisocial kid ever to attend a stodgy New England prep school where I broke every record for misbehavior—to a pretty happy fellow tooling along the main drag of my hometown. Like teenagers across America burning rubber from a stoplight, kchcheeeee! zero to fifty in three seconds gunning it down those friendly streets en route to a sorority meeting at Coralie Panducci's. Then the day came, too soon though many could hardly wait, for going away to college; or else on the honeymoon which simply could not be put off; and then came the decades of marital prose: earn living, raise kids, drink beer, watch TV. Hey. Others entered the military and were sent halfway around the world to fight in wars. Well, in the meantime I too would have my letter sweater and my first love, like an initiation: double date to the bowling alley and then Tony Eden's for the works; Sunday picnic by the river; high times at the drive-in movie; beach under the same blanket the day after Senior Prom. It was a brief springtime of happiness like none I'd know later. Soon enough the day would come when I said so long to friends and made a pledge to my high school sweetheart in tears. Before much longer our class of '61 would graduate and become a memory, our beings and doings a part of the town's unwritten history. But not quite yet. And now something had changed. After my sister's death I could no longer take our innocent Redemaine life at its face value. The detective story was more than a mystery, if you will; it cried out to be solved before I could move on to the next stage. Oh, soon enough I would go on my way—but not like Fran Fofanna when he tossed back his head with a laugh, and did his carefree duck walk into the sunset of America's adolescence. For I had a little job to do first. It was not one a teenager knew much about.

IX

I drove a half mile past the golf course and took a left onto suburban streets leading out toward Thorndale Avenue and the rural outskirts of Redemaine. Overnight those peaceful lanes had burst into bloom. Besides forsythia, golden bells, there were weeping cherry trees in a profusion of pink from yard to yard; there were kwanzan flowering cherries and white dogwoods; saucer and star magnolias; viburnums, flowering quince and shadblow; also, pistachio nut buds dear to Louie the Limp.

After the excitement Beth rested her head back on the seat and closed her eyes. She trusted me to choose a spot where we could park in security, and pet to our heart's content. But how did I repay her trust? Were her needs, her desire for safe intimacy the main thing on my mind? Hey, I was on the way up to Maldoror Drive again . . . And you, Reader, exclaim: No! How is this possible?! Boy, what are you doing? Is the idea to use your girlfriend as bait to catch the Maldoror Mon? You're really too much! What a maniac!

Calm down. For one thing it takes a maniac to catch a maniac. For another, there would be other couples up there enjoying the spring afternoon; and they'd cluster at the first circle, the scenic lookouts: not seek out a dirt turnoff hidden amid the trees where anything might happen. We would join the others. Thirdly, as an aspiring private dick (pun) I predicted The Mon's next move. If he struck again it would probably be elsewhere: Galen Street bridge over the parkway; high school couples also went there. But probably he would desist now: not too many mixed couples were forming up after what just happened to the first one. If he was out to kill teenage parkers and preserve our social mores: then Maldoror Drive in broad daylight did not lend itself. There were police on patrol from one end of the park to the other. They made sure another horse didn't get out the barn door.

X

I pulled into what after all was a secluded glade of West Hills forest, and turned off the Willys motor. I miscalculated: there wasn't a soul up here but us. Not cop cars, and not parkers. Silence. A breeze rustled in the sallow underbrush and branches of trees. Birds chirped.

–Thani?

She slept. Her breasts rose and fell beneath her blouse buttoned to the cleavage. I bowed my head and breathed in woman's fragrance. What a strange person–I thought–strange and different. Am I different too? Maybe this brought us together: in the last analysis it isn't about how beautiful you look, how cool you act, but who you are. She could not have wished to be more attractive: draw more eyes to her deep-zoned and graceful figure. She was a star at the high school. Her hold on me was so firm I just yearned to spend time with her, magnetized by an ancient need. Yet she was restless, teasing, sort of scheming, seeking to increase her power within the relationship, and guarantee it. Did insecurity begin when her father died? Would she ever be easy, feel safe to let things happen, and accept her place in nature and society? Maybe not. Maybe there was a contradiction between nature and society. Hm . . . to be so pretty, have such a way about her, yet need to prove it constantly; use wiles; wrest from the one who loved her what were better given freely. Hm. Such a combination of beauty and insecurity could hurt her in the long run: unless there was a man by her side who loved her all the way, and didn't mind dying daily. Would her man have the patience? strength? capacity to sacrifice on her behalf? Would I? Would she love such a man? We are not gods, far from it. And she, Bethany Engstrom, was a hell of a tease. Oh yes. She was like a woman with grave dignity who fears being taken for a piece of snatch.

So I thought, or felt: as we sat in a quiet spot on Maldoror Drive, after the Redemaine High riot, that spring afternoon.

I bowed to kiss her shoulder. A sacred act, or profane? Ever so gently my fingers traced the contour of Beth's breast–her breast so precious to me not because spectacular (what is nature?), a cynosure of eyes at the high school, but because hers. During our last date in the back row at the movies, I had begun to stake my claim, in a first exploration of that virgin territory. Now I wasn't just sneaking round other people's property where I had no right.

But I recalled the Cobra driver. Was he up here now? Was he coming toward us, slinking tree to tree in the shadowy forest? He drew closer, ever closer, ready to pounce . . . I glanced back. This was madness. I didn't even have a weapon. Well, a tire iron. But unlike Jame Hayes when he made his great mistake, I would stay by her side.

Even while casting glimpses at the sun-speckled trees, I caressed Thani and rhapsodized. Oh! What these women do to us: it's hypnosis. I wanted to go down on the Willys floor and kiss her queenly feet over and over, and pledge my love like the late, great Johnny Ace! What won't a man do let alone say once *she* holds out the hope he may one day, somehow . . . aïe!

I cooed, and said:

—Baby, you awake?

My whisper had a tremor as I kissed her hair, her incomparable neck, her blouse. This was living, after the long dark night of an all-male private school with only the masters' wives for sex-objects. Now I felt charged with desire after the cafeteria violence; now, parked in this lonely spot on Maldoror Drive, I felt we might finish what we'd begun in a few hot petting sessions at Lavater Field where I used to play Peewee League games. Was it possible? End two virginities at a go? Might we lose control and go all the way? What if I got her in trouble?

XI

I meant to wake her, tenderly, with my caresses. I meant to kiss and kiss her so she wouldn't ask where we were but only kiss too and one sweet thing lead to another. In my mind we entered not Maldoror Drive where an innocent girl was murdered a few days ago; but, rather, the precinct of lovers, where satyrs and nymphs entwined in the sunlit foliage. Play, Pan, your priapic pipe.

She came from her dream with a sigh, a low moan.

—Newell?

With a hand she brushed at my fingertips like cobwebs. I had to contain myself: so excited I could hardly breathe. My blood was in a riot. As we kissed, our lips, mouthes locked–I remembered what someone told me in the locker room after baseball practice one afternoon last spring. Thani English couldn't be called fast; no one said vulgar things about her: she does this, you know, she does that (never about guys of course–or it's a distinction for them). But she was a hot item who went out with senior athletes. You could ask Worley Morse, a catcher now in Class D ball, whether she didn't come a close second to Miss Jollymeier, homemaking teacher.

If you ever drove a Willys Jeep stationwagon, good for campers, you know the front seats recline. Holding Thani in my arms I let hers down notch by notch, and she let me operate. Hair dishevelled, short skirt ridden up, she said in a whimper:

–May I stroke you?

Her breath was hot when I breathed it in. She had been backed in the zone: defenses in disarray. And, hair in her face, blouse unbuttoned so she sprung boldly from the tight silken brassiere, Thani groaned, and waited. It was a feminine chaos, elemental, voluptuous, passive. Was this paradise garden: where pastoral swains tend their flocks, while playing a flute, and nature goes naked in her plenitude? Hey. Paradise or no paradise, it beat the hell out of hell. And now I had to have Thani Engstrom, gorgeous cocktease. Now I must take full advantage of this unique opportunity, never expected, much less deserved by the likes of me. Now, I thought, or maybe never. Oh, there is nothing quite like possession. Hey! So I, in my wisdom, reasoned.

She lay there at love's mercy: knees raised like floodgates. Eyes two slits, she stared. Lips parted, a strand of hair curled like a snake in between. I lowered my body onto her.

Forgive me, Reader. I don't know what got into me in those instants. Why go for the kill when we were both minors? Why not take it easy and have some more fun? Stay on alert, Bert. Keep your head, Ned. What's done is done, son. Why not try to learn a thing or two before burning childhood's bridges, and starting to go through the mill of adult life? But, you see, Thani was so damned alluring with her curves, her teasing manner like an incitement to riot in the nerves. I was shook up. How often our actions have the opposite effect to that desired? Maybe she only wanted to civilize me: I was pretty wild after that hyper-civilized prep school. But she created a monster.

XII

Now what to say on this topic which hasn't been said a time or two? At last we were in position. Our moment had arrived. On the verge I had a savage rapture. Good gracious! Has anyone else gone through such a thing? Beneath me she wriggled. In abandon, hands grasping air, she cried out my name . . . A few days before my sister died, Thani and I drove an hour to see a church. Protestant church in the New England countryside: it had the usual spire, and primitive stained glass. Springtime reflected on the white facade: pure green trees and shrubs, yellow daffodils. She took me there, and I wondered who took her before: how she knew about it. Maybe Nazzarro when they were going steady? For a few weeks I had tried not to show any suspicion, a demeaning jealousy. But I knew he drove by her house on Godsen Avenue in his 'Vette, and moved some furniture for her mom. Why not ask me to do it? I suspected she used the boy to have an effect on me. But why undermine my self-confidence, my goodnatured sense of things? Why mar the joy in our relationship these wonderful days and weeks? Unless . . . unless she was using *me* to attract Nazzarro Zummo on a deeper level?

Anything was possible with this girl whose charm, more than she needed or could use, might seduce her too in the end. And now I poised above her: ready for entry. In those instants I had such a need to prove myself before the proper time. So goaded on by her wiles: there was no question of better judgment. Also, in the rush of events after Evo's death, everything kind of went faster, like our hothouse desire. Events, reports, rumors flew about town with a new meaning to them, and urgency. I was a semiconscious teenager still enthralled with baseball, but awakening.

You ask how Maldoror Drive capers, an attempt on Thani Engstrom's virginity, tally with a resolve to find my sister's killer. Work for justice, do good; and deflower cute kids. Well, I was starting out in a quaint way, but my intentions weren't base. I loved her. Maybe, unconsciously, I felt: Let's create new life to replace the one that was taken. Maybe my spirit reacted in this wild way to such grief out of season? In any event, it was not a conquest I had in mind: not a male ego booster.

Hey, I was a teenager. But it would take more than a childish act to get life back on track, after our loss. Hope springs eternal; but it isn't always so easy to begin hoping again realistically. That must be planned, and struggled for. My sister was gone; she would never return to us. She lay in a cold coffin up on the windswept hill of Fenbrook Cemetery. We who loved her would remember Evelyne Gilbert's fine life: brief, brilliant, a blossom in spring. See how she tried to live? Principled. Now I must do the same. But first—

Well, how many have fought the bad business until the end, and tried to make things better. Some get nowhere. Others, worse off, pave the way to hell with their good intentions.

XIII

Suddenly Beth screamed. I thought: one of her wiles? At that point it wasn't easy for me to give pause and draw back to look over my shoulder. I was on course—levelled off, set in my coordinates, like a torpedo. So I didn't glance around and ask right away: why the shriek? There's no pain since I haven't gone in yet. Why cry out so shrilly her voice breaks? Does life without virginity loom as so appalling? . . . All this took a split second: the same instant I was about to take the plunge.

But I saw her terrified stare. And I couldn't help following it to the front windshield. Lifting from her, turning to look also, I saw— nothing. Leaves and sunlight.

—Newell, he's—it!

She was so afraid she couldn't speak. Unless she was playing? Creating a diversion, that is: so we wouldn't go through with this thing for which we were not prepared? I can't make love to you today, big boy, because the Maldoror Mon is right outside the car. The Mon is getting ready to attack!

I couldn't think what to say. So I said:

—For crying out loud . . .

And I made once again to go into my routine—not a routine, quite yet, since I'd never done it before, at least with another person. Being uncircumcized, I doffed my coat in the foyer, so to speak, and was getting ready to make myself at home: take up residence at that cozy hearth. It wasn't as hot as the pizzeria's 800° oven; but it did glow warmly, invitingly. No; Beth's body wanted us to consummate just then, if not her mind. So why did a cold shiver come over her? And then again:

—Ah!

Not so much a scream as a child's cry, desperately afraid—she turned her head toward the side window. Her features contorted.

Once more I followed her gaze, and—nothing.

—Beth, is this a joke? Are you okay? I feel a little crazy too, but this—

—Ho-o-o!

She sounded like someone on a rollercoaster ride.

—What?

—It's—it's it! Evelyne—

—You—

The sound of my sister's name brought me to my senses. At that point I could only think: there's something to this.

Again she screamed and cried out:

—The Maldoror Mon!

Again I looked over my shoulder.

Nothing.

—Aw, c'mon, Thani.

XIV

It isn't easy to act the lover—the first time, an amateur—when your partner yells *It's the Maldoror Mon!* at the top of her lungs in your ear. What to do? Let it go? Well, I must pull myself together and go take a look around. But once I disengaged, then goodbye to prospects for a successful outcome today. She would say she saw a ghost, and let's get out of here fast.

So, more gently, with a show of calm, I turned back to the task at hand. And, wouldn't you know it, just as I poised on the threshold, about to insert my key, she let out another bloodcurdling scream.

Beth didn't try to rise, and struggle out from underneath me. She just lay there, whimpering. She wasn't so pretty in those moments; not the hottest chick at Redemaine High. Oh no. She lay in disarray, blouse wide open, rumpled, skirt bunched over her waist, panties down. She was a poor kid who had seen a ghost, which, I knew from my efforts to see it too, was only in her mind.

I confess I didn't handle the situation well. Insensitive jock: at one of life's key moments. Her head jerked to the driver's side window this time; she let out another shriek, but this was the scariest of all, because silent. The thing hadn't gone away; it came closer, and so Beth's fear was too much for her vocal cords. She thought on what happened to my sister; though I had not left the car, and it was broad daylight. Really I didn't see what she had to worry about, since each time I looked, there was no Maldoror Mon but only a springtime afternoon filled with sunny leaves rustling in the trees. True, I was more intent on the glint of terror in my girlfriend's eye, as it related to the other small matter in hand. But if Mon was out there, Mon would have attacked by now and not played hide-and-seek like a six year-old in the windows of my Willys.

And so I drew up from her. Our fun was spoiled. I heaved a sigh of unsatisfied desire, and said:

—That does it.

XV

I poised above her. How anti-climactic. But what to do? Each time I set to work and tried to pay attention, she let out a holler.

Time to zip up the ball bag. Head for the shower—a cold one.

Then suddenly—imagine my surprise when, outside the Willys, a booming voice sounded, like a bear's. My heart was beating a mile a minute from non-Mon related activities. Now I lurched for the tire iron, in back by the spare, and didn't think whether I bruised Beth in the process.

But The Mon was saying something. Hey, it spoke human language. We heard it say clearly:

—*Are you decent? I am The Mon. Cover asses! Save skin! Do not dawdle any longer in that preposterous position! Nudity turns The Mon off!*

What did this mean? A practical joke? Was it Ray-Guy and Cuckoo dressed up like the four-legged monster on a comedy show? No, it was no joke: Beth had seen. And then I saw too. A grisly werewolf streaked with blood, sporting fangs, hulked and guffawed in the Willys back window. So was it, oh! was it our Redemaine High principal, Dr. Ewald Sangesland, called 'The Rhino', who cavorted out here in the woods? Our 'pal' was a bit stick-in-the-mud for such antics (I thought agoraphobic: the way he rarely came out of the main office). Would he put on a costume and scare young couples out of their wits as they made ready to pass a milestone?

Not The Rhino? Who then, as Guardian of the Public Morals? Maybe Souvarine, the French teacher, who also coached Drama Club? Well, I didn't think that prissy person would come gamboling through the forest in a werewolf costume. Hmph! . . . But who then? Tomao Simiglione? No; Mr. Mayor got his kicks in more dignified ways; besides, his voice was high and shrill when he made campaign speeches on the Town Hall steps. Well then Rune Roscommon, our noble Police Chief? Perhaps The Rune went mad from downing one too many shots and beers at his brother's restaurant and decided his true calling was not law enforcement but rather the Maldoror Mon. Neat idea, if this were a novel, and not a true account from our town annals. Besides, Chief Roscommon was kept busy changing all the locks at the police station, since the Mayor and Town Council wanted him out. Also he was too fuzzy most of the day, and too much the bureaucrat for deeds which will get you a felony conviction. His soul was no longer hardy enough for aggravated assault.

Well who then? Who was the Maldoror Mon, or else a Mon impersonator? Impersonator, you say? The word brings to mind our capable School Board Chairman, Donaldsen O. (Ottilia) Sorifa, who ran a red light late one night in February, and, when haled to the roadside by our courteous police, was found to be dressed up as a drag queen. It wasn't Halloween. But I'd say that act about leaves him out. I'm not too sure what the Maldoror Mon sees as his calling in life; but I do know what a drag queen is after.

Well then who was the Maldoror Mon? For all I know it was the stacked Mrs. Hebbel from POD class, or Miss Jollymeier whose style was cramped by homemaking; or even Penny Grich driven wild by her emphysema and the horror of conjugating Greek verbs. But did this hairy werewolf wear a mask sometimes and roam the Drive late at night in a black Cobra without license plates?

XVI

Beth and I, at The Mon's request, were buttoning up. Town cops could not have gotten a quicker response. I lunged to roll up windows, lock doors, and turn over the ignition. But just then on the driver's side: watch out! Mon's disgusting mug thrust up pointblank. It was a ravaged face, and the view put an end to this day's lovemaking. And then, and then . . . Do you know what happened next? Of course not because I haven't told you. And you won't find out from reading our history teacher Marsden Dale's *Annals of Redemaine Town: From Its Settlement in Colonial Times to the Present Day.* That Marsden Dale, so pale, elongated, with a grin: almost as anemic as his writing. What a guy! In seventh grade, at my first private school, I wrote an essay on 'Sherman's March to the Sea'; and, would you believe, I used it as a senior thesis, five years later, and Dale gave it a B+! Good as Trish Manteuffel! I cheated my way through his history class; but what could I do? It was so boring I couldn't stay awake. Say! You know what? I wouldn't be surprised if Marsden turned out to be the Maldoror Mon, because his lectures were a killer, and his tome on Redemaine was deadly. Well, he was a learned historian, and his *Annals* were commissioned by the Chamber of Commerce. Grandiose! The dignitaries sitting on that august body are the modern day equivalent of French Encyclopedists; as I believe our distinguished French teacher, Souvarine, would assert, if asked. Yes, one might rank palefaced Dale with d'Alembert and Helvétius. Bien sûr!

But where were we? Ah, the Maldoror Mon . . . He gazed sadly at something he would never have, namely Bethany Engstrom; while I fumbled with my fly, and also gazed sadly and thought: time to split!

XVII

I heard laughter. Maldoror Mon laughed, reached a hairy paw in the driver's side window, and—ffflip! snatched my keys! Then the big hairy fool went bounding away through West Hills forest. Please, sir, my keys! But sir! Mon gave a happy laughter and went loping back toward where he came from.

Hell, now what?

Beth was hysterical. I rolled up the windows, locked the doors, and moved to take her in my arms and calm her down. But she didn't want to start that again. There was mistrust between us now. Hadn't I brought her to the Drive as she drifted off to sleep trustingly, her head on my shoulder? She had no say in our travel plans. And then came an attack by a psychopath. And, although no one was hurt—not yet—how were we going to get back down the hill? Walk? Run like Jame Hayes that night . . . ? The Maldoror Mon was out there, and he laughed low and waited as he grasped my keys.

It was absurd that I didn't have a gun. Some private eye . . . The Maldoror Mon existed, and I had brought us up here and put us in harm's way.

What to do?

Hell—I shook my head—she doesn't trust me anymore. Adam and Eve sort of thing: the fall. I'm expelled from paradise and didn't even get to enjoy the fruit of knowledge.

XVIII

Get out and walk. Don't leave her alone as Jame Hayes left Evelyne. But we had to wait a few minutes before starting because Thani was trembling from head to foot. She had an attack of nerves, and said, hiccupping:

—Don't touch me, Newell!

Her shoulders shook. She cried. Exciting day: even more so than when she led cheers for the Redemaine Red Renegades. And it wasn't over yet.

For a half hour we waited there while she tried to calm down. Midafternoon had passed.

Then I perked up my ears. I heard someone whistling—free as you please, a top tune from the WRED chart.

—What's that? said Beth, and shivered.

—I don't know. Shhh.

She had the hiccups: loud ones.

—'cup! Cup!

Sure bet for Best Looking in Redemaine High Class of 1961 Yearbook (*Cupola*) looked like a poor thing just now. Tears on her cheeks, rumpled in her sheer blouse and short skirt, she retched hiccups.

I glanced back past the tailgate, then out the side windows, trying to spot the whistler. Who was it? The sound was so lighthearted and nice—Maldoror Mon in an upbeat mood?

Then I saw him: out the front window.

No, it was—why, the darn fool! How did *he* come to be around here just now? Well, at least we were safe and could get a ride home. We wouldn't have to walk and risk a Mon attack from the bushes.

Beth also saw, and came back to life, waving:

—Nazzaro! Over this way! . . . Open the window, Newell, quick! Open for Nazzaro!

Now really. It was Nazzaro Zummo alright. And do you know what he was doing? what had brought him up here on West Hills? Oh, he just happened to be in the forest that day, the same sector where the Maldoror Mon terrorized us.

Now he skipped and tiptoed amid the wildflowers, with a smile from ear to ear. He did a little dance and whistled his tune. Tra la la! In the mad boy's hand was a butterfly net. That's right. The big gorilla went frolicking in the springtime foliage. He laughed. In Italian he called to the pretty butterflies; no doubt they knew his parents' southern Italian dialect, and would all fly gaily into his net. How touching: St. Francis of Assisi.

Nazzaro Zummo looked so innocent, as he did a dance among the forest underbrush, and waved his butterfly catcher. Life was a lark to the boy. Hey. Never mind our scare, the real-life horror of Maldoror Drive—the curse that came to our town ten days ago.

By my side in the jeep Thani looked so relieved. Oh, him she could trust. She read in his eyes the adoration he felt for her.

She waved. Why certainly: Nazzaro hadn't spotted the car yet. She called his name.

XIX

What happened next was strange. I won't dwell on it, but a few words are needed. The Maldoror Mon had given us a jolt: the more I thought about it, the more upset I got. But . . . from afraid, then annoyed as hell . . . I, and Thani too, entered a land of enchantment. Yes, that's the word: a kind of idyll. Nazzarro knew the Drive and West Hills forest like the back of his hand, and he showed us wonders. I'd call him a naturalist, but that doesn't express it. He was part of the life up there. And they, the birds and small animals, wildflowers and trees, sort of knew the crazy guy as one of their own.

At Nazzarro's 'Vette parked on the Drive we found his pet raccoon seated patiently at the wheel wearing a pair of moon-goggles. Naz kept it on his lap as he drove. Then here and there we stopped, and he took us back in the woods to show us the secrets of chipmunks and squirrels; the mystery of fish eggs spawned beneath a rock in the stream. He knew where a fox hung out, lone survivor, and what that fox did each day. Nuthatches, cardinals, redwing blackbirds: he introduced us to birds. What a charm it was: what poetry in the unnoticed life around us.

Look at him over there: so tickled among his close friends the skunks, the earwigs, and sod webworms. He had a field day with chickweed and spurge. I did think of St. Francis as Nazzarro traipsed by sprawling birches with their three or four compound trunks, shiny leaves reflecting like sequins in the sun: the white trunks, the metallic leaves like droplets of opaque sunlight. Our guide posed against springtime's sallow green, its mauve mist. He was a tallish guy, gangly with Italian features, the bold nose, and fine expressive eyes. I remembered him from Peewee days: when the Spring Glen boys played that Lovett Hill gang up at Lavater Field in the first summer of the Town Fathers' new park.

Now Beth seemed so happy with him, but not with me: sorry she ever met Newell Gilbert. And, would you believe it, he even managed to find my Willys keys! Quite by accident: there they were beneath his feet; they lay by a path where a hilarious Maldoror Mon must have dropped them. What luck!

XX

In those moments Nazzarro Zummo knew he had won the day. His laughter was boyish, his manner engaging. Now he didn't have to play tough guy as ZBK leader.

I eyed Thani. She warmed up to him as a wilted flower revives in sunlight. On her better days she was too sensitive to things. Today she had been through a race riot, then nearly lost her cherry in a Willys Jeep when the Maldoror Mon saved her . . . hm!

Nazzarro cracked jokes. He said whimsical things, a comedian, and crackerbarrel philosopher. He put the springtime all around us through its paces like a magician. And this made Thani relax and have fun again.

What scenes those two played: worthy of old legends. What grand gestures, stilted language, knights and ladies. They were talented. I joined in, using nervous energy released by the day's ordeal. Hm, Naz and Thani made a handsome couple; they did honor to our school. As for me, I was good about it, but I felt like the wicked witch just then.

What comraderie, what nice hacking around. The day of disaster turned into a good time. And then Nazzarro offered to drive her home. I wanted to protest, but what could I do? She accepted his offer at once.

—Newell, you'll be late for work at the pizzeria.

Well, I had felt her need to play one guy off against another. There must always be a second suitor. She was very attractive, but so insecure. Feminine dignity, not snatch!

Now she seemed to recover. From Nazzarro's 'Vette Thani waved to me as, a bit stunned, I got in the Willys and revved 'er up.

Chapter Four

I

Redemaine High closed for a day and then reopened in a tense atmosphere. It had to, or else leave a vacuum which would cause problems. The School Board met in special session: still headed by Donny Sorifa despite his taste for women's dress. He provided leadership during the crisis.

Meanwhile the town's black community was having its own meetings: agreeing on demands, making these known to town leaders and Duggan at *Our Town News*. First they wanted an end to hassle by whites: arrogant treatment by whites so used to such behavior they didn't know they did it. Blacks in town were fed up with being jostled and called names and looked at that way and treated as second-class citizens. Oh yes. Then came the historic factors: their service to this country as soldiers whose red blood has flowed, young lives been sacrificed, during America's wars. Then there were the contributions made by black men and women to our cultural life; also, if truth were told, to every aspect of social life: in every role, every community where they were given a chance. Then, on the bottom line: this nation, history's wealthiest, became rich and dominant on the backs of black millions used and abused as slaves. They worked for free under the lash while producing fabulous capital for the masters, the slave drivers, plantation owners, Master Cotton, Wall Street.

This went on: as it might. Redemaine's black community was in
ferment and nothing would turn them around. Among the emergent
leadership was Rev. Charles Esmonde, blind pastor of Gordiane Baptist Church, and cheerleader Samantha Esmonde's dad. The minister
had preached a stirring sermon the previous Sunday: it mustered
Biblical versets for the black community's demands. Not only did he
roust 'em out saying black folks were sick and tired of racist stereo-
types, 'watermelon 'n shortnin" and the like, but he did this with a
scholarly flair. *Out of ashes his bread shall be fat, and shall yield royal dain-
ties (Genesis 49, 20).* Blacks weren't the first ones who shortened their
bread, or the last.

   —Maybe some of our white brothers and sisters think they are better than others, better than us. (Stirrings in the congregation.) I say in
that one aspect of their lives, their personalities, they are worse.
('Amen.' 'Tell it.' 'The truth now!') For let them know we are fed up
with racial epithets used to make us feel inferior and to justify injustice. ('Yes!' 'Yes we are!' Rumblings through the packed church.) We
are no longer willing to feel inferior or guilty for being black, for being brought here across the centuries against our wishes, for being exploited mercilessly and separated from our families and the land of
our ancestors. (Outburst. Cries. 'That's right!' 'Amen!' 'Let me hear
you!') We never asked to come here. The white speculators in human
flesh brought us! (Shouts; like an explosion.) They extracted every
penny of profit they could and this resulted in more millions of dollars extorted and more millions of valid black lives lost. And to sanc-
tify that unholy process they said this nation had a sacred mission, a
manifest destiny, chosen by God—why, to make them rich! But a
black man or woman's soul was not valuable. Not valuable! Well,
well, we know our worth. ('We do!' 'We do!' Cries, shouts.) We will
proceed to prove it. (Outburst. Feet stamping pews. Cries.) From cradle to grave we are made to feel inferior, feel guilty for sins committed against us: a sorry victim to be blamed, exploited, mistreated,
again, again, again! But I am here today to tell you I am not inferior.
(Pandemonium.) I am any man's equal. (Bleating, crying, shouting.)
I am not guilty for sins done unto me through the centuries. ('No!'
'No!' 'Not guilty!') But something deep in man is the true transgres-
sor: something erected into a system. (Shouts. Amens.) I tell you
from now on I'll fight against that something. ('Right, Sir!' 'Tell it!'
'Tell us!' 'True, true, true!' 'More! More!') I am not afraid to stand up
and fight and die if need be for my rights, my freedom, my dignity as

a man! (Pandemonium in the hall. Cries, shouts, a woman shrieks.) Freedom! I say. Say it with me: Freedom! Freedom! Freedom is our creed. Sing it: Freedom, freedom over me. ('Freedom! Freedom!') I'll never stop this fight . . . until the world respects my right! (The packed congregation produces a kind of thunder.) I'll never stop this fight . . .!
      Reverend Esmonde turned from the pulpit.
      Uproar.

II

      Meanwhile, across town, other meetings were being held. Of course everyone was talking over the recent events. It wasn't revolution; but neither was it last night's TV shows or the upcoming Pee-wee League season. No, you might almost say Redemaine's streets were in session. There was excitement. Casual words between acquaintances had an edge to them. Any lunch counter conversation might turn into political debate a bit more intense than 'I Like Ike' versus 'Halfway with Adlai'. Decades of prosperity after the Great Depression, plus the advent of television in the late 'Forties, had cast a torpor over public opinion. But now Governor George Wallace became a symbol: 'Segregation now, segregation tomorrow, segregation forever!' Now Bull Connor braced to meet Freedom Riders with brutality on Mother's Day: in a Birmingham renamed Bombingham due to attacks on Blacks. Now the Albany (Georgia) Movement was getting underway: there the people's will produced a mother lode of rallies and demos, protest, resistance. Pressure, pressure, pressure! Civil Rights groups were coordinating their efforts in Albany: where mass arrests occurred, and activists went to its jail, famous for lynchings and disappearances, by the hundreds. Police Chief Pritchett liked to say: 'You see, it's mind over matter. I don't mind, and you don't matter.'
      Hear that, Citizen? What do you think? Wake up, man on the street . . . Redemaine, asleep since its inception, gave a yawn, looked around with perplexed eyes, and said:
      —How do.
      There were whites in the poorer white sections who said:

—Look out. Blacks are going to want privileges and special treatment now: like we never had!

There were whites in the more middle-middle class sections of town who said:

—Pretty soon they'll be moving in here. Oh my property values! My daughter!

There were whites in the more affluent sections of town, so-called old families, business leaders, professionals, university liberals, who said or thought:

—Settle it before it spreads. What do they want? All charges dropped against black rioters? Okay. Black course curriculum at the high school? Okay. Black recognition? Black business? Black opportunity? Okay. Race is okay. Give them race, race, race. Race separates, money dominates. It is the question of class . . . which could threaten our ass.

Each day, as the conflict developed, the School Board met. Those were agitated sessions. The members sought to reach a cohesive position but were unable to control their emotions. For, in general, we may say that if black families in town were afraid of the new situation, then white families, parents, had a fear of those same Blacks which was mystical.

Anonymous phone calls flew around Redemaine, and irrational comments.

The FBI came on the scene. They talked to the School Board Chairman, and Town Attorney.

For now Mayor Tomao Simiglione stayed behind the scenes. He made no public statement. Why? Redemaine was a focus of attention. One article, in a national weekly, showed a dramatic photo of Thad Floriani on a table, hair wild, as he gestured and addressed the race riot across the high school cafeteria. But Mayor Tomao, an ambitious man with higher office in mind, did not come forward like a born leader and face the situation. Why? Some, in Redemaine, called this a failure of leadership. Others, contacts in the state capital, and Washington, D.C., termed it political savvy and an astute move. Well, a future statesman like Tomao bides his time; he cannot be swept away by events. Hey, if there's one thing Mafia life teaches you, it is this: Don't show your hand. Of course I am only surmising that Tomao and his dad Zu Girolamo were New England *mafiusi*. I never heard an adult in town say so. But Redemaine young'uns like

Thaddy and myself grew up with the pleasant idea that Simiglione clan were a bunch of gangsters.

III

Meanwhile, Police Chief Rune Roscommon made a public appearance. He was guest speaker at a patriotic function sponsored by one of the service clubs in town. His speech was much awaited, given 'the events'; it was likely to cause a stir. Unfortunately the good man was a bit under the weather; in fact, he stood at the podium looking a whit less dashing than usual. In the old days this man had a flair for public appearances. Rare the mane of chestnut hair in an officer of the law; it waved out romantically from beneath his cap. Also there was a fairness in his judgments, and a friendly twinkle in his blue eyes which was attractive to the youth in town like myself–quite unlike his underling Crumley who used to hound us out of the Water Company. Roscommon had served his community for a long time, and I think in the main he was a good man. Now his time was past.

First, he was under pressure to produce at least a clue in the Evelyne Gilbert murder. And then, if this didn't fill his cup, along came a riot at the high school: a thing never seen in *his* peaceful and law-abiding town (except for the Simiglione crime family known to whack people out in traffic). So Chief Roscommon was feeling the heat, and perhaps we may pardon his slight inebriety at the potluckical dinner. There were media outlets on hand, WRED, Hal Duggan of *Our Town News,* the two most widely distributed state newspapers; also one of the bigger boys from a magazine with nationwide circulation was on the case.

I too was there with Thaddy, and we both felt Chief's remarks had a touch of the bizarre. Like he was trying to hide something? As though he had some other role in all this besides that of assuring order? All in all it was strange; and yet I'm not quite able to say why,– or share a quote from his address that will leave you wondering as Thad and I were?

–Isn't it enough for all of us to be living in this great free land? I mean who else on earth has it so good? Our way of life is the best! So I say love it or leave it and to hell with Bolshevics. Let Beatnik intellectuals get a haircut and a job . . . But . . . but my hat is off to the humble, hardworking people who respect America and her laws. As long as our ethnic communities contribute and do their work, and don't become communist, threatening our democracy . . . why, as far as I'm concerned, they are as welcome here as my Irish ancestors . . . As for myself I have tried my best for long years to be a public servant and keep our streets safe and respond to people's needs and guarantee law and order. Maybe I have made a mistake or two along the way. Forgive me for this, forgive me, citizens. I always meant well by all of you, each and every one . . .

There was applause as Rune Roscommon sipped water, his hands trembling slightly with emotion, from a paper cup by the microphone.

One other distinguished town leader having his limits tested by events was the Redemaine High principal. Dr. Ewald Sangesland, 'Baby Rhino', had his complacency jiggled in those agitated days. The old-school aplomb got a bit ruffled at moments. He was starch incarnate; but his Germanic features, pink fleshy cheeks gave a quiver the day fistfights broke out all over Redemaine High.

The Rhino didn't go galloping into the thick of things, that noontime when the school cafeteria went berserk. Oh no. He stayed in the main office, calling for outside help, directing operations. In days following there were white groups, class officers, Student Council members, who came to him. I never heard he met with a black delegation.

And yet—should we classify him as a hardliner? There was a pathos to the old duffer when he said: 'They've thrown aside authority; they've spoiled the school year.' One morning he did find himself in the middle: when some black girls, militant, devil-may-care, started shouting at a white group including ZBKs in the main lobby. But through the crisis he clung to school routine: met with APs, guidance counselors; visited a class per day as in normal times; kept his door open to faculty and students.

A few days after the riot Baby Rhino called a schoolwide meeting in the auditorium. He asked for calm and said we must learn to discuss our problems. He made a bowwow speech about academic excellence and college applications.

There were those in town, liberal types like my dad, who considered our principal a bigot. Is this true? I don't think he talked any differently from what he was: an American fossil. The problem is that American fossils are still alive, to all appearances, and running around, in power.

Teacher since the early 'Thirties, he became a principal in 1947. Well before the Redemaine High Race Riot of 1961, control had been slipping away, authority cast aside; so he believed. And he had a mania about legality: can I do this? can I do that? Why, you need an in-house lawyer. Control, control; otherwise—anarchy, ladies and gentlemen, Beelzebub.

His flabby jaw might still give a tic at the sight of a Cuckoo Kiernan or a Ray-Guy Beatty. But theirs were adolescent pranks compared to what lay ahead for the world he had known till now.

IV

The bell rang ending afternoon homeroom. Mr. Gags had less students now. Mills Brooks, Francescuccio Camposoldana, Ray-Guy and Cuckoo, Smagowitz—they, like others in the past, disappeared from the homeroom of dropouts. No trace of Louie the Limp since February. A few black students had come and gone since September.

Down the stairs we went as the school emptied out.

I took the long ramp to the gym.

In the locker room the others were there: baseball players I'd known since childhood, when our sections of town played each other in Midget and Peewee Leagues. Chic, Franny, Bo Wurzel, the others: good buddies. I daydreamed about them when I went away to school, and my heart warmed to find them when I returned after four lonely years. They were the best of the year's crop, and I suited up too when spring came. But today I saw my childhood friends with other eyes.

So much, so much it had meant to me: just being in that locker room, chattering. Well, I played baseball with a difference. The year before, in my first start, I no-hit a non-League team; and then to be saluted and looked at along the high school corridor the next morning . . . Ah, ah. For I had been deep in shit as Buddha, spending my life in Saturday detention; I was the most wretched kid in a hellish private school named Ethridge. But I fought them, their system; I rebelled and suffered the consequences and made my way back to a place where people enjoyed themselves a little. So I believed. Now I was really in high school. I had a letter sweater. I had, for a few weeks at least, a high school sweetheart, a fine one. What? A cheerleader for the likes of me? Oh, I was accepted. Seventeen friends piled in my Willys, and we overturned 'er in the Mall parking lot in front of Tony Eden's. A hit! Sorority night at Coralie Panducci's: that was heaven. Good times. Feeling like myself again, I had a blast before high school years passed.

But all that was about to change: in a few minutes.

The handwriting was on the wall since the night my sister died.

V

Now what words can describe what baseball had meant to me since the dawn of consciousness? I was a boy collecting cards, stealing 25¢ from my mom's purse so I could buy five more packs, and maybe get Sibby Sistie, or Ed Pellegrini, which I needed for the set. I listened to Dodger games, and that was the last time I remember praying: so Campanella would hit one in the ninth. At age nine I threw my first pitches, which went out faster than they came in, against the James Street Jets, Franny Fofanna's team, and the great Cocò Arzigogolo long gone by the time we got to high school. Baseball and boyhood friendship kept me out of the house, sane in a crazy family, hopeful. Like every normal kid across the land I felt all-fire certain I would star at Ebbets Field. And, like all but the chosen, I was too small, too this, too that. Another few inches and I might have wasted all my life, not just ten crucial years: when I read little, and didn't care a plug nickel for education—if there *had* been a real, noncomformist teacher to further it by making me feel the connection of serious, sincere books and ideas to real life, to our destiny as a people.

Yet I might have guessed my lot: from a glance at my older brother, Joey, the thirdbaseman. He was cast in a different mold. He was big, first of all, and strong; catlike, graceful; the great young athlete who knew it. Down south at college now, setting records, he could sign at any time. As an athlete Joey was just so special, bigger, better; and every scout knew it, including Fran Fofanna's father, who fawned on him. Once, Evelyne and I wondered out loud whether our older brother hadn't been adopted. He took things in stride and succeeded at least in high school, and now college, with no sweat. But I wasn't like that. I've always had to work ten times as hard for the little I get. And so my own strong ambition, not yet in its proper element, had me practicing harder, longer, pitching nine fierce innings per summer afternoon against a rubber tire. If I wrestled Franny on the outfield grass because he said we were both 'a couple of high school pitchers', then this was because I knew it deep down, and had a dogged insistence with regard to baseball.

VI

Woolly athletic socks; then the thin white undersocks; then high-arched stirruped uniform socks of the Redemaine Red Renegades, plus garter. Lace and tie cleats with the pitcher's toe-guard—a ballplayer's footwear was complicated as Amiens Cathedral.

Cap, A-2000 glove, hanky, rosin bag in hip pocket—let's roll, hawn' you kid.

But I paused. I sat down on the bench by my locker, half hearing my teammates' banter about girls, or tomorrow's opposing pitcher. Maybe I looked up at their easy laughter, cut-off red sleeves, sunburnt napes. Hey, I'd always yearned to be the star—Chic was the star—but now, suddenly, this didn't matter. What had mattered so much, was that I played, participated, on the team. I was there.

But something had happened. And now, today . . . I bowed my head, and shook it a little. The thought I had then was like a yoke. I tried to shake it off like a sign from my catcher. I couldn't believe it.

VII

Outside: sunlight, bright green grass. Track and field team jogged the quarter-mile track. Ballplayers made their way past the pole vault area and broad jump pit, across the wide playing fields toward the baseball diamond. There were girls. Pretty high school girls sat in stands by the track and did homework or watched their boyfriends practice. Also, cheerleader tryouts for next year's squad were in progress. The girls' voices went lower, sort of comical, when they chanted. I gazed across and saw Thani among them. For an instant she looked back, but busily. Since our adventure on West Hills I hadn't driven her to school in the morning, loving the scent of her mothballs. We had broken, up, or she had, by telephone:

–Newell, I just feel . . . we need to date other people. We'll both know we . . . have a special feeling for each other . . . but . . .

Other people: Nazzarro, the Maldoror Mon.

I mumbled in the phone: alright. I didn't contest it, much less beg. Instead, I said sorry for my behavior the afternoon of the riot, when we parked along Maldoror Drive and got carried away. In this context she brought up Nazzarro's role: it was a good thing he happened by. Then I grew quiet, hearing the tease which was her trademark. I felt a sinking, a sort of giving way. My Redemaine High idyll was over. Yes, you could get bit by a snake here, too, in your high school paradise.

So my breakup with Beth jibed with a sense I had. Something was wrong, out of joint. Something old, ever accepted, was about to give way.

Now, headed out to baseball practice, I paused. Someone called to me; I hardly gave a gesture. Taking off my cap, I wiped my brow on my sleeve, and shook my head. What was it?

Always I felt, thought, acted like a ballplayer, a pitcher. This was my identity: the ticket to good nurse's office life. Acceptance. From class to class through the day I did wrist exercises for my hard curveball: thrown slider-wise, like a football, by an arm not strong enough for a real slider. I carried around an iron ball, like a shot-putter, hefting it to make a baseball feel lighter and give my smokeless fastball some velocity. Well, All State pitcher Chic Wieboldt was the success; I was just obsessed, a reliever who threw three World Series games per stint in the bullpen, and rarely saw action.

Now I wiped my brow, standing there, looking around a little. Franny Fofanna trotted toward me, whistling, head high, carefree, like a duck. Fran reached and poked my rib, but I didn't goose him back for fun. He cackled and strolled off in the sunlight. I stood staring in a daze out toward the playing fields where my classmates ran, jumped, waved their arms, called to one another, threw and caught a ball.

I didn't see Coach Wieboldt among them. He must still be in his office.

Blue sky, sunlight. Summery breeze. High school girls: our POD teacher's healthy daughter Bärbl Hebbel, co-head cheerleader, doing her stretch. Other students held their afternoon club meetings in the stands: Penny Grich's Aesthetes; Chess Club, Debate Club, Tomorrow's Homemakers grouped around Miss Jollymeier, Italian Club, Pep Club.

Bright sun. Not a cloud in sight. High school athletes, cheerleaders.

Warm day in May . . . senior year in high school.

Something wrong.

I turned around, and went back toward the gym entry.

VIII

Coach Wieboldt sat at his desk doing paperwork before he went out to baseball practice.

—Sir?

—Yes . . . Newell.

He looked up. In the years I'd known him, he didn't smile much. He had a sense of humor, but it was wry, like vinegar in a wood cask. From Peewee times—six, seven years ago—he had coached his son's teams on the other side of town; and they seemed older, stronger than Spring Glen boys. When I was ten, our Midget coach Raupach wouldn't let me pitch because I made a remark about 'needing more support in the outfield'; so he kept me in left field all summer; and, during the Midget all-star game, Coach Wieboldt's team had me running back to retrieve homeruns. Well, kids from Cedar Rock and Lovett Hill, the Greenwood working class section, could hit. Don't give them fastballs. By the way, there's a small monument to Coach Raupach and another 'town father' up there beneath the trees by the Peewee Field. Paul Raupach committed suicide.

—Newell . . . come in.

—Sir, I can't come to practice.

He gestured:

—No problem.

–Not today, or . . . tomorrow.

He heard the quiver in my voice, and looked up.

–Oh?

–I'm quitting.

–Quit? You're the relief pitcher.

–Chic doesn't need relief.

In three years as a high school pitcher he hadn't been taken out. It sounds far-fetched, but I seemed to serve some psychological purpose.

–We need a bullpen. You're it.

I shook my head, lips pressed.

–You've got Fran.

–Lefty starter. Why quit baseball, Newell? You're good.

–I have something else to do.

–Go do it. We have three weeks to the State Tournament.

Last year we lost in the finals. I'll never forget the bus ride afterward. You'd have thought Yahweh broke his Covenant. This year we were the favorites.

–No, Sir. It's . . . it has to do with my sister.

He looked at me.

–I understand your grief. We all share it: such a fine girl, so bright, positive. But life goes on. You must live it: use what you've got.

–This . . . this isn't my show.

I frowned and looked out the window. I bit my lip: in my mind was something I'd like to tell him. But it wasn't the important thing, and you don't say such things to a coach. Two nights before Evelyne died I had started the one League game I ever got to pitch: in a twinighter against the doormat. Into the fifth I had a one-hitter when Coach Wieboldt told me: don't throw curveballs. Bingo, there it goes: 3-run homer. We won 9-4; but why tie my hands? Why spoil my one chance? . . . Well, a week earlier some Town Fathers were at Tony Eden's one evening for an ice cream, and one said to me: 'It's not right, Newell. You should get starts too.' I shrugged and said: 'Chic's the best high school pitcher in the state.' And they: 'Wieboldt should pitch you more.'–Was this why Coach vetoed my curveball? It looked too good?

Now I met his gaze which had a glint to it. In his own playing days he was a tough sidearmer: knock you down soon as look at you. He went through life with that glint: like he was still pitching. It worked. I thought then: in this town with its Maldoror Mon, enigmatic Police Chief, mafia Mayor—here's a man haunted by winning baseball games, and by his son's career. It's a fixed idea. No wonder he got upset a year ago when the benchsitters voted for me, a reliever who never got in, to be team captain. (I voted for Chic.) How angry Wieboldt got that day at the team meeting. I felt on the spot when he said: Vote for a relief pitcher . . . Godsakes! Now, since I decided not to be part of it anymore, I began to understand. Well, well, I didn't get to play. I had my petty grievance like a few other high school athletes in America who will brood over it ever after. Baseball, sports ended soon enough, in most cases. But were those old times supposed to be the most exciting thing in life?

Another moment we paused in Coach Wieboldt's office. He stared at me. I think he couldn't believe I would hang 'em up. Win, win, win—that was the creed. But did he really think we benchsitters could feel deeply about the outcome? those who never got in a game? Come, now, we weren't put on this earth to sit and admire, even if our team was the favorite. We want our kicks too. I had an urge to tell him this, or something. But what for? A pitching rotation has nothing to do with turnabout fair play. Coach wanted a State Championship with Chic in the limelight, if possible. It was his dream and he'd do what he could to achieve it. Win. Never mind the rest. Yet he did mind, a little. Thus the bit about curveballs.

IX

For another moment I stood there, quietly, in his office.

From playing fields outside the window came sounds of a baseball being caught, its plock off the bat, infield chatter. The athletes' voices, calls mingled with cheerleader tryouts.

Coach said:

—You're a pitcher.

I frowned and looked down. What was I giving up? Tomorrow the school would know I quit baseball. Along the corridor between classes I'd recall the glorious day of acceptance, greetings from seniors I knew by sight, after my no-hitter last spring. Now the students, classmates, Bethany, would look past me.

—My brother is the athlete. Joey Gilbert . . . or Chic.

Coach Wieboldt straightened his papers. His mind turned to to-
day's practice. Case closed. Non-essential personnel. There was Fo-
fanna for the pen. There was a sophomore, talented black hurler.
Coach said:
—What are you going to do?
—When?
—Now—he said, with a little laugh, as though there might not be
life after baseball.
—I don't know, Sir. I have an idea in mind. Something real bad has
happened. It feels like there's a problem in our town . . . You know, I
just feel like asking a few questions.
—You're a bit young to play at detective.
—Yes, Sir.
—It isn't the town's fault. It's one sick person.
—Sick . . . But what made him do that?
Coach raised an eyebrow.
—What do you mean?
Foolishly, I started to talk. I said what came in my head:
—One reason, Sir, I need to leave baseball is . . . it takes so much
time. On a whim I took a book from my dad's study and started
reading. A serious book: sociology. It asks questions: what makes a
person act like the one who killed my sister. Okay, he's sick, that's
sure. None doubts it. And then? Can we pin the blame on one, and
forget it? Why did he do this thing? Hey, says Joe Blow, call a thing
by its name. It's clear; no one is fooled. But if Joe Blow is right, and
the truth goes floating by us on the surface: then why do we need
science? The town's upset about Evelyne's death; but what if . . . I
don't know how to say this. What if our town has . . . has depths we
ourselves don't suspect? What if, some way or other, we . . . we do
things in such a way that . . . we . . . —
The look on Coach's face made me lose my train of thought.
He said:
—Soon you'll sound like a communist.
—I don't know what that is.
—Somebody who wants to change our way of life.
—Can you be one without knowing it?
He thought a moment, and said:
—Maybe.
—Is everybody with a different idea a communist?
—No.

He straightened the folders on his desk and held forth an arm to usher me out.

−So . . . I shouldn't ask questions. Or spend time studying.

At this he gave the slightest jolt. Said:

−I wish you good luck, Newell. I'm sorry you've decided not to play. We try to do what's best. Right now I don't have time for an abstract discussion, but you might drive by and see Hal Duggan. He likes them.

−Does he?

−Duggan might give you some insight into the town's depths.

A note of irony?

−Thanks, Sir. Thanks for letting me be on the team. You'll win the State title, and pretty soon Chic will sign.

X

We went from his office into the afternoon sunlight. Pleasant commotion of track and field practice, ballplayers running around, cheerleaders leaping and doing splits. By the portable bleachers he shook my hand, and we parted ways. But he looked back and said with a grin:

−See you in gym class.

Varsity athletes were exempted from gym. I nodded, and then made my way, stunned by what I had just done, to the empty locker room. Hang up my spikes at age seventeen? Well, people must understand it was because of my sister. And I could play next year in college, if I wanted; at least keep the bullpen warm, since at that level there would be three or four Chic Wieboldts.

And that All-Stater's prospects? He might never sign a contract despite his amazing high school success. I remember the day in Peewees, at age 12, when I first turned my wrist−not straight-arming−before the delivery. All Big League pitchers do this, more or less: from the controlled Whitey Ford who almost didn't, to lanky hurlers like Gene Conley whose arm was tangled yarn. It gives speed, movement. But that first time I was so wild, hitting Bo Wurzel and Braggi in the second inning, the Spring Glen coach yanked me. Well, Chic Wieboldt, a near perfect pitcher at every stage, never turned that corner. He had the strangest short-arm delivery, sort of fetal, or like he was cradling a baby. Maybe his dad, and coach, didn't want him to change—moult—and jeopardize perfection: maybe lose a game or two. He was almost big enough, and gifted: what control! Everything low-outside. Yet it was hard to see how he had only lost one high school game in three years. He didn't look the part. Didn't extend. And no scout would sign him. Win, now. Success . . . But Buddha, as I said, must go in the shit before coming out shining.

And the State Championship? That year we didn't qualify for the tournament. My fault! Or, let's say, my ghost came back to haunt the Red Renegades. Fewer teams than usual, eight, were allowed entry; you could only have two losses in a 20-game schedule. Well, two were Franny Fofanna's: home and away one-run losses which he pitched brilliantly versus a team that socked righty curveballers like Chic and me. Their own mainstay was one. My last week on the team Coach had me throwing batting practice—curveballs all afternoon. Hey, all you want. And the third loss? I had sulked through the season's first weeks, and literally wouldn't speak all day: so depressed I wasn't getting a start. Then, after Coach made me pitch a jayvee game, a sort of re-tryout, I shut out a non-league team. Two weeks later he sent me to the mound against the same team, instead of the League start I yearned for. I couldn't get up for it: no challenge. The weak team beat us, on their diamond, in extra innings. Three losses.

Coach Wieboldt never believed in me.

XI

In a few minutes I had cleaned out my locker and put on street clothes. But, back in the jeep, I sat for a long moment staring out at the cheerleaders and baseball practice in progress. It felt strange and familiar: to be out of the flow again, like I was in prep school. At a stroke I just lost my status with the in-crowd: the jocks, the nurse's office. How nice that was: to belong . . . Oh, they'd be friendly; but, hey, I no longer needed my ankle taped. And Thani? Well, we broke up, and she was also lost, it appeared, to Nazzarro. From the Willys I looked at her, and felt I loved her; but she didn't glance back. So I asked myself: where to, Newell Gilbert? Will you spend your life as an outsider? Oh what a drag.

For a minute I thought about my mom. She was in a bad way, though she went through the motions. She had a thing about fixing our meals. I felt sorry since she'd begun to feel hope for me: not getting into trouble once I got my way and went to public school. Unlike my dad she loved baseball, and used to attend Joey's and my Peewee and Babe Ruth League games. I think it tickled her that I, so moody, unhappy often as not, could breeze through the days and feel good about life—even have a girlfriend, which she guessed because I picked at my food and asked for money. Pizzeria earnings weren't enough: I was spending hard-earned cash on some books I wanted to read, a damn fool idea.

Seated at the wheel I lingered, staring out. Goodbye, childhood. I couldn't believe baseball was over. The summer afternoons in Spring Glen were spent daydreaming about a game, or listening to the Dodgers in Brooklyn, that place of romance. Well, so much for dreams; let's go, reality. So much for high school larks, too: it was time to do what I said, and look for my sister's killer. Unlikely private eye, to say the least: a little more like Peter and the wolf. But a plan had started forming in my mind.

With a sigh I turned over the ignition—no smoke bomb this time— and backed from the parking place by the stands. Slowly, still grandstanding since a few eyes could be watching the Willys, I drove across the parking lot. The jeep stationwagon gave a low uneven rumble, a backfire in first gear: souped up out of its mind in the garage of Nazzarro Zummo. Slightly crooked, set high on its wheels, it put on a little show as I turned round the side of the big redbrick high school building and rode off—not into the sunset, yet.

XII

My plan to catch the Maldoror Mon needed help from childhood friend Thad Floriani. The scheme was ingenious. And demonic! It takes a devil to catch a devil. Famous policemen, the Vidocqs and Vautrins, were former criminals. Hey, you can ask anyone—any

adult—at the two elite institutions I had the honor to be kicked out
of: they'll tell you I was a little devil. Anyway, I needed Thaddy's
help to begin setting my trap; but right now I knew he was inside the
high school painting décor and designing costumes for a Drama
Club production. He'd gladly lend a hand, a master's; the basics
were his idea in the first place. But he was busy now, so I thought:
why not take up Coach's idea and call on the *Our Town News* editor?
Hal Duggan has his finger on the town's pulse—a rather fast, irregular
pulse in these times.

Along Gordiane I plunged into a new element, like some sort of
explorer. For seven years baseball was my life and my identity; hm,
no more baseball. I was Ulysses at Gibraltar, Marco Polo in China;
the first European risking a mystic river into the heart of the unknown. What did people do in life when they didn't play ball?

On a side street, Old Gordiane, by the Town Hall I parked and
locked the Willys.

—Mr. Duggan here?

His editorial assistant on this smalltown paper, Harriet Pulley, a
fun-loving spinster with wooden cheeks and balding red hair, said:

—Hi, Newell! Not playing ball today?

—I just quit.

Wide-eyed, I said it.

—Oh, dear. Why?

Her eyes showed surprise too, girlish. If only that was the way she
wrote, and lived. But her beat was marriages, births and deaths, local
charities, barn sales, news items from the neighborhoods—Centerville, Lovett Hill, Cedar Rock, Spring Glen, Harmonium—also a
4-page monthly supplement called *Good Times*. She knew me since I
came in during summer to write up a game I pitched.

—Kind of busy.

—Doing what?—asked the fond Harriet Pulley; there was a shy
mockery about her, a twinkle in her pale blue eye. But her face contracted:—Here I am forgetting to tell you, Newell, how deeply saddened I was . . . by your sister's . . . At the funeral I felt so sorry for
you, your parents, Joey and cute little Lemon.

—Thanks, Harr'. I know. Is Mr. Duggan on the premises?

—He's here. I'll ring him . . . I thought you loved baseball. Why
quit?

I had to chuckle. There was something in her: deeper, wilder,
though it's silly to say, if you ever saw her. She had something that

could never find a home in our Republican town. What? It's hard to pinpoint. For an old maid—and she was that: a graying, human splinter in her calf-length print dress which was also faded;—for an old maid she could sure look a babyfaced jock, or ex-jock, up and down. Eye his crotch! Scorch his butt with her tinder gaze, ow! Yet it wasn't only sexual. I want to use the word spiritual. Harriet had a fine racy irony that knew, but couldn't print, the town's secrets. Well, you won't savor Miss Pulley's je-ne-sais-quoi in 'Our Neighborhoods' or the *Good Times* section. Her body was fruit out of season; her mind had an untapped intelligence which, in another epoch, another place, might have put her in the front line shoulder to shoulder with Susan Anthony or Mother Jones, if not Louise Michel, Rosa, Kollontai. I liked the way she sort of teased and egged me on, as if I had one too (a mind); it made me want to tease her back and sniff around.

—Why I quit the team? Well, it's like this, Harr': when I was a child, I thought as a child . . . but now I'll try to become a man, by (my voice went low) . . . by finding the Maldoror Mon! (I leaned forward, a hand on her desk, and hissed in her face.) Do *you* know where he is?

—Goodness me! I really don't. Not in my boudoir, I hope.

She gave such a comical look then. But I also, in that instant, seemed to glimpse . . . what? Her intelligence again. She hid behind humor. She was afraid of something, but not the Redemaine Ripper.

—You know, I have my own theory. I think The Mon may be a woman: someone . . . like *you!*

She raised her arms and gave a flustered little shriek. Then said, calmly:

—Purely an external resemblance.

Our eyes met. For a second neither spoke.

But a door opened. Here came *Our Town News* editor from his office.

XIII

—Come in, Newell. Take a seat, I won't be a moment.

—Thank you, Sir.

—Harriet, let's make it snappy on that obit . . .

I nodded and moved past. From the cluttered outer room with its column of afternoon sunlight among bound newspaper volumes, old and dusty, I went into the chief editor's domain which faced eastward and had no sun at this hour. The windows opened onto a garden, green shades of shrubs and ivy. Birds chirped: what did they care if our town was going to hell in a handbasket? A dog barked in a backyard, as I stood breathing in the scent of lilacs. Harriet and Hal spoke low, in a mumble, discussing some layout detail. I turned from the window and scanned his bookshelves, comparing them to my father's. The editor came in and shut the door quietly.

—Newell. What can I do for you?

—Sir, I just talked to Coach Wieboldt. I quit the baseball team.

He blinked when I mentioned the baseball coach. Why?

—Really? They'll miss you.

His eyes, beneath bushy salt-and-pepper eyebrows, bored into me.

—They won't. That's just it.

—Will you play Legion ball this summer?

—I don't think so, Sir. You know, my mom's not feeling well. I should stick around the house a little more. Maybe do some studying on my own.

—Well, that's a good idea.

—I can pick up sports again in college. Or leave the baseball playing to my brother.

—Joey's a great one.

A silence fell between us. Birds sang. I gave a little headshake and said:

—These days I'm not myself, Sir. My sister's death changed things.

Hal Duggan nodded:

—We were all affected. We share your sense of loss.

—I know it.

He thought a moment, and said:

—It's true what you say. This town isn't the same.

The silence weighed his words. I said:

—When I was talking to Coach Wieboldt, he suggested I come and see you. He said you know a lot about what goes on.

Duggan smiled. But it was an odd smile, a sad one, tight-lipped.

—I'm always the last to know.

—Really? But you're a reporter.

—Especially a reporter. Listen, a small town leads two lives. There is everyday life, friendly enough, a cheerful routine.

–Until something happens.

–That's right. Redemaine has its placid surface. But there's a life underneath, which bubbles up letting us know it is there. Murky depths. This one does this, that one does that; a third had a nervous breakdown but let's not gloat over it. Such talk is taboo, like the word cancer used to be, or homosexuality. Uh-oh, the minister at Redemaine Congregational is having an affair with his assistant pastor's wife. Did you know that?

–No, Sir. But I heard his own wife ran off with a parishioner.

Duggan laughed.

–See that? And I still wouldn't know a thing except Harriet got wind. But she can't use such tidbits in her column. Keep it light! ... Well, it's too bad you're underage, Newell; you could make the rounds of our bars and get an earful. But when they see me coming, the editor, mum's the word. Afraid we'll print something indiscreet.

–Like the truth.

–So I stick to our public life, such as it is. I report the official story: what the big little boys tell me, Mayor Tomao at Town Hall, Rune Roscommon at the Police Station; Principal Sangesland and School Board Chairman Sorifa when it comes to our educational system. Though more voices are being raised over the racial business at the high school. In a crisis, a local earthquake, let's say, when the depths rise up and destroy the deceptive calm: then the community wants more of a say. Then they come to me. But in normal times no one confides in *Our Town News* editor. No, sir. So Harriet produces the 'Our Neighborhoods' column you see each week, the ladies' book club meetings and family visitors from out of town. I am told less of the juicy stuff about our ... (His phone rang.) I know less about the ... murky depths. Hold on. Hello?

XIV

I watched Mr. Duggan nod at what he was being told in the receiver. He said nothing. He listened, as the lines of his face deepened. What was it about him? ... Well, the same thing as the town, since my sister's death: there was a cloak-and-dagger note. I sensed both he and his assistant editor, Harriet Pulley, knew some secret that must be hidden.

So I looked at him. The tallish lanky man with a ruddy complexion had changed since I saw him at Evelyne's funeral service. In his late forties, well dressed, he was always clean shaven, fresh, relaxed. Not so today. Also, he had a small knob in the center of his forehead, by one eyebrow, maybe a lipoma, or old injury. This slight bump was more noticable and gave the respected editor a diabolical look, in my opinion. It seemed to tell of a dark fact he had learned; the truth come out not as ass's ears but in a tumor, if benign.

During a long and honorable career he had crooned a favorite tune: respect for his profession, all honor to the confraternity of journalists. They upheld the noble tradition of free speech in America. They kept to a strict objectivity while reporting the day's top news events. This was Hal Duggan's slogan: intellectual integrity, and impartial news stories. He used to tell me about it: when I came in dusty and sweaty from a Babe Ruth or Connie Mack League game, and sat down with the box score to write a few column inches.

As a young man out of college he worked as beat reporter for a city daily in the Southwest. Then he came to Redemaine in the early 'Forties to run our smalltown weekly. He married a local girl, and they raised four children while living in the affluent Crest Road section of Spring Glen.

Now, I knew he had been across the street to Roscommon's for lunch and threw down a drink or two. I knew because I was attuned to my dad's drinking habit, up a notch since grief came to our family, and my mom began to pine away. Neither man was a guzzler, a lush for all seasons. But in Hal Duggan's case you caught a moral whiff, and wondered if the man hadn't been tainted somehow. Perhaps his professional pride, that holy of holies, was tarnished?

In his editorials since the high school riot he committed *Our Town News* to a tough law-and-order stance, which blamed two small groups of students: one 'happened' to be white, the other 'happened' to be black. Well, I discussed Mr. Duggan's ideas with my friend Thaddy, and we both found them muddleheaded. While the rioters just happened to be black and white troublemakers, the rioting was said to be 'racial in the worst way'. So which was it: spontaneous? A personal grudge? Or socially, historically based? Mr. Duggan was an intelligent man, yet he avoided asking: *why?* Instead he vented frustration just like the rioters. He did this by blaming a 'small, loud faction of black girls using the foulest language . . . hysterical girls asking for trouble . . . They must be dealt with directly, firmly . . .' He went on: 'The vast majority of students are good, and revolted by violence. But there are a few irresponsible whites, militant blacks, above all those loudmouthed black girls, who are spoiling for further collisions'. Tough School Board measures—the 37 suspensions, each individual case to be reviewed closely for possible expulsion—such measures were correct, in *Our Town News'* view, if the dangerous course of events was not to escalate further, and go out of control. Then: anarchy at the high school. Anarchy among our youth.

Duggan played the 'individual guilt' theme once again in a closing paragraph: not whites, and not blacks, must we blame, but rather 'the bad ones' as proven by their actions; and 'it doesn't matter what the color'.

—I seem to detect some 'anarchy' in this editor's thinking—said Thaddy.—Once you place all the blame on individuals, then what? Remove them, and everything will be hunky-dory again. But have we reached a better understanding? Or will the same situation continue, minus those individuals . . . toward a bigger outburst someplace else?

To Thad and myself this 'individual' tack sounded like a case of denial. Forget about local history: we wondered if there were Ku Klux Klan in the area. Forget about national history: slavery, racism. No; the recent events in Redemaine were 'simply' a personal thing involving a few rotten apples. That's all. So punish, swiftly and sternly. Move on. Let's not talk about it any more than we have to; since we, the authorities here, don't reason with delinquents like Ray-Guy Beatty and Cuckoo Kiernan and tough black elements from across town. No, we don't cater to 'loud, abusive black teenagers . . . though they try to justify their misbehavior with accusations of racism. Come now: was slavery Redemaine's fault? Is it still an issue? Give me a break: slavery was abolished a hundred years ago. Rather, we must single out the culprits, black, white, or any other color, red possibly, and remove them. They have no business in our schools.'

Hunky-dory.

Thaddy demolished Hal Duggan's editorial entitled: 'In the Aftermath'.

But I—sitting in the writer's office while he took a phone call—I couldn't help asking, in my mind: Why, Sir? Why deny the facts?

Are you trying to hide something? Why, even I, with my senior thesis on Little Rock's Central High for Mrs. Hebbel's POD class: even I seem to know more about it. I can't understand why a smart guy like you writes such shallow stuff! Ah, you're trying to please somebody—our townsfolk perhaps? But your mission is to teach, enlighten; not foster hate. Or maybe someone behind the scenes exerts editorial control over a smalltown newspaper like *Our Town News?* Why let them? If our press is free, if our journalists are upright and honest, as you never get tired of saying: then why kowtow, Sir? Why lie, Sir? Does someone up the ladder, Mayor Tomao with his mafia ties, have a lien on Duggan's conscience? Will he break Hal Duggan's legs? Or is it a more potent force that leans on you and makes you write commentaries worthy of a foolish virgin? Thad Floriani and I see through them, Sir. We are disappointed. How are we supposed to admire and believe in our elders, if they lie?

Mr. Duggan swivelled behind his desk and noted my young gaze fixed on him. For an instant his eye met mine; but I turned away from that vision: the five o'clock shadow; the mesh of dark hair slightly awry on his forehead; the sweat on his brow this cool day in May; the loosened necktie, open collar, on his hairy chest.

I looked out the window and thought of my friends engaged in hitting and catching a baseball. They were happy, running about in the bright afternoon. I was not, inside this office.

Finally he hung up, and said:

—Sorry. Where were we?

—Murky depths, Sir.

—Ah, yes.

Curiously, he had spoken few words during the phone conversation. He nodded. He assented. Then, putting down the receiver, he gave a little shiver.

XV

—Ah yes, murk . . . —Duggan laughed without mirth.—We go along, you know, cordial in this town. Hail-fellow-well-met: to a latent suicide, like Paul Raupach, your Peewee coach. Nobody knew it;

we didn't learn till later, when it was too late, for him. Talk might have helped.

–Are there many suicides in Redemaine?

Again the little laugh. His eyes went wide, spooked. But maybe he was playing with me after I stared at him that way.

–If so, they're not the worst thing. But shhh. Why discuss such matters? Lighthearted, friendly on the surface: it's deceptive. The volcano has depths, you know. In normal times: a few sparks, bit of thunder. People try to keep still about their pain, pretty brave all in all. They don't carry on a lot.

–Me 'n my dad do.

–Do you? Get in each other's hair? Well, yell then, it's healthy.

–Everyday I rub him the wrong way. I guess it's my style. Sets him on edge.

–How so?

–I guess because . . . like you said. On the outside he puts on a show for the fans. Deep down it's something else. All my life he's wanted me to play along, sort of. But I can't see it.

–He's a great man.

–He's my Pa; at times a royal pain in the ass.

–Emory Gilbert. Some think it might help if he met with black and white groups at the high school.

–Why?

–Lend his prestige. Arbitrate.

–And will he?

–No.

–Why?

–Schedule's full. Your father's an important man. Big one.

–That's not why. See what I mean? Says one thing, but it's another.

–How so, Newell?

–Afraid he'll burn his fingers. Afraid they'll call him a name again: a red. Then the Eastern Establishment boys will shut him out.

–Hm, said Hal Duggan with a laugh. Eastern Establishment yet! Well, they play hardball.

Birds fluttered outside the window. Harriet Pulley, at her desk beyond the door, typed an 'Our Neighborhoods' column, omitting the week's scandals, incest cases, suicides, School Board Chairman Donaldsen O. Sorifa dressed up in drag when pulled over by town police.

Sweet scent of lilac, or was it rhododendron, drifted in the window as the afternoon wore on. Birds lilted, insects buzzed, flowers smelled sweet. Hal Duggan, whose real first name was Howland, expounded on our town's birds and bees.

—Eastern Establishment, ha ha.—He laughed more airily, like a man learning his betters were really no better.—You don't say . . . ha ha! You're quite a character, Newell. Next you'll be telling me adults are by nature two-faced, and don't forget 'the human condition'.

—No, Sir. I don't believe the School Board Chairman, what's his name, Porfiria?

—Donny Sorifa.

—I don't think he's two-faced. He's doing his best.

This time Duggan sniggered: xe-xe-xe. In front of my naive self he swallowed his glee, made a sweeping gesture, and said:

—I'll tell you about Donny. The day of the race riot, our School Board was in session by 5:30 p.m. All nine members, plus the Town Attorney. Extraordinary meeting. Until ten that night they thrashed it out; and, at 10:30, announced school cancellation for a one-day cooling off period. They heard testimony. Apparently black-white feuding led to a rumble up at Cedar Rock Field a few months ago.

—I heard about it.

—Before your sister's death, Newell.

—Yes, Sir.

—Those nine Board members worked like demons on a plan to restore order. The result? 37 suspensions, 27 whites and ten blacks. After the seven arrests.

—You wrote that you favored stern measures.

—Still do. 'A strict, comprehensive plan of curtailment on behalf of the innocent majority . . .' Official statement drafted, press conference held in Principal Sangesland's office: long live law and order. Civilization wins the day. Then they went home. Do you know what happened next? At 2 a.m. that same night?

—What, Sir?

I didn't know. But Hal Duggan's grin boded no good for the man named Sorifa. And, as I sat before the editor's desk waiting to hear yet another, if less macabre, town horror, I seemed to glimpse something. Let's say a moral fact. I had an aperçu—this man, Duggan, is haunted too! Coach Wieboldt was haunted by a vision of his short-arm son pitching in the Major Leagues: because he knew, deep down, it would not happen. Innocent enough! Editor Duggan was haunted by a vision of journalists telling the unselfish truth: because he knew, deep down, they did not do it. And there was the feeling, so thick you could cut it with a knife, he was holding back the facts, beating around the bush, as we sat and chatted. Neither man had anything to do with my sister's death; yet, in my grief, I sensed they had, somehow, not by commission but by omission. I sensed everyone had: every haunted person in this haunted town was somehow responsible for the tragedy of Evelyne Gilbert.

—Our School Board Chairman, man of the hour, was pulled over again, a *second* time in two months, by town police. Do you know why?

—Sir?

Duggan paused. I waited for the sky to fall on Mr. Sorifa's reputation: 'Donny', the sensitive mediator in events tearing apart our town. I saw him once or twice in the high school auditorium: the kind of guy you might like on the spot, and think, Now here's a grown-up I can talk to.

—He ran a red light.

Was he driving a Cobra? I asked.

One of the editor's bushy eyebrows went up. But that was all. He passed over the Cobra. Yet it seemed to jolt him.

—Do you know what Sorifa was charged with?

—No, Sir.

—Drunk driving.

I laughed.

—Big deal. Our Police Chief should arrest himself for that every night.

—Could be.—Mr. D.'s dark eyes narrowed beneath his salt-and-pepper eyebrows.—But do you know what *else* he was guilty of, this hero of our time? Though no formal charges were brought.

—Tell me. Maybe I've heard.

—Donny Sorifa, the School Board Chairman in charge of our children's education, was dressed up in drag, boy, a transvestite. And, get this, he likes girls, women.

—Me too.

—But you don't dress up in a reinforced corset for bouts of S & M. You don't sport fishnet stockings, garters, black nylon slit-panties with lace fringes.

—Not yet.

—You don't wear a bra stuffed with foam rubber.

–Hm. Murky.

I smirked.

–Murky as hell, boy. Depths. Our town has 'em.–He eyed me askance, and tapped his temple with one finger.–See this?

–What, Sir?

–It's a file. Filled with *their* comings and goings. For a quarter century.

–Who is *they*?

–My mind is a file which could damn all the upstanding citizens: all these infernal innocents who put on such a fine show. Well, I've never printed a word of it. I never will. Yet now I'm supposed to go public with this Sorifa business and discredit a sincere person. On May such-and-such at 2:33 in the a.m., Mr. Donaldsen O. Sorifa was stopped by police for going through a red light where Wilke Parkway meets Havilland Avenue. Allegedly drunk, he laughed in the officers' faces and said he was on his way home, if you don't mind, from the House on the Hill where he just gave his heterosexual perversity free rein.

–House on the Hill?

–Zia Grippina's, for those who know: a pleasure palace, second home for mafia husbands, in Spring Glen.

–Really?

–Up in the woods by Dyre Club Lane. And our own Donny Sorifa, whose nickname as a female is 'The Anvil', when he goes in for such activities: Sorifa told the officers they could 'jag themselves off' if they didn't like it. Moreover, they might take over as School Board Chairman if they cared to, since he was 'fed up to here',– pinching a colossal foam rubber falsie like a squirt gun, laughing: fed up with our school system and our ignorant civic leaders! Ha ha ha.

–House on the Hill . . .? Mafia husbands?

–Not only.

–You say up there by Dyre Club Lane?

XVI

Mr. Duggan gave pause. Mouth open, he stared at me. He looked haggard. The mesh was down on his forehead.

Silence flowed in the room. It was a palpable silence: as though our polluted Dray River might be the river of time, and rise up, and overflow its banks.

Clearly the newspaper editor was feeling pressure. Under the gun? He had forgot himself, and said a few things my alerted ears—a private eye's—had no business hearing. Hal Duggan gave off a scent of anguish in those instants. The man who knew too much didn't have a friend.

Even birds outside the window grew quiet: so it seemed. You fool, they chirped. You blab state secrets to a teenager.

I said:

—Does someone want you to hurt Mr. Sorifa?

—Could be.

—He's been working so hard, trying to help. Everybody says so.

—Donny's okay.

—Then you won't do it. You wouldn't ruin him by printing that smut.

Duggan screwed up his eyes so tight I thought his nose might fall off. Well, he had made a mistake. He shot his mouth off.

The gesture Hal Duggan gave then, palm upward, was like despair: a man driven to the limit. Watching him made me sort of grimace, like sour milk.

—Life is complex, Newell. You'll understand better when you've settled down, after college, and have children of your own. Then you'll know the need for security: when you marry a good woman, and pursue a career.

—Sir, I was wondering about something. In my POD class we've been reading up on the Ku Klux Klan. Do we have them in our town?

—No.

—Well . . . And what about the so-called Maldoror Mon? Does something like that exist?

—A fable.

—What about a masked driver up on Maldoror Drive, in a racing car with no plates? Have you heard about that?

The look Hal Duggan gave me then—make no mistake, it was fear. He looked away. He began to arrange his desk.

—Sorry, I haven't heard.

—Sir, I haven't either, but I have seen. In a Cobra-bodied sports car, up there by the relay tower where my sister was killed. And my question to you is: how does someone do that and get away with it? No plates. Yet he doesn't get stopped by the cops? No face, only a mask, as he rides around terrorizing people. Is this possible? —Anything is possible. Now, Newell, as you see I'm busy. I gave you what time I could, but it's Tuesday. I have a newspaper to get to bed.

He buzzed Harriet.

I left the editor's office. In my mind were the words: Verily this night, before the cock crow, thou shalt deny . . . But why were my steps so light? Passing by Harriet Pulley's desk I gave her a high sign and a little laugh:

—Take care, Big Harr'.

—You too, Cutie.

Chapter Five

I

−Hey.

−Art-boy.

−New-boy.

−Hey.

To my left Kilroyne decorated pies, taking a break from 130° heat by the oven while I relieved him as ovenman. He said hey to the tomatoes and mozzarella cheeze, hey to olives and scallions, hey to oregano, basil. Through the day it was hey, hey, hey, as he mixed some fifteen ingredients, zucchini and chopped onions, Parmesan, Romano, provolone and shredded caciocavallo, anchovies, peppers, minced garlic, sausage and mushrooms, to create the different combinations and pie styles: pizza bianca or classica alla Napoletana, al pomodoro, alla Siracusana, alla Ligure, all'Amalfitano, della luna, antica alia Frattese, Marguerita or della Regina; pizze rustiche also called pasticci, or tortini; foccace . . .

−Elijah was the first to eat pizza, Art-boy.

Talk about pedantry. Thus my late night studies. A little knowledge is dangerous.

−Hey, he said.

I worked busily with the thirty or so pies cooking, crisping. In

433

went a 12-inch pie on the broad wooden peel. Out came another on a metal shovel-like peel.

–'And as Elijah lay and slept under a juniper tree, behold, then an angel touched him, and said unto him, Arise and *mangia*.'

–Hey.

–'And he looked, and, behold, there was a cake baken on the coals, and a cruse of water at his head. And he did eat and drink.'

–Hey.

It was hot by that oven. My face burned red fit to burst. I was a devil quoting Scripture.

–Art-boy, pizza made Elijah feel better on his way to the mountain. Later on, the Romans decorated it with seeds and herbs, and called it *maletum*.

–Hey.

–There you have the sum total of what I learned in prep school: a little Latin. At least in high school I learned typing.

–New-boy, hey.

Art-boy's heys had overtones these fateful days. They seemed to say: big things, events, in motion. Hey. When I told him I quit baseball, he gave me an amazed look and said, you guessed it–

II

Beside Kilroyne stood tonight's pieman, Sali Degennaro, a quiet Sicilian in his fifties. He dissolved yeast and let it stand while putting flour and salt in the mixing bowl. Yeast, oil into the flour: turn it out on a board; then knead and slap the dough to a consistency, smooth and elastic, not too sticky. Degennaro didn't spend time philosophizing, like me and Arturo of the hundred heys; the pieman didn't quote *l'Arte di Mangiar* while gathering and flattening dough; instead, he said mostly one thing over and over: retire, buy a house in Trapani, enjoy life among his people, eating Indian figs at the harvesttime *festa*. Such was his dream. I don't know why our waitress, Arlene Facciuto, liked to tease Sali without mercy.

–Ha ha! That's what they all say. But when the time comes, bene, bene, me no go Old Country, addio Trapani.

Meanwhile I was sweating like hell. The 800° oven, with its 2500°

fire never put out as long as anyone remembered, used a ton of coal per week. I stood before it raking pizzas, alternating the two 12-foot peels, the way a devil piles and trusses sinners. At suppertime on a Saturday night I had many pies cooking fast; and they'd bubble up, brown and curl along the crust before I knew it, if my thoughts wandered. Yet my mind left the task at hand for Hal Duggan's unguarded statements, or something else I'd heard. Duggan might deny, but the mystery was there. Who killed Evelyne Gilbert? Was it an isolated crime? Was another girl, a Bärbl Hebbel, next in line?

I gave a sigh because, for one thing, the heat was getting to me. For another, not only my brawn but my brain too felt overworked. I was in high school, and out to have a good time, not think! Heaven help us when we begin to think. I was badly cast as a ratiocinative Dupin: solving the world's crimes by logic. Detective stories bored me: rigged, shallow. Why couldn't I just enjoy my last few weeks as a high school student? Why not go my way with a smile, like the carefree Fran Fofanna? Now tragedy had struck my family. Now Bethany Engstrom had shot me down, as the saying went; she and I hadn't spoken in ten days beyond a high along the hallway between classes. Now baseball, my reason for being since childhood, was ended. I felt like Job amid the ashes.

In the big oven pizza pies began to char, as my thoughts drifted and dwelt on my twin sister's death. Who could do such a thing: tear open a young life so all its beauty, kindness—my sister was kind—spilled out on the ground? Amid hectic weekend activity in the pizzeria, I mulled over clues, and tried to make a few jagged pieces fit a gruesome puzzle.

Late at night a masked driver cruised Maldoror Drive in a racing car with no license plates. A few days ago I asked Nazzarro, the expert, about Cobra automotive bodies, and he said you sent away for them from a catalogue; not too expensive, a few hundred dollars. Then you fit them over an engine. I asked Naz if he had done this; he paused and said:

—Never a Cobra.

Hm. I felt maybe he had.

And the medicinal scent? A familiar smell was on a leaf not far from the murder scene. I asked Lemon, my little sister, and she didn't remember the name either. I kept meaning to ask Thaddy, or go into Floriani's Drugstore and find out from his dad.

A Maldoror Mon snuck up on the Willys Jeep where Thani and I nearly went all the way in midafternoon. Then Nazzarro showed his beaming mug in a great display of catching butterflies. Lord help the poor girl if he was really The Mon. I didn't think so.

III

There were new facts regarding the case.

Another murder of a high school girl had occurred in Beulah, forty miles across the state. So far police were discounting a 'pattern theory' in the investigation. Though there seemed to be no racial angle, for them, in my sister's death; as there wasn't in the other.

One morning, during homeroom announcements, I had a chat with Paepe when Mr. Gags came in late and we were left on our own. Rawl Paepe told me about the pickup football game—arranged in advance: tackle without pads—played last winter between a black team and the ZBKs. It ended in a fight with police arriving at Cedar Rock Field, and arrests. But Biff Modena, usually a mute, chimed in to say a few whites played on the black side that day. So why the scuffle? Not racism? A need to work off teenage orneriness? Biff shrugged and said the thing got played up later in a racist light. It preceded my sister's death by ten weeks.

Also back in December—said T. R. Fallon, laughing—some black girls asking donations to buy Christmas toys for inner city kids 'got all excited' when white boys threw pennies at them.

There were other anecdotes of this kind, as I carried my investigation through the school day. But no one was more helpful about it, sensitive to my grief, than Mr. Gags' ragtag homeroom.

A prisoner had disappeared while on furlough from the State Correctional Institution in Condor, 25 miles from Redemaine. He was doing time for a murder committed at age 17 during a holdup. The police were seeking Jared Simms for questioning; though he wasn't seen as a suspect in the Gilbert murder.

A few cars seen at the 'first circle' on Maldoror Drive, the night of my sister's death, had been listed in *Our Town News*. Gold Thunderbird stripped of chrome; tan Chevvy Impala. But no plate numbers given. Also, at Police Department prompting, this week's *News* asked the public if any hunters had been noted in West Hills Park that day. Hunting was forbidden. There were few leads turned up by twenty town policemen assigned fulltime to the Evelyne Gilbert case. Over 750 man-hours had been expended so far on interviews. Didn't I need to cultivate those officers and consult with them the way private dicks do in the movies? Shouldn't I pay a call on Police Chief Rune Roscommon? Under such pressure these days to produce a killer, he might blab a mouthful if in his cups enough. His son Orin, a golfer, was my classmate.

IV

Thus my adolescent mind, carefree, fun-loving as Fran Fofanna's, was now filled up with clues and questions like a pizza with everything. I mulled over the race riot. I read and reread the write-up in a national magazine: 'Riot at Redemaine High: Disturbing New Dimensions'. I inquired about the highly regarded educator named Donaldsen O. (Ottilia) Sorifa, who dressed up in drag and frequented a mysterious House on the Hill in our quiet Spring Glen neighborhood. What was it? A mafia brothel? I intended to find out: thanks to a plan hatched with Thad's help. Had the New England mafia anything to do with Evelyne's death?

Hal Duggan said: no Ku Klux Klan chapter in our town. And nearby? I knew from my dad's files on race relations the KKK wasn't only a southern phenomenon; and such elements were apt to stir up trouble and racial hatred—Emmet Till, Medgar Evers, Evelyne Genia Gilbert. KKK did not care who got hurt.

So that was the pizza pie I had my finger in. That was how fate, or our destiny as a town, as a nation, had decorated it so far. Well, I didn't feel much like a *pizzaiolo,* a pie-maker, even when it came to a plain mozzarell'; I mean I just wanted to be a regular high school kid and have my fun. And even if I did solve the mystery, and find out who did such a terrible thing—what then? How could I make it count? The Mayor was probably mafia. The Police Chief was out to lunch. Who, in this 'murky' town, were the good guys capable of bringing the culprits to justice?

Hey, I was looking for trouble. When you hear our mad plan in a moment, you'll see I was right on course for it. And yet I only wanted good times, hanging out with Franny Fofanna in front of Tony Eden's, grading girls and talking rot and trading heys. Above all I wanted my sweetheart back: Bethany Engstrom the lovely, the laughter-loving, high school Aphrodite. Now she rode triumphantly to school in Nazzarro Zummo's 'Vette. Now he got to use her favorite nickname, Thania, like her closest friends. But I didn't.

V

One more thing before we leave the pizzeria for Thaddy's . . .

In and out I slid the pies, as 8 o'clock drew near. I sprinkled the farina as it browned, and my roasted head and bare arms as well. There was a moment, shortly before the stint ended, when I got distracted: like a red devil in a reverie of sinners. And so Art-boy who had an eye on my activity, gave a:

–Hey!!

One pie was charred. Kilroyne stepped in and saved the others.

–Sorry–I said, wiping my stinging eyes with the back of my wrist.

–Hey, he said, New-boy. H-hey.

I backed away, shaking my head. For, you see, I just had a vision. With a glum fascination I stared into that 14'×14' firebrick oven which never went out; but I no longer saw the pizzas under my care. Gazing in at the firebox, I made out a strange fiery landscape receding back among caverns, red and black perspectives of glowing coals. You'll say I was getting like Mr. Duggan under the pressure of events, when I insist that I glimpsed tiny figures, maybe hundreds, at a great distance moving around, way inside the oven. I blinked. Did the place need an exterminator? I stood there open-mouthed. Heat from the open hearth must be affecting my thoughts, my perceptions? And then, if that wasn't enough, I seemed to hear a thousand voices, a huge chorus: moans, howling, like a long lament of torture victims, so far, far away, yet close! . . . Well, I shook my head, trying to clear away the fumes. That was when Kilroyne stepped in.

–Art-boy–I said, frowning–do, uh, you see something in there? I mean besides pizzas.

He stood beside me, working the metal peel with vigor. For an instant he paused, looked in my eyes with concern, as if I'd gone round the bend.

–Hey.

Still I stared past Kil-boy into the oven. Still I saw those distances with the swarming little figures, cinders. I heard howls, far in the distance, so far away, yet near. Well, my nerves were overwrought. My five senses were overheated. Things weren't clear due to grief for my sister, and also losing Beth. Was I seeing and hearing things? Hallucinating? Or was Redemaine Pizzeria affiliated with another great pizza place, maybe a national chain of pizzerias: where the generations got cooked to a bubbly, blistery crisp; where human souls grew savory as a *quattro stagioni* topped with artichokes, sauteed mushrooms, raw mussels, clams, olives, eggplants, zucchini, onions, gruyère cheeze, ham, tomato fillets, diced mozzarella, minced garlic, and strips of prosciutto. Don't forget the oregano: it's good for you.

VI

What a nutty and brilliant idea it was–Thaddy's brainchild to catch a killer. And just like him too, extravagant boy! I guess the School Board Chairman's sexual adventures had inspired the young artist; though in truth Sorifa had nothing on Thad Floriani when it came to wild ideas.

The plan was this. Peter–cf. *Peter and the Wolf*–would dress up like Little Red Riding Hood. Why? Instead of Peter in the 'big green meadow with a birch tree', using himself as bait to catch a wolf, it would be Little Red Riding Hood making the bar and nightclub scene in Redemaine. There she would use her young self–namely *my* self dressed up in drag–to flush out a psycho killer.

Hey.

But how would this happen? How get a rise out of the Maldoror Mon?

Instead of Peter's Grandpapa, a fuddy-duddy (bassoon, maestro) cramping the boy's style, there would be another chaperone for the nubile Hood. This would be Thad also in disguise: his pink, pimply, ferret's face blackened like Al Jolson's.

—But you're too small for the part, Thad, I mean physically. You don't make a very good youngblood escorting a strapping lass like me on her romps from bar to bar.

He laughed:

—Ye of little faith.

He said he wouldn't try to impersonate a jock like Jame Hayes, a track star. Instead, he would now show the world his genius as a makeup artist. First: dye his bushy red hair to salt-and-pepper. Next: don a tuxedo, from trunks of snazzy clothes left by his Victorian grandmother, Rita Joy, in their attic. Find a pince-nez. Buy a carnation, like Senior Prom night.

—Well, can you tell me why the black grandfather of lily white Riding Hood, a perfect virgin like myself . . . why he'd want to take her in bars and have her toss down shots and beers while seducing our Redemaine rednecks?

—Not her grandfather.

—Who then?

—Peter's trying to catch the wolf, right?

—Horns, maestro.

—We must lure the Maldoror Mon out of his hideout and grab him by the tail. Shall we wait for our trusty Redemaine Police Department to arrive on the scene?

—Kettle drums, bass drums.

—I think we shouldn't. That could prove lengthy. I think we must catch the sucker in the act, and lead his young ass on a leash, like Peter's wolf, along Gordiane Boulevard for all to see.

With gestures he described the scene. He began to rant and grow exalted, race riot style.

—Uh, T?

—Yessir.

—Be cool.

—I'm cool!

—Then tell me this, please. How do you explain the presence, in Redemaine's bars or anywhere else, of an older black gentleman by the side of a young white woman? I hope you're not going to say he's her pimp.

—Good gracious!

—Well, what then?

—Listen. Do you suspect a racist motive in your sister's death?

–Sickness, either way.

–Let's say a deep, jealous, pathological fear leading to rage at Jame Hayes' daring to date Professor Gilbert's pretty white daughter. And I am banking on the idea that it was a lynching, whether a Ku Klux Klan attack, or a lone racist.

–But why my sister? Why the white girl, and not the black man, Jame, put to the knife?

–It wouldn't be so easy to kill him. But there was also Evelyne's nature. She loved Jame Hayes. She wanted to spend her life with him. It was the talk of the town, and they created something of a sensation. Who can say what rage of betrayal this gave rise to in the racist psyche . . . ? Of course, it may have been timing: he wanted both young lovers, but found her alone in the car.

–So you think by going out there, and making fools of ourselves in public, we'll get the psycho to strike again?

–Newell, I say it was the age-old fear of miscegenation at work in this case. We must target that. Send a clear signal to a maniac: here's another mixed couple for you, flaunting it in public. How do you like them apples?

–Make him mad.

–See red. Provoke his tight ass, or theirs. Work him up so he'll make a mistake. And then, when he comes looking for us up on Maldoror Drive–since we'll advertise it in the bars: Where ya' headed, kids? Oh, a little petting session in West Hills Park–then we'll be ready for him, and meet the onslaught.

–'Kids', you say?

–You'll be dearie, sweetie, Millicent, you name it. Juicy young thing.

–Hm. And you, Granddad?

–Not Granddad, but Uncle.

–Rather improbable, genetically speaking.

–Not your uncle, silly. Uncle will be part of my name.

–Uncle Tom?

–Yawsuh.

I shook my head.

–Give me a break.

–What could be more plausible than Uncle Tom wanting to marry white?

–A girl one-third his age?

—Well, you said I made a poor matinee idol. So I'll be a character actor. You and I, Uncle Tom Totem, and Millie LamOOre, capital O's, from down South.

—Down South.

—Of course! Why do you think we came North anyway? So we can be free and left in peace.

—Good luck.

—We're young lovers on Maldoror Drive. Ready Teddy.

I shook my head some more:

—Lure him. Bait the racist, in the bars. Let it be known . . .

—You want to catch the Redemaine Ripper. Well, you've been playing private eye, but that's all so far: play.

—No, Thaddy, it's just that I can't help thinking there's a little too much of you in this stew. You're a show-off. I think you'll show your way off to greatness someday. But right now you're a little too hot to dress me up in women's clothes, and put on a theatrical performance. My guess is that catching a criminal comes a distant second in your mind. You want to prove you're a genius. Look, Ma!

Thaddy laughed happily at that. A devil danced in his eyes.

—Come by Saturday night after work. I'll get things ready.

—Lord, what next?

—Ha ha!—He jumped around.—Jumpin' Jehosaphat!

—Heavens to Murgetroy, I said.

VII

And so it was. On an evening in late May, after my shift at the pizzeria, I drove toward the Florianis' place up the hill from our house on Santa Fe. What a warm, fragrant spring evening we had chosen for our escapade. And there was a full moon. Anything might happen before this night ended. All bar-loving Redemainiacs would be at their posts: at *Farrelly's Spa* on Gordiane, a second home for the less genteel elements; at *Redemaine Bar & Grille* on Havilland Avenue, where the sex appeal is a bit less direct; at the Simiglione family's *Dream Bar* on the outskirts, where the décolletage and flounces conceal a heater; at Roscommon's Tavern where our petty bourgeoisie convenes; at the mythical *House on the Hill* in Spring Glen, elite bordello, whose secret we will learn, vicariously if possible, during the after-hours.

I greeted Thad:

—Ready to roll, Uncle Tom Totem? Mojo working?

He rubbed his hands:

—Wait till you see. Neato! We will now proceed to nab the Maldoror Mon. I, director of Redemaine Vice Squad, vigilante division, swear you in young man, or young lady I should say, as my deputy.

—Duly sworn.

—In this operation you're engaged to marry Uncle Tom. You're a hot number, a cock-teasess in the grand style. Got that? As for me, I'm a bit old but still randy. I'm wise Uncle Tom Totem. Gray hair, mustache, twinkle in eye.

—Swannee.

—Why yes, he said, I'll give white society a try, but I don't forget my roots. Uncle wears an Exchange Club pin.

Then I drew up; grew silent; I said to him:

—Thaddy, can we do this? I mean can you?

—Do what?

—Go around like that, impersonating a black man? It's stereotyping, it's degrading. You'll just be a big fool, or worse. A racist yourself!

He thought this over a moment. He said more soberly:

—First of all I'm no racist, and I've got none of that poison in me.

—My dad says we're all racists: all white people are. Blacks face discrimination from cradle to grave, and they're as good and human as us. But we just run around like privileged characters and go about our business, and don't bother to think about what our black sisters and brothers have been through.

Thad knit his brow, thinking some more. Shook his head.

—And your dad says that makes us racists?

—At least by omission, he says, whatever that means.

—Hm, by omission, hm. Well, maybe. So we'll have to live in a way which puts it right. Ever heard of John Brown?

—No.

—Well, he did. One white man did, at least, though I admit it's not enough. He was hung for it too. So let's live like him.

—Oh, cool!

—The second thing I want to say is we're trying to catch a killer, and that's no joke; it's a war; you use any means, any weapon. Wit's a good one. We're trying to help everyone now, the whole town, starting with a talented black friend named Jame Hayes who's in despair and thinks people blame him for Evvy's death . . . So: your budding social conscience will have to put up with this awhile as we do our thing and catch the Maldoror Mon. Capisc'? We have to get attention and make a spectacle of ourselves; so Al Jolson make way for your betters . . .

I stared at him. And then he started laughing again and cutting up some more in his Uncle Tom Totem routine. All week he must've practiced it with glee before a mirror.

Well! I couldn't help staring at my childhood friend. It was like his mad behavior during the race riot, up on a table, screaming, gesticulating, exorting everybody to mind their manners—Peace, brothers and sisters!—while he's a regular dervish. You name it: the crazy guy will imitate Robespierre or an old lecher. He craved the spectacular: seize the moment! Fame his shtick. And then his picture appeared in a major weekly: arms windmilling, hair wild, face pimply, laughing as he harangued the masses. He playacted and made it look like his show. Great photo; but somebody should write the editor: please don't encourage him!

VIII

—Here—he giggled—try these.

His tone gave me a shiver. He was excited, and what fun! First act like a pair of wild-siders, con artists, ornament to any dive. Then go for a spin on Maldoror Drive and see if we can get attacked. Don't forget to visit Fenbrook Cemetery later: in case The Mon went in for molesting graves, or headstone-lingus. Work out! I mused: a second teenager may die before this night is over. Who?

—Lord, where'd you find them?

—Rita Joy's trousseau in the attic.

—Rita Joy. Who did you say she was?

—My maternal grandmother. Hot knickers, hot as hell.

I gave a blush, and turned from my friend to undress. With thumb and index I held up Rita's black nylon panties. Faded musk odor: the decrepit have sex. I guess my family was prudish; I never got such an unobstructed look at women's underwear before. Nothing like this! The mons veneris was quaintly fenestrated–drop in for a visit if you're ever in the neighborhood. Gold thread filigreed the padded crotch with a spider web pattern–overdoing it a wee bit, I thought. The sides were cut off: hips bare, the waist a glorified drawstring, or garter. Those panties sat high on the midriff.

Thaddy, impatient with my mincing ways, reached and yanked the drawstring.

–Ow!

–Go get 'em, kid.

He leered.

But there was worse. A lace ruche made a battlement to guard the most sensitive spot. Com'moan!

–Thad, I'm not so sure about your plan.

He snickered, and handed me more *objets:*

–Stockings. Honey, try not to make a run in them. And get the seam straight . . . Garters. Here, I'll help you.

–Thanks, I can do it. What's that?

–Your first brassiere.

–Isn't it sort of risqué? Are you debauching your teenage fiancée?

Thaddy looked me over. He mimicked a parent:

–Tsk. Today's youth . . . I don't know what this world is coming to.

–Who am I trying to please?

–The Mon.

–Ooh.

I thrashed about, trying to get into that bra like a boa constrictor's coils.

–Petticoat.

–Say, how much more of this?

–Corset.

–I'm not wearing that.

–You have to, dearie.

–Why? Don't call me dearie.

–First, you can't go out there with your brawn showing, now can you? Muscle-bound jock! You cute thing! I could 'rrrumph you.

–Please don't, friend.

–Second–

–Second what?

–It's armor-plated.

—A bulletproof corset?

—Let's say knife-proof. I put in padding, a coat of mail (pun) to fill you out. Spent half a day working up this contraption, so don't complain. Work of genius, like Michelangelo's fortifications.

—But I'll be hot. I'll suffocate in these layers.

Thaddy broke into a peal of laughter. Eyebrows raised, he glimpsed down, with a little kiss.

—M-muh! You are hot, dearie. Hot to trot with a Hottentot.

How embarrassing! Unbeknownst to myself I had sprung a frank, fullblooded, robustious erection, in those baroque panties. Rabelais never did better, let alone my humble self: limp as a wimp in a guimpe, ever since my hot date with Beth Engstrom up on Maldoror Drive, and Mon-related coitus interruptus.

—Alright, alright.

—You'll need the corset to protect others.

Thus Thad. But I was not giggling, and said:

—I'm supposed to be a private eye in disguise, not a female cathedral.

—Benedicite! Here, try these.

Heavens to Betsy! What a pair of falsies he thrust in my face, with another mad laugh. They were big, subtly flesh-colored. They coulda' fooled a few of our discerning men.

—You made these?

He glanced heavenward, crossed himself, and said:

—Thaddeus *fecit*. I played God.

—God makes falsies?

I got my Latin from prep school, Thaddy from a Catholic upbringing which he rebelled against. Now I wondered if I was hunting my sister's killer, or catering to the crazy guy's obsessions. Gravely, he said:

—And God saw everything that he had made, and behold it was very good. And on the seventh day, when he was resting, he clicked his fingers and said: Ah, I forgot false tits. Xe-xe-xe!

The little runt began stuffing my brassiere.

—Say, you better back off.

He gave a whistle under his breath:

—You're getting to be quite a piece of ass.

—Thanks, I'm sure. Ooh! Stop it, that tickles.

He insisted:

—As a guy, you're not easy to fetishize: third-string pitcher.

—*Ex*-third-string pitcher.

—Kicked out of schools.

—On principle!

—Wiseass kid. Don't amount to much as a hardass. But as a gal, whew! You look good enough—to goose!

—Stop that! Get back, Satan!

—Please look to your breasts, dearie. Those things need to be on straight.

—Okay, okay.

Rigged and harnessed like a mare, I pulled at them. I growled:

—Stay put, you.

—Like sacks of wheat, he said.

—I don't see how women do it.

—Not for pleasure, dearie. Profit. It seems society sets the rules. Stick to 'em, or else. Still our ladies wait for some nice guy, or semi-nice, lawful spouse or otherwise, to come along and bust them out.

—Shining armor type thing. Thaddy, are you and I going out on the town like this?

—Yes, dearie.

—Please stop calling me dearie.

—What should I call you, Miss Hood?

Humming a tune—'*All of me, why not oh-ho! all of me . . . ?*'—he went to the closet and brought out an evening dress: good for a whore specializing in nostalgia. I saw he was excited by the thought of pouring me into that sheath. For a week he'd been working on this project, rummaging among Rita Joy's chests, taking in, letting out hems, cleaning, pressing, revamping these feminalia. I had told him of my chat with Hal Duggan, and the House on the Hill—which seemed unlikely to us both. What? A tenderloin in the heart of our own Spring Glen? where we had played so happily, so innocently all through childhood? explored every street and lane on our bicycles? . . .

Last week, along the corridor between classes, Thad whispered his ideas in my ear. He was a born leader, in his way, and I went along. He got things ready for our sortie on the trail of a killer, using my young ass as bait—in the same spirit he'd make breathtaking décors for our Senior Prom and Class Night activities before graduation. He was just being his ingenious self, using what he had, as an artist. But he could only bring off such stunts on one condition: he feared nothing, capable of anything. Now he hummed:—'*You took the best . . . now why not umph! the rest . . .?*'

What a struggle as I thrust and wriggled my way into that tight dress. Straight black affair with some paisley trimming at the corsage, quite fetching; a slit up one leg. My left breast was still off kilter; my right arm, the former Redemaine Red Renegade relief ace's, was larger than the other. Two little details, or big ones, which could give the game away. Thad wrinkled his nose at my loppy teat, and Bob Feller right arm.

—Still hanging your curves, eh?

—What! I said, offended. Coach said I couldn't throw any curves; otherwise—

—Forget it, kid. Let it go. Over-the-hill gang!

Forty years later that homerun spoiling my one-hitter would still tweak. But right now it was my bra, aïe!

Thad went in his mom's bedroom and came back.

—What's that?

—A mantilla. Here, cover up, Miss Low-Slung.

Then came the wig: blond, parted down the middle, with two braids. Then makeup: rouge, mascara, lipstick, pizza with the works, but touched on finely by an artist.

Thad lectured:

—Cleopatra used kohl as eye makeup, and henna in other places.

—Spare me that.

—Greek women went in for charcoal, rouge, a poisonous leaden face powder. Maybe Roman ladies took the cake: they had slaves working all day on their faces, so they'd be devastating by night.

He applied a greenish eye shadow from his mother's arsenal.

Then came a pearl necklace.

—Real ones?

—Fake, dearie. You don't wear the real thing to Farrelly's Spa.

Then earrings.

—Are you mad? I asked. Skull-and-crossbones earrings?

—I made them.

—Good, but what's the point?

—Well, what do you think, Newell? This isn't the cotillion. We're going out there after a killer, a real one.

—Why advertise it?

He touched his temple.

—Psychology, Watson. It takes one to know one. I want our Maldoror Mon to feel at home.

Finally, my Victorian Granpapa fiancé, Uncle Tom Totem, sprayed me up and down with a musk perfume. Now I understood why the world keeps turning. Anything can happen when you go all out, and our women do it everyday! No wonder we yearn to submit to them, and be at their feet—and then rebel when they take us seriously.

Whap! He slapped my derrière.

—Ha! ha! ha! Sorry. You're so cute.

—Look, Uncle Tommy. Let's get one thing straight between us.

—Please do.

—I'll put you under a cold douche if you don't behave.

—Won't happen again, I hope.

—Please remember yourself out there. I'm a lady.

—You are, dear'—I mean sweetie.

He laughed some more. I was no lady, but a tart for all the world. In a few minutes I'd be the most luscious piece of tail ever to strut into Farrelly's of a Saturday night looking for a beau. In fact my main rival, Donaldson 'The Anvil' Sorifa, couldn't hope, though he did hope, to match my superabundant if somewhat lopsided bosom, and stunning rump. If only the erection would go away. No normal girl wears a codpiece.

—Step into these.

—Now, really!

Rita Joy's high heels. I felt I was at the rink, and tried not to sprain my ankle. While Thaddy suited up in his outfit, a process that would need *longueurs* to describe, I practiced walking. Girlish curtsey for the bartender, as I entered. With my luck Fran Fofanna would be on hand, and see through the makeup and layers. First I quit the team, and now—

An astounded Gertruda Floriani watched her blackfaced son, and that bad boy Newell Gilbert, scourge of the neighborhood since age four, swing through her kitchen like a prostitute and her escort on the way to work.

—Say hey, Moms.

Thad gave his mother a high sign.

—What's this about?

—Masquerade party. We'll be back.

—When?

Wobbly in the high heels, working my arms and grunting with the effort to walk, I tracked up her newly waxed floor. Hands on hips she eyed me and Thaddy, and looked confirmed in her worst thoughts. For years she and her husband, Big Jim, the pharmacist and leader of town Democrats, had worried about their nonathletic son. They didn't understand him, a little imp with a brilliant mind, who looked a situation in the face.

Watch out, Maldoror Mon, here we come.

IX

By the garage stood my friend's motorcycle: smallish, 250 cc. Beezer. In a high, scratchy, rustic voice, supposedly Uncle Tom's, he said:

—Now saddle up, young'un. We're gun' fer a ride in the cy-unt-ry.

I laughed, but it hurt to laugh. Tight brassiere, corset hooks, garters, those lace panties dug into my skin. How did Donny Sorifa do it?

—Uncle, we can't both fit on that. You stuffed my butt so full, I feel like a truckload of potatoes. C'mon, we'll take the Willys.

—Now, young'un, would 'dat be wise? De' whole town knows yo' mad ve-hickle: tilted up like a box kite, an' fartin' thundeh'. Dead giveaway.

—We'll park a few blocks away. Let's go, and get this ordeal over. Hell, how will I ever make it through this night?

With a bow, Thad held the door for me. He tried to find the right accent:

—Come hyair, dearie . . . our dear, sweet little Millie.

—That's me, Millie.

—Millicent LamOOre. Way'ell, yer' poor m'uether . . . God rest her sweet soul, she died, you know, an ice-skating accident in de' deep South. Fell through a fishin' hyole in de' ice, she did. We found 'er 'mains de foll'n spring: had de same dress 'n all. Town fisherman thought he done hooked into a mighter' big'un.

—How nice. She named me Millie?

—Way'ell! Had some he'p from yer' no-account white trash Paw: mah would-be fodder-'n-lore, if'n we knew whar' de dern critter done got to, prob'bly de state pen. Anywar' 'dey called yer sweet l'il ass Millicent, an' you's de luv uh mah laf'. Yer' m'uether entrusted yuh to mah care.

—Did she now. I see. And you think in the deep South they'd let an Uncle Tom—

—Doctuh' Uncle Thomas to you, honey. I gots mah' docter-ate.

—Sir Doctor Uncle Thomas then: you think they'd let you court my lily pure butt as big as a barn?

Thaddy worked his facial muscles beneath the makeup. He cleared his throat, and went on, in the high grating voice:

—Court yer' two bezoomies too, dearie, big 'z a Hinder'burg blimp. Cain't never tyell whar' laf'll lead us to, sweetie, mebbe' de lynchin' tree. 'seh beech', laf'.

—Pretty philosophical, aren't you, Uncle?

—Way'ell! Fer' mah' docter-ate I done studied Gene-Jake Trousseau. Got mu' larnin' fum' m'udder nechur down on de fyarm, ah'z dood. Fuh'! I ain't lak' none dese' shaller techno'rats, dese' ac-nedemtricks 'n sich trash, we got roun' hyair' tuddeh', Oxturd 'n Came-in-Britches. Xe-xe- xe. Naw, sweetie, I done studied de good ol' boys down on de' farm, de Sebben Sedges o' Grass' doncha' know, 'doze ol' pre-Sickratic boys, Thales o' Miletus 'n Anaximander 'n Anaximenes 'n 'der laks, ol' Heraclitempedoparmellisus' type o' thang!

—Pretty pedantic, aren't you, Totem? I mean for a tuxedoed hustler, my fiancé, bar-hopping as an Al Jolson Uncle Tom type thing? I wouldn't have thought that'd get you very far.

—Xe-xe-xe. Ah' been stoodyin' up: gitten' ready fur de day, doncha' know, when ah' bikkems uh true Uhmurrikn gen'us. But say, yuh'z uh geuyill, aincha'? S'pose t' talk sorta' high up lak', girlie talk, 'n sich, aincha'?

X

We drove toward Farrelly's Spa. With luck no town cop would spot us, and take us into custody, like our School Board Chairman. I tried out a falsetto voice, then an alto. I mimicked my mom's southern accent. No go. It sounded male. So I'd be a deaf-mute and use sign language: just sit on my bar stool and look sexy with my made-up face, bushel breasts, and rigging. Smile.

Thaddy said:

—Ah've got somethin' fer yuh, Millie.

—No thanks, Uncle.

—You c'ud be in a way ter' needin' it, Sweetie, 'fore 'diss naht's out.

—Oh yeah? Hold on to your rubbers. No hardass is going to have my virginity, and that includes you. Even if we are engaged.

At a red light he nodded toward his lap. I expected to see a full-blown Uncle Thomist boner in those moments before we went into action. Instead, from under his silk cummerbund, he produced two weapons. One was a stiletto, whetted razor fine, reflecting the stop-light as he slid back its sheath. The other was a .32 caliber pistol.

Thaddy sang out, screechy, in his yokel's voice:

—'Ah didn' knyow . . . de gyun were lyoaded . . .!'

—I'll take the knife.

—Too long fer yer' bra, dearie.

—I'll put it in my garter.

—Wayell! Hyere 'den: 'case any o' thiss' ol' crackerbarrel philoso-phyers fum Grik' 'iniquiteh gits t' probin' a l'il too close intuh' laf's sucrettes. But trah' nat t' deflower yerself widder', missie.

XI

—*Benone!* Alright then, very well!—cried Bill Civitello, his wavy hair flame-like as he shadowboxed.—Come on! I'll split your head open for you.

—Ha! ha! ha!—Jay Bryant, tall, gangly, gestured contempt.—Try it, you little fart. See how far you get.

Inside Farrelly's Spa the two had squared off for a fistfight, but halfway across the floor. They made a formidable pair, titans. So much so that an older guy, Rube DeLuca, strolled through the no-man's-land between them with a shrug. Casually, raising his beer mug, DeLuca ordered the bartender to fillerup.

I saw them as, wobbly on my heels, like walking on a mattress, I entered Farrelly's behind my escort who almost came up to my chest.

Civitello and Bryant, Redemaine High Class of 1960, pulled this same stunt during their Senior Prom a year ago, at Frankie's Villa Pompei out on the Post Road; and the cops came and led their drunken asses away, stranding their dates. Now they both stood in place, dancing a little like boxers and working their arms. They called insults across the floor while a few others, more or less wasted by ten p.m., egged them on.

–Skinny Minnie!–Civ bawled, punching air.

–Go get 'im, Skivvy!

–Yeah! Show him who's boss.

–I dare you to try it–said Bryant.

– *'In this corner, wearing a plaid shirt and faded bluejeans with a hole at the knees, Billy . . . Civitello!'*

–Ra-a-a-ahhh!

A guy I knew because he used to umpire Peewees, Paulie Mc-Manus, imitated the Friday Night Fights, Don Dunphy at ringside:

– *'And in this corner, his opponent for tonight's 15-round title fight in the three-sixpack division, John 'The Human Stringbean' Bryant!'*

–Raa-a-ahh, ha ha ha!

The two heavy punchers were ready for the opening bell.

But then I walked in. All eyes turned.

XII

With our outmoded costumes we might have felt at home, almost, in Farrelly's Spa. Since the 'Forties a resort for Greenwood section workers, after the day's toil to fatten factory owners' billfolds: this bar in Gordiane's tougher blocks had not come up in the world. Once it had a propriety: Sligo pub with an ironic dignity. Now it was shabby: the long counter, beer taps, bare wall with liquor license, jiggered bottles standing at attention, a wood cash register and spewing High Life ad. The worn floorboards were unvarnished for a long time. Now and again the jukebox took a notion and played hit tunes from the 'Fifties. Strangely, no stools lined the bar: you got soused standing up, like at a party. And no pool table in back; just a few streaked tables. Farrelly's was a wide room where mostly men, lumpen elements, high school dropouts, a rough crowd came to let it hang out. There might be a few underage students, Ray-Guy and Cuckoo types, eternal truants, since the bartender hardly bothered to check a draft card. Mainly the place catered to guys a few years out of high school, still single or else not doing too well at marriage, 'real life', and needing to blow off steam.

All in all this was the Tony Eden's of dropouts—young men, also a stray woman, in and out of a workforce they hated since for them it led nowhere. But whereas Tony Eden's at The Mall was an upbeat hangout, high school kids showing off cars and dates, having their ice creams while talking over a hundred things to do with the future—Farrelly's gave off a whiff of life forces beginning to turn. Boy, you may as well join the Service; otherwise, you'll never settle down. Oh, man! Submit to this shit, bit by bit? For the moment Farrelly's steady customers couldn't do it: not able or willing to conform. And, not far under the surface, the carrying-on fuelled by triple shots, there was anger about the way things seemed to be turning out. So they guzzled. They mulled over the fell ways and means of the other sex; also the speed-up greed of bosses, fury of foremen, the 'efficiency experts' and Taylorism as they knew it firsthand in the factories.

For some this was new and not what they bargained for: not like the old high school life which they couldn't wait to leave. So they sipped liquor and threw down beers; they jug-jugged, but not like nightingales. One or another grew boisterous toward midnight after whining a same complaint for hours, brooding a gripe. The real world: what a place! Women . . . pfah! But that was when someone chimed in with the greatness of the nation, America the beautiful, my country 'tis of thee, mom and apple pie, and for all its faults ours is the world's best way of life, the biggest, richest, with a divine mission of bringing freedom and democracy to the barbarians who don't appreciate our efforts, and hate our freedom: especially that godforsaken little place way over there in Asia, what's-its-face? Vietcom or something like that where President Kennedy said we had to send our boys . . . Oh yay, we are tops! But why must the ungrateful wretches keep flooding our nation with workers, more unwanted labor taking away our jobs? And why do they insist on making so many babies? Oh! the 'wetbacks' and 'Chinks' and 'Ayrabs' and . . . what next? They'll infest the place with a mess of commie rats before they're done . . . In the meantime, see how all fired-up they are to work long hours for pennies and take good American jobs away?

Why does the Government permit this? Hey! We're a free country! Even the furriners is free to work for a song in Uhmurrikuh; and that song is: 'My country 'tis of thee, sweet land of liberty, of thee I sing . . .' But say, you know what? (Shh . . .) The races ain't supposed to mix no way. Bible said so! You know that, don't you? I hope you know it by this late date . . . You saw what happened to that high school girl, didn't you? Well, didn't you?! . . . Look, I've thought the matter over quite a lot the past few weeks and I'm real sorry for her parents but that was God's punishment for too much freedom. Understand? I say stay away! You over there, me over here . . . 'cause, you see . . . the races ain't supposed . . .

On and on. Nightly it was the same bolero, or almost, depending on the day's events. The beer was laced with patriotism and hatred for the outsider. The world went from bad to worse as midnight drew nigh but especially it grew sloppier. A good guy got drunker, and skunker. And, as this went on, the bare walls at Farrelly's Spa made a vista which seemed immense of young vital life going to waste. More on weekends. On Saturday night—forget it! The week's full cup of frustration, silent humiliation, needed hardly a jolt to spill over in loud curses, insults, threats, worse.

XIII

Our arrival at the bar, Uncle Tom Totem in the lead, caused a stir. Here silence was sensational. You might say the bottom dropped out of the collective jaw. Too much! A few seconds' silence, the first since D-Day I think, became an ooh! and an aah! and a ha-ha-ha! The fists of Civ and Slim, dread pugilists, revolved slower and then hung suspended in midair. You knew we made a hit because of the strange effect on this place which was all show and worldly facade.

—Psst! Ginoli, you see what I see?

—I see it, Vin, but I don't believe it.

There was a low whistle as they looked over my nibs. But I think the astonishment at Uncle Tom went even deeper, since Blacks did not come to this night spot for reasons of health. I guess we hadn't considered that aspect—Thad Floriani, future great painter, might have his eyeballs punched out before he could copy old masters in

the Great Hall of the Louvre. Thaddy was such a fanatic in everything he did. He was so engrossed for the moment in his Al Jolson
role, he read books for it: *Black Like Me;* a biography of Edward Wes-
ton 'Daddy' Browning, and his Peaches; a few of the better detective
writers whom he termed insipid. He leafed through a criminology
textbook. But, in preparation for our night on the town, a beating at
the hands of redneck racist elements never entered his perky head.

    —B'B'Braggi! You see th' that?

    —Them thar' . . . No, Ray-Guy, I don't see it. It's a dream.

    —A wet d'd'dream. Whew! Look at them t't'tits!

    —Drink your beer like a good boy.

    —I d'don't need b'beer. I need a c'c'cold shower.

    Thar' we blew. The two of us sidled up to the bar, in limelight of
the High Life sign. I was at wit's end in my high heels, tight garters
cutting off my circulation so my feet went to sleep, stays which
didn't stay, and that corset! Despite my sex change I felt ready to start
a fight. Girls' night out! In one week I had gone from respected Red
Renegade hurler to Victorian tart with extra whipped cream. Not
bad! This eunuchdom jarred on my male ego. I stood there smiling
from ear to ear, like a dumb broad with a difference. I rested my forearm on Thad's shoulder while he went into his Uncle Tom from the
Platonic Plantation routine.

    —Young man, make that two beers on tap. Nice and frothy, if you
please. Millicent here—he raised his voice over the jukebox—*my fiancée,* Millie LamOOre, likes 'em frothy. By the way, young man,
could you indicate *the way to Maldoror Drive?*

    —Who wants to know, Pops?

    —Millicent here, *my betrothed,* you know, and myself. We just got
off the Parkway, and we'd like to be alone for a nap before she takes
me to her parents.

    Ridiculous? You wouldn't have thought so: to see the way they
gaped at us, Rube DeLuca and Debevoise, Worley Morse, Sim Curtis, Paulie, among those I recognized. Ginoli Delfini, Vinny Resca,
ZBKs still at the high school. But most were older, in their twenties,
and I didn't know all of them. They were bad boys maybe despite
themselves, by force of circumstances, and hanging on the fringes.
They pumped gas and checked oil; they washed dishes and served
fast food; they worked at the sorry jobs, parking lot attendant, security guard, handyman. They were cogs in the private sector: moving
men, tilers and carpet layers, stock boys—non-unionized, paid by the

hour and going nowhere. I recognized the latest in a long line of ushers at the movie house by the bank on Gordiane; also Mr. North's current soda jerk from North's new candy store, in a lower rent district, since the Health Department had closed down the Glendower some years back. One sensed that from this crew would come tomorrow's drifters, vagrants, men filling the chinks and crevices of society, with perhaps a criminal recidivist or three. They were our town's lower depths.

Some talked big. All had plans. Hopes soared, a rough-grained poetry. Fame, fortune, here I come. Hey! It's the land of opportunity, ain't it?

I glanced around for Franny Fofanna. I wanted to hang out bad, in those instants.

Mostly I stood fluttering my eyelashes caked with mascara at the lovelorn hardasses, who wore libido on sleeve, since they lost high school sweetheart's trust some time ago.

And they stared back beady-eyed, thinking I looked pretty fresh for a prostitute. Fair game. They also heard what Uncle said; they got the message: the way to Maldoror Drive. Dig it! But I thought the response might look like a funeral procession; and it could prove hard to tell The Mon from all comers.

Their eyes fell less and less abashedly on their humble servant, Millicent LamOOre, and her accoutrements. But I'll tell you one thing: it is strange to be a woman. Our ladies, whom we love and admire, must go through life finding the world an unsubtle place. Well, it has an ulterior motive, which is: to perpetuate itself. At least that's the end; though the means may seem a bit more queynte.

Now I was on the other side of things. This gave me some insight into my behavior with Beth Engstrom. A cad! Taking advantage of her moment of weakness, her vulnerability, the day of the riot. No wonder she traded me for Nazzarro Zummo, a wildman who became a puppydog in her presence. I gored her. He adored her.

I guess most of us men don't know it. We just do it.

XIV

With a lipsticky grin I invited that bar crowd for a ride on Maldoror Drive. Alongside me the Negro gentleman in a tuxedo, gray-whiskered and -bearded, in ruffled blouse and cummerbund, held forth with a perky wit. When he told our plans for all to hear, I guess they took him for a distinguished pimp. But he just went on talking a lot of bookish stuff and calling this and that one 'young man' and using words they didn't know. Without blinking he said we were en route for Harvard where he would receive an honorary doctorate and deliver the commencement address; though it was hard being in such close proximity with one's *fiancée*, hour after hour on the Parkway, and not take a moment for rest and relaxation. And so we needed to know the way *to Maldoror Drive*.

Sweetly I smiled into that popeyed masculine mass, which ogled my bosom. Get a load of her! I breathed deep and drew in my stomach. Talk about overkill! I grinned broad as a bawd when she's pawed. And then, leering down at Uncle with lusty eyes, I went into the sign language routine we had agreed upon.

—Say! Is she givin' us the finger?

—Can't say for sure, Arch. Maybe deaf-mute talk.

—First mute woman I seen. Where you think she comes from?

—Paradise, said Worley Morse.

—Could be a snake in it.

Morse shook his head:

—There's fruit.

—Righto, said Arch. But is it forbidden?

—Baw' . . . , said Paulie. Those are some fine tits.

—Hey, Worl', do they beat the homemaking teacher's, Miss Jolly-meier's, your old flame?

—By about a pint.

Arch scratched his head:

—They're big.

—Big.

—Look a little uneven to me.

—Well, Arch, if you had that much: could you keep track of it all?

—Guess not. But look how she's dressed: like she just stepped out of a trunk.

—There's something strange about her, that's for sure. Say, maybe she came out of a coffin!

—Naw, Worl'. Dead women don't have such big ones. And look how rosy cheeked she is, despite the powder.

—Must be a mystery.

—I'll tell you one thing: I wouldn't mind getting to the bottom of that mystery.

Meanwhile, Uncle Tom was displaying his erudition. By the bar he bowed, scraped, scratched his head a little, and quoted Latin: 'dulce est desipere in loco'. I kept reeling off sign language, and looked around. Probably no one, in town, would have called Farrelly's clientele a mess of poor suckers headed nowhere. They weren't pampered by society; but hey, they partook of the 'biggest, richest, bestest way of life ever', our American middle class after all, without troubling their heads much. The only problem was that among the innocent assortment—older guys I grew up around, now working construction or public works, driving trucks, putting in time by day then carousing by night—among them might be a murderer. And so Thad and I put on a show, with a racial twist in case this was part of it. We played our roles to lure my sister's killer up to West Hills Park where we would catch him in the act, flagrante delicto, carried away by my charms. Then I would rip the mask off his face if it was the last thing I did.

But whoever it was, lurking in an unmarked Cobra at the scene of Evelyne's death: the boy probably didn't stem from the Crest Road section, polite society, though you never know. I only surmised he might spend his happy hours, undisguised, at a dive like this.

And so it was that Uncle with his book larnin' and big words, and me with my fast fingers, sighs and grunts, my buttressed butt and shocker knockers, went out there that night to entice a psychpath. We intended to mystify him. Step right up, young man: meet Millie LamOOre, my sweet, innocent fiancée.

We stood by the long bar in that beer joint which reeked of it—reeked, I mean, of something wrong—and spoke a lot of hocus-pocus. Uncle and I talked bull with them while seeming to breathe in mystic essences, love on a night in springtime, here in the grove of Academus.

XV

Tell me now, you Muses that dwell on high West Hills! Who captained the contingents of drinkers from Galen Street, Harmonium and Lovett Hill, that night when destiny, like Zeus the Thunderer, came to Farrelly's Spa? For as the many tribes of wingèd birds, wild geese, cranes and long-necked swans on the wide Western meadow by Dray River in Redemaine—and they fly this way and that, glorying in their pinioned strength, as some dart forward, drawing the hosts over the plain, Lavater and Cedar Rock Peewee Fields, with a clamorous din:—so the heroes flocked here for a beer after their softball game. From Muldaur Street, from Greenwood sector and Centerville they came, and the night honked dreadfully to their epic chant, as young men revved up their Chevvies. Toward the windy Ilian towers of adult life they made their way. And huge would be the onslaught, huge the carnage, in the flowery grasslands at Farrelly's. Here, there, a great-souled leader rolled down the driver's side window, and sang out hit tunes with his car radio for the fragrant May evening to savor, and wonder at. Lo! Like leaves and flowers in season were the numberless young studs armed in dazzling youth: and the chrome lines and grilles on their modified coupes gleamed terribly, like Apollo.

Muses! Fling wide the gates of Helicon, and wake your song! For you know all things, while I am a poor high school transvestite, a mere mortal trying to finish his bloody term paper for the P.O.D. teacher, Mrs. Hebbel, famed for her footnote format.

Daughters of Zeus! What Stentorian mufflers farted? What Thunderbirds, 'Vettes (and one Willys Jeep) ground gears, dropped transmissions, threw rods, en route to Farrelly's Spa? Intent on bane, they burned rubber and roared down Gordiane Boulevard toward the high-greaved garrulous brawl. O Goddesses: though I had ten tongues, and lips unwearying, and the heart within me were of bronze, I could not recall all the warriors, fostered of Zeus, that assembled beneath the High Life ad.

Yet I sing their decade-long patience, great-hearted, in wasting their lives. I sing the grandeur they showed for that noble cause. Truly they suffered pains grievous as Philoctetes, skilled in archery, who stank the morning after.

Of all those that dwelt about grassy Cedar Rock, rich in vines, the co-captains were Ginoli Delfini and Vinny Resca, ZBK members, famed for their spears. But Ginoli had no business being here at Farrelly's. For he was on juvenile probation after pleading guilty to vandalism counts: what time he and Nick Tanzone sacker of cities, stole most of the town's traffic and real estate signs to decorate Ginoli's basement where they lifted weights. But you, daughters of Zeus that beareth the aegis, heard only rumors of those direful events, since the youthful heroes were given a sealed indictment.

From the well-built citadel of Galen Street School, sacred as Euboea rich in sanctuaries, came the Leopardi brothers, Jamie and Danny. Peers of Zeus in counsel, they both dropped out of high school. They did not attend graduation. But on Saturday nights you could find them here at Farrelly's, swilling nectar and ambrosia, on draft. They were like Castor and Pollux drunk on Milky Way. Lordy, those two could drink, and piss too: to equal the fair-flowing stream of lovely Peneius, tributary to Styx, dread river of oath.

From Mt. Sorrel with its many ridges came wind-footed Worley Morse, former Redemaine High baseball captain, now home from the Minors. For Worley, warrior that bore the mask, chest protector and shin guards, more dread than mighty Achilles' shield, never made it out of Class D ball. He couldn't hit the curve; though he liked to stare at curves—mine, that is, LamOOre's, rival of Miss Jollymeier's, famed for her homemaking, but she never married. Give The Worl a high hard one and he knocked her out of the park, ding! like tonight's Twilight League game where he starred for the Townies.

By Worley's side stood Archie O'Shea, who marshalled the Harmonium hosts. Also a catcher, preeminent in eighth grade, Archie O. was a grammar school god when he caught pitches one-handed, and snap-threw a pick-off at first. But Coach Wieboldt cut him from the high school team, because The Arch boasted he could pitch too, and better than Chic. And the gods heard, and saw his one-handed hybris with the mitt, and stunted his growth because he smoked, too.

From vine-clad Lovett Hill came the delinquent Ray-Guy Beatty, whom immortal Poseidon begat—Lord of the sea, earth-shaker, what time he entered into Gren (Grendale) Beatty's skin, and possessed that clod. And he slept by the lovely Aunt Maisy Beatty, née Mickiewicz, daughter of Aphrodite, the laughter-loving. But Gren Beatty was long gone from Redemaine, having abandoned his beloved family. Now his putative son, Ray-Guy, reckless of speech as Thersites, mocked the high-greaved heroes to his peril. But he came to Farrelly's underage.

From Muldaur Street, haunt of doves, fair-founded with its many ravines, came Debevoise, confident in his zeal, who wore a gray meter reader's uniform from United Power.

And they that held Greenwood workers section, bristling with spears, were led by Mal Dallai, dear son to Aglaia Dallai, the resplendent Aglaia, a single mother; and by Sim Curtis, bravest in war of Redemaine captains. This warrior, skilled in close combat, was the same who loved deep-zoned Makarie Straiton in vain for years, and so he vowed to 'mess up Spring Glen'—like Persian King Xerxes, pounding with an oar the sea that sunk his fleet. But Curtis had calmed down a bit by now, in his mid-twenties; and queenly ox-eyed Makarie, comeliest of Spring Glen's daughters, had gone to her destiny of wedlock with another. As for Neddy Parigi, Patroclus to Curtis's Achilles, he was not on hand at Farrelly's this evening. For he, Parigi, had bethought him of dolorous war, of furious valor, joining the Marine Corps. And so he flew high and far away, affrighting the blue billows, cutting through briny clouds with a brazen beak: on his way as a military adviser to Vietnam, where his unit was stationed in the Central Highlands.

From flowering Spring Glen, between the fair-flowing brook and craggy Crest Road, famed for its walls, came Harkins and Whittington, two flits, just home from freshman year in college. Crewcuts being no longer cool, they sported a casual prep style now, not parted but brushed. They came to Farrelly's fending off the mighty boredom, and looking for an easy lay; since it was still a bit chilly to wile away days and nights at the beach club. Now Randy and Ritter—Ritter N. Whittington conceived when Ares lay with his honored mother in secret, entering her upper chamber, and the boy became such a flit he skipped a grade—: now the two captains stood by the long bar, their spears poised to rend corselets about the breasts of the foemen.

From prophetic James Street came Rube DeLuca, uncouth of speech, a bulwark; and by his side Cocò Arzigogolo, who hit the longest homerun in Peewee League history: parked one all the way out by the brick outhouse, on the grassy bank in left field, before the official Peewee field existed. But Arzigogolo faded from the baseball scene.

Lastly, Woodeye Street was led by Biff Modena and Smagowitz, since Nazzarro Zummo, good at the war cry, was off somewhere parking with my girl, the flashing-eyed Bethany Engstrom, daughter of Aphrodite. Those, then, were the captains. Of warriors they were by far the best, that night at Farrelly's Spa, among the sons of Redemaine. And when they sang out, or stomped their feet to the rhythm of the juke-box, the floorboards groaned greatly, as though all the town were swept with the scourge of war.

XVI

Those were the guys I recognized that night, besides Civitello and Bryant no longer squared off, gathering round with the gapers. Not Mother Mary, you might say, but a pair of falsies had interceded to bring peace. A couple dozen other hard drinkers, and livers, I didn't know at least by name; which was good since I could make eyes at them more easily than at Worley, who had been my catcher in the past. I had to watch myself: if Morse's gaze met mine romantically, I could start laughing. He might take that amiss.

Uncle Tom asked directions for Maldoror Drive.

—Why up there? said Biff, wide-eyed. It's dangerous.

—Now see hyar, young'un—said Tom, fussing about: afraid the beer would mar his makeup job.—If you had a sweet thang as luvabubble as mine: would you be afeared? Or would a' want a nice dark place to be alone?

—You can come to my house, said Debevoise. It's dark.

—Young man! How cu'd ah thunk o' imposin' on yer folks' hos-pertaliter? But thanks fer de kine offer . . . Nossih, Millie LamOOre 'n me got'r hearts set on Maul'er Drive. Doncha' know.

I stood by the bar looking pretty: gave it some more handjive as though I thought in sign language. When Tom mentioned The Drive, my fingers moved quicker. Was Beth up there with Nazzarro at this moment? There were only so many times you could go bowl-ing, or to the movies, or Tony Eden's for a butter crunch cone. I didn't think she would be safely in her bed of a Saturday night; and my mind was on her, like much of the time these days. But, standing there, I also wondered if Farrelly's Spa, in its pristine innocence, might be home away from home for a psychopathic killer. Could the Maldoror Mon be here, among us, right now? There was a withdrawn guy with a dark gaze, named Mervin Schlosser, hanging by the back wall: I knew him because he never missed a ballgame at the high school. We, the benchsitters, might make a crack at his expense, and send a ripple of laughter through the dugout. For one thing, he didn't keep his eye on the ball, but on a certain Redemaine High senior, lately my girlfriend, where she sat in the stands. Could The Mon be Mervin Schlosser? Or was it another—a masked murderer on hand in casual dress this evening, among us?

XVII

Rube DeLuca, with an unassuming look, edged closer; and after a moment he entered the charmed circle. Looking seriously interested in Millicent's person, The Rube ordered a refill, and said to her escort:

—Look, Grandpa—

—Uncle, not Grandpa.

—Uncle then. You must be nuts to come in here.

—Why so, young man?

—Do you see anyone else here that's your color?

Now, what Uncle Tom did next was kind of crazy, and it had consequences. Uncle, or Thaddy, was unlike any other childhood friend of mine. He had a thing the others lacked: sympathy. On the one hand, he suffered so much from his mother, Gertruda 'La Furia'; on the other, his dad, Big Jim Floriani, the pharmacist, was truly a good man, who stood by his elder son right or wrong, and even against the wild wife. So Thaddy knew emotional pain as a boy, with a face full of bad acne to show for it. But he also had strength to master his pain: get over resentment that mars a personality, a life. Only the strong have real sympathy, their sincerity all of a piece. Thad was that way. But he could also show another side: a contempt, like no one else I ever met, if he didn't like someone. And so it was now, feeling an instinctual dislike for Rube DeLuca.

In his scratchy, pedantic voice, Uncle Tom said:

—Well now, young'un, do ye think we Uh-h-murreekins live in a free que'entry?

—Yes, I do, old'un. And I am free to throw you out of here.

—Way'll, dat's mahtih fine o' yuh, dats follers. But listen tuh yer' Unc-Unc'. 'Dat 'dar 'z spatio-temporal freed'hum, so tih speak. But do yuh' thunk U-h-h-murrikuh knows 'erself, young'urn?

—Yep. And you'll be sorry you ever knowed me, Grandpa, in about thirty seconds.

—Way'ell 'den, let's foller dis'ere sillerjizz'm to de bittry end. Know 'dyself, young man! America don't know 'erself, and you don't know yo'self.

—I don't?

—No.

—Well, one thing I do know, old man. Your ass is grass. Get the hell out. But the chick can stay.

Then my friend did a mad thing.

Without turning his head he sent his pupils to one side, down the bar: so the whites of his eyes stared in The Rube's face. That was strange, and rude! Well, he didn't like him. He'd stand there and talk to the boy but not look at him.

—No Uncle Tom—said Thaddy, with a little laugh—no future mom.

XVIII

DeLuca was in his late twenties. Mean guy, no gentleness in him that I saw; maybe worse with those he loved. I knew him because he worked for the Parks Department, and I helped with a playground program last summer. We had a run-in over lawn mowing: he told me to cut and trim a difficult bank, his job. Plus I used my glib tongue to tease someone like The Rube. Once I caught him wiping his eyebrows on a handkerchief, and laughed: 'You use eyebrow liner? Why not lipstick and rouge too?' Chaotic, bad tempered, he threw his weight around, and one afternoon we almost came to blows in the shed. I just don't have much patience for his sort: maybe since my old man is such a heavyweight. Ruby, as might be expected, had woman trouble in a big way; he paid for his youthful passions with alimony times two, and grumbled he got 'blamed for the whole rotten mess'. How he despised the wives who had taken him for a ride! And then the cost, and the guilt, were all his. Even worse, he believed it, deep down. Hey, why complain? I told him, rubbing salt in the wound. Change your name and move to another state, Rubester.

Now, sipping foam, DeLuca stared down at Uncle Tom's eyeballs.

Thaddy, like that day in the high school cafeteria when violence erupted, showed no fear. He stood there and stared with his eye-whites, weirdly, at the first-class cad.

In those instants The Rube had an evil eye: a racist's, KKK maybe. But a Maldoror Mon's?

Just then the focus of attention was not Rube and Uncle. It was me. My magniloquent titties, slightly off kilter, had that bar in thrall, and don't think I exaggerate. A few other women in the fairly crowded space—fishing for husbands?—had to take a back seat and could only stare glumly at the big blond in braids with larger-than-life boobies, lipsticky grin, gobbed eyelashes risking a blink per minute or so.

Thad, scratchy-voiced, mocked The Rube:

—What say, young man?

—I said get ready for the old heave-ho. No coloreds, comprende?

I had to create a diversion before Ruby made hash of my best friend. So I gave another flurry of sign language.

Uncle Tom took due note, and said:

—'Dat so, Missy. 'Dat 'm so.

—What'd she say? asked Rubeth.

—She sayed, young faller, if yih' 'jackerlate me f'um'n 'dese hyair p'emises, who'll translate fuh' yuh'?

—What I got to tell Missy don't need no translator, Pops.

XIX

By now a crowd had gathered round and trapped us against the long counter. I made more signs, but almost blew my cover by saying hi to the two guys from my homeroom, Biff and Smags. Unlike Thad and me they weren't underage. Ringers: all the stay-backs went to Mr. Gags.

Someone said:

—She needs to go in for balancing and alignment.

On lopsided, I admit. But the hardasses didn't mind. My chest bulged, and their eyes bulged.

Rube insisted:

—You heard me, Grandpa. Git! If not, I'll grind you to a divot.

—Don't do that, young man.

Flurry of sign language.

Rube:

—What's she saying now?

Thaddy:

—She says if you don't leave me alone, she'll kick your sorry ass.

—Ho! said the bully, laughing. You can't stay here, Shorty. This place is for men.

At eleven-thirty that tipsy male crowd eyed me with a dogged fixity. What a trip! I felt a little impatient since for one thing I needed to pee. Also, it seemed to me these hard-ons didn't give a hoot if I could talk or not, or whether I had a brain in my head. So this is the plight of women! I considered telling the machos a thing or two; if DeLuca felt mean, I could feel mean too; but there went our plan to lure Evelyne's killer onto Maldoror Drive, once I opened my mouth. It was so hard not to talk.

—Ouch!

—Hey, said Ginoli, wide-eyed. I thought she couldn't talk.

—She cain't, said Uncle, but she cain say ouch.

I didn't appreciate Debevoise's gesture. He had reached round and pinched me, viciously, between corset and brassiere. That about did it for me: those tight garters biting into my thighs; that bra with its wire stays grinding my sides; that blond wig giving me an itch, so I felt a big need to lift it and scratch; those high heels making my ankles ache, and want to cave in, sending the entire godawful contraption—overstuffed falsies, black lace panties, stockings, corset, petticoat, skintight evening dress, makeup, jewelry, perfume—the whole shebang collapsing in a heap on the beer-stained floor at Farrelly's Spa . . . Get along with you!

Debevoise and Ginoli, Smagowitz, Curtis, Resca, the Leopardis, even the more dignified Worley, were roaring with laughter at

Thaddy's saying I would kick DeLuca's ass. But, you know, I sized him up and asked myself if I wouldn't try to achieve just that. Without question I needed an outlet for frustration that had been building in me since the night my sister died.

XX

I didn't want to leave Thaddy by himself among the rowdy crowd. He was so free and flippant they might lynch him to the nearest tree. But by now I had to pee bad, so I went into my dactylogical act to make this fact known, and say it was time for us to split the scene. We'd made our message clear. Mon, see you on Maldoror Drive.

Uncle Tom paid me no mind. Chattery, dominant with his bookish words and turns of phrase, having himself a fine time, he ran rings around the dull-witted Rube done in by life's dilemmas.

—Young'uns! Me 'n Miss Millie LamOOre hyar' . . . mah' feeyancih' . . . we jes' kem' off'n de Pahkweh lookin' fer some hos'paliter, doncha' know. We'z feelin' uh mahtih' th'ust fer beer, nigh untuh dypsomaniacality! Now we is on'r way t' Millicent's folks, up thar' in Came-in-Britches, doncha' know, whar' she'll pissent ma'r sweet ayse t'er p'ants, Ma 'ner Pa LamOOre, doncha', 'ner we means ter git hitched . . . quick.

DeLuca:

—You old rascal, you ain't gettin' hitched to nobody. I'm marrying Millie tonight.

—Tonight? But she don' wantcher', young man. She warnts mar divotered arsk.

Furious barrage of sign language.

—What'd she say?

—Says she wouldn' feel raht' comfu'bubble murryin' uh skunk lak' you. Says she thunks you de Maul'erer Mon.

—Ha ha ha!

Roar of laughter from the crowd around us.

Sign language, slowed down. I gave Thad glimpses: be careful. But he was so into his act, he threw caution to the winds.

—Young man, Millie says yuz' porbubbly de rat 'dat kulled Ev'n Gibbet 'dat naht up on Maul'der Drahv'.

–I did not!

There was a kind of hush in the barroom. For a moment the jukebox had fallen silent. In a pause all eyes fixed on me and Uncle. And then . . . do you know what came over that motley crew? It's hard to describe, let alone believe. Sympathy–something like sympathy: not directed toward me of course; what was Evelyne Gilbert to Millie? But a touch of collective grief, mixed in with drunken sentimentality, seemed real more or less. Briefly we shared a sadness for the brilliant girl who lost out on her life. That lasted barely ten seconds: bad for business. A hit tune blared forth from the nickelodeon, and more rot got talked, like people rubbing their own noses in it. Once again there was that age-old foolishness in the air: all about 'Chinks 'n furriners takin' over our jobs' . . . and: 'Beatnik intellectuals infesting the world's greatest nation' . . . and: 'Harry Truman hit the bullseye when he dropped the bomb on all them Chinks . . .' at which Thaddy said: 'Those were Japanese, sweetie' . . . and then: 'Well, we ought to blow that other country sky-high too, what's its name?' . . . and Curtis supplied the name, Vietnam, because his friend Parigi was stationed over there. But despite all the 'Chinks and Japs, kikes, frogs, krauts and what have you, wops, Ayyyrabs and Mooselrams, greasers 'n Spics, homos, commies, and cunty women'; despite all the sweet land of liberty and God bless Uhmurrika–something else snuck in Farrelly's Spa for just an instant there. It was a pause, like a hush, in memory of Evelyne Gilbert. Something good had gone to waste.

Someone, I think Mal Dallai, said:

–That Jame Hayes could run.

Arzigogolo:

–Pride of Redemaine.

Not the Black of course. But the Olympic runner, who wouldn't be.

Morse:

–Too bad.

The Arch:

–A bitch.

XXI

Meanwhile my bladder had reached its limit. I'd have to leave Thaddy alone. In a groove he held forth, and it was fascinating. Fussy, filled with wit and big words, he treated the boozers to an accent, a dialect made up for the occasion, spiced with Latin quotes, and used by no one in the deep South or anywhere. He called them young man, or Sonny. But he only had eye-whites for Rube DeLuca.

—Sonny, move back a step thyar'. Millie needs air. She's got a pair of lungs on her. Young man, don't push. Miss LamOOre's dainty!

Someone, unknown to me, said:

—Gilbert kid shoulda' watched her step.

—You can say that again, said Whittington, chortling in his beer which sprayed his eyes, the flit.

—Not even the President can do anything he wants. For the love of Mike don't go making out up on West Hills with no . . . And I don't care if he is the best athlete in the state.

Ray-Guy:

—Ki'k'kind of asking to h'have her h'h'hash s'settled.

Smagowitz:

—Her brother's in my homeroom. What a nut! That Newell Gilbert is a real loser.

Millicent, a good kid if there ever was one, did not like to hear this kind of talk. For an instant she looked sadly at The Smags, and gave sign language to the contrary. But she did a little dance, like a monkey in high heels to a hurdy-gurdy, because she needed to peepee.

Biff Modena, also one of Mr. Gags' greats, said:

—Newell's regular.

—Regular? said Smags. You're bats too if you say that. Look at the car he drives: no one ever souped up a Willys Jeep! Did he or did he not turn it over with seventeen people inside at The Mall in front of Tony Eden's with a crowd watching? Did he or did he not quit the baseball team and break up with his steady, Beth Engstrom, hottest chick at the high school? That's nooky! You gotta' be flipped to turn your back on that kind of nooky. Regular, you say? The boy's a regular madman, and you should have your head examined too.

Biff:

—Aw, Newell ain't so bad. Just got a little tetched in the prep schools he went to. Tell you so himself.

Smaggeth:

—His parents sent him away. They couldn't stand it no more.

Ray-Guy:

—If he's s'sane, then why does h'h'he hang around with that h'h'huh!homo Flo F'F'Floriani?

At this Uncle Tom's eye-whites flashed. He forgot his accent:

—What?! What did you say, young man? That is sacrilege! Why, you must mean the famous and remarkable Thaddeus Floriani, whose photo appeared in a national magazine recently. Didn't you see it?—Tom peered into the distance, raising an arm.—Oh, just look at that noble individual, prince of teenagers, the same Thaddy we all love and admire. He's like Mozart! Look at him standing tall with the help of a coffee table as he speaks out for social justice, racial tolerance, love, brotherhood. And you call him a homo? Why, yang' faller, you were misinformed. You ought 'ter respect yer' betters. The said Floriani, nicknamed Flo, is a very great man, peer of Da Vinci, Rembrandt, Cézanne. You'll see! And who will decorate the hall for your upcoming Senior Prom, if not him? Who will make the stunning décor for your Class Night activities? You call the universal genius Floriani a homo? Pshaw! For shame, young man, fie! Fie!

—I only m'meant . . . I d'd'didn't—Ray-Guy stammered.

Ginoli:

—Evvy Gilbert shoulda' watched herself, dating a Black.

—Hell—said Bill Civitello—with a brother like she had . . . musta' been off her rocker too.

Rube:

—You can say that again. I almost had to teach Gilbert a lesson, little wiseass. One day last summer we were working at Roquefort Field and he got in my hair. Always making remarks, you know. Said I better do a little work for a change, or maybe I could find a new job using my ex-wives as references. Man, I came within an inch of smashing his skull.

—Get this! said Smagowitz. I heard New-Boy got it on with Miss Grich after one of the Greek Club meetings she holds at her house. He's turned on by her cigarette breath. Used that snotty hanky she always takes out of her brassiere during class for a rubber.

—Gossip, said Worley.

—Ha ha! said Archie O' Shea. You should talk, Worl. Fess up, you spent senior year in private t'ittering with the homemaking teacher. I bet Miss Jollymeier taught you a few spicy recipes, baw'!

Resca, thoughtful:

—That Penny Grich has some nice little ass on her. Too bad she smokes and coughs all over herself.

Ginoli:

—Pair of little titties, too.

Skivvy Civitello:

—Gimme' Ma Hebbel anyday. Two for the price of one.

Ray-Guy:

—M'Ma's got s's'size alright. B'B'B'But I can't take the n'n'neck wrinkles, and p'p'powder. S's'smells like my g'g'grandma's b'b'b'-bathroom.

—So drape a flag over her head—said Debevoise—and do it for Old Glory.

—How flattering—said courtly Tom.—She's a nice lady.

—Listen, said Smagowitz. I happen to know it's true about Gilby and Miss Grich.

—Aw, c'mon, said Biff.

—Naw, I got proof! Look, he goes around with Flo, right? And what do those two douche bags do all day long? Talk a lot of bullcrap in Latin. You can even hear those homos at it in the hall between classes.

—What's the big deal? said Biff.

—And what sort of bullroar do you think he mouthes off at Greek Club: before he gets down to the real business on the agenda, and mouthes her doosits? At Greek Club they speak Greek, do they not? Well, what more proof do you want?

—Greek ain't the same as Latin, said Biff, frowning.

—Almost!—Smagowitz brought down his palm on the bar, a pool of run-over foam, which splashed.—It almost is! Suck pussy in Greek or Latin, what's the big diff'? Proof!

—A sillerjizzm, said Tom. Socrates is mortal.

In back someone raised a screechy voice:

—We're the richest goddamned country on this goddamned earth, goddammit! Fuck 'em.

DeLuca nodded his head, pondering:

—I guess the Gilbert girl asked for it. Hell, screw 'er. Screw all'um.

Coming from him, that sort of talk didn't surprise me. What did, was Vinny Resca, when he said:

—You halfass moron. How can you blame a girl who died?

—Blame all'm, dumb cunts.

Same voice in back:

—Shut your trap! You Sheenie intellec(hiccup)chal, you dud! . . . I'll kick your royal heinie right outa' this bar! Love 'er, I say, 'er leave 'er . . .! 'For spacious skies, for(hiccup) . . . ever . . .' Hey, buddy-boy, how's that song go? Sing along wid' me.

DeLuca sneered down at Vin:

—You talking to me, Shorty?

Resca—muscular, a football guard:

—Yeah, you, Longy, you longeared donkey. Respect the dead.

DeLuca grinned:

—What the hell, if you say so, kid. Hey, you're okay.

Screechy, over the jukebox:

—I said mind yer' manners! We're number one, you cow-pie! Furriners out, fuckem, 'Uhmurrrikka . . . Uhmurrrikkkuh . . . God shed his grace on thee . . . And crown thy good with bro-otherhood . . . from sea(hiccup) . . . to shining . . . sea . . .' Thank you, thank you.

XXII

Now by this time I couldn't hold it any longer, not thirty seconds; so clear the way, big bruisers, or there'll be a small pool of something besides beer on the floor at Farrelly's, and it won't be that small. Thus I, ladylike, if you please, hustled my young ass plus false hips back to the collective potty. Oops! Watch out, hon', almost went in the men's room. Then, with feminine grace and a show of nonchalance, I crossed the threshold of a ladies room. Lawsy! What an inner sanctum, what accoutrements. I shook my head and wondered what this or that thingamajig was for.

But I was not on my own in there. Which fact could impede my flow; that is, if my bladder hadn't jammed from the pressure so I'd have to get pumped and cathetered in the emergency ward. Think of that! Also, it was no waltz getting into position to pee. With so many

blooming layers of lacy undergarments I needed an oil rig. I wondered how Thaddy's grandmother, Rita Joy, managed to urinate in
the old days without the help of servants.

And then, alas! in such an all-fired hurry: I left the door to my
stall ajar. As I was beginning at last to enjoy the pause that refreshes,
a woman behind me, peeking in her nose where it didn't belong,
screamed.

—She's standing up! She pees on her feet!

Well, you try relieving yourself sometime amid such a ruckus.
Come on! Hurry up! I tried to finish before the Fire Department
arrived.

Right off, a couple other gals rushed in the loo to watch me pee-
ing on my feet, or, I should say, Millicent LamOOre pissing in her
panties. It was a miracle I could perform at all, under such pressure:
still fumbling with that pantie girdle. Then I turned around to pull
the stall door shut, and this caused more shrieks, shouts, a bathroom
pandemonium. Hands to temples those three women wailed in horror as I stood there nursing a thin dribble.

XXIII

Out of the ladies room I came on shaky steps. On those giraffe-
like high heels I wobbled along, my confidence shaken, and confronted a barroom full of fuzzy faces. It was after midnight by now,
and I was thinking our farce had gone far enough. Then I saw
DeLuca had Thaddy by the collar and meant to lift him off the
floor—lynch a wriggling Uncle Tom in his bare hands. But everyone
turned and gawked at my approach. One of the women came on
pointing at Millicent, and hollered:

—It's a man! She pees like one, and she walks like one!

No need to sound so terrified, lady.

Drunken men looked stunned. Bill Civitello's moonface, Bryant's
long doleful chin, Ray-Guy's smirk like he swallowed a mouse
drowned in his beer, which was why he stuttered; Merv Schlosser's
depressive scowl, Vinny Resca's mug: they gazed, like fish in an
aquarium, at the female impersonator. Such disillusion! The hard

drinkers leered amid shadows tinged by the High Life sign with its diagonal beams over Milwaukee. Suddenly I wasn't tired anymore—only afraid for Thaddy who didn't look too good in DeLuca's clutches. The bully in his anger, made a fool of by a girl, Millie, didn't know his own strength. And so I moved forward across the streaky floor: like a tall ship in Rita Joy's ten layers of rustling silk, flounces, brocade, straps, stays digging my skin, fenestrated panties like a museum case, black lace ruche dewy after my trip to the toilet. I marched up to The Rube, and—

Boomah!

My first punch landed square on Ruber's bony nose, which splotched red.

Thaddy slumped to the floor. He crawled beneath our feet in his tuxedo.

XXIV

All hell broke loose in Farrelly's Spa.

—Look at her fight!

—It's Marciano in drag, ha ha ha! Hey, Roxanna!

What struck me was the violence of it. Where did such viciousness come from? No one seemed to care just whom he was pushing, punching, pummeling. That random hate was summoned from way back in a bad childhood. It was triggered by a black man coming to a redneck bar, by a transvestite mocking the male egos: those grown men ogling fake charms. But the crowd violence seemed to flow forth from some ancient cistern, frustrated life force, poisoned dreams: the place where devils drink and gain strength. Take care! It isn't far beneath the surface; it will rise up like a flood. When the hour strikes, the dark forces flow over into everyday life. For they must have an outlet, war, racial hatred; never mind how many innocent people have to die, women, children, the old, innocents. Suddenly it happens: Rome under Sylla, massacres, never seen before, here. A society whose mainspring is competition, individualism, and 'freedom' rises more, ever more toward the top, while the rest cope with pressure as best they may—such a society erupts. Macro-violence on the world scene, Vietnam. Micro-violence at Farrelly's Spa, in the heart of Redemaine.

XXV

No need for a blow-by-blow account. The joint was jumpin'. Guys waded in, guys flailed, guys grappled other guys down on the greasy floor. Ladies shrieked. Cries grew more guttural as bodies jumbled, mauled, crashed across the cluttered space. Beer mugs flew, conked. Ritter Flittington fell unconscious. Smagowitz, laughing wildly, went from table to table grabbing up pitchers of beer and showering the fighters.

There were no lines drawn. It wasn't like that time eleven of us climbed in the Willys and drove down to *Mack's & Jack's* in Portchester and I asked a local chick to dance and her boyfriend got excited when I went on my knees in front of her looking for a contact lens that popped out of my eye while she did The Twist with her back turned and so the boy thought I meant to offend his girl and he tripped me on the way back to our table and Chic Wieboldt threw a punch at him and *Mack's & Jack's* became a brawl between Portchester and Redemaine but Franny Fofanna didn't take part because he was on probation. It wasn't like that.

Farrelly's, that May evening in 1961, was all against all, a free-for-all. Make hay!

Only I had a plan. Give Thad Floriani, future artist, time to crawl out the door and then make a beeline for the exit myself.

Debevoise took advantage of the mêlée to feel me up. He still hadn't caught on, though those things had gone almost vertical. Well, the boy was not himself. But did I show any mercy? I did not. Take your grubby mitts off my false tits! I decked him.

That wise sucker Beatty leapt up on the bar and began calling the fight from ringside:

—Resca a right to D'D'Dallai's jaw, oh-h-h! D'Dallai on the canvas ... t't't'two, three ... C'C'Curtis b'b'body-punches Rand H'H'Harkins, p'p'prime cont-cont-contender from Sp'Sp'Spring G'G'Glen! ... C'Coc'co Arzig'g'g'og'golo has B'B'Biff Modena on the ropes, ag'g'gainst the b'b'bar ... one-two! one-t't'two! work'k'king B'B'Biff over . . . Oh! oh-h-h! Kid Millicent and that shaggy b'bear D'D'DeLuca are in a clinch . . . Hold on, boxing lovers! Are those t't'two-tit-two heavyweights still fighting? Is that a nosebleed D'DeLuca's having, or an org'g'g'gasm? Oh-h-h! Ha ha ha! He c'c'creams K'Kid Millie and her w'w'wig f'f'flies off again. S'say! She needs a t't'trainer just to k'keep that w'w'w'wig on! Oooh! D'DeLuca d'd'delivers a B'B'Bobo Olson b'b'b'bolo p'p'punch and Millie's left t't't'tit flies up in her f'f'face! A knockout punch for a knockout b'b'broad, sports lovers. But she's not d'd'down yet, just a b'b'bit s'saggy. Say, R'Ru'Rubester, was that a low b'b'blow? Seems your op'p'ponent for this cham*penis's*'ship b'bout has b'b'brassiere p'p'problems: slung mighty low! P'P'Put up your d'd'-dukes, Millicent LamOOre! You'll need some b'b'bra adjustment in your c'c'c'corner between rounds. Ouch! Millie's h'h'h'hard right to the jaw stagg'gers D'DeLuc'ca. But The Ru'utube c'c'counter-p'punches to the midriff, heu! K'K'Kid Millie's face wrinkles with p'p'pain as the sweat flies off, sp'sp'poiling her makeup'p'pup. Rur'rhby is b'b'bleeding p'p'p'profusely; and if this is K'K'Kid Mill's t't'time o' the month, she'll b'b'be b'b'b'bleeding t't'too, ha ha ha!

Funny guy.

Farrelly's bartender watched the donnybrook. Blasé, he'd seen a few. Which is why they kept the place so bare, no décor, trimmings, nothing to tear up. But I feared he might call the cops; and then Duggan would have to make a decision about ruining my reputation like Sorifa's. Also we were underage.

One of the women cried:

—That cunt can throw a punch! Pees upright, and fights like a guy too!

Smagowitz:

—She should take out a patent on—

But just then Danny Leopardi conked Smags' forehead so hard, the boy fell back on the seat of his pants. I saw it and thought: good for the snide, backbiting, envious gossip Smagowitz, teenage bureaucrat. There's some justice in the world.

My wig flew off again, but what the hell. I just picked it up, put 'er back on, and back into the fray. Most guys on hand, Worl and The Arch, Ginoli, Resca, Leopardis, kept their distance and wouldn't hit a woman. They just rocked and socked each other some more and enjoyed their giving as well as their receiving, like Christmas.

XXVI

It hit the spot. That's right. You heard me. I sort of took it amiss the good ol' boys wouldn't hit Millie. Knock 'er for a loop! For weeks the depressive grief over my sister's death; the frustration from losing Beth Engstrom to Nazzarro; the sense of failure and letdown now baseball had ended: what! I will not play in the Major Leagues?; also my mom being sick in the hospital, we didn't know why yet, and my dad's heavy drinking, every night in his cups, and short-tempered–I guess it all just built up until I enjoyed a barroom brawl.

At Farrelly's it was a ritual. Hey! I'll take a Saturday night riot over Sunday school anyday for therapeutic value. Because what kind of future could the Redemaine greats look to after graduation? 'Shoot the shit, grab a little ass', as Ned Parigi once said profoundly. Boring, low-paying job: to underwrite the boss's yacht or private plane, fancy hobby. As for marriage, it had loomed as somewhat more romantic in the high school sweethearts stage. You can ask Rubric. Day after day, month after month: must your life force go to a draggy routine, Big Worl, now the thrills and achievement of Class D ball are done forever?

Here, there, 'Fifties conservatism was beginning to hit the fan. But Beatnik nonconformism, deep chatter in the cafés; Civil Rights struggles; 'Sixties movement ideas and trends would hardly make a dint in the lives of those at Farrelly's Spa tonight. Vietnam, yes, but not hippiedom. And yet they were young.

Nope. It was fun, an adventure at times, growing up here in Redemaine. Of course there were hard things too. Families are no joke. But there was a sense . . . as summer began: oh! the warm sunny days with nothing but fishing and swimming in store . . . freedom.

Now that was gone for the most part. Drink, and fight stupidly, with friends, if you want to feel free. For things weren't working out according to plan. Disappointment, frustration. Now depression, anger, betrayal. Now rage, violence, a good old-fashioned bloodletting from time to time. Hey!

That's life.

Hey, Art-boy.

New-boy.

Hey.

But I couldn't help wondering for just a moment: even as I stood backed against the bar, trading punches with good ol' Redemaine boys. It came in a flash, and I thought: Could it be the Maldoror Mon feels this way too?

XXVII

By the door Thaddy bobbed up—sort of like a cork on choppy waters. I wanted him out the door and away from the madness.

But he was still playing. Hand to his heart, or the black velvet lapel of his tux, he sang out:

—Come away, Millie dear. Sweet Millicent, ah' reckons tits' tahm' we'z retirin' fer de evenin'. Innih'whore 'zeez fu'ks don' appreciate us hyair'. We ought'ter go whay we's luvved 'n 'spec-torated, dear. Le's go up ter Maller Drahv' 'n mek' out!

Even while jabbing at DeLuca I made some sign language.

Thaddy opened the door:

—Yers, yers. Le's go, honey, fo' de cops arribe.

And so I ducked a punch, and managed to dance and weave my way toward the door.

Millie LamOOre followed Uncle Tom Totem through the front entry of Farrelly's Spa.

We both went tumbling out, me more wobbly than ever on my high heels, but exhilarated by the frank exchange of opinions; Uncle a bit ruffled after being manhandled by DeLuca, but still dignified.

We got out of there. We made our way, costumes rumpled and grease-stained, back to the Willys. Time to call it a night? Hey, go on home and lick our wounds. We blew it at Farrelly's. Those big bruisers deduced that I was a bruiser too.

Oh well, set the trap better next time. But first take a rest. Sooner or later we would hit The Drive, and I would act as jail-bait.

Chapter Six

I

A few days went by, into midweek. I tried to rest: rubbed my sores. Not Thaddy though; he had a demon in him, ever active, working afternoons on the Senior Prom Committee even as he mulled over our next move, and pushed me toward another foray into Redemaine's night life. Raring to go, he rubbed his hands, and said:

—We're on the tracks of a killer. Peter bags wolf. We catch Mon.

But I saw no tracks: none since the night I went to the scene of my sister's death; and met a masked driver in a Cobra-bodied racing vehicle; and smelled a scent which I couldn't quite place, on undergrowth up there by the radio relay tower; and saw the killer seemed to have taken out his rage—before or after?—by hacking up some shrubs.

The Thursday after our fiasco at Farrelly's, I found myself decked out as a dame once again. Wired padded buttressed: I was dressed to kill so Millie and Uncle could take a ride along Maldoror Drive. This time we drove not Willys but Mrs. Floriani's green Pontiac.

At nightfall we entered West Hills Park. Last rays of sunset cast a tragic light over the hillocks and stretches of forest cut through by the winding Drive. We passed the first circle emptied of high school couples. No one came to park and make out these evenings. That hadn't ended at once after my sister's death, but did after *Our Town News* reported Jared Simms' escape from the State Prison in Condor. Then we came to the high tower with its two red lights seen across the county. And there, by the base, I told Thad my idea of the murder. We walked through it; we reenacted Jame's movements, and the psychopath's, and Evelyne's. As always Thad went about fussily, inspecting, asking questions; he kept up Uncle's pedantic chatter, in that accent like no one on earth, but only a stereotype. He gave a shrug and laughed, happy as a lark. And there you have genius: it soars on strong wings, with an eagle eye, above sorrow.

I stood to one side in the darkness and let him talk. He puttered about the base of the tower, thinking out loud. But for me this field trip was painful.

My first time here, you'll remember, was during a numbness: the zombyish half-life which is grief trauma. Now the numbness had long worn off; my moods swung strangely as I felt the thing itself: pain, loss. To understand this you need—well, to have experienced something like it; but also I'll say, in my idealizing, to have seen Evelyne Gilbert, and known her. She was very beautiful, high-cheekboned: with an oriental note like our paternal grandmother. It wasn't only I who said Wilhelmina had Cherokee blood in her: from some crossroads way back when. I called her an Indian to scandalize my dad, who knew it and denied, the snob.

Lady's eyes were dark yet bright, alert to the world around her, responsive. She was kind, as I said before: a trait I find rare, and not only in teenagers. At times she might look surprised: maybe at a thought, at something inside herself. Who knows what she might have done if given time? I won't say become a politician or diplomat, in our day. But she was a born leader, Student Council President; her presence gave life to afternoon activities, clubs.

She combined opposites in the way of great people: stern and gentle; serious, cheerful; pensive, outgoing; proud, whew, so proud, and humble. I know you think I am overdoing it—well, go to our town and ask them. She was gracious, sweet, but she could frown too, and such a frown: like Beatrice once, displeased with Dante, as he passed by. Above all, not one iota of false pride or pretentiousness in her, that I ever saw, no jot of conceit. Like our mother in this. Her nature seemed to know the art of living: good to be around, also like our mother, but with less effort, and maybe on a grander scale someday.

She liked sports but only to play: no time for cheerleading, or joining in Pep Club type stuff; she went to the games because it was fun, exciting in parentheses. Small, though few knew it. I should tell you she loved Thaddy as a close friend; those two had many good times together, ever since childhood. They shared interests and sense of humor.

Oh how our parents loved Lady. How my older brother Joey showed deference to her, a protectiveness in little things, or big if necessary. How our younger sister, Lemon, adored Evo and wanted to be like her. And how I loved her, my own, own sister. Still do. Always. Always will.

Anyway . . . no masked rider or Mon rose to the bait during our cruise on the Drive, and two hours spent by the towers. I tried to locate the scent of a killer again, on a leaf, a blade of tall grass—so my partner might identify it. But the chemical smell was gone: washed away by the rain.

II

Our Senior Prom was ten days away, and I didn't have to ask Beth Engstrom who her date would be. Well, need I complain? Nazzarro was her steady before I came into the picture. He got her on the rebound when I blew my shot.

—You don't respect me, Newell.

So she told me on the phone one night.

—I only love you.

—Maybe. But you make it seem more like play. A spoiled prep schooler on an adventure.

—Really?

—You'll risk everything on a throw. That's your way. Why did you quit baseball? I see you with Thad Floriani in the hall. Tell me the truth: don't you like being with him better than me?

—No, Beth. But we're trying to do something important.

—Ah, but what you and I did together wasn't.

—It was and is! But . . . we're trying to find my sister's killer.

Such a statement was not the way to win Thani Engstrom to my cause. She was a decent person who shared our grief, but she didn't want to discuss that horror any more than other students at the high school, or most Redemaine adults. There was so much we needed to talk about: so much she didn't understand. I felt she didn't want to. Then I had an idea which gave a pang, in my grief. Had Evelyne's death led to our breakup? It would be understandable if the lovely and vulnerable Beth Engstrom wanted to distance herself from the tragedy. I asked myself: What is better, beauty or character? But you don't fall in love with character—not at our age.

Hey, I had my moment in the sun: an outsider dating the 'finest chick' at the high school. I should feel grateful. Yet, in my dejection, I felt: Why go to their old persnickity Prom? So I can stare at Beth and Nazzarro in their happiness?

III

Those were sunny June days, as the Prom and graduation exercises approached. Springtime with its cooler days and thundershowers was moving toward summer's hot sun, skies a paler blue adrift in humidity. Beach days were on the way, and later bedtimes, and summer baseball though I would not play. There was a promise of summertime fun in the warm fragrant air, wildflowers teased by a breeze; murmurings of the brook which ran through Spring Glen. This year I hardly noticed.

Had the baseball team made the state tournament? Would Beth get Best Looking, or Cynthia Landis? What popular singer would croon at The Prom? What student would be elected valedictorian?— Important questions. I couldn't have cared less.

A few friends were touting me for Best Sense of Humor; that is, Class Clown, or: Thani's Clown. I declined. In those days I was serious, a bit withdrawn. I was going through a change.

Even amid grief, misery, there are new perspectives. To defend myself against sadness I began taking volumes from my dad's library. Unheard-of! A deep-dyed anti-intellectual like myself? A self-respecting jock? or ex-jock. I stayed up late at night reading, studying on my own. What a thing it is to use one's mind. It changes life.

My real education began: on my own! I had put it off too long: partly because Emory browbeat me all through childhood. Read a book! he thundered when I was bored, instead of dealing with my needs a little and giving me attention and being the dad I needed. He was using books as an excuse, an evasion.

Remember your first reading binge at age nine or ten? That was healthy, exhilarating. Today: TV addiction, computers, video games–sick, stunting. Way back when, as a fifth grader, we read a book a day: children's versions of the classics, *Iliad* and *Odyssey*, *1001 Nights*, *Monte Cristo* and *Three Musketeers*, *Ivanhoe*, *Sherlock Holmes* . . . ; or else Landmark Books, extolling the nation's heroes, J. Edgar Hoover.

Now I began to read again, but with something new in mind, a purpose. I asked my pa:

–What are the Devil's favorite books?

–The Bible, he said, laughing.

–Ooph, I don't like it. Too much moaning and whining.

–Hold on, Bub. Goethe called it the great folk book, the book of the people.

–Who is Goethe?

–He wrote *Faust:* another one Satan annotates. What devil doesn't like to read about himself?

–Have you got it here?

–Of course. Hold on, here's a translation, but it's worthless. Learn German!

–Give me a primer. What others?

–Dante, Shakespeare: his private stock! The cheap stuff, commercial trash is good enough for humanity on its way to damnation. But the Devil wants to improve himself, and develop: strengthen his game against a worthy opponent. He studies Marx-Engels' forty-seven volumes.

–Who's Marx-Engels?

–Two German devils who also went for the jugular. Marx was mankind's greatest thinker; though most don't agree with a word he says. Satan does though; he reads those two in the original. He thrills to the ambiguity in Man's future.

–The Devil speaks German?

–Are you kidding? His mother's milk! But an American accent comes natural too.

–He's bilingual.

–Polyglot!–my father laughed.–Here, take these: Tasso, Hölderin,

Nietszche, three geniuses who went nuts. The Devil's playmates. And take this play called *Penthesilea.*

Now I got so involved with Mephistopheles, I was turning into a little devil myself. I didn't eat dinner, and then Lemon, my good l'il sis', came up the attic steps with an ice cream stick as the Good Humor Man jingled through Spring Glen in the twilight.

—Here, Newburg, munch on this.

As a boy I loved my attic room. It held a fascination for me with its pennants on the walls, desk where I played electric action games, bookcase with my favorite books, and window overlooking Santa Fe. Now it was outgrown; though I'd have smaller rooms before my student days ended, and beyond. But I used it for my first hours of serious, non-school study.

My poor dad, fuzzy with drink, his alcoholism on the march, trudged up the stairs and looked at me. He was haggard after his day at the office, and worried about Mom in the hospital again for more tests. He was lonely. By this time Lemon had gone to bed. Joey, my older brother, spent a few days in Redemaine last week: in transit from college down South to the Cape Cod League.

—No more High School Harry? asked Pa.

—Naw.

—Where's Beth lately? No hot dates?

—Naw.

—You prefer spending your time with the Devil?

—Naw.

—No baseball practice even? No joy rides with your friends?

—Naw.

—Is that all you can say: naw?

—Na'—hey c'mon, Dad! I don't come bugging you when you're working.

—What mischief are you getting into this time?

—Look, you're the one who always says: Read a book! Now I'm doing it: see? Read a book! Xe-xe-xe.

My turn.

—I didn't say all day and all night. It isn't normal for a teenager.

—Naw.

—*Faust, Macbeth* . . . the Bible . . . Don't tell me you've got religion.

—Naw.

—You gave up church for Lent when you were eight years old. A regular little devil, and proof of the Tempter's existence. What's going on, Newell? Why the half-baked theology?

—I'm trying to put myself in Satan's place.

—A good way to go crazy.

My eyes went wide:

—It takes a devil to know a devil, and catch one!

—You are half-crazy. Say, you better leave that to the police.

—I'll tell Chief Rune Roscommon you said so.

Then Emory, the professor, began a lecture. He wouldn't go away and leave me alone. All my childhood he was busy and I was bored, so he said: Read a book. Now the tables were turned.

—The Devil is a symbol, Newell, of negativity in man. He expresses socially conditioned forces, envy, greed, lust, and the rest. The Devil, so to speak, can get into a person, a town, a nation like Nazi Germany, a system, culture . . . But we create a Satan tailor-made from our own imagination . . . or from our needs, let's say. Maybe we call him: God. And one day all hell does break loose. And then the Devil take the hindmost.

—Reet.

—Or, let's say, if socioeconomic relations are the roots, stem and branches, then the Devil is the blossom. And bad life the fruit. Something like that.

Well, it beat his maudlin monologue on Mom's illness at least: and how 'we're going to see her through this, don't worry, son, we'll get her squared away . . .' At night the noted academic got soused after 'a life of working myself to the bone, so you, Joey, and Lemon could have every advantage, the best education available . . .' And on, and on.

At length I gave a sigh, and said, softly:

—Dad, can't you see I'm busy?

IV

So I stayed up reading half the night, and went bleary eyed to the high school at midmorning. I checked in the nurse's office where Mrs. Aylmer gave me a pass.

Thaddy buttonholed me in the corridor between classes. He outlined our second foray as private eyes:

—On Friday night we'll go to Roscommon's Tavern, again in disguise. I'm the distinguished black educator, Zeb Scott of Tuskegee, dressed in tweeds with a pipe, and goatee.

—Won't you be hot?

—Never mind. Give my all for science. Gentlemen, I am a bonafide sociologist, here to investigate race relations in the famous town of Redemaine, written up in a national weekly. In particular I want to interview the world famous Thad Floriani, that superman.

—I'm sure the good people will appreciate your interest.

—Righto. And by my side tonight is the cute, petite Nilda, a doctoral candidate who is my assistant. Nilda, as you can see, is white, tinged with pink.

—Outside and inside. But I thought Tuskegee Institute was for Blacks.

—Predominantly, sir, but not all. And it is coed. So we are mentor and student, maybe a little lovey-dovey as we sit in tête à-tête by the bar. Our togetherness should get a rise out of The Mon.

—What do I wear this time? More false this and that?

—You just stepped out of the College Shoppe, dearie. Or I should say: associate.

I glanced over Thaddy's shoulder: at Beth and Nazzarro by her locker along the hall. The leader of ZBKs stood attentively by the lovely cheerleader; he held her books as they lingered there, and she rummaged for something. He looked sweet as pie by her side; no more wildman, no more big guffaws and scratching his armpits, showing off. What a hypocrite!

I sighed:

—Alright then Zeb and Nilda. Here we go again.

V

In Centerville section of Redemaine, a few doors past the Town Hall, stood Roscommon's Tavern owned and operated by the Police Chief's brother. The place was a far cry from Farrelly's Spa, but not swanky like Mayor Tomao Simiglione's Dream Bar located on the outskirts. Roscommon's was staunch middle class: the active bar frequented by business people, professionals, townsfolk on their way home from work. They came here to meet and greet, have a few drinks, unwind while hearing the latest.

The bar area was all mahogany and brass. Amber lighting flickered with TVs above either end. You felt a prosy abundance. Conversation flowed with the cordials: pleasant, in a groove, and tonight was Friday. Laughter came easy, a bit more raucous, in discreet bursts, as the evening wore on.

Small trophies, mementoes, certain homey artifacts hung from a kind of canopy pole, knobbed, looking medieval, over the well polished and stately bar. Whereas Farrelly's had a bare look, as if nobody cared, this establishment seemed to run over with life's good things. The amber light gleamed amid ranks of liquor bottles, and framed photos of celebrity clientele, politicians, football captains and other of the chosen, along the wood-pannelled walls. There were scenic views from Ireland, a clear blue lake in County Limerick, white surf round a cove in the Ring of Kerry. At the center of this cozy décor was a majestic cash register, the pride of some Sligo pub upon a time; its gilding still brilliant, with rococo keys, where it sat enthroned like a queen behind the bar, so that the bartender turned his back when he rang up a sale. There was no music for the moment; only talk, talk, more talk by townspeople, men in their thirties and forties mostly, who had known each other for a long time. Maybe they went away for a few years, college, military service, broader job horizons; but they came back home to settle down, and didn't feel too cramped.

Adjoining the bar was a spacious restaurant area where the food was ample, quite tasty after a few appetizers, good for the price. Middle-aged couples came here year in year out, to drink and dine. Through entries at both ends of the bar went the good citizens, men in business dress, women in nice outfits. They went toward their dining pleasure. And a couple hours later they came out again, redfaced, ready to let their belt out another notch, sated. Beaming benignly by the exit someone called a loud goodbye to a friend still seated by the bar. He raised a hand and waved, like a blessing on Roscommon's Tavern.

VI

Our entry caused no sensation as at Farrelly's, not even a stir. It was Thaddy who raised an eyebrow, and said under his breath:
—Oh yeah, suckers? We'll see if you sit up and take notice.
I chuckled, but I also shook my head. Tonight we must try to start the Maldoror Mon, like a pheasant, not with spectacular effects but by polite conversation. That wouldn't be so easy. Professor Zeb Scott might be ignored, even if he was believed, by these business types mixing work with play, talking over the day's market report.
Also, we didn't feel last Saturday's exuberance. At Thaddy's, donning our disguises, we hadn't hacked around and behaved like a pair of crackpots. This time we got ready quietly, like athletes before a big game. Fake eyelashes, lipstick, smooth my skirt; check purse with weapon . . . No, we weren't brash and filled with laughter tonight, adolescents on a lark; but only worried about being ignored at Roscommon's, making fools of ourselves among that older more settled crowd. We could fail pitifully.
Destiny was a twitter in my gut, as I suited up: not sexy as all get-out, à la Millie the Mammary, poured, false hips et al, into Rita Joy's seven veils; but conservatively, tastefully, for the nonce.
Something else made me thoughtful.
Thad's older sister Lalla, away at college, left garments behind which she had outgrown; and they didn't fit me, they didn't appeal. So tonight I was wearing a prim outfit selected from Evelyne's wardrobe, straight skirt of a fine gray material, white blouse with brocade by the collar. My twin sister would have taken these things to college with her in September.

VII

Thaddy, face blackened again, hair fringed with gray, gave a grin at no one in particular.
—C'mon, Nilda . . . I'll call you Nilly for short. C'mon, Nilly, let's imbibe while discussing sociology.

And he marched forward, little guy in bulky Harris tweeds, which his parents brought him from a trip to Scotland, where his paternal grandmother's clan, Menteith, still existed. He took an absurd pipe from his mouth and gestured with it, leading on my perky self in tow. His shirt collar wasn't tucked properly: up in back, as if he bristled. But that didn't matter; he confronted the crowd like a honcho before camera lights. Luckily there were two free seats, bar stools with armrests, toward the middle.

Maury Potter, longtime fixture behind Roscommon's tap, showed the true discretion of bartenders by not laughing, or asking a fifty year-old Negro and his pretty young consort for their draft cards. Maury only worked his lips a little, dubious, as he put down the coasters.

—What'll it be?

No 'young man' routine, no absurd big words, from Professor Zeb Scott. He nodded:

—Martini on the rocks. Nilly, name your poison.

Sign language.

—Tom Collins, straight—said Zebby.

Maury stared at me an extra second, then back at my escort, and picked up a cocktail glass carefully.

The well-known academic took a wrinkled twenty from his lapel pocket and made to spread it on the counter. But I gave a gasp: my eyes went wide as a southern belle's when she sees a guy's fly open. I launched into sign language but then took the professor's hands in my own and whisked them toward my lap as though I meant foreplay. For I saw now what I did not see in the dark car on our way over: Thaddy's white hands. He forgot to blacken them too. So he'd have to sit at the bar all evening hands in pockets. What if we had another fight?

VIII

I sat on my barstool looking kind of pretty if I do say so myself—the kind of chick I might dig in a big way. But also sad, dragged down, because I felt—well, I felt like Evo might have been sitting here, staring out at this sweet life.

Professor Zeb Scott went on at some length listing the reasons why he didn't like to imbibe. He asked me to help nurse the martini. What a fund of profound comments the man was: facts, figures, smut about the New England town called Redemaine as compared with *Middletown, U.S.A.,* which we studied last semester in Mrs. Hebbel's P.O.D. class.

Looking around I blinked, wide-eyed, like someone with an eyelid condition. I dug the man's act and tried to show interest, the way poor women do across this wide earth, while sustaining a toothy smile.

The place was full on a Friday night. At the long bar, sitting and standing, maybe thirty people sipped appetizers and talked over the week's events while waiting to go in for dinner. Some I knew to say hi to, others by sight only. Curious thing: the familiar faces were like exceptions to the solid mass of insurance and real estate brokers, town merchants and small business owners, contractors, salesmen, professionals. Many were in the service sector, as agents and middlemen of one kind or another. They spent their lives selling something; and spent free time, until the liquor released their nerves, talking business. Here it wasn't the deep-voiced bravado with guffaws of the dive, Farrelly's beer joint: not the litany of grievances against a boss bent only on speed-up and docking your pay for a minute's slackness; on strictly regulated coffee break and bathroom time, or else your ass was fired. Next! Why, pay attention there, no talking in the shop. I pay you, now work—have your life's marrow extracted, in value . . . No; here at middle class Roscommon's the dollar was the only boss; and 'How may I serve you better?' the only slogan: whether it was about a magazine subscription, a new hairdo, or customized business forms for your firm. Over drinks men discussed the situation; the more enlightened went over market trends and sought to forecast tomorrow's climate, investor confidence, and talked about The Fed. All wanted better information, acumen, a way to make decisions which beat the competitor.

IX

Down the bar sat Mr. Zwergli, Bobby Zwergli's dad. Careful! I almost nodded at that friendly man; he'll think I'm giving him a tumble, and, driven here by the vicious cycle of a nagging wife, take me up on it. Mr. Zwergli ran Home & Garden Center there on Havilland Avenue beside Spring Glen Grammar. It didn't matter what you said to him: he stared at you and repeated your words, solemnly, with a nod. 'I'm reading the classics of Western literature in order to enter the mindset of a devil who murdered my twin sister, Mr. Zwergli.' And he would look at you, and wait patiently until you finished, and then say: 'So you're reading the classics of Western literature in order to enter the mindset of a devil who murdered your twin sister . . .' Now I thought Bobby's father couldn't really use the drink in his hand, since alcohol kills brain cells.

My gaze was drawn to a mid-thirtyish woman sizing me, the more youthful rival, up. Adele Fitchew smiled alongside her current admirer, a portly man in three-pieced suit. Bit past her bloom by now, Adele was still poured into her dress, like molten sex, 'ooooooeee! . . . But I won't tell you what happened to her son, Hershell, who kidnapped the Williams' small child that time . . . There's enough sadness.

I saw the Mount Sorrel Radio & TV repairman, Will Rinse. He wanted 20 dollars to get ignition static out of my car radio: housed in the Willys glove compartment. Seemed a bit steep: I got the old thing in a James Street junkyard for a buck.

Hey! There's Jocko Hake from our local radio station, WRED. 'The Loner' does a late night talk show with call-ins and Make-Believe Ballroom type music. Get with it, Jocko!

I recognized the proprietor of Plaza Bowling Academy, oh la la!, in other words the old duckpin alleys, which I found exciting as a kid. He was talking to his counterpart at the Music Box—next door along Redemaine Plaza arcade—where I, poor kid home for a rare weekend from prep school, once saw Cynthia Landis buying rock 'n roll records.

Sperling & Nussbaum's Department Store manager was also on hand. He worked his way up: used to fit me with sneaks every few weeks when I came in the store with my mom.

Oops, look out! I almost cried out, 'Hi, Mr. P.!' to Rolly Petrocchi who teaches biology and coaches tennis at the high school. He runs a small printing business from his home: 'Wedding Invitations, Graduation Thank You Notes, Liberal Discount, Personal Service', his ad would say in our Class of 1961 Yearbook. Hey, wait a minute! That's the sprightly if pre-lung cancerous Penny Grich by his side, on an off-night from Greek Club meetings. I wanted to tell Miss Grich I had started reading like ten libraries—hold your horses there: you're a deaf-mute scholar named Nilda, not the apostate Newell Gilbert, former Redemaine Red Renegade hurler, third-string.

Art Kilroyne's pa was a steady customer at Roscommon's: in his cups, I'm afraid. Hey. Last summer a few of us hung around his house on Gordiane—Chic, Franny Fofanna, John-O Kogan once in a while. Others dropped by. In those days Wil was lovelorn because Charlene Buffe, the Twirler, B-, did him dirt. Hey, Art-boy. Kilroynes' was cozy: front porch with rockers looking out on the avenue, games of pinochle and cribbage, Art's ma served us snacks. But one day Mr. Kilroyne put me out of the house when I quaffed a triple-shot glass of 'perfectly good whiskey' which he set on the counter for himself. I was laughing when I left, but I didn't go back.

One individual stood out because he looked so alone, oddball with highball. He didn't belong in this place, where you could always find him, or any other place. His presence heightened the sense of 'identity in non-identity' to that Friday night gathering: inhabitants of my hometown who had known one another since childhood. Each was an exception, each a personality so familiar to me, with foibles, like a rough sketch—if not a human wreck, or borderline psych case. But together they made up something more imposing: namely the American middle class I grew up among. Taken as a whole I guess they seemed unfamiliar to me, alien, deceptive . . . Anyway, the man's name was Murray Morton. His vocation was to compose strawberry floats, frappes, root beer ice cream sodas (brown cows), vanilla sodas with milk, or curdling raspberry ones. He did this for thirty years. I knew him since he worked for Mr. North at the Glendower. Oh! what silent disputes, what a frenzied ill-will between those two, barricaded behind the luncheon and candy counters when they got in each other's hair. No wonder Murray Morton took a bus routinely into the City, where he found relief from life's bed of nails on the somewhat softer, if lumpy, pallet of a Times Square prostitute. Get laid, Big Murr'! Brrr. A bundle of nerves even in his prime—with his sparse curly black hair, cheeks never quite shaven, thick glasses, fingers atremble as he spooned malt into a milkshake tumbler—now he was retired early due to a neurological disorder. So he told me one day when I saw him at a bus stop and pulled over to give him a ride. Syphilis? One wouldn't deem hard liquor indicated for a man in his state.

And I recognized a few others: Town Fathers who coached baseball teams in the different leagues. Also, some softball players came in after the big game. There was no dress code.

X

At half past ten things weren't going too well for the private eyes in disguise. Bar-goers ignored our act after a second glance. This wasn't Professor Zeb Scott's element—except for Miss Grich; and her intellect was like a wilted flower in Mr. P.'s lapel, as they went in for dinner. She was into her third pack of the day, and wracked with coughing, as he patted her back.

Then Thaddy almost blew it. He tried to barge his way into a real estate conversation going on beside us. Rots o' ruck! Ever heard one? It's like the Sirens' song heard by Odysseus: once you start with real estate, then good night to higher interests. On the day you die, you'll be trying to flip your plot in the cemetery.

Hey, what else is there to talk about? Nothing. The planet isn't beginning to wilt and die, and us along with it, from pollution. Right?

On the other side of us: two men talked over male-female relations. Birds, bees. There was chatter about 'building trust', 'timing', and 'exquisite sex'. It wasn't the real estate paradise—or was it? Hey, Adam and Eve, read your lease.

Sports talk. Celebrity talk: under the auspices of two TVs above the bar. Politics: distrust of young Kennedy in this Republican town. Snatches of local gossip; but no word, that I heard, about my sister or the Maldoror Mon.

Strange thing about our town: it has taboos. For instance: people vote for Mayor Tomao, but don't like to talk about him. Why? As I said, we grew up thinking the Simiglione clan was New England mafia; old stories, Zu Girolamo and Company lead to this conclusion, plus the long list of their area holdings: factories, warehouses, stores, public relations firm, truck rental and leasing, food processing, the town's only refuse haulage (how they got started: intimidation and worse, driving others from the field), Redemaine Dairy, Redemaine Construction. Then, after serving you in so many aspects of life, the Simigliones are there in death too, at Redemaine Funeral Home managed by Zu Girolamo's younger son, Dominic. Like clockwork the older son, Tomao, defeated Big Jim Floriani in the race for mayor. Why? Hey, we're Republicans. You don't like it? Lump it. Sound irrational? Hey, cash in, in full. But don't ask us to talk about it in public: like advertising our net worth.

Intermittently, through the years, townspeople did take notice of feuding between Simigliones and the prominent Irish family of Roscommon. In these weeks, after Evelyne's death, then violence at the high school, there was pressure on town authorities to find a killer. Was it the escaped convict: Jared Simms? The forces of law and order must stabilize the situation. But it wasn't done yet. And now new hostilities had broken out between Simigliones and Roscommons. By tonight, as Thad and I sat in the latters' restaurant, things had come to a head: Mayor Tomao named a replacement for the longtime Police Chief. But Rune Roscommon refused to leave, and he had backing too. Plus he had all the locks changed at Redemaine Police Station . . . Good idea!

So it was a standoff, sort of dramatic, and you might have thought: on people's minds.

Nope. They didn't go into it, that I heard. Instead: chatter, chatter, and more chatter. It was the American perpetual motion machine of smalltalk fueled by good life and comfort, satiety. Shallow, citizens, shallow. Why, you could wait till Doomsday and never hear a word other than self-interest, money and sex, sex and money. Pragmatic jabber. Or else a profound analysis of the current baseball season, latest box office hit at the movies, some TV show, the new restaurant just opened on Gordiane, food and more food. Gimme' a refill. Let's keep company.

Listen, Mac, we're everyday folks, we don't put on airs. Go with the flow! Hey, it's a free country, last I heard, I'll say what I darn well please. Let freedom ring, and let tongues wag. Until now no Hitler with his gang has come and pulled the wool over our eyes. Heck no. You can still speak your piece in the world's greatest country. Right? Am I right? Just take it easy.

As eleven p.m. approached, my eyes questioned Thaddy's. I gave a yawn, groggy from his martini. Also, I had to weewee again, like at Farrelly's; oh no, I wasn't going to risk that move. Prim Miss Nilda slips outside in the bushes? As for the sociology professor: if he kept his hands in his pockets much longer, the good people would think he was doing something fishy.

Call it a night? We were on the verge of bolting, admitting defeat. Then we caught a break.

XI

Professor Zeb Scott fell silent.

Looking around, I thought: time to mosey. This is getting us nowhere slow. My eyes flickered from TV back to drinkers and palaver along the bar. And, would you believe it, I had the strange feeling again: sort of blaming those on hand for my sister's death . . . I mean as if it happened *because* they were all happy as pigs in shit, squealing and grunting their pet idea, and that was what counted in life. But I was wrong. Forgive those words: they sound bitter.

Then I saw something: a vision. There was a man standing apart at the far end of the bar, the street side. He had on a dark blue uniform with two gold stripes at the cuff, and a red strip—town color—down his trouser seam. A policeman's cap sat high with a silver eagle pinned over the visor.

I nudged Ned with my elbow; whispered:

—What's this?

—Oh ho!—My friend gave a laugh.—Look at his eyebrows.

Come to think of it: those were the highest eyebrows I ever saw, halfway up his forehead, above two tiny eyes, like dots. Nose a squidge, red at the tip, in the pale pasty flesh. Nostrils tight: he wasn't in love, for all the redolent springtime; mouth, lips just a slit: did he breathe air?

Police Chief Rune Roscommon stood in full regalia, all in blue with gold buttons and a white silk tie. Well, he couldn't spend all his life barricaded inside the Police Station. He was a weighty man, burdened with the day's concerns, lock changing at Buckingham Palace, He waited to be recognized for what he was: a creature from a higher sphere, law-and-order heaven, where men like himself hover on eagle's wings. He looked so tense, uptight outa' sight. There was a killer on the loose who might strike again, and who was his responsibility. There was a town shaken by unrest. A week ago last Thursday, the top cop had sat as panelist at a Town Meeting alongside School Board Chairman Sorifa, Principal Sangesland, Rev. Charles Esmonde of Gordiane Baptist Church, an envoy from the Mayor's office, and the Town Attorney. Another riot almost broke out, like at the high school, but this time adults. Chief Roscommon's remarks fanned the flames.

A stirring account appeared under the headline MOB MEETING, and Hal Duggan's by-line, in this week's *News*. Shouts, boos, jeers, people out of their seats like a classroom in disorder; and too one-sided, the white perspective. Poor Sorifa sat petrified and would have decamped if he could. "Commie! Krushchev! Resign!" The blind Reverend Esmonde sat stonefaced. "Resign! Resign! Resign!" As one the hall rose and hollered at the top of its lungs demanding a capitulation from the School Board Chairman who stood for forbearance, negotiations to include all parties, fair play for black students. Rune Roscommon sat solemnly among the town leaders; he spoke once or twice; he looked tight as usual. Violence seemed likely despite the police presence. It was a community going wild. When Sorifa told the audience black people were 'just tired of Jim Crowism', and mentioned a Black Fathers Association's demand of $100,000 liability insurance per black student in Redemaine's public schools, there was such an outcry spectators made threatening gestures and rushed up on the stage. "Jew! Go back to Ausschwitz!" someone shouted; I don't know who. "Commie! Trotskyite!" Then Reverend Esmonde's plea for tolerance and brotherhood, speaking from his pain as a black man, met with more taunts and jeers; though some, wrote Hal Duggan, felt uneasy.

–Zip it, Blackie!

A blond woman shouted:

–Listen, you! I'm Treasurer of Galen Street PTA and I got a say in this! He's a red, and that's a fact. I know his kind. It's an international communist conspiracy to make our schools atheist!

–Yeah!

–She's right!

–Yeah!

Someone else stood up, waving:

—And what about that paranoid black kid who beat Ralphy Penna's son almost to death? The rules don't apply to him I guess!

This had happened: a bad incident after school. And reprisals were feared. Maybe another Emmett Till . . .

Back and forth the accusations flew. Now the black community was talking boycott, demonstrations, self-defense. They would send a call to national Civil Rights Movement leadership in the South: come help us, come open a northern front in this hell of a Rede-maine . . .

At the Town Meeting an enraged parent got up and yelled:

—I'm waiting for this rotten School Board to make one fair decision. Always Blacks this, and Blacks that, and Whites come in a distant second!

Then an Italian man stood up and bawled out:

—And they won't even make Columbus Day a school holiday!

Shouts, curses, more bleating cries:

—Curtail Sorifa's service!

—Commie! N–lover!

—Ayrab lover!

—Indian lover!

—Out! out! out! out! out! out!

Foot stamping.

XII

So it was: the Police Chief came to his brother Kenny's restaurant. On home turf he took his case to the people. Maybe he sought an informal vote of confidence. For in these days Mayor Tomao, a past master at manipulating public opinion, was using the chaotic situation to further his political ends. A 'Mayor's Committee' had been set up to consolidate Simiglione power in town, and remove the one real source of opposition to his policies: not the Democratic Party led by Thaddy's dad; but, rather, Police Chief Rune Roscommon.

For a good minute nobody noticed him. But then the bartender, Maury Potter, turning with a broad smile from the cash register, hailed the Chief.

–Ha ha! Look who's here, everybody! I propose a toast to a bonafide hometown hero. What'll it be, kids?

Chorus of hellos. Some clapping.

Professor Zeb Scott rubbed his hands.

–Time to make hay. Watch this.

But I hissed, appalled by his white hands:

–Put those back! Crazy fool.

Good thing all eyes were on The Chief.

–Shush, Nillie honey.–Professor grinned.–Now if the big man will just come within range. Lord, look at him: like Maurice Chevalier stuffed with straw.

XIII

Make no mistake: that Rune Roscommon was some consummate politician. He ventured a zombie grin: drunk as a skunk in a spelunk, of a Friday evening, beneath the unruffled exterior. When the law is blotto, it looks like this: a granite facade. Sober in the presence of police. Instead of engaging conversation with the enthusiasts nearest him, Chief opted to move along the bar greeting all and sundry. But he couldn't really bear that freight, so tanked up, and beaming, as he handed out executive handshakes. The effect was rather condescending, so the good old boys turned back to the business at hand.

Rune kept on coming: toward us. And Thaddy pounced:

–Police Chief! Hello, Sir! Over here . . . I'm Professor Zeppelin Scott from Tuskegee! Sociologist, Sir, egghead, you know the kind. Hm. We, my assistant Nilda Nightshade and myself, are here in Redemaine studying race relations, Sir, the recent events. That we are, hm. You won't mind if I ask you a few questions, Chief?

Well, this tirade seemed a bit impertinent. The town's highest ranking police officer looked at the nodding black scholar in tweeds. Unforgettable. Chief's eyebrows soared higher, higher toward the silver eagle insignia on his cap. His bunghole of a mouth grew smaller, tighter, and emitted what seemed the day's order:

–We are urging calm, restraint.

–Yessir! Makes sense. Festering situation, hm, outside agitators and all that. Rabble rousers from the Urban League.

Meanwhile I tried to blink coquettishly at the middle-aged man in uniform. I gave that male specimen my most seductive grin, and he stood there looking dour. I always liked him as a person.

—Who is . . . she?

—Like I said, Sir, Nilda Nightshade. She's a doctoral candidate, in criminology, and my capable assistant. Stone deaf. Right, Nillie?

The lawman asked:

—How can she be deaf and going for her doctorate?

—She's one of the most brilliant minds in Alabama.

I threw in some sign language to prove it.

Roscommon looked me over, and said, with a touch of brogue from his faroff Irish boyhood:

—Is she now.

—Chief, Sir, is it true the Mayor wants your job, but you changed all the locks at the Police Station?

—Who said so?

Professor Scott laughed, and rolled his eyes upward.

—Tell the truth, Chief, no forked tongues. Who's to blame for what is happening in Redemaine? Is it the Blacks, or the Whites?

Now people were more interested. There was a hush along the bar, as a couple dozen customers tuned into our conversation, and a thoughtful Maury Potter turned down the ballgame from the West Coast on two TVs. All awaited Chief Roscommon's answer. That man of integrity looked some more at his black questioner, then at his white constituency, and said:

—Blacks . . . in part.

—Sir, I thank you for your candor. But why say Blacks?

—They provoked it.

—How?

Till now Chief's replies were brief and to the point, like belches. But he felt himself on the hot seat with everybody watching. He began to heat up:

—Black girls, taunting, squaring off in the high school lobby. Hard to control.

—What about ZBKs in their frat jackets, Sir?

—What about them?

—Seven, eight abreast along the school corridor: vigilante patrols.

—Emotional kids.

—Well what about the Town Meeting last week? I heard it was you who got emotional, Chief.

–Doing my duty.

–You said to a Black in the audience, a respected educator like myself: 'Now just a minute, sonny boy'.

–He was yelling at me. I don't like being pushed around. –Rune Roscommon looked ever so fed up, even threatening, for an instant. –Do you?

–No, Sir! –said the 5'3" professor. –What was he yelling?

–You're not sensitive to this, to that . . . Whites did this to my daughter, they did that . . . Give us two black members on the School Board at once, or else!

–Ay, and then you told the man, a teacher at the junior college, to shut his face, or else! 'I'm the Police Chief, I'll have your likes arrested.' Did you, Sir? Do I misrepresent?

–He made accusations. Racism, police brutality. I don't like it! He said I 'called out the canine corps'–

–Did you?

–It was the needed thing. Crowd control, a visible show of force. Take statements, make arrests: put some fear of God into those crazy tecnagers.

–Hm! said Professor Zeb Scott. Good thing there are no crazy teenagers around here right now. They might take it amiss, Chief.

–Let them! They make a powder keg out of their own high school where they go to study and learn. Skirmishing all day long, and it still goes on. And all the time our Mayor won't have the schools closed, or either of the junior highs, where it's hot too. No cancelling a school day because it could reflect badly on him. And he must cover his ass of course. Wants to be Lieutenant Governor someday. But not only him: the town as a whole wants to sweep this mess under the carpet and deny reality. And so the school administration goes on putting up with students' brashness, intimidation tactics. Why, they wander the halls unchallenged while scared teachers run into the faculty lounge. Security remains lax. Outside agitators come in and have a field day. Commies! Hell, we ought to load the disruptive students in buses and send them home with a police escort.

–Home? Or a concentration camp?

–Look, Smarty: if you insist, it could come to that.

–Sir, I believe it. You lost your temper at an innocent Town Meeting.

–Innocent! They were reds, troublemakers.

–Blew your cool. Shook up.

—Agitprop, a commando! Knew what they were doing too. One stood up and pointed a finger: 'All the racist Bull Connors ain't down South in Birmingham!' That's what he said, accusing me in front of everybody. I couldn't let it pass.

—Good for you.

—Look here, I'm no bigot. Never been a bigot in my life! It's just that all these people moving out here from the City got to respect the law, and stay calm. They're not the bosses, not our Commissars, not yet! We gave them a piece of Harmonium section, or they took it, flooding the town. There's plenty in Greenwood, too. Next thing they'll want to live in Spring Glen!

—Perish the thought. Spring Glen a Gold Coast.

—Look, just don't come around here upsetting decent folk with a lot of Smarty-pants talk, insults, demands. Stay put, or else. Mind your own beeswax!

Applause at the bar.

—Hear hear!

—Sock it to 'im, Rune.

—Got a rocket in his pocket!

—Agitators, 'er just plain 'tators? Ha ha ha! I'm a funny guy!

The Police Chief nodded, on the verge of turning away. Clearly he wanted this unprogrammed interview to end. In a moment the official pose could collapse: no more questions like a wrecking ball on the granite facade.

I saw Professor Zeb hadn't done yet, but meant to poke the good man's ribs some more, jarring his pose. So I put the martini glass to my mentor's lips and made him sip—an act Roscommon watched with interest.

XIV

The visiting scholar gave a low, mocking laugh.

—Say, uh, Chief—

—What now?

—We're thankful for your frankness, and taking time today. There's just one other little item.

Frowning, the bulky law enforcement officer glanced around. Yes, a bit more of this grilling by a black man, an intruder, and he would run short of patience. Who's in charge here? . . . So I smiled coyly at the handsome devil. And then, turning to my teacher from Tuskegee, gave Professor Zeb a tweek on the cheek. Baby, we could get ourselves run out of here on a rail, or start another brawl like at Farrelly's.

Then, just my luck: a bit of Thaddy's blacking, a smudge came off on my southern bell fingers. The lawman saw, and his eyebrows went up another notch, if that was possible. His tiny eyes spoke volumes: who the *di*vil are these two jokers? FBI in disguise, dressed up like a couple of maniacs, and here in Redemaine to investigate *him?!* Chief's face went pale; he looked at us with more interest. Now maybe he would cooperate.

Professor Zeb Scott never noticed. He just kept on asking fussy questions, a regular interrogation, Police Chief on hot seat. And why? Again he meant to place a racially mixed couple on public display, and lure a lone killer from the psychopathic lair. But he also got carried away. Oh, it wasn't the first time I'd seen Thad Floriani thrilled by his own act, on a high horse. Now he waded in and stirred up the usual manias. In that Roscommon's crowd there were phobias as old as the genocide of indigenous peoples, and beginnings of black slavery: four centuries ago when the European psyche came up with racism to sanction economic exploitation; and from one generation to the next the cultural aspects were developed. No wonder our culture at its best is a blighted affair. Small. Accept oppression, serve the system, conform—or die in silence. You want to be a sincere writer? Principled? Tell the truth? Good luck to you. Someday the American stables will be cleaned; but for now, tonight at Roscommon's Tavern, the same ancient hatred threw off sparks. A volcano sputtered beneath the everyday, hail-fellow-well-met surface of things.

XV

—Well then, Sherl' . . . I mean Mr. Chief Sir: what can you tell us about the Evelyne Gilbert case? What light can you shed? Are there clues? Has progress been made?

—Progress.

Chief worked his lips.

—Is Jame Hayes under suspicion?

—N-no.

—Will the mystery be solved?

—We have extra funds, and a special task force working fulltime.

Under the bar stool I gave Professor a little kick, love tap, with my pump. We were treading on thin ice. I wasn't sure why, but this new tack by Zebbeth, more than questions about race relations, caused a tension and seemed to ruffle our Redemaine Police Chief.

—Can Jared Simms have done it?

—Who?

—The escaped prisoner from Condor.

Listening to them, I threw in my two cents of sign language. This caused a man named Holt Nairn, local landscapist—not painter but lawn mower, weeder and hedge trimmer—to stare at me and scratch his head. He piped up:

—Say . . . She's supposed to be deef.

—What's that, young man?—said Professor Zeb, a third Nairn's age.—Don't worry, she's deaf as a stump. Aincha', Nillie? But she reads lips, and wants to tell us something. Tell you, Chief, in particular. I know you aren't deaf and dumb. These past few nights Nill and I have been conducting research on Maldoror Drive. And we saw something strange up there: a masked man driving a Cobra racing car, without license plates. Any comment, Chief?

At this Roscommon seemed to buck, slightly. Why? His eyes, two black dots, narrowed:

—Where did you say you're from? Zebulun—

—Professor *Zep*pclin Scott of Tuskegee. You know what, Sir? I've reached the conclusion your town is a mess. All 35.5 square miles of it. Just look! Frustration in the black community: it reaches a boiling point as kids have no hope, and adults feel their upward mobility is thwarted by skin color. No opportunity! And white youth too: if not college bound, then where? The high school is overcrowded: how many young souls get lost in the cracks? Blacks are like an island in a hostile sea. Black girls get abused. A white student cried 'Black bitch!' at a girl he felt up in passing along the hallway. And that isn't the ugliest epithet being flung around. What about this, Sir? With due respect for your position: are you on the case? Or do you deny, like other honest citizens, that Blacks are the historic victims, and they are being revictimized right here in our town? Yes or no? . . . And so I ask you: might the Gilbert murder have a political motivation? Not merely some psycho knifer but in fact done on purpose to stir up racial hatred, and put the onus of blame on Blacks; though to suspect Jame Hayes is absurd, if only subconsciously; blame the black community; blame the entire African race; that is, blame the victim. And then rub it in: call 'em names, sonny boy, Shortnin', watermelon eater. It's embarrassing, vulgar, offensive. It's shameful! Try to take a man's dignity away, and make him hate too! Divide and conquer. And the thing was done by a white provocateur . . . Is it possible, Sir? Will there be other murders, Sir, one more grisly than the next? Can it be? Last week the good Hal Duggan at *Our Town News* put forth a 'pattern theory' in his editorial, saying this could be a serial killer. Which is it: the Redemaine Ripper? or a white racist conspiracy? The plan was hatched by the Ku Klux Klan perhaps: as a way to keep us all hating, separated, unable to love worth a damn anymore, unable to unite, unable to help one another out, and fight the bad thing, side by side. For it is here among us, in our system, like mosquito bites, like Erinyes, ha ha! Know what that is? Ha ha! Yes? No? And the KKK did it, or some other philanthropic group. Say: are there KKK in this state, Sir? We got 'em down in 'Bama, Sir, got 'em bad down there, yep, you betcha'. Whole state's infested. But what about this New England town? What about these upstanding citizens sitting here in this bar tonight? All these undiluted Americans, white as a sheet with bleach: are there Klan members sitting quietly among us? No? Yes? Ha ha!

XVI

Well, I was kicking Scott of Tuskegee pretty hard by this time. I kicked to the rhythm of his lofty phrases, which might get us in a peck of trouble. You'd think I was spurring a horse: the way Professor Zeb talked louder, more recklessly, as I kicked. Why, that gentle little guy, a mumbling academic who spent his life in libraries: he fairly shouted at Rune Roscommon. But I felt so sorry for the poor Police Chief in his cups—if you saw him just then, grayish, bloated up, with shaky hands, and that childish look of alcoholics . . . Just his luck to cross Professor's path tonight when Zebby was on a soapbox.

Whew! That Professor Zeb Scott of Tuskegee was something else! I'll tell you one thing: he had a demon in him. It reminded me of Thad Floriani's harangue from a cafeteria table while a riot was in progress: gone kaflooey, and to hell with it. The fool puffs himself up on matters of principle. Look at him: how he plays the hero by telling the truth. Hardly your typical FBI; no, not like a G-man at all, with this fun and games approach.

I think many found his words shocking.

When he finally paused for air, there was a burst of protest:

—No! No!

—That's not right!

—All wrong, you nitwit!

—Cynic!

—Shut your frigging mouth or I'll shut it for you.

—What a dimwit, psss.

—What's the little twirp saying now?

—Insulting Rune.

—That so? I'll break his head open. Hey there, numbskull. Pipe down!

—Yeah, shut yer' trap.

—Too many words. I can't stand all those words. Hey, Maury, put up the TV a little, willya'? My nerves can't take all these words.

—Who let the communist in here?

—Goddamned atheist. Sounds like one.

—Hey, Maury! I said turn the TV up louder. Cripes, turn 'em both up. All this claptrap is worse than my wife! Damn words, can't stand it.

—Claptrap, you can say that again. You there! If you don't like it, you can stuff it.

—Go back to Moscow. Damn Trot.

—Yeah, zip it, or I'll clip it.

—What's he got to gain by insulting everybody?

The hard drinkers sang their Hallelujah Chorus.

And do you think this—the implicit threat, the sheer volume—could daunt or deter the eminent scholar? Was Professor Zeb Scott of Tuskegee a scaredy-cat? Guess again. He waited with a little smirk on his pouty face: oily pimples aglitter through the charcoal makeup. He looked like he swallowed a mouse. Then he took a

hand out of his pocket, raised his arm toward them and, pointing, said calmly:
  —Know thyself.
  —Huh?
  Murmurs.
  —You don't know yourself.
  —We don't?
  —You aren't what you seem.
  —We're not?

XVII

A gasp.
Gasps.
Sodden heads raised. Bleary eyes went wide.
The dialogue died abruptly. For Thaddy, so intent on making his point, had let the cat out of the bag.
All stared at his white hand.
He stared at it.
He pulled out the other: as if he couldn't believe it either. He compared the two.
So . . . white hands. So it was all a trick: to put one over on honest citizens.
  —Hm, said a surprised Zeb Scott of Tuskegee.
  —Hm, said the thirty dedicated drunkards in Roscommon's Tavern.

XVIII

There was silence. I waited, aghast, to see what would happen next.
Then Rinse, the Mt. Sorrel electrician, shook his head and said:
  —C'mon, boys. Let's ride these two no-good polecats out of here on a rail.

And Bobby Zwergli's dad, from the Home & Garden Center near Spring Glen Grammar, said:

—So you want to ride these two no-good polecats out of here on a rail.

Mr. Zwergli nodded thoughtfully. I think the last thing he needed was a drink.

But Professor Zeb Scott said:

—Now, fellas: respect your elders.

Down the bar Murray Morton, syphilitic soda jerk, said:

—Elder schmelder.

Professor:

—You wouldn't hurt a girl, would you?

Nairn, the landscape gardener, said:

—Come to think of it, I'll bet you she ain't a girl. I been sniffing something funny all night. And maybe she can talk too!

He reached over and pinched me.

—Ouch!

—See that? said Nairn. She can talk too.

Rinse:

—I think these two dirty dogs need to be tarred and feathered and carried to The Dump. Toss 'em there for the rats and vultures. You know what I mean.

Mr. Zwergli:

—So you think these two dirty dogs need to be tarred and feathered and carried to The Dump and tossed there for the rats and vultures. I know what you mean.

Jocko Hake, 'The Loner' from WRED, got off his barstool with a healthy burp, and, yawning and stretching, said:

—That's a good one. Dagnabit, that one's on us. Well, folks, I have a radio show to do. You men keep it in your pants: I know you all got the hots for Miss Nilda here.

—See you later, Jocko!

—Hey, babe, catch you on the airwaves.

—Golly!—said the Sperling and Nussbaum Department Store manager, Mr. Schultheiss, who looked me over.—Boys, I never saw a real live drag queen. Is it the School Board Chairman?

Will Rinse had an evil leer:

—Maybe it's his sister.

By the exit Jocko waved to his fans, and called back:

—Whatchoo' think, Rune? That sexual pervert why our schools in shambles?

Then—there's one in every crowd—somebody I didn't know said: —I don't mind your everyday n——s, some'ums okay. What I can't stand is a white one.

Things were bad enough without Thaddy just asking for it. He stared in Rinse's evil eye, and said:

—You KKK, boss?

Rinse:

—PhD., we're going to put you and Pickadilly Nilly in the back of my van, trussed like two hogs for the slaughter, and drive you to The Dump and incinerate you with the rest of today's garbage.

—So you're going to put PhD. and Pickadilly Nillie in the back of your van, trussed like two hogs for the slaughter, and drive them to The Dump and incinerate them with the rest of today's garbage.

Then Thaddy did another unwise thing. He shook his hands in Rune Roscommon's adipose face, and said:

—Do you see these, Sir? They're the same color as KKK hands, and I'm ashamed of them.

Will Rinse had a pair of white hands too. And, rising, with a nod at Nairn, he made a neck-wringing gesture at my friend.

You know, I think they meant business. Rune, the fuzz, was looking on, but what of it? Varmints aren't protected by game laws.

Luckily the bartender, Maury Potter, was at his post, and said: —Now now, Will . . . Holt . . . —He turned to Professor Zeb Scott and Miss Nilda Nightshade, doctoral candidate, and told us:—It's time you two lovebirds flew the coop. Run along now if you know what's good for you.

Rinse, serious:

—Cut out your gizzards!

In a grand finale of sign language I urged my mentor to think it over. Would you believe he still seemed unready to leave? So my hands dropped the dactylological baloney (!) and went for the scruff of Professor Zeb Scott's neck. There were cheers, a chorus of good old boy laughter, as I set the little man with the big mouth on his path, and rode him like a dogey out the door.

We made our graceful exit.

Behind us: a roar of laughter.

—Ha! ha! ha! Lookatemgo!

–Ha ha! This one's on us, Jocko! Ha!

–What a scream! You see those two rascals hightail it outa' here? Ha! ha! ha!

–Too much!

–Where'd they come from anyway? Hey, Maury!

Finally Rune Roscommon broke a grin, and said:

–Set 'em up, bartender. This round's on me.

More laughter, jeers, more sarcasm at our expense. Nervous energy releasing.

And yet ... The laughter didn't sound all that easy to me, back there, inside Roscommon's Tavern. Not your typical case of the giggles; a bit forced–so I sensed, as Thad and I walked toward the car, and their squawking, like crows enjoying a bawdy story, still reached our ears. I guess when you're that tight, it can hurt to laugh.

XIX

I report facts. How I give them–form, central conflict, theme–is my business. But you must believe every detail in my hometown story is true. There is no image, incident, scene, quote, that did not happen exactly as I tell it. What would Plato say, after he banished lying poets from his own hometown, if he caught me in a fib? No way. I invent nothing. Nor do I embroider.

I say this because what comes next is so utterly bizarre, macabre, disgusting, if you will: a psychopathologist will believe it, but not Gentle Reader. Such a thing has no more place in conscious life, our polite society, than in healthy art, which this is. But what can I do? I am bound by the facts to tell what happened: not parrot the official account, *Redemaine Annals* by that historiographical titan, Mr. Marsden Dale, who gave my senior thesis, written five years ago in 7th grade, a B+.

No, sir. If you want the truth you must leave the learned Dale to his shelf, and read Newell Gilbert's *récit* which doesn't tidy up things.

And that, as you shall now see, is the understatement of the year 1961.

XX

As midnight neared Thad Floriani and I rode along Havilland Avenue toward Spring Glen in his mom's green Pontiac—which dropped its transmission that time we drove into the City after telling people we would 'pick up some chicks and have a blast'; but we spent the evening looking for a mechanic.

Now passing the Grammar School we laughed like a pair of hyenas: I guess because we made it out of Roscommon's on our feet, not a rail. And we weren't ignored. Blowing our cover as an interracial couple wouldn't help lure my sister's killer back to Maldoror Drive; but hey, we got our kicks, and made a point or two. The look on Rune Roscommon's face was simply precious.

Thaddy was the excitable type on his better days. And I wasn't likely to have my beauty sleep after nearly getting tarred and feathered. So we cruised around the quiet Spring Glen streets. By the brook on Santa Fe we got out and breathed in the air laden with suburban vegetation, rustling trees, shrubs, flower beds; dewy grass with long night crawlers that come out easy if you squeeze them, and make good bait for the Water Company. The brook gurgled its way through backyards, past patios, gardens of the affluent neighborhood. The night air was so fragrant and inviting: you wonder how such a kindly environment could produce the horrors that were a few minutes away.

Then we rode slowly up Santa Fe Avenue—not an avenue, but a homey street on a hill, overhung with elms and maples. We passed the sacred precinct dedicated to Artemis of my first crush, Gemma: a large Tudor house up there on Lorelei; then over to Spring Garden where my piano teacher, Miss Romney, had me in a love-hate relationship for four long years—hate for her piano lessons, 'Knight Ruppert' and 'Für Elise', and love for her homemade cookies.

On up the hill we went and turned left along Crest Road where the millionaires live: stingiest of the stingy at Halloween. What they need is a good trick.

XXI

And then . . . Leave it to my strange friend. He turned off Crest onto Fenbrook Terrace. This street, rarely visited by Spring Glen boys on their bicycles, looked out over The Dump aglow in the distance: our town junkyard lit here and there with fires like the Greek camp on the plain before Troy. Fenbrook dead-ended at the older, more pretentious of our cemeteries with its monuments and la-di-da mausoleums. My sister was the first Gilbert buried here: our parents being Southerners who came North during the 'Thirties. But my mother wanted to be buried in the South.

I jolted forward.

−Look!

−What?

We had turned and were going slowly alongside the cemetery. I put a hand on Thad's arm, and said low:

−Just keep on.

−Why the−?

I pointed.

−That's his car.

−Whose?

−My masked driver, Maldoror Mon, whoever he is.

The Cobra sat there, sleek, without plates. It was parked by the chest-high barrier of old, dark red bricks covered with ivy.

We approached and rode by: nobody at the wheel. Did The Mon live around here−not in a West Hills cave? He wouldn't leave an illegal vehicle parked by the sidewalk . . . Was he paying a visit to the graveyard at midnight? If so, he would see passing headlights, unless too busy−doing what?

Thad turned left at the next corner, coasted half a block, parked, doused the lights. It was quiet up there. Had The Mon heard us?

−Shhh.

How to open a car door in the late night silence and not make a racket?

Out we came, like paratroopers, on the driver's side. It seems nearly being lynched by the mob in Roscommon's was not enough for one night. We must also check up on a homocidal horror moonlighting as a body snatcher.

By the brick wall I cupped my hands like a stirrup for Thaddy. He slipped over. How little he weighed. For me, in a straight skirt, it wasn't so easy. My kingdom for a pair of gym shorts and sneaks. Geez! I got a run in my stocking . . . Well, have at 'im: the interracial couple takes it to the racist killer haunting Fenbrook Cemetery at midnight–where he went fascinated by his victim? Care to dance?

I touched the sheath knife in my garter, and whispered to Thad:

–Gun cocked, youngblood?

–It is, dearie.

Ow! Smack against a tombstone. Good thing I had on a jockstrap over my rayon panties.

We went in the dark graveyard.

XXII

From tomb to tomb I took the lead as my mentor in criminology hung back a little. A lonely church bell tolled across the sleeping town. Someone died tonight? Crouched forward we moved on my twin sister's fresh grave, and I felt a tinge of hatred in my resolve. Not quite like Detective Johnny Dollar: 'I hate hard . . . and I hate killers!' When I thought of Evelyne's murderer as a sick person, and not a devil, I couldn't hate. Then I hated, let's say, a relation. Reality is a bit more complicated, than a radio show.

Over there, in the cool earth, my sister lay in her coffin.

Who is to blame?

Behind me Thaddy barked his shin on a headstone, tripped, cursed in a whisper. Here come the citizen arresters: me in my skirt, blouse, pumps; Big T in his tweeds, cordovans, pinstriped poplin shirt with sleeve garters and suspenders. Hey, this wasn't the Debate Club. Skinny academic kicks rump.

At first we didn't see our prime suspect. Maldoror Mon, Jared Simms, whoever you are: come out of that grave with your hands up. And the question remained: did Cobra like to visit my sister? A hot date! If so, then he's the one? Prove it. Perhaps he had an innocent crush on her. Many did, you know, among the vocational training students: kids with police records, on down the social ladder. They loved Evo. Mills Brooks for one, the scion of Ojibwa, had it bad for

Evelyne Gilbert; and so he hung all over me with his cigarette breath in morning homeroom. Even Ray-Guy was sweet on her; it made him stranger. Others. As for this off-hours visitant, psycho in mask, he may have fallen in love with the dead girl *qua* dead; there's a name for that. He made sentimental journeys to the cemetery. But what does it prove?

As we drew near, a stone's throw away, I stopped and sniffed. There it was: same scent as at the radio relay tower, on a leaf of shrubbery a few nights after her funeral. Pungent smell, pharmaceutical. In my mind came images of summer, the beach, a tan, a sunburn . . . your body hot and cold later. What did you take from the medicine cabinet?

Nearing the grave we couldn't make out what was happening. Sort of filliping my nose, I wrinkled it. I put a hand to Thad's panting chest: so cool at Farrelly's and Roscommon's, a little shook up now. He murmured:

—Skin cream.

Sure, skin cream. So this ghost went in for sunbathing. Maybe he took off his mask at the beach club, jiving honies.

XXIII

We drew closer. In the darkness we still didn't see movement. But, a few plots away, I knew her grave was open: an oblong hole, black, not grass . . . This gave me a sinking feeling. On the verge of action I thought about my mother: we feared her test results would say cancer. Through boyhood I hardly gave my mom a second thought. Took her for granted. Why? Because she loved me, she was sure. She stood by us through childhood: when I was wrong, and when I was right. Now who would stand by her?

Creeping forward, closer, we lurked behind a marble slab adjacent to the one that read: GILBERT. I wanted to tell Thaddy: watch it, he has a knife. But we were too close to whisper.

Then we saw something . . . yes, uncanny, not nice. But what? Darkness made it hard to tell. The near-full moon hid its face behind a high-riding cloud: like a child in a movie theater when the scene gets too scary. Something unearthly was going on at Evelyne

Gilbert's grave. What was it? A romantic individual? Necrophilia anyone?

I rose, and peered over a wide marker by the neighbors' plot. There was movement in the grave. The soil had been dug out and heaped to one side; and the digger, in the hole, was hard at work. A grave robber? Was the coffin open? Seemed a bit late to take the corpse's organs gone stale, in death, for dissection or resale. Maybe this ghoul had a scientific bent?

Arms moved in the dark. A huge maggot worked away, doing its filthy business on a saint. So my beautiful sister was subjected to some further outrage as this vermin made little human grunts, and ate. Raid the fridge! Make yourself at home. But were those sexual huffs and puffs? Not precisely. They had a job to do, though not normal business hours.

Well then . . . what? Just keep my distance, stay put, while he did that to Lady?

No.

XXIV

Now I had the knife in hand, unsheathed; and the time had come to use it. Knife the knifer. And never mind what happened to me after: the legal consequences. He was in our grasp.

So I stood up, crept forward, closer, toward the rim. Heu! Stubbed my toe on the plot's corner stone.

The grave robber's head looked up, over the edge—the mask! What a case of nerves he had: like a wild animal in man's backyard, which is deadlier than the jungle.

I had my own wildness. Maybe it confused The Mon to see a young woman, in a white blouse, skirt ridden up over her knees, come leaping in the open grave on top of him. Maybe he hadn't read *Wuthering Heights* in Miss Grich's English class. He stared as I plunged my knife and it glanced off the mask like armor and flew out of my hand.

Arms strained. Fists flew. Oh, what a thing it was to grapple with that iron body in black leather. A weight lifter? Lifeless mask, mad eyes: one sparkled, the other a blank. He gained the upper hand and pinned me against the squooshy substance in a gown which was once my sister.

He tried to pin me, the woman, down, and mount. Was this to be a rape by proxy, as the living stand in for the dead? We'd better let the experts tackle psychological aspects.

—Shoot him! Shoot the monster!

—I could hit you!

Up above Thaddy jumped around.

—Never mind! You've got the gun: use it!

—But I can't see!

Maldoror Mon gave pause. He looked over his shoulder at the black man peering down at us, and the pistol. He was trying to grab my neck in a stranglehold, but he had to fend off punches. In those instants I fought in a frenzy.

Valiant Thaddy dove in too, on top, cuffing with the gun butt to no effect. But the black face scared The Mon, who roared like a wounded bear. This madman could fight furiously, but could not stand to be touched. An elbow thrust, upward, on the solar plexus, winded my friend and hung him out to dry.

But this gave me a chance to counter. Instead of kicking, throwing body punches, writhing beneath The Mon, I changed tactics. I clutched at the mask.

My fingers couldn't get a grip. Was that a mask? It was on tight. Tight. Then, as the moon came out, I saw better and caught hold of its rim and held on. As the monster turned from Thad to pound me some more, I hollered and endured. I dug my nails beneath the expressionless mask, and yanked it off.

Oh! oh! oh!

I yell at the top of my lungs writing this, at the memory. Oh! oh! But that night, struggling wildly in my sister's grave, I grew quiet at the sight, and shuddered. A tingle of horror went down my spine when I saw what surpasses my capacity to tell.

It was a badly burnt face, but not only. It was a face burnt beyond recognition, and plastic surgery, long ago, all hard interlacing scars now—which *also* had a massive tumor roiling from within and distending it. The face had become a tumor: not smooth but lava-like, in layers. It went beyond everything: the guts of the monster, on display. The one good eye stared pointblank into mine. Oh! How I wanted to put the mask back on him. But I held onto it with both hands: grasping the nasty thing for dear life, sticking it in his ugly face, using it to parry his punches.

And what did I do then? Believe it if you can. I laughed. I laughed loud, mad, at that craggy mess. I hooted, shouted:

–Go on, you big pizza pie face! What horror are you going to cook up next because someone did this horror to you and so you hate life and people and anything beautiful and loving, like my sister! You weenie! You freak! Nature hates you and wishes she never had a date with you. Ha ha! I give you Worst Looking in the Redemaine High Class of 1961 Yearbook! Ha ha ha ha! I laugh right in your grouchy sourpuss, your bare mask beneath a metal one. I hate– not you, you noodge, you're not worth it–I hate what it was that did this to you!

I ranted what came into my head. I screamed for the silent cemetery and Spring Glen, my hometown and all America to hear. And then I laughed again and–and put his mask on my own face!

I stared up at the Maldoror Mon who had stopped pounding me. Grown thoughtful. And his response?

I wouldn't give him back his mask. I laughed low, devilish, from inside it; and then sang out the way kids do when they tease:

–Nanh-nanh-nananhnanh!

That ought to spook the sonuvabitch. Give him some of his own medicine.

And what did he do?

With a backward sweep of the arm he cleared Thaddy from his path. He struggled up, and got his bearings. I don't know why he kicked back dirt clods on me, and Evelyne Gilbert's open coffin. And then, turning away, baldfaced as hell, an eyesore for our universe, he ran.

XXV

There he went vaulting among the tombs. Lickety-split he made a dash for the Cobra. Oh, he could knife an innocent girl to death; he could do that; but the sucker couldn't stand up and face reality. Ran away. In denial.

I climbed out after him. Pulling up my rumpled skirt like a girl who means business, straightening my stockings which had a run like the Mississippi Delta, I made ready to give chase. Ollyollyinfree! But first I shook a dazed Thaddy by the shoulder and barked:

–Get the car! Go get it! Bring it round!

Hell, we should have checked whether that loser left his keys in the ignition, and swiped 'em. Gotcha' back, serves your sorry ass right.

Up ahead I saw the fellow move amid tombstones like a dolphin in the moonlight. But he fell and went sprawling. Hurt himself.

I trotted along in my skirt and torn blouse. In the scuffle I had taken hits on my face. Later I would feel and show them. Right now I just felt pounded, and worked up, with a taste of blood in my mouth. So I came up and started kicking The Mon where he lay stunned. I wished my lady's pumps were heavy boots to kick his face in; but, you know, it was already done.

That was his fear too. To the face. Now he was more afraid than I was, and made noises like a child. With difficulty he was getting up. My hunter's instinct, unleashed, wanted to kill the killer! I could have kayoed him then; but from–what? deep disgust, or dare I say pity? I did not want to touch him, much less sink my fist into that putty face. If I had a club I would have brained the boy. Put him out of his misery.

Then off we went again: him in the lead. We ran the broken field among those headstones. Ow! Barked my shin . . . He drew away, but I needed to stick near him: Peter had to catch this wolf. I didn't know what I was doing just then, or how to go about it. Kind of awkward running the hurdles while holding up your skirt, dearie, stockings bunched on ankles.

By the brick barrier I latched on and tried to haul him back, while he flailed and sort of whined. Still he hadn't uttered a human word. Also: not having his mask sort of took the fight out of him.

–Not so fast, Bub. Just simmer down. You and me got a date at the police station.

–Roarrrr!

The Mon's face went up, like a bear stung by a bee on his penis, and he roared. Wide-eyed he looked at me: the girl who fought, and talked, like a guy. What's this world coming to?

As for myself, I stared at the spectacle: his porridge face.

–RoaOOrrr'!

I shook my head:
—So that's all you've got to say for yourself?
Did the cancer make him unable to talk? For an instant I thought
that mishmash was a mask as well: his ugly mug tinted grayish-pink
by a streetlamp, and disfigured by sarcoma. What made it worse was
that he had no hair, no eyebrows.
Now we stood there like a pair of old acquaintances. He clambered up. I dragged him back. I should've taken a brick and conked
him one. Out. Then at our mercy. Instead I delayed his getaway
while Thad provided valet service. Mistake! Mon swung round and
caught me on the neck. I fell to one knee choking. He had a right up-
percut like Kid Gavilan.
Over the ivy-covered wall he dove. And I went after: even as I up-
chucked popcorn and pretzels munched on when nobody would talk
to us during happy hour at Roscommon's.
On went the Cobra ignition.
Round the corner, bright lights blaring, came Thaddy in his
mom's Pontiac.

XXVI

Lights off, the Cobra slid away like a snake in the dark.
With a screech we pursued and went careening through the Spring
Glen streets at one p.m. Down Old Farm Road we flew and past the
ritzy sector with its homes set back from Crest Road under the tall
oaks. Then we swung onto Dyre Club Lane. As a boy I liked to ride
these blocks on my bike, feeling free. Now look what a thing had
grown up in our midst.
Suddenly, in front of the country club, Cobra hung a sharp left.
The sportscar entered a driveway. House on the Hill!
We sped past. It took a moment to turn around. And then, as we
tried to follow and gain entry—too late! A metal gate barred the way
to that place, the former Shetland Estate.
But he entered. Did the Maldoror Mon live here?
Also: what was the music we heard? Strains of an old 'Twenties
tune, Rudy Vallee wafted to our hearing the length of the long driveway overhung with trees.

Maybe The Mon was going dancing? He had activated the electronic gate, and withdrew behind it, like a rat in its hole. Rather fancy, luxurious, for a rathole.

XXVII

By now Thaddy looked a bit the worse for wear. He shook his head and said:

—Nilda dearie, let's call it a night.

But he was the rotogravure compared to me, face swollen, body battered, bruises.

—No, sir.

—No?—Thad gave his goofy stare.—What next?!

—You go home, partner. Take a rest. I have to restore my sister's grave, close her coffin, put back the soil and grass. How can we leave her that way? We have to . . . make her comfortable.

Then side by side, with a flashlight, we worked in the deep night. It was the only time I ever saw Thad Floriani cry: when he gazed a last time at what had been Evelyne Gilbert, his childhood playmate.

And what did we find there? What was the Maldoror Mon's purpose in life?

Teeth.

That's right: teeth. It seems Mon was an amateur dentist. Inside the opened coffin lid we picked up two molars and a bicuspid. We also found an oral surgeon's forceps, extraction tool, and a scalpel for incising the gums.

—Who'd do this? I asked.

—Someone with training. Or knows a dentist.

—Why? It's sick.

—An obsession, said Thaddy.

—I'll say. To break into a coffin . . . isn't it hard to do?

—For the layman—he yawned.—They're hermetically sealed. You have to know how.

—Hm, Redemaine Funeral Home. That's Simigliones, right? Mayor Tomao's brother runs it.

—Dominic.

I thought a moment.

–Don't they own House on the Hill, too? That woman . . . what's her name? Hal Duggan said it.

–Her name is mystery.

We found a few of Evelyne's teeth. What to do with them? I took one, and gave one to my friend. As for the others–Thad had an idea.

–Let's use them to make an oath, then bury them with Lady. Let's pledge to live a certain way: not for money, careers, so-called success, but for higher things: intellectual truth, and truth in art.

–Brotherhood, I said. Social justice.

–Friendship, said Thaddy. Sympathy, every day, and until the end, among us two.

–True love, I said, for one woman. One other person, until death.

–The highest things.

–This is a pact, I said. But how do we seal it?

–Each takes this eyetooth, Evelyne Gilbert's, in his mouth: first you, because you were closer to her, then me. Nine times we must roll it around with our tongue, and then take it out, and say: I promise. And a promise is a promise; it means: I said, and now I will do.

I laughed:

–No need for rigamarole, Tom Sawyer. But okay. Why nine?

–By my count the grave robber took away nine of her teeth: pulled them before we came and scared him. Look–

–N-no.

I couldn't stand shining the flashlight in my sister's face.

–Also, nine was the miracle number in Medieval times. Beatrice said she was 'a nine'.

–Who was Beatrice? A cheerleader who rejected her boyfriend?

–Sort of. The poet Dante's girl; but they didn't date here below. They went to The Prom in heaven.

–Oh. Why is 'nine' important?

–Because we need a miracle.

We worked through the night. We talked in low voices, and wondered why The Mon had done this thing. Why? There was no gold. My sister's fine even teeth didn't have time to develop cavities.

–Read Freud, said Thaddy. Teeth are symbols.

–Who's Freud?

Dawn was rising far across the flatlands, beyond The Dump at Sackett's Point, as we did some last gardening and sprucing up. We tried to make what was a terrible gash, a few hours before, into a place where a modest yet highly talented, life-loving, sympathetic teenage girl might rest—long, half a century, before she had any need or desire for such rest—in peace.

Chapter Seven

I

Senior Prom was on Saturday. And then, ten days later, a Wednesday, graduation exercises.

There was the small matter of term papers and final exams. I could be bothered. No teacher would flunk Evelyne Gilbert's brother headed for one of the elite campuses.

The weather grew warm after a rainy spell in early June. Summer was around the corner. Then weekday trips to the shore; afternoons wiled away at a beach club talking of sports, girls, college in the fall. The wide world seemed to beckon.

The fragrant late spring went by in a waltz for Redemaine High seniors in the college prep classes. With some excitement the high school sweethearts looked forward to Prom night. It was a tradition: after the dance, teenage couples spent the early hours together parked in a dark lane, or leafy niche along Maldoror Drive. Then breakfast; home for a rest; and, in the sunlit afternoon, to the shore where weary lovers lay under the same blanket and murmured of future like the plash of Long Island Sound waves. But the water was too cold for a swim.

We were into our final days as high school students.

I would not be going to the Senior Prom. Beth Engstrom was Naz-zarro's date, not mine. And that felt right, almost.

Why?

Among our classmates she passed for a deep one. Once a mutual friend told me: 'We were waiting for you two to start going out . . .' Thani with her vulnerability, at moments, had a strong response to romantic poetry and music. She craved it but gave a quiver—of fear even, mistrust—when it worked on her nerves. So she turned toward jazz and the hip subjectivity of the new decade: drives to the city for poetry readings at a Beatnik café; an affected introspection; existen-tialism; first dabblings with pot. She had a date with the 'Sixties era and made plans with Nazzarro to check out Provincetown in the summer.

From Thani I first heard, even as we went parking and made out, that clowns are sad; that beauty and death go together; that Euro-pean movies are deep and help you grow: it was worth reading the subtitles; that the best thing in life is to be perceptive. Perception can be painful, she said, and many shun such pain. But it nourishes in-tellectual development. Personal growth is the name of the game, not sports, or butter crunch. The great men and women of history were not crazy about baseball.

From one day to the next in our brief springtime, she looked at me and noted a change. Classical music, not rock 'n roll; books which are real, serious, about something, not the shallow trash I car-ried around in my back pocket; thoughts, conversations toward in-sight, not the usual gossip, chatter, 'rambling' as she called it: these were her tenets at age seventeen. Anything worth doing takes work, she said, good faith, and discipline. People seek the easy way.

During our dates, en route to and from school cach day, she got me started intellectually. Hey! You mean such things, books, art, ideas, have to do with life? Amazing. Grow up, young man. And then there was our initiation into love, the caravan of fingertips across a virgin continent. O wonderful intimacy. All this was inno-cent. It was pure. Well, Thani Engstrom was your everyday high school girl, a pretty cheerleader filled with pep, but not only.

Vaguely, in those days as our high school career moved toward its close, I felt she belonged to a former life. She was part of the 'happy' American adolescence I had lost, in essence, when Evelyne died and I got involved in this struggle I'm telling you about. I had fallen. Sometimes I shook my head and tried to figure out what ever possessed me that afternoon I took her up to the Drive, where my sister perished, and put the heavy make on her, the way adults do it. Luckily Nazzarro happened by before I could take Thania's virginity. But why did I do that? I'm not sure. Maybe I wanted her to fall with me, share the fig leaf, and the struggle. For I was no longer innocent, I felt, but she was.

At school I wasn't 'in' anymore, nor could I be. Evo Gilbert's brother didn't spend half his life at the nurse's office chewing the cud with other athletes while Mrs. Aylmer shaved and taped our ankles. I could hardly get a pass from class and enjoy life with a shrug the Monday after my tussle in the graveyard: when I came at midmorning looking totalled, and sat in class scowling at Miss Grich with her 'Murder in the Cathedral', epitome of stupidity, like a fart in a parlor. No; things had changed. Now I was 'an aesthetic wolf on the outskirts of society . . .' Hey, don't laugh.

Oh, there was a timid suggestion, among friends, to get me fixed up for The Prom—Fata viam invenient—with a junior twirler, Dee Sapegno, broken up with her abusive boyfriend. But I said: uh-uh. Thani was a hard enough act to follow without getting involved in other people's love spats.

No, I wouldn't be going to the Senior Prom on Saturday.

I would be going somewhere else.

II

Thaddy, among other chores for the Prom and Graduation committees, was getting up one more costume for me. Quitting baseball I had thought: done with uniforms. Chucked out of prep school I believed: no more of the most profoundly distasteful, deadly, conformist of all uniforms: the formal jacket and necktie. For ever and ever! Now I'll go through life in the costume of a poor student . . . But there was to be one other costume.

Also I needed information: before this next adventure.

Thaddy for the disguise.

And for the lowdown on House on the Hill—Hal Duggan.

Our Town News came out each Wednesday. So I guessed the time to find him more relaxed, with a few minutes to shoot the breeze, was that evening. Run by the office; then, if he's not there, try his home.

As the sun went down I sat by the window in my attic room. In my hand I held: the mask. I thought I knew our town, and its people. Not this guy . . . Who was he? What was he looking for at my sister's grave? Poor Yorick? A bargain on partial dentures? Why did he light out for House on the Hill? And what was his relation to the Simiglione clan? These were questions I had to ask Hal Duggan; but would he know? Would he talk?

For a long moment I sat staring at the mask: its contours, features, straps. Of resilient plastic, finely worked: this was no five-and-dime affair to go trick or treating at Halloween. It was a prosthesis done by a medical professional. But it also seemed to suit the mood of a psychopath, smirking at a girl's murder.

Why, you may ask, didn't I do the obvious thing and take this mask, along with my observations from Maldoror Drive and Redemaine Cemetery, to Chief Rune Roscommon who I know inspires your confidence no less than mine?

I answer with my own questions:

—Why was an unlicensed Cobra allowed to roam the town freely without being pulled over, ticketed, if not confiscated? Do you think the Maldoror Mon had a valid driver's license? At all hours the Drive was patrolled by squad cars, and staked out by unmarked vehicles: some posing as high school kids parking. Why wasn't The Mon arrested and taken to the Police Station for questioning? Why wasn't he committed to a hospital or longterm treatment facility? How could he live this shadowy nocturnal existence, invisible to the everyday life of our people, if he wasn't let alone and even condoned by local authorities? I mean who ever heard of such a thing. They must know who he was . . . Put him away! This situation could affect anyone's life, at any time, in a tragic way. And yet it was permitted to continue: left alone to grow wild, like a horrendous tumor; denied, apparently, by those in high places. I repeat: why wasn't this man, so ill it's a wonder he could still walk, never mind terrorize a town: why wasn't he put in an institution where he'd get the treatment he needed, even if too late? Was he real? Was he the latest thing in robots?

Hear no evil, see no evil, speak no evil.

Meanwhile, as we head toward catastrophe, nothing is done.

III

From my attic window I gazed out over trees lining the cozy street where we lived. The dark contours of West Hills Park stood out far across our town settling in at nightfall. From my bedroom, gazing across the valley, I saw the two red lights of the radio relay tower.

With a sigh–for Thania Engstrom, the Senior Prom, my lost high school paradise–I tucked the mask in a drawer, and put on jeans, t-shirt and sandals.

On the way out I kissed my mom home from the hospital: quiet now, sort of shrinking into her skin with its ruddy or patchy tint. Such a good kid of a mom: she did her best and gave her all, for others. She might have loved her four children a different way, and made them more dependent. But that wasn't her nature.

Now I leaned to kiss Anne Gilbert where she sat thoughtfully in the living room with my kid sis' to keep her company.

I said:

–I love you, Mud.

Such was the nickname I gave my mother: Mud. How cute. I felt like patting her on the back and telling her: Good game, way to play, you babe. But that wasn't the note. It would sound like the game was over. A few hours ago she looked too pooped to pop; so I told her to take it easy: just hang out while I fixed dinner. This went over like a lead balloon. She got angry at my generous offer, and had a frown like ox-eyed queenly Hera. Hey! I was only trying to be nice. Well, I'm no great shakes as a cook, but I boiled an egg once, and we had a good game of handball with it after. Once I baked a chicken, and then gave it to my friend Thaddy to make his drawings *au fusain*, charcoal.

Lemon said:

–Where to, Newbeth?

–What's it to ya'?

–Just asking.

–Well then: to the market to buy a fat pig.

–Oh.

–Which goes to show it's for me to know, and you to find out, Limoni. But I'll bring you something.

—Really, Dada? You gonna' bring me sumpthin', you gonna'?

—Sure.

—Like what?

—A dead skunk.

—Hey, great—said The Lem—just what I always wanted.

—How about a melted creamsickle?

—What flavor?

—What do you care, if it's melted?

—Could matter a lot to my dolls.

—I see.

—Said the blindman, when he didn't see at all.

—Hm. Well, I've got to run. Tata.

—You can bring me the stick, said Lummox. I'll file it to a point on the sidewalk.

—What for?

—That's for me to know, and you to find out. Something to do with my dolls.

—Say, you're regular obsessed with those dolls of yours. Tell you what: I'll bring you a cracked 78 rpm recording of 'Transfusion'.

—Ick!

—How about 'Ghost Riders in the Sky'?

—Oh, Nuisance . . . how outdated.

—Well then, I'll bring you something even nicer. 'Cause you're number one on my hit parade, you and The Moms here.

—Outdated, said Anne Gilbert, with a smile.

IV

Who knows why I thought Mr. Duggan might be in his office at this hour. Parking my Willys I knocked on the front door—waited, heard steps. Slowly, someone opened: the man himself. But he looked . . . different, under the weather; also, like he was expecting someone else. Face flushed, darker, but not hale and hearty; maybe I should say: afraid. The knob on the bridge of his nose was more pronounced, shiny. And the eyes—his eyes—spooked, staring through me.

—Mr. D, can I have a word with you?

−Come in.

He didn't open the door wider, but stepped aside.

Back in his office I came to the point.

−Sir, I need some information. A few nights after my sister's death I drove up to Maldoror Drive for a look around. What I found was a masked driver sitting in the dark, headlights off, in his Cobra racing car with no plates. Who is he, Sir? Someone in this town must know. I thought maybe he lived in a cave, Cobra and all, and came out at night to get some exercise . . . But last Friday, after midnight, Thad Floriani and myself found that same masked driver robbing a grave in Fenbrook Cemetery. Do you know whose? My sister's . . . He had the coffin open when we came along, and he was . . . he was extracting her teeth. I kid you not; he had dentist's tools. So I'm here to ask you why. Can you tell me why anyone would do such a thing? After I saw his car parked by the cemetery, we snuck up and surprised him, chased him away, and then followed him through the streets of Spring Glen. He went to a place you mentioned last time we spoke, the House on the Hill, and disappeared behind the high gate. So now I ask you, Sir. Can you shed light on this? Who is the masked driver? Did he kill Evelyne? Why does he want her teeth? What is his connection with House on the Hill? Does he live there? Help me, Sir. I'm trying to solve this mystery for our noble police department before someone else gets hurt. You're a reporter, and you must have an idea what's going on. Dominic Simiglione could have taught the boy how to open a casket; but is there a dentist in the Simiglione family?

−There is everything in the Simiglione family.

−Is there? How does it all fit together, Sir? Please tell me! Will the Maldoror Mon, or whoever he is, strike again?

V

I poured out my story while staring at Hal Duggan. Amazing how he had changed in a few weeks. Now he peered back: the way a gazelle might do, wounded, unable to move, if you came near it. Duggan's mouth, I noticed, had a strange shape: sort of twisted, reflecting his thoughts, his reaction to my outpouring, and life. What a dilemma. I asked him for the plain truth, and his lips convoluted. Answer my five questions please. Now was the moment to uphold his journalistic honor; but at the risk of his skin?

Silence.

Then, after a time, he stood up: a tallish man, bit gangly. He went to his file cabinet, opened the second drawer from the bottom with a key on his chain, and took out a folder.

—See this?

—Yessir.

—Know what it is?

—Nossir. Material for Harriet Pulley's 'Our Neighborhoods' column?

The old manila folder, with green reinforcements at the corners, sat on his blotter. There was a red-bordered label marked: 'Macro'. He tapped it: sort of strummed it.

Silence.

Now that executive office, with its framed diploma from a prestigious school of journalism, plus a few civic awards; also the op-ed piece which may have been his first publication: now his office looked changed also. Not so nice anymore, not so prim, innocent. A strange force seemed to radiate from the 'Macro' file on his desk. I thought of magic, an alchemist's retort.

In those instants Duggan's face was grim. It looked twisted a little, haggard. I realized we were sitting there almost in the dark. He tapped, and said:

—It is the political file. I could ruin them.

This sounded like big talk: 'Macro', or macaroni, talk? So I stared in space, and thought: Is everyone in the town going crazy?

VI

He said:

—You're a teenager. Must be fun: play sports, see your girl. Darn pretty girl, Beth Engstrom, star cheerleader. Then, next thing you know: no more sports, no more girl.

—What's that all about, Sir? The masked driver—

—Something went wrong. It can, you know.

The way his eyes darted in the half-light, the mesh out of place on his forehead, unlike him—Mr. Duggan looked haunted.

—I pulled off the mask. I saw.

—You know, Newell, our town is good in the main. I've been pleased to have its school system, Spring Glen Grammar, Wyatt R. Krayling Junior High, Redemaine High, for my kids. My wife and I always felt at home here, and *Our Town News* is part of this town's life, and history. I try to report fairly on our local scene, struggles, small successes, the comings and goings of well-meaning people.

—Yessir.

I was in no mood to yawn, on the eve of risking my neck. But something came over me, and I did yawn. Duggan took this in, and nodded—to himself. During the interview I seemed to count for little; though I had come to his office with a bombshell. No; the newspaperman wasn't too eager to ask me *his* five questions, and play investigative reporter, while I sat there before him with a scoop. I had happened by when his thoughts were at fever pitch, his nerves ready to snap; so he talked more or less to himself, still trying, despite everything, to keep the lid on things. No doubt there was a notion of propriety at work: how much truth do you tell a teenager when the words may be unsafe for speaker and hearer? How many adults, let alone minors, are ready for the 'Macro' facts? . . . Still, he seemed to take my yawn as a hint—he could bore everyone to death, literally, while the truth went packing.

Duggan said, in a trembling murmur:

—I could, yes, ruin a few of them.

—A few, Sir? Which ones?

—The ones who came to our town and ruined it. The little boys, I call them, the 'micros', if you will, whom the bigger ones sent here to steer the course for their profit. That's right; oh, not so much you'd feel it just yet, maybe a pinch. You don't hear news about them.

—Not in *Our Town News?*

He had said it, but he winced when I did. Took him aback. What? You mean our free press is bought and sold?

—They own it, he mumbled.

He leaned forward and took a copy of this week's issue. I didn't know what the talk about macros and micros meant, at that point; I didn't pick up on his pet conspiracy theory. But I sat forward alerted by the tense tone.

—Yes, Sir?

—There are corrupters, who send them. Harder to get at, roots deeper.

—Like teeth?

—Listen. When Jim Floriani made his second challenge to the present mayor, a few years back, someone said to me: Howland, a man like Big Jim couldn't win around here if The Pope came and campaigned for him. Why's that? I asked. First because he's a liberal Democrat, always a bridesmaid in Redemaine; second because you have to talk to someone. Oh? I asked; and who's that? But the person bending my ear thought better; he laughed, and kept mum. Well, it didn't take me forever to find out.

Duggan tapped his file.

I said:

—Did you have to talk with him for this job?

He gave a laugh, which seemed to echo, in a cavern.

—I would if I misused it.

—Does that person control things in our town?

—In a sense, yes . . . most.

—Does he know who killed my sister?

Duggan stared at me, thinking, and tapped the file.

VII

Mr. Duggan turned; his swivel chair creaked, like a cry of pain from beneath the flooring. He gazed toward our lamplit reflections in the bay window—shying, I sensed, from his own. Then, ominous, he said:

—A fine girl, your sister. A dream of a girl, son, now you'd better let her rest. Your actions don't go unnoticed.

He held forth his hand. Interview over? Time for me to leave? I didn't take that handshake. I wasn't ready to clear out yet.

—Kind of hard to rest, don't you think, when a monster comes and raids your coffin? Who is it, Sir? Who does such things in Redemaine, and whom may I talk to about it? You haven't told me.

—Nor will I, Newell.

—Could you tell me who the masked driver is? I'm asking you because I need to know, and without your help things can only be harder, get worse. Please, Sir, tell me that much at least.

−Not now, I . . .

He looked away. There was a pause. In the stubborn silence I thought: how to make him talk? Call him a coward outright for not answering? Say there's a lie in the air: what he's lived and known for a long time is not what he reports or will talk about? No, don't say it, but imply it.

−Mr. Duggan, if you'll give me that name, I won't say where I got it. Never. Not under torture. But if you don't, I'll have to go elsewhere, and then, yes, I'll need to mention you. Even, if necessary . . . say you sent me.

The newspaperman's pupils sort of jittered, back and forth, quickly.

I stared, persisted. I tried to fix him in the sights, so to speak, of conscience. No way out, this time, old fellow.

Maybe he didn't like that silence. He realized I wasn't going to leave. So he sighed, with a shrug, and said:

−Alright. His name is Ripoli.

−Ripoli?

- I don't know the family name. He probably goes by Zia Grippina's.

−Zia . . .

−Zu Girolamo's niece.

−Ah. A Simiglione. And who would the proud father be?

Duggan paused−such a pause, I thought he must be in catalepsy. He froze: maybe a good minute. I waited. And then his eyes went heavenward, and he said:

−Rune Roscommon.

−Ho! I thought Simigliones and Roscommons had a vendetta.

−Lifelong.

−So it's like Romeo and Juliet?

−Not quite. But that's how the hate started.

−How did it, Sir? Please go on.

−No, I've said enough.

The way he looked at me then: I had my hands full trying not to laugh. He saw a horned devil−none other than Newell Gilbert, the virgin.

−Go on, Sir. I won't leave until you tell me. You'll have to call . . . Rune Roscommon! to haul me out of here. In the paddy wagon I'll ask him about it, and say you told me to.

Duggan threw up his hands−the reins.

−Tst. Roscommon seduced and then dropped the striking Zia

Grippina twenty years ago: when she was young. New arrival from the Old Country, she didn't speak English, but what matter.

—And?

—He was a young buck then, handsome man, on his way up. And, well, she was a woman. Genre of Gertruda Floriani, southern Italian ragazza, breathtaking. But Gertruda is crazy with a heart, Zia has a steel trap.

—With teeth?

—I think to control her better, fill up her time, give this restless woman something to do, they started House on the Hill. She is Madame—they call her Madonna—at one of the more elegant whorehouses, qua exclusive men's club, our Eastern Establishment has to offer.

—How can such a thing be hushed up? And in our own Spring Glen! Why no traffic tie-ups, late-night revellers, tussles?

—Please ... This is a high-class joint: successful men in their fifties, with plenty to lose from publicity. They don't go gamboling along the brook like hamadryads in their drawers. As for traffic: go stake out Dyre Club Lane at midnight. You'll see the taxis pull up, and limousines slip in off the Old Turnpike, via Crest Road.

—But why do we never see the women? And all this time I've had to concentrate my fantasies on Adele Fitchew of Dorsal Drive ... Why didn't I know about this at puberty? I could have asked my dad for a raise in weekly allowance. Think of it: a brothel not ten blocks from our house on Santa Fe!

—Sancta simplicitas. There are still one or two things you don't know.

—Gee! My dad would blow his top if he heard about it. Southern gentleman, you know, defender of womanhood.

Duggan gave a low chortle:

—With all respect to your eminent father—

—What, Sir?

—N-never mind.

—And the police know nothing? Do nothing?

—Ha ha ha !—Duggan laughed like a devil, and he looked like one, in the dim light from his desk lamp.

VIII

—But Ripoli . . . How did he get burned? His face—

—Another aggravation. No doubt it goads Grippina's hate. The thing happened inside House on the Hill. It is said . . . sounds a bit gothic to me . . . that as a child Ripoli had a puppy he loved, cocker spaniel. Zia Grippina, in one of her fits, flung it in the fireplace. That fireplace, by the way, is a monument to sexual love: marble relief with Eros and Aphrodite figures, Priapus, Bacchae shouting with hands upraised, in ecstasy. It's so lurid you wouldn't see it in a museum; but it rivals Indian sculpture, and erotic prints by the Japanese, for explicitness. Also, unlike them: here Woman has the upper hand; this heightens the . . .

—Sir?

—I don't know how to say it.

—Oh well. Then tell me about Ripoli.

—Legend says he went in after the pup. Maybe ran forward, tripped, and fell face down into the flames. Either way: his cute chubby face, a true Cupid's, got maimed. Who knows what really happened.

—Grippina knows.

—He went in. Can you guess who pulled him out?

—Madonna?

—She wears black gloves at all times.

—Got her fingers burned . . .

—By love. And let that be a lesson to you. But those skeletal claws, charcoal broiled, still have a fiendish strength. She uses them to . . .

His words trailed off in a chuckle. Duggan's eyes were dreamy. I thought he must be among Madonna's admirers, seeking her intercession too.

—Sir?

—Whip.

—Whip?

—She totes a lady's whip in the folds of her black skirt.

I gave a whistle:

—Madonna with the whip, by Raphael. Well, it beats a lasso.

—She doesn't do it downstairs of course, in the restaurant. There she is elegant hostess.

—Hostess with the mostess.

—You must penetrate the inner sanctum if you wish the full treatment.

—Sanctum?

—The third floor: sex club proper. Then there's a room in the attic. They call it Seventh Heaven . . . This paradise has its levels.

—Strange theology: hell is heaven.—I sang:—'Hell is up, heaven is down . . . Redemaine . . . it's a wonderful town . . .'

—Only in America . . . At age thirty-nine Grippina is still a stunning woman.

—You bet.

—Rich and influential men, financiers, the merchant bankers, corporate big boys and government officials—

—And newspaper editors—

—They come to call. From New York, Washington, Europe, they arrive wanting this woman's personal touch.

—Claw-woman.

—There's a long line.

—I guess poor Sorifa'll have to wait his turn.

—Oh, she wouldn't say boo to Donny O. One of her girls, and not the freshest, does him.

—In the attic?

—Or a closet.

IX

We fell silent. Outside his office window the town hummed: cars along the two main drags, Gordiane and Havilland, which intersect at the Town Hall. People lived their lives unaware of what went on in their midst. I sat amazed, and asked:

—Did Ripoli knife my sister to death?

—No proof. You say he was in the cemetery?

—Why kill her? What's the motive? Because his mother threw his puppydog in the fire? Because he's sick unto death himself, his face a worm-eaten mess?

—That or . . . macro.

Duggan's features, when he said the magic word, looked so mysterious—almost comical.

—Macro?

—Orders.

—Orders? From what headquarters? Orders to kill an innocent girl?

—One thing always struck me about your sister, Newell, when I used to see her here and there, at the high school games. Yes, she was beautiful, but . . . in an exotic way. She had high cheekbones, an oriental note.

—From our paternal grandmother, Wilhelmina. Down South they say she got it from a Cherokee ancestor. This riles my pa. But you say orders, Sir? From where?

—I don't know. All we can know is: it's about power, and money. And it's complicated, one long intrigue, up there.

—In Seventh Heaven.

—But probably it was only Ripoli, after all, acting alone.

—He sucked in hate with his mother's milk, so Evelyne Gilbert has to die.

Duggan thought aloud:

—If you look at Grippina . . . she has them too, high cheekbones.

I frowned:

—Well, this explains why he's still on the loose. His kin are the powers that be. And then they give us a cock-and-bull story about the escaped convict, Jared Simms. And you report it too, and pull the wool over everyone's eyes. Why, Sir? Why lie?

He gave the wriest grin: like a schoolboy caught with an inkwell full of spitballs.

—Once you start it's hard to stop. There's a wife with expectations. There are kids, mouths to feed. A man has to make his mark. It's our way of life.

—Lying as a way of life?

—Yessir, said Hal Duggan.

—Lord, what a mess, Sir! How did we get ourselves into such a mess?

—Pragmatism. Do what works best—line of least resistance . . . But you don't know the tenth of it, boy, not the hundredth, and I can't tell you. State secrets. I never should have said this much, blabbing to a teenager. You do not need to know, and you do not want to.

—The 'macro' facts of life?

—Of our society. You don't want to know them, Newell; that is, if you like living, and plan to enter college in the fall. Forget it, son. Go on to the next stage.

—Of the lie . . . Well, I wouldn't mind. But you see, Sir, my sister is dead, and this seems kind of unfair to me. Not you?

—Yes, yes, unfair. Life is unfair. And yet . . . hey.

—The great secret you can't tell me, Mr. Duggan, the reason of reasons, and cause of my sister's death: is it in your file?

—On page one.

He tapped the folder.

—And you say you could 'ruin them'?

—A few. Not the big fish, long as they have control.

—Mackerels?—I paused, nodding at him, in thought. Then I said:—There's one more thing.

—What now?

—Are you a member, like Sorifa?

He gave an offended look:

—Who, me?!

—Ho! So you are. Tisk, Sir—I rubbed my finger at him—but you're forgiven on one condition. You must know the code.

—What code?

—For the outside gate. For entry into House on the Hill.

—No, no—Duggan stood up.—Time for us both to go home, boy. Now that's it!

—It isn't, Sir. It isn't quite it. I won't leave here till you give me the code.

—No. Go along. Scoot.

—Tell me, then I'll go. Not before.

—I won't.

—Why not?

—I can't.

—You can.

—No, all who enter need clearance. Serious offense to crash that party. Important people go there.

—To a whorehouse. My important sister went to her grave at age seventeen.

—No. I can't tell you.

—I need the code, Sir, and I need it now. I'll never tell a living soul. But if you don't, if you refuse: then I'll make a few calls and tell

everything you said tonight. I'll reveal your 'macro' file, and we'll see how you like it when you go join Evelyne. I'll talk, I'll blab, I swear to you I'll go on a campaign. Tell all and say you said so.
–Don't.
–I'll use your bi-line. By 'Macro'. Macro-fish!
–I have a family.
–Tell, and I won't divulge my source.
–Two grandchildren.
–Adorable; but you must tell, Sir, or else! I won't leave. I'll . . . I'll call the police! Ha ha!

It took a barrage of pleading and threatening, but he told me the code–scowled, like he swallowed something nasty, and spat it up. At last Hal Duggan came forth with the hocus-pocus known only to Zia Grippina's distinguished clientele. What gobbledygook really: worse than the Freemasons said to be so influential among business elements in town. Duggan sang, if you please; he looked deranged in those instants: even produced a Bible and made me take an oath not to speak, in my lifetime, those few damning syllables.

So I can't record the code here. So much the better! I don't want to corrupt you, Reader. This isn't the cheap fiction that corrupts–pay your money, waste your time, and when it's over you're a little worse. The way things are going: if I told you Grippina's code you'd probably drive to Redemaine tonight and try it out. But I need to keep one last illusion: that there is still an innocent person left in America–my Reader.

X

Then it was Senior Prom Saturday. A good time.

As my classmates, Nazzarro Zummo included, spent the day picking up rented tuxedoes, buying corsages, waxing and vacuuming their cars, I lay in bed reading and waited for Thaddy.

While the Class of '61 got ready for all-night petting, parked in lonely spots so the Maldoror Mon might claim a second victim: I thought over my date with Zia Grippina.

Her manicured claws scratched my nape, and drew blood, as we danced cheek to cheek to a slow tune. She raised her 'lady's whip' over my head, and said icily: Kneel, slave . . . ! Frankly, I don't know if my pen, a high school senior's, is up to describing an S & M orgy in House on the Hill. Maybe I'll serve up 'Sherman's March to the Sea' again, since Marsden Dale, historian laureate, regards my seventh grade production so highly. You'd like that better, wouldn't you? I know you've no interest in an ultra-voluptuous sadist and what she did to—shhh! hush up! libel!—the national figure strapped on a bed in the attic, Seventh Heaven. You have no brief for such savage sex acts, a blow-by-blow account with detail worthy of the naturalists—do you? What say? You *do?* Oh! Friend, you let me down after I just called you innocent. Alright then, here it comes: the gooiest dessert on the menu, stuffed down your throat for you—ah! ah! you know you love it! Ahhh! shouted the venerable U.S. Senator, presidential timber.

As for myself: I had to go in there and get proof Ripoli killed my sister. I had to find out whether he acted alone, a sick and solitary psychopath, or else in concert.

XI

Thad was headed for The Prom with a fellow committee member; but mainly he was in charge of technical aspects, décor, sound system and the like: overseeing the event. How he had time to work for me too, I do not know, but in late afternoon he brought by my costume. It wasn't a tuxedo.

—What the—? I stared at it.

—This is the ticket, he said.

Black leather it was. But it had strips, or vents, let's say, of military camouflage at the armpits, and down the pant seams. Looked amphibian, winged.

—It's what The Mon wore in the cemetery. To a tee. It wasn't easy to do, and you owe me some dough.

—No sweat, I'll hit up The Pops.

While I put on the replica of Ripoli's uniform, and then strapped on the mask, Thaddy watched. He made a few adjustments; fit my

hair in a silk hairnet since The Mon was perfectly bald; and then plunked down a pair of army surplus boots to complete the outfit.
–Good luck!
Then he was gone: off toward his responsibilities to our high school class, and the memorable evening.
Then I was alone: with my mission.
I had to gain entry into House on the Hill. I had to case out the unnatural habitat of a psychotic killer. I had to put myself in his place and try to find out what lay behind my sister's death. Also, I had to be nimble, quick, in the event he was there: for we two would make a strange effect in the same room together. This said and done: I must keep an eye out on this night of nights, dog his steps, since on The Drive and around town there'd be easy pickings, if he had acquired a taste for blood and meant to strike again.
It was my show now, and I would play it to the end. I felt a sinking.
A few hours remained before nightfall. So I went downstairs and played 'ouiji board' with my little sister. Spooked out! In a low voice I asked the board:
–Will I make it through this Prom night?
Impish Lemon steered the ouiji marker and also said low, voice aquiver:
–No-o-o . . . hoo! You wo-o-on't.
Then I raided the fridge since Mom was upstairs in bed too sick to serve us anymore. Dad the world traveller was off on one of his jaunts. The current housemaid, Bowman, had left a lamb cake for us; so after taking a bite I went outside and romped with my dog, a collie-husky named Pyggie, in the yard.
And then, as night fell in a blaze of red over West Hills Park, old gold and crimson, it was time to suit up.

XII

Spring Glen takes its name from a cheerful brook which flows through backyards, and a few underground ducts, among the hilly streets filled with trees and sunlight like a glen. The source may be Dyre Club Pond, I don't know; and from there the brook wends gurgling and purling through the one Spring Glen area reminiscent of wilderness: the old Shetland Estate. The place has Revolutionary War cachet: a cannonball in a sturdy oak cornerpost of the mansion, once Gruby's Tavern where General Washington paused for refreshments, now House on the Hill.

As boys we made forays up into those jungle-like grounds overlooking Wilke Parkway. I had my bicycle accident as a ten year-old: ran a stop sign, blam! hit by a car. Woke up in the guest bedroom to hear Dad calming The Moms in the kitchen: Now, Doll, his leg isn't broken . . . A rotted tree trunk bridged a ravine gashed in the hill, as with clayey bubbles the pond water tumbled down that rugged terrain.

There were snakes. We caught garter snakes, and waved them like a lanyard in Lil Berryer's and Betty Lundgren's face: waylaying a hot chick who came late from after-school activities at Spring Glen Grammar. Soon enough we outgrew the garters, and went about with a canvas pack and switchblade stalking the deadly copperhead: until Ronald Kong got bit by one and had to go to the hospital. Then we didn't play there anymore. One day we moved on, Thaddy and Otter, Willard Steuart, Haas and Bobby Zwergli, The Mooch: like Schiller's *Robbers* making our peace we met at Lavater Field for our first organized baseball games, in the Midget League.

I don't think any of us, Spring Glen boys, ever got a close look at the great house. It was set back beyond a high fence in its quiet domain of tulips and azaleas, oak and maple trees. It always had a mystery; but I couldn't get over Mr. Duggan's story of such goings on up there now. Hey, since age eight I knew Spring Glen like the back of my hand. Didn't I?

As night fell I got into the tight costume. Whew, the leather was hot, this balmy night. Sexy! Ask Thaddy for a favor, and it got done right. I'll say that for the boy. But now I had to wear a straitjacket and mask all night. Dammit, my Senior Prom . . . Maldoror Mon . . . Beth and Naz. Dammit all.

What weapon to take? If they catch me with a knife they'll think I'm The Mon. Take the gun.

In my attic lair I paced back and forth another moment. Devils in hell must have made the pattern for Ripoli's skintight outfit.

Well, time to split the scene.

Over the leather I put on a trench coat: in case my alert kid sister saw me, sneaking out.

She did.

—Where to, Chewy Nougat?

—Nowhere fast, Pipsqueaketh.

What a good kid she was, and what a brat!

XIII

In the garage I pulled Willys' choke and turned 'er over. On came the staticky radio in the glove compartment, since Will Rinse wanted 25 bucks to fix it. That old hit tune about Dracula and Transylvania: sung with a warpy voice. Oh great. Get me in the mood for my Prom date with Zia Grippina, and her whip.

I threw Willys in reverse and began backing into the alley— boomah! Forgot to pull up the garage door. Splintered it. Now my dad'll hit the roof as usual, and not fork over for Thad's expenses.

In second gear I taxied the back alley which halved our block between Ridgewood and Spring Glen Terrace. In ten minutes I might have walked to Zia Grippina's, but I wanted my horse hitched nearby to make my getaway. I imagined House on the Hill as a squalling madhouse where the Sexual Inquisition tortured its three-piece suit conformists, heretics of inhibition, who were repentant. (!) More, Zia, give me more. Whap! . . . Whap! . . . But what was Ripoli's role in all that? I had to imitate his behavior.

Now a few more blocks . . . to the end of the known world. Where Spring Glen Terrace dead-ends on Dyre Club Lane, I parked my car and got out.

Onto the grounds I snuck the way we came the other night. At the front gate I did just what Hal Duggan told me—and entered.

There were shiny cars, like he said, lined up along a drive before the house. I walked the picturesque lane bordered by linden trees, like a Russian manor house, nest of gentry, and thought: Strange. Is it another planet? Among those sleek automobiles, stretched out like a long copperhead in the moonlight, I didn't see Ripoli's Cobra.

Night had fallen. For a minute I paused outside in the dark: not too late to turn back! At half past ten a full moon straddled the clouds, like a masked rider. I saw the big three-storey structure loom, in its own lurid glow, beyond the neat rows of trees. The broad Victorian porch, forming a semicircle at the front entry, extended round the side. This was a great mansion from the 1700s—when the colonial Governor made huge gratuitous land grants to the feudal lords in each region. It looked like a New World château: its underlying colonial or Federalist architecture overlaid by Victorian features. So large, isolated on its hill beneath the night sky, like the mysterious Grippina herself; so weird with its windows seeming to flicker candlelight: it soared amid the cupolas and gables of 'Seventh Heaven'. The place was not homey and inviting, like a New England inn. It had a hostile beauty, which was intimidating, as hell. It had come a long way from George Washington to Zia Grippina.

XIV

Through the front entry, a double door of heavy oak, I went in House on the Hill. My chest heaved as I tried to breathe and thought what a mad act this was—by that wiseass teenager, myself. Inside stood a tall rough-looking bouncer type: but well oiled in his wide-lapelled suit, black with snaking pinstripes. In a later age Al Capone's bodyguard became Cerberus, offspring of Typhon and Echidna, taught his manners by the capitalist Hercules. From beneath the mask I beamed a honey cake smile on the boy, and met his humble if steely gaze. He knew Ripoli. His lips sketched a wry grin.

And then I was in. What to do? How to make myself unseen, a listening post? Slowly moving forward I took in the place, a Roaring 'Twenties décor. I heard a tinny radio from the past; it was the Happiness Boys crooning on an antique Florentine cabinet set. The front room made a lobby with reservations desk, plush furniture, an attractive receptionist. The wall hangings, paintings—a hunting scene, an artist's atelier—were racy with taste, and showed a golden age of promiscuity. Sex was a reward for middle-aged men who had gone by the book, worked doggoned hard, and come to the astounding conclusion that you can't take it with you. Now the money burned a hole in their large plaited pockets. Here, at House on the Hill, it was the myth of a carefree age.

Three young women fluttered past: very pretty. Good as Beth? Dressed as '20s flappers they wore sleeveless outfits, summery, light

as crinoline; seamed stockings rolled below the knees; more makeup than they needed, rouge, etc., or so it looked from a distance. They didn't act like flappers, free and flirtatious with a twist of irony. No; they looked . . . purposeful. One glanced back and said:
 —Hi, Rippie.
 I nodded.
 —What's with The Ripper tonight?
 They disappeared in another room.
 Quite nonchalant in my mask which all took in stride, I poked my nose past a first door. It was the restaurant: a pleasant room, spacious, maybe fifteen tables; a conservative affluence aged in the oak panneling, in a Venus and Adonis tapestry; in the marble hearth (mentioned by Duggan) with its erotic bas-reliefs which, truly, beckoned for a closer look. Here was a superior depravity; as gaslights had a luster, and made for that flickering aura, seen outside, in the darkness.
 Getting into my role I gave the hostess, another very swell young woman—did they play two parts in this comedy?—a high sign; strolled to a table for two by the window; and seated myself. This amazed her. She stared at me. With every move I showed them a new Ripoli: has the Revolution come? For all I knew he was a handyman around the place, and this was off limits. But what to do?

 Settling in, I had a strange sense . . . It was breathtaking as I risked my skin, a promising future like my twin sister's. What I felt is hard to say: in this 'old money' setting with its Jazz Age touches. But let me try. Some evenings, lately, with Mom ill and Dad drinking too much, I would know they were sitting in the living room and wanted me to come in. But not for a few minutes; no, at least an hour, two hours, all evening. Sort of a stand-in for Evelyne who was so kind to them, so helpful. Well, the idea of going in that room and sitting with them—I'm selfish, that's for sure, but I couldn't do it. Why? Such a loneliness they had managed to generate, between them, across the decades: it was like carbon in a motor, like Freud's death principle. Kids grown—Lady dead; Joey gone South to college, myself on the way in September, though not far; Lemon unable to fill such a vacuum: no one could. And there were no new ideas, greater community relations, vital struggles to take the children's place, for Mom at least; no renewal. It was still the old way, behind the times; and, as such, a kind of breakdown of the social being. I felt my parents' neediness of life, movement, reality; and I felt they would eat me alive if I went in that room.

And so, also, it was here in House on the Hill. No matter how decolletée the women were, how appetizing the 7-course menu, how elaborate the dessert! This was a vacuum that could suck you right up. Oh yes. Make no mistake: the posh establishment was dedicated to serving old men, I mean mentally, morally old, regardless of age.

In this place where the wildest most perverted and repressed instincts were lured out of their den and catered to for a price, a high price: there was a sense of limbo on the rez-de-chaussée. Quite unlike Farrelly's lumpen dive, or Roscommon's home away from home for shopkeepers and the service sector. Here was our financial aristocracy working out the kinks in the deal—say a nightly Predator's Ball—and they brought their deadly boredom in with them. Even the gorgeous 'girls' I had seen looked like female automatons; they were personified genitalia bereft of self. There was a dread spirit of conformism ready to eat you alive, like Cyclops. Make a ruckus, brother, and you'll be expelled by my bouncer friend over there with as quiet, measured, well-mannered a response as possible. This whorehouse was very comme il faut.

So I sat alone at a table by the window, and gazed on those two extremes: a wrought-iron protocol in the low voices, the quiet steps, nostalgiac music piped by the A & P Gypsies; and a threatening, an explosive sexual violence just beneath the surface, most appropriate here, awaiting its cue.

XV

Staff knew me. Waiter, busboy, they gave me no nod, but traded glimpses. Ripoli's acting up? They eyed the receptionist: go tell Zia. He can't sit here. Oh, what a grim thing to be Grippina's bastard; it gave me the shivers. On the edge of my seat, staring at the dark window, I thought what to do next. Wander around? Retreat upstairs? Wait here until that woman came? She would tell me where to go.

Toward eleven p.m. there were a dozen or so still at dinner. Demure gentlemen, graying, middling, they sat with a gravity in their tailored suits. They were important men in banking and business. Pissers. Two sat with their dates to The Prom, lovely creatures, paid escorts if I'm any judge—of prom dates—; though far be it from me to say the word: prossies. An elegant diner shot a glance at this devil who had come on the premises, and looked away. My mask smirked back; it marred the illusion of a romantic soirée.

Two tables away sat a few colleagues. One I seemed to know, as I settled in and got my bearings: pending my trainer's arrival with her whip. There, in profile, sat Mayor Tomao Simiglione, of the Simigliones, and he was worked up about something.

I gazed out the dark window, trying to spare them my mask. But I listened as they talked over a Nightly News report on our local Channel 6. A scandal was brewing about the town snowplows. On the threshold of summer? Well, it was a Democrat conspiracy . . . to defeat the incumbent Mayor in the next election.

The three men discussed the issue in lofty terms: I thought they must be Roman senators. After a moment I realized one was the State Commissioner of Motor Vehicles, Guigacks. The third I also recalled from somewhere . . . ah! It was the young State Representative, Jer' Cacciatore, who grew up in Lovett Hill section and had a fine future surely. Redemaine High '51. I once got roused by Jer' with the other rabble in our high school auditorium.

—Grant, it's politically motivated! I tell you it's ridiculous. One of the trucks was on a lift being fixed.

Mayor Tomao, a man with higher ambitions, Lt. Governor or a U.S. Congressional seat, was usually cool as a cucumber. But he had a strange trait: if you pushed his button, if he got excited, then watch out. His face and slight frame seemed to fly off the hinge. The man became one vast spastic tic.

Meanwhile I listened. For eavesdropping it was kind of neato in a mask. I didn't budge. I sat wondering what took Zia Grippina so long, upstairs.

Grantland Guigacks waxed poetic:
—The implication is a continual crisis in the body politic: autumn leaves, snowdrifts, sand, and grass.

Tomao:
—So a sweeper is back in the shop: on a hoist getting an air-conditioner installed. Pollution laws require this.

Jer' shook his head, and made weight beside the two heavies:
—'Deadlined inoperable': now I ask you!

—Grant! I've known you and observed you a long time. I respect you. You criticized your own Party and that takes courage. But I have indignation against these manipulations. I've been too honest. Nice guy gets used. Petty things are made important for political points.

At dinner the orators were impressive. With cocktails they passed from local matters to 'law of government . . . laws of man, country, civilization . . .' Then back again to brass tacks:

—I mean really—Tomao's large, sensual mouth nearly swallowed his face.—A reflector missing: how scandalous. Dirty marker plates: Christ! They're supposed to get dirty, for Chrissake! Grant, we are both honorable men, and I must tell you that your department is being used politically. We've always dealt with one another in a civilized manner. And now hear me when I say: it's morally wrong. I can respond to this sort of thing if I have to.

Guigacks:

—When I was Mayor at the state capital . . . such situations occurred, often enough: usually instigated by a labor union, to tell the truth. I can't get into details from 169 towns; but the vehicles must be inspected. Then each communality sends us a letter so they will look good.

Representative Cacciatore:

—The Dems got hold of the checklist: 15 pass, 44 warnings, 14 grounded.

Tomao:

—I would have called you myself, but I was out of state.

—Just send me a letter with the check-off list.

The Republican Representative:

—Nightly News called Mayor Simiglione's office asking for a press release. They were put on the trail by our enemies. 'The Public Works Investigation.'

The Commissioner looked around:

—Alright, gentlemen, enough. Or do we have to talk about this all night? Just act civilized, and let me help you. You come to me with a preconceived idea.

—It's my political career! said Tomao.

Jer':

—The report was made public before the Mayor even had it.

—Nothing under the Bureau of Information Act obliges you to release a report . . .

Back and forth they tossed the football. What a momentous political issue: snowplows! Pots and pans . . . and their exalted careers. Tomao Simiglione framed his accusations in noble periods, and forms of address worthy of Plutarch. He said: snowplows are the pivotal issue this summer. But I thought: a brilliant teenage girl lies in her grave; and racial hatred tears the town apart; and a war heats up in Southeast Asia where many will die. I sat there listening: it made me forget my role and begin to get angry. Why, it's all just a game to these animals! They pose and make promises in public, but they care nothing about other people. They only love other people's money, OPM. All they say and do is for their own enrichment and self-gratification. Unprincipled, opportunists to the core, Tomao and Guigacks and Jer' would rather lose an election than risk making waves about a real issue, 'dividing the public'. Oh, oh! Revolution! Horrors! Scary! Scientists, not religious prophets, could be telling us the world is ending, our planet poisoned by corporate pollution; but since the mighty corporations control U.S. politics, buy and sell all the Tomaos, such fearless leaders, Micro and Macro as Duggan called them, would not lift a voice or raise a finger. Hourrah! What a band of petty gangsters these U.S. politicians. What epitomes of mediocrity.

Grantland Guigacks:

—Control yourself, Mr. State Representative.

—But the report is by Democrats! Do you hear? Nothing too conspiratorial or insidious for them! Big Jim Floriani just wants to be Mayor of Redemaine, that's all. He's behind this.

Tomao touched his young crony's cuff with a wise paternal hand:

—Good, Jer'. That'll do for now.

XVI

That did do, because suddenly there was a hush across the sedate dining room reminiscent of an alumni club. The dozen or so patrons lingering over dinner turned their eyes to Zia Grippina hands on hips in the entry.

She glared at me.

It seems her son was not the apple of her eye: judging from contempt written all over her spectacular person. But I was not her son. I was Peter in the wolf's lair. I was Newell Gilbert going in there after my sister's killer: trying to come up with conclusive evidence before I went public; trying to find out if Ripoli acted alone, on his own initiative or following orders. (So far no white KKK hoods inside House on the Hill, that I saw, among the very important people.) But Mayor Tomao's bad faith, his shallow conversation had got my dander up, such as it was. An adolescent doesn't know the ropes, but I was learning. So I didn't like being looked at by Zia that way, and made the mistake of looking back, fresh kid that I was, from beneath the mask.

It was hard not to.

Now, in the instant before she beckoned—Come here you!—I have the task of describing her. If Zia were my muse, she might whip my inspiration into shape; then my words would fill the bill. But she didn't specialize in muse-like activities.

First: was she angry? Was she an Allegory of Anger, as she stood there, so statuesque, and larger than life? Not exactly. Anger is relative; but what her fine, classical features expressed was an absolute. It was a kind of cast-iron nihilism, which made men—men besides Officer Roscommon, that is, who had known her when—want to grovel.

Second, if such a thing could ever come in second: she had a courtesan's fabulous body—large, of course, the breasts a fortress, but also perfectly proportioned for, let's say, very excessive pleasure. Oh! not the wet dream of some poor boy who loved her; but a deluge to flood away the Eastern Seaboard, with its financial elite, its ruling class that came here for diversion of a Saturday evening, after the week's boardroom meetings, puts and calls. And look at the exquisite dimples on her rear end, beneath the fine taut fabric, which the world's richest men loved to go on their knees and kiss. But as for her hands, oh dear, who would kiss them?

XVII

I stood up slowly. I walked toward her, and she . . . gave a little hitch: the closest that woman came to showing emotion. Didn't I carry myself quite like her son? Ripoli the deformed, body and soul; Ripoli the sneaky coward, who would knife a girl to death in the dark . . . Or was it my eyes? He had one good eye, while the other twittered, off on its own, in the land of cancer.

Before my trainer I tried to look shy, but it wasn't what I felt. Into those pallid eyes, her gray-blue eyes, I gazed, and waited to hear my fate.

She spoke. Italian? It was dialect from the hills of Sicily: like I heard in Mr. Gags' homeroom between Francescuccio and Rawl Paepe.

I shrugged. My purpose gave me presence of mind.

Zia nodded. You, boy: out. Up. Go upstairs. There she would deal with me for coming where I didn't belong: the restaurant off limits. She wasn't used to such a thing, and she wasn't fooling. I would catch it later. With her black gloved hand she gave my mask a fillip. Plup. I blinked.

XVIII

Okay, Ma. Scat, get a move on. Hustle my butt up to the second floor . . . And then? What would I find there? No point asking the staff for directions, because dollars will get you doughnuts my voice was not like Ripoli's, if he still had one. Did the boy live here? Did he have his own room? What did he do all day? Had he ever been to school? Did he exist legally? Did the Maldoror Mon have a birth certificate? . . . Apparently he kept a backup mask: Grippina made no comment on my costume. I wondered if he ever took his off in order to wash that terrible face, or when he slept. I wondered if anyone knew or cared he was so sick . . . Judging from the way employees took me in stride, Rippie must be a fixture here. Menial work? Help with lifting: receive deliveries, move things. Clean up: after the distinguished clients and their dates made a little mess. Take a hand in groundskeeping . . . Maybe the Cobra was a birthday present so he could unwind sometimes; get his kicks one way or another; stay out of his mother's and the VIPs' hair? But then he couldn't take driver's lessons like a normal guy.

Benone. Just guessing. Let's go check out the rest of Shangri-La.

Behind me someone said:
—What's got into him tonight?
—Drunk! said doorman Cerberus.
Laughter.

Up the red-carpeted stairway I trudged looking at lewd finials on the banisters: carvings of naked nymphs, and fat satyrs lipping grape clusters. Okay! House on the Hill! Let's go. Not my Senior Prom tonight? Then this hell which takes itself for a heaven.

A wainscoted landing without windows served as foyer to the second circle. Standing there I saw four doors. One was ajar; and from it came the 'Twenties music I heard downstairs. Nostalgiac strains of Roxy and His Gang wafted on the romantic evening.

Inside the open door I found a nightclub space. To the right a bar: the woman bartender served a few gentlemen on stools, also couples at candlelit tables beyond the dance floor. On the far side stood a raised stage, where a DJ spun platters piped into other rooms; and there was sound equipment for live performances. I guessed a couple of large bedrooms had been joined to make this cozy space.

A portly gentleman and his young lady with her hair up—all youngish, these women, till you get close—fox-trotted cheek to cheek. That didn't seem so bad to me. If I had to spend my life's day slave-driving my wits to make a pile, and then another pile on top of the first pile, here a pile there a pile, until a golden pyramid with my name on it rose up to high heaven? if I had to make money instead of tooling around in Willys and going to the beach and having fun and not, ever, wearing a necktie: then I wouldn't mind somebody's tender touch at night either. Even a paid stranger's.

XIX

No time to tap Croesus on the shoulder and take a spin round the hardwood floor with Miss Thousand-and-One-per-Night. Zia Grippina would be here looking for me in a minute, and she was hot. I needed to avoid her, plus lady's whip, at all costs so I could see what I could see and find Mr. Ripoli's den. Sooner or later I had

to ask him a few questions: Did you kill my sister? Why? On someone's orders? Would you please give me back her teeth–if you don't
mind! . . .

So I exited the House on the Hill nightclub, and left the volup-
tuaries to their foreplay. I was thinking: My friends are at The Prom
dancing the night away, Thaddy, Chic, Franny Fofanna, guys I pal'd
around with and played sports with since childhood and Art-boy Kilroyne and John-O Kogan, and Cynthia Landis, and my homeroom
greats, those who were still among us, and Nazzarro, and Beth . . .
They're having a good time, as teenagers should, a night to remember; but I have to risk my neck finding a madman, solving a mystery
which the cops, it seems, don't want solved. Where is Ripoli right
now? Cruising the Drive to select his Prom night victim? Does he
have a date for The Prom too: up there on Maldoror Drive beneath
the WRED radio tower?

Now I wondered what to do. The three other doors were shut. Try
one? I opened . . . hey, the movies. A mini-cinema. So the second
floor, this main deck of the Good Ship Sybarite, was dedicated to
such nice things as dancing, moviegoing, polite entertainment. And
what was the feature this evening? Home movies? Not exactly . . . Before the screen were a dozen comfortable seats; in the back row two
velvet divans for some petting to the audio-visual. There in the flickering darkness sat a few more staid executive types; they were well-
behaved beside their winsome dates, as their sexual drive got a
booster from images on the screen. Hey! One's libido is a bit sluggish after moneygrubbing for half a century. It takes some high-
octane porn, fuel-injection to boot, if you want to get those old
bone-buggies rolling again.

The couples sat like good children. Sagely they held hands, pawed
a little, maybe gave a glancing kiss while their eyes stayed on the
movie. And what screen classic was being featured? No ordinary skin
flick, I can tell you, at these prices. It was a lively orgy: behind the
scenes at a semiannual festival in ancient Athens. Stilted manners
succumbed to drunkenness. Flesh peeped beneath the frippery, chi-
ton, peplon, himation; and not a drachma of talent. Actors and ac-
tresses played their parts stiffly under a long festive table as the
voyeuristic camera followed. But before I could tell apart those hot
throbbing orifices, those purple priapic penises, Plato's included:
one of the movie buffs snapped a finger at me:

–Git! Psst! Out!

Have fun, Pops. You creep! So I almost said to that captain of industry: but kept my mouth shut, since I came here tonight with a higher purpose.

XX

Outside again, I stared at the two other doors, and thought: What next? Then I opened one, peeped in, and gave a gasp beneath my mask.

This was a small theater in the round, a performance area. A raised platform in the center had a wing chair, an overbed table, commode with towel rack. On a nightstand was some gear. What gear? To me the sex toys, S & M paraphernalia, were sinister, as was the heavy scent of musk perfume.

For the audience there were chairs and sofas with cushions. The stage was lit in a way that separated, while onlookers seemed to recede, in the anonymous dark.

I peered in. Ah so! . . . On stage a buxom blond was eating dinner. Upbeat, smiling with pleasure, she gave proof of a healthy appetite. She had the élan, the joy in excesses, of superior pornography.

Meanwhile a second woman . . . or was it? No! I couldn't believe my eyes, and held both hands to my mask in horror. For *that* was Donaldsen O. (Ottilia) Sorifa, 'The Anvil', our School Board Chairman, devoted husband and father of three; the only man in Redemaine who went around saying he loved his wife. Did he work here too? Moonlighting after his School Board day? His photo had been in *Our Town News* lately due to his work as mediator in the high school race crisis. And now, beneath the makeup, his identity shone through—in an ecstasy of self-abasement. For just what, dressed up in drag as usual, was our top educator and het-perv doing here? Some volunteer work? If you will! . . . He was ***

Well. I guess the elderly gents needed novelty, extremes. And complicated, duly twisted: they were the female sadist, they were the

---

*** Censored.

male masochist. For an epoch these big boys went out and beat the world everyday; but a time came when they turned into their opposites; other instincts clamored for a chance. But they were long gone. I hadn't seen nuttin' yet. This was only the second floor. Up in the attic, Seventh Heaven, there could be such convoluted sex acts it would take a Graham McNamee ('Twenties sports announcer), if not a Hegel, to call the play by play.

Hey.

Quietly I closed the door behind me. I drew back from the mad scene.

XXI

Uh-oh, watch out. It's Zia.

I heard her metallic voice give an order at the foot of the stairs.

What to do? Hide? With a frown I stared at the mysterious fourth door. So quiet in there: what's going on? Should I open? Go on in? Hurry up, ex-Red Renegade hurler, decide.

Here came that female demon, taking the steps. In the worst way I wanted to open the fourth door and have a glimpse. No, sir: take the wiser course, decamp. So thanks to Zia Grippina I'll never know what they do in Room Four. Open season for sex? Wall Streeters on their knees before an idol even more compelling than Mammon? The President as Pan, pastoral god of fertility, plays his syrinx while the Cabinet Members as wood nymphs cavort in a choreographed orgy. Oolooloolooloo! But there's no time to see such wonders because here comes that woman.

Hold on—hold it! The fourth door is opening. What's this I see? A wedding procession!? The music segue'd to the Wedding March but jazzed up 'Twenties style. And here they came: solemn, in full regalia. There was an adipose banker type in tuxedo, red face fit to burst after his seven courses. And, by his side, went the bride: an Asian girl maybe thirteen years old, or twelve. To say she was angelic in her lavish white wedding gown, with bouquet and long train, would be a gross understatement. She was worthy of legendary Chinese beauties from the Palace of Han; but around here Big Bucks did the honors for the Son of Heaven. Then one of the house staff–gad! was it Harriet Pulley gathering material for 'Our Neighborhoods'?–read out a wedding account as the bride and groom made their way up to the third storey orgy chambers. The music changed: bridal chorus from Lohengrin; and the woman recited:

–'The bride was strikingly beautiful in a Chanel model of capusin lamé, cut on princess lines. The gown featured long sleeves, with cuffs of kolinsky fur, a high neck, and a plaited train. Her hat, an imported French model of brown tulle, was trimmed with dark brown sequins, and had a small nose roll. She carried a shower bouquet of bride's roses . . .'

So the portly partner had his extravagant fantasy: to debauch a pubescent bride on their 'wedding night'. Nice. But I wondered how much it cost him–or the shareholders–to simulate in such a detailed and elaborate way. And, too, I asked myself what came next, and had a sinking feeling. For the girl actually had a first night daze about her–just disembarked on these shores to a life of prostitution?

She was an exquisite girl, tender, aquiver with a childish life. What was happening to her? Since then I have heard a human rights report: 65,000 children, many younger than this one, arrive in New York City as port of entry each year and are sent out to staff the brothels and high-priced call girl operations of America. Millions of children across the earth serve as sexual slaves. It is called white slavery.

The procession paused before the stairs, as the reporter read on:

–'The maid of honor was gowned in a Chanel model of seagreen crinkle crepe and carried a shower bouquet of Talisman roses . . .'

The portly, red-faced CEO or investment banker, beaming and at the same time grave, like in a boardroom, led his prey upstairs to debauch her. It seems our capitalists like to invest in 'first night' futures. Jus primae noctis.

I slipped past them out of Zia's grasp. On cat's paws I took the stairs to the third floor. Up I went to the promenade deck.

There was a door at the top of this flight, and I tried the knob. Hell, it wouldn't turn. Locked. But wait–ah! The door wasn't quite to. I pushed, opened . . . then shut it behind me.

Here the layout was different. I found myself midway in a rather narrow corridor. Not four wide catty-corner entries, but eight doors on either side: a hive of private rooms tucked among the great mansion's gables. There was more oak paneling between wall hangings, and gilt-framed reproductions of Venus and consorts. Lamps on two hall tables shed an amber light shadowy at the far end. The plush quietude lent an exclusive sense. There were no rhythmic shouts, groans, squeals of protest, I can tell you that. Indeed this whorehouse was like a boardroom.

My next move? If Ripoli had his digs up here, then Zia, in her icy fury, would make a beeline and not stop on the second floor. And now, yes, those grim steps . . . on my trail. Such a zombie anger, I thought; such cold cruelty in her movements, her measured footsteps. What ever had been done to the poor woman? Ripoli-boy, you are in for it now. And because I had a father who also went for the jugular, not physically but verbally, which is worse sometimes, I felt a strange fellow-feeling for the prime suspect in my sister's murder. I had commiseration with the Maldoror Mon.

Here she came.

Where to duck from view in this maze? Find a vacant room? As midnight approached the cubicles must be filled with lovers in their stages of rapture. If I opened doors I might catch some of the state's, the nation's more influential men with their pants down. Barging in on one at his capers was not the thing to do if I meant to get ahead. If I got an eyeful of the naked deity, he could call downstairs on the intercom system.

I glanced around. Another few seconds and terror in an evening dress would come through the door. Where to, New-boy? And the exit leading up to the attic?

Scampering to the end of the hallway, I saw it turned right toward a door in the corner. Back stairs to the attic? Locked? Lunging from view I knelt and peered down the corridor of sin with its reddish aura from two shaded lamps.

Grippina emerged. Here she came; and behind her: the wedding procession.

Full speed ahead she moved in my direction. Oh yes, she knew where she was headed . . . So they had video cameras as part of their security system; and, following Rippie's movements, they thought he had gone nuts?

XXII

The attic entry looked much used. I jumped for it and turned the knob. Open! Up those old steps I vaulted three at a time.

The attic ceiling sloped low on both sides. You could unbend toward the center. I looked about—the wide space beneath the roof, used to store things, stock supplies, was unlit except for one bare bulb, red. Darker and darker, this symbolic house, as you went up. The place was pretty cobwebby to be calling itself Seventh Heaven.

What was it I heard? Voices. Not free ones, with live accents, pauses; but the canned accents of TV. Too many at once: a game show's phony happiness, a TV drama's fake sentiment, a newscaster's noble emotion as he presents his corporate employer's lies as objective reporting; a talk show's smug, fulsome tone. All jumbled together.

Here came Grippina. Her steps, on the attic stairs, plodded. She did not like having to come up here. Suddenly I heard—whap! Ooh! That smarts. Not a friendly gesture, as she gave the stairs a rap with her lady's whip. It boded no good for someone; and I'll bet you my agate for playing marbles against your ball and jacks that the person about to be flogged was a male. Come to poppa!

At the far end was a half open door. I fairly dove for it since the poppa about to get popped was me. I wasn't ready to be a poppa; I just wanted to say bye bye to this madhouse and take off the suffocating mask and, back inside Willys, drive to the place where my classmates were holding a Senior Prom tonight, though it was almost over. I wanted to gaze my fill, poor guy, at Beth and Nazzarro dancing cheek to cheek in this life's only real Seventh Heaven, perhaps: namely first love, adolescent happiness, but it doesn't last long.

I went to the door at the far end, tiptoed inside, and—well, you've heard a few gasps in these pages, lovers' gasps, naïveté's gasps; but this time I gave a quadruple, no, a sextuple gasp, though silently, as I crouched inside the door unnoticed. For in this room a tall blond man, not so old, lay across a king-size mattress on the floor, and he took things to the limit. Was the tall blond man, corporate executive or famous politician, in his birthday suit? Almost. Was he grandly erected? Maybe, but that's complex. Were these Buddhist breathing exercises he was doing: Zen meditation, yoga for the initiates? I don't think so, but he was in Seventh Heaven nevertheless. Had he memorized lust's catechism? Yes.

I know what comes next will be hard to believe. It is like allegory, a Lecher's Progress. Also, I don't want to make my true story too unreadable by showing a lot of unholy filth. But what can I do? Here's the reality. Cry, or deny. The more graphic it is, in this case–the more adequate.

The gentleman's tailored suit of finest cloth, his linen, vest, suspenders, silk necktie, personal effects, were neatly arranged in the space provided. No disorder, no messiness. Enjoy yourself.

Two handsome ladies straight from an English sitting room, as overclad as Queen Victoria, though without panties, were giving the good fellow his money's worth. They wheezed, they grunted a little, at their task, like an infernal punishment. But did they really want to hurt and humiliate the famous man, one of our most respected public servants? I think if they'd had their druthers they might have chosen another way to make a buck. This was just plain hard work, not pleasure, for them.

One sat on his . . . on his . . . countenance, pardon me. She reached back and gave his thighs, and contradictorily stiff prick (I'll explain) brisk taps with a leather crop, as though riding a mule, geegee!

The second gal whose charms I also viewed from the rear might have lost thirty pounds without lessening the effect. Kneeling, she had the client's downy legs slung round her hips. All her strong body rocked as the lower torso drove some sort of prosthetic device, a plastic phallus strapped to her vagina, into his anal cavity. She had a plodding rhythm, like a well handle.

I describe this without verve: the way a doctor charts a patient. But in the orgy chamber I gazed like a scientist on the verge of new worlds. It was all new to me, though vulgar enough, everyday stuff in House on the Hill. Crouched by the door I watched them work out, pumping flesh, getting in their reps.

Then Zia Grippina crossed the threshold.

She cut a stately figure as she unbent toward the center. She had the whip in her hand. I feared she would come this way and find me; but it seems she did not share my interest in the sexual excesses of Seventh Heaven. Instead, she made for the other side where the TVs were playing.

The two prostitutes, hard taxed, didn't note Zia's arrival. Facing the other way they went through the motions of rapture, and chatted a bit:
—Twenty more minutes of this.
—Christa's got her cramps.
The offhand tone only fortified the masochist's illusion. He groaned; he managed a little whimper. Spurred on by his lovers' nonchalance, the idea they did this for money, his superb body gave a shudder. I thought in a minute he might sing out: aïe, Maria! Mommy! But he was a well brought-up boy and didn't speak with his mouth full.
—Cramps or no cramps she better get her butt up here. Jeannette too, the bitch.
Pause.
Ah! . . . pfslüsk . . . ah! . . . pflsoooss' . . .
—Christa could be in for a career change.
—Whuz' she care? . . . Gawd, what a tight arse this one has . . . Think it'd get easier after . . . (She checked her watch.) After forty-three minutes.
—'s a shame though, goodlooking kid.
—Sure, sure, fit for a lord. Dame Christa, heh-heh.
—You're hard, Minnie.
—No, I'm soft. That's my problem. If I had an iron cunt this dildo wouldn't make me sore.
—Shh.
—Good grief, I can't wait to go douche. This character has a der-rière on him like a brick.
—Hush, he'll hear.
—Of course he'll hear, and he digs it. Right, Sweetie?—Minnie went on satisfying the customer: like a hackney driver at an amble.—I'll tell you a joke. What has more fun than a barrel of monkeys?
—I give.
—The asshole of flunkeys. Ha ha ha, get it? Not bad.
The one sitting on U.S. Senator's face gave a laugh: sort of a girl-ish giggle at the humor.

XXIII

Big Minnie glimpsed her wristwatch again and said:
—Shit.
By the door I chuckled. I'm a fool. But it was funny the way she sodomized the great man, so casual.
Minnie turned and screeched:
—Ripoli! Are you bats? Get the frick out! La Grippe will have our asses if she catches you in here.
The other swung round, lifting from her saddle. And that's when I saw two things. First, the cunnilinguist's face: those noble features awash with vaginal secretion. He was happy. He beamed. And why not? It was a gift for the man who has everything; and this man, ***, Jr., already had fame and fortune not as Senator but Governor of the great state of ***. Shh! Not a word! He also had a nickname, Timber, or Tim: whether because the press said he was 'Presidential timber', or because his doctoral thesis, published and recently reedited, was on conservationist history and issues. *Almanacs and Timberjacks* is the work of a scholar, not a bad book, if we are to believe my P.O.D. teacher, Mrs. Hebbel. But it seems Gov.***, Jr., went the way of all elected officials and became an absolute imbecile once in office.
Now someone will ask: What are you saying, Newell Gilbert? Do you imply that every such leader of U.S. society, from the President on up, does his kinky business with the big corporations, those whorehouses? That the United States Government itself is nothing more or less than a . . . Seventh Heaven?
No ticky, no laundry.
The second thing I noticed, before I had to scoot, was this: Mr. Governor wore a black leather doozy, like an athletic cup, tied tight over his dingle. Did it protect him against taps from the rider's crop? Pain was the name of the game; but let's not get carried away and injure the national figure. Also, I guess he wore that doodad to keep from orgasming after two minutes and wasting a lot of precious time, for the trip down here, and money; so he wouldn't come to his senses, and miss out on the fun. So it was a sort of bridle on that proud pizzle: that thoroughbred racer kept in the starting block. In other words, this foolishness must go on until tomorrow morning, as the civil servant put in overtime without a break for coffee and

doughnuts, but only a change in shifts so Minnie could go douche. Good deal! Isn't this how things should be in Seventh Heaven? I think I'll just stand up and recite 'Ode to a Grecian Urn' from memory: a poem much praised by our English teacher Penny Grich, future old maid if she survives lung cancer who may not find a man good enough for her, unless it is our tennis coach Mr. Rolly Petrocchi, 'Mr. P.' to you, and he proves willing to help her out pretty soon. That could be; it might even come to pass tonight, since they were chaperoning the Senior Prom together at Frankie's Villa Pompei, and could hit Maldoror Drive later on; unless, as adults, they skipped the secondary stuff and made 'the shortest line between two points' straight to our biology teacher's bunk, where a few organisms have been investigated, the makeup of their parts, long 'ere this. 'Forever shalt thou love, Mr. P., say hey! and Penny Grich be fair': if Miss G. just wouldn't smoke and was a little more stacked; if she wouldn't cough all over the classroom pulling a hanky spasmodically from her bra, Miss Emphysema in our Class of '61 Yearbook, while she recited Johnny-boy Keats, as Byron called him, if not that farce 'Murder in the Cathedral'.

But enough meditation. Minnie is screaming for me to leave, and it's high time I evacuated Seventh Heaven. The coast is clear, Zia Grippina has gone into a room across the attic, and I must scram while the scrammin' is good.

And Gov.***, Jr.? He'll be here till dawn: taking on Minnie, Christa and colleagues. The great man is like the Roman emperor's wife who visited the city's tenderloin from time to time, and took her place in one of the prostitutes' cages.

XXIV

I was at the attic door and on my way. Screw this! But I heard someone crying, a distressing sound, along with that strange Babel of TV sets. What was it? I love children and didn't like to hear one squawking, bawling his head off, being abused. Whap! The whip came down. Momma! Don't! . . . Whap! Please, Mommy, no! I'm sorry! . . . Whap! . . . Now what further craziness was going on inside House on the Hill? A little kid being whipped? Ripoli-boy, you sure knew how to choose them when it came to mothers.

Something in me snapped. I saw red, and didn't know what I was doing just then. I made for the room on the far side.

In there I found Zia Grippina lashing not a child, not physically one at least, but the real Ripoli. She came down on him with all her might; and this time, for once in his life, Rippie was innocent. He cried out and writhed under his mother's vicious, pitiless whacks. To his face, also.

—No, Mama! Ow! . . . It wasn't me. Ow! ow! I won't do it again. I promise! No-o-o!

Don't ask me why, but I advanced on Zia from behind and grabbed the whip just as she poised to strike again for all she was worth. The timing was such: her raised arm must have wrenched out of its socket. She sent up a howl and fell backward, at my feet, cradling the arm or maybe dislocated shoulder. Had enough?

Well, she couldn't believe her eyes and neither could her bastard son: seeing *a second Ripoli* in the room with them. One of him was enough! A little terror! At sight of me they both stared and looked mesmerized. But I couldn't help them. There wasn't time to explain. Half out of my own wits after the dullsville night which I should have spent like a normal teenager at The Prom, even if it was with twirler Dee Sapegno, I took out my frustration on Zia. Sorry about that. I hit her when she was down, lying on the floor in pain; otherwise I couldn't have handled her. Did she care if she whipped her son's cancerous face into a bloody pulp? No. Did she pull her punches?

Ripoli got up, grabbed for his mask, and ran out. But, escaping, he yelled not in a child's puling whine like just now, under the gun, but in a gurgle, maybe his everyday voice:

—I'll kill her. Kill! Kill! I will.

He disappeared through the attic door, and I turned to Big Zia. On one knee I grabbed, hoisted her up, by the arm, and positioned her over my other knee. Indelicately I yanked down her panties: not a cagey black lace affair like her dress, but a prosaic beige as though after all sex wasn't her brand. And then: I let 'er rip—a lady's whip for a lady. Whap! Blip! Ah, that feels good. Ha ha! Want more? Whup. Aïe! . . . As you see I was out of my mind. I gave Grippina the good spanking her first lover should have given her; but Rune Roscommon didn't love her, or himself, enough to do that. Love is needed to take someone on, their pride and errors, and all that nasty chaos inside us, the personhood for better and for worse. A real, risky, until-the-end love is required. I guess our Police Chief didn't have it in him: those days when he and Zia found bliss in the sack. Hey, one or two don't.

What happened next will sound kind of wacky. So be it. Lately in raids on my dad's bookshelves I had found the great Russian novelists: now why did our learned teachers never have us read them? Too real? . . . So now I tried out my Dostoyevsky on this fallen woman: since Newell Gilbert hadn't found himself yet, but was looking among the Karamazovs.

I eased Zia off my knee, onto her side. Enough rough stuff for one day! But the way she looked at me then: as if I gave her a taste of what she craved; and would I please serve up the second helping? Ah! that's more like it . . . Finally! She sighed with a frank invitation to the hard-guy detective, Johnny Dollar, who messed up her hairdo; and I had a notion to finish what I started with Beth Engstrom on Maldoror Drive, a few weeks ago, when Nazzarro happened by catching butterflies. Only thing, there wasn't time right now to get myself deflowered. I had to go after Ripoli. The boy was in such a state, he might claim his next victim, Thania, Penny Grich, whomever, before this night ended.

Still I knelt there staring in Zia's strong, handsome face gone soft for the first time in a long time. Eyes wide, lips parted, she held out a gloved hand and sort of scratched my pants leg. I took that hand . . . grabbed the wrist . . . and pulled off the glove! Oh, oh! Her hand was a gristly, tendonous claw. And do you know what I did? A Dostoyevskian impulse came over me, and I bowed to kiss that ghastly talon; at least the intention was clear as I held it to my Ripoli-mask. And do you know what Zia's response was to my saintly gesture? She laid a fart. So you see here I must part ways with Fyodor Mikhailovich. From her shapely bum, with red stripes, came a lengthy and sonorous aporrhea . . . Take that, Father Zossima.

Well! I must say: her bullet made sad work of my caresses. Maybe that was her mating call; there were some strange auk squawks here in House on the Hill. But I preferred perfume to passing gas; so if I did have any designs on Grippie's person, I dropped them on the spot. Ah me, where would we be without the animal in us? But it can be pretty pitiful.

XXV

I stood up. I paused over her, and laughed, low. Not at her. At myself.

Before going I glanced around.

Ripoli's room.

Creepy! And my sister's teeth?

There was a shelf of cosmetics: a few different facial creams. I saw no medicines, no pill bottles. So the thing was left untreated? . . . I had a friend who complained of headaches every night: his family never noticed that his eyeglass frames were badly askew. But maybe the sarcoma was Ripoli's secret, among other secrets, beneath his mask? Zia knew.

I said to her:

—Your son needs treatment. That's cancer on his face.

But, of course, Ripoli couldn't go see a doctor or enter a hospital. For this he would have to join the human race: exist legally.

—Who are you? she said.

On the wall I saw two framed pictures of Evelyne Genia Gilbert. One was clipped from *Our Town News* during the period when she, a ten year-old, got her fifth grade friends together and formed a Disaster Relief Committee (her name for it) after the 1954 hurricane. The kids canvassed Spring Glen and made phone calls; they raised over 2000 dollars, some money back then. Evo was like child Mozart with his opera for children.

The other photo, published after her death, showed the high school senior. Beautiful and strange: her dark eyes so alert, her hair cut short; her high cheekbones like Granny Wilhelmina's, a trait coming from contact with a North Carolina tribe generations ago.

I looked around. In the heat of action we weren't watching television, but now I saw seven, eight TV sets spaced along the walls and playing all at once: every channel beamed to Redemaine. So this was the life of Zia Grippina's sick son: boob tube all day long, like a living death. Not one show but eight at once were required by such an addiction. Then at night he went out to cruise in the Cobra, prowl, maybe imitate the violence he imbibed like mother's milk from television. And so his life became a hate-filled fantasy of the whipping mother: this furthered by TV programs the best of which are antisocial, a toxic pollution. Could it be that we, as a people, if we watch enough TV, and believe the lies we are told, all corporate lies meant to program us and control our minds, make us individualistic and sociopathic as Ripoli: could it be we will end up living like him, in our more subtle way, and become a nation of hate?

I left Zia there on the floor, panting like a wounded animal, and ran onto the attic stairs after my double.

XXVI

Back on the third floor I found such a silence. Were the rooms soundproofed? Hm. Was something unsavory in the works: like the marriage of a depraved magnate to a girl sold into slavery? Hush up, you! Cover it up! . . . And I thought: who knows if my sister's death wasn't planned in one of these rooms? And the conspirators, KKK, State Security for all I knew, simply made use of Ripoli's hatred of women? . . . For there were those who feared Evo's relation to Jame Hayes; they despised it as a bad example, and saw its destruction, and hers, as a way to stir up racial division. Divide and conquer. When the people start getting together, their rulers begin to quake.

In my grief for Evelyne I was ready to suspect the jokers who paid visits to House on the Hill: all the big men on their knees before a whore called Capital. It must excite them a lot to pay money and commodify love. The Midas touch! Their hearts, or their peckers, a better investment, are commodified too in the process. But that was done long ago. Now staid banker and fancy courtesan were ready to sell life itself. And so they met at the cash nexus, where opposites interpenetrate.

Well, I had to go. But why not give these johns, or John Birchers— or birchees—something to think about? Why not create an uproar and make my getaway in the confusion?

XXVII

Along the plush corridor I went opening doors to the inner sancta. This side and that I flung them wide. Now there were sexual grunts, love taps and slaps, whaps, slurps, laughs, laps. It should have been a lovemakers' symphony to encourage the world; instead, it was like canned audience responses. Sounds of sadomasochism, rapt sighs, cries, wafted along the stuffy hallway. I went about harrowing hell, and singing *Reveille* at the top of my lungs. You gotta get up! You gotta get up! You gotta get up in the mo-o-orning! . . . I gave the old boys a jolt in passing; I made them raise on an elbow and say: huh? it's the cops? and think it was time to bolt. Lust's hard labor, love's locomotion, pain's pleasure, passion's protest—the hypocrites—torture's transport, ah! Voices, whispers, murmurs, exclamations. Bleating, purring, pleading. Besides the squeals, fake cries of outrage, there may have been angry reactions to my prank. I couldn't tell the difference.

I went along laughing and yanking doorknobs. And now, in my wake: here came society's leaders in their briefs. The crème de la crème, creamed and creamy, in hell. Men with bellies too big for their spindly legs, financiers, top executives, government officials: all stood grimacing, and fingering their G-strings. Ho! One had his partner's panties round his neck. Another poor specimen, with a tuft of white fluff on his sunken chest, made you wonder if the place had wheelchair access.

No sign of our noble bridegroom with his child bride. He must have rented the executive suite, tucked in a secret fold among the mansion's eaves, where he could be certain his dirty work would go undisturbed.

Like Christ in the temple I rousted out those parasitic bandits, those CEOs, and they came forth squinting into the dim corridor. Is it the Revolution? Now tycoon and Street hotshot, sound businessmen all, solid names, pictures of probity, stood in their underdrawers staring after me. They looked mighty piffed. Glum as scum. Perhaps it had been that magic instant, for them, when nature seems to recollect an ancient secret, and a shudder passes from the man to the woman . . . The one they paid for. And at such a time Grippina's mad son comes along and upsets the applecart. Get the hell out of here, young skunk! Piss me off!

XXVIII

I erupted onto the ground floor gripping Thaddy's gun in case the big bruiser by the door had orders to block my exit. A good thing he just stood there and gaped at Ripoli II. I was pretty wound up and capable of anything.

—Forgot my car keys!

I tried to talk Rippie's gurgle-talk.

People in the front room looked at me, then each other, and wondered.

Someone said:

—What's taking Grippina so long?

It occurred to me: there could be pressure on her to get Ripoli out of House on the Hill. Have him put away.

Past the pert receptionist, past the doorman and through the front door I plunged into the Spring Glen night . . .

Phew! What a relief to be out of there. What rotten loneliness . . . ! What sorry behavior on the part of those big boys! Tomorrow they'll strut about like paragons of virtue, but tonight they pay top dollar to go on all fours and lick Folly's feet. Stimulation! Shake 'em up! Old bag of bones! Why, I think I'll just give a hearty rendition of 'Cigareets and Whuskey' right now in their honor. C'mon, Reader, sing along with me:

> *Cigareets 'n whúskey*
> *'n wild wild women!*
> *They'll drive you crazy,*
> *they'll drive you insane,*
> *pum, pum . . .*

> *Cigareets is a blight*
> *on the whole human race,*
> *pum, pum . . .*

XXIX

Off came the mask.

Back in the Willys I drove beyond Spring Glen and through the sleeping town. Streets empty at three a.m.; all my classmates gone to their petting nests. Along Havilland a few night owls made their way home.

By Redemaine Mall I hung a left and then turned on Thorndale Avenue. There was a dewy fragrance in those wooded stretches as I made my way toward the Maldoror Drive entry.

Silence. Maybe a lone cricket. And no street lights, way over there, on the outskirts.

Senior Prom '61 had ended. I missed it, and for what? A few weeks ago I had a notion to ask Samantha Esmonde to go with me: a junior, the high school's first black cheerleader. Pretty girl, so bright. But I hardly knew her.

Slowly, I drove up the approach road onto The Drive. But I paused and stepped out to take a deep breath, freshen up a bit; get my thoughts in order. I breathed in the sweet night air, let my eyes adjust to the darkness, and then got back in the jeep.

Headlights off, I started along Maldoror Drive.

At the first parking circle, lookout area, half a dozen cars stood side by side. In the backseats were my classmates. It was the chapel in the moonlight.

I drove past them, slowly, in the Willys.

—Hey, Gilby! What's the word?

What fool was that calling out? Ah, Fran Fofanna, lefty hurler, in his dad's Plymouth. He was with Filomena Ornata who worked after school at the Music Box. Not bad.

I cruised, lingering a minute. It was nice to see stars twinkling over the town. What got me was the moon, big, overripe, how it hung low toward the horizon and looked so near.

There were more cars, couples. High school girls would brave the Maldoror Mon, telling their parents some story or other, to go where their boyfriends led. Try to tell a normal teenager there's some chance we may die one day—much less today. Crazy kids, good kids. The Maldoror Mon and/or escaped inmate Jared Simms could go jump in the lake, or Water Company, for all my classmates cared on Prom night '61. Anyway, they weren't interracial couples targeted by a killer with a fixation . . . Also, it was good the way they grouped together, and had an eye out; though I wouldn't have wanted to be in the car at either end.

XXX

Roaming deeper into West Hills Park, I saw no more cars. Only darkness. It wasn't easy to drive lights off. Not far from the radio relay tower I switched off the ignition and coasted down a slight incline. Did I hear voices?

Then, on my right, maybe a hundred yards before the WRED tower, there was a dirt road leading beneath the trees. Nazzarro's father, Giovanni Zummo, Town Comptroller, had been able to acquire a small plot here; I don't know how, since this was public land. There was some talk about zoning law infringement; but they let his son build a cabin up here in the woods to keep the restless boy out of mischief. (!) Talented Nazzarro might have become a naturalist, an engineer of some kind, but he had a phobia to sitting in a classroom.

Now I glimpsed right and thought I saw something, by the moonlight in among the trees. Pulling over the Willys I got out and ran half crouching down that dirt road. By the cabin two cars were parked, Nazzarro's 'Vette, and—the Cobra!

So Ripoli came here after running out of House on the Hill? What was he doing with Naz? Did he return to the scene of his crime again and again: seeking to feel that charge again, the thrill of killing an innocent girl? . . . Did it release him for an hour from the anguish of being himself?

Was Beth inside the cabin with them?

XXXI

A candle flickered in the window. There were low voices: the way whispers want to become louder. Yes, I heard Thani Engstrom's voice, as she seemed to protest. What was going on? But before I could hear more, and get the drift–a powerful flashlight shone right in my face.

–Newell? said Nazzarro through the window. What are you doing here?

I pointed at Ripoli.

–Following him. Will you turn that off?

Nazzarro lowered the beam and said:

–Okay, it's good you came . . . Thani, go with Newell till this is over. He'll take you home.

–N-no.

–Go on.

She was dressed not in her Prom gown with corsage, but slacks and a blouse which looked rumpled. What had they been doing? How far did they go? . . . I looked at her and thought: all the way. But why on earth was Ripoli here–the Maldoror Mon become their best man?

Nazzarro said:

–Don't worry, I'll come by in the morning.

Hands on her shoulders, he turned Beth and marched her toward the door. And I thought: yes, they slept together, for him to look so cocksure of her. She is putty in his hands. But somehow or other I felt: it is right. And just then I didn't hold it against him, or her. By Nazzarro's flashlight I saw she didn't look too perky. Had she been crying?

Meanwhile the other, masked, stood there, like a dark statue. He looked on: amazed by my bizarre costume, just like his own? Ah, ah. He waited.

XXXII

And then we were headed back toward the Drive entry, Redemaine side. I still didn't know what was happening. Lights on, as dawn approached, we went like a funeral procession: first the Cobra, next the 'Vette, then Willys. Was Nazzarro taking him in: to the police station? Better yet to the hospital? I had a hunch the theatrical and strong-willed Naz was showing off as always: as when he rode past Tony Eden's in a sort of Roman triumph–seated at the wheel of his trailored speedboat, wearing a pair of great Moon-Goggles, while a friend drove; or when he and his pet raccoon went on a boisterous drinking bout and painted the town; or when he donned a Maldoror Mon disguise and made forays to scare people: myself and Beth, for instance, the afternoon I poached on his territory . . . and then he had us hiking through the forest so he could point out its wonders. Well, he had finished what I started. But where to this time? Had he convinced Grippina's son to confess and turn himself in? Or else be admitted, late in the game, for medical treatment? Perhaps Ripoli only came to ask Nazzarro–who assembled his Cobra and souped it up like my Willys?–ask the master mechanic to work some more on his car.

The three hot rods rolled on with an ominous rumbling, as if something dramatic was about to happen, past the first circle.

I broke the silence:

–Will you please tell me what this is about?

By my side Beth didn't speak. She seemed distant, not crying, but needing to pull herself together. Hysteria lurked. It was in the situation. I felt such a tension without knowing why: also, there was a strangeness between the two of us, finding ourselves side by side again, on Prom night.

I asked:

–What is that . . . that guy doing here?

In a weak voice she said:

–When he's upset, he comes to see Nazzarro.

–They know each other?

–Childhood friends.

–Ah, so he knew him . . .

–Long time.

–Where are they off to now? Please clue me in.

–They're going to race.

–At this hour?

–Ripoli's been begging him to have a drag race.

–What for?

–To see who's got the fastest car in town.

–Say, that's important.

–It counts.

–Who will know? Or care? *Our Town News* doesn't report drag races.

–I'll know, she said. You'll know. He's got us in position to watch.

–That's all? So you and I will know? What ambition. Anyway he's already got you, he's won.

–There arc stakes, said Beth. If Naz wins, Rip goes to the hospital for treatment. Now, after the race. That's the bet.

–And if Rip wins?

–Then he's the fastest. And Naz will pay for some sort of newfangled Moon-Goggles gear.

–The Cobra's already modified out of its mind. IIell, what will such a race prove?

–Who's the fastest.

–I don't like it.

She gave a gesture, and said:

–Join the club.

I paused. Then, grimly, took a plunge:

–Seems a bit anticlimactic . . . when you consider Ripoli's a psychopathic killer. He murdered Evelyne Gilbert.

Beth shot a glimpse. It was the first time her eyes met mine.

–That's a big statement. You have proof?

–Not hard and fast, yet. Everything points to it.

–I don't believe you. The escaped prisoner from Condor . . . what's his name?

–Jared Simms. Scapegoat.

–But why Ripoli? she said. What's the motive?

–Hate.

–Of Evelyne? He never met her.

–Yet her picture is on the wall of his bedroom: two of them, blown up life-size. I just now had a look.

–What?

–If he'd known her maybe he wouldn't have hated. What he can't stand, what he envies . . . is life. Beauty. Love. Things he can't have.

–How do you know this? Did you ask him?

–No.

–Then, said Beth, you don't know.

–I know what I saw tonight: his mother named Zia Grippina thrashing his tumor-face, up in House on the Hill, where I snuck in. I'll grant you he doesn't chat much. But I've had a look beneath that mask.

I grinned, and showed her *my* mask–reached around and took it from the backseat. Held it up.

–Oh!

–His face isn't pretty, not a joy forever. Advanced sarcoma–what my mom has, now, but it doesn't show, yet. And the characters he lives with aren't pretty either. Simigliones. And Zia too: Mafia Ma. I talked to Hal Duggan at *Our Town News;* and Duggan hinted at a conspiracy in my sister's death. Ku Klux Klan, or others.

–Really now. In Redemaine?

–KKK, maybe with 'macro' backing. Up the scale.

–Macro?

–Do you know about House on the Hill?

–What?

–You don't. In Spring Glen: the old Shetland estate. I just spent my Prom night there, and who do you think I danced with cheek to cheek?

– . . .

–Ripoli lives there with his mother, Zia Grippina of the Simiglione mafia clan, and . . . others.

–Tomao Simiglione is not a crook. Tst, I think you're getting a bit carried away, Newell. Like the things you told me about your private school: your imagination working overtime.

–You believed me then . . .

Well, I didn't insist, but only laughed, low, and kept my eyes on the road. It hurt. In her eyes I was a dropout: after we broke up, and I quit baseball, said so long to the in-crowd at the high school. And yet she was the one with a weakness for Beatniks, introspection, the new '60s life waiting in the wings. In words, for her, okay, but not in deed–Beatniks, sure, but . . . go steady with one? Marry one? That was a contradiction in terms. Well then: what she didn't know, I couldn't tell her.

Anyway we had reached the end of Maldoror Drive, and the two sportscars made their turn onto the runway.

What a night ... 'Oh What a Night', by The Dells, on the ***
record label.

It wasn't over yet.

XXXIII

Slowly, the other two moved out into Thorndale Avenue. Ripoli
slipped into the safer right lane and waited as Nazzarro lined up on
his left. Then both hot engines stood idling, jumpy, splut-grrr, fsplutt
... I drew up behind them.

I nodded and said to Beth:

–This is foolish. A drag race at 4:30 in the morning. But tell me
something: are you two engaged?

–Not formally. College first. But we're a couple, Newell.

–College for Nazzarro?

–First the community college. He'll settle down.

–Wild child takes Psych 101.

–Remember, I was dating him before you and I met. When Naz
and I couldn't make it, the first try, he got wilder.

–Why did he send you with me now?

–In case anything happens.

–Why ask me to drive you home?

–He trusts me. Believes in me.

–Sure, I know. But also–

–Also what?

–Less weight in the 'Vette.

–Come now. Really, Newell.

I stared ahead, and gave a poor excuse for a grin.

From the Drive entry Thorndale Avenue makes a long downward
bend, like a toboggan run, which has always attracted drag racers eager to test-run their creations. This strip was not much travelled, and
fully visible from either end: a good mile and a half. That was the
beauty of it. But way down there the dividing lines closed; it became
dangerous to stay in the passing lane. The road wound leftward beyond a treeline so you had little warning if a car came the other way.
Of course this added to the fascination: it was like drag racing the unseen, death in the lefthand lane, as crazy kids roared into the blind

curve. One must let up on the accelerator and accept second place or else take what may be a fatal risk. I guess if this was only about being fastest that wouldn't have been enough. Even speed begins to bore in the long run. Now, for example, I could have gone to the finish line, using the Willys headlights to start the race and then hitting my brights if a car came from the far side. But it was too late. Anyway Nazzarro would have vetoed such ground rules.

Screeeeech! Ripoli floored the Cobra leaving a wake of rubber as flames purled on his rear tires and flung back smoke.

Screeeeeeech! Nazzarro's 'Vette leapt forward burning rubber and cutting the other's head start since the Cobra fishtailed.

Screeeeechch! I rammed down the Willys pedal and haulassed after them since the fumes in my face were a taunt to my male ego and sent my saner instincts out the window.

Beth gasped as the jeep stationwagon, perched high and slightly lopsided, jumped, bumped, clunked through its gears and lunged forward like a big jack-in-the-box—not low and sleek, made for racing, not hugging asphalt like the other two, but jolting itself along, a loping hunchback.

Midway on the drag strip we were pushing top end but curiously my car had power to spare, and, decreasing their lead, might have made a bid to pass if there was room. All three cars were souped up to the limit in Nazzarro's garage; and only he knew what each had under the hood. It seemed he had chosen a clumsy green Willys to produce his masterpiece.

Down the raceway we flew eastward toward a patch of purplish red sky beyond the dark trees. Dawn began to rise over the New England town in slumber. Phrphrooom! This was the first time I ever opened 'er up and I thought: what did the boy put under my hood? No wonder my mom got the willies that day she went in the garage with her grocery list and turned over the ignition and then shook her head and said in her whiny southern accent: Newell, you damn fool. But my little sister, Lemonie by her side in the car, said: C'mon, Ma-babe, Newby's ruined this one too; let's crank up the Packard.

Along Thorndale Avenue we three went screaming like eagles after the same rabbit. Up ahead the frontrunners were dead even, full throttle in a bottle, while I stayed on their tail for the fun of it. Thani sat staring forward, almost in shock: like the time I took her on the rollercoaster and she came away deeply shaken—hip-swinging cheerleader on the outside, sensitive plant within. I shouldna' scared her then, or now . . . but hell, I was feeling pretty loose after Zia, and House on the Hill.

At the yellow and black sign for a curve in the road, reflecting our headlights, and as the dividing lines went solid saying: stay in lane—those two kept on racing neck and neck. Nobody ever died here that I know of; though Clay Vorhees from our class now drag races in a wheelchair; and Ricky Graybeal in the class ahead of us, mound ace before Chic, screwed up his legs in an accident on Thorndale Avenue.

Suddenly Nazzarro went into his run. He gave it the gas and tried to pass.

No! no! no!

Here came a car rounding the curve: at high speed as its headlights shot through the trees. A drunk driver? Didn't he see both lanes occupied? Didn't he see four lights rushing toward him? He kept on coming. Maybe it was our School Board Chairman, on his way home from House on the Hill: out here dragging in drag . . . ? Donny, haven't you had enough kicks for one night? Thus I joked to myself, with a chuckle, since it is human nature to think nothing bad can happen.

Nazzarro still had time to let up and ease back in behind the Cobra—accept defeat with a good excuse, and race another day. I braked to give him room. But, as the leader of hot rodders in Rede-maine, he had to win. Thani and I were watching him. Also, he wanted his childhood friend to enter the hospital for treatment: that was the deal. Though Ripoli would probably kill himself if he lost this race. His car was his god.

Oh! oh! oh!

Not only would Ripoli not give way and let Nazzarro pass—oh! oh! now he slowed when his opponent slowed, and wouldn't let him get back in the right lane! At the sight I gave my car the gas to jolt that Cobra's tail out of the way. Too late! The other came on, came on, blaring its horn, beginning to brake but not willing to take his car over the road shoulder and into a tree.

For a breathtaking few seconds it could have gone either way. Nazzarro wavered. The 'Vette veered. At the last instant he might have got back in. He was trying—but then, oh! Ripoli gave him a lit-tle bump, fender against fender, bump, sparks. That rascal kept him out there in the passing lane. The devil! Oh! Devil in hell!

Bbooooooooommmmmmmaaaaahhhk!!!!!!!!!
Head on, grill to grill doing over a hundred Nazzarro smashed into the oncoming sedan which went airborne and flew up over the windshield of my Willys and back behind us with sparks showering in the darkness and then flames bursting up. Missed us by a hair! Beth was shrieking as miraculously we rolled on. But the 'Vette shot sideways darting, rolling over and over like a toy matchbox car on a rug; it hurtled into the forest on our left-hand side and exploded in fire.

Live fast, die young, and have a mangled corpse burnt to a crisp.

The Cobra never looked back. It zipped free as you please along lower Thorndale Avenue, and ducked into a side street.

I headed for the nearest house and a telephone.

By my side Beth Engstrom laughed hysterically.

Dawn was rising as the sky turned crimson over the town.

Chapter Eight

I

Nazzarro's death sent shock waves through Redemaine. More than Evelyne Gilbert's: for she was daughter to a university professor who used Spring Glen as a bedroom, while Nazzarro was the Comptroller's son, his family a fixture in the life of the community. Also, this being the second tragic teenage death in ten weeks: people asked what the world was coming to. What next?

On a Sunday morning in June the neighborhoods came out for the funeral service like a public event. The largest Catholic church, Saint Rita's, could hardly hold them all. Local and state officials offered condolences. They sat up front. The Italian community came en masse and shared their grief. Classmates were there; the ZBKs came as one to mourn their leader. But Bethany Engstrom was in the hospital.

I remember Nazzarro's mother in her stately robe as she entered church from the bright sunlight. Her dark eyes glowed. One day, visiting their house while Naz worked on my car, I saw those dark eyes sparkle as she admired her favorite who had such talent, such promise. He held up his bristling pet raccoon and shook it a little, and laughed. Now those maternal eyes shone like smoldering coal, but they didn't sparkle. There was a pall over that exaltation.

Everyone felt a sincere grief. Something very good, though left to run wild, had been taken from us. Lost. The people knew it, I mean the *people*-people, working districts and their children, who came out that day and didn't need fine words and gestures to show their big heart and their sympathy. Some I knew since Peewees and had seen here and there over the years. Also I saw former classmates, all but forgotten, from Mr. Gags' homeroom of dropouts. Louis 'The Limp' Trecastagne was on hand with his parents, and Mills Brooks, Francescuccio, Biff, Rawl Paepe. There were so many familiar faces. But one student, alumnus from the class ahead of us, I wouldn't see again: that was the other driver, Mervin Schlosser, tooling around drunk in the predawn hour after another night boozing at Farrelly's. He was killed.

II

I found a place at the back of the church. I had been in the news as one present at Nazzarro's death: a drag racer too, a crazy teenager. And so Evelyne Gilbert's brother all but made a second focus of attention. I didn't try to hide, but stood by a pillar with my head up. The town had known me through the baseball years; they understood I could be a little wild, and lately rumors went around about my and Thaddy's pranks. But I don't believe they thought I was bad, capable of anything base. Mainly I was the bane of my poor folks, my mom sick with cancer.

No need to get into legal aspects. The matter was dropped the moment Beth seconded my story: that Nazzarro's rival on Thorndale Avenue had been someone else. Do you think Ripoli ever got brought in to answer questions? Guess again. The devil has connections. It might not be easy to arraign someone who was the shame personified of our civic leaders, and therefore not admitted to a legal existence. So Ripoli would keep floating around, out there, like the town's evil genius. He was exempt. In vain did I and then Beth Engstrom identify the drag racer whose tire marks stood alongside the 'Vette's by the Maldoror Drive entry. Nobody cared to hear: not town officials, and not Hal Duggan or the reporters. Rippie never got mentioned in *Our Town News* and broader news outlets following the fate of Redemaine.

There were those who nodded and said hello to me inside Saint Rita's. Among them were the Blacks in attendance. Sammy Esmonde, the cheerleader, smiled nicely toward me and said a word to her father who was blind, Reverend Esmonde from Gordiane Baptist Church. He also sketched a smile. Then my Babe Ruth League coach from the Greenwood section gave me a nod. And others had signs of sympathy for the family of Evelyne Gilbert dead like Nazzarro at an early age.

But I must say the majority disapproved of my presence at the funeral. They stared or looked away, if they noticed me, which most did. First there was my role in his death, though suppositious. Next there were the escapades with Thad Floriani at Farrelly's Spa and Roscommon's Tavern, bruited about town by now since sooner or later people see through disguises. The story was embellished. Ah! The pair of spoiled brats, headed for Ivy League in the fall, like to mystify the citizenry. Our town will be better off without them . . . And so forth. Though I declined the Class Wit honor in the Yearbook, I was unofficial Town Rebel.

Standing against the pillar at Nazzarro's funeral service, I felt a bit less sensitive to people's glances than St. Sebastian. Who frowned at me were the staunch middle class elements: among them the same Town Fathers whose sense of fair play had been offended by my rarely getting to pitch. Now they treated me like a pariah not welcome here; why, I didn't even wear a necktie. Also, Willys was famous by this time; it too didn't belong here, parked outside with the others.

Well, so be it. I knew the plight of outcasts from four years in elitist private schools. Strange though: I was a bad boy, riling people up, but I had tears in my eyes for Nazzarro.

In front Thaddy sat among the dignitaries: his dad Big Jim was leader of town Democrats; his mom Gertruda striking in her show of sympathy. Mrs. Floriani cordially despised my humble self, and feared my influence on her son. Thad laughed and told her he had corrupted *me* even though I was The Incorruptible.

III

And then, after a eulogy by Mayor Tomao, and more solemn music, the pallbearers brought the dead boy down the aisle and carried him out into the sunlight. We were in the first hot days, on the threshold of summer; and Nazzarro seemed to be passing over that pleasant threshold only to find he wasn't headed in his speedboat for the seashore. He went from our lives as showily as he entered, and into our memories.

As I said: Thani wasn't there.

Ripoli saw fit not to attend his best and only friend's funeral.

Then the long motorcade wended its way toward the graveyard. A few hundred headlights in the brilliant midday sunlight—it moved, slowly, along Gordiane Boulevard as far as the Town Hall, then turned right on Havilland Avenue, left on Wilke Parkway, and made its way up the hill, along Dyre Club Lane past the old Shetland Estate, to the cemetery on Fenbrook Terrace.

We went up to the breezy heights above the town. And there the mortal remains of young Nazzarro Zummo were laid to rest a few rows over from my sister. Standing at their grave sites one gazes far across to West Hills and the radio relay tower, two red lights at night, while on the other side behind the cemetery is The Dump at Sackett's Point. And down there in the valley: Redemaine spreads like a big arena for everyday life where, as in a few thousand other such towns, the fate of a nation is sifting, sifting. Streets, houses, schools, factories, parks, playgrounds, Dray River, the Water Company, the high school in the center with plazas and shopping malls in a Miracle Strip on either side: all this one sees from Fenbrook Cemetery. On the hottest summer days a wisp of breeze moves through the grass and few shade trees past the marble headstones.

Family members, squinting in the bright sunlight, tossed first clumps of earth down onto the coffin.

IV

There were a few more school days left to my high school career. On Friday: commencement exercises, then a farewell dance at the Lawn Club where I once attended Capers dances. I had missed school off and on since my sister's death. It was strange going there in the final week, walking along the corridor between classes and to the cafeteria at lunchtime, sitting in the auditorium, as we rehearsed the graduation ceremony.

There was a poignant sense. This place let me convalesce after the sick years in private school. Here I found my friends again. Here I got back into the good town life, sports, adolescent adventures, and pal'd around with kids I knew from the youth leagues. All this was pure. Then I found a fine girl to date long enough, at least, for a tender initiation. Thani renewed my faith in myself and the future.

At the same time I was bitten with grief for my twin sister. I wouldn't mind saying goodbye to faces and places seeped in this sorrow. Here at the high school, in Redemaine generally, there was such a bustling young health and activity—but mixed in with something quite different, unhealthy I think, not so nice. On the surface: pleasure, brightness, hi! with a smile, the smile of America. Let's go to Tony Eden's! But below the surface: undercurrents, a darkness, denial, mute.

Now along the hallway students talked lower and gave a glimpse as I passed by alone. Hardly like the fine morning my junior year after I pitched a no-hitter, and the senior Krzhizhanovsky, football tackle, said: Hello, you! . . . No; now at the finale I felt close only, besides Thaddy, to my homeroom. Mostly those were kids from the poorer sectors; a few dozen came and went during the two-year period. They knew the meaning of neglect—on the fringe of so much prosperity. Soon they would be draftees, cannon fodder for Vietnam; but for awhile I still saw them, the dropouts, around town, and exchanged a friendly word. They wedged their way into the work force, but it wasn't an easy fit. They were doing the shit jobs no one else wanted, for minimum pay, pending word from Redemaine Draft Board.

After the April race riot there were black students who softened toward me. At a key moment I took their side, a few hits of the kind they get all their life. And they responded with a nod. Of course since boyhood sports had brought us more together; also my sister dated Jame Hayes, a milestone for the town. I now believe life's crises and milestones must forge unity if we are to hope for survival. Love, suffering, death: the most serious things cross color lines; and a great redemptive force, a capacity to respond, comes out of tragic black history.

But what of my former teammates? What about the in-crowd?

It varied. Some still hung loose, say hey along the hallway, what's the latest and the greatest. Social issues were not their department, but at least they didn't change toward me. Others did, and grew reserved: in this category I place the wafflers; they kept me guessing a moment. Yet others, a few, ignored me when I greeted them, once.

And the teachers? Quietly hostile; perhaps a remark to this effect. Penny Grich, the nervous wreck with her cigarettes, looked sorry for me, and asked why I missed Greek Club. Mrs. Hebbel, the blousy P.O.D. teacher with the G-man husband, showed a certain ironic interest; she gave my term paper on Little Rock an A, but C for the format, footnotes. History teacher Marsden Dale, author of *Redemaine Annals,* kept the Olympian distance befitting an intellectual giant, and gave 'Sherman's March' a B+.

In the guidance office Mr. O'Donnell fielded questions about college with a smile. But there were a few others, like Souvarine the French teacher—so wrong, I thought, so ignorant of the facts, yet self-important. Once I refused to conform in some small class matter; and that man, Souvarine, said brusquely: 'Suicidez-vous donc!' Any slightest departure from accepted norms was inconceivable except as a kind of suicide.

Regarding our principal, The Rhino, he kept to his office as usual; he was not my pal.

As for the whispers, sidelong glances, an impatient gesture here and there—'Segui il tuo corso, e lascia dir le genti.'*

---

*Dante: Go your way, and let the others chatter.

V

Then we sat in the auditorium practicing for graduation. As it happened I was seated next to a black student named Booker Best. His entourage called him Porky; but the rest of us: Booker T., of course. Who in Redemaine school system hadn't read the Landmark Book on Booker T. Washington?

Booker Best made almost perfect grades and might have got Valedictorian or at least Salutatorian. Pep Clubber, track team manager and close friend to Jame Hayes: he was the guy you find around athletes. Chunkily built but spry, clever and quick-witted, helpful, he was a positive element if snide and bitingly humorous; maybe a little bitter. His parents were Jamaican, father a factory worker at United Tool & Die there on Gordiane. Booker had gained early admission with a part scholarship to Howard University for next fall.

Assistant Principal Kurt Bergan explained things from the stage before putting us through our paces.

One classmate, a gung-ho twirler, sniffled: her emotion hinted at the general mood. Evelyne Gilbert, honorary Valedictorian, would not be on hand to make a speech and receive her high school diploma. Nazzarro Zummo, also a star during our brief time together, perhaps a force to be reckoned with someday—gone also. And Bethany Engstrom, Best Looking in the Yearbook, was locked in a mental ward where she fought for her sanity. All this was astonishing, and very sad.

VI

Booker, without turning his head, said in a low nasal voice:

—Can you come to a meeting after school?

—S-sure, I guess. What meeting?

—Shh.—He glanced around from beneath his brow.

—What meeting? I whispered.

The way he scrunched his nose, and peered out with beady eyes, was certainly conspiratorial. Thani would have given her in-the-know, teenage sophisticate's laugh, and arched her fine eyebrows.

Again, nasal, twangy:

—I'll meet you by the bleachers after school. We'll take your Willys.

—That'll throw them off the track.

And so I went to my first 'political' meeting. It was secret alright: held not in the booths at Tony Eden's, but Gordiane Baptist's basement where I once attended a church supper with my dad. In the black section therefore; but not only Blacks were present this time. Besides myself there were two whites: Momino Postella, a guard on the football team, quiet kid, famous for looking out the window during class; and rough, wiry Vinny Resca. This surprised me: ZBKs.

There were two black students besides Booker. One: Whit Wendell, weight-lifting halfback and discus thrower, a Mr. Gags great; and a girl, or young woman. She came in bobbing her shoulders pleasantly as she held up a refreshment tray. She acted like she lived there, and she did: it was Reverend Esmonde's younger daughter Samantha. Smart, pretty, Seven Sisters bound, she wanted to be a doctor.

Chairman Booker got us started in a serious tone:

—Newell, the people you see here form an ad hoc committee. This is our first real meeting, but we've been talking to each other. All of us think something is wrong, and it must be settled before more people get hurt.

Samantha said:

—Jame Hayes is our friend and brother. As you know, some people in town still think he caused your sister's death.

Her tone when she said Jame's name—I hope someone feels that way about me someday. She was ready to help.

—He's innocent, I said.

—We know, said Booker. But who did cause it?

—I can tell you, I said.

—What?!

—You know? . . .

They chorused.

—99% sure. No final proof, yet.

—Who? said Booker.

—The same person who caused Nazzarro's death. But in Evelyne's case I think it isn't so simple. There are the racial overtones: so maybe a conspiracy.

—Well, who? said Samantha.

—Maybe KKK was behind it. That exists in this state, though some deny . . . I know somebody who knows, or seems to: hinted as much. But so far the person won't tell me. I intend to go for another visit and ask again.

—Who's the person? said Booker.

—No, I'd better not say that name, yet. But I can tell you the killer's: the one who did it.

—Who? said Sammy.

—He's called Ripoli. I don't know his last name. His mother is a Simiglione, and his biological father: the Chief of Police.

—What?!?

—You mean Roscroppit? said Whit Wendell, who had a high cutting voice, a competitor's.

—The suspect is very sick physically. I mean his face looks like a . . . sorry, like a raspberry soufflé. But cancer can't stop him; it makes him more desperate. So he goes on late night forays in a black Cobra sportscar, without license plates, up to Maldoror Drive, or my sister's grave in the cemetery. His whole life is like that: unlicensed, running wild, sick.

—Why not take what you know to the authorities? said Booker.

—The Police Chief is his father. Tomao Simiglione is his uncle.

Now I told the story of Nazzarro's death again, and this time I was believed. Hal Duggan never came to interview me about it. A few others did, and printed nothing of what I said. When WRED declined my offer to come to their studios, and tape an interview, at least a news segment, I called in to the late night talk show of Jocko Hake. But 'The Loner' said I was raving and cut me off after thirty seconds.

Momino scratched his nose:

—What if we caught the killer, took him somewhere, and made him talk?

—That's kidnapping, I said. Let's do it. Anyway you can't kidnap somebody who doesn't exist.

—Oh well—Whit gave his high laugh.—We're minors, we'll only get reform school.

The pastor's daughter, eyes atwinkle, said:

—Not the Ivy League for Emory Gilbert's son, but reform school. That's a good one.

—At least there I'll learn something.

—It's time the Maldoror Mon went to church, said Vinny Resca. We'll give him catechism on the balcony while Samantha plays the organ to drown out his hollering.

She sang, a sweet soprano:

—'Then my living . . . will not . . . be in vain.'

—Wait, said Booker. Let's get serious. There's no way around it: we need to catch him in the act.

Whit Wendell held up a make-believe camera:

—Take photos.

I looked at the camera, and said:

—How?

Booker looked at me:

—This is why we invited you here. Do you have a date for the graduation dance?

—N-no.

In my daydreams Thani and I still made a couple.

—What about Sam here?

Booker Best and the others waited for my answer. She worked her shoulders again like a dancer, and gave the nicest laugh.

Timidly I said:

—Isn't Jame going?

—He'll go alone, said Whit.

—I understand. Alright: what's the plan?

Booker took over:

—Guys, catch this. Tonight and tomorrow night, Newell and Sammy go public. They put on a show: interracial couple parades through Redemaine. Drop in at Tony Eden's. Make rounds at the Plaza and the Mall.

—Take a walk on Dyre Club Lane, I said.

—Bullseye. Plaster it around for all to see. It's the talk of the town: black girl and white boy hand in hand, gaga. Have fun, kids. And then, after the graduation dance Friday night: it's up to Maldoror Drive with you. In fact: go up there tonight, after dark, for practice. Cruise it but don't stop. We'll have someone close by, the whole time. There are others in this conspiracy.

I said:

—So on Friday after the dance we hit the Drive, and park by the radio tower?

—For a petting session—said Booker, scrunching his nose, as if he'd never done it, then leering.

–Without the petting, said Samantha.

–Shucks, that's no fair.

I clicked my fingers.

–She's pettable–said Vinny Resca, and gave the wink of the Italian male.

–So it's playacting, I said, wistful. And then?

–We'll be there, said Booker. Staking out the Drive, in strategic positions: we'll be hiding, waiting. You two behave like a pair of turtledoves. Let us do the rest.

–Not exactly, I said. I'll have a gun.

Samantha:

–You'll have to walk up by the radio tower, like Jame did.

–Leave you alone?

–Yes.

–We'll have witnesses, and pictures, said Booker. We'll grab The Mon and take him somewhere for questioning.

–Get ready, I said. He's strong, a weight lifter, and slippery in the black leather outfit he wears. Also, I should tell you he can't stand to be touched, not at all; and has only one functioning eye, the right one.

–We'll touch him, said Momino.

–And take him where? I said. To the authorities? Rune Roscommon and Tomao Simiglione, righteous men?

–No, said Booker. We'll use Nazzarro's cabin off the Drive: where the ZBKs hold, or held, their meetings. Vinny has a key. There we'll keep the boy overnight for questioning; then it's to Town Hall for a press conference on the front lawn.

–Saturday? I said.

–When we're ready. It'll cause a sensation. We'll make press calls: I got a list. Our area, in fact the whole state is fixated on the Maldoror Mon: afraid they'll be next. The nation even knows about it from nightly news coverage. And now we come along and say: We caught The Mon, we have him, come and see. We'll start by calling Mr. Duggan at *Our Town News*.

Thus Booker.

–Rots 'o ruck, I said. Also, Rune with his cops and Tomao with his mafiosi won't like this.

–Then they can lump it. We'll take The Mon hostage and grill him, all weekend, for a week if necessary, and get his confession on tape. We'll make him tell us if he acted alone, or on orders, such as the KKK's. And then Evelyne Gilbert's killer will be put on public display. Our photos will be blown up to life size, because a member of this team is in the Photography Club.

—Widespread conspiracy, I said.

—And getting wider, said Booker. Soon we'll be a movement.

—Hm, so that's it, I said. So . . . I take a walk to the tower. Ripoli attacks.

—And we're on him, said Whit.

—And he's on Samantha, I said.

—But we're quicker, said Booker.

The pretty cheerleader, Sammy Esmonde, stared in space. She gave a little laugh, and a shudder.

VII

We did as told. We put on a show. Holding hands we strolled into Tony Eden's, high school hangout, for a cheeseburger special on toast with mayonnaise, then double scoops of butter crunch. In the warm June evening we walked around Redemaine Mall, then the Plaza, looking in at The Music Box, the bowling alleys, clothing stores. We let the town see us in case anyone cared to know we were going out together. After dark we cruised Maldoror Drive; and, in low voices, went over Friday night's plan. No sign of the Cobra.

On Thursday, after my last day of classes at the high school, Sammy and I had supper together. We raided the ice box at my house after visiting Mom in bed upstairs. We had a fine time with Lemon who nearly set the place on fire making crepe suzettes.

Then, drunk from the suzettes, I took my date to a movie called 'La Notte' at the one art cinema in the province.

—Wow! Some sex, man.

—No petting! said Samantha out loud.

—Yeah yeah.

We read subtitles.

Afterward, we went for ice cream again, and a walk along Dyre Club Lane. Then to the Drive a last time before the real thing.

No Cobra.

VIII

At commencement exercises on Friday I was handed my own diploma, and a second one, which read: **𝕰𝖛𝖊𝖑𝖞𝖓𝖊 𝕲𝖊𝖓𝖎𝖆 𝕲𝖎𝖑𝖇𝖊𝖗𝖙**, in gothic letters. Through the afternoon I sat beneath a tree in our backyard, reading, and then rode through the twilit town to pick up Samantha at the church.

The graduation dance was a subdued affair. We mulled awhile and said hi to people, and bye.

—Hey, Franny! What's up?

Fofanna the high school pitcher:

—I signed this afternoon.

—Really! Where to?

—Boondocks somewhere. Midwest. I can't remember the name.

—Hm! Will they give you a plane ticket?

—Bus, I guess.

—Well, don't get lost, buddy. Good luck!

—Sure. Wha-choo doin' this summer?

—Oh, you know. Hit the beach clubs, maybe read a little.

—No Legion ball?

—Naw, that's it. High school pitcher, like you said.

—Me too, said Fran. But I can hit.

I noticed a few classmates leaving the dance early, Booker and Whit, Momino, Vin, Jimmy Bella. With handshakes they made their way to the exit.

Thaddy was kept busy as usual: a sort of marshall for the affair. After awhile our paths crossed.

—Brother, where to in September?

I laughed. He knew perfectly well where I was headed: same dump as himself.

—Think I'll try New Haven for the hell of it.

—Et tu? Oh no! Another four years together? What larks! . . . But is it all set, Newell? Suite mates, right? And your prep school friend, Boz?

—My dad says it's arranged.

We embraced. He was called away.

Well, I had dropped by the Guidance Office one afternoon—

before Evo died and the roof seemed to cave in on usual things–and
handed Mr. O'Donnell my college applications. Not that I cared
about higher learning; but only thought I might play some baseball,
take things easy, socializing and whatnot, a few more years. College
isn't exactly a factory–or is it? My grades through three secondary
schools were up and down; and the idea of more boring teachers, yet
another private school, left me cold. But my dad wouldn't leave me
alone, or my mom: so finally I said: Hey, Art-boy Kilroyne, I'm to
this verdammten manor born; I'll go to their Ivy halls if that'll please
my mother. Kids in Mr. Gags' homeroom and across the nation try
and try, and never make it to State University. Once I read only 12%
ever enter college in the U.S.

IX

There was a flurry of goodbyes, and bittersweet yearbook signings.
All best wishes to a swell kid. Where to in September? So sorry,
Newell, so sincerely sorry about your beautiful sister . . . Don't ever
lose your smile and unique sense of humor! Always remember good
times at the nurse's office, and that famous night outside Tony
Eden's when we overturned the jeep. Oh my God! Every success in
life to the brother of the nicest most caring girl I ever met . . . May
you have the best of luck in college and in the future, you devil. It's
been great knowing you these years at RHS; no words could express
what I feel about your sister . . . Never forget our wild jeep ride to the
haunted house on Hardin Avenue. Why not let's all go pile in the
Willys, seventeen of us, and go turn it over again like that unforgettable night. What a shot! Talk about cheap feels! . . . All my sympathy . . . Please accept my sincere condolences . . . Happiness and success be yours, dear Classmate, as you pursue your way in life. May
your every dream become a reality. All *worst* wishes to the great
beach lover of Meg's Point. I feel deep sorrow writing this in your
yearbook, Newell . . . You're a great Red Renegade! For the guy I had
the honor to beat every time playing dots in Marsden Dale's deadly
boring history class, ick! Take care of yourself, old teammate since
the days of Spring Glen boys in Peewees. Head up as you go out into
real life. All best wishes, Newell, really, though I know you'll get into

a peck of trouble no matter what because you've got some glib tongue on you. You always were a sassy-ass since the days of kindergarten and Miss Hetherington, always talking back! What a rascal, what a rascal, I can only shake my head as I write this and think what the future holds in store for you ... Goodbye, fellow student, remember the good times. I will never forget your sister Evelyne and am truly saddened, I always will be, by her passing ... Chin up! March! Into the future, hup-two ... !

By the door there were more farewells. The classmates wished one another the best and said so long and drifted out into the night.

In the Lawn Club parking lot Samantha and I stood breathing the fresh dewy air. There was a tear in her serious eyes. Evelyne, Nazzarro, Beth, Jame Hayes whom she loved: she might have cried for them, but it wasn't the time for crying.

–Let's go, she said.

We hugged. Who knows? Maybe the Maldoror Mon wouldn't show up tonight. Then we'd have to go through this again, and keep getting keyed up. But how long would the team stay together?

I had to admire her courage, and her love. She meant to clear Jame Hayes: so there could be no slightest doubt about his innocence. So he could move on. She wanted him to have life again, and play track and field in college, and beyond.

X

Once more we rode through the town we grew up in.

Beyond the Miracle Strip I turned left and went among the quiet suburban streets to Thorndale Avenue. We passed the spot where Nazzarro died. We made our way along the slow upward bend toward the Drive entry. Tire marks from Nazzarro's last drag race snaked under the headlights as I slowed to turn left into West Hills Park.

Neither of us spoke. At the first parking circle there were no cars. Nobody here tonight, except Booker and our guys in place already. They waited. Hopefully The Mon hadn't made his rounds early and spotted them. Slowly I drove, headlights on bright like an advertisement, the few winding miles of Maldoror Drive toward the radio relay tower.

We arrived. I turned right, up the bit of gravelly driveway overgrown with weeds, and killed the motor. We took our place in the same spot Jame and Evelyne parked that night in April.

Off went the lights. I leaned and put my arm around her. We waited, our heads together, like we were necking. I had an eye on the darkness this side, she on that. A lone cicada fiddled its one-note tune in the silence; and, as we sat there poised, ready to be attacked, it was hard to believe anyone existed in the world but us, and—the Maldoror Mon whether Ripoli, escaped convict Jared Simms still on the lam, or someone totally unexpected. The Mon filled up the quiet night with his threat of terror. We waited. We thought: who? Whose dark figure will come out of those bushes and move toward us? Who will show up now and start the horror again? Who does such things to people?

A half hour went by. Is he here? Can he see us? Will he attack? Sammy made an effort not to tremble.

She whispered:

—It's time. Go on.

I said:

—We better stay together. I won't leave you.

—No, no. Stick with the plan. You walk to the radio tower like Jame did.

—Sure?

—Very sure.

Another moment I paused. Whispered:

—I'll leave the keys.

—Good. Go.

—Remember . . .

I took her hand, kissed it, and then touched the glove compartment. Thad's revolver lay by the radio. I had the sheath knife.

XI

I stepped out of the car, and closed the door, loud enough. I stood sniffing the air and listening. Could anyone besides us be here? For a moment I felt anguish, catching my breath, and had little faith in

Booker, Whit, and the ZBKs. Well, what if I didn't do as instructed? What if I doubled back along the gravel path, and crouched peering past shrubs into The Drive? Would I see the dark Cobra sitting there, lights off, like a beast ready to strike? . . . But no. I must do as the plan said—do what Jame did: leave her alone in the car. The Mon must see me walk away casually so he can move in and try to stab another innocent girl. Come on, coward, into our trap. And then we're all over him, grappling him down, snapping photos. What if he wasn't human and had super strength? I thought he was human.

My steps crunched as I made my way to the tall tower with its two red lights. There I stayed five minutes, ten, hard to say. Wouldn't he sense an ambush—here ? He would do what he was—

There was a scream.
Samantha screamed.
I started running back to the car.
There was a male scream. Guttural sounds, grunts. Struggle.
A flash bulb exploded in the dark.
Shouts, screams.
—Ah! Cut me.
Vinny Resca—
—Hold him! Take him down!
—Goddamn it!
—Ah-ah.
—Slippery devil, stay put!—
—Pin him!
—No!
—Oh, oh!
—There he—

As I got to the Willys an engine started. The Cobra. Resca lay on the ground with two of our guys bent over him. Samantha leaned below the dashboard holding her head and breathing in spasms. Was she wounded?

I jumped in the driver's seat.
—Are you bleeding? I said. Did he get you?
—No, she choked.
I reached to close the other door even as I turned over the ignition. Willys gave a jolt and went plunging backwards out into the Drive.

Lights on! I saw the Cobra wriggle and scurry as it took the first curve back toward Thorndale. I heard my name called and caught sight, in the rearview mirror, of two, three figures running the other way.

If, once in their car, they came in pursuit, then who would take Vinny to the hospital? I couldn't hang around to find out: if I braked, Mon escaped.

Not this time.

XII

Once again I didn't care what happened to me personally. College in the fall? It didn't count. I wanted to catch this madman now, and put him out of his misery.

The chase was on: down the same track again, and around the curve. Ripoli streaked twenty car-lengths in front; it was him alright, in the Cobra. But headed where?

He fled. Where to? Home again home again? The House on the Hill? I thought he was scared, zooming for dear life. We almost had him. More people knew about him now: more outsiders in the know, against him.

Had he left his stinger in Resca back there? Now no weapon? Just a sick young man in a mask—sick unto death.

I flicked my bright lights at him, up, down, up. I harrassed him, and closed the distance between us. Across the front seat Sammy sat head bowed, rubbing her face. She sniffled and tried to regain her senses.

Then we left Thorndale and went careening through the streets asleep at two a.m. We swerved into a deserted Gordiane—now to hell with red lights. We raced past the turn he'd have taken for Dyre Club Lane, and flew by the high school, then Walpole Street on the left which meanders through the Water Company. Where was he going? On down the town's main drag, past the street by the bank building where Thani lived with her mother, we sped with a roar.

And then the Cobra lurched to the curb, skidded to a halt as its tires shrieked, and Ripoli hopped out.

Redemaine Pizzeria!

He ran forward as if his life depended on it and hurled his body at the locked entry and burst open the door.

Jumping from my car knife in hand I watched him fall forward, get on his feet slowly, and go inside.

I was right behind. I leapt at the masked man and, an arm around his neck, held the knife between his shoulder blades. I shouted:

–Wait up, you abomination! Why? Tell me why!

His voice was a gurgle:

–I killed her, and now I'm going to die!

–But what for? What did Evelyne Gilbert ever do to you?

–She said hi! She talked to me. Damn her. By the brook when we were children . . . she was nice!

A shiver went through him. For an instant he paused, gone limp, and I upended and pinned him on the floor. His back was bleeding: not greenish slime, but a deep and streaky red in the oven glow. Whit, Booker, are you coming? Did you lose the trail? We need witnesses to his confession!

–Now tell me why you did it or I'll slit your throat.

–Good.

–Why did you kill my sister?

–I loved her.

–You loved her? That's some love. You'd make quite a brother-in-law.

–I didn't want to. No way.

He gasped. Was he dying?

–Then why?

–I can't tell you.

–Was it KKK?

–Kay who? I'm glad it didn't work tonight with the other one. But now I've got to die.

–Just hold on. You're not dying yet. I asked you why my sister. Because she dated a Black?

–No. What they say, I do. That's all.

–Who's they?

–You don't need to know, and you don't want to, haha.

But suddenly he swung, hard: an elbow on my solar plexus. He sprang back, and the knife went flying. Oh-h! I couldn't breathe. Easily he threw me off and was able to turn the tables.

Sweaty, filthy, slimy, he stank. Unable to take care of himself any longer? Zia Grippina sure as hell wouldn't do it.

Then from under his leather suit he took something–a necklace. Of teeth! It was strung with teeth, my sister's teeth. And with that weapon he began strangling me, pulling tighter, tighter, ahhh! In a minute I, not he, would have to die.

XIII

Now it was I who gurgled:
–How's it feel . . . to kill an innocent girl . . . you loved?
–Good.
–What's it . . . like . . . to kill your best friend . . . your only . . . friend?
–Good! Now you, too. Enemy.
I felt my neck veins ballooning. My face would burst apart in an instant. Few more seconds–the end.
–Ahhh . . . !
I was losing consciousness. But I heard a yell as someone came storming in: Booker! and behind him Jimmy Bella the ZBK, Samantha, Whit.
Ripoli let go his grip. He dove away yelling at us:
–Die! Haha! You suckers! Hate! Die!
He threw himself toward the oven.
On one elbow, trying to rise from the floor, I watched the others go for him.
But he yanked off his mask. This disarmed and sent a shudder through the pursuers. It made them pause: touch that? Oh, oh! Ripoli's face had gotten worse, if that's possible: blue-grayish, necrotic, bloated beyond recognition.
He flung the mask back at us–laughed, shouted:
–Bye bye! Haha, I'll be back! Hate, everybody! Die! Hate! Haha!
And then, laughing madly, he vaulted up into the 14x14-foot firebrick oven. Crouching, he went in toward the 2500 degree fire which never goes out. He entered it on all fours. He kept on, crawling forward even as his monstrous distended head began to flare, and then his limbs. Incandescent bits detached and drifted upward, in wisps, from the body growing molten. And still we heard his savage laughter and his: hate! die! haha!

I struggled up and watched as Ripoli tossed something at us from the flames enveloping him. He threw back Evelyne's teeth.

Shreds of charred flesh peeled off and flew up from his receding form. Cinders darted like wasps about the oven.

—I'll be back!

Ripoli's words echoed. And, as we drew nearer, feeling the great heat, and stared after him: it seemed a whole red and black world existed deep in the big pizza oven which had never extinguished for decades. We seemed to see his flaming figure grow smaller, wade in further, take its place among a multitude of other devils. Flames crackled and danced. Tiny figures moved about busily in the far distance of a bright orange hellscape. It was like an optical illusion: dots, swarming, in an infinite mass, amid the coal and the fire. Toward the front a few sparks spiralled up as though nothing had happened: a human being hadn't gone mad and crawled into a coal-burning oven to commit suicide. Nothing was left of Ripoli: not a trace, except for the television sets and greasy porn magazines, in the attic at House on the Hill; and the necklace he had worn to signify his love for the girl he murdered, his hate—the girl whose pictures, blown up life-size, were on his wall.

XIV

They were around me, great guys, saying:

—You okay?

—I am. And Vinny?

—Momino drove him to the hospital, said Booker. We had to bring them to the Mall where Momino left his car. That's what took so long.

Then they wanted to see me home.

—No, I've got one more thing to do.

—Isn't that enough for one night? said Whit, and laughed.

—You guys take Sammy home. Check on Vinny.

—I go home, she said, when everybody else does.

For a few minutes I sat in the Willys. Head bent over the wheel, I tried to pull myself together. I guess I was crying.

XV

With a sigh, and with grim determination at this hour, I returned along Gordiane Boulevard toward the Town Hall. Before the crescent called Old Gordiane I turned left and, driving round, parked a block from Roscommon's Tavern. Then I went through backyards, hoping for no dogs, and made my approach unnoticed. I had flashlight, gloves, the couple tools needed for an act of burglary.

Was there a light on inside *Our Town News,* or was it a reflection? Trotting across the lawn I tried the back door. Left open! Not pulled to . . . Now that was strange at three a.m. I had expected to break the window, pull out shards and hoist myself over.

A cat met me inside; it hissed and arched its back. Frazzled, porcupiny. Something strange going on here too, little buddy? In the outer office I switched on my flashlight and saw Harriet Pulley's desk, also the metal shelves with bound *News* volumes. The cat's eyes glinted.

I moved toward the editor's office and Duggan's file cabinet, thinking to pry it open with my crowbar. I was after his so-called 'Macro File'. I wanted it! I needed to know who *they* were: the *they* mentioned by Ripoli before his last sordid act in life.

With each creak in the floorboards I winced; though no one else could be here at this hour. Turning the knob on Hal Duggan's door I recalled our meeting ten days ago, his mood of gloom and doom: eager for the interview to end, nervous, since he had said too much.

Slowly, I opened the door, as it creaked on its hinges.

The manila folder with green reinforcements at the corners; the file that would 'ruin them'—was it here?

XVI

For a moment I stood in the doorway and sent my flashlight beam from corner to corner in the editor's den. Silence. The old house stirred a little in its sleep. The cat hissed again. Small night sounds. But why did I have a sixth sense I wasn't alone?

A bit of breeze played in the window casements. A branch brushed against the eaves. Spooky in here . . . and, yes, I heard something stirring upstairs.

Now I went straight to the file cabinet and tried the second drawer from the bottom. Open! That is, all were locked except the one I needed, and a nudge would lock it too.

I had made a mental note that day when Duggan took out the dossier labeled 'Polit.' Now I leafed through the rack, file after file, and didn't find it.

Prying open the other drawers I went through them also. Then desk drawers, bookshelves, closet: I spent a good while among *Our Town News* accounts, subscriber lists, advertising invoices, editor's correspondence, old page layouts, mechanicals, decades of editorials, notes and jottings for 'Our Neighborhoods' . . . They kept everything here except the essential.

The 'Macro File' was missing.

XVII

Creak . . . I heard a sound upstairs, too random for somebody pacing, who would have sensed an intruder and kept still to listen.

I left Duggan's office and paused at the stairway. Cre-eak . . . Gloves off, flashlight also off, I took the small pistol from my belt, and started up. I had come here to find a mystery file; now, my search frustrated, the same impulse sent me up the steps, slowly.

—*Sssss!*

Woops, almost lost my balance. At eye level, on the landing, that damned cat arched, gave a hop backward, then scooted away in the upstairs darkness. Why was its fur bristly? Seen a spook, little critter? Just what *had* it seen?

On the second floor I stood and listened. The creaking came from the attic.

XVIII

Up a second flight–then, turning the knob, I pushed open the attic door.

I saw.

A street lamp glimmered through a gable window. And by that light I saw a dark figure hanging beneath a roof beam. The man's neck, wrenched by a wire noose tied to a heavy looped screw, looked like a hump. From cartons filled with paper came a storage mustiness, laced with an acrid scent, in the first hours of death. The body had begun to bloat, and bulged his business suit. A dapper suicide; though the shally bowtie wasn't quite on straight, and the jacket was drawn up showing a line of white shirt puckered above the belt and low-slung trousers. I don't know why his shoes, in particular, gave him a pitiful, a childish look.

There was a bound *News* volume beneath his feet. The cordovan shoes were only a few inches off the floor, but those few were enough.

I stood in a spell, and stared at the man's head turned the other way. Then I took a few steps and–not with my hand, but the revolver, turned him. Cree-e-eak! So loud, in the predawn silence: it was like anger.

Hal Duggan swung around, as though facing his accusers. But he didn't look them squarely in the eye, any more than he had me during our meetings. No, his head was turned to one side, evasive. He stared out from beneath his bushy eyebrows, the knobby lipoma on his brow more pronounced in death; and his soul seemed to glint, like the cat's eyes, in points of reflected light that were his pupils. Oh, he had never been any kind of crusading editor; but he looked pretty ferocious right now, and pointed a spastic finger at society. His clenched gaze had a pugnacious note. He had just fought a scuffle, and lost; so his graying hair was a little unkempt. And, forgive this indelicacy . . . in death he was erected.

What should I do? Take him down? Pick up the phone and call the Police Station? Bright idea! And what was I doing here in the first place? Looking for a file that would ruin the Police Chief? destroy a few reputations, our town bosses', and their betters in the State Capital–if not in Washington, D.C.?

So I stood there staring in Hal Duggan's eye: as if asking him one last time what he knew about my sister's death, the KKK in our town, the conspiracy of power on local and national levels. But he didn't answer. He chose the Fifth Amendment. Oh hell, Sir! If you're going to die anyway then why not do it right? A principled death, at least, since you no longer have anything to lose? Why not tell the guilty ones a thing or two about themselves before you go? Why not help out? . . . But no: we die the way we lived. You keep it all bottled up inside, and finally the Angst gets out of hand, and then—

Tsk-tsk. This suicide business seems sort of selfish to me: alright for the poor Ripolis of the world, if you will, but hardly in character for an editor-in-chief with an ideal of objective news reporting to uphold.

I turned away toward the stairs. But I glanced back when the suicide, at the end of his rope, revolved a little and made his sound.

—Oh, dear. So you don't want me to leave you alone up here?

In response he laid a loud fart, smelly as hell, which made me recall the beautiful Zia Grippina.

And then he creaked some more—like the mooring line of a boat, when it tugs a bit at the dock, dreaming of sea lanes.

XIX

All quiet at *Our Town News*. Hal Duggan had written his last article, and he wouldn't be putting this week's issue to bed. Too bad: he had a scoop.

On my way downstairs the thought struck me: what if this wasn't a suicide? Hm.. Back door open. Key file missing. So somebody knew . . . ? But . . . just by waving the sensitive material in front of me, recklessly, during our second interview: wasn't he saying he hardly cared anymore? Well, he cared enough to brag a little, if only a hint: about what a brave investigative journalist he might have been . . . if he was brave. And yet—

Naw. That's it.

Hey! I've had enough playing amateur detective for one night . . .
Wouldn't you say? Enough for a lifetime!

Anyway, if you want to know who *really* done it, then check the
newspapers. Local, state. Check out *The Times.* Perhaps the truth of
the matter will be found in there someday—Section H, page 37 or
thereabouts, the fine print.

I walked to the jeep yawning, drove home, and slept all day.

Chapter Nine

I

That summer I went to the beach clubs. I swam and sunbathed, hung around, chatted with friends. On my beach towel I lay reading and half heard the songs on other people's radios. It was good to talk about college coming up in the fall; about people and things and the world; about Beatniks. Organized baseball used to fill up my summers, but now it was over. They called me to play Legion ball, and I said: no, sorry. I had a chance to go pitch in the Cape Cod League. Uh-uh. So I slept good and late, and drove to the shore each afternoon, and then read far into the night. There was a new loneliness, or maybe the same old one, which I'd almost forgotten during two years in public school.

In August I ran into Beth Engstrom. Behind the high school she was helping the new cheerleading squad practice cheers: they jumped, did splits, waved their pompons like a bunch of bacchantes. Harry, Harry, he's our man! If he can't do it, Jerry can! It seemed a long way from there to a Beatnik café, in the nearby city, where I met Thani another time. Whew! That was all new to me, weird stuff—the deep talk, the strange-tasting tea, the guys with beards and girls with low voices tuned in to their own vibes. I found it all fairly pretentious: hey, I made an unlikely Zen Buddhist. Also I didn't pick up on too many literary allusions. But there was a siren singing in the new introspective mood.

Then, one evening in late August, Thani and I went to an outdoor concert together. She had called me. And now I saw the change in her: still lovely, a feminine force; but the blossoming that brought her Best Looking honors in our class yearbook had begun to pass. She was less lively; she was self-consciously arty like the Beatnik café, and talking about a trip she made with a friend to Provincetown. During the concert she sniffled over 'When Sonny Gets Blue'; but she'd also developed a temper, and let me have it once when I said a dumb thing. After the concert we sat in my car outside her mom's apartment. We held hands and kissed nicely; not the rabid desire of last spring, but tenderly, easily. Those were goodbye kisses before our leave-taking in different directions. College soon. They were also postmortem kisses because the vital thing we had to do together, in life, was over. Nazzarro had loved her the way a man loves once; but I loved Thani like a high school sweetheart: for a wonderful initiation, which restored my balance after private school. Nazzarro gave her all power over him; but I was always so restless, heart and mind casting about, asking myself what I was supposed to do next.

So we kissed again and said we'd write often and see each other at homecoming. Thanks, dear, thanks so much for the good times, and the innocent sex. What a swell kid you are, what a teenage beauty . . . Those were thank you kisses.

II

A few days before I left for college, I drove fifteen miles with Dad to visit my mother in a longterm care facility. Sort of a halfway house, you might say. By now it was early September, and my little sister was back to school: in fifth grade.

Outside Mom's window the late summer day shone brightly, pearly, with its warm colors after two rainy days. Nature was flush that afternoon in the New England countryside. Emory and I had sat quietly for once, not arguing, while we enjoyed the ride.

But inside Anne Gilbert's sickroom it was winter. The white sheets, the pale lemon walls, my good kind grayheaded mother grown old before her time . . . She could hardly sit up anymore. So pretty when I was a boy, and spunky (Beth's word for her): now a poor desiccated stick of a woman. All her life dominated by her mother, who treated her like a child: Anne carried her big famous baby of a husband emotionally for thirty years. She gave our family the glue, the love-glue that kept us—six individuals living under one roof, as someone said—more or less together. All her adult life she worked and worried for her family: a demanding husband, four children brimming over with life, energy, squalls and departures. She had a dream of peace and family harmony, but it was not meant to be. And the dream cost her daily, a daily death, since she found herself amid conflicts, pressures, and played her stressful negotiator's role to the end. My dad and I for the longest time had all-out verbal brawls: since I was a kid and began to feel his anger. Anne had to swim against the current, day by day, year by year; and she wasn't a strong swimmer. Father-son conflict, other secondary conflicts, plus nicotine addiction, drinking at night to keep her husband company— in her early fifties she was spent. Cancer overran her.

Well, Dad was under the influence that day we visited The Moms. Chevalresque, like the southern gentleman he was, Emory Gilbert raised his dying wife's hand to his lips, hurting her, and then said:

—Don't worry, Doll. We'll get you squared away.

Ah me. The thought is what counts.

But I wanted a moment alone with my mother. And, mirabile visu, Dad actually showed tact for once. When our visit was over, he went out in the hallway leaving me the field.

I don't know what got into me then, but I went to the bedside and gave my mom a hug. With my cheek to hers I said:

—I'm sorry I hurt you!

That's all. It wasn't much: less than a Mickey Mouse wristwatch after a lifetime of service. But it was something. Anne gave a little jolt forward as tears welled in her eyes. Good mothering is a thankless task, boy. And if ever a kid took his generous no-apron-strings mom for granted, I'm the one. She was Mud to me—with a nod of the head and a cocky little laugh as I strolled out the door to go find my friends. She gave her all and saved me from 'Dad's wrath', in this family epic, and made me free as you please to neglect her. Another woman might have rationed the good stuff out, and bound me to her heartstrings.

Well! Who can say what awful pressures from the past, like a curse, are brought to bear on families? What converging tides sink the Good Ship Family Happiness. Besides the stock Oedipal complex, child competes for Ma, there is the Laius complex: Pa responds defiantly, perhaps violently. And there's Jocasta's complex too, completing this trinity. For the mother fears she may be left out, discarded after use. Unconsciously she calls on her feminine power to set husband and son jousting for her, at one another's throats. She is seductive toward her son, thinking to shore up love for the future; also compensate for the fact that her spouse, a known quantity, is not after all the godhead she married so virginally, so hopefully; while her son, a little chaos as yet, at least lets her imagine. Anne's father, like Beth's, died when she was young: she had more space to idealize, in her struggle to engage the male . . .

Gracious! And, if that wasn't enough, the experts tell us all softs of unsavory drives are the norm in the bisexual subconscious of families. But all that is too deep for me. That's Beatnik talk.

At my mom's bedside I blurted:

—I'm sorry I hurt you!

This meant: by my arguments with Dad. And such a statement was brand spanking new in Gilbert annals. And she started to cry.

Way to go, Momma. Hey, you babe! I award you MVP and Rookie of the Year posthumously. You are 'Most Sincere' in the Class of 1961 Yearbook of Moms.

Then I went from the wintry sickroom to go pack things for college.

And Anne Gilbert was left there alone, by her menfolk, to face the disease and pain, her fate.

III

On the eve of departure I spent an hour with Thad Floriani. My dad had arranged for us to be suite mates in New Haven along with a friend named Boz Krips from boarding school days.

After talking things over with Thaddy, excited about our new adventure, I left him and took a ride around. It was one of the sunlit crisp September days, and I drove to Spring Glen Grammar for a walk in the Water Company down the hill.

The kids were back in school, and my prodigious little sister was in there with them. I lingered in the playground listening to their chirpy voices, having a blast at their lessons though they didn't know it.

Autumn already? The leaves weren't turning yet; but I recalled fall days of my childhood when leaves were shimmering in sunlight as they floated down. Those were the year's last warm days, World Series weather; we ran about during recess waving our arms, signalling for the catch of a certain leaf, like outfielders; or maybe just dove in a crinkly pile for the hell of it. Mm, what a good smell. Hey! Get the hell off, Otter! Stubborn guy! That's *my* leaf!

I walked around the Water Company for awhile: where we, illegal boys, spent our summers swimming and fishing when we weren't playing ball up at Lavater Field. Me 'n Thad, Otto 'n Bungya, Bobby Zwergli, Willard Steuart, Haas, Lenny and The Mooch to name a few. Eh, those were some times—summer days after Otter and myself acted up in Miss Kenny's class, hiding in the closet when we thought we might get left back. What? Not get promoted to Mr. Pyat's sixth grade free-for-all with Lily Berryer, and Janie Gluck also called 'The Pain'? With The Lunger and Terrible Typhoid and El Neuterman?

Then I rode around some more: by Coralie Panducci's house, where the sorority meeting was held in fall of my junior year, and I felt so happy being in high school, part of it, after all. At last I had what I needed, the people: since I was not some kind of prep school aberration, in my own eyes, but a people too.

IV

Then I went by Redemaine High: not inside to the nurse's office, Mrs. Aylmer's, or seeing teachers; but out back where I took a seat in the portable stands by the football field. I sat there frowning in the sunlight while breeze stirred leaves on the high embankment adjoining Redemaine Plaza. I was thinking about Evelyne and didn't hear when someone approached.

—Newell?

It was Penny Grich, the English teacher.

—Hello, Corinna.

We each took a heroic name in Greek Club.

—Hello Teiresias! I'm in a prep period, and saw you pass by. Such a dreamer, Newell . . . watch out, you'll fall into a well. But what are you doing here? Not off to college yet?

—Tomorrow. Orientation week.

—So you came for a goodbye?

—Sure, and thinking about something.

—What, if I may ask?

—Well . . . I just can't get over the way our town voted a Tomao Simiglione into office. Mafia for Mayor?

—Shh—Miss Grich giggled, girlish; but then started to cough up her guts, like she was retching.

—I mean . . . how does a person like that win people's trust?

—Self-interest, Newell. He favors the business class. But he also may have cheated: there were rumors of electoral fraud.

—How so?

—Oh, have people in the right places, controlling things.

—Control a town?

She laughed:

—Town, country . . . In Chaucer all Brittany was hypnotized, remember? Money and connections work wonders.

—But what about the law? The U.S. Constitution?

Penny Grich shrugged, coughed; took the eternal crumpled hanky from her blouse.

—Our Constitution is a great document for private property. But it can't plan. And apparently it can't set healthy limits. Individuals, corporations get too big for their britches.

—Big selfish babies, I said.

—Too big to spank!

Again she gave one of her deep reverberant coughs, like a signature. She was too young for emphysema. Then she took out her cigarettes, lit up, and sucked in, deep.

I frowned, watching her, and thought of my mother.

—Where does it end? I said.

—Abuses, corruption—she said, spitting a tobacco spec to one side.—The system, democracy, deteriorates, like Rome due to the patricians' greed. Listen: a German writer in the 'Forties wondered how a band of putchists could gain control of a nation.

—Putchists?

—Power grabbers. Usurped the leadership. At first they failed, but then the voters elected them, if there was no fraud. The incumbents, liberals, weren't much better, in their way. And the best people sat by and watched, while the masses grew wildly jubilant, not all of course, but enough: believing in such leaders, eager for any sacrifice. They would make war against the world . . . Well, Germany was led on a journey through hell, where 'thundering flames danced round', as the writer said, poetically. And he called the Nazi chiefs: Abschaum.

—Abschaum?

—Scum.

—Ah. Scum rises, type thing. But why the fuss? I mean do they enjoy life, with all their money?

Miss Grich puffed, gazed across the wide playing fields, sighed, coughed.

—I guess people like that have a devil in them. A devil called: System. The rewards are high, so they'll tell any lie with a straight face, say or do anything, to win.

—Monsters.

—Sure, she said. A sleeping people produces monsters.

—Our nation has its KKK. Redemaine produced a Maldoror Mon.

—True.

—But, Miss Grich, I don't understand Thaddy's father. Big Jim was favored to win, as Tomao's opponent in the mayoral race. So if they did steal the election, then he was like the Germans: just sat back and let it happen. He never fought back. Why? Is he a coward?

—Oh, I don't know. Big Jim Floriani? . . . There are enough cowards to go around; but most folks just tend to accept things. They've got a few problems of their own. And all along the Abschaum see life as fair game. They do not care. They want no limits set on their so-called freedom.

—Freedom, I said, to become savage beasts. And my sister died . . .

V

We sat there. Last class was ending. Now students would wait in afternoon homeroom for the dismissal bell to send them home, or to extracurricular activities, sports.

–Good luck to you, Newell, truly. You know–she gave a throaty laugh–I feel a twinge of envy.

–Envy? Why, Miss Grich? The whole thing bores me. College will be like another prep school . . . strike three, for me. What I'd like to do is chuck the whole thing, and go out on the road, hitchhike, with Beatniks!

She laughed.

–Now now, take it easy. Go on to Yale, Newell. Even there you can learn something. You'll have a chance to develop what's in you, maybe fulfill it someday, which is rare. You're going out toward the great world, and I say bravo.

–You sound romantic, Miss Grich.

–So be it: romantic. Life!

My English teacher looked pensive then–thwarted, in her 'small' world. Three packs a day had left their mark on her intelligent features. I wondered how she and our tennis coach, Mr. Petrocchi, were doing as a couple. But I didn't ask.

–Isn't life here, too?

–You know, we're only a few hours from the City. But those few hours are an age . . . Well, we stay here, in this small-minded place; we're dependent on 'reactionary' forces which eat our minds alive. I guess I would say that. If you don't have a strong will, then good night. Narrow, petty, these relationships, after all: TV is culture, church on Sunday is spirit. Small everyday squabbles and intrigues, yick! Sick of it! (She coughed.) It . . . it deadens instead of rousing to resistance. Small relations, narrow childish views on life, in the nursery of Redemaine. Who can see past his nose and keep the greater currents, the life of the nation and wide world in view? Who doesn't wind up in a smug self-complacent 'objectivity': the most limited subjectivity parading as wisdom, even as thousands of our town dwellers share it? For the public struggles here in Redemaine are small and stupid, Newell, pots and pans, or snowplows; not the people's great struggle for social justice: the workers oppressed by the bosses, capital; the nation trying to survive long corporate abuses to our social fabric, and now our planet . . . That broad world historic struggle is the one that never deadens, but ever awakens, teaches, and gives an ever new and vital energy. But it hasn't come here yet.

I stared at her a moment in silence, and then said:

–Why don't you teach the way you're talking now? It would be so interesting.

–How long do you think I'd last in this school system, if I stood in a classroom quoting Engels?

–Who's Engels?

She laughed:

–You'll find out in college; though you could spend a dozen years at Yale, Harvard and Princeton, and never really learn about Fred and his buddy . . .

I thought a moment, and said:

–At least you've got Greek.

–A hobby. Greek isn't the essential thing.

–What is?

–I think a destiny. And it doesn't matter how much you have to suffer, or lose for it. The main thing is to keep fighting.

–What?

–The bad thing. The cheating Tomaos, their system. Earth could be sinking into a poisonous morass, and they'd speculate on that real estate. Just gimme the money! And, yes, for a long time our Town Fathers will still be talking sports, as though such and such a pro ballplayer were their macho peer, and a sportscaster's lofty words conferred dignity. And meanwhile we're all halfway to hell in a hand-basket, like Germans in the 'Thirties, only worse this time . . . But wait: when it's *our* children who are suffering, and fearing for their fair share of life: then, at long last, maybe we'll start to wake up, and produce the needed men and women.

–Too late?

–Maybe.

–You sound like my father, Miss Grich. Convincing; but I never know if he means it.

–If I meant it, I'd try to do something about it.

She laughed, and puffed, then coughed again, convulsively.

At halftime during basketball games she filled the gymnasium with her imitation of a certain male crooner. That was funny. I almost enjoyed a moment or two in her English class; though I couldn't swallow most of it. Too boring! Now and again one of her vocational training students would drop by the classroom and say hi, still shy, grateful to Miss Grich, years later.

Another moment we sat there, side by side, in silence.

Then she walked me to my car.

VI

I went home to Spring Glen and packed a few clothes and books for tomorrow's getaway. Then another crazy meal cooked up by Lemon standing in for our mom. I tried a few bites, but my dog, Pyggy, was the one who chowed down, and made out like a bandit.

Then, as night fell earlier now in September, there was a last place I wanted to visit. Not Maldoror Drive. Hey. And I'd already been to my sister's grave that morning: thinking how so much had happened since her death; and how I 'fell' from baseball, Beth, and being an adolescent.

What I wanted now was not at Redemaine Pizzeria, a pizza in hell seasoned à la Ripoli. No, I had a yen for an ice cream cone at Tony Eden's. So that's where I went.

And whom do you think I found there as always? Fran Fofanna, hanging out.

—Franny kid! Back from the Minors?

—You see me.

—They ran your stats here in the newspapers. You were connecting.

—I poked a few.

—Yeah! Long ball too, a few four-baggers. Well, you headed up in the system? Spring training with the parent club?

—Naw, don't think so.

—Say what? Not going back?

—Naw, that'll do.

—But why? You were hitting; even had a streak.

—I signed because my dad's a scout, and he wanted me to try. But I'm a high school athlete, maybe some semipro, no more.

—C'mon, Franny. What happened down there? Homesickness, that it? Never been away from home before. Couldn't take the bus rides and bad hamburgers, so he comes running back.

—You're a wiseass kid, Gilbert, always was. Like the time you called out 'Let's go Mouse!' at me during a game. Piffed 'cause you didn't get to pitch. You think I like having that for a nickname? But if you bug me any more, right now, we'll have to tangle.

—Remember in Midgets when the James Street Jets beat the Spring Glen Boys, 17–0? Cocò Arzigogolo poked that long homer.

—Sure. Well, when you leaving for college?

—Naw. Ain't going.

—What!

—Think I'll get married and work full-time in an insurance office.

—Cut it out, Gilb. You go to work? Ha ha ha!

—No, really, Fran-kid. I'm a quitter, see. Insurance agent, some real estate deals on the side: that's my speed. Or maybe open a bar on Ferry Street. Bikini'd waitresses, you know the deal. Or else refuse! Yeah, I'll get into junk: there's some loot in that. If only those Simigliones didn't have it wrapped.

I nodded at him.

For ten seconds he stared at me. Then he looked around a little. And then, head high and tilted slightly to one side, whistling a tune, Fofanna turned away and duckwalked into Dominic's Billiard Parlor there alongside Tony Eden's.

—Good luck, Fran-boy!

—Hey, you too, Gilby. Go get 'em.

—Hey! I will.

He waved and said:

—Half-price drinks at Farrelly's tonight. You goin'?

—Naw.

1964, '76, '92, 2004–6